THE YELLOW
FRIGATE

INTRODUCTION.

INTRODUCTION.

IN that broad and magnificent valley which separates the chain of the Grampians from the Ochil Mountains, close by the margin of the Allan, and sequestered among venerable trees, lies the pleasant and peaceful little village of Dunblane, in Scotland's elder days an old cathedral city. Northward of the limpid Allan lie purple heaths, black swamps, and desert muirs. An old bridge which spans the river, and was built in the time of King Robert III., by 'the Most Reverend Father in God,' Findlay Dermach, bishop of the see, with a few ancient houses, having quaint chimneys and crow-stepped gables, that peep on the steep braeside from among the shady beeches, are all that survive of Dunblane; but over those remains rise the grey ruins of King David's vast cathedral, of which nothing now is standing but the roofless nave, with its shattered aisles, and the crumbling but lofty Gothic tower.

The gleds and corbies that flap their wings between the deserted walls; the swallows that twitter on the carved pillars, or build their nests among the rich oakwork of the prebends' stalls, with the grass-grown floor and empty windows of this magnificent ruin, impress the mind of the visitor with that melancholy which is congenial to such a place. But it is neither the recumbent figure of a knight in armour, with his sword and triangular shield, marking where the once powerful Lord of Strathallan sleeps, nor the burial-place of the Dukes of Athol, blazoned with the silver star of the Murrays, that are the most interesting features in this old ruin.

It is not the fine west window which overlooks the wooded path that winds by the river-side, and is known as 'the Good Bishop's walk,' nor the ruined shrine where sleeps

St. Blane of Bute—he whose boat sailed upon the Clyde
without sail or oar ; he who (as the veracious Breviary of
Aberdeen tells us) struck fire with his fingers when the
vesper lights went out ; and who raised from the dead
the English heir of Appleby and Trodyngham, that attract
most particularly the attention of visitors, but *three plain
slabs* of blue marble, that lie side by side on the grassy floor
and nestling, as it were, together, as if to show that those
they cover had loved each other in life, too well to be separated even in death.

The fall of the ponderous and once magnificent roof, the
action of the weather, and the footsteps of visitors, have
defaced the legends that were originally carved there ; but
the memory of those who sleep below these marble slabs
yet lingers in Dunblane and Strathearn.

Under the first lies the affianced bride of one who was a
good and valiant soldier, and faithful to his king.

Under the second lies the betrothed of a stout Scottish
mariner, as brave a fellow as ever faced salt water or cannon-
shot.

Under the third sleeps the youngest—she who perhaps
was the fairest—the wife (but not the queen) of one who
in his time was the most gallant and magnificent monarch
that ever wore the Scottish diadem.

These three ladies were sisters ; and their story is a strange
and a dark one.

History, tradition, and an old manuscript, that was
found (no matter when) among the Records of the Scottish
Court of Admiralty, have enabled me to lay their lives and
narrative before the reader in the following pages.

CONTENTS.

CONTENTS.

CONTENTS

THE 'YELLOW FRIGATE.'

CHAPTER I.

ON BOARD.

BY the fragment of a log-book, which was found among the MSS. just referred to, we are informed that on Beltane day, in the year of Grace 1488, two Scottish ships of war, the *Yellow Frigate* and the *Queen Margaret*, were lying becalmed off the mouth of the Tay, about seven miles from the Gaa Sands, and three from the Inchcape Rock, the large bell of which was heard at times, as its sonorous notes floated over the still bosom of the water. An abbot of St. Thomas at Arbroath had hung it there, on a wooden frame, to indicate by night that ghastly ridge, so long the terror of mariners; and thus as the waves rose and fell, they swung it to and fro. Water will convey sound to a vast distance; thus, in the noon of a calm May day, the notes of the Inchcape bell were distinctly heard on board of the two ships of his Majesty James III., although they were three miles distant from the reef.

A groundswell came off the dangerous sands of Abertay; the sails of the caravels flapped lazily against the masts, as the hulls rolled from side to side slowly and heavily, for there was so little wind that neither would obey her helm, but lay like a log on the water.

The fertile shores of Fife and Angus were shrouded in hazy summer mist, above which peeped the bare scalp of the Law of Dundee. Noon passed, and still the swell came rolling in long, glassy, and monotonous ridges from the land, while the burnished sea seemed smooth, as if coated over with oil. The ships lay about half a mile apart ; and the *Yellow Frigate*, with which we have more particularly to do, was nearest to the shore.

A young officer who was pacing to and fro on her poop gazed frequently and impatiently at the mouth of the river, and after wearying himself by whistling for the lagging wind, tossing splinters of lighted wood into the water, and watching anxiously the direction taken by the puffs of smoke or steam, he suddenly clapped his hands. ' Ahoy there, mizen-top ! Barton,' he exclaimed to an officer who had ascended into the mizen-rigging, ' there is a breeze setting in from the east.'

' Right, Falconer,' replied the other ; ' I can see it curling the water over the Inchcape ; and it comes in time, for I was beginning to bethink me of some other trade, for this of sailor requires overmuch patience for me. So-ho ! here it comes ! ' he continued, while descending the ratlins with the activity of a squirrel. ' See how the sea wrinkles before it ! '

' Now the canvas fills,' said Falconer, looking aloft.

' The *Queen Margaret* has caught it already, and now old Mathieson squares his yards. Aha ! he is an active carle ; always on the lookout, and his messmates jump like crickets when his whistle blows.' The person thus eulogized we find to have been Sir Alexander Mathieson, a rich merchant-skipper of Leith, who had become captain of a king's ship, and won the name of *King of the Sea*.

' Keep her away, timoneer,' said Barton ; ' keep her away yet—a point or two to the south.'

' Why so,' asked Falconer, ' when she lies so well ? '— ' Because, in entering the harbour of Dundee, we must keep the north gable of St. Clement's kirk upon the bar, and on the north-west, right over against Broughty, else we shall run upon the Drummilaw Sands ; and then not St. Clement himself, nor his blessed anchor to boot, would save us. Master gunner—Willie Wad—please to inform Sir Andrew that a breeze is springing up ; but that I see nothing of my father's ship, the *Unicorn*, at anchor in the Firth.'

' Art thou sure ? ' said Falconer, anxiously.—' Sure ! I would know her by her red poop-lanterns and square rigging among a thousand ships.'

Robert Barton, who was captain of the ship, hastened to get sail made on her ; and as the breeze freshened, the yards were almost squared, the notes of the Inchcape bell died away, and both vessels stood slowly into that beautiful estuary formed by the confluence of the Tay with the German Sea.

The sailors, who, during the calm, had been lounging lazily on deck, or basking in the sunshine between the brass guns, exchanged their listlessness for activity; a smile of satisfaction spread over their weather-beaten visages, and a hum of gladness arose from the ship.'

' Now, timoneer, the breeze is more aft,' cried Barton; ' steer dead for the harbour mouth.'—' So-ho ! ' said Falconer, ' the *Margaret* is coming up with us, hand over hand.'

' Fear not,' replied Barton, joyously, ' we shall soon leave her far astern. Thou knowest, Falconer, that this good caravel was built under Sir Andrew's own eyes at the New Haven, near Leith,' continued the captain, surveying with a seaman's proverbial delight the lofty rigging of the frigate.

' Yet she is but a cockle-shell to the great ship of Hiero, anent which Father Zuill, the chaplain, told us so many wonderful things after mass yesterday.'

' If you had seen how beautifully she took the water, diving deep with her stern, and tilting up her bow like a swan. She is sharp as a lance at the bows below the water-line—bold above it; straight between poop and forecastle—clean in the counter, and bolted with copper. By the faith of Barton, there sails not such another ship in all Scottish waters; and I marvel mickle, if either French Francis, or English Harry, will ever build one like her.'

The ship which Captain Barton eulogized so highly would create no small speculation in Bonnie Dundee, if she and her consort were seen standing before the wind, right up the Firth of Tay, in this year 1855 ; and we may imagine the criticism of the rough old tars, who usually congregate about the piers and rocks of Broughty Ferry. Her whole hull was painted *brilliant yellow :* hence the name, that has won her a place so conspicuous in the histories of the period.

Both vessels seemed comparatively low in the waist, for their gigantic poops and forecastles rose like wooden towers above the sea ; and to render this simile more complete, were furnished with little wooden tourelles at the inner angles. Elaborate carving and gorgeous gilding covered the hulls above the water-line ; and amid this grinned the great carthouns or forty-eight pounders ; the brass culverins and falconets, tier above tier. The port-lids were painted a flaming red ; three gigantic lanterns, with tops of polished brass, surmounted each of the poops, which had round their sterns and quarters a gaudy row of painted shields, bearing the armorial blazons of the gentlemen who served on board. Round the butt of each mast stood a rack of long Scottish spears and hand-guns, into the tubes of which were inserted the hafts of Jedwood axes.

The *Yellow Caravel* or frigate carried fifty guns; the *Margaret*, twenty. Both were ship rigged, with three masts, each of these being composed of two long tapered spars, fidded at the tops, which were clumsy and basket-like enclosures, surrounded by little embrasures, from whence the cross-bowmen, pages, and arquebussiers, could gall the enemy in security. From the carved bows, the bowsprits started up at an angle of forty-five degrees; and each had rigged thereon a lesser or fourth mast, having a great square spritsail before. At the yard-*arms* were iron hooks to grasp an enemy's rigging. All the sails were large and square. At her mainmast head, each vessel carried the flag of the admiral, a golden tree in a blue field; while at the stern waved the blue national ensign, with the great white cross of St. Andrew extending from corner to corner.

The summer sun of this fair Beltane day shone joyously on the glassy water, on the glittering hulls and snow-white canvas of these stately caravels, as they neared those green headlands which form the entrance to one of the noblest of the Scottish firths.

On the south the shore is bold and rocky; there, round its old peel, now in ruins, clustered the little village of Port-on-Craig, whose population lived by fishing and managing the boats of the ferry (the oldest in the kingdom), which plied between Fife and the opposite point, where, on a bare and unwooded promontory, stands the Royal Castle of Broughty, a strong, square tower, then surrounded by a barbican and other defences, which frowned towards the ocean on the east, defending the narrow strait from hostile fleets, and on the west, towards a dreary salt-marsh, that stretched almost from the outer walls to the gates of busy Dundee.

The dresses of the officers and crews of the ships of James III. were as remarkable as the aspect of their craft; for Robert Barton, who was sailing master or captain, and Sir David Falconer, who was captain of the arquebussiers, wore doublets or pourpoints of grey velvet, cut very short, with slit sleeves, to show the loose white shirts below: their shoulders were padded out with *mahoitres*, or large puffs; they wore tight hose of Flanders cloth, with long boots that came up to their knees. They had swords and daggers of great length and flat blue bonnets; at the end of his gold neckchain, the sailor carried a whistle; but the soldier had a cross and medal; and, as a protection from salt water, each wore an overall, or rough surcoat of Galloway frieze, trimmed with brown fur.

The sailors wore gaberdines of the same coarse material, with fustian breeches, blue bonnets, and shoes of undressed deerskin, which in those days won us the strange appellation of *rough-footed Scots*. Willie Wad, the gunner, and Archy of Anster, the boatswain, only, wore doublets of Flemish cloth, edged with silver lace, and with the royal crest, the crown and lion *sejant*, embroidered on the sleeves thereof. The arquebussiers, of whom there were a hundred and fifty on board, wore steel casquetels, with large oval ear-plates, buff coats, and broad military belts, which sustained their dirks, priming-horns, bullet-bags, and the spanners of their long-barrelled arquebusses.

Such was the general aspect of the ships and crews of his Majesty James III.

Barton and Falconer were both stout and athletic young men, but were somewhat different in aspect and bearing; for the former, who was the son of the admiral, Sir Andrew Barton, or Barnton, of that Ilk in Lothian, the wealthy Leith merchant, who had acquired a splendid fortune, and purchased a fine estate, was a florid and jovial-looking young seaman, with something of the Cavalier in his aspect; but Falconer, who had no fortune but his sword, had been introduced to the royal favour by the late Earl of Mar—the murdered favourite of James III., who knighted the youth for his valour at the siege of Dunbar in 1478, when but a stripling. Thus, though a knight, and captain of one of the king's bands, he was but the son of a poor merchant-skipper of Borrowstounness; yet he was a handsome and a stately youth; his eyes, hair, and complexion were dark, and his sharply pointed mustachios stuck fiercely off on each side of his mouth.

'A boat has shot off from Broughty,' said he, shading his eyes with his right hand; 'and two stout fellows are pulling for the ship as if their lives depended upon their speed.' —'Keep to larboard of the *Margaret*,' cried Barton to the timoneer; 'for she draws less water of course, and we require all the fairway to ourselves. Keep her away—see how the surf curls on the Gaa Sands!'

At that moment a door, which was studded with iron nails like that of an old tower, opened in the after part of the poop, and the sentinels saluted with their arquebusses as the admiral stepped on deck, and first cast his eyes aloft and then ahead.

'Keep her full, Barton,' said he, 'keep her full. So, the old Tay now opens her arms to us! and now the spires of St. Clement and St. Mary are in sight again. Gadzooks, I can see the Rock of St. Nicholas, and if I had thine eyes, Falconer, I might distinguish the great house of Stobhall.'

Falconer only twisted his mustachios, and smiled, but with a sombre aspect. 'How, Sir Andrew,' said Barton, 'you think the eyes of a mariner——'

'Are but green glass when compared to those of a lover —yea, I do,' laughed the good old admiral, as he walked to the quarter, looked over the side, and whistled to the freshening breeze; thus he failed to observe the ill-concealed gesture of impatience that escaped Sir David Falconer, and the bitter smile he exchanged with Barton.

Sir Andrew Wood of Largo, admiral of the fleet of James III.—the Scottish Nelson of his time—was originally a wealthy merchant of Leith, where in early life he was as well known in the Timber Holfe as at Sluice and the Dam. He had first been merely a merchant-skipper who fought his own way at sea, but he had done so with such signal success, and had so frequently defeated the fleets of Edward IV. of England, and of Alfonso, King of Portugal, and the pirates of many nations, that he was knighted on his own deck by James III., who never omitted an opportunity of distinguishing that rising middle class which the feudal barons viewed with aversion and contempt. James further bestowed on him the noble barony of Largo, in Fife, and he held it by the tenure that he should at all times be ready to pilot and convey the king and queen to the famous shrine of St. Adrian, on the Isle of May. His Castle of Largo, a pile of great size and strength, he built by the hands of several English, French, and Portuguese pirates whom he had captured at sea, and whose hard work he made the price of their liberty.

Thus he, who had commenced life as a poor sailor boy of Leith, found himself, before his fiftieth year, a Scottish knight and baron of Parliament; the founder of a noble family; the possessor of a stately fortress, Laird of Largo, Easter-dron, and Newbyrne; with a coat of arms, bearing two ships in full sail under an oak tree, in memory of his defending the

Castle of Dumbarton against an English fleet in 1481, and defeating another near the Bass a few years after—But we anticipate.

Now, his caravels had just returned from Sluice, where he had been on an embassy, concerning the quarrel then existing between Scotland and the Flemings.

He was rather under than over the middle height, and somewhat stout in body, with a round good-humoured face ; his complexion was fair, but burned to a dusky red by exposure for nearly forty years to the sea air in many climates ; his beard and mustachios were rather full, and the former fringed his face all round, mingling with his short-cut hair, which, though it had been dark in youth, was now becoming grey and grizzled.

On his head was a cap of maintenance, adorned by a short red feather ; he wore a rich military belt, and a jazarine jacket of the fashion of the late King James II. ; a gorget of polished steel, having escalloped edges, and a magnificent poniard, which he had received from Bartolemeo Diaz, the famous Portuguese navigator, who discovered the Cape of Good Hope. Buff-coloured hosen encased his sturdy legs, and he wore plain knee-boots of black leather, with high red heels. The only indications of naval life about him were, his silver whistle (in those days the invariable badge of rank on the ocean), with a consecrated medal, bearing the image of Clement, the patron of mariners ; and more than these, that unmistakable roll in his gait, which is peculiar to all those brave and honest souls who live by salt water.

' And so, Barton,' said he, returning from the starboard quarter ; ' there is no sign of thy father's ships in the Tay. We expected to have met them here.'—' It is indeed most strange ! ' replied Captain Barton, giving a last and anxious glance up the broad and shining river that opened now before them ; ' but assuredly I can see no more ships in the Firth.'

' Not even from the mast-head ? '—' Nay, though I could see the river as far up as the Pows of Errol.'

' Some service must have turned up in our absence, and while we lingered at the Sluice,' said Falconer. ' And if service was to be found,' said the admiral, with honest emphasis, ' my brave auld messmate, Sir Andrew Barton, would be the last man on the Scottish waters to keep his anchor down. But, ho ! gadzooks, here is the captain of

Broughty beginning to waste the king's powder.   Archy of Anster, order a yeoman of the braces to lower my pennon.'

At that moment a puff of white smoke broke over the black ramparts of Broughty, as the cannoneers saluted the admiral's well-known flag, which was thrice lowered in reply to the compliment as the vessels swept slowly past, and entered the broad bosom of that magnificent river.

The tide was now beginning to ebb, and those dangerous shoals, known as the Drummilaw Sands, were gradually appearing.

Under these heaps lie the wrecks of those Norwegian galleys which were destroyed in a storm in the days of Duncan I., after his general had defeated the soldiers of King Sueno in the Carse of Gowrie.   There they sank, and there the shifting sand rose like a bar at the river mouth above their shattered hulls.

CHAPTER II.

THE SWASHBUCKLER.

By this time, the boat which had shot off from the promontory on which the fortress is situated was alongside the *Yellow Frigate*, which was moving slowly, almost imperceptibly, up the river, and was now some hundred yards ahead of the *Margaret*, which was but a dull sailer. As the boat neared, the song chanted by the two rowers was heard on board. It was a dull and monotonous chant, the constant burden of which was :

> Hey, the canty carles o' Dysart !
> Ho, the merry lads o' Buckhaven !
> Hey, the saucy limmers o' Largo !
> Ho, the bonnie lassies o' Leven !

' 'Tis the boat of Jamie Gair,' said Barton ; ' the bravest fellow that ever dipped a line in salt water ; let a rope be hove to him from one of the larboard ports.'

This was immediately done ; the boat (which was one of those strong clinker-built fisher craft, which are peculiar to the Scottish firths) sheered alongside ; and the two fishermen who rowed it, together with a gentleman, enveloped in a scarlet mantle, who had been lounging in the stern, ascended to the maindeck, and from thence the latter climbed by Jacob's ladder to the lofty poop, where the admiral, his second in command, and the captain of the arquebussiers, were surmising who the visitor might be.

' Pshaw !' said Sir Andrew, as they all retired aft ; ' 'tis Sir Hew Borthwick !'

' But we must not forget ourselves altogether,' urged Robert Barton ; ' the man is a visitor.'

' True,' said the admiral ; ' I forget.'

' Welcome,' said Falconer, as this visitor, not in the

least daunted by the coolness of his reception, approached
them jauntily, with a tall feather nodding in his bonnet,
and an enormous sword trailing at his heels ; ' welcome on
board the *Yellow Frigate*.'

' A dog's welcome to him,' muttered Robert Barton,
under his thick mustachios ; ' for he is the falsest loon
in all broad Scotland. Dost thou know, admiral, that
'tis said, this fellow, with two brother villains in the English
pay, betrayed Berwick to the King of England ? '

The admiral nodded a brief assent.

Borthwick's appearance was somewhat forbidding. He
was past forty years of age, and had black, glossy, and
fierce-looking eyes ; a mouth like an unhealed gash ; ears
set high on his head, black teeth, and a stumpy beard.
He wore a faded doublet of figured satin with *mahoitres*,
that had once been cloth of gold ; his feet were encased
in English boots of that absurd fashion then called duck-
bill, as the toes were like beaks, and five inches long. A
purse hung at his girdle, and a chain encircled his neck ;
but rumour wickedly averred that the former was frequently
distended by pebbles, and that the second was only brass.

When he removed his bonnet, the remains of a tonsure
were visible ; for Sir Hew (the origin of whose knighthood
was somewhat obscure) had formerly been a prebend in
the Cathedral of Dunblane, but forsaking the cloister at a
time when the ecclesiastical rule was considerably relaxed,
he had espoused the more congenial occupation of sharper,
bully, jockey, and swashbuckler. Always obsequious to
the rich and noble, but supercilious to the poor and humble,
or brutal whenever he dared venture to be so, he hovered
like a vulture wherever the ambulatory Court of James III.
chanced to be residing.

' And, now that all ceremonious inquiries are over, may
I ask, *Master* Borthwick, on what devil's errand thou hast
boarded us ? ' bluntly inquired Robert Barton, who, being
less good-natured than the bluff old admiral, was at no
pains to conceal his scorn for the swashbuckler.

The dislike was quite mutual ; thus a malicious gleam
lighted the eyes of Borthwick, as he replied :

' I came on board to learn that which is of much importance to the jovial gallants about Court ; (nay, nay, Sir
David Falconer, do not laugh quite so loud if *you* please !)
whether our good friend the admiral has been successful in
his embassy to the Flemings ; for since the interdict of '66,

when our vessels could no longer trade with the ports of the Swyn, the Sluice, and the Dam, wine hath been so bad, and so dear——'

' That you must e'en content your noble self with plain usquebaugh,' interrupted the admiral, laughing outright at the idea of communicating the result of his important mission to a pitiful fellow like Borthwick. ' But canst thou tell me, sir, where are the ships of mine old messmate, Sir Andrew Barton, and where is he ? "

' The ships of Sir Andrew,' replied the swashbuckler, slowly, and with another malevolent glance at Robert Barton, ' are anchored safely by the walls of London Tower.'

' And Barton——'

' Is at the bottom of the sea, I suppose.'

' Borthwick ! ' exclaimed the admiral, in great wrath ; ' if thou hast come on board to laugh at us, by Heaven's mercy, thou shalt find none here, for I will rig thee by the earrings to the spritsail yard.'

' He dare not trifle with us,' said Robert Barton, in a thick hoarse voice, as his swarthy cheek grew pale ; ' be patient, Sir Andrew, and let us hear what he has to say. Hew Borthwick, thou art poor, and lovest gold, like thy own life-blood. I will give thee a hundred crowns if thou speakest the truth ; but I will poniard thee on this deck, sirrah, if thou liest ; so spin thy yarn, then, hand over hand ; be a man for once. 'Tis a son who asks for tidings and the safety of his father.'

' Quick ! ' added the testy admiral, stamping his foot ; ' for my arm is somewhat longer than my patience, sir.'

' Hearken,' said Borthwick, with deliberation. ' On the very day you sailed for Sluice, three months ago, the Provosts of Aberdeen and Dundee appeared before the Parliament at Stirling (where the king was biding) making doleful complaints anent the great loss their burghs had suffered from the pirates of Portugal, who had seized many of their ships and barbarously murdered the crews. In five hours thereafter Sir Andrew Barton put to sea with the *Great Lion*, the *Unicorn* and *Little Jenny*. He sailed towards the Tagus, and by a herald's mouth demanded immediate justice from the Portuguese. Alfonso V. delayed ; then stout old Barton lost his temper, and after firing a few shot at the castle of Lisbon, put to sea. Falling in with the identical ships which had committed the outrages complained of by the two Provosts, he captured and sunk them, sending the heads of their crews, daintily salted in beef barrels, to the king at Stirling. Being somewhat soft-hearted, James, as you may believe, was no way delighted by the present; but Sir Andrew, after cannonading every town on the coast of Portugal as he passed it, and after destroying every ship of that nation which he met on the high seas, bore away for Scotland. Alfonso complained to his good ally the King of England; the latter made inquiries as to the most likely route to be chosen by Sir Andrew Barton on his homeward voyage, and despatched his high-admiral, the Lord Thomas Howard, and his brother Edmund, with a strong fleet of the best ships London could produce, to the Downs, as these Southerns call that part of the north-sea——'

'I know, I know, off the south-east coast of England, on the Kentish shore,' said the admiral, stamping a foot impatiently; 'go on, man—go on!'

'After sweeping all the shores of Portugal, and after escaping a frightful tempest on Saint Swithin's day, he was descried by the English fleet, breasting gallantly up the Channel, with all sail possible on the *Lion*, and the *Jenny*, too, which bowled on alongside, like a little gadfly, all legs and arms, with sweeps out, and every stitch of canvas set.'

'Ay,' said Robert Barton, 'she was a noble little sloop, built under my father's own eye, poor man! Well.'

'The English fleet came on in the form of a half-moon, each vessel with a large white rod at her bowsprit, in sign of amity; but Sir Andrew knew the Lord Howard of old; and undaunted by his array, came on with his guns double-shotted, and all his ports open; but failing to break through, he engaged the English admiral. A desperate conflict ensued, for the *Great Lion* was hemmed in on every side, and boarded at both stem and stern. Through the joints of his armour, Sir Andrew was shot by an arrow when about to retreat by the rigging into the main-top on his decks being taken; and just then, as he was falling, a cannon shot swept both his legs away. His brave crew fought round him in a circle, and he continued to cheer and encourage them, by blowing his whistle to the last, until they were all slain, or taken and disarmed. Edmund Howard, with three ships, pursued the *Jenny*; dismasted her, and shot her sweeps away; then she struck, and the survivors of both crews—only one hundred and fifty poor seamen in all—were marched in chains through the streets of London, as a spectacle to the exulting citizens. They were then flung, like felons, in the fortress which they name the Tower; but after being instructed to implore their lives from the English king, they were dismissed; and now, *Master* Robert Barton, your father's noble ships, the *Great Lion* and the *Unicorn*, have the honour of being esteemed the best in the navy of England, and display St. George's red cross where St. Andrew's blue ensign waved before.'

'And what says *our* king to all this?' asked Barton, in a voice that was rendered hoarse and tremulous by grief and passion.

'Ay,' added the admiral, with a terrible frown; 'what says King James?'

'He despatched the Rothesay Herald to Windsor Castle, demanding redress, and threatening war.'

'And the Englishman answered——?'

'That the fate of pirates should not occasion disputes between princes.'

'*Pirates!*' exclaimed Robert Barton, whose rage at such an epithet surmounted even his grief for his father's death. Borthwick's sinister eyes were brightened by a grim smile; but mutterings of anger were heard among the officers and seamen, many of whom had crowded round to hear the news from shore; and many a swarthy brow was knit, and many a hard hand clenched: for old Andrew Barton, like his compatriot and messmate, Andrew Wood, had long been the idol of the Scottish mariners. '*Pirates!*' reiterated Robert; 'dared the English king stigmatize by such a name a gallant merchant mariner, who, by noble valour and honest industry, has won himself a fair estate and spotless reputation—a knight, who received his spurs from the hands of a queen—an admiral, second only to the Laird of Largo!'

'Second to none, my brave boy,' said Sir Andrew Wood, clapping Barton on the shoulder. 'Thy father was second to no man that sails upon the sea; but he hath found a sailor's grave, so rest him God! As for pirates—Heaven will know best whether kings or those who live by salt water are the most honest men. Every dog hath his day; and just now Lord Howard hath his. Be patient, my boy, until our new ship, the *Great Michael*, is off the stocks, and then we shall see whether the Scottish or the English cross shall float highest above the water. But tell me,

Hew Borthwick, what hath been the result of all this; for among these lubberly Flemings we learned no Scottish news?'

'You all know, sir, of course,' resumed the swashbuckler, assuming a lofty and impertinent air of consequence, as he stuck his left hand into the hilt of his sword, 'that the king's eldest son, James Duke of Rothesay, was at his birth betrothed to the Princess Cecilia of England, daughter of the late King Edward IV.; that his brother, the Duke of Albany, was to marry King's Edward's fair young sister, the Dowager Duchess of Burgundy; that our adorable Princess Margaret was to marry the English Duke of Clarence; that every one was to be married to some one else, except myself, who, in all these illustrious alliances, had been strangely overlooked; when lo! the brave Archibald, Earl of Angus, who is now Warden of the East and Middle Marches, grew weary of all this traffic with England, and the long truce to war. To square accounts with Henry VII. for barton's loss, he marched ten thousand of his vassals across the Border, and ravaged all Northumberland. So thus, for the present, have all these royal marriages ended—in fire and smoke—bloodshed and cold steel.'

'So may they ever end when our kings look for alliances elsewhere than on the Continent,' said Sir David Falconer.

The admiral paced up and down the deck, in a bitter and thoughtful mood, grieving for the loss of his oldest and earliest friend; one hand he thrust into the breast of his jazarine jacket, the other rested on the pommel of his poniard.

Relinquishing the ship to the care of others, Barton stood apart, gazing dreamily upon the shining river, with his heart full of sad and bitter thoughts, while involuntarily he clutched the mizen rattlins. His eyes were swimming; but he bit his bearded nether lip till the blood came. Suddenly he raised his eyes to a large mansion, which was looming high above others, through the summer haze in which Dundee was sleeping; and then a smile spread over his broad and thoughtful brow.

At that moment a hand was laid upon his shoulder, he turned, and encountered the ship's chaplain, Father Zuill, a Dominican.

'Relinquish these bitter thoughts, Barton,' said he; 'and come below with me to my cabin. There I will show thee an invention that will avenge thy father more surely than all the cannon in Scotland—yea, a burning-glass, that will consume a ship at the distance of a hundred leagues.'

' Right, Father Zuill,' said the admiral, who did not hear, or mistook, what the friar had said. ' God may listen to the prayers of an honest sailor, when He turns a deaf ear to those of a king.'

A few minutes after they had gone below, the friar re-appeared and ascended to the ship's waist, where Sir Hew Borthwick, notwithstanding his knighthood, was comfort-ably regaling himself with Archy of Anster and Wad the gunner on salt beef and spiced ale at the capstan-head. Zuill placed a purse in his hands, and said,

' Here are the hundred crowns which Captain Barton promised thee.'

' A hundred crowns ! ' stammered Borthwick ; ' 'tis an enormous sum, good father.' (And so it was in the time of James III.)

' But Barton hath a noble heart and a princely fortune,' said the chaplain, retiring hurriedly, for he had neither respect nor admiration for an apostate priest like Borthwick.

' Ah me ! ' muttered the latter ; ' where shall I conceal this, and what shall I do with it ? I never had such a sum before ! What a thing it is for a poor devil, who has not had even a black penny for ten days, to find himself suddenly the king of a hundred crowns ! I' faith ! ' he added, while concealing his prize, ' 'tis well that fiery birkie Barton knoweth not by *whose* information the Lord Howard knew that the Scottish ships would pass the English Downs about Saint Swithin's day.'

CHAPTER III.

BONNIE DUNDEE.

IN that age of cold iron (for indeed we cannot call it a golden age), when the potent and valiant knight, Sir James Scrimegeour, of Dudhope and Glastre, Hereditary Bearer of the Royal Standard, was Constable and Provost of the Scottish Geneva, the unexpected appearance of Sir Andrew Wood's two stately caravels created no small commotion within the burgh. No sooner was notice given from the Castle of Broughty that the Laird of Largo's ships had been seen off the Inchcape, and were now standing up the Tay, than it spread from mouth to mouth, and passed through the town like wild-fire.

Though now the shapeless façade of many a huge linen factory, and the tall outline of many a smoky chimney, over-shadow the ground that was covered by green fields and waving coppice in the days I write of, ' Bonnie Dundee ' still merits the name given it of old by the northern clansmen—*Ail-lec*—the pleasant and the beautiful.

Spread along the sandy margin of one of our noblest rivers, and nestling under the brow of a green and conical mountain, it was without walls in the year 1488 ; but at each end had a strongly embattled gate, which defended it on the east and west, while its castle, of the eleventh century, which stood on an immense mass of steep rock that overlooked the Tay, gave it additional strength, and added a military character to the naval importance which the burgh was acquiring by the shipping that usually crowded its harbour. This castle is now removed, and a broad street has been hewn through the heart of the rock which it crowned.

Its quaint thoroughfares contained then many beautiful

chapels, convents, and monasteries; and the stately hotel
of many a noble family, with turrets and turnpike-stair,
embattled porch, and armorial bearings. These towered
above the timber-fronted and arcaded houses of the Flucker-
gaitt, the Overgaitt, and other venerable streets, whose
appearance was more picturesque than their names would
import. There our kings had a mansion named the White-
hall, the vaults of which are yet remaining; as also had the
Lords Drummond, the Scrimegeours of Dudhope, the Barons
of Strathmartine, the powerful Earls of Angus, and the
great Earl of Crawford, who, for his valour at Blackness,
in the recent struggle between the king and nobility, had
been created Duke of Montrose, and Lord High Chamberlain
of Scotland. Many great barons of the Carse of Gowrie
also resided in Dundee, where Parliaments and Conventions
have been held; and which could then boast of the Mint
of King Robert I.; and the palace of St. Margaret, the
Queen of Malcolm III.; but its proudest objects were that
broad river, which from the hills of Strathfillan and Glen-
dochart rolls its mighty current to the German Sea; and its
ample harbour, crowded by the high-pooped and gaudily-
painted ships of France and Norway, Sweden and Flanders.

On the afternoon of this bright Beltane day, the return
of the great naval hero from the shores of Flanders caused
an unusual commotion and satisfaction in Dundee. The
whole inhabitants were ' on tiptoe,' and a joyous murmur
spread along the Mole when the well-known caravels of
Wood were seen to enter the river; for now, though the
admiral was a knight and baron of Parliament, who fought
under the king's pennon, he still dabbled a little in mer-
chandise, which gave him additional value in the estimation
of the thrifty burgesses and merchant traders of the town.
Thus, every ship in the harbour, from the great argosie that
traded with the Levant down to those little crayers or
lowbuilt smacks which are still peculiar to the Scottish
firths, hoisted her colours. The bells in the vast tower of
St. Mary rang a merry peal; groups of old weather-beaten
tars, wearing broad blue bonnets, gaberdines of Galloway
white, and enormous boots of rough skin, assembled on
the rock of St. Nicholas, and on the Mole, which then lay
to the westward thereof, to observe, and exercise their
nautical criticism on the aspect of the tall ships which,
before a gentle eastern breeze, were slowly coming abreast
of the town. There are bluff old fellows of this kind—

half man and half fish—who, in all ages, have haunted the piers of seaport towns, and are great, pugnacious, and, moreover, obstinate authorities, in all matters appertaining unto salt water.

Amid all the dense population so interested in the arrival of the admiral, there were none who bent their eyes more eagerly on the coming ships than five fair young girls who were seated on the bartizan of a large mansion, which (after surviving nearly all its baronial contemporaries) still stands at the corner of Fish Street, and the Flesher Row, which were then, as they are yet, the busiest part of all Dundee, and contained some of the finest examples of old Scottish street architecture.

This mansion is large and square, like a great bastel-house; and at three of its corners has broad round towers, which are strong enough to turn cannon balls. The whole superstructure rests on an arcade composed of finely-moulded elliptical arches, that spring from fluted pilasters.* Its arcade is partly sunk into the earth, and it is further diminished of its original height by a slate roof sloping down upon the walls, which of old were surmounted by a bartizan, from whence a view could be obtained of the river to the south, and that quaint old thoroughfare to the west, where two hundred years before, the schoolboy *William Wallace* slew the son of Selby, the English governor; but to the north the lofty mansions of the Nethergaitt shut out the view.

In the time of our history, this stately mansion, the stone panels of which were covered by coats-of-arms bearing a Sleuth-hound and shield, with three bars *wavy*, was the town residence of one of Scotland's most powerful peers, John, Lord Drummond, of Stobhall and that Ilk, who was Baron of Concraig, Steward of Strathearn, Privy Councillor, and had been Ambassador of James III. to England, three years before, concerning the marriage of James, the young Duke of Rothesay, to a princess of that kingdom; an embassy on which he mysteriously failed.

The five fair girls who were watching the ships' approach on this bright summer evening were his daughters, now left entirely to their own control; for Lord Drummond was with the king at Scone, and their mother, Elizabeth Lindesay,

---

* In 1808, two hundred silver coins of James VI. were found imbedded in the wall of this fabric, which is now named King James's Custom House from the use to which it was last applied.

of the princely House of Crawford, had been dead three years, and lay entombed in Dunblane.

Euphemia was twenty years of age ; her sisters, Sybilla and Margaret, were respectively nineteen and eighteen ; but Elizabeth and Beatrix were little girls, and of them contemporary history has recorded little more than the names.

Lady Euphemia was a very handsome girl, with fine hazel eyes, and glossy dark brown hair, which was entirely confined in one of those cauls of gold net by which the Scottish ladies had gladly superseded the fontanges of the preceding reign. Over this floated a white kerchief of the finest texture, edged with gold fringe. Her nose was straight ; her well-defined eyebrows expressed decision; her complexion was clear, but pale ; her bust and figure were unexceptionable, and the very elegant costume of the court of James III.—an ermined jacquette of black velvet, with spangled skirtle and yellow mantle, displayed them to the best advantage. She wore scarlet gloves from Perth, and shoes of crimson tissue. Her whole appearance was gaudy and brilliant ; while her air was lofty and reserved, for it was an age when pride of birth and station were carried to an absurd extent; but in her beauty there was something noble and majestic ; and her dark hair imparted to her skin a pure and transparent whiteness that was very striking, even in a land of fair women.

Sybilla was just a second edition of Euphemia, but with a slight rose tinge in her cheek, and a stature somewhat less. Perhaps the most charming of the three was Margaret, who was then barely eighteen, and had soft blue eyes, a pure and delicate complexion, a profusion of that beautiful and brightly-coloured hair for which our Scottish Mary was so famous ; and her face (though less regular than her elder sisters) had the sweetest expression that ever Raffaelle conjured up in the happiest moments of his artistic inspiration. There was a dash of thought or sadness (which you will) in Margaret's winnings mile that fascinated all, and she was the favourite of the proud and ambitious old lord, her father.

Lizzie and Beatie were both fair-haired and happy little girls, who inherited from their mother the blue eyes and dazzling complexions of the Lindesays of Crawford. The three elder ladies occupied tabourettes ; their two younger sisters alternately romped round the bartizan with a wiry otter terrier, or nestled among the embroidered skirts of Euphemia and Sybilla.

The rich attire of these five girls, the abundance of satin, velvet, jewels, and embroidery which they had about them, betokened wealth; while by their air, the carriage of their heads, the chastened expression of their eyes, and above all by the beautiful form and whiteness of their hands, any one might easily perceive their birth was noble; yet their father (although the heir of a long line of chieftains) was the first of his race who had worn a coronet.

' Oh, look at the caravels ! ' exclaimed little Lizzie to her sisters, who had been doing little else for the last hour ; ' look, sister Margaret,' she continued, clapping her pretty hands, ' see how one gay flag runs up after another ! Dost thou see Captain Barton yet, sister Euphemia ?—or thou, Sir David Falconer, Sybilla ? '

' How should we, if thou dost not ? ' asked Euphemia, with some asperity.—' Because you are older and bigger than me, and should of course see farther.'

' Hush, child,' replied Lady Euphemia, who had frequently found little Lizzie's powers of observation somewhat provoking ; ' but I *do* think,' she added, turning to Sybilla, ' that I can distinguish Falconer and Barton on the poop.' —' At this distance ? ' said she, shading her fine hazel eyes by a small white hand.

' Dost see a white feather waving there ? '—' Euphemia, Falconer always wears a red feather in his casquetel,' replied Lady Sybilla.

' We shall have good Father Zuill, the chaplain, visiting us ere long,' said little Lizzie, ' to read us some of his wonderful stories out of that great book, in which he writes down the miracles of St. Clement, the mariner's patron.'

Be it known, that though these charming girls could write, not one of them ever read a book in her life ; for the simple reason, that there was not then a printed book in all the realm of Scotland, where the noble art of printing was unknown till twenty-two years later—being fourteen years after it was known in England.

Here little Lizzie, after terrifying her sisters by a large wasp, which she thrust before them on her fan of feathers, threw it over the bartizan. ' 'Tis the first wasp I have seen this year,' said Euphemia ; ' thou shouldst have killed it, child, for that would have freed us from foes till the end of December.'

' Father Zuill told us not to believe in that superstition,'
said Margaret, gently.—' Yet he believes in beads that cure
blindness,' said Sybilla.

' And burning-glasses that will consume a fleet at the
horizon and further,' added Euphemia ; ' but lo you, now,
the ships are about to anchor ! '

The sun was now in the westward, and a bright flood of
light was poured along the broad and beautiful river, the
green banks of which lay steeped in purple haze. The *Yellow
Frigate* and her consort, towering above all other craft in
the harbour, were now abreast of the mansion from whence
the five daughters of the Steward of Strathearn were observing them ; and being distant only a bow-shot, the
words of command issued through the trumpet on board
of both could be distinctly heard.

There was a light wind, thus the vessels were under a
press of canvas, and formed, indeed, a noble sight, with
their snow-white sails shining above the mirror-like water,
and their many-coloured pennons streaming in the sunny
air. They elicited frequent bursts of nautical rapture from
the old Tritons who were clustered on the craig of St. Nicholas,
a sea-beaten rock, that took its name from a small chapel
dedicated to that saint, which crowned its summit.

' To your quarters, yeomen of the sheets and braces ! '
cried a clear and distinct voice from the poop of the
frigate.

' This is *his* voice—that is the voice of Barton ! ' exclaimed
Euphemia, a glow of joy replacing the paleness of her fine
face to hear again the familiar accents of her lover—even
in the hoarse words of command.

A moment after the courses were hauled up, and the
light breeze swept through the rigging ; boats were now
putting off from the shore, and the high gunnels (or *gun-
walls*) of the caravels were crowded with glad faces, and
hurried but hearty recognitions of friends were interchanged.
The seamen, clad in their grey gaberdines (each with St.
Andrew's cross sewn on the breast thereof), and their flat
blue bonnets, were seen swarming up the shrouds like
bees, and displaying themselves upon the sharply braced
yards ; and then, as if by the wave of a wizard's wand,
the great canvas sails disappeared, landsmen scarcely knew
how, as they were neatly and compactly handed and laid
in, revealing the taut black rigging and ponderous top-
castles of the frigate—nor was Sir Alexander Mathieson,

in the *Queen Margaret,* an instant behind the admiral in his manœuvres.

' Stand by the anchor, lads ! ' shouted Barton, with a voice like a trumpet.—' All clear—yare, yare, my hearts ! ' replied the boatswain, Archy of Anster, from the forecastle, while as the frigate rounded to, her great blue ensign flapped in the wind.

' Then let go ! '

A rushing sound, as the thick rope cable swept through the hawse holes, and a heavy plunge, as the ponderous iron anchor disappeared into the calm flow of the river, announced that the admiral's ship swung at her moorings in the harbour of Dundee, from whence, four months before, she had sailed for the coast of Flanders, as we have already mentioned, anent King James's dispute with the merchants of the Sluice and Dam.

At that time no man was so popular in Scotland as Sir Andrew Wood, unless we except Sir Andrew Barton ; but now he was gone to his long home, and the people looked to his old messmate to avenge him. Three loud cheers were given from the shore as the frigates came to anchor ; and from aloft and alow their crews responded, with the deep and hearty shout that can only come from the throats of those who are incessantly combating with the waves and winds.

' See, dear Lizzie,' said Margaret, who, though usually silent and languid, had partaken of the excitement and bustle caused by the admiral's arrival, ' a barge is leaving the side of the *Yellow Frigate.*'

' Oh, the bonnie little barge ! " exclaimed Beatrix, dancing about her, and comparing the sixteen-oared boat to the towering caravel.

' Two gentlemen, clad in grey doublets, are in it.'

' Margaret, 'tis Barton and Falconer—thou seest *his* red feather now, Sybilla,' said Euphemia, as she flushed again with pleasure.

' They will bring us pretty, pretty presents, will they not ? ' said the younger girls, clapping their hands.

' Father Zuill promised you each a box of sweetmeats,' said Margaret, with one of her sad kind smiles.—' Captain Barton promised me a silver collar from Bruges,' said little Elizabeth.—' And David Falconer promised *me* a carcanet of pearls, with a hood and veil,' added Beatrix, who was a year younger.

' Thou—child ? ' said Euphemia ; ' and what would *you* do with a carcanet, a hood and veil ? '

' Wear them at mass, and in the Highgaitt, to be sure,' retorted the little dame, testily ; ' no one fell in love with you, sister Euphemia, till you exchanged the coif for a hood and veil.'

' Nor with Sybilla, either,' added Beatrix, making common cause against the elders ; ' and as for poor sister Margaret, no one has loved her yet.'

Lady Margaret grew ghastly pale, and turned away. Sybilla, who did not perceive this emotion, laughed ; but Euphemia, who had now the place of mother over them all, said gravely,

' You are overforward, imps. Eight years hence it will be time enough for Lizzie, and for you, Beatie, to think of lovers, and talk of hoods and veils. Marry come up ! child, thou canst not spin yet ! But see—Barton's boat hath reached the Rock of St. Nicholas.'

' Alas ! ' said Margaret, sadly, ' what evil tidings we have to give him of his father's fate.'

As the two friends sprang ashore, the old seamen who were clustered by the chapel wall all doffed their bonnets, and murmured a hearty welcome.

The rock was the ancient landing-place, and lay to the westward of the old harbour. It was there that David, Crown Prince of Scotland, landed on his return from the Crusades ; and there that, two hundred years after, the good Sir James Douglas embarked for Jerusalem, with the heart of Robert Bruce ; for ' bonnie Dundee ' is a place of many old and many stirring memories.

' They are coming this way,' said Sybilla, in a flutter ; ' we must hasten to receive them.'—' But lo !—what scurvy companion do they bring with them ? ' added the haughty Euphemia.—' Sir Hew Borthwick,' said Lizzie, ' who cheated our butler at dice, and stole the gateward's bugle.'

' *Sir !*—how can you thus pollute the title of knighthood ? ' asked the eldest sister.—' But do not the people call him so ? ' said Margaret.

' He is a mansworn priest,' continued Euphemia, ' and I marvel that the Lord Bishop of Dunblane permits him to be at liberty. Was not Father Arbuckle built up in the gable of Gilston kirk for the same crime—abandoning his cloister ? '

' Oh, frightful ! ' said the gentle Margaret, with a shudder ;

' 'tis so unlike *you*, dear Effie, to urge such an expiation ; moreover, I do not believe it.'

' Not believe !' repeated Euphemia, as they all descended from the bartizan by a turret stair ; ' has not our father told us that he saw it done—yea, and guarded the kirk with the lances of the stewardry for ten days ; and there, in the wall, the bones of the friar, poor man ! are yet remaining. But, hark ! there are our visitors.'

At that moment Sir David Falconer blew the copper horn which hung at the tirling-pin of the house door.

CHAPTER IV.

THE SISTERS.

In an apartment which had three large windows overlooking the river, the ladies seated themselves in a group to await their visitors; and two, at least, were flushed and palpitating, for they expected acknowledged lovers. The younger girls were all expectation too, anticipating certain gifts or presents; Margaret alone was, as usual, pale, calm, and quiet—even sad.

The lofty walls of the chamber were hung with pale brown leather, stamped with rich golden figures; the ceiling was covered with grotesque gilding, and upon every available place appeared the sleuth-hound of the Drummonds, with their motto, *Gang warily.* A magnificent Dutch buffet, having bulbous shapen legs, and deep recesses, stood at one end, and was surmounted by a large hound in delft ware; a gift by which Barton, whose father brought it from Flanders, first made an impression on the old lord's heart. The chairs were of oak, with crimson cushions; but the floor had no other carpet than a matting of plaited straw. There was a high stone mantelpiece covered with carving; an iron grate, the enormous basket of which (the season being summer) was filled with sea-shells, and on each side was a sculptured niche or armbre, so common in old Scottish houses of that age.

'Heaven be praised, our anchor hath again hold of Scottish ground!' said Falconer, as a page conducted him and Barton upstairs.

'How so—thou art either more of a lover or less of a sailor than I, David?'—'Nay, I am not less of a lover, but more of a soldier, perhaps,' replied the arquebussier, 'or more of a landlubber, if you will.'

'Now then, little marmoset,' said Barton, who perceived the page listening, 'heave ahead, if you please.'

The captain of the caravel and his companion were attired just as we have seen them on board, save that the latter had adopted an embossed helmet, with a plume of feathers, a bright gorget, and long steel gloves. He looked very handsome, gay, and glittering; but honest Barton, in whose heart the recent tidings he had received sank deep, looked grave and grim, though a sad smile spread over his brown and weatherbeaten face, as he took both Lady Euphemia's hands in his, and greeted all her sisters with warmth of heart, though perhaps with less of formal courtesy than Falconer, who had served in the King's Guard, and was one of those fine handsome fellows whom all women unite in admiring; for he had a superb but native and inimitable air. While his friend, inured to a life of hardship on the ocean, at a time when the infancy of science trebled its dangers, was perhaps less easy, he was not a whit less noble in manner or aspect; and the name and wealth he inherited from his gallant father, the fighting merchant-mariner of Leith, had gained him a place among those proud barons, who, but for the valour by which old Andrew Barton won his spurs, would heartily have despised the magnificent fortune and estate acquired by his probity and care.

Poor Falconer was wont to say, that all *his* father had left him consisted of a rusty coat of mail, two old swords, and four or five cordial hatreds, or feuds, to settle; all of which he had settled honestly and manfully, twice over, on the street, or the highway, wherever and whenever he chanced to meet with the creditors; and now he owed no man either a blow or a bodle.

'Welcome, Robert Barton, my dream is read,' said Euphemia, rising up with a bright expression in her beautiful eyes.

'And what was thy dream, dearest Effie?' he asked in a soft voice.—' 'Tis of an old saw, told me by Jamie Gair.'

'The fisherman of Broughty—he boarded us as we passed the auld craig—but what of his saw?'

> 'To dream of a ship sailing on the blue sea
> Is a sign of bright joy to thy kindred and thee;
> But to dream of a ship that lies bulged on the strand
> Is a sign that dark sorrow is almost at hand.

Now last night, Robert, I dreamt of thy yellow caravel

sailing on the sea (said I not so, Margaret ?) ; and lo, thou
art here ! '

' And my friend Falconer, too ? '

' He is, like thee, most welcome,' said Lady Euphemia,
offering her pretty hand, which Falconer timidly raised
to his lip, and then approached Sybilla ; but on receiving
from her a significant glance, full of prudence and love,
he sighed, bowed and remained aloof ; for the passion of
these two was as yet secret, or merely a matter of jest with
some, and of speculation with others.

Falconer, brave to a fault, was poor, and had only his
spurs and his sword. He knew this but too well, and
Sybilla did not forget it. He had long concealed his passion ;
but she had soon divined it ; and now they treasured up a
secret thought in the depth of their hearts, like a dream that
might never be realized ; for Lord Drummond was ambitious,
and had many a time sworn, that at least ' four of his daughters should *die countesses.*' Thus Sybilla and Falconer had
found their best resort was patience or hope.

The eldest sister was a happy, rich, and beautiful *fiancée ;*
Sybilla was a timid girl, loved by one who dared not avow
his passion to her family ; and Lady Margaret was sad
and melancholy, loved, the people said, by many for her
goodness and gentleness, but by none for her beauty—save
one, of whom more anon. After the first compliments,
inquiries, and congratulations were over—

' Ah ! I had almost forgotten thee, little one,' said Barton,
kissing the pretty Lizzie, whom he now observed hovering
about him ; ' but here is thy promised necklace.'—' Oh,
joy ! ' said the girl, skipping among her sisters, on receiving
a beautiful collar of Bruges silver, with a pendant of opals ;
' now I am not less than my cousin Lady Egidia Crawford, who is so proud because *her* mother was created a
duchess.'

' By my faith, Barton ! ' said Falconer, ' thou givest such
magnificent presents to Lady Lizzie, that to keep Beatie's
favour I shall be a ruined dyvour.'—' With all the rings and
blessed medals these children have got, they might open a
trinket shop,' said Sybilla.

' And hast thou nothing for me ? ' asked Beatie.—' I
have the most beautiful veil that the nuns of Sluice could
work ; but unfortunately it is still on board the frigate.
To-morrow I shall remember it better than I did in the
hurry of to-day.'

' To-morrow the king arrives,' said Barton.—' Nay—we heard nothing of it,' observed Sybilla.

' Sir Hew Borthwick, or the man so-called, informed us that the king was coming hither from Stirling on the morrow with the young Duke of Rothesay, and all the court.'

Lady Margaret's colour heightened at this intelligence, and to conceal her emotion she hastened to say, ' If Borthwick said so, it must be true, for he is one who is never far from those parasites and flatterers who crowd the court at present.'

' Moreover, he told us that certain ambassadors from France, who are now at the constable's house in the Carse, would be presented soon after.'

' And on what mission have they come ? ' asked Sybilla.

' I know not ; but our right honourable informant, the worthy swashbuckler, hinted—and really this fellow often knows matters which are far above his position—that they had come anent some royal marriage, as the young prince's proposed alliance with the House of England has been so fortunately broken off since my poor father's battle in the English Channel.'

Margaret trembled so excessively as Barton said this, that had the four lovers been less occupied with each other than they were, and had the children not been engaged with the silver collar, some of them must have observed her singular emotion, which however fortunately passed unnoticed.

Restrained by the presence of others, the conversation of Sybilla and Falconer (who, had the world been his, would have given it for liberty to press her to his breast) was confined to the merest commonplace ; but Robert Barton and Euphemia, who, by Lord Drummond having consented that their marriage should take place in autumn, were under very different circumstances, had retired somewhat apart. She had passed her arm through his, and clasping her hands upon it, was looking up fondly in his sunburned face, and was telling him in a low and earnest voice of all she had learned concerning his father's death off the English coast ; how she had prayed for him, and had masses said for his soul ; and with an air, in which sternness, bitterness, and tenderness were curiously mingled, the heir of Sir Andrew Barton listened to her ; for his thoughts hovered between the bright eyes and soft accents of the fair girl by his side and the carnage of that day's battle in the

Kentish Downs, when he would have given the best ten years of his life to have stood for an hour on his father's deck. In these thoughts, and in those of future vengeance, he almost forgot that this untimely event (though it put him in possession of a princely fortune, an estate in Lothian, and a mansion like a baronial castle in Leith) would necessarily delay his marriage with Lady Euphemia for many months to come.

' How happy thou art to be rich, Robert,' said Falconer, as they descended to the street, after lingering long and bidding the ladies adieu.

' Wealth does not always bring happiness, David,' replied the seaman ; ' and just now I am miserable, when I reflect on how my brave old father, and so many fine fellows, have been flung overboard, to feed the hungry serpent of the sea.'

' The ocean is wide,' replied Sir David ; ' but thou mayst meet the Lord Howard on it yet.'—' And he is not the man to avoid me.'

' I would give my right hand to be, like thee, Lord Drummond's friend,' said Falconer bitterly, and still thinking of Sybilla.

' Without thy starboard fin, David, thou wouldst be of little use in this world ; and mayst yet be the Lord Drummond's friend without so great a sacrifice ; besides, I can foresee, that between intrigues, mayhap invasion from abroad, and domestic rebellion, the loyal and the good in Scotland will ere long require all their hands to keep their heads on their shoulders.'

' Dost thou think so ?' asked the arquebussier, with kindling eyes.

' Yea—a child that knoweth neither how to pass a gasket or knot a reef point might see it.'

And though no prophet, but only a blunt and plain-speaking seaman, Robert Barton spoke of coming events with more foresight and acuteness than he was perhaps aware of possessing.

CHAPTER V.

JAMES III.

NEXT day, the second of August, the sun rose above Dundee in the same unclouded splendour, and again the green hills, the ancient burgh, with its spires and castle, the bannered ships, and all the wide panorama of the Tay, were mirrored in its clear and waveless depths.

Bells were tolling merrily in the tall spire of the great church, then designated the Kirk of the Blessed Virgin Mary in the Fields, as it stood without the portes of the burgh; and a wreath of those sacred lilies which still form the armorial bearing of Dundee encircled the now mouldering statue of our Lady, which, with the little infant Jesus in her arms, has survived the storms of seven centuries and the rough hands of the Scottish Iconoclasts, and still adorns the western gallery of that stupendous tower which overlooks the '*Gift of God.*'

Almost drowning the peals that jangled from the belfries of the Grey Franciscans in the Howff, the Dominicans in the Friars Vennel, the Mathurins, and the nuns of St. Clare, the great bell of St. Mary (which was rent when too joyous a peal was rung for Prince Charles, in 1745) rolled a flood of iron sound above the town, and summoned all the burgesses to meet a monarch whom the people loved, but whom the nobles hated—James III.—who was now approaching by the road from Perth.

Beyond the western porte, and all the streets that led thereto, this road was crowded by the populace; and there might be seen the merchants and burgesses, clad in plain broadcloth, with steel-hilted poniards in their girdles. By law, neither they nor their wives could wear scarlet, silk, or furring, and the females of their families were restricted to short curches with little hoods, after the Flemish fashion;

and the ladies of poor gentlemen, whose property was under forty pounds, had to content them with the same. There, too, were officials of the church, doctors, and gentlemen (having two hundred marks per annum) in cloaks of scarlet, laced and furred; and labourers, who had exchanged their work-dresses of grey frieze and Galloway white for the holiday attire of red and green.

From the eight stone gurgoyles of the market-cross, which, as usual in Scotland, was surmounted by a tall octagonal column, bearing the unicorn *sejant*, resting its forepaws on the imperial scutcheon, wine was flowing, and a noisy contest waging among the young *gamins*, seamen, and others, who struggled and thrust each other aside, not always with good humour, to fill their quaighs, cups, and luggies with the generous Rhenish and claret, which gushed forth alternately from the mouths of the dragons and wyverns; but order was stringently kept by the Constable of Dundee, Sir James of Dudhope, who had brought into the burgh five hundred of his troopers from the Howe of Angus—all sturdy yeomen, who wore black iron casquetels, with oreillets over the cheeks and spikes on the top, and were armed with that deadly weapon the ghisarma, which had been but recently introduced.

Escorted by a numerous retinue of well armed serving men, all of whom had *the sleuthhound* embroidered on the sleeves of their gaberdines, and were accoutred with jacks and bonnets of steel, two-handed swords, and wooden targets covered with threefold hide, the daughters of Lord Drummond, with their aunt the Duchess of Montrose, the Lady of Strathmartine, and many other noble dames from the Carse of Gowrie, were grouped together on horseback, awaiting the king. Robert Barton, Sir David Falconer, and other gentlemen, attended them on foot, and held their bridles, having assigned their own horses to the care of the pages, who carried their swords and helmets,—for a page was at that time indispensable to every gentleman of pretensions.

Conspicuous amid all was the old Duchess of Montrose, a tall and noble-looking matron, whose height on horseback when her stupendous coif was added, became almost startling; for, like old people generally, ' being behind her age,' she still retained one of those enormous head-dresses which our ladies had copied from the French, and which had been introduced by Isabel of Bavaria, consort of Charles VI., who had to enlarge all the doors in the Palace of Vincennes after the arrival of his bride.

Nor must we forget that redoubtable Knight of the Post and Chevalier d'Industrie, Sir Hew Borthwick, who loitered near, bowing and smiling to people who knew him not, or knowing, who disdained him. After completely failing to attract the attention of Falconer or Barton, he swaggered through the crowd, clinking a pair of enormous brass spurs, and exhibiting a new scarlet cloak, which he 'ad procured by the recent replenishing of his exchequer ; he tilted up the tail of this by his long sword, pointed his mustachios, and from time to time turned up his eyes complacently, to watch the nodding of an absurdly long feather that drooped from his head-dress ; and the latter being a velvet hat, like that of an Englishman, the people murmured, and made angry observations about it.

The undisguised aversion and fear with which the crowd made way for him wherever he went were a source of satisfaction to this barefaced charlatan, of whom we shall hear more than enough, perhaps, in time to come. He found ample occupation in observing the brilliant group which surrounded Margaret Carmichael of Meadowflat, the Duchess of Montrose, and in surveying the brilliant colours of those splendid costumes which exhibited all the frippery, extravagance and coxcombry of the time of James III. Gold and jewels flashed on everything, from the ladies' fair fingers to the bridles of their palfreys ; but by far the greatest number of diamonds and pearls glittered on the long stomachers and among the braided hair of Lord Drummond's three beautiful daughters.

Finding himself bluntly repulsed by Captain Barton and the arquebussier, Borthwick had actually the assurance to address the admiral, who came through the archway on horseback, surrounded by his barge's crew, who had no other weapons than their poniards and boat-stretchers ; but a determined and hardy-looking old bodyguard they were, with swarthy visages, long grisly beards, and broad blue bonnets.

' Your humble servant, Sir Andrew,' said the impudent swashbuckler, elbowing a passage through them ; ' I dare say the folks will marvel at this—a knight like me on foot, and thou, a seaman, on horseback.'

' And how came this to pass, Sir Hew ? ' asked the admiral, who, being older, had, perhaps, more complaisance or less pride than Barton or Falconer. 'My favourite horse was shod in the quick by a villanous smith, who is now dreeing the reward of his carelessness in the jougs at the burgh cross.'

'I congratulate you on your good fortune,' said the admiral, endeavouring to pass; 'by your scarlet cloak I perceive——'—'That I have now more per annum than the Apparel Act requires: so far right, Sir Andrew; but, alas! an ancestor of mine lost a noble estate by one act of indiscretion.'

'Ah! How?'—'By eating an apple,' replied Borthwick, with one of his hideous grins; 'but so thou art come hither among *us* courtiers, admiral, to steer by the royal smiles.'

'The sailor's best compass is his conscience, messmate, and by that I steer,' retorted Wood, as he gave a peculiar wink to his coxswain; then the Knight of the Post was gently put aside by the barge's crew, and the old admiral alighted on foot by the side of the Duchess of Montrose.

Around this noble matron, who was then the second lady in the realm, the conversation was very animated; and, notwithstanding the awful exclusiveness with which the Scottish noblesse in those days chose to hedge themselves about, it was evident that the venerable Wood, the gallant Barton, and the handsome arquebussier, were three centres of attraction.

Margaret Drummond, still sad, pale, and thoughtful, paid little attention to the buzz and bustle around her; she gazed anxiously at the vista of the road which stretched westward past the convent of St. Mary Magdalene and the Tower of Blackness; a page held her bridle; but the horses of her sisters were each held by their lovers, with whom they were conversing in low and earnest tones. Falconer spoke little, yet he was, perhaps, the happiest man in Dundee, for now he was by the side of Sybilla, and could converse with her untrammelled by the observation of others; and as the only matron who could control her actions knew neither of his hopes (or, as she would have termed it, his presumption), many little attentions were unheeded or unseen.

A cloud of dust that rolled along the road announced the approach of the king, and soon a troop of nearly a hundred and fifty mounted men was seen approaching at a rapid trot. This cavalcade was well mounted on horses of a breed which at that time was famous, a baron of

Corstorphine having improved the high Lanarkshire horses by the introduction of some sturdy Flemish mares ; thus, for hacks and chargers, these large animals were esteemed as superior to any of the four distinct breeds of horses belonging to the country. All their steeds were brilliantly caparisoned with rich saddles, housings, and bridles, covered with fringes and tassels of silk and gold embroidery, gilded ornaments, and armorial bearings.

On approaching the west porte of Dundee, the king and his attendants slackened their speed to a walk, but their horses continued tossing their proud heads and flinging the white foam from side to side. The monarch was unaccompanied by his queen, Margaret of Denmark and Norway, who had departed, with many of her ladies, on a pilgrimage to the famous shrine of St. Duthac, in Ross, then esteemed a long and arduous journey.

James III., a tall, handsome, and athletic man, was then in his thirty-fourth year ; his complexion was of that deep brown tint which is not usual to the islanders of Britain, and his hair was black and curly. When in repose, his mouth expressed the utmost sweetness of expression, but there were times when it curled with bitterness and suppressed passion. His beard was closely trimmed ; his air was soldier-like ; his manner dignified, at one time cold and reserved, but at others sad, even to despondency, for he was the most unhappy of kings.

On this day he wore a doublet of rose-coloured satin, embroidered with damask gold, cut and lined with rose-coloured sarcenet, and fastened by twenty-four little gold buttons. Over this he had a riding surtout of green velvet, laced. On his dark locks he wore a black velvet bonnet, with an embroidered band, a St. Andrew's cross, and white plume ; he had long riding-boots with embroidered velvet gambadoes and gold spurs.

James, the young Duke of Rothesay, then in his seventeenth year, also tall, and a very handsome youth, inherited his father's dark eyes and hair ; his straight nose, with its fine nostril, and his mouth, which was like a woman's, but over it a dark mustachio was sprouting. The dresses of the king, the prince, and all their suite, were nearly alike in fashion, colours, and richness, unless we except the Lord High Treasurer, Sir William Knollis, one of the most upright and valiant men of the age, who, as Lord of St. John of Jerusalem, and preceptor of the religious knights of Torphichen, wore the black dress and eight-pointed cross of Rhodez. Around this ill-fated king were many who were his friends, but many more who were his most bitter enemies, and whose loyalty or treason will all be revealed in future chapters; to wit, Sir James Shaw of Sauchie, who had been made governor of Stirling because his father had been slain by a cannon shot at the siege of Dunbar; Evandale, the Lord High Chancellor; Sir Patrick Gray of Kyneff; the Lord Drummond; his brother, Sir Walter, who was Dean of Dunblane and Lord Clerk Register; the Duke of Montrose, who was Master of the Household and Great Chamberlain of Scotland; Lord Lindesay of the Byres, and Archibald, *the great Earl* of Angus, a noble then in his thirtieth year—one whose fierce and restless ambition, indomitable pride, and vast feudal power, made him a terror to the good king on the one hand, and to the oppressed people on the other. Then, he was popularly known by the sobriquet of Bell-the-Cat, from the quaint parable spoken by him at Lauder Bridge in that memorable raid when he hanged every favourite of James III.; for, in his eyes, Robert Cochrane, the eminent architect, was but a stone-cutter; Sir William Rogers, who composed many fine airs, but a fiddler; Leonard, the engineer, was but a smith; and Torphichen, the fencing-master, a miserable fletcher—men who disgraced James III. by the preference which he showed for them over a proud, barbarous, and unlettered nobility, whom, like his father, he resolved to spare no pains to curb and to humble.   Vain thought !

This Lord of Tantallon, who was Warden of the East and Middle Marches, and a chieftain of the powerful House of Douglas, overshadowed even the throne by his power; for the King of Scotland was but a laird in comparison to the great military nobles.   Angus was dark and swarthy as a Spaniard; his hair and beard were sable, his eyes black and sparkling, with a keen, restless, and imperious expression.   Like his father—that valiant earl, who with ten thousand horse covered the retreat of M. de Brissac and the French troops from Alnwick in 1461—he constantly wore armour, and was now riding beside the Earl of Erroll, Lord High Constable of the kingdom, who had come with a few lances from the Carse of Gowrie, to escort the sovereign to Dundee.

As this brilliant and illustrious cavalcade passed through the old moss-grown and smoke-encrusted archway which

then closed the end of the principal street, a general uncovering of heads took place, and loud and reiterated cheers
greeted James, who was beloved by the people, especially
in the towns where there was now rising a wealthy middle
class, who had no sympathy with, and who owed no fealty
to, the great barons, but were rather at enmity with them.
He who cheered most lustily, in forcing a passage through
the gate with the courtiers, was the soi-disant Sir Hew
Borthwick, who endeavoured to place himself as near to
the king or prince as Lord Erroll's lances would permit.

On passing Sir Patrick Gray, he exchanged a glance of
intelligence. '*To-night*,' said he, in a whisper.

'*Where?*' asked the Knight of Kyneff. '*On the beach
near Broughty*,' replied Borthwick. And here the crowd
pressed between them.

The king, still young and handsome, doffed his bonnet
to the tall duchess and her fair companions, and the young
heir of Scotland, whose spirited horse curveted past them,
bowed again and again to his saddle; and though he looked
anxiously amid all that glittering group for one beloved
face, by some fatality he never observed it, and caprioled
through the archway by his father's side.

Margaret Drummond, the foremost of the group, and
almost unconscious of where she was, had watched the
approaching party in silence with a beating heart. The
shadow of her hood and veil concealed her pallor and the
sad and anxious expression of her fine blue eyes. Amid
those hundred horsemen and more who swept up to the
gate, she had soon distinguished Rothesay, and held her
very breath with joy as he passed, but alas! without
observing her; and her young heart sank as he did so;
for though none knew it, save one old priest and two other
persons, the crown prince of Scotland was her wedded
husband—wedded at the altar of St. Blane with all the
solemnity of the ancient faith—but in secret.

Barton and Falconer were now compelled to leave the
ladies, and with many other gentlemen sprang on horseback,
to accompany the admiral, who had now joined the royal
cavalcade.

The king received the fine old man with unfeigned expressions of affection and joy; for grief soon discovers true
sympathy, and misfortune readily discerns the difference
between flattery and devotion: thus James III. always
felt stronger and more confident when such men as Sir

Andrew Wood, or Lindesay and Montrose, were by his side;
but such nobles as Angus and Lord Drummond were his
horror and aversion.

'There are times, my faithful friend,' said he to Wood,
as their train fell back a little on entering the narrow Nethergaitt, ' when I envy thee and thy honest hearts the free
and happy life they lead upon the open sea.'

'Yet a sailor's life hath its troubles and its crosses too—
witness the fate of Barton, my gude auld messmate.'

'Of that, and of thy Flemish mission, we will talk at
another time,' replied the king; ' let us not mar the happiness I feel at seeing thee, honest Wood, the dearest and most
faithful of my people, by allusions to such cold and bitter
subjects.'

'God and St. Andrew bless your Majesty!' said the admiral, whose eyes and heart overflowed as he spoke. ' I
have never done aught more than my duty to Scotland
and my king, as man and boy, for forty years, since first
I trod a deck—a puir sailor laddie, in the *Peggie* of Pittenweem. I would run my head into a cannon's mouth, if
by doing so I could serve your Majesty; and that, I believe,
is mair than half of these gay galliards ahead and astern
of us would do; natheless their long pedigrees and their
dainty doublets, with white lace knuckle-dabbers at the
wrists.'

'Some day I shall go to sea with thee, Wood,' said King
James, with a melancholy smile; ' for by the soul of Bruce!
I begin to tire of this trade of kingcraft.'

'I like the land as little as a fish; but should a day of
foul weather ever come, when your Majesty is safer on
salt water than on Scottish earth,' said the admiral, more
than divining the secret thoughts of the king; ' remember,
there is a ship's company of five hundred good men and
true, under the flag of the *Yellow Frigate*, every man of
whom hath a seaman's hand and a seaman's heart, solid
as a pumpbolt, and not like a perfumed and painted
courtier's, hollow as a leather bottle, or rotten like an old
pumpsucker. Gadzooks! I would like to see a few of these
braw gallants drifting under close-reefed topsails, with a
wind blowing hard from the east, and the craigs of Dun-
nottar on their lee!'

The king sighed, and allowed the reins of his horse to
drop upon its neck. 'Your Majesty is troubled,' resumed
the honest seaman; ' but if any of these dogfish barons

have been at their auld work, just let me ken, and, by all
the serpents in the sea! they shall feel the weight of
my two-handed sword, or I shall pipe away my barge's
crew with their boat-stretchers, and they will soon clear
the causeway of every lord and loon in Dundee.'

The king laughed. 'Thou art indeed an honest heart,'
said he; for he found that they could converse freely, as
the incessant exclamations of the people, as they pressed
along the crowded streets, concealed their conversation
from such jealous listeners as Angus and Drummond.
'A process so summary might destroy thee, admiral,
and thy barge men too. But indeed, Sir Andrew, I am
sick of this ferocious loyalty (if I may so term it) by which
the nobles encircle me like a wall of iron. Though short,
my life has been a long and dreary labyrinth of intrigue
and civil war, of crafty councils and infernal suggestions—
a struggle between a tyrannical feudal peerage and a gallant
people, who would, and by St. Giles's bones, shall yet, be
free! The nation has placed upon my brow a crown of
gold; but the nobles have engirt my heart by a band of
burning steel!'

As the king spoke in this figurative language, he glanced
about him uneasily, almost timidly, and encountered the
dark and stern visage of Angus, and the proud, inquiring
eyes of Drummond; but they had not heard him, or, having
done so, did not comprehend.

'I speak figuratively, admiral,' said he; 'but do you
understand me?'

'Perfectly, your Majesty,' stammered Wood, as with
some perplexity he rubbed his grizzly beard; 'but come,
come, Sir Hew,' he added, on perceiving that worthy close
to them; ''ware ship—give us sea-room here, if it please
ye.'

At that moment the report of cannon on the river announced that the *Yellow Frigate* and her consort were firing
salutes, as the king and his train halted at the old palace
of St. Margaret, where the Duke of Montrose, as Master
of the Royal Household, and the Constable of Dundee,
had already alighted, and were on foot to receive him.

CHAPTER VI.

THE PALACE OF ST. MARGARET.

THIS venerable royal residence was situated at the head of a narrow street, opening off the great thoroughfare, then called St. Margaret's Close, though by mistake the civic authorities have now given that name to another alley in the Nethergaitt, where stood an ancient chapel, dedicated to the Saxon Queen-Consort of Malcolm III., who had her dowry lands in the adjacent Howe of Angus.

By her numerous virtues, the sister of Edgar Atheling was so endeared to the Scottish people, that every spot connected with her presence is still remembered; thus her name was long and indissolubly connected with this little palace at Dundee. It was a gloomy and massive building, which stood within a court or cloister, and had over the central door, and all the windows, deep and low-browed arches, covered with a profusion of catsheads and grotesque sculpture. These arches sprang from short, round and massive pillars, having escalloped capitals and zigzag mouldings. The deeply recessed windows were all barred with iron, glazed with lozenged panes, painted with coats of arms and brilliant devices, designed by Robert Cochrane, the royal architect, an artist of great taste and talent—one of the murdered favourites of the king, who in his foolish generosity had created him general of artillery and Earl of Mar.

It was in this palace that in the year 1209, Alan, Lord of Galloway and Constable of Scotland, espoused Margaret, niece of King William the Lion.

Soon after the entrance of James III. the bells ceased to toll, and the ship guns ceased firing; the wine and ale still poured at intervals from the stone spouts of the Cross; but the acclamations died away in the Nethergaitt, and soon a stillness reigned around the small but crowded residence of the king. A stranger could not have imagined that a monarch and a court were there—so ominous was the silence in that grim old Scottish palace; for James mourned over the caprices of his nobles and the insults he had endured from them, during his nine months' captivity in the Castle of Edinburgh, from which he was not released until Richard III. of England interfered in his behalf, at the head of 30,000 men. Young Rothesay mourned over domestic troubles, and a secret marriage which he dared not yet avow; while a crowd of cunning favourites on one hand, and of ambitious nobles on the other, watched like lynxes for the turning of any scale that would prove of advantage to themselves.

Discontent was apparent everywhere in and about the court of James III. It was visible in the face of the king, for the recent slaughter of his courtiers by Angus and others, against whom he was nursing secret plans of vengeance; it was visible in the stern eyes of the noblesse, who, by a royal edict, had been desired to forbear wearing swords within the royal precincts—an order which they observed by arming themselves to the teeth, and doubling the number of their mail-clad followers; it was visible in the faces of the merchants, *anent* the twenty-one years' quarrel with Flanders; and in the faces of the people, because they saw a disastrous struggle approaching between the feudal nobles and themselves—a struggle which the field of battle alone would decide for their future good or evil.

That evening the king gave a banquet to his false courtiers, and to Admiral Wood, to Barton, and Falconer. Lord Drummond was grand carver, Angus grand cupbearer, and the Laird of Kyneff grand sewer, or *asseour;* but Rothesay stole at an early period from the table, and reached his own apartments unperceived. There he exchanged dresses with his faithful friend, Lord Lindesay of the Byres; and putting on a mask, with a shirt of mail of the finest texture under his doublet, issued by a private gate into the main street, just as the last shadows of the mountain that overhangs Dundee were fading away upon the river—or rather becoming blended with the general obscurity of the summer gloaming.

The young prince wore a casquetel, and had his sword and dagger under the scarlet cloak of Lord Lindesay, for whom he was mistaken by the pages, yeomen, and archers, in the neighbourhood of the palace, as he passed into the burgh.

'Oho, my merry masquer!' said Sir Hew Borthwick, who had been loitering near the king's residence for the livelong day, in the hope of finding some one to drink or play with him, or from whom to pick up any stray intelligence concerning the admiral's embassy to Flanders, and the errand of those envoys who were now at the house of the Provost in the Howe. 'By the Holy Kirk! I should know that dainty red cloak; now, were those locks black instead of brown, and had that casquetel a feather, and those boots silver spurs instead of gold, I would say this gallant was my good friend Lord Lindesay of the Byres, and *not* the young Duke of Rothesay. But to the proof! On my honour, I'll follow him; and if he is bent on the errand I suppose, this night may bring another thousand of King Henry's English pounds to my purse.' Walking very quick after the young prince, who was carefully keeping himself under the shadows of the darkest and least frequented streets, the spy cried aloud,

'Soho! sir—I crave pardon; but can you tell me what's o'clock?'

Annoyed by this impertinent interruption, the prince paused and laid a hand on his sword; but being anxious to avoid a brawl, turned and walked on at a quicker pace. Borthwick, who was now close at his heels, came abreast of him just at the corner of Fish Street, which was then quite dark and destitute of lamps.

'Sir—thou with the mask,' continued Borthwick; 'when I ask questions I expect to receive replies. Will you please to give me one?'

'*There*, blockhead!' retorted the prince, furiously, as he gave him a blow with his clenched hand which levelled the intruder in the kennel; and as it was dealt skilfully, right under the left ear, it was a full minute before he recovered.

Then, from the muddy street, Borthwick rose with a heart full of rage and vengeance. His first thought was of his soiled cloak; his second of something else.

''Twas the prince's voice!' said he; 'I was right! Oho!—let me watch, and watch well. How fortunate! the more so as I keep tryst at Broughty to-night.'

After knocking this fellow down, Rothesay hurried along the street in the twilight.

Borthwick saw him cross it near the great mansion of
Lord Drummond, which, with its dark façade and round
towers, overshadowed the narrow way. There he disappeared under the arcades, but whether he was lurking
among them, or had been received into some secret door,
Borthwick could not discover ; yet for more than an hour
he lingered there, watching to make sure that Rothesay
had really entered the house, which he dared not approach,
lest a thrust from a sword, unseen, might reward his im-
pertinence, from behind one of the columns on which the
superstructure stood.

At last eleven tolled from the tower of St. Mary's Church,
and remembering his appointment, of which more anon), the
swashbuckler muffled his cloak about him, and set off at a
rapid pace along the eastern road, which by the margin
of the river led towards the Castle of Broughty, the lights
of which could be seen twinkling on the low flat promontory
that approaches the mouth of the Firth of Tay.

CHAPTER VII.

MARGARET DRUMMOND.

In a small round chamber, really 'a secret bower,' of her father's house, Margaret Drummond was seated alone. She was half kneeling and half reclining in an old *prie-dieu* of oak, for she had just concluded her prayers; and a missal, bound in velvet and gold, with a rosary of bright amber beads, lay in her lap.

In a large holder of carved wood and brass work, two tall candles lighted this apartment, which was hung all round with dark red arras. Here was a little bed, raised scarcely a foot from the ground, canopied by a gilded cornice with plumes of feathers, with a small niche over the pillows, and within it stood the prettiest Madonna that ever came out of Italy, with a little font, which always contained some holy water.

This was Margaret's little bower, and at times her sleeping-place.

As she lay half reclined in that old and grotesque *prie-dieu*, with her soft sad features partly hidden amid her clustering hair, her long lashes downcast, one white hand supporting her temples, and the other drooping by her side, she would have made a beautiful picture. She was still as death, as she listened for every passing sound; but all was quiet in that vast mansion, whose inmates were now retired to rest. For more than an hour she had watched and listened, without hearing anything, for the old walls of the house were several feet thick, and, together with the wainscoting and tapestry, nearly excluded all external sound, even by day. At last she raised her head and listened, while her fine eyes sparkled with animation.

St. Mary's bell struck ten. '*Ten*—and he comes not yet!' said Margaret, rising, to sink again with a sigh into the *prie-dieu*, but almost immediately a knock was heard at the side of the apartment, and a soft voice sang the burden of that beautiful old song:

> Oh, are you sleeping, Maggie,
>   My ain, my dear, my winsome Maggie?
> Unbar your door, for owre the muir
>   The wind blaws cauld frae Aberdaggie.

An expression of joy spread over her features; her eyes sparkled again; her cheek flushed, and springing from the *prie-dieu*, she raised the red arras, opened a little door by withdrawing a bar of oak, and stooping low the young Duke of Rothesay entered from a secret staircase, to which he alone had access, and which communicated with the lobby of the house and its arcades below.

'Tears?' said the handsome prince, taking her tenderly in his arms, and kissing her on the lips and on the eyes. 'Dearest, why this emotion?'

But Margaret only sobbed, drooped her head upon his breast, and wept. 'It was my happiness to see you; but you did not observe me to-day.'

'See thee, dearest Maggie,' said the prince, throwing aside his casquetel and rich mantle; 'I looked all amid the glittering crowd that stood by the western gate for thee, and thee only; but, whichever way I turned, could see nothing save the enormous fantage of Madam the Duchess of Montrose. I vow it looks like a kirk steeple! But now,' added Rothesay, with a smile of inexpressible tenderness, 'thou forgettest, I have one other little mouth to kiss.'

Margaret drew back the curtain of an alcove, and there, within a little couch, canopied by rich hangings of rose-coloured velvet, lay a pretty child of not more than eight months old, plump, fair, and round, with its small face and cheeks, tinted like rose-leaves, encircled by a lace cap. Two hands were also visible, so small and so very diminutive, that but for their dimples they might have passed for those of a fairy. The prince knelt down, and while his heart rose to his lips, kissed gently the soft warm cheek of the sleeping baby that in after years was to be Lady Gordon of Badenoch; and after gently closing the curtain, again he pressed Margaret to his breast, and seated her beside him.

'Life is so sweet!' said he, 'when one has something to love, and is beloved again; and you, my Maggie, are a diamond among women.'

'And thou wilt never tire of thy poor little Margaret?'—'Tire of thee?' sighed the prince, smiling; 'dear Maggie, since I knew thee I have only begun to live—to know joy. To me it seems that we have but one heart, one soul, and that without thee I should now have neither. And thou hast confided to me thy life, thy love, thy destiny, and this dear infant, the pledge of them all. Oh, Margaret, without thee, how dark would this world be to Rothesay!'

'And yet, prince, for one long month we have not met.'—'Why call me *prince*? Dear Margaret, here there is no prince.'

'Nor princess!' she sighed.—'There *is*—for thou art Duchess of Rothesay, and shall yet be Queen of Scotland—even as my ancestress, Annabella Drummond, was before thee.'

'Alas, but for our unfortunate consanguinity through her, we had not been wedded in secret, or been driven thus to commit a mortal sin. I had not borne this poor child unknown, or carried under my bosom a load of grief and shame.'

'Shame,' reiterated Rothesay, kissing away her tears. 'Ah, Margaret, have you forgotten that night in the cathedral of Dunblane, when we were so solemnly united, as Father Zuill and the cathedral registers shall yet bear testimony in Parliament. Ere long the Bishop of Dunblane will bring from Rome the dispensation that shall clear us all, and then I shall *again* espouse thee, Margaret, with such splendour as Scotland has not seen since Mary of Gueldres stood by the side of James II. at the altar of the Holy Cross.'

'But till then, I must live in terror, and love in secret. Oh, prince, had I loved thee less—had I known or foreseen—but I must not weary thee with unavailing reproaches, prince——'

'Prince again! Now this is most unkind. Dear Margaret, why call me otherwise than James Stuart—am I not thine own James?'

'Thou art, indeed, and my beloved one!' said Margaret, laying her beautiful head on the breast of her handsome lover with one of her sweetest and most confiding smiles; 'but do pardon me, if I say, that there are times when

I look forward and tremble—look back and weep. There is something to me so terrible in the renewal of the old strife between the king and the nobles. My father, the proudest among them, is ever muttering deep threats of vengeance against the royal favourites, and in the quarrel which I see too surely coming, if all the pride and ferocity of the peers are unchained against the throne, what may be the fate of thee, of this poor tender bud, and of myself? Oh, James, think of the many who wish for the English alliance, and who would brush me from their path like a gossamer web!'

'Thee!' exclaimed the prince, clutching his poniard; 'not Angus himself, even in the heart of his strongest fortresses, or amid his twenty thousand vassals, dare harbour an evil thought against the lady Rothesay loves. Nay, nay, Maggie, thou art sorely in error.'

'At a wave from the hand of Angus, all the troopers of the east and middle marches are in their helmets; then think of the hatred of Shaw and Hailes—the treachery of Kyneff—the mad ambition of them all! They are brooding over revolt—one day it will come. Would, dear prince, that we had never met, or rather, that I had never been!'

'Still regrets,' said Rothesay, impatiently.

'Pardon me, dearest, if I weary thee—I do not regret, but I fear.'

'What glamour hath possessed thee to-night, Margaret? for, by the Black Rood, I never saw thee so full of dolorous thoughts.'

'An evil omen, perhaps,' said Margaret, with one of her faint smiles. 'This morning, when looking for the prayers prepared for those who are in tribulation, I thrice opened my missal at the burial service for the dead.'

'And what then?'

'Madam my aunt, the Duchess of Montrose, told me, to-day, 'twas a sure sign of coming evil.'

'Your aunt the Duchess of Montrose is an—old fool!' said the prince, bluntly.

'Strife is coming—I know it,' continued Margaret, emphatically; 'for I have read it in the face of my father and the faces of his friends, when Angus, the Lords Hailes and Home, and Shaw of Sauchie, are with him. I have heard it in their deep whispers, and seen it in their dark and angry glances, when Lindesay or Montrose, Gray, Ruthven, Grahame or Maxwell, Wood of Largo, Falconer, or Barton—any who are the king's known friends—are mentioned.'

'And what matters it to us if all these high-born brawlers cut each other's throats? The peers of Scotland are her curse, and in all ages have been her betrayers, and will be so until the detested brood are rooted out. A few names less on the peerage roll will better enable the grain to ripen in harvest, and the people to live in peace. My father, the king, has taught me this lesson, and I will never forget it. War will come—I know it; for if we do not fight with England, we must fight among ourselves, just, as it were, to keep our hands in practice. But fear not for me, Margaret, and fear less for our little babe, for I can protect both, and must do so; for my soul is but a ray of thine—my life, the breath of thee. My castle of Rothesay is thy proper dwelling, and I will place young Lindesay in it, with five hundred of his men-at-arms.'

The young prince left nothing unsaid which he thought might soothe Margaret's fears, and remove those dreary forebodings of coming evil in which she had indulged, and by dwelling as long as possible on the expected return of the Bishop of Dunblane from Rome, with the dispensation of Innocent VIII., he completely restored her to cheerfulness; for that venerable prelate was in their secret, and had undertaken to remove the only obstacle that prevented the public or *state* espousal, which Father Zuill (who, being partly a seaman, and not over particular) had anticipated by performing their marriage ceremony in secret, and thus ending for ever all those deep intrigues by which the three Kings of England, Edward IV., Richard III., and, lastly, Henry VII., had each in succession striven to have the Crown Prince of Scotland wedded to a princess of their families.

Though thus espoused, Rothesay and Lady Margaret were still lovers, for both were so young, that long and frequent absences, with the secrecy they were compelled to observe, lest the politic king on the one hand, or the imperious Lord Drummond on the other, should discover their union, all tended to increase rather than to diminish their tender regard.

The prince remained by her side until midnight had tolled, and their conversation was all of themselves; for so it is ever with lovers, who would cease to be so if they tired of their theme, which 'is ever charming, ever new.'

Promising to return at the same hour on the second night following, James kissed his beautiful princess and her infant daughter, wrapped his scarlet mantle about him, and raising the arras, slipped down the secret stair, the concealed door of which Lady Margaret immediately secured.

'She hath spoken truly,' muttered the prince, as he turned the buckle of his belt behind him, brought the hilt of his sword round, and looked cautiously up and down the dark, silent, and deserted street for the interloper by whom he had been formerly followed. '.She hath, indeed, spoken truly. A strife approaches that will drench the land in blood —a strife which even I cannot avert. This secret marriage may destroy us both. Dear, dear Margaret! Like my father, a fatality pursues me, and those who could guide us both may be the innocent cause of undoing us all.'

He hurried along the narrow and quaint old street, and, favoured by his disguise and the watch-word, passed the sentinels, and reached the Palace of St. Margaret unknown and undiscovered.

The unfortunate relationship which rendered a papal dispensation necessary in those days, was caused by Rothesay's descent from Annabella Drummond, queen of Robert III., who was a daughter of Margaret's great-great-grandsire, Sir John Drummond of that ilk. In her own time, this queen had been justly celebrated for her loveliness; for, as Camden says, ' the women of the family of Drummond, for charming beauty and complexion, are beyond all others.'

Other writers amply corroborate this, and add, that three girls more beautiful than Euphemia, Sybilla, and Margaret Drummond had never graced the court of a Scottish king.

CHAPTER VIII.

A CHEERFUL fire burned on the hearth of Jamie Gair, the fisherman of Broughty Point, and it seemed to burn brighter as evening deepened on the land and sea. The cottage, which stood within a kail-yard, the gate of which was a pair of whale jaw-bones, consisted of a butt and a ben,—i.e., an outer and inner apartment,—the latter, serving as a kitchen, had a floor of hard-beaten clay; the walls were lined with wood, and in the rafters were a vast quantity of lumber boat-gear, oars, sails, fishing-creels, bladders, floats, and other apparatus stowed away aloft. Half a cart-wheel felloe formed a fender (such as we may yet see in Scottish cottages), but the fire of bog-fir was blazing on the hearth-stone, for iron grates were then an article of splendour and luxury. On the wooden shelf above the fireplace stood a little image of St. Clement, the mariner's patron, with the anchor of his martyrdom hung about his neck; and on the back of the door a horseshoe was nailed, with a sprig of rowan-tree, the usual precaution against witchcraft. From a rafter an egg was suspended by a rope-yarn. This was the *baby's-egg*, the first laid by a pullet, the gift of its granny, and carefully preserved, as a source of good fortune to it in after life.

By the bright red light of the fire (which shone through a little window upon the waters of the ferry) Jamie Gair sat mending his nets, and affixing various large brown bladders thereto. A red night-cap was placed jauntily on his round curly head; the sleeves of his blue flannel-shirt were rolled up to the elbows, displaying his brawny arms, and, where his thick beard and whiskers did not conceal it, his face was browned to the hue of mahogany by exposure to the weather.

Mary, his wife, a buxom dame of six-and-twenty, wearing one of those long-eared coifs, which are still worn by old women in the Lowlands, and a short skirted jacket, was fondling their son and heir, a baby about a year old, to which she was merrily *lilting* in that manner peculiar to the women of Scotland, when a song is hummed and half-sung, while a dish of stappit-haddie (i.e., a haddock stuffed with oatmeal, onions, and pepper) broiled before the fire for breakfast next morning, as Jamie had to start early, and now sat late in the preparation of his nets.

Jamie had not sailed that day to the fishing-ground for various reasons. He had passed a stray pig on the beach; and, moreover, he had on a pair of new boots—both ominous of a bad day's fishing, and, perhaps, of greater evil; so he had spent the noon and evening beside his red-cheeked Mary at the cottage, mending and thoroughly repairing his nets for the morrow; for he believed as implicitly in these augurs of evil as in the mark of St. Peter's thumb on the haddock, and in the wonderful story of the twenty-four beautiful mermaids who swam round Inchkeith, and sought in vain to tempt Abbot William of Holyrood, who dwelt there as a hermit, to trust himself afloat on their tails, which, happily for himself, the Abbot politely declined to do. Mary was pleased that he was at home, for the night was fitful, and dark masses of cloud crossed the face of the moon, which rose slowly above the ness of Fife. The wind swept in sudden gusts down the ferry, and the surf hissed as it rolled on the outer beach; for the sand was thickly strewn with enormous whin boulders, and was not a pistol-shot from the cottage door.

Three strange ships had been visible in the offing all day, and, as evening fell, Jamie had observed them stealthily creeping towards the shore; and when the gloaming came on, the headmost vessel was perhaps not three miles from the Gaa sands. When Jamie had scanned her last with his nautical eye he observed her laying off and on, but without manifesting any intention of entering the harbour or requiring a pilot, as she never fired a gun or showed her colours. Not a vessel had passed the ferry that day; all was quiet in the harbour of Dundee, for the old superstition about the ill-luck of sailing on a Friday was still devoutly believed in.

The hour was now verging on midnight. Jamie had mended the last hole in his nets, and the pretty Mary looked very sleepy and coy. 'Hark, gudeman,' said she, interrupting her lilting, 'some one tirls the door-pin.'

At that moment a loud and reiterated knocking was heard, and the door-latch was shaken violently. Jamie relinquished the net for a boat-stretcher, lest the visitor might be, as he muttered, 'some ground-shark, or uncanny body,' and angrily opened the door, saying, 'Wha the deil's this, makin' sic a dirdum at my door at this time o' nicht?'

'Sir Hew Borthwick,' replied that personage, with gruff hauteur; and Jamie perceived that he and two companions were well muffled in cloaks, beneath which he saw their long swords and spurs glittering. The two gentlemen were masked. 'Thou knowest me, Jamie Gair, I think?'—'Ay, Sir Hew,' replied the fisherman, doffing his night-cap, while something of a leer twinkled in his lively grey eyes; 'I took ye on board the *Yellow Frigate* yestreen, for which——'

'I owe thee half a lion; here it is. Now, art willing to earn another honest penny?'—'Troth am I, sir,' replied Jamie, throwing on his storm-jacket; 'I've my gudewife and a bonnie bairn to provide for. In what can I serve ye, sir?'

'Take us on board the vessel that is nearest the shore, and thou shalt have an angel.'

An angel was thirteen shillings Scots—but now Jamie paused. 'A Louis, then? Plague on't! thou sailest nigh the wind, man!'

'Come, come, fellow,' said one of the masked men, imperiously, 'do not trifle, for we have not time to chaffer with such carles as thee. Besides, this place hath a devilish odour of tar, wet twine, and old fish baskets——'

'Wow, sir, but you've a het tongue in your head, and a dainty nose on your face. But it's no the money that I tak' tent o',' replied Jamie, proudly. 'The craft that was close inshore, and hugging the land a' day, never showed her ensign; but three times lowered her boat, and three times hoisted it on board again. Her forecastle guns are levelled owre the gunnel, and not through portholes, wherefore I opine she is English; so, gentlemen, I crave your pardons, but I likna the job.'

'Jamie Gair,' said one of the strangers, in a hoarse whisper, ''tis on the King's service we are boune; here are six golden lions; art satisfied? If not, I would not be in thy tarry boots, fellow, for all the Howe of Angus!' This man's voice

startled Jamie, for he now recognized Sir Patrick Gray of
Kyneff, captain of the adjacent Royal Castle of Broughty
—one with whom he, a poor fisherman, dared not trifle for
a moment.

'I will do your bidding, fair sir; but my neighbour is
away to the fishing-ground; whilk o' ye can handle an oar?'

'I,' said Borthwick.

'And I,' added Gray of Kyneff; 'so let us be off, for I
have not a moment to spare.'   'Gudewife, thou wilt pardon
us taking Jamie away for an hour or so; and bethink thee,
dame, how many braw gauds and new kirtles these golden
lions will buy.'   And with these words Gray placed in
Margo's hand six of those large gold coins of James II.,
which bore on one side a lion rampant, and on the reverse,
the St. Andrew's cross.   Jamie put on one of those broad
blue bonnets for the manufacture of which Dundee was
even then celebrated, and, after kissing the sleeping baby,
said, 'Now, Mary, let me kiss thee, lass, frae lug to lug.'

'To spare time, I shall be glad to save thee that trouble,
Gair,' said Sir Patrick Gray.

'Mony thanks, my braw gentleman,' retorted Jamie,
twirling the boat-stretcher in his brawny hand; 'but
there are some things I like to do for myself, and *this* is
ane o' them.   Keep a cog fu' o' het yill on the hearth for me,
Mary, g in the time I return; and now, sirs, let's awa'.'

As they stumbled along the beach to the rude stone pier,
where Jamie's clinker-built boat was moored to an iron
ring—

'Dost see anything of those ships?' asked Sir Patrick
Gray, whom Jamie was careful not to recognize.

'The headmost craft wasna a mile frae the Buddon Ness
when the gloaming fell,' replied the fisherman, looking
keenly to the eastward; 'the wind was off the land then,
but it veered round a point to the north.   Wow but the
moon bodes a grand haul o' herrin' off St. Monan's the
morn!   I wish I had gane to the fishing-ground——'

'And lost these six lions—eh?   But here is thy boat,
grumbler,' said the third personage, who as yet had scarcely
spoken; 'now let us shove off.'

'If these are English ships, sir,' said Jamie, as he assisted
the three to embark, and cast off the painter, 'I marvel
mickle at their impudence in being off the Tay, while Sir
Andrew Wood is at anchor in the Firth.'

'Marvel at nothing; but keep thy wind for cooling thy

porridge, or for better uses,' retorted the haughty Gray, rolling himself up in his mantle, and his companion did the same, while Borthwick and Jamie shipped their oars, and turned the boat's prow to the sea.

When the shadows of the land and the square dark keep of Broughty, with its broad barbican and flanking towers, were left behind, the night (even while the moon was enveloped in clouds) was not so murky that objects could not be distinguished; yet the three voyagers looked in vain for a vestige of the ship which they expected to be nearest the shore. A pale stripe of white light edged the horizon, and between it and the boat the waves were rising and falling, like those of an inky ocean; and in that streak of sky, and between the flying clouds, a few red, fiery stars were seen to sparkle at intervals. Cold currents of air swept over the estuary, bringing that peculiar fragrance which a night breeze always bears off the land; and the hoarse roar of the heavy surf, as it bellowed on the rocks of Broughty Castle, and rolled far inland upon the shingly beach to the eastward of it, could be heard distinctly, as the boat of Gair was pulled directly out to sea.

'Tarry a moment, Gair,' said Sir Patrick Gray; ' now where are those vessels—eh ? '—' You'll see them, sir, when they are lifted into the streak o' light; there they are! awa' doon to windward.'

'But what the devil is windward—which way ? ' asked Borthwick.—' Well mayst thou ask that, for it seems to be whichever way I turn my face ; but oho ! I see them now ! ' added Gray—as the dark outlines of two vessels, with all their sails set, appeared in the distant offing, between the black vapours that seemed to rest on their mast-heads and the darker ocean on which they floated. ' 'Sdeath ! they are ten good miles off.'

'Outside the Inchcape, at least, I should say,' added his hitherto silent friend.

'But where is the *Harry*—this devilish craft, which Gair says was visible near the Buddon Ness ? '—' I'll soon find out.'

'What was the signal agreed upon ? ' whispered Gray.

'*This*,' replied the other, discharging a hand-gun in the air.

Almost immediately afterwards, two sparks appeared about half-a-mile off; they brightened fast, and then two pale blue lights were seen burning close to the edge of the water.

' 'Tis the *Harry !* Give way, Jamie—give way, Borth-wick ! ' said Sir Patrick. The oars dipped into the water, and the sharp-prowed boat shot over the waves towards the lights, which soon faded away and expired. The night was now intensely dark, for not a vestige of moon was visible ; but soon a noise was heard above the incessant dashing of the sea. It was like the flapping of a sail ; and then one faint blink of moonlight, as it broke through an opening in the clouds, showed, close by, a large and high-pooped vessel coming suddenly to the wind, as if the watch had descried the boat upon the water ; and this proved to be the case, for almost immediately, a voice in English cried out,

' Boat, a-hoy ! '

Gray, who answered the hail, and held the tiller, passed the fisher-boat under the towering stern of the English ship, and sheering sharply round on her larboard side, the little craft was soon made fast ; but Jamie was commanded to remain in her, while Sir Patrick Gray, Borthwick, and the third personage, who proved to be no other than Sir James Shaw of Sauchie, governor of Stirling, were introduced to the state-cabin, where, with some reluctance, we are compelled to accompany them.

CHAPTER IX.

THE BANE OF SCOTLAND.

FOR many hundred years a curse, or rather a fell spirit, hovered over Scotland, and time seems never to have lessened its force, or the evil produced by the blighting breath of that *yellow slave*, of which he who found a grave so far from her shore—poor Leyden, one of the sweetest of our bards—has sung, in his beautiful Ode to an Indian coin of gold. This curse has been the mal-influence of a party within the Scottish nation, whose interests were separated from its common weal, who throve on its ruin and disgrace, and have ever been the ready instruments of oppression, neglect, and misrule: I mean that party distinguished in the darkest pages of our annals as *the English faction*—usually a band of paid traitors, whom even the Union could not abolish; men who surrendered themselves to work out the evil, disastrous, and insidious projects of the sister kingdom, for the purpose of weakening the power of the Scottish people; and thus, as Schiller says, 'never has civil war embroiled the cities of Scotland, that an Englishman has not applied a brand to the walls.'

To the patricidal efforts of this faction, which for many hundred years proved the bane of Scotland, our historians lay the blame of every dark and disastrous transaction that blackens the page of Scottish history.

Their intrigues brought on the troubles of Alexander III.; the betrayal of Wallace; and that long war, which even Bannockburn did not end; the early misfortunes of James I. and those of James III., when England intrigued with Albany to gain the town of Berwick, and marry a prince of Scotland to Margaret Tudor. We recognize the same corrupt faction in those ignoble peers who pledged themselves to the English king after the fight at Solway Moss, and thus broke the heart of James V., the most splendid of our monarchs; who plunged Scotland in bloodshed under the Regents Murray, Mar, and Morton; who betrayed Kirkaldy of Grange, and, after a life of woe, surrendered their sovereign to the axe of an English executioner. Again we recognize them, when 'the master fiend, Argyle,' and his compatriots, betrayed her misguided grandson to Cromwell, and when their more sordid successors sold their country at the Union; when they betrayed our Darien colonists to the Spanish allies of England, and the Macdonalds of Glencoe to the barbarous assassins of William of Orange.

Sir James Shaw of Sauchie, Sir Patrick Gray of Kyneff, and the despicable swashbuckler, Borthwick, in the days of James III., represented the ignoble Scots of 1488. They were conducted by a page to the great cabin of the English frigate, in which several gentlemen, all richly dressed, were lounging on the cushioned lockers, and drinking Canary and Rochelle wine out of silver-mounted horns. A lamp, having a globe of pink-coloured glass, swung from a beam, and diffused a warm light around the cabin, which was all wainscoted, and hung with armour and weapons of various kinds.

On the entrance of the three visitors, all the English officers withdrew, save Edmund Howard, the captain, who wore a scarlet cassock coat, richly furred with miniver, and a diamond sword-belt; and his secretary, Master Quentin Kraft, a London attorney, who was attired in plain blue broadcloth, trimmed with black tape, and who immediately produced writing materials, clean drinking horns, and more wine.

'Welcome on board the royal ship *Harry!*' said Edmund Howard, bowing, without rising, while a sneer of ill-disguised contempt, curled his handsome mouth, over which hung a dark mustachio; for, like a noble cavalier and honest mariner, he had an unmitigated aversion to the duty on which King Henry had sent him, and for the three Scotsmen, with whom he had to conduct a court intrigue, 'I am glad you have come off at last; but why all rigged in armour—aloft and alow, from head to heel, eh?'

'In Scotland, men go not abroad without their harness,' replied the Laird of Sauchie, haughtily.

'By St. George,' said Howard, 'four hours ago I was sick of knocking about in the offing, and then having to creep in, like a thief in the nightfall, between the Inchcape

Rock and yonder devilish sands. A fine business 'twould have been to have found myself beached in the shoal water, and just after this hot affair of ours with Sir Andrew Barton in the Channel. Be seated, Sir James, Sir Patrick, the Canary stands with *you;* come to anchor, Master Borthwick—cannot you find a seat? By the bye, talking of Barton, I owe thee a hundred crowns, Borthwick. Kraft, hand this gentleman a hundred crowns, and be sure to get his quittance for them, ere they are stowed away.'

While this transaction passed and the price of Barton's blood was being paid to Borthwick, the two rebellious barons divested themselves of their ample cloaks and masks, and each presented an athletic figure, completely cased in iron, save the head, and armed with daggers and long swords of a famous kind, then made and tempered at Banff.

Shaw of Sauchie was older, less bloated, and less dissipated in aspect than Gray; but he had the same cunning eyes, large mustachios, and bullying or imperious aspect.

' Now, then, Captain Howard, let us to business,' said he, filling his wine-horn.—' Ay, to business,' added Borthwick, filling his, and imitating the nonchalance of the baron.

' Well,' said Howard, ' how does his Grace of Rothesay's amour proceed (for of *that* we have heard at the English court), and what chance is there of his ranging up amicably alongside of a fair English princess, yard-arm and yard-arm, with Cupid ahead ? '—' Very little, I fear, since this affair with Barton.'

' Barton was a brave seaman, and man of honour,' said the Englishman; ' but,' he added, contemptuously, ' I have just paid for that piece of sport.'

' You have paid King Henry's spy,' retorted Sir James Shaw, warmly; ' but remember that King James, and more than he, old Andrew Wood, and Barton's eldest son, will amply avenge your battle in the Channel, unless we have them both fettered, or disposed of otherwise.'

' Then dispose of them, in God's name, and as many more angry Scots as are in the same unruly mood; for King Henry wishes no more of this work; and indeed, ere long, an ambassador will leave London, to clear up the story of our conflict with the ships of Barton, against which, I think, *we* may fairly set off Lord Angus's invasion of Northumberland.'

' Well, but what is King Henry's new proposal ? '—' Simply this, Sir Patrick; that by force or fraud we must either bring off the young prince and have him wedded to the Princess Margaret Tudor, in terms of their betrothal, or we must kidnap the young Dame Margaret Drummond, whichever your most worshipful knighthoods think can be most easily accomplished, for we have undoubted proofs that Rothesay loves her.'

'Ah!—is it so?' said Gray, with a dark frown: 'but what does Henry VII. propose to do with her? for I would not have evil done to the maiden.'

'He would shut her up in some remote Welsh castle, or perhaps the Red Tower of the Dudleys near Wem, where she would never be heard of again. Like a wise old fellow, King Henry knows well that love is fed by the society of lovers; but that, in absence or separation, the fire goes out, and the passion dies. Thus, if we could spirit this dainty dame on board the *Harry*——'

'Easier said than done. I have reason to believe,' said Borthwick, 'that the young prince loves her better than life, and would never survive her loss.'

'I have heard it said that thy mother was a witch, Borthwick,' said Gray, tauntingly; 'I would we had the old dame's aid to-night.'

Borthwick darted secretly at the speaker one of his sinister and ferocious glances, for this taunt stung him deeply.

'The prince is only seventeen—a chit, a child—and may yet love twenty better than little Margaret Drummond,' said Sir James Shaw; 'but to engage in a plan so desperate, I would require King Henry's written assurance of a safe sanctuary in England, for myself and friends, in case this plot were blown and we obliged to fly; moreover, I would require another written assurance that, if all succeeded—that is, if Lady Margaret *disappears*, and Rothesay marries your Margaret Tudor——'

'Princess,' suggested Howard, stroking his mustachio.

'Well—well—your Princess Margaret—that Henry will use all his influence with Rothesay and the king to have my lands of Sauchie, in the shire of Stirling, created into an earldom, together with a gift of two of the best baronies now possessed by the Duke of Montrose, supposing that by the same happy intrigue the said dukedom is abolished, Angus made Lord Chancellor, and the Lindesays driven to Flanders or the devil!'

'Um—um—Flanders, or the devil,' muttered Master Quentin Kraft, writing very literally and very fast.

'And I,' said Sir Patrick Gray, 'require the same royal assurances, with Henry's recommendation to have my barony of Kyneff and estate of Caterline created into a lordship, with the captainrie of Broughty to me and my heirs, heritably and irredeemably, and the salmon's cruives of the Dichty, now pertaining to the Laird of Grange, who must fish for his salmon elsewhere.'

'In all these particulars, if Henry's interest fail not, you shall be perfectly satisfied. Write carefully, Master Kraft.'

'And I——' began Borthwick. 'Shall have two hundred crowns yearly, to be paid by the English ambassador. Ah! your eyes open like port-holes at that!'

'But suppose there is no ambassador, which happens very often, Captain Howard?'—'Ah! to be sure; then the Governor of Berwick shall pay thee.'

'But how are we to have this pretty maiden brought on board an English ship?' asked Howard. ''Tis the most difficult matter of all. A dose of poison might serve us better, and obtain our ends without much trouble,' suggested Borthwick.

The ruffian barons eyed each other, but did not speak.

'Nay, nay,' said the gallant Howard; 'by Heaven, fellow, if thou makest another suggestion such as that, I will order the boatswain's mates to fling thee overboard in a hencoop! In the king's service I have usually carried more sail than ballast—but poison! a sailor's curse on't! Egad, 'tis a word never mentioned to a Howard, and moreover,' he added, with a furious glance, as he rose from the table, ''twas a villan's thought in thee!'

'Softly,' said Sir Patrick Gray, with alarm; 'let us not quarrel, Captain Howard, about poison or abduction; none of us are severe moralists——'

'Scot—you speak for yourself, I presume.'

'I would rather marry the damsel myself than that we should have high words anent the disposal of her. Bethink thee, Englishman—'tis as much as your life is worth to be this night within gunshot of the Scottish shore; and this gentleman——'

'What—Borthwick?'—'Yes, he——'

'Might inform Sir Andrew Wood, you mean to say,' continued Howard. 'Well, I should like to see your admiral's *Yellow Frigate* come out of the river, with all her iron teeth bristling; for now that Barton is gone, he is the best and bravest seaman that treads upon a deck. Nay, nay, none of you will betray me unless King James pays better than King Henry.'

Gray and Sauchie were stung by this bold remark, and the former hastened to say, ' How know we not, but the prince may have wedded the Lady Margaret Drummond ? '

' Pshaw ! what would it matter if he had ? She is only the daughter of a subject—a baron ? '

' Captain Howard, you talk like an Englishman, who knows not the temper of our Scottish barons. Her father can rouse all Strathearn, and set Scotland on fire. Beware lest the flames roll over the border.'

' Master Borthwick, you did not inform me that the Lord Drummond was so powerful, or this amour so dangerous.'

' If King Henry had written to me——'

Here the Englishman burst into a loud fit of laughter. ' King Henry write to thee ! By Jove, I like this impudence —it amuses me excessively ! '

' So it seems,' growled Borthwick, every glance of whose sinister eyes indicated the restless and evil soul within.

' Bah ! people don't write that which is more safe when borne by word of mouth. Henry might hang me, or the King of Scots might hang us all, for letting our gaff too loose— our words would die with us ; but letters will endure while ink and paper last. Yet where is our *bond in cipher*, of which King Henry has the key—we cannot do without that. Master Kraft, is it ready ? '

' Here it is, sir,' replied the little secretary, laying a piece of parchment on the cabin table.

' Then, sirs,' said the English captain, ' when you have signed it, this shall acquaint King Henry that ye are his liegemen, and pledge yourselves, with life, limb, and fortune, to further the English alliance of His Grace the Duke of Rothesay, on the understanding that Henry, by his new ambassador, urges your claims to the peerage, and that, on the espousal day, you each receive the sum of twenty thousand English crowns.'

' It is agreed,' said Shaw of Sauchie, as he and Gray touched the pen of Kraft, who wrote the names they were unable to sign ; but Borthwick, having been educated as a priest, wrote in a bold hand, amid a multitude of flourishes, *Heu Bortwyck*, knyt, at the bottom of this precious document.

' From the Inchcape, gentlemen, we must run over to St. Abb's Head ; and after hanging off the land for a day or two, we will stand again towards the Tay. Here, on the evening of the 10th—St. Anthony's Day—we will be in the offing ; if by that time you can give me this dainty dame to stow under hatch, all your fortunes are made.'

'Enough—we shall see to it, Captain Howard,' said Sir Patrick Gray, resuming his mask and cloak.

'Remember this, sir captain,' said Borthwick : 'the king's chaplain, James, Bishop of Dunblane, who is returning from Rome, will pass through England in disguise. I would recommend his capture, and the seizure of whatever papers may be found in his possession, for they may prove of much service to Henry, your king.'

'Another thousand crowns to thee, Master Borthwick ! Zookers ! man, thou wilt die rich as a Jew of Lombard Street ! Now then, Kraft, hast thou scribbled all this into thy devil's log-book ? '—' Yes, sir,' replied the secretary, securing his volume by a curious lock in the iron band which encircled it.

'Then fill the wine-pots. Take another cup, gentlemen,' said the Englishman, with that contempt for his guests which the necessity of pandering to the snake-like policy of his court could not repress. ' 'Tis time we were all in our hammocks, and your boat is waiting, sirs.'

Shaw and Gray, who knew very well that they were in his power, gave him dark and savage glances ; and as they left the cabin they heard him issue orders to ' Lower away the port-lids, larboard and starboard ; to run back the culverins —lash and make fast ; to stand off before the land breeze ; for,' said he, ' we must make the offing ere daybreak—ay, and be hull down, if we can.'

They left the English ship, just as the bell rang the middle watch, and the hoarse voice of the boatswain was heard ringing in prolonged echoes between decks. Howard, who mistrusted his visitors, by an after-thought, came in person to see them over the ship's side, and into their boat.

'Fare ye well, gentlemen,' said he, in his jibing way. ' Adieu, noble Master Borthwick—I beg pardon—*Sir Hew.* I hope you will not forget your visit to Ned Howard and the good ship *Harry.* I pray it may not shorten your cruise for life.'

'Hush, hush !' said Shaw, as the oars plunged into the water.

'*Howard and the Harry !*' muttered Jamie Gair, under his thick beard, as he bent to his oar and slued the boat's head round towards the land, where the bright red light of his own cottage window was streaming on the water, and while the English ship filled her headsails, and stood off towards the sea. ' My certie! but this *will* be braw news for Rabbie Barton and auld Sir Andrew! Here's been some fause wark; but I'll spoil your sport, fair gentlemen, lord barons though ye be; for the admiral shall hear o' this, though I should hang ower Broughty tower for it.'

The mast was stepped, a sail set, and before the south-east wind, that blew from the Fifeshire hills, the boat glided over the starlit water like a wild sea-mew.

CHAPTER X.

THE BOATSWAIN'S YARN.

JAMIE GAIR had the stroke oar, and Borthwick the other; they bent all their energies to the task of pulling the boat against an ebb-tide, which was fast leaving bare and dry the Drumilaw Sands, and the long stretch of desolate beach at the promontory known as the Buddon Ness. Jamie kept his ears open to catch any passing remark from the high-born traitors who occupied the stern-sheets of his boat: but, full of their own dark thoughts, they remained silent until she was within a bowshot of the beach, when the Laird of Sauchie said, 'So, on the evening of the 10th, we must have this dame sailing merrily at sea! A perilous promise!'

'Perilous!' said Gray gruffly; 'how so?'—'Ken ye, Sir Patrick, what the law saith anent trysts with Englishmen?'

'I ken little, and I care less,' replied the Knight of Kyneff, doggedly; 'but what says it?'—'That if any Englishman enter the kingdom of Scotland without the sign-manual of the king, and is found at kirk or market, or in any other place, he shall be the lawful prisoner of whoever chooses to seize him. That the Scot who brings an Englishman to tryst, shall be committed to ward, and have his goods escheat. For such are the laws of James II. and his parliament of 1455.'

'Well, we who are barons of parliament, and make the laws, have assuredly the power of breaking them. Besides, he who can lead a thousand lances to the king's host, can make laws to suit himself.'—'But how know ye not, Sir Patrick, but this fellow Borthwick may betray us.'

'He dare not mar his profit and our own,'—'The boatman, then—he might suspect us—yea, might speak.'

'Assure me of that,' hissed the low, deep voice of Gray, 'and I will drive this poniard into his brisket.'

Jamie's heart leaped, and he grasped his oar tighter; but at that moment the boat grounded on the beach, and, while they sprang ashore, he hooked his kedge-anchor in the sand, placed the oars on his shoulder, and doffing his bonnet to his honourable employers, turned away towards the red light that yet streamed from his cottage window.

'Be discreet, good fellow,' said Shaw, in an impressive whisper, as he placed a coin in Jamie's hand. 'Now, fare ye well, carle, and God speed ye.'

'Be close as a steel-vice, Jamie Gair,' added Borthwick, 'lest I tell the Lord Chamberlain that there is a rookery in the trees at thy kailyard, and thou shalt be sorely fined, and mayhap imprisoned in Broughty; for Beltane time is past, the corn is ripening, and thou knowest the law.'

With these warnings they left him, and, muffled in their cloaks, strode hastily along the beach, towards where the outline of Broughty, square, black, and grim, on its rock that jutted into the ferry, rose between them and the starlit sky—for now the clouds had disappeared, but the moon had waned. Jamie turned to look after the English ship, but though almost shrouded in haze, he could perceive her standing off towards the south-east with all her sails set.

'An angel—a golden angel!' said Jamie, turning over the bright coin in his hard hand. 'By my saul, there maun be some dark plot in the wind when these limbs o' Satan pay sae weel! Jamie Gair, Jamie Gair, tak ye tent; for this braw fee may never bring aught but dool and sorrow to thee and thine. Now to kiss my doo Mary, and then, ho for the admiral! for he shall hear o' this hellicate job, though I should never see another sun blink down the Carse o' Gowrie.'

Entering his cottage softly, this honest fellow found his blooming Mary asleep by the warm ingle. The fire had smouldered on the hearth, and the stappit-haddie had been allowed to burn; but the bicker of spiced ale stood yet by the wooden fender. Jamie took a long draught, wiped his mustachios with the back of his brown hand, kissed Mary, and awoke her.

'Where awa' noo, gudeman?' she asked, perceiving that he took up his walking-staff.—'Dundee, lass.'

'Dundee, at this time o' the morning, when you should be beside me in your bed. And mind, ye maun awa' to the fishing-ground by sun-rise, Jamie.'—'Na, na, lass, I have other bait to my line. There has been foul treason on the water this night, Mary, and I maun e'en seek the admiral; but, 'odsake, say nae word o' this to the neighbours, or the hellicate Captain o' Broughty may mak ye a widow before your time, lassie. In a siccar place, put by the braw gowden fee, till we see what comes o't, lest dool and disgrace fa' on us. And now, lass, fare ye well," and pulling his broad bonnet over his face, Jamie departed for Dundee.

The keep of Broughty was reddening in the rising sun, as the fisherman passed it, on the landward side, for safety and concealment, keeping as much as possible among the whins and other wild bushes that grew on the margin of the wide salt marsh which then stretched from the barbican of the fortress round by the hill of Balgillo. The tide had ebbed; the sands of Moniefreth and Barry were dry, and the bare promontory of the Buddon Ness stretched far into that blue sea, on which the three English ships were then diminished to mere specks. Jamie gave a last glance to ascertain their course, and hurried on towards the town.

The summer morning was beautiful; the Tay lay in its basin like a sheet of glass, on which the ships, the town, and sunlit hills were mirrored. The midsummer flowers were mingling with the bluebells, the crimson foxglove and wild hollyhock; the hill of Balgillo, with the desert muirland that lay at its base, were waving with purple heather-cups. The fisherman's heart expanded joyously with the beauty of the opening day; and after hurrying past the old castle of Claypotts, then a seat of the Abbot of Lindores, he reverently said a short prayer to St. Peter, the patron of his craft, in the little chapel of St. Rocque of Narbonne, which stood without the Cowgait Porte, on the east side of the Bitter Burn. This little fane, like all other holy edifices in that age, remained open night and day; and in the principal shrine stood an image of the saint, having the left breast marked by the cross which appeared upon his bosom when born into the world. A little burying-ground encircled the cell. From thence a narrow lane, causewayed with large round sea-stones, and encumbered by outside stairs which ascended upward to the houses or descended downward to the cellars, where the merchants were beginning to display their wares, led to the centre of the town, and to the Kirk of St. Clement, near which another narrow lane then led directly towards the harbour.

The streets were then unpaved, and were full of gleds and

corbies, which squattered and fed on the offal of the narrow
wynds and fleshers' stalls.

Some of the loiterers at the Craig of St. Nicholas readily
permitted Jamie to use their boat, and in a few minutes he
found himself on the ample deck of his Majesty's *Yellow
Frigate*, which was riding with her head to the stream, her
yards all squared to perfection, her black rigging all taut as
iron rods, and her broad blue ensign and pennon flaunting
in the morning wind.

The watch on deck crowded about the early visitor.
'Welcome on board, Jamie Gair,' said Master Wad the gunner,
who was in charge of the deck, and was a short-legged personage, with a red visage, enormous black beard, and
stunted figure, encased in a rough grey gaberdine ; 'whatna
wind hath blawn ye here betimes ? Are ye tired o' your
lubberly trade o' fisherman, and come to take service under
the broad pennon o' the admiral ? I marvel muckle ye
havena tired lang syne o' sailing ilka morning to that weary
fishing-ground, like the son o' a shotten herring. I would
rather drink bilge-water a' my days, than turn fisherman
again.'

'My best anchor—my bonnie Mary—is still at hame,
Maister Wad,' retorted Jamie ; 'but we a' ken how your
Tib broke from her moorings and went adrift, naebody kens
where.'—'Tut—I have ten Marys as gude as yours,' replied
the gunner, 'forbye a Meinie and a Peg to boot.'

'I have nae time for daffin the noo, Maister Wad. Is the
admiral on board ?'—'No—he is at the king's lodging, and
has no' come off yet ; but what would ye wi' *him ?*'

'That which you maunna hear, Willie. Then, is the
Captain Barton on board ?'—'No—he, Sir David Falconer,
and a' body else (but the chaplain) are ashore at St. Margaret's.'

Gair stamped his foot, and scratched his beard impatiently. 'Can ye no tell us what's in the wind, man ?'
asked the seamen, as they clustered about him, in surprise
at his excitement.

'Come,' said Cuddie the coxswain, 'what can *you* have
to tell the admiral that we canna hear ? Out wi' it, hand
owre hand, man.'—'It's something that will find ye a' work
for a week to come, something that may knock the harns out
o' half your heads,' replied Gair, angrily.

'I have seen foul weather in my time, brother,' growled
Archy of Anster, the boatswain ; 'and I have seen some gey

het work, too, between the English Channel and the Rock o'
Lisbon ; but I marvel what the deil ye drive at, Gair !'

'May I never drink aught but black bilge-water, if I
dinna think him clean daft,' added the gunner ; 'but he
canna see the admiral till mid-day, when the king's counsel
breaks up ; sae, Jamie, after Father Zuill hath piped all
hands to mass, you had better just take your breakfast wi'
us, like a douce man, and meet the admiral after, when tide
and time suit.'

Aware that he could not entrust his secret with the seamen, among whom it would have spread like wildfire, and
cost him, perhaps, his life—for a word from Sir James Shaw,
or the tyrannical captain of Broughty, would be sufficient
to hang a poor fisherman among the rooks that Borthwick
spoke of—Jamie was obliged to exert his patience, and join
the seamen at their mess of Lammas ale and porridge in the
forecastle, where, after this humble repast was over, Master
Wad produced his fiddle, and, after mass was done and the
chaplain gone ashore, sung the famous ditty, still known to
our fishermen, of the

> Four-and-twenty mermaids, who left the port of Leith,
> To tempt the fine auld hermit, who dwelt upon Inchkeith ;
> Nor boat, nor waft, nor crayer, nor craft had they, nor oars or sails,
> Their lily hands were oars enough, their tillers were their tails, etc.

'I could tell ye something mair wonderful than the mer-
maiden's voyage, brother,' said the grey-haired boatswain,
who dearly loved to spin a yarn whenever he could get
listeners. He was a rough-visaged Scot, with two great
red-spotted cheekbones, a nose that had a sword-cut across
it, and which stuck out between two enormous whiskers
that mingled with his grisly beard. 'Our gude chaplain
thinks to discover a process whereby he can make ships proof
to the shot of culverins—for so he told me yesternight.'

'By my faith, old Ropeyarn,' said Cuddle the coxswain,
who was his exact counterpart, 'that will be better than
muddling his brains in trying to mak burning-glasses that
will set a fleet in a bleeze at a league's distance.'

'Brother,' said the gunner, striking his large-jointed
hands together emphatically, for between such inventions,
it seemed not improbable that his profession would prove a
useless one ; 'brother, I ken navagation as weel as maist
men ; I have run all Europe down twenty times, frae the
North Cape to the Gut o' Gibraltar—ay, I have seen the Rio

Grande, and the great peak o' the Fortunate Isles, that rises right out o' the sea like a spearhead, and flames like a torch; I have seen the sea-devils that swim round the Cape de Verde, where the glinting o' the moon makes men mad, and where St. Elmo's light dances like a will-o'-the-wisp on the main-mast heid: yet it is a blessed light, for it ever precedes a calm; but may I ne'er drink aught but bilge, if I can swallow a yarn like yours. I have seen muckle in my time, but never saw I a ship's side that would turn a cannon shot, or a sail that had a hole burned in it by a mirror ten miles awa'; yet our chaplain pretends to ken o' baith. My word on't, lads, he sails beyond his commission, and will be brought up all standing, some day, by the bishops, for sorcery, maybe.'

'He is as gude a man as ever trod a plank,' said the coxswain, 'but his noddle hath as many crotchets as the dog-star hath rays. Minnows and mackerel! to believe in shot-proof ships!'

'Why not?' asked the boatswain, gruffly. 'I'll tell ye what I have seen, messmates—a shot-proof *man*. Now what think ye o' that? one, at least, who was proof to steel.'

'I'll tell ye when I hear, brother,' replied the seaman: 'was it one o' the antipodes, who walk on their heads?'

'Weel, I carena if I spin the yarn before the watch is called,' said the boatswain; 'but first, here is to the gude saut water, and a' that live on't!' and he poured down his capacious throat the last of the ale, and after wiping his mouth three or four times with the cuff of his gaberdine, spitting twice through an open port, and fixing his eyes on the beam overhead, he thrust his hands into his pockets, placed his legs on the deck, his back against a gun-carriage, and began thus:—

'Ye maun ken, messmates, that after leaving the Gut o' Gibraltar, we were beating westward against a head-wind. Our craft was the *Peggie o' Pittenweem*, homeward bound from Barcelona, for Leith, wi' a mixed cargo o' wine and oil, fruit, cork, and hides, and Sir Andrew, the admiral, who was then but a sma' merchant-skipper, had ten brass culverins in her, forbye some braw pateraroes along her gunnel, for the behoof o' the heathen Moors o' Barbary if they daured to meddle wi' us. After losing sight o' the Castle of Gibraltar, and the chapels of our Lady of Europe and our Lady of Africa, that stand on ilka shore, the wind veered round to the north-west, and we were obliged to bear right away before it for well nigh a week, till we had mony fears o' being blawn round Cape None, or getting into the downhill currents, that bear ships away to the southern pole; or, what is waur, being blown off the earth a'thegether: for the warld is round, ye ken, just like my bonnet,' continued this ancient mariner, balancing the article named in his hands; ' and flat, as ye may see, for the sun dips down to port at night, and then comes up to starboard in the morning, rising at the edge, like this penny piece. Weel, ye wad flee owre its margin if ye stood on owre long wi' your canvas set, and so be launched out into space like a hoodie craw. The ship o' auld Sir Patrick Spens was ance a' owre but the waist, when the current swept her back again, and then she hauled her wind. At last we saw the high peak o' the Fortunate Isles rising frae the sea, vomiting fire and brimstone, its side covered in one place wi' glistening snow, in another wi' a forest o' green laurel bushes, wherein the yellow birds o' the Canaries built their nests in the warm sunshine.

' The gale deid awa', and the sails flapped against the masts and rattlins; the sea became like glass, and there was sae little wind that the *Peggie* wouldna answer her helm; but it mattered little, for Sir Andrew and auld Gibbie o' Crail had been in these seas before, and we kent our whereabouts. We were within less than half a mile o' the shore, but in fifty fathoms water by the line. There was nae current, and the ship lay like a log, wi' her decks blistering in the sun. Sir Andrew thought it wad be a gude time to get fresh water, for our last pint was in the scuttle-butt; sae we hove up twelve casks, the crews o' the yawl and pinnace were piped awa', and cheerily we shipped our oars, and pulled for the shore, as I weel mind, singing merrily the auld ballad:

> Oh, who is he has dune this deed,
> And tauld the king o' me,
> And sent us oot at this time o' year,
> To sail upon the sea?

Every man o' us had a durk and gude braid Banffshire whinger in his belt, forbye ten that were armed wi' crossbows, for Sir Andrew kent of auld that the Guanchos o' the Fortunate Isles were unchancey chields to warsle wi'. Gibbie o' Crail, wha had served wi' the Spanish buccaneers under the Captain Bocca Roxa (he whom Barton slew off Cape Ortegal), tauld us that they had once landed there, and put

a hail village to fire and sword, and that wi' his ain hand
he had killed the prince o' the place by a slash *across the nose*
wi' his boarding-axe.

'We landed at a sma' bit creek among black rocks,
covered wi' ashes, dust, and pumice-stane; but among them
grew the green sugar-cane, the olive, and the bonnie cotton-
tree. The wee birds wi' their gouden wings flew aboot frae
branch to branch, singing in the bright sunshine. A' the
sweets o' summer were there, and they wiled mony o' our
messmates awa' frae the wark o' filling and bunging the
water-casks to stray in the laurel woods that grow on the
base o' that tremendous peak, which is five leagues high frae
the water-line to the Deil's Cauldron on the tap, where the
red brimstone burns day and night. Ay, Jamie Gair, ye
think muckle o' the craigs o' Dunnotter; but I wish ye
saw Adam's Peak, in the Fortunate Isles!

'The fresh water was delightful as milk, and the grapes
that hung owre the pumice-stane rocks were sweeter than
heather honey; and sae, despite Sir Andrew's orders, twa
or three o' us, including Sandie Mathieson, a Leith man,
strayed a mile or mair into the island, flinging our braid
bonnets after the gouden birds, eating grapes and wild
honey in some places, tumbling knee-deep in soft sulphur
and spongy pumice-stane, until we found the entrance o
a cave, for a' the warld like ane o' the weems in the Fife
and, sailor-like, we scrambled in to see what was there, and
my faith, messmates, we saw a sicht to mind o'!

'In that cave were mair than twa hundred deid corpses
a' rankit up in rows against the walls; for it was a buria
place for the Guanchos, who, instead of putting their dei
like Christians into a grave, bathe and parboil them in butte
and wild lavender, black gum and wild sage—for sae Fathe
Zuill told me; and after drying them in the sunshine i
summer, and the cauld breezes in winter, they sow them u
in goatskins, and then the mummies are hard as a ship
figure-head, yea, and harder, for they will never decay
and there they stood, twa hundred or mair, wi' their tanne
visages and sichtless eyen, their hair and beards all brushe
and plaited, and as if they yet lived; and oh, there was a
awesome grin on their shrivelled maws!

'It was a sight even for a sailor to scunner at, and w
glowered at them for awhile, ilk ane o' us ashamed to be th
first to put up his helm and be off. At last Gibbie o' Cra
an auld sea-horse, that feared nocht, and had mairowre

gude dram under his hatches, began to examine them, in
the hope of finding some braw goud or trinket; and solemnly
Mathieson and I warned him to let the deid corpses alane;
but he laughed, and tumbled them owre like nine-pins.
There was ane, a great stark and brawny corpse, wi' a lang
scar across its nose, and twa precious stanes, like emeralds,
glinting where its eyen should be. Gibbie said, wi' an oath,
that he was sure it was the prince o' the Guanchos, whom he
had slain twenty years before, and wi' a dab o' his jocketeleg,
picked out ane o' the emeralds. But lo!

'At that moment the jaws opened, and there came frae
them a yell that shook the dust frae the cavern roof; that
seemed to mak the corpses start, and made Gibbie spring
ten feet awa'; and then we turned and fled, wi' every hair
on our heids bristling; and without ever daring ance to
look astern, we cam' plunging doon the side o' the peak,
through the laurel bushes and owre the sulphur banks,
till we reached the creek, where the yawl and the pinnace,
wi' the last o' the water-casks, were about putting off, and
mair deid than alive wi' terror, we sprang on board. We
were just in time to reach the boats and get a rope's-ending
for disobeying orders; for though Sir Andrew was but a
skipper then, as I tauld ye, he kept a tight hand owre his
crew.'

'May I drink bilge if ever I——' began the gunner.

'That evening a favourable breeze sprang up, and we
bore away for hame: but as the gloaming fell that breeze
freshened to a gale, the rain sowed the sea, and the red
lightning flashed at the far horizon. Gibbie, Mathieson, and
I were on the first nicht-watch; we were restless, and fearfu
o' coming evil, and we nestled in our storm doublets under
the lee o' the foremast; and though we would a' hae fain
spoken o' that awesome adventure, we never once referred
to it; but sat listening to the dreary wind, as it whistled
under the leech o' the foresail, or watching the waves that
ran past us, like lang black ridges o' ink. A' at ance an unco
blast took us a' aback! Sir Andrew jumped on deck in a
moment, and ordered us to double-reef the mainsail and fore
topsail; and after this it became sae dark and eerie, that
we couldna see a crossbow-shot ahead.

'Amid the soughin' o' the wind and the hiss o' the waves
we heard a strange cry rising from that terrible sea—a cry
that made our blood curdle! We rushed to the weather-bow,
and after a time could discern a man's head, as he rose at

times, bobbing like a fisherman's float upon the crests of the foaming ocean, or as he sank doon into its gloomy trough ; but again and again the eldritch cry went past us on the gusty wind.

'"A man overboard!" cried Sir Andrew through his trumpet ; "and in sic a sea! Forecastle there—see ye anything, lads ?"

'I kenna what possessed us, but none o' us made any answer. To back the foreyard or render any assistance were, we thought, impossible ; but Sir Andrew, wha does mony a thing other men would never think o', on hearing the first cry, knotted a line to a handspike, and getting a glimpse o' the man in the water as he was swept past our bows, flung it right at him like a harpoon, and we saw him catch it—yea, almost without an effort, as it seemed. Then the starboard watch, who had come on deck, towed him aboard, and he cam' up the ship's side by the main chains, like a cat or a squirrel, and stood dripping wet among us, a strong and sturdy child, wi' a brown skin, and grisly and matted hair. Gibbie held up a ship's lantern to tak' a view o' his face, and then I saw that he was almost bare bones, brawn, and skin, wi' a long scar *across his nose*, and but one eye, that glittered like green glass, while the other socket was *empty*, like a walnut shell. We felt as if the deck would open under our feet, for we knew it was the dead Guancho !

'I could feel puir Gibbie tremble as we slunk forward, leaving the skipper and crew to question the stranger, whose answers satisfied them, I suppose, but we couldna hear them for the lashing o' the sea and roaring o' the wind, as it soughed through the rigging. A can o' usquebaugh was offered to the Guancho, but he shook his head ; and then clothes were offered him, but he preferred his ain, a pair o' goat-skin breeks with the hair on the outside. The wind shifted— the squalls cam' oftener, and in a wee while Sir Andrew had stripped the *Peggie* to her staysail and trysail ; we sounded the pumps, and had twa men at the tiller ; all hands were on deck, and though the crew muttered doubt-fully and fearfully under their beards to ilk other anent the strange loon that had come on board in sic weather, there were none that shared the terror o' Sandie, Gibbie, and my-sel', for in our hearts we kent that a deid corpse was sailing wi' us on that mirk midnight sea, and that the ship and a' its companie were doomed ! The wind was still roaring, and about three bells in the middle-watch the staysail gave way, and I heard Sir Andrew shout through his trumpet, "Yare, yare, my lads! down wi' the staysail—bend on the sheet and right it again."

'We three rushed to obey the order, but the ship broached to, and before we could recover her again, and while that devilish Guancho uttered an eldritch yell, a sea took her right on the broadside, and burst over the decks, sweeping boats, booms, scuttlebutt, skylights, and four men overboard; but the masts o' pine frae Falkland Woods stood brawly, and then we let her drive before the storm. We were certain the *Peggie* was a doomed ship now, unless we got rid o' the fiend that was aboard o' her; and we three consulted in what manner it should be dune. As yet the nicht was dark as pitch tar; no' a ray o' light was glimmering, and we saw the Guancho standing by the weather fore-rigging, wi' his one eye shining at times like a green star. Gibbie, who was a ferocious auld buckie, proposed to gie him a cloure wi' a capstan-bar, or a dab wi' his durk, while we should chuck him overboard; and wi' our hearts fu' o' fear and hatred, we resolved upon this, for we dreaded sairly lest our crew should be washed awa' man by man, and we be left alane wi' the Guancho, and led to destruction. It was an unco wild night, and noo the lightning glinted between the scudding clouds and breaking sea wi' a green and ghastly glare.

'Wi' muckle o' fear and mair o' desperation in our hearts, we drew near the Guancho, who stood by the gunnel grinning at the passing waves. None could see us, either forward or aft, for the crew were busy enough, and kept aloof frae the stranger.

'"Heave, Gibbie, heave, and wi' a will!" cried I, as I grasped him by the breeks. Gibbie took his heels, and we shot him richt owre into the deep black trough o' the hungry sea; and then on swept the ship, like a shot frae a culverin, and as if relieved o' half her cargo.

'"Mony hands mak' licht wark," said Sandie.

'"But the Lord forgi'e us if we hae dune wrang," quo' I, taking off my bonnet at His name.

'"Wrang!" growled Gibbie; "wrang to drown a deid man! I could swear that his ankles were but dry banes as I hove him owre the bulwark."

'The *Peggie* laboured hard and creaked in a' her timbers, the wind howled, and now a wave like Ailsa Craig came roaring after her.

'"Beware, my lads, beware fore and aft!" cried Sir Andrew through his trumpet. The three of us grasped the starboard rattlins, and at that moment another heavy sea poured like a torrent owre the decks o' the *Peggie*. Our mate, Mathieson's brother, and another seaman were swept away; for a time, the ship trembled and was settling down. By my life, had one more wave like that rolled on her, she had gang doon into the trough and never risen mair; but the water ran off her; she swam like a duck, and again shot on, though the foresail was splitting to ribbons.

'"St. Clement be near us!" whispered Gibbie. "Look, Archy—look, Sandy!" and there, just where we had pitched him owerboard, was the Guancho, standing by the starboard gunnel, grinning and laughing as before. Naebody on deck had missed him, and nane but oursel's kent that the same sea which had swept awa' our mate, had washed the storm-fiend on board again.

'Towards morning the gale subsided, and the grey daylicht cam' in through a mirk and louring sky, to brighten a rowing sea. We were cheerless and sad. The men muttered among themsel's, and were aye in pairs, keeping aloof frae their unco shipmate; and even Sir Andrew liked him but little, and promised that he should be set upon the first land we came to. For five days we drifted about, and wist not where we were; for, as the sun was hidden, our captain couldna win an observation wi' the cross-staff. He asserted that we were blown right out into the Atlantic, where never ship sailed before; but Gibbie, wha kent these seas o' auld, averred that we would sune mak' the coast o' Mogadore, which belonged to the king o' the Moors. Yet our brave captain proved to be right.

'For these five days and nights, the Guancho did nocht else but mope about the deck, and grin whenever Gibbie cam' near him; but our men worked hard to repair the damage o' the gale. We bent on four new sails, reeved some o' the rigging anew, shipped a new foretopmast, and, after taking an observation, bore away for Madeira.

'Gibbie aye gied the Guancho a wide berth on deck, and kept as much aloft as possible. For three hail days he sat perched in the craw's nest; and three times I took the tiller for him at night, as he was ever in mortal terror when the awesome thing cam' nigh him. We crowded every stitch o' canvas, carrying mair o' nights than the skipper kent o'; and twice nearly ran the *Peggie* under water, in our eagerness

to reach the land. A' this time the Guancho ate little or
nocht, but a grain or sae o' maize; and mony o' our men,
wha, owercome wi' weariness, had slept on their watch, had
frightfu' dreams, and averred that the Guancho pressed
their throats in the night and sucked their blood; for they
fand bite-marks about their necks in the morning;—but
then the *Peggie* was swarming wi' Norway rottens. The
terror increased; men spoke in whispers; and day by day,
this awsome Guancho sat in the lee scuppers, motionless as
if deid, and only moved and girned when Gibbie drew near
or passed it, which he aye did sidelong, wi' his hand on his
durk; and three times the thing pointed to his eyeless socket,
from whilk Gibbie had howked the shining stane.

'On the fifth night o' this horrid voyage, Mathieson and
I had the foretop. We were on the look-out for land. The
Peggie was going free, about eight knots or sae; and having
now to take his helm, Gibbie stood by the binnacle, and, Gude
kens, we watched the deck mair than the horizon for four
hours o' that dreary night. The Guancho sat, as usual, in
the lee scuppers, and a wet berth it was. About the middle-
watch, we saw him rise and creep towards Gibbie, whose een
were fixed on the sails—for he was a gude steersman, and
aye loed to keep them full. I think I see him noo, as he
stood wi' his siller hair and red face glinting in the light o'
the binnacle lamps; his feet planted firm on the deck, and
his hands gripping the lion's head that was carved on the
tiller-end; and he sawna the fiend that drew nigh him!

'"Deck ho!" I shouted. "Gibbie, man—mind your-
sel'!" but the wind swept my cry to leeward; and a' at
ance the Guancho sprang upon the puir helmsman—there
was a despairing cry, an eldritch yell, and the demon
dashed him against the larboard stanchions, a breathless
and a brainless corpse.

'Wi' the wild cry that rose frae the deck a' was owre!

'Unhanded, the tiller swayed frae side to side; the vessel
fell awa' round like lightning; her canvas was a' taen aback,
and her topmasts went crash to leeward by the caps. We
were a wreck in a moment.

'In a trice Sir Andrew was on deck. Sandy and I cam'
doon the backstay by the run, and "out hatchets" was the
word to clear us of the wreck; and under the foresail,
mainsail, and gib, we entered the roads of Funchal, and
anchored off the Castle of St. James, to refit, procure fresh
water, Madeira, hock, and provisions.'

'But what o' this deevil wi' the green ee?' asked Willie Wad, impatiently.

'Anger got the better o' our fear. We sprang upon him the moment the ship was safe; a desperate tulzie began, for every blow o' his bony hands was like a cloure frae a smith's hammer, and he knocked our best men owre like ninepins; his eldritch yells were like the whistling wind, and he laughed and kicked, when at last we laid him sprawling on the deck, and, while our hearts boiled wi' fear and fury, lashed him hard and fast by neck and heels to ringbolts. Some proposed to heave him overboard, wi' a shot at his craig, but Sir Andrew wouldna hear o' that; and as soon as we dropped anchor at Funchal, the Guancho was handed owre to the Dominicans and the Commander of the Order of Christ, who put him in a vault o' the Castle of St. James, to thole a trial for sorcery and murder. Our story filled a' Funchal wi' terror and consternation. A lang procession o' Dominican Fathers, carrying relics, crosses, banners, and holy-water pots, marched to the Castle o' St. James, to exorcise the demon; and the holy water, when it fell frae the asperges on his brown hide, hissed as if it sputtered on iron in a white heat, and he girned at the priests like a marmoset. At last, finding that exorcism and blessed water were used alike in vain, the Portuguese Dominicans and the Knights of Christ betuik themsel's to prayer, and after solemn high mass in the great church, visited the Guancho again.

'They found him free o' his fetters, and laughing like a wild imp, while he gied the finishing strokes to a great galley or boat, which he had chalked, wi' its sails set, and twenty rowers at their paddles, on his dungeon wall. They marvelled sairly at this strange employment, for one wha's funeral fire stood burning in the castle yard; but a glamour was owre them, and nane dared approach him.

'Then the brown deevil drew the waves below the galley sae lifelike, that *they* seemed to roll and *it* to heave, while the rowers began to paddle, and a low wild chant was heard, as they a' paddled and kept time. Then he drew a ladder, wi' two perpendicular strokes and sax horizontal ones; and then he *stepped on board*, wi' anither o' his eldritch yells. The rowers began to paddle harder than ever, and while their sang died awa', it sailed clean off the wall wi' him, and left ne'er a trace behind.

'A Knight of Christ sprang forward, but the place was

empty, clear o' its evil tenant, and no' a vestige o' the fairy ship remained upon the dungeon wall. Noo, what think ye o' *that* story, messmates ? '

' By my faith, I would rather drink bilge a' my days than once sail the sea wi' a deevil in the ship's companie,' said Willie Wad.

' Puir Gibbie o' Crail ended his life, as I told ye, and sleeps in his hammock among the mermaids,' said the boatswain, rising from the gun-carriage ; ' but Sandy, our messmate, hath left me a lang way astern, for he is now Sir Alexander Mathieson, Knight—*the King of the Sea*, and captain o' yonder gallant caravel, while I am only auld Archy the boatswain. And, see, yonder his barge is shoved off frae the Craig o' St. Nicholas, and pulled straight for the *Queen Margaret*.'

' Which shows that the king's council maun e'en be owre, and 'tis time I were awa' to the Admiral,' said Jamie Gair, as through an open gun-port, the gilded boat referred to was seen to leave the rock of St. Nicholas, with a banner waving at its stern, where three or four gentlemen, wearing rich dresses, were seated ; and, with sixteen bright-bladed oars flashing in the meridian sun, it was pulled across the shining river directly towards the consort of the *Yellow Frigate*.

CHAPTER XI.

CHAINING THE UNICORN.

WHILE the boatswain was spinning his incredible yarn in the forecastle of the frigate, the king, after being at mass in the chapel of St. Salvador, which stood near the palace of St. Margaret, on a rocky eminence to the north side of the High Street and Overgaitt, proceeded to the hall of this ancient residence, where the great officers of state were to assemble, and where he was to receive the ambassadors of Louis XI.

This old apartment was of great height, and was lighted by six round-headed windows; its roof was an arch of solid stone, spanned also by six sculptured ribs, that sprang from capitals, the floor was of oak, which had been split into planks by wedges, in the old Scottish fashion, roughly dressed by the axe, and secured by large-headed iron nails. The hall bore the impress of the architectural genius of the early part of the Middle Ages; the mouldings, the corbels, the flowered bosses, the ribs and mullions of the windows, were bold and massive, and the subdued light of a calm bright morning stole softly through their painted lozenges and crimson draperies. Old tapestries of green and amber colour, representing in quaint and misshapen figures the virtues and miracles of St. Margaret, the valour and death of her husband, clothed the walls of this sombre hall. The fair fingers of six Scottish princesses, viz., Margaret the Dauphiness of France, Elizabeth of Brittany, Jane of Huntly, Elinor of Austria, Mary of Campvere, and the Lady Annabella, all daughters of James I., had woven, in Dunfermline Tower, the stern romances which hung on tenter-hooks of steel around those ancient walls. At the lower end was a buffet, on which stood a gigantic thistle, with its stamens, composed of English swordblades, and its bristles of poniards, all gathered from the victorious field of Sark; at the upper, was the large fireplace, surmounted by the royal arms, and from each of the antique crowns by which the supporters—the white unicorns—were gorged, there depended a gilded *chain*.

This new and most remarkable addition to the imperial arms of the kingdom was soon remarked by several of the nobles, who muttered together, as they gathered in groups, awaiting the entrance of the king.

' It is significant of the chain he would bind around *us*,' said the Earl of Angus, with one of his dark and bitter smiles, as he thrust his furred cap of maintenance over his dark and shaggy brows.

' But 'tis a chain the sword can easily sever,' added Sir James Shaw.

This trifling affair shed a gloom over all the courtiers, who were rapidly assembling, all clad in rich and magnificent dresses. Accompanied by Sir David Falconer, Captain Barton, and Sir Alexander Mathieson, a wiry old seaman, the admiral arrived, and many of the proudest peers felt themselves constrained to greet the brave old man with courtesy and outward respect.

' My Lord of Angus,' said Robert Barton, frankly, kissing the hand of Scotland's greatest noble, ' God bless thee for avenging my poor father on the Howards and their Northumbrian kerne. From my soul I thank thee ! '

' Thank me not, good Robert Barton,' replied the earl, with coldness ; ' for though but a trader, thy father was a true Scot, and a brave one.'

At this reply Barton's eyes flashed, and Sir Andrew Wood bestowed on the speaker a frown.

' This haughty admiral does not bow very low, I think,' whispered Sir Patrick Gray of Kyneff.

' He who can stand upright in the presence of *honest* men needs not to bow in the presence of *great* ones,' retorted Sir Andrew, who overheard the remark.

At that moment the curtain at the lower end of the hall was drawn aside, and the king entered, preceded and followed by a brilliant retinue of ladies and nobles ; Colin of Argyle, the Lord High Chancellor ; Knollis, the Lord High Treasurer ; the Bishop of Dunkeld, who was Secretary of State ; Patrick Leith, a learned canon of Glasgow, who was Lord Clerk Registrar ; Sir William Halkett of Belfico, the Judge of Justiciary ; the Great Chamberlain, the Master of the Household, the standard bearer, and a crowd of other courtiers and favourites followed ; among them were many ladies, but those who attracted most attention were the Duchess of Montrose, with her conical headdress, and Margaret Drummond, yet pale and sad, and, as such, contrasting with her sisters, who were all brightness—beautiful and blushing with pleasure and excitement,—especially little Lizzie and Beatie, who wore their rich gifts, the silver collar and veil of lace.

The Duke of Rothesay, whose only attendant was his friend the young Lord Lindesay, kept himself a little apart from this variously attired crowd, which divided in two as the king assumed his lofty chair, which was placed on a carpeted dais, and under a cloth of estate, or canopy of purple velvet, which was then the royal colour in Scotland.

The king bowed and smiled to all around him ; but under those smiling acknowledgments there was, too painfully visible, that thoughtful expression which resulted from those bitter dissensions and civil broils that in past years had wrinkled the handsome face and seared the generous heart of James III.

He wore a jacquette and tight hose of white satin, embroidered with Venetian gold, and over the former a loose surcoat of blue velvet, without sleeves, but furred with miniver ; his sword, dagger, and belt sparkled with jewels, and around his neck were the orders of the Thistle and St. Michael the Archangel. His blue bonnet was borne by a pretty little page,—a royal protégé,—who was the son, not of a noble, but of some poor mendicant, who had attracted his notice, one day, when passing the Bridge of Dunblane. His hose reached to his feet,—for stockings, apart from hose, were then unknown. The first pair ever seen in Britain were worn by Henry VIII. of England, who obtained them from Spain, and his little successor, Edward VI., was solemnly presented with a pair by Sir Thomas Gresham.

Angus, Lord Home, Lord Hailes, Sir James Shaw, Sir Patrick Gray, the Laird of Keir, and others of that fierce noblesse, who never laid aside their iron coats, and who despised the almost effeminate dresses, the laces, ruffles, and ribbons of the courtiers, stood in whispering and observant groups. Apart from these and such as these, who too often the curse and betrayers of their country, were grouped a few of those learned men whom, like a true Stuart, the king loved and cherished.

Among them were three Benedictine priests, viz., John Abercrombie, a vigorous writer against the dawning heresies in the Church; Alexander Barclay, the translator of Sallust; and Robert Henrison, author of the *Bluidy Serk* and *Ye Burrowstoun Mouse and ye Landwart Mouse*; Father Zuill, the learned chaplain to Sir Andrew Wood; John Bellenden, then the greatest poet in Scotland, and afterwards Archdeacon of Moray; the learned Andrew Forman, the Protonotary Apostolic of the kingdom, in after years the most famous of our churchmen, and the mediator between Pope Julius II. and Louis XII.; David Steele, who wrote the *Thrie Priestis of Peblis*, and many other poor poets, who subsisted on the good king's privy purse, and wrote odes, ballads, and songs for a small yearly fee and the gift of a camlet gown, a bonnet and shoes, at St. Martin's-Mass and White Sunday. In the bearded visages of all these sable-gowned and black-capped literati, there were plainly visible a peculiar mixture of self-conceit and pedantic pride, tempered by an unpleasant timidity; for some of the smaller satirists, like Steele, were eminently obnoxious to the nobles; yet it was to this group that the impolitic king first addressed himself.

'Come hither, Father Barclay,' said he to the gifted translator of Sallust; 'I have just read thy noble satire, *The Ship of Fools*, and owe thee a chain of gold for it. I prefer it to thy *History of the Jugurthine War*; but we must imprint both, if we can get those newly invented iron letters from Germany. By my honour, Barclay, a scholar such as thou—or one like thee, Abercrombie, or any of ye —might well become the mentor of a king! I may mistake,' he added, turning to his gloomy-eyed peers, 'but I assure you, my lords, that nobility of mind is more acceptable to me than nobility of name.'

With a grotesque mixture of fear and pleasure, Barclay kissed the hand of the king. Angus glanced scornfully at his friends, and Kyneff whispered,

'Thou seest, my Lord Earl, how this doting king hath not even policy enough to gild the chain by which he would fetter the unicorn.'

Wood now approached and presented to James his three favourite officers—old Sir Alexander Mathieson, Sir David Falconer, and Robert Barton.

'God's benison on thee, my old king of the sea,' said James, clasping the hard rough hand of the venerable captain of the *Margaret*; 'and on thee, too, Barton. To thee I leave the duty of avenging thy slaughtered father. His estate of Barnton shall be created into a free barony, and his services shall never be forgotten. But come *thou* hither, Davie Falconer,' added James, who, to mortify his nobles, never omitted an opportunity of distinguishing one of the people. ' I owe thee something for that brave fight with the Spanish caravel in the English waters, but I know not what it may be—unless this trinket, for the time '; and taking from his finger a ring, he presented it to the arquebussier, whose heart swelled within him with sudden gratitude and joy ; and then his eyes sought those of Sybilla Drummond. His heart leaped anew, for it was full of all that a strong and beautiful passion can kindle in a profound and sensitive nature.

' Sir David,' continued the king, ' thy father died on the deck of his ship for mine ; and to feel that I have such subjects as thee and Barton, is to feel the true pleasure of being a king. Go—from my soul I love all such brave and honest fellows ! '

' 'Twas I who first made men of them both,' said Sir Andrew Wood, ' and who gave them a relish for gunpowder and salt water. Gadzooks ! confess, Robert Barton, when first thou camest aboard thou couldst neither hand, reef, nor steer, clamber aloft, grease a mast, handle oar, culverin, or caliver. All these I taught him, your Majesty, and made a man and a sailor of him ! '

' This day makes poor David Falconer the envy and the hatred of the nobles,' said Barclay the translator to Father Zuill.

' 'Tis false, sirrah,' growled the laird of Sauchie, who overheard the remark, which was made a little too audibly ; ' he is a brave fellow, who has won his spurs as he wins his daily bread by knight's service and the sword. Were he a cutter of stones, like the umquhile Cochrane, a fiddler, like William Rogers, or a useless scribbler, like thee, I would care little to see him gang the gate those loons were sent at Lauder.'

' Alas, noble sir,' urged the Benedictine, submissively, ' Cochrane was a most unfortunate man——'

' He was a villan,' said the Earl of Angus ; ' a dyvour who had turned heretic in his heart, and carried a Bible at his belt by a silver chain—a Bible printed in black letters by a German sorcerer, even such as the king would employ to print thy written book. Enough, sir ! '

After this, the priest had nothing more to urge.

'Father Zuill,' said the king to the chaplain of the *Yellow Frigate,* 'I am glad to see thee, and have received thy learned treatise on the burning glasses of the ancients, which I hope to peruse with pleasure; though I doubt mickle if you will ever supersede our cannon-balls. I have desired his grace of Montrose to present you with a copy of Virgil, by Caxton the Englishman.'

Confronting the lofty and arrogant eyes of the nobility, Falconer, who was armed like themselves, but less richly, retired towards the curtained doorway, where his arquebussiers were stationed, with the Montrose Herald and Garioch Pursuivant.

'This protégé of Wood,' said Sir Patrick Gray, 'is a coxcomb, whose profound admiration of his own person——'

'Is only surpassed by his profound loyalty and respect for his native monarch,' said Lady Euphemia Drummond, bluntly interrupting him, as she and her sisters drew near their father. Sybilla, who blushed with anger at Gray, gave her tall, pale eldest sister a glance full of gratitude; but the governor of Broughty, whom the words *native monarch* had stung deeply, bit his white lips with sudden anger, and relapsed into silence.

'How the devil doth it come to pass,' said the imperious Lord Drummond, 'that this churl, Falconer, who hath neither lands nor rents coming in, wears a scarlet mantle like a landed baron?'

''Tis the growing insolence of the class he springs from,' replied Sir James Shaw, haughtily, drawing his own rich mantle over his breast.

Poor Sybilla put down her fine face with timid sorrow, on hearing her lover spoken of thus.

'Well, my Lord Angus,' said Drummond, as they all drew a little apart into one of the deep windows; 'by your presence here this morning, am I to conclude you have become a faithful counsellor of the king?'

'As *you* have, my lord,' replied the dark Angus, with a courtly but crafty smile; for each was quite equal to and understood by the other.

'Your followers have valued lightly the new edict anent wearing swords in the king's vicinity!'

'As Scottish men should ever value such infamous edicts,' replied Bell-the-cat, with a dark frown; 'I have five hundred lances from the Howe stabled in the close of St. Salvador, and should like to see any one enforce the edict on them.'

'Angus,' said Drummond, with a deep glance, 'where will all this loyalty and this disloyalty, this open flattery and secret discontent end?'

'*On the field of battle*,' was the hoarse reply, whispered through a thick and wiry beard; and the timid Margaret Drummond trembled as she heard it, and drooped her soft, dark eyes, on finding the keen glance of Kyneff fixed as it was from time to time upon her with mingled curiosity and pity,—if in such a heart as his there might be pity.

Amid all this court intrigue and sea of plotting but aloof from it, stood the Duke of Rothesay, conversing with his friend and follower, the princely heir of Crawford. He saw only Margaret, whom he loved with all the heedless ardour of a boy, and was quite oblivious of the many fair ones, possessing no ordinary amount of charms, who were clustered around the Duchess of Montrose; and there were not a few who whispered into each other's pretty ears many a compliment on Rothesay's handsome figure and face. On this morning he was dressed almost entirely in white satin, slashed with blue and edged with gold. Margaret Drummond was attired in the same colours, which so well became her fair complexion and blonde hair. In the presence of the king, though he seldom addressed her, she always felt a dread, as of one against whom she had committed a wrong in becoming the wife of his son. She was ever apprehensive that his calm, inquiring eye might read her secret. She was pale as marble; and from time to time applied to her little pink nostrils a gold pomander ball, which was filled with scented paste, and such as were then used before the introduction of pouncet boxes. This had been one of Rothesay's earliest love-gifts to her.

Kyneff and Sauchie had been closely watching Rothesay and their beautiful victim, but found themselves completely at fault, and unable to discover any glances, signs, or tokens of intelligence passing between them; and Kyneff, who, although he could be politic and wary at times, was generally coarse, reckless, and bold, resolved to probe the matter at once, and dared to do so in the following manner: 'I have a boon to beg of your highness this morning,' said he, in his easiest and most familiar tone.

'A boon—thou?' asked the prince, with the coldness of instinctive distrust. 'Well, Sir Patrick?'

'I have taken the liberty of addressing your highness on

the dearest secret of my heart,' said he in a low voice, and twirling his mustachios, while he drew the prince aside, and with his stealthy eyes bestowed a covert glance on Sir James Shaw; 'I crave your influence with one of your most favoured courtiers—for—for——'

'For what—do not be *bashful*, Sir Patrick—his purse?'

'Nay his daughter's hand.'

'I crave in turn to be excused, for I would be exceedingly loth to assist a fowler so deadly as thee in meshing a poor little dove.'—'But I am one of the most faithful servants of your highness and of the king.'

'Well—and you are in love?'

'Prince, I have just had the honour of saying so.'

'But with whom, Sir Patrick?'

'A woman——'

'Of course, I took that for granted. Well; and this woman——'

'Is, beyond all compare, most beautiful!'

'Pshaw! Sir Patrick, money-bags were more to thy purpose. Is she rich?'

'Yea—as a queen in charms.'

'Twere better in crowns for thee. But who is she for whom I am to act a proxy lover?'

'Lady Margaret, the Lord Drummond's younger daughter.' As Kyneff said this, his keen grey eyes were fixed with an intense scrutiny on the clear hazel eyes and open brow of the young prince, but nothing could he detect, not even the slightest start; for although the hot heart of the impulsive Rothesay vibrated at that dear name, so admirably had he schooled himself to encounter the base plotters of his father's court, that he betrayed not the smallest outward sign of inward emotion; and with all his cunning, the traitor was completely baffled.

'I have but little influence with that family, I assure you, Sir Patrick Gray,' replied the prince, with a smile; 'and still less in the quarter you indicate; yet such as I have is yours. When shall I address the Lord Drummond—now?'

'Nay, nay, not just now,' said Kyneff, hurriedly, and confounded by the prince's perfect facility; 'but on another opportunity; and I beg of your highness to accept of my profound gratitude.'

'Doth this villan laugh at me, or hath he already divined our secret?' thought the startled prince, as the conspirator withdrew to the side of his friend and compatriot, the governor of the town and castle of Stirling.

The great chamberlain now approached to lay several complaints before the king, who by a power which had come down from those good old patriarchal times when the Donalds and Constantines dispensed justice from the mote-hills of Scone and Stirling, could yet hear the complaints of the most humble of his subjects ; but so crippled was his power, that James III. was now approached in vain. Then there were no courts of session or justiciary. Territorial jurisdiction was vested in the barons and provosts of burghs, from whom the appeals of vassals might be made to the sheriffs, to the royal justiciar, to the parliament, or the king —and from burgesses, in the first instance, to the chamberlain-ayre and court of the four burghs : but generally the people loved better to prefer their prayers to the ear of an indulgent prince, who regarded them all as his children. Thus, after Sir Andrew Wood had related that his embassy to Flanders had proved futile in clearing up our quarrel with the sturdy citizens of the Swyn, the Sluice, and the Dam, and that all trade with them would still be interdicted, the loyal and venerable Duke of Montrose said, in a most impressive manner,

' I grieve to say that complaints against the nobles have been pouring into your Majesty, and everywhere the people murmur against their oppression and misgovernment. Here,' he continued, consulting his notes, ' is a certain bondsman of the Lord Angus, who hath bought unto himself a burgage in the royal burgh of Dumfries, and is consequently a freeman, enjoying the liberty of that provostry ; yet, without a crime, he has been manacled and thrown into the dungeon of the castle of Thrieve.'

' What say you to this, my Lord Angus ? ' asked James.

' That I have hanged the frontless loon for complaining to his grace the chamberlain,' replied Angus, tightening the buckle of his gold waist-belt.

Montrose and the king exchanged impatient glances.

' Another complaint hath been made against Sir James Shaw of Sauchie, governor of your Majesty's castle of Stirling, for seizing and slaying several swine belonging to burgesses in the Braid Wynd ; and moreover, emptying eight byres and twelve henroosts in one night.'

' This is only according to law, duke,' replied Shaw ; ' for the king's castellans may freely slay all swine that are found straying upon the causeway; and may also exact kain thrice in the year: at Yule, Pasch, and White Sunday.'

'But not at Bartilday and Martin-mass too, Sir James,' said the chamberlain.

'Refer this to the judge of justiciary,' said the king.

''Tis long since syne, sirs,' urged Shaw, doggedly; 'besides, the burgesses of Stirling have ever been contumacious villans, and utterly unworthy of all belief.'

'Lord Home hath seized the leper-house and hospitium of Soltra,' continued the chamberlain, again glancing at his notes; 'his friend, the Lord Hailes, has stormed the knight of Ravelrig's castle, and burned his three farm-towns. The Steward of Menteith, with five hundred redshanks, hath forced himself upon the burghers of Auchterarder as provost, at the same time sacking them of armour, furniture, and all manner of gear.'

'Incited by ane auld witch carlin,' replied the steward, a grim-looking old man, who wore black armour and a kilt of blue and purple tartan; 'they ground their wheat wi' handquerns instead of coming to my new milne on the Ruthven water, quhilk is contrairy to the nineteenth chapter of the Statutes of Gild, and I swore that carlins should weep, and bearded carles should dee for't. Let them appeal to the General Convention of Burghs at Edinburgh, if they choose.'

'Nay,' said the king, in great anger; 'let them rather appeal to arms.'

'Be it sae,' said the savage old steward, with a laugh like a growl, as he rattled his long two-handed cliobh on the floor; 'what the deil care I? By a wave of my hand I could quench every fire between the muir of Orchill and the kirk of Aberruthven, if they winna thole my yoke.'

'Upon Rood-day, in last harvest,' resumed the chamberlain, 'the Constable of Dundee cruelly slew, under solemn tryst, the laird of Fetter-angus, at the glack of Newtyle.'

'Wherefore?' demanded the king, starting from his seat with irrepressible indignation. And the constable replied:

'A year before he harried my lands in the Howe; but I have made amends by paying an ample bludewit and by founding in the chapel of St. Blaise the martyr of Armenia, here in the Thorter Row of your Majesty's burgh of Dundee, an altar, where the priest for the time shall annually say for ever, until the day of doom, on the anniversary of that unhappy hour, a solemn mass for the soul of the umquhile laird; and on that altar lies the sword wherewith I slew him.'

'Tis well, constable,' said the king; 'may some good spirit do as much for thee. What, Montrose, is not this catalogue of crime exhausted?'

'The Heritable Forester of Drum,' replied the duke, closing his notes, 'hath seized a hundred head of swine belonging to the citizens of Aberdeen.'

'Because they declined to pay *pannage*, the usual duty levied upon all porkers that feed on mast and beech-nuts in the royal woods,' replied this baron, whose badge of office was a magnificent silver bugle.

'By the holy kirk, thou art a faithful subject!' said the king, scornfully.

'Something *must* be done,' resumed the Duke of Montrose, looking at the group near Angus, 'to repress this growing spirit of outrage, and to bring the complaints of the people before parliament; or, as my lord chancellor will agree with me, we cannot warrant peace among them for three months longer.'

'Montrose,' said James, in a soft, but bitter voice; 'well awa! I remember the raid of Lauder Brig, and am now, as then, powerless.'

'Lauder Brig,' reiterated the remorseless Angus, who had caught the words, and, whispering, turned to those around him; 'by St. Bryde of Douglas! I was beginning to think thou hadst forgotten that day, when we strung thy base mechanical favourites like a devil's rosary over the Lauder stream.'

Such were the peers of Scotland in the year of grace 1488.

CHAPTER XII.

EMBASSY OF THE SIEUR DE MONIPENNIE.

WHILE these accusations had been made by the lord chamberlain, and proud replies given by the noblesse in question, Rothesay had drawn near Margaret, and smilingly, and in whispers, related to her his conversation with Sir Patrick Gray, and the suit which the knight had requested him to urge. She grew, if possible, paler at the relation, for in her secret heart she feared that even were this new suit not urged for some dark and ulterior object, it might afford her great cause for uneasiness, and perhaps lead to the discovery of that private union, which, as a deadly secret, she treasured in her timid heart; for well she knew that the jealousy of the greater nobles at such an honourable alliance formed a *second time* with the House of Drummond would fan the flame of many a feud yet slumbering in its ashes.'

In the group near the Duchess of Montrose, Captain Barton was conversing softly with her sister Euphemia; and poor Falconer, from the foot of the hall (where a few of his soldiers supplied the place of Lord Bothwell's guard, who were then at Stirling), glancing anxiously at Sybilla from time to time, and sighed when reflecting that all the gold *he* possessed was on his spurs and doublet. A flourish of trumpets in the court-yard, and a glittering of pike-heads and heralds' tabards between the festooned curtains which shaded the lower end of the hall, announced the arrival of the new French ambassador and his train, and then all became hushed, save some such scraps of conversation as the following:

'Sybilla Drummond,' said the Duchess of Montrose, 'remember ye aught of the splendour in which the Lord Stuart d'Aubigne, Mareschal of France, came here in 1483?'

' As ambassador of Charles VIII. ? '

' To renew the ancient league.'

' Ah yes, madam ; how could I forget it ? My dear brother, who was killed at Naples by Gonsalvo de Cordova, was captain in one of the eighteen Scottish companies whom he took away with him to the Italian wars.'

' My puir nephew—he was indeed a brave gallant ! ' said the old duchess, with a sigh.

' Yet, madam,' resumed Sybilla, glancing through the painted window near her, ' I think the train of this Lord of Concressault every way inferior to those of the Mareschal d'Aubigne and of the papal ambassador, who came soon after from His Holiness Innocent VIII.'

' In the following year—the Lord Bishop of Imola : I remember me, child.'

' He succeeded in procuring a three years truce between King James and Richard of England,' said Barton, ' who sent his despatches sewn in the stomacher of Muriella Crawford.'

' Ah, that woman became a Lindesay by marrying into our family,' said the haughty old duchess, applying her pomander ball to her nose.

*   *   *   *   *

' My Lord Drummond,' said the swarthy Earl of Angus, glancing grimly at the king, who was sitting with his fore-head resting on his hand, and buried in thought, while the Chancellor, Treasurer, Secretary of State, and other richly dressed courtiers, hovered near him ; ' it would seem as if we peers of Scotland had become mere grooms and pages in the eyes of this king's new pimps and puppets.'

' By the fiend, yes ! Only conceive again what we have just heard—Hailes, Home, the Steward of Menteith, and the Forester of Drum, being thus arraigned at the instance of a few wretched burgesses ! '

' Yea, and before some of those we spared at Lauder Brig—men who are yet unhanged,' added Angus, with one of his darkest scowls.

' There now, not a yard from the king's chair, is a bal-ladeer, the son of a sword-slipper in the Shoegaitt of Perth, who hath exchanged the file and hammer for a sword and Parmese poniard—his canvas gaberdine for a dainty doublet of cramosie, because, forsooth, he is master of the king's music, and Margaret of Denmark loves to listen to the twangle of his viols and ghitterns—faugh ! '

'Men say he will be made a knight and privy councillor.'

'If so,' said Sauchie, 'by God I shall forswear my spurs for ever!'

'I knew such another clown who was made an earl,' said the Steward of Menteith, who had given his tent-cord to hang Cochrane over Lauder Bridge.

'There are Falconer and Barton, too, whose fathers were but merchant-skippers!'

'But the former is a brave gallant, and the latter is my particular friend,' said Drummond.

'Well, well,' resumed the discontented Angus, impatiently; 'but think of him whom I saved at Lauder, when *your* tent-cord was twisted round his neck—John Ramsay—a mere bonnet-laird, who is now, forsooth, *Sir* John Ramsay, and Lord of Bothwell, Baron of Balmain, Flaskie, and Pitnamore, with the Captainrie of the king's guard. Yet, by St. Bryde, this springald dared but yesterday to pass me in the Baxter's Wynd at Stirling—me, Archibald of Angus—with head erect, and without beck, bow, nod, or recognition!'

'The brose these loons shall sup is thickening fast, lord earl,' said Drummond, with a dark smile, as he spread his silvered beard over his steel gorget, 'and ere long our lances will be at their throats.'

At that moment the Montrose herald, an officer of the Lyon Court, who had been recently created in honour of the Crawford dukedom, exclaimed, 'Place for the ambassador of his Majesty, the King of France!'

'Sweetheart!' whispered Rothesay, pressing his Margaret's trembling hand, as all eyes were turned towards the entrance, 'this is, indeed, a critical day for us! Should my father depart on his long-proposed pilgrimage, I shall be regent, and he must grant us pardon ere he go. If he stays, we shall then be condemned to linger on in secrecy, but only a little longer.'

'Until the good Bishop of Dunblane returns,' said Margaret, with one of her dearest smiles.

During the reign of James III. there were an unusual number of solemn treaties and splendid embassies passed between the court of Scotland and those of Louis XI. and Charles VIII. of France; Alphonso *Africanus* of Portugal, Ferdinand V. of Spain, Christian of Denmark, and Charles *the warrior*, Count of Flanders, by means of nobles, prelates, and heralds. Some of these were exceedingly magnificent, for under the care of kings who were far in advance of their times, Scotland was rapidly rising in the scale of European nations. But on the present occasion the special envoy of Charles VIII. was attended only by two esquires and two pages, who bore his helmet and braquemart, or short French sword.

The Sieur de Monipennie, Lord of Concressault, was a Scotsman, a cadet of the family of Pitmilly, long naturalized by residence in France, in the armies of which he had served for thirty years. He commanded four thousand archers in the war between the Charolois and the Lords of the League, and at the battle of Montleri had slain, with his own hand, Pierre de Breze, the grand seneschal of Normandy. At the left clasp of his cuirass dangled the gold cross of eight points, worn by the chevaliers of the Order of St. Etienne, and the Cross of the Immaculate Conception. In aspect he was venerable and soldierlike. His armour was black, edged, studded, and engraved with gold : his boots had those long toes or *poleines*, of which we may read in the chronicles of Monstrelet : his beard was white as snow, but his dark grey eyes were bright and keen ; his features were severe and somewhat harsh, but a smile of pleasure and loyalty overspread them as he approached his native monarch, and, full of honest enthusiasm, knelt down to kiss the hand of James, who immediately raised him from the dais.

' The last time I had the happiness of seeing your Majesty,' said he, in a voice that was strongly tinged by a foreign accent, ' was about thirty years ago, and ye were then but a halfling laddie.'

' At the funeral of my mother, of royal memory, in the collegiate kirk of Edinburgh,' said the king.

' I mind it weel, as if 'twere yesterday. Woe is me ! but the cares of manhood have been written deeply on your Majesty's brow since syne ; yet ye *do* remind me of the king, your father, when I saw him last in '58 at the Castle of Stirling. He was ever a good friend to me and to my house.'

The eyes of the veteran suffused with emotion as the recollection of years long passed came gushing back upon his warm and generous heart.

' I rejoice, indeed, to see you, my Lord of Concressault, and am all impatience to hear the message of my cousin of France.'

' It is simply concerning the proposition formerly made anent the invasion of Brittany. He has been pleased to **desire me to urge** your Majesty to invade and take possession of that dukedom, promising, at the same time, to make over to the crown of Scotland all right and interest France may have in its five bishoprics of Rennes, Nantes, Saint Malo, Dol, and Saint Brieuc. He would advise your Majesty, as more fully set forth in these papers which I shall have the honour of laying before your council, to promise to the Bretons that their states-general and all their ancient privileges shall be retained as inviolate, subject, however, to the modifications of the Scottish Parliament.'

'What say you to this, my lords?' asked the king, as a murmur of varying opinions rose among the nobles.

'I say nay,' replied Angus; 'the poor Bretons have never wronged us, and by St. Bryde! why should we invade and dispossess their duke, to please a King of France or to avenge his petty piques and jealousies?'

'The King of France requires no man to avenge his quarrels, Earl of Angus,' retorted the Scoto-French Lord Concressault, turning abruptly round.

'Drummond,' said the king, 'what sayst thou?'

'I agree with Angus,' replied Lord Drummond. 'Why should we imitate England of old, by waging wanton wars, and violating the rights of a free people?'

'There are some fine harbours off the Breton coast,' said Sir Andrew Wood; 'gadzooks, Robbie Barton, we know Nantes well, with its castle at the mouth of the Sevre.'

'King Charles desired me to say,' continued Sieur de Monipennie, without heeding the nobles, 'that twenty thousand men will be sufficient to reduce the Bretons, with such French forces as he would send against them by the way of Maine and Anjou, together with all the Scottish troops now in the service of France—to wit, Sir Robert Patulloch's gard du corps Ecossaises; my thousand lances of Concressault, and those of John of Darnley, the mareschal Stuart d'Aubigne, who has just been created Comte d'Evereaux; and those would enter by the way of Poitou, as these letters will show.'

Whatever James thought of this splendid offer from the wily ministers of his cousin Charles the Affable, who was then in his eighteenth year, he had not time given him to say. In 1471, the proposition had been made before, and he had then intended to annex Brittany, at the head of 6,000 Scottish infantry, but the Parliament opposed it; and now nearly with one unanimous voice, the nobles said, and perhaps with some feeling of justice—

'Not a man of us will draw a sword or lift a lance in this cause!'

'The Bretons have never wronged us,' added Lord Drummond; 'and woe be to those who wage an unjust war!'

'You forget, my lords, that the barons and burgesses are yet to be consulted,' replied the king, with rising anger; 'and if *their* voice is for the annexation of Brittany to our realm, by the Black Rood of Scotland, I will march without my recreant nobles, or create *new ones* on the field!'

The peers on hearing this rash speech smiled at each other contemptuously and incredulously while the Lord of Concressault gazed at them in astonishment; for though he knew well the stubborn pride of his native chiefs, he had but recently come from France, where he had seen the iron rule of Louis XI., his fortresses of Loches and Montilz-les-Tours, with their trap-doors and gibbets, for the proud and refractory; his atrocious bastille, with its vaulted hall, and those cubes of masonry and iron which stood therein, and were called the king's little daughters, and in the heart of which some men were pining and had pined for twenty years, like frogs in a marble block! He had seen all France tremble at the nod of the decrepit little tyrant who espoused Margaret of Scotland—and now he gazed with ill-concealed wonder at the effrontery of these Scottish nobles. And James, though his generous nature was ever averse to injustice and oppression, merely to oppose, and if possible to mortify them, seemed not indisposed to undertake the conquest and annexation of this then independent dukedom, which was not united to France until 1532.

'Immediately after the meeting of Parliament, before whom your papers shall be laid, I will send to France my final answer,' replied the king; 'and now, my Lord of Concressault, you can favour me in a very particular manner. You are, of course, aware, that since 1477, now eleven years ago, I have been bound by a solemn vow to visit the shrine of St. John, in the great Cathedral of Amiens.'

The ambassador bowed; Rothesay pressed the hand of Margaret Drummond, who hung upon his arm, and stepped forward a pace to listen. A deep stillness reigned in the crowded hall; even the nobles seemed to hold their breaths for a time.

'On this pilgrimage I was to have gone, accompanied by a thousand gentlemen; but the arrival of a legate from his Holiness Sixtus IV., the siege of Dunbar, the revolt of my

brother, the Duke of Albany, and those events which bro
on the—the fatal raid at Lauder, with many other eve
have totally precluded the fulfilment of this most holy pled
I therefore entrust to you, my Lord of Concressault, this ho
medal, the gift of our Father Innocent VIII.,' continued James
taking from his neck a large and heavy gold medallion.
' This I beseech you to present in my name to the shrine of
St. John, as at present I see no possibility of my leaving
Scotland, even for the short period of three months.'

The Sieur de Monipennie knelt to receive the consecrated
medal, which he kissed and suspended by its gold chain at
his neck. It bore an image of the Virgin, and was encircled
by the legend,—

Hail, Mary, Star of Heaven, and Mother of God!

This medal was afterwards conveyed to the Shrine of St.
John at Amiens, and there it hung until the plunder of the
churches during the French Revolution.

Rothesay gazed on Margaret tenderly, and in silence, for
the king's sudden and unexpected abandonment of his long-
projected pilgrimage removed, for the present, all hope of a
fortunate or happy revelation of their rash and secret union.
Rothesay sighed with disappointment, and Margaret's
timid eyes filled with tears ; for had James actually departed on this pilgrimage, the rules of the Church would have
compelled him to forgive all who had offended against him,
or his journey would have been deemed a false and futile
pretence.

Distinguishing from among the nobles the stout and
portly admiral, whom he knew by the silver whistle which
hung at his neck, the venerable ambassador of Charles VIII.
entered into an animated conversation with Sir Andrew
Wood, which was a fresh source of irritation to some of the
jealous peers, who thereby felt themselves slighted. The
hum of voices again pervaded the large and stately hall,
and James, after exchanging a few words with the Duke of
Montrose, reclined his brow upon his hand, and with his face
overshadowed by a bitterness which he could not conceal,
at the affront so publicly given to him by the nobles, suddenly
and abruptly arose to withdraw. Angus, who at times was
not ungenerous, perceived his deep emotion, and as the acknowledged leader of the peers, approached and said in a low
voice :

' Your Majesty may feel that we have wronged you ; but

I beseech you to rest assured, that at heart your nobles love you.'

'And hate all else who have a claim on my friendship,' replied James, bitterly, ' or all who deserve my affection ; is it not so, lord earl ? '

'Yes, if bestowed upon the ignoble and unworthy,' replied the earl, haughtily, while his deep, dark, glassy eyes bestowed on his sovereign one of those daring, fixed, and penetrating glances which even he at times found almost insupportable.

'Yet would I hope, Angus, that with our great banquet in the Castle of Edinburgh—that friendly feast of which I have spoken so often—all these feuds and bitternesses will cease,' said James, as he bowed low to Concressault, the ambassador, lower still to the ladies, and retired, leaning on the arm of his most faithful friend and counsellor, the Duke of Montrose.

'Poor king ! ' said the admiral to Barton, as they also departed ; ' between his peers and his people, he is like one between the devil and the deep sea.'

CHAPTER XIII.

TO SEA!

On leaving the hall, Sir Andrew Wood was received at the palace-gate by his usual bodyguard; the crew of his barge, under the command of Cuddie, the coxswain, armed with their boat-stretchers, and clad in their spotless white gaberdines, girdled by broad black belts, in which each had his Scottish knife or dudgeon-dagger, and all wearing broad blue bonnets, having red cherries on the top and white St. Andrew's crosses in front. They were sixteen of the smartest men in the ship's company, and Cuddie—or Cuthbert—the coxswain, marched in front.

As the admiral, thus escorted and accompanied by Falconer and Barton, proceeded towards the landing-place down Tindall's Wynd, a narrow thoroughfare, then paved by those round stones such as may yet be seen in the streets of Arbroath and other seaport towns in Angus, he perceived a seaman making various efforts to attract his attention, by coming close to the barge's crew, and always touching his bonnet with profound respect whenever his eye fell on him.

'Ahoy, brother!' said the admiral, 'what cheer? Do you wish to speak with me? Ha! Jamie Gair—is it thee who art backing and filling thus, as if I were some great lord? Put on thy bonnet, man. But why art not away to the fishing-ground? Are there English cruisers off the coast?'

'Ye have guessed aright, Sir Andrew,' replied Gair; 'and I crave the honour o' a word wi' ye apart.'—'Well, say forth.'

'Captain Howard, the *Royal Harry*, and twa other English ships, were off the Firth last night.'

'What dost thou tell me?'—'Sure as I am a living man, sir—inside the Inchcape bell,' continued Jamie, in a low anxious whisper.

'Lubber and loggerhead! And thou only tellest me now!'
—'Wi' the first blink o' dawn I was aboard the frigate, Sir
Andrew, but ye werena there; and I hae been haudin' off
and on about the palace door since syne, in the hope o' seeing
you. But oh, be wary, Sir Andrew, and ask me nae mair,
for I am but a puir fisherman, wi' a wife and a bairn to feed
and to cleed——'

'Wary—what mean ye, Jamie Gair?'—'Your word as a
knight, Sir Andrew, that you will never repeat what will
assuredly be my ruin.'

'Messmate, thou hast my word as a seaman. Well?'—
'Last night three gentlemen, in masks, went off to the *Royal
Harry*, and remained two hours aboard.'

'About what time was this?'—'Mirk midnight——'

'When honest men are swinging in their hammocks.
Well?'—'When day broke, she and her twa consorts were
bearing awa' south and by east.'

'Three gentlemen, wearing masks,' said the admiral,
keenly scrutinizing the honest brown visage of the fisherman;
'ken ye their names?'—'No, Sir Andrew,' replied Jamie,
looking down, for he trembled for his wife and child, if
exposed to the vengeance of Gray of Kyneff.

'By every shrine in Largo kirk!' said the admiral, 'I
would give my starboard fin to know who these villans
were. Ho! Robert Barton, I have news for thee,' he added,
with a grim smile; 'the English *Harry* and her consorts are
off the coast.'—'Edmund Howard—he who with his brother
slew my father in the Downs?'

'The same, my lad; and while we have been loitering in
smooth water among those gilded sharks of courtiers, they
may have escaped us.'

'Edmund Howard—oh, David Falconer, hearest thou
that?' said Barton, with fierce joy; 'come, admiral; if
he escapes us now——'

'May we never go to sea without a foul wind, or come to
anchor without a rotten cable. Away to your arms—to your
cannon—the English fleet is off the coast!'—'Bear away,
then, Cuddie—heave ahead, my lads! hurrah!' cried
Barton, waving his bonnet, and the whole of the barge's
crew ran down Tindall's Wynd brandishing their boat-
stretchers, and springing on board, shipped their oars.
Wood and Falconer leaped into the sternsheets, and
Barton grasped the tiller.

'Give way, my braw lads, give way!' exclaimed the

admiral, as Cuddie shoved the boat off; the sixteen oars were dipped into the water; the crew bent to their task, and almost lifted the light shallop out of the river, as they shot her round the Craig of St. Nicholas, where the nautical loungers bestowed a farewell cheer in honour of old Sir Andrew. Jamie Gair was left in the middle of the Wynd, where he stood for a time, irresolute and half repenting the interest he had taken in affairs of State, and dreading that the gold he had earned might bring him naught but sorrow.

'Give way, callants—give way!' continued the brave old Laird of Largo; 'see—the tide is ebbing, and there is a fine breeze blowing down the Carse o' Gowrie! Give way merrily, my hearts—pull with a will!'

The old man was all impatience; the crew of the barge caught his enthusiasm. They bent to their slender oars with all their muscular energy, and the light boat was shot over the waters of the Tay, which parted before its bows, and curled under its counter, in the bright sunshine, in long lines that were edged with bells of snowy foam. Like an arrow, the long sharp boat sheered alongside the towering frigate; the oars were unshipped from the rowlocks and piled along the thwarts, while Cuddie the coxswain caught an eyebolt with his boathook. In three minutes, the admiral, his officers, and the crew were all on board and the boat was dangling like a toy from the davits.

'Run up the signal for sea,' said the admiral; 'Master Wad, fire a culverin to let Sir Alexander Mathieson know what we are about. Boatswain, pipe away the yeoman of the windlass, and heave short—cast loose the courses; trip the anchor, and prepare all for sailing.'

The greatest alacrity followed these rapid orders. Archy of Anster was as active as if the one-eyed demon of his extraordinary yarn was after him: he hurried from poop to forecastle, growling, shouting, swearing and piping away between decks.

'Willie Wad—quick wi' your gun!' he cried; 'or we'll serve ye wi' a stoup o' bilge in guid earnest.'

The little blue flag, which, from time immemorial, has been the signal for sailing, was run up to the foremast head, where it fluttered in the wind; one of the starboard ports was triced up, and a great cannon-royale sent its report like thunder over the calm still flow of the shining river; and immediately a commotion was visible on board the *Queen Margaret*. The flag of Sir Alexander Mathieson was displayed from her mainmast head, and the shrill whistle of her boat-swain was heard, as he piped all hands on deck.

As to referring to either king or council, lord high chan-cellor or secretary of state, for orders to put to sea, such an idea never entered the head of stout Sir Andrew Wood; who sometimes was not over particular, for it is recorded that once during a private quarrel with the Provost of Aberdeen, he sailed up the Don with the king's ships and bombarded the granite city in a fashion which its citizens never forgot or forgave.

Falconer stood on the poop looking regretfully at the house of the Drummonds, with its large round towers, which were then almost washed by the river; but Barton was all life and animation; and with a celerity astonishing for an age when every species of mechanism was rude and in its infancy, the ships of war were got under way. The boatswain manned the windlass, and after a few hard tugs with the handspikes, they tripped the anchor and turned

> The engine round,
> At every turn the clanging pauls resound;
> Uptorn reluctant from its oozy cave,
> The ponderous anchor rises o'er the wave.

Its square stock appeared above the surface of the water, and then Barton seized his trumpet.

'Hard up with the helm, timoneer,' he cried; 'fill the head sails—on board with the foretack! haul out the spanker and set the spritsail. Forecastle, there—cat and fish the anchor!'

'Quick, my lads!' added the boatswain; 'yare, yare—mony hands mak' licht wark.'

'Sheet home,' said the admiral, stamping his feet as he walked up and down the poop impatiently, and at every turn looked aloft; 'sheet home! Barton, hoist the top-gallant sails! Gadzooks, but it *is* a brave breeze this! Archy of Anster, send your sharpest man to the crow's nest as a look-out, and see that he kens a fleet of ships from a flock of gulls. By the whale of Jonas! I will give a hundred golden angels to the first man who discovers these English pirates!'

Cuddie the coxswain scampered up aloft, and perched him-self in the main-cross trees.

As the great square mainsails of the frigates fell, they began to feel the full pressure of their canvas and gathered way; the transient bustle subsided, and as the broad sails swelled out from the yardheads, and the glassy river rippled beneath their sharp and lofty prows, they stood noiselessly down the opening Tay, with the ebbing tide, and a western wind, right aft to bear them onward.

With evening a soft opal-coloured light stole over the summer sky. The heat of the day had subsided, and a light breeze stole along the water, wafting from the shores of that majestic river the rich fragrance of the apple bowers, the ripening grain, and the thousand plants that flourish by its margin.

The great square tower of St. Mary, the pointed spire of St. Clement, the Rock of St. Nicholas, and the little burgh—for it was then indeed but a small but beautiful Dundee—became shrouded in the haze of the warm summer evening, as the frigates, keeping straight in the fair way, rounded Tentsmuir Point, the sands of Abertay, and then bore away a point or two towards the south, with the western wind upon the quarter, when the sun's rays were fading behind the undulating coast of Forgan, or, as it then was named, St. Fillan.

People supped early in those days; thus, an hour after sunset, the bell in the great cabin announced that the evening meal was ready.

'By Heaven! admiral, I have an appetite for the first time since my father's death!' said Barton, as he took his seat with a flushed brow.

'Gadzooks, Robbie, if Cuddie descries those Englishmen——'

'I will add two hundred angels to thine, admiral, and rig him a crayer of his own—and she shall be the best that ever was launched on the Forth or the Tay!'

Father Zuill, the chaplain, who sat on Wood's right hand, blessed the viands, which consisted of a platter of fried garvies fresh from the Tay, two great pies, one called a gibelotte, which the Scots had adopted from their friends the French, and have now abbreviated into *giblet;* and the other a tower of paste, containing all the odds and ends the cook could collect in his larder. This was designated a double-decker. There were pies of quinces and orange marmalade for dessert, and cases of sack and canary for those who sat above the salt; with a great leather jack of ale for Archy the boatswain, Willie Wad the gunner, Cuddie the coxswain, the captains of the fore, main, and mizentops, who sat below this line of demarcation, and who, instead of supping off plate and a silk-edged table-cloth like the officers, were bound to content

them with a plain bare table and wooden tree plates, with
horn-handled knives and spoons. The conversation was
general and animated, for it ran chiefly on the merits and
death of Sir Andrew Barton, the probable strength of the
enemy, and the chances of overhauling them. When supper
was over, Sir Andrew desired all to fill their cans, for the
toast which he invariably gave every night, at the same hour
and in the same place, when on board, and had done so for
the last thirty years.

'The gude Port o' Leith, messmates—God bless it, and a'
our Scottish ships at sea!'

When again they came on deck, the ships were off the
Eden mouth, and the waves of St. Andrews stormy bay were
rolling their crests away to windward. As the light breeze
swept over them, they were tinted with a thousand prismatic
hues by the broad white summer moon, which rose in her
clearest beauty from the German Sea. Falconer's thoughts
were then of Sybilla, whom he loved so well and perhaps so
vainly; and abandoning himself to the fondest reveries, he
brooded deeply over his passion amid the majestic silence of
the sea that swept around him, and the distant land, whose
headlands jutted into that shining mirror in bold but hazy
outlines.

Barton loved Euphemia Drummond not a whit less than
the captain of arquebussiers loved her younger sister; but
with the secure feeling of a fiancé, for the present he dismissed
her fair image from his breast, and gave full play to those
high hopes of fully avenging his gallant father on the very
men who had slain him, and whose ships he knew were on
those moonlit waters, which he was incessantly scanning
with eagerness and impatience, but with his unaided eyes
alone; for telescopes were not invented for nearly a hundred
and twenty years after.

The old admiral, who burned to punish the slayers of his
venerable friend and messmate more than to avenge the
temporary disgrace—if disgrace it was—cast by the Howards
upon the rising prowess of the Scottish mariners, shared all
the impatience of Barton, and together they trod up and down
the weather side of the poop, frequently hailing Cuddie, who
was still perched at the crosstree, to be assured that he kept a
proper look-out.

The night stole on; the moon began to sink; the frigates
were still going free with the wind upon the quarter; Fife-
ness, with the dangerous Carr Rock, arose on the starboard

bow, and the old admiral, who knew every part of the coast as well as the features of his own face, now looked from time to time at the compasses which stood in the lighted binnacle, or as the seamen then named it, *habbitacle*—i.e., a small house, for there were two—one for the steersman and another for the gunner who was conning.

The *Margaret* was now a falcon shot astern, and the great poop-lantern of the *Yellow Frigate* was lighted ; but this precaution was needless, as her cloud of snow-white canvas and all her taut black rigging were as visible to her consort under the clear blue sky of night as if at noonday.

' Fifeness in sight, and no sign of them yet ! ' muttered the admiral ; ' square the yards, Barton, and stand right away before the breeze.'

The temporary bustle of this manœuvre soon subsided ; the rope-ends were again coiled away, and, save the watch and some of the crew, who were listening to another of the boatswain's incredible yarns in the forecastle, all the ship's company had turned into their hammocks. About the middle watch of the night, Barton, who was still impatiently pacing the deck, heard the man (who for a time had replaced the coxswain) at the masthead hailing the deck.

' Poop, ho ! '

' Hallo,' answered Barton, instinctively grasping his trumpet, which lay on the binnacle; 'are *you* aloft, Dalquhat?' —' Twa sails are in sicht, sir.'

' Where away, my old Carle ? '—' On the larboard bow.'

' What are they like ? '—' Ilk ane is a three-masted ship. Ane has a poop lantern, the other is hull doon ; but we are coming up wi' them hand owre hand.'

' Look hard, shipmate, and mayhap ye may see another,' said Barton ; ' Falconer, call the admiral. Yeomen of the sheets and braces, to your quarters : up with that fore-top-gallant-sail a bit, and fill the heads of that sprit-sail yard. How does she steer, Wad ? '—' Like a swan,' replied the gunner ; 'a wee bairn micht keep her full wi' a silken twine.'

The admiral now came on deck, and with a beating heart the gallant Barton sprang away aloft, to have a look at the vessels ahead, and praying as he went, that they might prove to be those of Captain Edmund Howard.

By this time the silver moon had waned, and the hills of Fife were melting into the darkened sea and cold, blue, starlit sky astern.

CHAPTER XIV.

THE OGRE OF ANGUS.

THE gun which was fired from the *Yellow Frigate* before she sailed from her moorings at Dundee attracted the attention of many in the town, and among others Hew Borthwick, who, at a bench outside the gate, had been teaching the constable's men-at-arms, who loitered about the king's lodging (as St. Margaret's Palace was sometimes named), various tricks with cards and dice. Hurrying down St. Clement's Wynd with others, to the beach, he saw the frigate under full sail, standing down the river.

'What the devil's i' the wind now?' was his first thought; 'if Sir Andrew encounters Howard on the high seas, our special plan will assuredly be blown up like a soap-bubble! Can Gair have suspected us? Impossible! the fellow knew nothing, save that we boarded a ship—and what of that? Well, well, let those laugh who win this desperate game. But it looks ill, yonder old grampus putting to sea in such haste,' he continued, after a pause; 'I must e'en hie me to Broughty, and see Sir Patrick.'

In those days there were but two hostelries in Dundee, and as neither of these had confidence enough in human virtue to entrust our worshipful knight with a horse, he was obliged to depart on foot for Broughty, passing out of the town by the shore instead of the Seagate and market-place, for which he had a decided aversion; and, indeed, wretch as he was, he could never pass through the latter without a shudder, as it recalled certain passages in the history of his family, with which we may now acquaint the reader.

In many ancient records, but chiefly that old and quaint chronicle of Scotland written by Robert Lindesay, Laird of Pitscottie, we are informed, that about thirty-eight years before the time of our story, there was a strange being named

Ewain Gavelrigg, who dwelt among the Sidlaw Hills in Angus, and who with his whole family was accused of the strange and horrible crime of eating human flesh!

At the foot of the mountains, he occupied a small hut, walled with turf and thatched with heather, at a place called Uach-dair Tir—now *Auchtertyre;* but his chief haunt was that savage pass in the Sidlaws, known as the Glack of Newtyle, where he waylaid, robbed, and slew the solitary travellers who chanced to be benighted in that wild and lonely district, which then lay between Dundee and Strathmore. Several who had escaped him, and reached either the Castle of Baille-Craig, which was close by, or that of the Constable of Dundee, related how they had been encountered by a man of frightful aspect and vast stature, armed with a great mace and poniard. All accounts of him were similar. He was entirely clad in homespun grey, with rough deer-skin shoes and galligaskins ; a broad belt of cowhide encircled his waist, and his head, which was ever destitute of bonnet, was protected by a forest of matted black hair. A blow from his clenched hand was sufficient to brain a mountain bull, or smite a charger to the earth; and those who escaped from him, averred that they saw him sucking the blood from the wounds of those he had slain, and rending asunder their limbs like the branches of a withered bush, while he picked their bones, as a marmoset might pick those of a chicken.

In that age of credulity and marvel, such stories made a terrible impression on the people. The whole of Angus rang with them—and others were constantly being added, each more startling than the last. The men of Strathmore, the light Lindesays, the vassals of Glammis, and even the valiant Sutors of Forfar, never ventured abroad after night-fall, save in parties of three or four, and always well armed, with their quarter-staves or two-handed swords.

Twice had men of undoubted valour and veracity averred that they had slain him ; one an arrow-maker of Dundee, by a wound he had given him in the throat ; another who was a sword-slipper of Banff, by a thrust he had given him in the breast ; but they were taunted as bootless boasters, for this strange and uncouth being was still haunting the pass of the Sidlaws.

A succession of these incredible stories excited the wonder and kindled the chivalry of Sir James Scrimegeour of Dudhope, the young Constable of Dundee ; and attended only by Lord Drummond—then Sir John of that ilk—well mounted and in full armour, on St. John's night in the year 1440, he rode to the Glack of Newtyle, and there, like a paladin of old, blew three blasts with his bugle-horn. The night was unusually dark, and the broad sheet lightning was reddening the sky behind the black peak of Kinpurnie, which is eleven hundred feet in height, and is the highest of the Sidlaw range. The narrow bridle-path which led through the Glack was buried in obscurity, and clumps of stunted firs which grew in the morasses waved mournfully in the wind that sang down the mountain pass and through their wiry foliage.

With their chargers shod with felt, the knights rode softly on, and as challenger, Scrimegeour, the royal standard-bearer, was a bowshot in front of Sir John Drummond.

By the first blast of his bugle the erne was roused from its eyry among the cliffs of Kinpurnie; by the second, the warder at Baille-Craig was wakened from his sleep, and the hirsels lowed on the hills; but the third had scarcely been tossed among the mountain echoes by the wind, when between him and that midnight sky, which every instant was reddened by the bright but silent lightning, the valiant Scrimegeour saw a gigantic figure arise as if from the ground, with its long hair waving wildly, while it brandished a mace, which was furnished with a studded ball of steel, that swung at the end of an iron chain.

'Ewain Gavelrigg—man or fiend—come on!' exclaimed the knight, and though every pulse in his body for a moment stood still, he dashed forward to the combat.

By one blow of this iron mace, which descended like a thunderbolt, the brains of the horse were dashed back into its rider's face, and the rider himself hurled prostrate on the path. Then the vampire or demon of Uach-dair Tir strode over him, brandishing his tremendous weapon, and uttering a succession of wild shouts of laughter. Grasping by the throat the half-stunned Constable of Dundee, and compressing his gorget of steel as if it had been a lady's ruff of lace, he would have slain him there but for the valour of his companion, and a vow he had made to build a chapel in honour of St. John, if he escaped. Moreover, it is related, that he was almost suffocated by the inconceivable odour that pervaded the body of his herculean conqueror. While the latter, exulting in his victory, and laughing like a hyæna, was half strangling and half dragging the discomfited Scrimegeour towards the pine woods, he neither heard nor saw Drummond, who with his light Barbary courser, shod by soft felt, ad-

vanced over the velvet sward that bordered the wayside,
but noiselessly, like the tall shadow of a man and horse.

The long sharp lance of Drummond was in the rest, and
urged by the full force of a galloping steed and the thrust of
a powerful arm, the head of steel and a yard of the tough ash
pole were driven through the body of the midnight marauder,
who expired with a frightful cry.

When day broke and the body of this strange man was
examined, it was found to be vast in its strength and pro-
portion, but terrible in aspect; and multiplied by a hundred-
fold, the odour of dead carrion pervaded it. When stripped,
it was found to have *four* wounds, from all of which the black
blood had been freely flowing; viz.: those where Drummond's
lance had pierced the back and breast, and those inflicted
by the barbed shaft of the arrow-maker and the sword of the
dalmascar.

Two wild and haggard-looking women, his wife and
daughter, came from their hut at Uach-dair Tir, and as a
boon begged to have the body for interment, and as a refusal
would have been deemed unknightly, it was freely bestowed
by the valiant Laird of Dudhope, who first hewed off the
hand which had grasped him by the throat, and nailed it
on the western gate of Dundee, where the skeleton fingers
were to be seen in the days of James IV.

In accordance with his vow, he endowed and dedicated a
beautiful little chapel to St. John the Evangelist, which he
built at the Sklait-hewchs, upon a rock near the burgh;
but the walls of this fair oratory had barely been raised three
feet in height, when again the travellers, who in that unruly
age were hardy enough to traverse the wilds between Dundee
and Strathmore, were found murdered and mutilated;
children disappeared, desperate conflicts were fought and
pools of blood found in the Glack of Newtyle, and all Angus
was stricken with consternation by tidings that the wild
man of the Sidlaws had come alive again!

By sound of trumpet at the burgh crosses, Sir Alexander
Livingstone, of Callendar, governor to the young King James
I., proclaimed a general crusade against him. The hut at
Uach-dair Tir was levelled and destroyed, when, in a chamber,
or vault below it, there were found an incredible number of
bones, which the credulity of the time magnified to a perfect
hecatomb of human remains. Dudhope brought a hundred
lances on horseback, the Lindesays of Crawford and the
Abbot of Aberbrothwick a thousand each; the Laird of

Baille-Craig brought a band of gallant archers; a general hunt began; the whole country was searched between Stenton Craig and Edzel Kirk, till, deep in a chasm of the Sidlaw hills, the sleuth bratches of Dudhope discovered Ewain Gavelrigg, who made a desperate and frantic resistance, slew eight men and three horses—after threatening all the rest with dire vengeance, even if he should be slain; but he was at last overborne by blunted spears, for the knights wished to capture and not to slay him; and for a charm each had tied to his lance's head a rosemary branch, with a twig of the rowan tree.

Having but *one hand* to fight with, he was soon bound hard and fast by cords and chains, slung under a horse's belly, and thus conveyed to Dundee, where he was sentenced by the constable to be burned at the market cross, together with his wife, daughter, and son, a little child, to make sure that none of a brood so terrible should ever come alive again.

Jellon Borthwick, a prebend of Dunkeld, pled hard to have the child delivered to him; and his boon was granted; but the others were burned in succession: first Gavelrigg, then his wife, and next their daughter, who was also accused, whether truly or falsely, we know not, of having eaten the flesh of many children.

'When she was coming to the place of execution,' said Robert Lindesay in his Chronicle, 'thair gathered an hudge multitud of people, and especiallie of vomen, cursing her for being so unhappie as to committ such damnable deidis; to whom she turned with an ireful countenance, saying:

'" *Whairfoir chyde ye me, as if I had committed an unworthie act? Give me credence and trow me, if ye had experience of eating of mens and womens flesch, ye wald think it so delitious that ye wald never forbear it agaen!* "'

'So without any signe of repentance,' concludes the historian, 'this vnhappie traitour deid in the sight of the people.'

Her ashes, with those of her terrible parents, were scattered on the waters of the Tay; and a black whin-stone in the causewayed market-place long remained to indicate the spot where they perished. Hew Borthwick was the child whom the priest saved: hence it was that he shuddered to pass through the central street of Dundee. The good old prebend, who had given him his own name, reared him for the Church, in the hope that through his piety and prayers the atrocious lives of his parents might in some measure be atoned for : but Hew broke his vows, and came forth into the world, to fulfil the terrible mission for which fate seemed to destine him.

The people of Dundee and Angus knew not that he was the rescued child of the terrible Ewain Gavelrigg, the ogre of the Sidlaws : for the secret was known only to the prebends of Dunblane ; and animated either by pity for the wretch himself, or a sense of shame that their holy cloister had once been desecrated by his presence, they locked the secret in their own breasts,—unfortunately, we may add, for many of the actors in our drama, and most unfortunately indeed for the whole of Scotland, as the event proved.

An hour's walk along the rough and shingly beach brought Hew Borthwick to the gates of Broughty, the strong walls of which, when occupied by a gallant garrison, twice defied the Regent Arran with eight pieces of cannon and eight thousand infantry. The barbican, with its flanking towers and strong curtain wall was then well mounted by heavy culverins of yetlan iron, to sweep the river ; but the smaller guns, which faced the salt marshes on the north, and the links of Monifieth on the east, were composed of iron rings, enclosing malleable iron bars. Like other royal castles, it was garrisoned by a company of the king's *Wageours*, as the people named the enlisted soldiers of those military bands by which James III. at a time when standing armies were unknown, with a foresight far in advance of his age, provided for the security of the kingdom ; especially towards the frontier of England.

Thus, in addition to the troops in the five great fortresses of the Lowlands, and to five hundred soldiers maintained in Berwick until its loss and betrayal by the Duke of Albany, James, with consent of his Parliament, made the Laird of Glengilt captain of a hundred archers and lances, who kept the castles of Blackadder, Hume, and Wedderburn ; the Laird of Edmeston commanded as many royal archers and lances in the castles of Cessford, Ormiston, and Edgerston ; the Laird of Cranston, a hundred lances and archers, in the Border Peels of Jedburgh, Cocklaw, and Dolphington ; the Laird of Lamington had a hundred troopers under his orders in Hermitage ; the Laird of Amisfield a hundred more in Castlemilk, Bellistower, and Annan. In Broughty, Kyneff had fifty archers, and fifty pikemen. All these troops, like the arquebussiers of the king's ships, were uniformly clad ;

the horsemen in steel jacks, and the infantry in blue sur-coats, having St. Andrew's white cross upon the back and breast; under all these captains were lieutenants, who received from the exchequer, as the daily pay of their soldiers, eleven shillings and sixpence for every spear and bow. This organization was one of the many wise measures taken by this good king to ensure the safety of his southern frontier; but such a permanent force, however small, was eminently ob-noxious to the feudal nobles.

The sentinels at the gate of Broughty, who knew that Borthwick, though a sorner and blackleg, was a dependent or follower of their captain, admitted him at once, and he was conducted up a bare stone staircase, through the large bleak and ill-furnished hall to the great tower, to an apart-ment, which was hung with arras, that had once displayed bright stripes of alternate crimson and gold, now faded to rusty green and sombre brown. A straw mat covered the stone floor; the furniture consisted of a buffet, encumbered by flasks, bowls, and drinking horns, swords, poniards, cards, chess-men, hawks' hoods, dog-whips, and a hundred other et-cetera, covered by dust; four clumsy arm-chairs, as many tripod stools, and an oak table, at which Sir James Shaw and Sir Patrick Gray were drinking the cheap Bordeaux wine which was then brought in by the Eastern Seas.

'Ho, ho! speak of the devil!' said Gray, as Borthwick entered; 'welcome! thou art the very man we have been wishing for,' he added, kicking a stool towards him uncere-moniously with his foot; 'close the door and drop the arras, for we have something to talk of that others may not, must not, hear.'

'The king's intended banquet to the nobles at Edin-burgh?'

'Nay, nay; fill your horn first, my fine fellow,' said Sir Patrick Gray; ''tis a thirsty affair, a walk in the sunshine along yonder sandy shore.'

'Thanks, Sir Captain—devil! I *am* thirsty,' replied Borthwick; so he quaffed off a pot of wine; 'I had not my purse at my girdle, and the rascally hostler in the Seagate would trust me with nothing more than a cup of cold water, and on that I lunched.'

'So the Laird of Largo has sailed,' said the Governor of Stirling, knitting his brows inquiringly.

'I ken not on what errand, sirs.'

'If yonder villan of a boatman hath proved false, we shal

all have to mount to ride, like Bordermen, when the spurs are on the platter and the houghs i' the pot,' said Gray.

At this surmise they all changed colour, and Shaw looked as yellow as that English gold for which so many Scottish traitors were ever ready to sell their services and their souls.

' Well, I care not,' said Gray ; ' for every man in this tower, though drawing the king's pay and drinking his ale, are mine own true men to the backbone ; vassals of my barony, who will fight only under the banner that I choose to follow.'

' I may say as much for his Majesty's garrison in Stirling,' said Sauchie ; ' but I would that Angus and Drummond were come hither ; for now since this plebeian king of ours will neither march to fight in Brittany, nor to pray at St. John of Amiens, we must e'en devise other measures, or our pretty bubbles may be blown, if yonder old sea-horse, with his devilish *Yellow Frigate*, encounter Howard on the high seas.'

' Then I trust in God that the Englishman may sink with all his papers, for he can never captuie Wood ! ' replied the Captain of Broughty with fervour. ' A startling affair it will be, if Sir Andrew finds all the secrets contained in the iron-bound book of Master Kraft, the London Attorney, and lays them before King James and our enemies of the Privy Council.'

' But our *Bond* with Henry is in cipher.'—' Those shaven monks and cunning clerks who write to James in Greek, Hebrew, and other damnable languages, will soon find a key to our ciphers, believe me, Sir James.'

' Then something *must* be done, for we know not what this night may bring forth,' said Shaw, refilling his wine cup ; ' where are Wood's ships now ? '—' Hull down, already,' replied Borthwick, looking from a window which faced the Firth of Tay, whose blue waters were beginning to redden in the setting sun.

' By my soul ! I could have laughed outright at the gravity with which Rothesay acceded to my proposal for the hand of Maggie Drummond,' said Gray.

' What if she accept thee ? ' asked Sir James Shaw.— ' Right well knew I there is but slender chance of that ; but Borthwick, have you examined all the avenues to this damosel's chamber, so that we may have her by the time Howard returns ? '

' By to-night I will have made sure, Sir Patrick ; but if

Howard is slain or taken by Sir Andrew, what then ? '—' We must devise other means,' said Shaw, with one of his deep, fierce glances ; ' by St. Andrew, I would give three of my best tenements in Stirling to have this suspense brought to an end.'

' For *one* of these tenements,—yea, the smallest, Sir James,' said Borthwick, ' I will write such a letter to Montrose as shall dethrone the king.'—' To Montrose——'

' Yea ; but the letter must go to Angus.'—' Doth the Lord Angus read ? ' asked Gray.

' A little ; I saw him spelling over the legend on the castle gate.'—' A letter !—and who will sign it ? '

' I——'—' Thou ! Borthwick ;—fellow, thou laughest at us!'

' Under favour, Sir James, I never was more in earnest in my life. I will write, and sign it with the king's signature, and seal it with his seal, in such wise that not even he could detect the hand of a forger ; then how much less the half-lettered Angus ? '—' With the king's seal, say you ? '

' His private signet, which I found this morning at the gate of St. Salvador's chapel, where the king must have dropped it, after mass.'—' And this letter——'

' Will kindle a blaze through all Scotland.'—' Art thou sure of this ? ' asked Shaw, with a grim joy that was blended with incredulity and contempt.

' Let the deed show.'

' Hew Borthwick,' said the traitor Shaw, ' I know thee to be subtle as that serpent which of old beguiled our mother Eve. I know thee to love money, even as thine own soul, and I swear to thee by my part of Paradise, that if thy boasted letter achieves the promised ends, thou shalt have not one, but three of my best tenements in the Broad Wynd of Stirling, held of the Burgh by an armed man's service.'

' 'Tis a bargain ; and thou, Sir Patrick Gray, art witness,' said Borthwick, rising with joy beaming in his atrocious countenance.

' In that inner chamber are pens, parchment, and wax,' said Gray ; ' away to thy clerking, for here come the Lord Angus and his friends.'

As Borthwick retired to compose one of the most villanous forgeries ever made by a traitor's hand—unless we except the contents of that silver casket so famous in the history of Mary or some of the letters of Secretary Stair— a train of brilliant horsemen rode up the ascent to Broughty, and dismounted in the waved barbican.

CHAPTER XV.

CONCLAVE OF MALCONTENTS.

SIR PATRICK GRAY and Sir James Shaw rose with much real and more feigned respect, as the swarthy Earl of Angus, still clad as usual in his armour, the statesman-like Lord Drummond, wearing a suit of black velvet edged with corded gold, the Lords Hailes, Home, Stirling of Keir, and the Hereditary Forester of Drum, all partially clad in buff and steel, and the grim old Steward of Menteith, with his long Highland cliob, and portentous beard that reached nearly to the top of his kilt, entered the apartment, making a great clatter with their long steel Rippon spurs, and those enormous swords, for the manufacture of which the sword slippers of Banff bade fair to rival those of Cologne and Toledo, and which were of such preposterous length, that they were generally worn across the back, with the hilt at the left shoulder, over which they were unsheathed when necessary.

Now, since James had declined his pilgrimage to Amiens, and Angus, leader of the peers, was quite averse to the invasion of Brittany, to destroy Montrose, Wood, and other favourites of the king, there seemed to be no other resource but a general appeal to arms ; and yet the malcontent barons were perhaps loth to engage again in a project so desperate.

' I ken o' nocht for us but an open raid and massacre o' the king's garrisons, if they hauld aloof,' said the stern Steward of Menteith. ' Those paid soldiers are but an insolent curb upon the auld and inborn power of the nobles.'

' Massacre ! ' reiterated Angus, with one of his dark smiles ; and what then, Steward of Menteith ? The king can readily find new garrisons, and new favourites, who will again keep the power in their own hands, to the exclusion of our interests.'

' Then let us dethrone the king,' growled the Forester of Drum.

' And crown young Rothesay in his stead, whether he will or not,' added the Laird of Keir.

' I like not the project,' said Drummond, who was the most politic and least violent noble there ; ' *dethrone !* it hath a new and strange sound, sirs, to a Scottish ear.'

' Dethrone—and why not, my lord ? ' asked Sir James Shaw, who was now flushed with wine ; ' in our past history there are precedents enough even for the most unscrupulous. Without going back to that barbarous age when Fergus II. restored the monarchy, have we not had Constantine I., who was slain by a Lord of the Isles ; and Ferquhard I., who fell into the errors of the Pelagians, and for his contempt of all holy rites was dethroned by his nobles, and cast into a dungeon, where he died like a Roman of old ; Malduin, who was strangled by his queen ; and the son of Findon, who was shot by an arrow ?   Had we not Ewen VIII., " *who was slain for having wicked favourites,*" all of whom ended their lives on a gallows, around which the people held jubilee as round a maypole ?   And did not Eth, Malcolm I., and Colin, all die at the behest of an insulted people ?   And last of all, was there not Duncan II., whom the Earl of Mearn slew by one stroke of his dagger ? '

' The last you have named reigned four hundred years ago, Sir James,' replied Lord Drummond coldly ; ' but I do hope in my heart, that the measures which suited the thanes of the eleventh century and their more barbarous predecessors, are altogether antagonistic to the sentiments of the Scottish peers of James III.'

A partial murmur of pretended assent responded to this reply, and thus encouraged, the old lord continued—' When I remember the love of this young king for me, and how he placed a coronet on my head, I feel something of remorse when men speak as thou, Sir James, hast spoken.'

' My lord,' retorted the fiery baron, ' in this desperate game the man who feels remorse is lost ! '—' Alas ! I fear me it is but too true.'

' Remorse ! ' added Gray ; ' pshaw ! 'tis but weakness of mind and narrowness of soul ! '

Lord Drummond made an impatient step forward, but Angus grasped his arm. ' Knight of Kyneff,' said he, with a reddening brow and quivering lip, ' I can afford to pardon this rashness of speech, which a younger man and soldier would be compelled to resent.   I am an old man now, sirs, but while this dear Scotland of ours required my sword, was never allowed to rest in its scabbard ; and if it is for the good of the people, whose natural head are the nobles, I will unsheath it against a corrupt court, as readily as against our hereditary foemen of England or elsewhere.'

'In this hast thou spoken well ; for by one grand stroke must this corrupt court be swept away !' said the Earl of Angus, who as yet had not spoken much, but in whose breast was concentrated all the pride of feudal nobility, and the memory of a lofty ancestry, whose origin was lost in the dark ages of Scottish antiquity, and whose military glory was incorporated with the past history of the nation. 'My lords and gentlemen, I will appeal to you, whether it is not an intolerable thing that I, who am lieutenant-general of the kingdom, must receive orders and edicts from this new-fangled Duke of Montrose, whose ancestry were but Lairds of Crawford and Glenesk when mine were Earls of Douglas and Lords supreme of Galloway ?—men who, since the days when Sholto the Swarthy won the Dale of Douglas by his valour, have been foremost in every field that is honourable to Scotland,—men who bore on their shields the red lion of the Galwegii at the battles of Largs, Theba, and Northaller-ton, and whose war cry, six hundred years ago, found a terrible echo in the ranks of the Longobardi ! I will rather die, as many of them have died, on the red field of battle, than stoop their honoured crests to this ignoble yoke ! Aid me to drive these tawdry courtiers into England or the sea, and I will make thee, Drummond, Great Chamberlain of Scotland.'

'It would appear to me,' said Sir James Shaw, who was blinking over another pot of wine, 'that thou, my Lord Hailes, art better fitted for the office of treasurer than yonder old Saracen, Knollis, the Prior of Rhodez.'

'Yes, and we shall make his good friend Home lord privy seal, in lieu of that old foutre the Provost of Lincluden,' added Sir Patrick Gray, half in jest.

'Accept my thanks, sirs,' replied Home ; 'but are there no pretty places you could choose for yourselves ?'

'Why, let me think,' muttered Gray ; 'I have some old feuds in the Howe of Angus—feuds which have been standing over since my father fought Huntly at the battle of Brechin, on Ascension-day, in '53, and I would like for one month—only a month, sirs—to be judge of justiciary, with a com-mission of fire and sword against all malcontents.'

'Right,' hiccuped Shaw ; 'by St. Beelzebub ! and thou shalt be clerk of justiciary too, instead of that painted fop,

Halket of Belfico, and I shall be lord clerk register. The Laird of Baille-Craig hath a pretty young wife and a cellar of pretty old wine ; we shall confiscate both, Sir Patrick— for he is a malcontent, and master of the king's hounds.'

During this, the Earl of Angus, who had been whispering aside with the politic old chief of the Drummonds, now stepped forward with a peculiar smile on his dark visage. It almost amounted to drollery, if such an expression ever lighted up that swarthy and stern, yet handsome face, before which the sister of Henry VIII. of England quailed when his bride at the altar, and knelt down in the dust at the castle gate of Edinburgh, thirty-six years afterwards.

' My lords and gentlemen, I crave your attention,' said he ; ' the Lord Drummond, although Steward of Strathearn and head of his house, does not feel that his family is suffi- ciently powerful to take the field formally against the court. His coronet is somewhat newer than mine, and consequently seems to him, perhaps, of greater value. Thus he proposes to strengthen himself by two alliances in marriage, through which he calculates on having at least, for the security of himself and his cause, six other castles, well furnished with men and artillery, and four thousand border horse and Lothian spearmen. His three daughters are beautiful, and as we know, my lords, are *peerless* (in more ways than one). He therefore proposes to make you, my Lords of Home and Hailes, his sons-in-law, giving to each a good slice of his arable land in bonnie Strathearn, and three of Montrose's best farms in the glen of Kincardine. Now, my lords, you have a noble chance to win earls' coronets, with fair countesses to share them. By St. Bryde of Kildara ! ' he added, turning to Stirling of Keir, ' were I not espoused to your dear daugh- ter, Sir William, I would lay my heart and sword at the feet of one of these beautiful Drummonds.'

There was a general, but very subdued titter at this pro- posal ; Shaw and Gray laughed so immoderately that Lord Drummond grew red with anger, and tall Angus bent his formidable gaze inquiringly upon them. The fierce old Steward of Strathearn stroked his white beard (which seemed the exact counterpart of his Highland sporran), and adjusted his belted plaid, with the air of a man who was about to say something for himself if the younger suitors declined ; though he had already handfasted by force the fair daughter of a cock-laird in Glenartney. There was a momentary pause, for the two young Southland peers were confounded by the sudden proposition, though such hastily conceived alliances were by no means uncommon in those days, when the Scottish nobles availed themselves of every means of strengthening themselves for those sudden raids and revolts which were the ruin of the national strength, and the terror of the rising middle-class.

'For my own part,' said Hailes, hastening to break the silence, 'I beg to offer my most dutiful thanks to the Lord Drummond, and to say, that I will consider it the task—or rather the pleasure—of my life to love his fair daughter Sybilla, and if he will honour me with her hand, two thousand of the best lances in Eastern Lothian will follow his banner to death! Alexander Home, what sayest thou?'

'All that you have said, I too am ready to perform—excepting that instead of spearmen, I bring two thousand troopers from Tweedside and the Merse, for I have long admired the Lady Euphemia Drummond, and would soon have learned to love her, but feared she was betrothed to the rich heir of Sir Andrew Barton.'

'Robert Barton is a brave, good fellow,' said Lord Drummond, 'but a stanch king's man.'

'And the son of a merchant skipper,' said Angus; 'so it is your bounden duty, Home, to save a noble lady from such a misalliance.'

'I place myself at the complete disposal of her father,' replied Home, whom, like Hailes, the dazzling beauty of the proffered bride had made completely tractable; 'but what shall we say if each of these fair dames assert a woman's right of choice?'

At this idea Lord Drummond laughed aloud, for that was a *right* which was but ill defined in Scotland till the middle or nearly the end of the last century.

'Wine—wine! more Rochelle and Bordeaux to drink to these fair brides and facile bridegrooms!' cried the half-intoxicated Governor of Stirling, as he thundered on the oaken table with a silver drinking-pot. 'Gray, is thy devil of a butler deaf, or is the cellar empty?'

'We have three butts of Rochelle, a bombarde of Bordeaux, and Lammas ale enow to swim the *Yellow Frigate*,' replied the chatelain; 'but, on my soul, Sir James, I think thou'st had enough before dinner.'

'More wine, I tell thee, thou inhospitable! Bring up the bombarde, and I will teach thee an infallible thrust, by which thou wilt always kill an adversary, even though girded in a

triple coat of mail. By my faith, old Drummond, thou art
a wise carle! Take lords, while thou canst get them;—
better have eggs to-day than hens to-morrow. Ha! ha!'

    *   *   *   *   *

    Altogether unaware of the troubles in store for them, the
three daughters of Drummond at that very time were seated
on the bartizan of their ancient mansion in Dundee, watching
the white sails of the *Yellow Frigate* and her consort, as they
shone in the setting sun, and diminished on those waters
which the western light tinged with a golden glow.

    With anxious eyes and saddened hearts, the dark-haired
Euphemia and hazel-eyed Sybilla gazed after them, for they
knew not on what errand the ships had sailed so hurriedly;
and there they lingered long after the summer sun had sunk
beyond the beautiful Carse of Gowrie, and its rays had faded
from the green conical hill of Dundee, which was then girded
by the ruined ramparts of a castle, averred by history to
have been the habitation of Catanach, King of the Picts,
and afterwards of Donald I. of Scotland.

    By their side sat Margaret, pale and thoughtful as usual,
with little Lizzie and Beatrix nestling by her side. The
ocean became a darker blue, and blended with the sky;
bells rang for vespers in the many ecclesiastical buildings
of the town, which then possessed four great churches, five
convents, and thirteen chapels; and reluctantly and with
silent anxiety the three fair girls withdrew from the proud
bartizan to the chamber of dais below.

    By this time their politic—perhaps we are not wrong in
saying cunning—old father was leaving the tower of Broughty,
accompanied by his two intended sons-in-law, and two
gentlemen, both Drummonds of Strathearn, who were his
constant attendants, and were constantly armed to the
teeth. Borthwick, who had finished his letter, and was
loitering in the archway, beckoned to his lordship, and uncovering his head with great respect, craved a word with
him, for he had not forgotten the punch he received on the
head from the fiery young Duke of Rothesay, and his heart
yet burned to be revenged for it.

    ' Well, good fellow, what would you with me?' asked
the noble, as he checked his horse, for he was in excellent
humour at the prospect of two such powerful alliances for
his daughters.

    ' I am one who has a sincere friendship for your lordship
and a regard for the honour of your family,' said Borthwick

in a whisper; 'and I beg to warn you, that by watching well, there may be discovered a certain masked man, wearing a scarlet mantle, who visits your mansion under cloud of night—generally about the hour of ten—and who enters a postern by the way of Fish Street.'

The old lord glanced hastily at Home and Hailes, but fortunately they were beyond earshot; so he turned sternly to Borthwick, and said,—' Fellow, art sure of what thou tellest me?'

'Sure as I have now the honour of addressing you.'

'A scarlet mantle, say you—the Lord Lindesay wears one;—'tis like his insolence. Well, this eavesdropper shall die! But who art thou?'

'A friend and follower of Sir Patrick Gray, who will vouch for my veracity.'

'A most worthy recommendation!' said the old lord, ironically; 'but I thank you, sir, and will watch, believe me. This muffled man may find it perilous work, and that he had better, as our motto hath it, *gang warily*, or byde at home. Carnock—Balloch!' he added to the two gentlemen referred to, 'come hither.'

They cantered up to his side; and with all the ardour of vengeance, Hew Borthwick watched their chief as he repeated the information just received, and no doubt gave them the necessary instructions how to waylay and discover this unknown interloper.

'So much for thee and thy blow,' said he, with one of his hyæna laughs; 'and *this* for thy simple father.'

For a moment he contemplated his letter, which was written on the coarse grey paper then coming into use, folded square, pierced at the corners with blue ribbons, which were tied saltirewise, and sealed with purple wax like a royal letter,—sealed, moreover, by the king's own private signet, which Borthwick applied to this most infamous use.

The traitor gazed complacently at his handiwork, and then concealing it under his scarlet mantle, he returned to the tapestried room, where Kyneff was still drinking, and Sir James Shaw was now lying prostrate on the matted floor, and completely intoxicated.

CHAPTER XVI.

ANOTHER SON-IN-LAW !

NEXT day was Sunday, and, as usual in that age, the people of Dundee, after mass, were shooting at the butts with arquebus and bow ; for, by the same act of the Scottish legislature which abolished the games of football and golf, targets were ordained to be set up by the sheriffs near every parish kirk, where, busked as archers, all the young men repaired to shoot at least six arrows, each a clothyard long, under fine of twopence ; and thus in every town, however small, there was an arrow-maker who drove a thriving trade, though firearms were rapidly superseding the more ancient weapon, in the use of which the Lowland Scots never equalled the English or the Highlanders.

The Duke of Rothesay, with Lord Lindesay and other young courtiers, mingled with the burgesses, and took shot about in their turn among the sailcloth-wabsters, bonnet-makers, and baxters at the butts ; for it was one of the greatest charms, and the leading wish of the Stuart princes while in Scotland, to be considered a part of the people, rather than as jewelled demigods enthroned on pedestals, and placed above the lot of common humanity. On this morning, it was remarked that the young prince did not shoot as was his wont, that his arrows fell wide of the mark ; that he was abstracted, careless, and fretful ; for overnight a trooper had arrived from the captain of the king's band in Annan, stating that there was a rumour of the old Bishop of Dunblane having been wantonly seized on the high seas by Sir Stephen Bull, an English captain, who had carried the reverend lord a prisoner, with all his papers, to Henry VII. at London.

Tidings like these spread like wildfire among the people, aggravating the angry bitterness occasioned by the assault on Barton's ships in time of peace ; the English faction, and those who, for their own infamous ends, were anxious to further Rothesay's marriage with Margaret Tudor, hung their heads; while the national party, whose eyes were always turned towards the Continent for royal alliances, openly exulted, and expressed the utmost resentment at an insult which yet required confirmation.

The first thought of the young prince was his Margaret, and of what *her* emotions would be; for on that kind bishop's return she had garnered up the inmost hopes of her heart. Oh! how he longed for evening, and cursed the lagging hours!

Evening came at last, and then more sombre night.

Masked, muffled in his cloak, and armed with his sword and poniard, Rothesay again left the little provincial palace of St. Margaret by the private door, and proceeded to the house of Lord Drummond. As he traversed the dark and narrow Fish Street, he did not perceive three watchers, who were also disguised, for they wore short black cloaks and iron salades, which completely concealed their faces, having only a horizontal slit for the eyes; they wore boots with felt soles, and had long swords at their girdles.

These were Lord Drummond, and his clansmen Balloch and Carnock; none of them recognized Rothesay, who, without perceiving the three figures which glided after him like dark shadows, reached the northern arcade of the old house, and by his master-key opened the private door which led to the secret stair (the entrance and windings of which Lord Drummond had hitherto supposed to be known to himself only), and ascended straight to the bower of his mistress. While his heart swelled with rage and astonishment, the chief resolved to discover the masker, and to probe the affair to the bottom. He drew his sword, and, desiring his friends to keep sure watch in the street, followed cautiously, but noiselessly, behind the young prince.

On that evening Lady Margaret had heard the rumour of the old bishop's capture, and, with a heart that was full almost to bursting, she sought the little oratory—every house had one in those days—to pray and weep; but it was already occupied, for her sisters Lizzie and Beatie, who had the special charge of the altar, were industriously dusting the cushions. and preparing all for the morrow's mass, after which they knelt down together, to pray and invoke the protection of St. Margaret, with whom their ancestor, Andreas Dromond, had come out of Hungary into Scotland.

'Pray for me, dear Lizzie,' said Margaret, in a tremulous voice, as she paused at the altar-rail.

'I pray for you all—my father, Euphemia, Beatie, and Sybie,' said the little girl, in a whisper, as she tied up a bouquet of white roses, 'and for my new doll, when it is good, and for kind Robert Barton, and Sir David Falconer, when they are on the sea. Do I not, sweet mother?' said the child, looking up at a beautiful white image of the Madonna, which, with the infant Jesus in her arms, stood above the altar draped by a veil, and crowned by a circlet of gold.

'Oh, sister Lizzie,' whispered Beatie, 'is not that a dear, dear wee baby?'

'How I should like to have just such a baby, for my doll fell and broke its nose,' responded the other; 'if you had such a baby, would you not love it, sister Maggie?'

Margaret thought of her little baby that slept in the secret alcove and her tears fell fast.

'Say one prayer especially for me, for indeed the wishes of such pure souls as yours must be like unto those of angels,' replied Margaret, as she kissed her pretty little sisters on the forehead, and lest they should perceive her tears, though the oak oratory was but dimly lighted by a silver lamp suspended from the roof, she hurried away to her own apartment, where she found Rothesay hanging over their sleeping offspring, which lay within its curtained alcove, like a waxen doll.

She threw herself into his arms, and gave vent to a long and passionate fit of weeping; Rothesay did all in his power to console her, and after a time succeeded. Rousseau remarks, that to the woman who loves truly, there is no *man* in the world; for to her the object is *more*, and every other less; and such was sweet Margaret's love for Rothesay!

As they sat with their arms as closely entwined as their hearts,

'Dearest Maggie,' said he, gazing tenderly and conscience-stricken upon her pure and pale Madonna face, and with that expression of eye that speaks of a love verging on idolatry, while he smoothed the thick tresses of her rich soft hair, 'dearest Maggie, I must end this painful and unmanly secrecy, by avowing my passion, and our marriage to the people.'

'Alas! then how shall I, a poor weak girl, withstand the power of two ambitious kings?'

'Thou wrongest my good father, dear Margaret. His heart is as free from ambition as from guile!'

'But not from the cold policy that would wed you to a princess.'

'I am not the first of our royal line who has wedded the daughter of a baron.'

'No—but from that I can gather but little hope,' sighed Margaret.

'David II. married Margaret Logie, the daughter of a simple knight.'

'Ah! and how fared she? Repudiated by her husband when his love grew cold—banished from his court, penniless and poor, she sought the protection of Urban V. at Avignon, and died of a broken heart among strangers; so that we know not where she, a queen of Scotland, found a grave. Better far, had she wedded in her own degree, to die beloved, and sleep among her kindred in the old chapel of Rattray.'

'But this was more than a hundred and thirty years ago; and since that time Robert III. married Annabella Drummond, of your own family.'

'Alas, again! was she happy?'

The prince was silent, and Margaret continued. 'Does not rumour say that she died at Inverkeithing of sorrow for the misfortunes that had descended upon the grey hairs of her good husband, and for the loss of her sons; and then there was Jane of Somerset, who received into her body the same sword that pierced the heart of her husband, James I. If no better fate is in store for your poor little Margaret than fell to the lot of those queenly dames, better it were a thousand times, dear prince, that you had never seen—had never loved her.'

'But the king, my father, must and shall remember that love levels all distinctions, and indeed knows of none,' replied the prince, impatiently; 'thy love for me, Maggie, raises thee to my rank, and mine for thee brings me down to thine, if indeed there is a difference, for a lady by birth is the equal of a king! But why those sad misgivings? and why look back to Margaret of Logie, to Euphemia of Ross, to Elizabeth Mure, to Jane, or Annabella, the queens of barbarous times, when our kings wore shirts of mail, drank out of pewter, and kept their courts in Scone or Rothesay? Be confident, little one, for I love thee with all the depth of a young and honest heart—yea, Margaret, with all the strength of a burning soul! Thou shalt yet be Queen of

5

Scotland, for if my father, or others, drive me into this hateful English marriage, I will join with the malcontent nobles, and when the cubs turn upon *the Lion,* woe to Scotland then ! '

The prince kissed her with ardour. Then Margaret sprang to the little alcove, and noiselessly lifting out the rosy cherub, which lay with its tiny hands folded under its dimpled and double chin, she placed it, still sleeping, in the arms of Rothesay, and knelt down at his feet, yet half reclined upon his knee, to contemplate their child, the dear idol of her affectionate heart—the pledge of her pure virgin love—nursed as it had been born, in secrecy ; the only solace of many a lonely and many a bitter hour. The young pair were full of ecstasy, and oblivious of all but themselves and their beautiful babe. To them it was a reverie, a joyous waking dream ! How happy they were, with their bright young eyes bent over that small plump sleeping face and rosebud chin, while the rich brown locks of Rothesay mingled with Margaret's still darker curls, as with all the expression of a Madonna she hung over her infant, with her soft eyes full of tears, and joy, and holiness.

' If my father saw this beautiful child,' said Margaret, ' I am quite sure he would forgive me.'

' *Be not over confident, Madam !* ' said a stern voice behind them.

A faint cry rose to Margaret's lips, which, like her cheek, grew ashy pale ; and with one hand round the infant, and the other on his sword, the bold prince sprang up, to be confronted by the tall dark figure of Lord Drummond, leaning on his naked sword, which was at least five feet long. He was contemplating them with an expression of eye which it would be difficult to determine or analyse. He had overheard the whole interview ; astonishment had given place to indignation ; indignation to grief and anger ; and these had in turn been supplanted by gratified pride and ambition.

Shame crimsoned the cheeks and terror sealed the lips of poor Margaret ; while confusion, with something of anger at being surprised, reddened the haughty brow of Rothesay, and for a moment there was a painful silence on the lips of all.

' Your Grace of Rothesay has wronged me—deeply wronged me ! ' said the old lord, with a terrible gravity of manner, as he struck his sword into the floor.

' Had I words, my lord, to extenuate the offence I have

committed against you,' replied the young prince modestly, as he cast down his eyes, and clasped in his the hand of the kneeling Margaret, ' I would explain and apologize for my seeming misconduct; but at this moment there is no coherence in my mind and I only dread to rouse your already too just indignation.'

' And *thou* too, Maggie!' said her father, reproachfully and with bitterness; ' it was very bad of thee to deceive me, for thou hast ever been my favourite child, and none but the blessed God can know how much I loved thee.' Then, raising his voice, he added passionately, ' By the Lord of heaven and earth, my daughter, prince, must be the acknowledged Duchess of Rothesay, or I shall slay thee, even as the Lord Athole slew thy grandsire James the First!'

Margaret's sweet pale face became convulsed by grief, and she wept bitterly; but still her father's brow grew darker, and his eye rested on the little babe in Rothesay's arms.

' Am I to understand that you have ignobly made a Highland wedding of it, or been handfasted by some hedge priest or tramping pardoner, to the foul dishonour of a house as yet unsullied by a stain? Answer me, Duke of Rothesay, for even were you heir to a thousand thrones instead of only one, I would not have the honour of my daughter and the honour of my name trifled with even for a single hour.'

' Alas, my lord,' said Rothesay, ' why do men, who, like yourself, are no longer young, forget that they have ever been so? I have loved your daughter long, yea, since I saw her first attend my mother's court in Stirling, a little demoiselle of the tabourette. Your lordship knows the hateful scheme of having an English wife for me, and how in my cradle I was betrothed to the Princess Cecilia of England, and thereafter to Henry Tudor's daughter. My heart, my after-life and happiness, were bartered away like a useless isle or frontier town by cunning ambassadors and cold diplomatists; but as I grew older I revolted at such a state of tutelage, and in spurning the future soon learned to love the gentlest of your daughters. She knew how I was circumstanced, but spare her, and spare me, the recapitulation of all I said and did to procure the honour of her hand; for in secret we were espoused, eighteen months ago, in the cathedral of Dunblane, as its registers yet can testify—espoused by Father Zuill, the admiral's chaplain, and with consent of my good friend, the Lord Bishop Chisholm, for whose return from Rome with a papal dispensation we have waited long and wearily. And here, to all unknown save to her nurse and me, Margaret bore and nursed this babe—and oh, my lord, look gently on it, for it yet may wear the crown of a hundred gallant kings.'

'Prince, thou amazest me!' said the old lord, with a tone of severity; 'this secrecy——'

'Think over it, my dear good lord and father,' resumed Rothesay with energy, and in his most winning manner, for he felt that he was advocating the cause of the shrinking Margaret, rather than his own. 'Had I openly espoused your daughter, taunted by the English faction, a hundred ambitious nobles had felt themselves and their daughters insulted; had I obtained the consent of Parliament for such a marriage, then long ere the dispensation for our consanguinity arrived from Rome, by poison or otherwise the subtle Tudor had swept our Margaret from his daughter's path; for alas! my lord, too well do we know that ever since the wars of Bruce there hath existed among us a faction of traitor Scots, each of whom for English gold would sell his dearest brother into slavery, even as Joseph was sold by his brethren—if by doing so place or pelf could be secured; *and this evil spirit will never die!* Reflect upon these things, my lord—reflect upon them—pardon and advise us, for I am the son of your king, and Margaret may yet be Queen of Scotland and the Isles.'

Though Lord Drummond maintained an outward aspect of severity and offended dignity, he was very far from feeling it in his heart, and indeed was at no small pains to conceal the real gratification afforded him by this discovery of a *third* son-in-law, and by the prospect that if this secret marriage was properly brought before the king, the parliament, and country, his daughter would, in the first place, be hailed as Duchess of Rothesay, and if she survived James III., would assuredly be queen consort of the realm. He saw the rival house of Crawford eclipsed, his enemies in Strathearn crushed, the house of Drummond placed on such a pedestal as it had not occupied since the days of Robert III. and Queen Annabella, and the golden shower of honours, titles, perquisites, and everything that ambition could desire, descending upon his old and politic head. Even Hailes and Home, with their earls' coronets in perspective, dwindled down into mere nothingness before an alliance such as this; and as for poor Robert Barton, he was no more thought of at that moment than an old piece of ropeyarn! Lord Drummond raised his daughter and kissed her with great formality, upon which she threw herself into his arms in a passion of gratitude and joy.

'Come to me, dear Maggie,' said he; 'I forgive thee; but secret as ye kept this matter, be yet more secret now, I pray you, until the time appointed for revealing all. Ye have been standing, as it were, upon a precipice, for royal alliances and a noble's honour are not to be played with like gems or gawds; for men—even the wisest and greatest —neither make nor mar them at pleasure. Be secret still, I implore you, keeping this unwary marriage from others, even as ye have kept it from me. The bishop has been seized, and Henry of England, for purposes of his own, will destroy the dispensation; but we will have a sharp war anent it, and then all hope for the English match will die amid the crash of swords and lances, the boom of cannon and the flight of flanes. But come, prince, the night waxes apace; the morrow is a new day, when I must, in the first instance, confer with the king your father, and in the second, have this little babe—this poor wee imp of love, perchance of wrath—committed to some of my surest vassals in Strathearn. Come, Rothesay, come.'

'Adieu, Maggie,' said the prince, as he kissed her hand and retired by the secret door; 'adieu, my best, my first, and dearest hope!'

And as the Lord Drummond hurried him away, he saw poor Margaret, as if overcome by the whole interview, sink down, pale, breathless, and exhausted, into her *prie-dieu*, with her face buried in her hands.

He gave her an anxious and impassioned glance, the *last* he was fated to bestow on Margaret Drummond for many a long and many an anxious day.

CHAPTER XVII.

THE WARLOCK OF BALWEARIE.

WHILE these events were occurring in bonnie Dundee, Sir Andrew Wood, intent on avenging the fall of his friend, Sir Andrew Barton, but no way dreaming that the fate of two affectionate hearts, perhaps the fate of two rival kingdoms, depended on his severely overhauling the ships of Edmund Howard, was cruising with his frigates on the German Ocean.

The two ships, in pursuit of which we left the *Yellow Frigate* and her consort some pages back, proved to be only large three-masted caravels, belonging to the Prior of Pittenweem, laden with wheat and malt for Denmark; and when hailed through the trumpet, if they had seen aught of three English ships, their skippers answered in the negative. This discovery proved a source of great satisfaction to Cuddy the coxswain, who had feared that his messmate Dalquhat was about to gain the promised reward. He took his place again in the main-cross-trees, and had not been there long before he reported other two sails in sight on the starboard quarter.

Barton eagerly mounted into the mizen-top. The upper sails of the distant vessels were then visible, even to his unassisted eye, for they shone white as snow in the light of the morning sun, which rose in unclouded brilliance from the eastern sea; and the shore of Fife, with the bold bluff Isle of May, were dimly mellowed in the morning haze.

'How do they steer, Cuddie?' asked Captain Barton.

'Dead for Dunbar Harbour.'

'Have they any colours flying, dost think?'

'Nane, sir.'

'One is a large three-masted ship, with her mainmast fidded at the topcastle,' said Barton, as he reached the deck; 'her fore and mizen are in one spar each, but with every rag of canvas set aloft; the other is hull down yet, but I take her to be a small merchantman.'

'It matters not,' replied the admiral; ''bout ship and overhaul them.'

The frigate was put about, a manœuvre immediately followed by the *Queen Margaret*, and both steered for the Isle of May : by this time the two strange sails were placed upon the lee-bow. The bustle caused by this manœuvre brought on deck Father Zuill, the ship's chaplain, a grave but kind old man, whose brains were so much steeped in abstruse study, lore, and scientific vagaries, as to be of little use either to himself or others. To defend him from the cool, fresh air of the morning sea, he was well muffled in a coarse blue over-coat, shaped like a cassock, with wide sleeves, and a cowl which fell behind ; on his head was a coarse blue bonnet. A cord encircled his waist, and thereat hung his cross and rosary, with a pocket-dial, or perpetual almanack, of brass. In one hand he had a pen, in the other a little volume, bound in vellum and clasped with gold ; he had been studying it overnight, till his eyes became red and inflamed, and he had applied himself to it immediately again, after morning prayers.

It was one of this good man's crotchets to imagine that, by discovering the true burning-glasses of the ancients, he would supersede the use of cannon and gunpowder, and this idea being ever uppermost in his head, he saw everything through its medium.

'If these should be English ships,' said he, 'have you no scruple, Sir Andrew, anent fighting on Sunday ?'

'Scruple! gadzooks, no—the devil a bit! There is no Sunday in five-fathom water ; and here, I believe, we have somewhere about seventy by the line ; besides, Father Zuill, bethink thee of the saw—" the better day, the better deed." Barton, run out that spanker-boom, and sheet home the foretopsail ; keep all hands on deck.'

These orders were obeyed in the time I have taken to write them.

'Hast thou heard, father,' resumed the admiral, 'that Vasco da Gama, a certain valiant mariner of Portugal, hath sailed from the Rock of Lisbon to reach India by weathering the Cape of Storms ?'

'Yes—but he will never do it,' replied the friar, emphatically.

'I fear me so, for the good Bartholomew Diaz—he who gave me this Moorish poniard—tried it with two fair barks of fifty tons each, four years ago, and failed completely.'

''Tis because of an evil spirit who dwells on the top of the Table-Mountain,' said the chaplain; 'a spirit whose angry breath can whelm the largest caravel in the ocean.'

'Yea, father, the Storm Fiend,' replied the admiral; 'old Diaz told me that he saw his shadowy form in the clouds, overhanging his mainmast head, for many days.'

'But Da Gama hath received from his king a consecrated banner, having in its centre the white cross of the Military Order of Christ; and, moreover, he hath a letter to Prester John, of the Indies.'

'Would that I were with him!' said Sir Andrew.

'By my faith, laird of Largo, thou art safer within a league of the auld Isle of May,' replied the chaplain, who was somewhat piqued by the admiral's general unbelief in burning-glasses; 'for I verily believe that none can inhabit the torrid clime beyond Cape Non, which lies in twenty-nine degrees north latitude.'

'That maintopsail shivers, Barton,' said Sir Andrew, stamping his foot, as he gazed alternately aloft and at the yet distant ships, which they were approaching by crossing their south-east course; 'this devilish breeze is failing us already.'

'Would that I could give you the winds in a bag,' said the chaplain, 'like the heathen, of whom we may read in this little book.'

The admiral, who had no great love for the chaplain's books, which he thought savoured overmuch of sorcery, glanced suspiciously at the little tome, which was no other than ' *The Boke of Eneydos*, made in Latin by that noble Poete and grete Clerke, Vyrgyle, and newly translated from the Frenche into Englishe '—a gift from James III. to the chaplain, who continued:

'Ere long, Sir Andrew, I may serve you in other ways, and now I have a notable opportunity for experimenting.'

'What, with thy devilish glasses again!' exclaimed the admiral, as the chaplain descended the ladder and entered the door of the poop without replying.

Almost immediately afterwards he reappeared bearing in his arms a machine which very closely resembled something between those now used by a photographer and the theodolite of an engineer, for it consisted of a little oaken box, containing a long brass tube, with a multitude of little mirrors, screws, and glasses, concave and convex, the whole being propped on three legs, triangularly, and forming their apex. For want of a better name, this mysterious apparatus was christened by the unlettered crew, ' Father Zuill's hurdy-gurdy,' and it was a source of secret ridicule with some and of curiosity with others; for whenever he was seen to level his lenses at distant objects, there was a confident expectation that they would go off with a report like a brass cannon. The Romans used movable types for stamping their names upon cloth and vessels of clay; thus they were very near discovering the whole art of printing. Father Zuill used lenses, and was quite as near discovering the telescope, yet no such idea ever occurred to him. Considering the whole affair as a mere whim-wham or harmless foible, the admiral, Barton, Falconer, the boatswain, and gunner, watched his operations, and made a covert joke upon them; but the crew, who had long since tired of experiments which ended in nothing, were grouped forward watching the approaching ships, or dozing away the hours on the sunny deck.

Father Zuill levelled his lenses and arranged his glasses in such a way that the bright morning sun, then straight astern, shone full upon one end, while the other was pointed at the headmost ship, which was now on the lee bow, and beating hard up against a head wind.

' Sir Alexander Mathieson will never sail ahead of us in a sunny day, Father Zuill,' said Falconer, laughing; ' for he fears your operating on his canvas, and burning holes in it;—what he calls your " damnable hurdy-gurdy." '

' Now, Father Zuill, dost thou really believe in the power of these bits of looking-glass ? ' asked the admiral; who, with an incredulous smile on his honest face, and his hands thrust into the pockets of his gaberdine, had been watching the futile attempts of the chaplain to ignite the white canvas of the head-most ship.

' As truly as I believe that Archimedes burned the Roman fleet with glasses at the siege of Syracuse ! ' retorted the chaplain. ' He used concave mirrors; and if I could only construct a parabolic speculum, the focus of which would reach three bowshots off, and burn there, does it not indubitably follow, that by increasing the scale, I might construct another which would consume a city at three leagues, and scorch to death all who were in it ? Hear me, sirs. If *one* mirror will light a spot one-fourth of its size, at a certain distance, assuredly we may presume that the reflected light of a *hundred* mirrors, all bearing on the same spot, will render the heat unbearable, and bring the light to that refulgent point at which it engendereth fire. So sayeth Anthemius, who used hexagonal mirrors surrounded by others ; and so say Tzetzes, Zonaras, Lucian, and others. We read in ancient history, that the ships of Marcellus were consumed to ashes at the distance of a bowshot when the sun's rays were at noon. I have heard of as much being done by two concave specula composed of polished brass. A little study, admiral, would make plain to thee (who use the cross-staff for striking the meridian), the geometrical mode of discovering the rectilineal propagation of heat and light, as it was understood by Eustathius and Ptolemy. Thou understandest me ? '

' May I never more go to sea, if I do,' replied the admiral, scratching his beard in sore perplexity. ' I think all this sounds as like sorcery as one ropeyarn seems like another. No, no! the gunner to his linstock, the steersman to his helm, and the cook to the foresheet. Thou to thy book lear, and I to my seamanship. By my father's soul! I would put more reliance in a good cannon-royale with a smooth bore, and a calm sea under the counter, than in all the glass hurdy-gurdies that ever were seen ! '

By this time the *Yellow Frigate* had the wind upon her beam, and she was close upon the two vessels, which proved to be merely merchant-traders of Blackness, whose crews had seen nothing of the English ships in question ; and the admiral was beginning to fear that Jamie Gair had been mistaken, or that he had been sent on some false errand for purposes unknown. His ships then stood close in shore, and steered again for the Tay, under easy sail ; and as they were near the dangerous rock named the Carrwick, Master Wad, the gunner, took the helm, and steered on the spire of the old Cistercian kirk at Crail.

' I agree wi' the admiral, Sir David,' said the boatswain to the captain of the arquebussiers, as they leaned over the larboard bulwark, gazing at the coast of Fife, which was then sparkling under a brilliant noon-day sun ; ' and I believe there is mickle mair o' sorcery than theology in Father Zuill's box o' glasses. I never kent o' man, wife or bairn that throve under the influence o' sic fause con trivances.'

' Yet it may not be magic,' replied Falconer ; ' for the same thing was thought of our mariner's compass when it was invented. For there are many things in nature, Archy which such simple fellows as thou and I cannot comprehend.'

'I ken this, Sir David,' replied the boatswain, 'that I never heard o' a skipper buying a fair wind frae the witches o' Pittenweem or Anster, but was laid bare on his beam-ends some day. I would rather hear the close-reefed foresail blawn to ribbons, and feel the saut spray hissing owre my head, than resort to siccan contrivances, and I could spin ye a yarn that would let ye see, Sir David, how puir mortal men should just content them wi' whatever God is pleased to gie.'

'Spin away, then, boatswain; out with it, off the reel, while the line will run.'

'It was told me by my father, puir auld bodie, who is now keeping his deid reckoning in the kirkyard o' Anster Easter, where he has been aground these thirty years and mair. Weel, sir, it was this :—

'In the days when the last King Alexander kept court at Scone, and whiles in the auld Castle o' Crail, the ruins o' whilk ye may see through the simmer mist on yonder hazy headland, auld Sir Michael Scott, the warlock, byded at Balwearie, near the Linktoun o' Kirkcaldy, where his great castle is yet to be seen; and where, on the anniversary o' the night on whilk he was summoned awa' frae earth, as men say, the shadow o' a great hand, wi' a forefinger as lang as the spritsailyard, appears on the wall; thrice in the moonshine it beckons an unseen spirit awa'; and when the bell at the Abbotsha' tolls one, it vanishes. Being a Fife man mysel, though frae the East Neuk, I ken the place as well as the trout-holes o' the Dreel Burn. I have seen the gate where, when Sir Michael stamped his foot, the deevil came up in the form of a black Barbary courser, with a silver bridle and saddle o' crommosie, the same on whilk he was carried to Paris in one night, and whilk, by every stamp of its foot, made every bell dance in the kirk of Notre Dame. I ken the window, where, by a wave o' his hand, Sir Michael raised the storm that rolled the German Sea upon the Links o' Forgue in Aberdeenshire, and there they will roll for ever; that tore the Lang Craig frae the Inch at Leith, and swallowed up the boat wi' the dead body o' his mortal enemy, Sir Alan Mortimer, when, at midnight, the monks, wi' tapers and torches lighted, wi' censers smoking and choristers chaunting, were rowing the funeral barge wi' muffled oars, frae the

Castle o' Aberdour to the Abbey of St. Colme; and there, where the yawning sea engulfed the Crusader's corpse, in its leaden coffin, cross-legged, with sword-at-side and spur-on-heel, men to this day call the place the *Mortimer's Deep;* and deep it is, I trow! for ye may pay out a thousand fathoms of line, and never reach the bottom. On that awesome night, the Donjon o' Aberdour was rent frae cope to ground-stane, and Sir Patrick Spens,

> The best sailor
> That ever kens the sea.

was weel nigh wrecked at St. Margaret's Hope; for his topsails were blawn clean out o' the boltropes; and the Laird o' Hartshaw, as he walked on the deck, was brained by a flap o' his mainsail.

'In these days there was an auld fisherman, called Logan o' the Weem, who served King Alexander wi' fish, when he byded at the Castle of Crail. Logan and his gudewife, Mysie, had ance seven sons, but six o' them had perished off Elie, in that fearfu' storm after which the herrings forsook the coast, and there wasna a fish to be had in a' the fishing grounds between Kinghorn Craig and the Red Head o' Angus. The time of Lent was at hand, and then King Alexander, wi' a great train o' lords and knights, auld Bruce, the pawkie Lord o' Annandale, the Earls o' Mar and Buchan, true Sir Thomas the Rhymer, and mony mair, were to keep the festival at Crail; and a helmetfu' o' bannet-pieces were offered for a creelfu' o' fish.

'On the first day o' Lent, Logan o' the Weem, a dour and determined auld carle, presented himself at the Castle o' Balwearie, and begged permission to see Sir Michael Scott; and, without muckle ceremony, but wi' a beating heart, he was ushered into a wee dark chalmer, like a coal-sloop's cabin, where, chin-deep amang great books, wi' a globe on ae side o' him, and a stuffed monster on the other, Sir Michael, a' dressed in sable taffeta, sat reading by the light of a lamp, which threw nae shadow behind him, for the warlock knicht had *nane.* Aboon his head, a blue star burned on the tapestried wall, and Logan could scarcely keep his eyen off it, for it glinted and shone, as it grew sma' and broad, and flashed and shrunk, by turns.

'Auld Michael's hair was white as the thistle-down, his beard descended to his girdle, on whilk was graven a row of shining letters. His head was bald, but his eyen shone like two diamonds, or like those o' the black cat and white owl that sat on the back o' his chair, from whence the one spat and the other whistled like the de'il in a gale o' wind, as Logan approached bauldly, but wi' his braid bonnet in his hand.

' " Well, Carle Logan," said the warlock, sternly, " what seek ye here ? "

' " Fish," quo' Logan, trembling a wee.

' " Dog ! dost thou take me for a fisherloon ? " asked the Knicht o' Balwearie, wi' a terrible frown.

' " No," said Logan, growing desperate ; " but I tak ye for a mischievous auld warlock, that will ruin a' the fishertouns o' Fife, by scaring the herrings frae every firth and bay ; and I've come to beg as a boon that ye will tak the spell off the water, so that the herring draves may again come back to Crail and St. Monan's."

' " Sayst thou that I have layed a *spell* upon the water ? " cried Balwearie, furiously.

' " I do—ever since the night when Mortimer's corpse was lost."

' " Then I tell thee thou art a presumptuous liar, whom I shall yet see hanging in hell by the tongue ! " cried the warlock, rising, while the cat flattened its ears, erected its back, and spat again ; the owl croaked, whistled, and ruffled its feathers, and the blue star on the tapestry flashed wi' sparks o' fire ; but Logan never flinched, for he remembered that his gudewife, and the gudewives o' many, were starving at hame.

' " Thou hast a son ? " asked the warlock.

' " The last, Sir Michael, that you and the storm have left me—alake ! alake ! "

' " Carle Logan, thou hast dared to do what never mortal man has done before ; thou hast bearded Michael Scott under his own roof-tree in the Castle of Balwearie, and it is but fair that such insolent courage should have its reward. To-morrow, at midnight, commences the Feast of St. Adrian, the martyr of the May, launch then your boat alone, and cast your line in Mortimer's Deep, and thou wilt see what will happen then. Bid your son, at sunrise, drop his nets off the Cave of St. Monan, and he will have in it such a strange haul as never fisherman, since the days of the blessed St. Peter, brought out of the great deep before ! "

' On this the cat purred, the owl whistled, the star flashed fire, and wi' a surly laugh the warlock received the thanks

o' auld Logan, who was right glad when he found himsel'
clear o' the great Castle o' Balwearie, and hurrying alang
the bright green links o' Kirkcaldy, when the summer sun
was setting behind the Lowmonds o' Fife.

'The morrow's midnight came; the Feast o' St. Adrian
was held in a' the fisher-touns o' Fife, and the priests o'
Pittenweem were saying solemn mass for the souls of him,
of the Bishop Stalbrand, and of the six thousand six hundred that perished wi' them when the heathen Danes
sacked all the Isle o' May and the towns o' the East Neuk.
Logan's gudewife, Mysie, as she lay alane in her warm
box-bed at Pittenweem, put up many a prayer to St. Adrian
o' the May for her puir auld fisherman, who had launched
his boat alane, and sailed to the Mortimer's Deep. The
night was calm and clear; her son was away to the fishing-
ground off St. Monan's Cave, and there he was to drop
his nets, as the warlock had said, at the uprising o' the sun.

'It was about the middle watch o' the night when
Mysie dreamed that she saw her gudeman's boat wi' its
lugsail floating on the dark waters o' Mortimer's Deep.
A bright moon shone on the Isle o' St. Colme, and the abbey
lights were glinting on the water; but the great Castle
of Aberdour, and its wooded beach, cast a gloomy shade
on the place where Logan's boat was drifting, and where
the dead Crusader lay. She saw him drop his line, and
stoop owre the gunnel; then she saw him bringing it in
hand-owre-hand—for all in a dream passes quick; he
had caught something! Was it a fine fish, for which the
chamberlain would gie a golden price at the Castle o'
Crail? Up it came, slowly and heavily, and lo! a mailed
hand arose from the water, it grasped her husband by the
throat, and dragged him down—down beneath the sea—
and the empty boat drifted awa' in the munelight, with
its lug-sail flapping in the wind.

'Wi' a shriek—a wild despairing cry in her ears, the
fisherman's wife awoke, and before her on the wall there
glinted a *blue star*; afar off she heard the splash o' water,
a hissing, gurgling sound, and the voice of her gudeman
moaning as he drowned, *thirty* miles awa'. The star faded,
as the awesome sounds sank, and mirk darkness, terror,
dool, and silence fallowed! . . .

'But I maun e'en be quick, or I'll hae to pipe the larboard
watch before my yarn's spun.

'The sun rose brightly frae the sea, and Mysie's son,

when the first blink o't glittered along the water, lowered his nets into the clear green waves that danced off auld St. Monan's; the kirk windows, the steep red streets and rocky shore were a-shining in the glowing light. Young Logan let his boat drift by the net for a wee while; at last the floats began to bob and sink! ha! there was something heavy in the net at last, and he dragged it in, thinking this braw haul would be brave news for the auld couple at hame. Hand-owre-hand he brought the wet twine, floats, and bladder on board; and then he could see something glittering in the net as slowly it rose to the surface. Up, up it came at last, and lo! there was not even a codling in the net—but there was the dead body o' his puir auld white-headed father! And surely, never fisherman had such a haul before. Now, Sir David, what think ye o' that yarn o' sorcery and devilry?'

'That, if true, boatswain, it is more wonderful than the story of the Imp that strangled Gibbie o' Crail, for stealing his toplight.'

'True! by my faith, Sir David, it is as true as that mermaids sing when the wind rises, and drag doon drooning men.'

The frigates continued their course, and keeping outside the Inchcape Rock, passed the broad estuary of the Tay about sunset. Sir Andrew then gave orders to keep them away 'north and by east,' and still in search of the Englishmen, they stood along the coast as far as the Red Head of Angus, favoured by the strong current, which there runs alternately south-sou'-west and north-nor'-east. In his impatience he carried all the sail he could crowd, till the masts strained, and he ordered the watch to heave the log every quarter of an hour, to ascertain the ship's speed.

At this very time, and favoured by the same wind, the three vessels of Captain Edmund Howard were boldly, and under cover of the descending night, bearing straight for the mouth of the Tay, with topgallant-sail set, a fair breeze, and a smooth sea.

CHAPTER XVIII.

FATHER AND SON.

Two days had elapsed since the prince's last visit to Margaret Drummond, and her father's discovery of a union which, ambitious as he was, had been altogether above his dearest hopes, and beyond his most daring schemes; and true to his plan of having it regularly announced to the nation by the voice of a *new* chancellor, when the Parliament assembled in the capital, he did not breathe a syllable of the important secret even to his most faithful friends or followers, or to his daughters, Euphemia and Sybilla, who were sorely puzzled to find that the two young Lords Home and Hailes were likely to become constant visitors at their house; that in two days each of these nobles had paid them four visits, and that beautiful hawks, with scarlet hoods and silver bells, had been presented to them; that elaborate little cases, containing gloves of Blois trimmed with miniver and perfumed to excess, Turkish fans edged with swansdown, and Cordovan slippers beautifully embroidered with gold and seed-pearls, had come to them, they knew not from whence; and that the sudden admiration and regard expressed by their father for these two border lords was unbounded, while he seemed to be ever in the best of humours with himself and with every one else; and guessing wide of the truth, because such thoughts were farthest from their own hearts, the timid girls believed and dreaded that this sudden and unwonted friendship was but the sure forerunner of some desperate raid against the courtiers of the king.

During these two days Rothesay, with Lord Lindesay, Sir Patrick Gray of Kyneff, Sir William Stirling of Keir, and others, had been hunting on Montrose's estates near the Braes of Angus; consequently, when he returned, on the morning of the third day, he knew nothing of the storm then gathering at court where Lord Drummond had imparted to the king the secret he had discovered.

Laying aside his hunting costume of green cloth, Rothesay was equipped by his pages in his favourite gala dress, which was blue velvet, slashed with cloth of gold and tied by aiguilettes and three hundred little trefoils of gold; for he had now resolved to pay openly a visit to Lord Drummond's family. The last point of his elaborate costume had just been trussed, when John Ramsay, Lord of Bothwell, the young captain of the Royal Guard, appeared, and said that the king required his presence in his private cabinet.

With an unpleasant foreboding of what was to follow, and with a beating heart and flushing brow, the young prince hurried to the presence of his father, whom he found seated in a little wainscoted room, the windows of which faced the sunlit Tay and the opposite coast, where the rich corn-fields of Fife lay ripening and basking in the noonday sun, and where the waving woods of Balmerino, Monkquhannie, and the Peak of Craigsanquhar blended the golden grain with emerald green. The ceiling of this apartment was profusely decorated with coats of arms and gaudy ornaments; the floor was of oak, polished and varnished. Books, globes, musical instruments, hunting-whips, handsome swords and ivory bugles, were strewn about the chairs and side tables; but the principal object was a grotesque and venerable buffet, which had belonged (as tradition said) to Saint Margaret, and thereon were placed six ancient silver goblets, which had belonged to King Robert I.; and above them hung the shirt of mail worn by him at the Battle of Bannockburn; seven valuable relics treasured by James III. with peculiar care, and which, long after his death, were preserved in the Castle of Edinburgh.

The king was clad in a plain dressing-gown of green silk, the open breast and loose sleeves of which displayed his rich shirt, with its diamond buttons; his vest and hose were of grey velvet, and his boots of soft white leather, with scarlet heels. A great ruby ring was on one of his fingers, and Father Zuill's pedantic *Treatise on Burning-glasses* lay open beside him.

By the aspect of severity which clouded the usually open and kind face of his father, Rothesay perceived in a moment that his secret was known to him. Reclining back in his armchair, with a hand resting on each of the carved arms, James III. gazed with calm but stern eyes on the young prince, and said:

' Shame on thee, Rothesay, for thou hast deceived me, who have ever trusted and yet love thee so well! But worse than that, thou has deceived the people thou mayst one day govern. Alas! the Lord Drummond has told me all.'

'I did indeed deceive you—but how was I to act? The intrigues of England, my successive betrothal to two princesses of that nation, my relationship to Margaret Drummond through our ancestress Queen Annabella, and the necessity for a public dispensation, must all plead my excuse for her; for myself I make none; upbraid me as you may, I feel that I deserve reproach for deceiving those who loved me, but not more than Margaret Drummond.'

Rothesay gathered a courage as it were from desperation; and aware how much the happiness of the future depended on the effect produced at this first interview on the subject, he endeavoured to rally all his presence of mind.

'This John Drummond,' said the king, bitterly, 'when only Laird of Stobhall and that ilk, was a good man and true; but in the same evil hour when I created John Hay, Lord of Zester, Robert Crichton, Lord of Sanquhar, and John de Carlyle, Lord of Torthorwald, I placed a coronet on his head, and immediately his heart became infected by the ambition, corruption, and falsehood which make the peers of Scotland a curse to the nation and to us. I could read the inmost thoughts of that old man's hollow heart, when smiling he stood before me, and told how the crown prince of Scotland had in secret wedded his daughter; and while affecting to reprehend such secrecy and disobedience in proper terms of severity, he could but ill conceal the joy with which he contemplated a second daughter of his house sharing the honours of an imperial crown.'

'The Lord Drummond,' urged the prince, 'is the most faithful of your Majesty's subjects, and his forefathers have all been true to their country; one fought by Bruce's side at Bannockburn, and destroyed the English horse by the Calthrops, with which he strewed the field; another was slain at the battle of Durham; a third took Piercy prisoner at Otterburn; and the present lord is a venerable and upright noble.'

'Do not deceive yourself,' replied James, still more bitterly; 'grey hairs do not indicate a wise head or honest heart, any more than bright armour indicates a valiant soldier; besides, I ever think meanly of him whose sole merits are based on those of a dead ancestry. Drummond will prove true to the innate principles of that high-born but hollow-hearted class who are at all times ready to betray their country. But listen to me, Rothesay,' continued James, impressively, ' the public duty and the common weal, your own honour and justice to the nation, to say nothing of simple prudence, require that you must conquer this most unfortunate attachment, and repudiate this irregular marriage, which the Church can and *shall* dissolve ; till when, I require you to see no more the too willing and too artful daughter of this ambitious and designing lord.'

Rothesay was thunderstruck by these words. ' This severity will distract me ! ' said he, clasping his hands,— for he loved and revered his royal father with a love and reverence that were never surpassed ; ' my dearest—my unfortunate Margaret ! Thou too willing—thou too artful ? Alas, you know her not ! A sweeter nature, a fonder heart, a purer or a nobler love than hers, never warmed a human breast ! It is I who have been criminal. It is I who have been false, artful, and beguiling ; and most justly to me she looks for reparation, vindication, and redress. She is my wife—wedded in the Cathedral of Dunblane—wedded solemnly before God and man, and is Margaret Duchess of Rothesay, Countess of Carrick, and Lady of Renfrew.'

' Prince ! prince ! ' urged the gentle king, overcome by the fiery energy of his son, remember that these Drummonds are only Barons of Stobhall.'

' Father,' retorted the proud young prince, ' do you forget that we Stuarts were *once* but thanes of Strathyryffe ? '

' I do not,' said the king, rising ; ' and by that proud memory command you to renounce this woman ! '

' Impossible ! mortal man may not now put us asunder.'

James III. grew pale with anger. ' If, like King Duncan, thou hadst openly wedded the miller of Forteviot's daughter, I could have forgiven it ; but the secrecy, the deceit of thee, and of this Lord Drummond, whose friend and benefactor I have been, sting me to the soul. He has but wiled and intrigued with thee, that his daughter may be a queen, and I dethroned, even perhaps before my wretched days are numbered. Now my own son conspires against me ! ' added the king, wildly, as he covered his face with his hands ; ' for I have fallen on evil times. Ah ! woe is me ! '

' I beseech your Majesty to pardon me ! ' said Rothesay, who was crushed for a moment by the grief and bitterness of his father.

' Promise me, first, the renunciation of this artful woman ! ' said the king, looking up imploringly.

'Rather than conceive a thought so base, I will take my sword, and, renouncing the Scottish crown in favour of my little brother the Duke of Ross, or even of the exiled son of my uncle Albany and Anne of Auvergne, I will enter the service of Charles VIII. to fight against the Breton lords, or of Ferdinand the Catholic, to fight the Spanish Moors; I will go wherever my sword can find me bread, and leave this land for ever!'

James III. grew pale again, for he knew well the rashness of which Rothesay was capable. 'Another menace such as this,' said he, snatching up a silver whistle which lay on the table, 'and I will send thee under guard to the Tower of Lochmaben or the Castle of Inverlochie. Inconsiderate boy, this rash espousal is every way illegal, for ye are both related within the third and forbidden degree of blood!'

'The Lord Bishop of Dunblane——'

'He has been captured on the seas by English pirates.'

'Alas! I know, but he was bringing our dispensation from Rome.'

'Ho! what is this thou tellest me? A dispensation! Could Henry VII. know of it? Impossible; yet why seize the poor bishop and destroy his papers.' James bit his lip, and, smiling disdainfully, added, 'This wily Tudor toils hard to have his daughter wedded to a Stuart—but Barton's bones are yet unburied, and his kinsmen will yet avenge his death. But do, dear Rothesay, pause, for it seems that this frantic love hath bewitched thee.'

'I have no reason to blush for it. Have not the bravest soldiers, the wisest philosophers—yea, the most virtuous saints—been vanquished by its power? Think over it calmly, my dearest king and father, and say, wouldst thou have me to deceive one who has trusted to me, and whose love for me is not second even to thine.'

'No, on my soul, I would not have thee to deceive her; but oh, Rothesay, I would rather have lost ten lowland earldoms than the hope of such an alliance for thee as Charles VIII. of France or Catharine of Navarre could have offered if this one with England failed. But leave me now,' added the good and indulgent king; 'a time may come when I shall forgive you, but not just now.'

The young prince's heart danced with joy; tears started into his fine hazel eyes, as, with a burst of affection, he kissed the proffered hand of his father, and hurried away to visit Lord Drummond's house, while James prepared

for that daily council or levee which was one of the tasks
our sovereigns had to undergo during their annual progresses through the kingdom.

Leaving the Palace of St. Margaret by the principal
entrance in the Nethergaitt, the happy prince, without any
followers or attendants, hurried along the crowded and sunny
street, and turned to the right, down the quaint old wynd
of St. Clement, where he was suddenly met by Lord Drummond, who was coming up hurriedly, and followed by his
constant attendants the Lairds of Carnock and Balloch.

' Your servant, my dear lord,' said Rothesay, uncovering ;
' you are abroad betimes this morning.'

' Prince, thou hast wronged and deceived me most foully ! '
said the stern noble, in a voice rendered hoarse by passion,
as he unsheathed his long sword ; ' I am an old man, but
beware, for not even a prince of the blood shall insult me.
My daughter Margaret—where is she ? '

' Where ? ' reiterated the prince, with confusion and
alarm.

' Yea, where—speak, speak ! '

' Is she not at home with you, my lord ? '

' With me—no ! All last night her chamber has been
vacant, her bed unslept in ; the window of her turret was
found open ; the tables overturned, the hangings torn ;
her babe half dead by cold ; a rope ladder dangling—yea,
it dangles yet—from the window that faces Fish Street.
My daughter is gone, none know whither, and her poor
babe mourns and whines for her in vain. Prince, by this
abduction thou hast doubly disgraced and insulted me.
Say, where is my daughter—this best beloved of five ?
—say, say, lest my too just indignation turn this sword
against thee—prince royal though ye be ! '

' My lord,' said the prince, clasping his hands, ' I swear
by all my hope in Heaven's mercy, by that blessed altar
before which I received her hand, and where I gave my solemn
troth, that I know not where she is ; but will spend the last
drop of my blood to discover and to save her.'

' Go to ! ' said the enraged father, hoarsely ; ' dost think
I will believe all this ? 'Sdeath, he who deceives me once
may readily do so again. But I will have vengeance sure
for it. Every man in Strathearn shall be in his helmet
ere the morrow's sun sets, and I will nail my gauntlet on
your father's palace gate in token of what a Scottish peer
may do.'

On hearing this threat, the two Drummonds, who shared all the indignation of their chief, twisted their shaggy mustachios, and played with the hilts of their long iron-hilted swords, in their fiery impatience.

'I am as little accustomed to deceive, my lord, as I am to be disbelieved or misunderstood,' replied the prince: 'and again I swear to you, by all we hold most sacred, that I have spoken to the verity, and the verity alone. My Margaret——'

'Behold the only trace of her,' said Lord Drummond, as he roughly grasped Rothesay's hand, and drew him a few paces down the wynd, to where they could see the northeast tower of his mansion. There Rothesay's eye first caught sight of Margaret's well-known window. It was open; the fragments of a rope ladder were yet streaming out upon the wind, and various passengers were grouped in the street below, conferring and surmising, with upturned faces, on what had happened there overnight. On beholding these ocular proofs of some terrible catastrophe, the prince lost alike his patience and presence of mind. He unsheathed his sword and exclaimed,

'We have been discovered and betrayed!'

'Thank God, this emotion seems genuine!' said Drummond, as he leaned on his long weapon, and grimly scrutinized the prince; 'betrayed, sayst thou? but by whom, dost thou think?'

'By some of my father's favourites.'

'Right! by the hand of St. Fillan, I thought these varlets had something to do with this outrage. Can the king know it, think ye?' asked Drummond, with a terrible glare in his eyes, as he turned to his kinsmen, Balloch and Carnock, who both drew their swords, as if by instinctive use and wont.

'Alas, I said not *that*,' replied Rothesay, giving way to tears; 'but my mind is a chaos—I can no longer think.'

''Sblood—act, then!'

'How now, my lord—your highness—gentlemen, what is astir?' asked Sir Patrick Gray, stepping out of a daggermaker's shop at that moment; 'beware, sirs—and up with your swords; remember that it is an act of treason to draw within four miles of the king or the lord high constable, and both are now in our burgh of bonnie Dundee.'

'D——n the constable, and the burgh of Dundee to boot! My daughter Margaret has been carried off by violence;

there hath been hership and hamesücken overnight, Sir Patrick, and as a knight and gentleman, and moreover as the king's good soldier, I claim your assistance.'

'Carried off !—the beautiful Margaret !' exclaimed Gray, with well-feigned astonishment; 'by St. Mirran! there hath been foul play, then; for alas, my lord, as last night I rode along the beach to Broughty, I heard shrill cries, as from a woman on the water.'

'Kyrie Eleison !' ejaculated the prince, trembling, and growing paler than death, at the terrible thoughts this information suggested, and he wept aloud.

'Some of James's courtly minions——' began Gray.

'Have been at work here,' interrupted Lord Drummond, passionately; 'thinkest thou so, too? Then the king shall do me justice, or this right hand, which has so often fenced his father's throne, shall be the first to thrust a lighted torch under it now. Come with me, sirs,' he added, hurling his long sword into its sheath of crimson velvet; 'come with me, the king is now in council.'

As they hurried up the wynd, taking the bewildered Rothesay with them, they heard the clatter of many hoofs, and saw the Earl of Angus sheathed in complete armour, and attended by not less than five hundred spearmen on horseback, all heavily accoutred, pass at a hard gallop along the Nethergaitt, towards the king's residence.

'Now, what may this portend ?' asked Carnock and Balloch together, with surprise.

'Heaven only knows,' said Gray, laughing under his thick beard; 'but the Douglases never mount without good cause, be assured, sirs. How this plot thickens,' thought he, as he looked towards the dim blue sea; 'and how readily this muleheaded old lord, who hath no ideas of his own, adopts the good or evil suggestions of others. Now, Sauchie and I have them all, like puppets, in our grasp ! But I would fain see the mouth of yonder fellow, Borthwick, stopped with earth for ever !'

At that moment they entered the palace door, and followed Lord Angus straight to the presence of the king.

CHAPTER XIX.

In fulfilment of his boast made in the Tower of Broughty, Borthwick had fully examined 'all the avenues' to the chamber of Lady Margaret Drummond, preparatory and previous to her abduction. By inquiries cunningly pursued among the domestics within, and by observations made from without, he had discovered the exact locale of her bed-chamber, and her hour for retiring, and now, being aware that the prince was hunting in the Howe of Angus, he resolved to make the attempt at once.

As yet there was no appearance of the Laird of Largo's dreaded ships returning; but the evening of the appointed day closed darkly and hazily in, and the three vessels of Captain Howard had been descried by Sir Patrick Gray from the Craig of Broughty, as they crept slowly and stealthily in shore.

It was one of those evenings when the chill east wind brings a thick *haar*, as the Scots name it, from the German Sea, when the moon veils her head in the clouds, and a murky gloom envelopes everything.

It was one hour past Margaret's usual time for retiring, yet she was not in bed. During the whole of that day and the day preceding, the new joy which had replaced her usually sad and quiet demeanour, the light that sparkled in her calm soft eyes, and the buoyancy of her spirits, were remarked by her sisters; but they knew not that Margaret was happy because her important secret was shared and approved of by her father, who had ridden away to Dunblane, accompanied by Carnock and Balloch, to examine the cathedral registers, and assure himself that nothing was wanting but the Papal dispensation to make all clear, on announcing to Parliament, when it met in the metropolis, that his daughter was Duchess of Rothesay, and the mother of a little princess who yet might wear that crown of thorns which was the inheritance of the Stuarts.

The fact of a priest and bishop being cognizant of a marriage within the degrees forbidden by the Church affords a strong proof that the corruption and neglect by which that Church was crumbling down in Scotland were beginning a hundred years before the Reformation was achieved by Knox and his followers.

Margaret was happy, too, because she would soon be able to impart to her dear sisters, whom she loved so tenderly, the perilous secret, which she was ever upbraiding herself for having withheld from them so long ; and she imagined how great would be the astonishment of Euphemia and Sybilla when her baby would be shown to them, and the joy of little Lizzie and Beatie finding themselves aunts to a real live princess.

Wearied with long surmises and thoughtful reveries, and with fondling her pretty little Margaret—for it had been named after herself and the queen-mother—and with hushing those feeble cries which as yet had never gone beyond the thick stone walls of the tapestried room, nor been heard by any one save her faithful old nurse and constant attendant, the beautiful young duchess had fallen asleep on her bed, partly undressed, and with the babe nestling in her bosom. On the inside her door was secured by those complicated bolts of wood and iron with which all internal doors were then fastened in old Scottish houses, but her window, which was in the round-tower at the street-corner, *still* appears never to have possessed a grating.

Twelve tolled in the tower of the ' Blessed Virgin-in-the-Fields.' The mist was thicker, and the night darker than ever.

Margaret did not hear the sound of feet in the narrow street below, for the lurkers there trod softly ; neither did she hear their voices, for they spoke in whispers ; but there, masked, muffled, and disguised as peasants, in broad round bonnets, frieze gaberdines, and deerskin boots, were the governors of Stirling and Broughty, with *Sir* Hew Borthwick ; other followers they had none, for this expedition was so desperate and daring that they could trust none, even from among the many well-chosen ruffians with whom the two chief traitors had garrisoned the royal castles committed to their care.

Margaret did not hear the jarring of two long lances, tied together, against the panes of glass, as by this means they affixed the iron hooks of a rope ladder to the stone mouldings of the tower window-sole, and then held it firm and steadily at the foot, while Borthwick clambered to the casement, which (although the it twenty-five feet from the ground) he reached with ease, and raising the sash entered softly. He then stood within the apartment, with two naked poniards in his belt, for defence, in case of surprise or attack.

All appeared just as we have described it before—the rich little couch, the carved *prie-dieu*, the Venetian mirror, with its bottles of rose-water, pots of essence and other appurtenances, and the thick dark tapestry. The wax tapers in the silver girandoles on the dressing-table were dimly burning and flickering, for the wicks were long, and snuffers were *not* invented until the epoch of James IV.

Margaret lay on her couch, fast asleep, with one white arm extended on her pillow, and the other round her infant, whose little head reposed on a luxuriant mass of her thick brown hair, which had escaped from that golden net or caul, then worn by the ladies of the court, and was streaming over her pillow. The ribbon points of her long bodice were partly untied, and on the dressing-table lay a multitude of those skewers of gold and silver tags and clasps which noble dames then used, before the simple invention of the *pin*, which was first adopted by Catharine Howard, an English queen. The rosy and dimpled hands of the infant, like its round and sleeping face, were nestling in the bosom of its young and delicate mother.

It was a touching picture of perfect innocence and love reposing together; but it affected not the sensual and cowardly heart of the ignoble Borthwick, or of Sir Patrick Gray, whose black head, through the mask of which his fierce and sinister eyes, that gleamed like two evil stars, might have been seen peering over the window-sole into the chamber of the sleeping girl. Something that glittered in the mouth of this baronial bravo, a nearer inspection would have shown to be a dagger, which he held between his teeth.

' Well, 'pon my soul, the prince's taste is not bad ! ' grumbled the other ruffian (who was flushed with wine, as he contemplated the beautiful girl, whose soft and regular breathing was the only sound that broke the silence of the sanctuary on which he was intruding his unhallowed presence. ' A baby too ! Oho ! now, whose brat may this be ? '

Margaret turned her noble head, parted her fine lips, and smiled tenderly in her sleep.

Borthwick thought she was about to waken, and shrunk

irresolutely back; but the dreams of such innocence as hers are ever pleasing and gentle, so the young girl still slept on. 'Donnart fool! why dost thou tarry?' asked Gray, in a hoarse whisper. 'Be quick!'

His voice half wakened Margaret, and she moved her head again, and a sigh escaped her lips.

Borthwick drew from his breast one of those large and gaudy Dutch cotton handkerchiefs which were then common in Scotland, and with brutal energy tied it completely over the head of Margaret, and tightening it across her mouth, muffled and stifled any cry she might have uttered; but the slightest sound was impossible, for sudden terror deprived her of all power of thought or action. He then raised her in his powerful arms, even as he would have done the wakened infant, which now began to raise its plaintive little voice, and which he shook roughly off, as it grasped its mother's thick soft hair. He bore her to the window, and thrust her through it, upon the right arm of Sir Patrick Gray, who grasped with his left hand the rope ladder (which was firmly secured below by Sir James Shaw), and which he descended in safety to the ground.

Borthwick sprang after them, but as Shaw lent his assistance to bear off Margaret, the light ladder swayed about in the wind, which dashed the growling and enraged conspirator against the rough wall like a plummet; by this means it snapped, and he fell heavily to the ground, but he hurried after the two barons, who were bearing Margaret down to the beach, which was then within less than a pistol-shot of the house.

As she had now freed her head from the muffler, she uttered a succession of shrill and piercing cries; but none heard or attended to them, for the stillness and darkness of midnight rested on the mist-shrouded town and river. In that 'good old time,' when the country houses of the Scottish gentry were manned and moated garrisons, or towers that were entered at an upper story by ladders, which the careful inmates drew up after them; when their towns had walls with barrier-portes, and their streets had neither lights nor pavements, but when every window was grated, and every close and wynd secured by a massive gate; when people carried lanterns at night, and every one went armed to the teeth, as a security against every one else—the clash of swords or the cries of fear and danger excited but little interest. Thus, without suffering the least interruption, the knightly ruffians and their accomplice reached the beach, where, within a bowshot of the chapel of St. Nicholas, Captain Edmund Howard, with a well-armed boat's-crew of picked English seamen, awaited them in the yawl of the *Royal Harry*.

'Do not be alarmed, fair lady,' said he, as Margaret was borne over the chafing surf, and placed in the stern-sheets of the boat by a man who grasped her with the tenacity of a vice, and who whispered huskily and impiously in her ear,—

'Be not afraid of me, lady, for I am innocent as the Paschal Lamb, and as gentle to boot.'

'By that blessed name,' she implored, 'I conjure you to tell me the meaning of this? and who you are——'

'I am Sir Hew Borthwick, knight of an unfortunate ilk, but your most devoted servitor, lady.'

'O, heavenly mercy!' she murmured, on hearing that terrible name, and believing that all her old forebodings were about to be realized, immediately fainted, or became powerless, and had no longer any capability of coherence in speech or thought.

'Devil be thanked—now we shall have no more trouble with her,' said Borthwick, as Captain Howard kindly spread his own velvet mantle over her.

'Poor little thing,' said he; 'she has fallen among evil hands; but, thank heaven, this dog's duty will soon be over. To-night she will swing in her hammock, aboard the *Royal Harry*.'

'And to-morrow may mingle her tears with the waters that bear her to English Harry's prison,' added Sir James Shaw, laughing.

'Hold water a moment, my lads,' said the English captain, as he flung a purse to Borthwick, who caught it as a hungry dog does a bone. 'Master Hew, this is the last largess of King Henry's I hope you will ever receive from my hand.'

'Thank you, Captain Howard—life is a race, and money the prize. In this world we always scorn honest poverty and worship gilded crime.'

'Philosophy in a cur's throat,' muttered Howard. 'Adieu, gentlemen; when next I unfurl St. George's cross in these waters, I hope to do it in fair daylight, when bringing to your shores a bright-eyed English queen. And now give way, my hearties,' he added, as the oars were dipped into the water, and the boat was slewed round—' give way for life ! '

' Or death,' said Borthwick, with a chuckling laugh, as he concealed the heavy purse in his broad leathern girdle. ' Farewell, sirs.'

' Farewell,' cried Howard, with one hand grasping the tiller and the other placed at the side of his mouth to convey the sound—' and may the great devil go with you for a rascally Scots pirate and ground shark.'

Margaret lay in a death-like faint, and this gallant English gentleman, while commiserating her fate and cursing the secret duty on which his subtle king had sent him, still urged his men to *give way*, and at every stroke their fourteen oars almost lifted the light boat out of the water. Howard raised the mantle repeatedly from the pale face of his prisoner, and the soft beauty of her features served every moment to increase the disgust he felt for himself and his Scottish colleagues.

The tide was ebbing fast, and as the river was running like a millrace, they soon reached the *Royal Harry*, which, with her consorts, was abreast of Broughty Castle, laying to, with her fore and mizen yards aback; but it was not until she was placed on one of the cushioned lockers of the great cabin, where proper restoratives were kindly and judiciously applied by two pretty young female attendants, whom Howard had brought for her from London, that poor Margaret began to recover from her first shock of terror, and to become aware of where she was.

With the wind right ahead, the *Harry* began to beat out of the narrow channel, on each side of which are broad and dangerous sandbanks, which then were alike destitute of lights and buoys; but a quartermaster was in the fore-chains, constantly heaving the lead. The night was misty, for a thick eastern *haar* yet floated on the bosom of the sea. The moon, now full-orbed and brilliant, was shining, like a lamp-globe of obscured glass, shorn of its beams, which lent a palpable whiteness to the mist they could not pierce. As the wind freshened a little and made gaps through the fogbank, the moonlight played along the waves, which followed each other in long white lines of glittering foam.

The English ships heeled over as the breeze freshened, for they were now always close-hauled. The stately *Harry* rode gracefully over each long rolling swell that curled under her prow; but Howard thanked his good angel when he was clear of that dangerous estuary, and when his next larboard tack enabled him to run far beyond the shoals of the Buddon-ness.

At times the mist was so dense that the two consorts of the *Harry* could not discern her top-light ; the watch rang the ship's bell every ten minutes, and they responded. This monotonous ringing continued for nearly two hours, when suddenly the watch of the leading English ship was started by the report of a heavy culverin, apparently only a few fathoms distant from their weatherbow, or so close that the red flash was seen through the white and moonlit haze.

All hands were piped, and with alacrity the seamen stood to their quarters, but in considerable excitement, for *Andrew Wood* was murmured along the decks as the ports were opened and the loaded guns run out, while Howard hurried Margaret Drummond to a place of safety below the water-line. But in accordance with King Henry's express orders, he was resolved to avoid hostilities if possible, and if the stranger should prove to be the famous Scottish admiral, to deceive him by answering his hail in *French.*

CHAPTER XX.

WOOD MEETS HOWARD.

AFTER running along the coast of Angus so far as that remarkable promontory named the Red Head, which rises to the height of two hundred and fifty feet on the southern shore of Lunan Bay, Sir Andrew Wood had put his ships about, and under easy sail bore back towards Dundee, without seeing any trace of the strangers he was in search of. From the tops the light had been discerned in the *Big O* of Arbroath, as the seamen named the great circular window of St. Thomas of Aberbrothwick, which was then illuminated at night by the charitable Benedictines of that magnificent abbey; and it formed a glorious landmark for those who traversed the German Sea, from whence it could be seen shining afar off, like a vast moon resting on the sloping promontory.

About midnight the vessels were creeping along the sandy shore of Barrie, where the waves rolled far upon the level beach, and chafed against the heaps or tumuli which cover the graves of the Danish invaders, when Master Wad, who had the middle watch, pricked up his ears on hearing the distant sound of a ship's bell. The silver mist was still so thick, that when viewed from the stern, the ship's head, and even the mizen crosstrees, were involved in obscurity.

' I hear a sound,' said Falconer, who, loverlike, was still loitering on deck, and restlessly musing over the hazel-eyed Sybilla, from whom he calculated he was now only about eight or ten miles distant. ' Willie,' said he, ' that sound is like the ringing of metal, or is it the deid bell in my ear ? '

' I would hope not,' replied the gunner; ' for if it is sae, some o' us will be slipping our cables before day-dawn.'

' There it is again—no imaginary, but a solid bell, and it rings in the mist. Can it be the Inchcape ? '

' Nay, Sir David; the moon is in the west, and the tide

is ebbing, so by the soundings we should ha'e the Buddonness about three miles off on our lee-bow.'

'And the Inchcape Bell ? ''

'About eight miles to windward. Ewhow, sirs! there are the top-gallant sails of a large vessel glinting in the moonlight and aboon the mist like snaw on a hill-top; a pint o' sack to a pint o' bilge, it is the English captain! Call up Robert Barton—pass the word to the admiral!'

The arquebussier who stood on guard near Jacob's ladder passed this intelligence through the door of the poop, and in a moment Captain Barton and Sir Andrew came on deck. As all sailors, do, they first glanced at the compass, and then cast their gaze aloft, to see that all the sails were full.

'How does she bear ? ' asked Sir Andrew.

'About a mile off, on the lee-bow, between us and the Gaa sands.'

'Gadzooks! her draught of water must be small.'

'There she's noo, sir, wi' top-gallants set aloft, for the wind is but light.'

As the gunner spoke the canvas of the strange vessel was seen to glitter like snow in the moonlight; but for a moment only, as she was again immediately shrouded in mist.

'What dost thou take her to be, Robbie ? ' asked the admiral.

'English,' replied Barton, · tightening his waist-belt, 'English by the rake of her masts and fashion of her top hamper.'

'Art sure ? '

'I got a full glisk of her just now, as she shot out of one fogbank into another. Hark! there goes her bell again!'

'Master Wad, get ready a gun there, for on the next tack we may fall aboard of her; I do think she is English, though there was no red-cross on her fore-topsail. But clear away for battle, Barton, for if it is the gallant Howard, we shall avenge thy father's fall, and make such a din on these waters as will scare all the fish between Fifeness and the Carlinheugh. Take in sail, and beat to quarters.'

The kettle-drum rolled and the trumpet was blown; in three minutes the ports were opened; the sails reduced by the watch; the magazine opened by the gunner; the arquebussiers of Falconer manned the tops and poop, and flinging aside their bonnets and gaberdines, five hundred seamen, grasping the rammers and sponges, the linstocks and tackle of the cannon, stood in fighting order, while

Master Wad fired a gun, and ran a red lantern up to the mast-head, to let Sir Alexander Mathieson, who was half a mile astern, know that the admiral had cleared for action.

' Sail ho !—here she comes again ! ' cried a hundred voices, as the gigantic outline of the English ship, looming like a great cloud through the mist, approached on the opposite tack, and within pistol-shot. Both shortened sail by backing their fore and mizen-yards. By the line of lights that glittered along the stranger's deck, her crew were evidently standing by their guns, and all equally prepared. Trumpet in hand, Barton, whose heart was brimming with fiery joy, sprang into the main-chains on the starboard side.

' Silence fore and aft ! ' cried he ; but the warning was needless, for then one might have heard a pin fall on board the *Yellow Frigate*.

' Ho—the ship ahoy ! '

' *Hola-ho !* ' replied a voice from the waist of the stranger.

' French ! ' muttered Barton, in a tone of disappointment ; ' what ship is that ? '

' The *Sainte Denis*, caravel of Monseigneur the admiral of the galleys to his Majesty Charles the Affable.'

' This is the *Yellow Caravel* of his Majesty the King of the Scots. We knew not that the admiral of France was in these seas.'

' We are in pursuit of three English ships commanded by Captain Edmund Howard, brother of the lord admiral of England.'

' So are we, and would give all the teeth in our heads to overhaul them. Sir Andrew Wood craves leave to pay his respects to Monseigneur d'Esquerdes, admiral of the galleys.'

' Monseigneur the Laird of Largo is welcome.'

Archy, the old boatswain, was piping away the crew of the barge, when the pretended Frenchman, having no desire for such a visit, hauled his wind, braced up his yards, and stood right away into the mist, with his topsails glittering, after which Sir Andrew Wood saw no more of him. The ports were lowered, the culverins secured ; Master Wad locked the magazine with a sigh, as he reflected there was no chance of fighting ; the hammocks were piped down ; the yards were squared ; and with no ordinary feelings of disappointment, the crew of the *Yellow Frigate* found themselves once more silently passing the Tower of

Broughty towards their former anchorage off the craig of St. Nicholas.

Intent only on reaching England without perilling the crooked measures of his sovereign, Captain Howard was glad that he had succeeded in ' throwing dust,' as he said, ' into the eyes of old Andrew Wood,' and when sorely importuned by his officers and crew to fight the Scots, is reported to have lost patience, and said,

' God confound ye, fellows ; dost think I will carve out my coffin to please you ? '

But fate, however, and the waves and wind were against him ; for before daybreak the mist was swept from the German Sea by a sudden and heavy gale from the south-east, which nearly threw the *Harry* on her beam-ends, and compelled her to run before it, in the very opposite direction from that which Howard wished to pursue. He was driven along the dangerous coast of Kincardine ; and before the second day's sunset, instead of making the coast of England, as they had hoped, the crews of the three English ships were straining every nerve, and using all the art of seamanship to weather the dangerous Cape of Buchanness, [nearly ninety miles northward from the mouth of the Tay.

How it fared with Margaret Drummond in the meanwhile will be related in another chapter of this history.

CHAPTER XXI.

THE PRICE OF THREE TENEMENTS.

A FEW pages back, we left the Duke of Rothesay, the Earl of Angus, and Lord Drummond seeking the presence of James III., all in a high state of excitement. They soon reached the hall (already described) where, during his annual visits to Dundee, the king received petitions and heard complaints, or held council, with what success we have already shown. It was, as usual, crowded by courtiers and nobles, with their armed followers and dependents; and Hailes, Home, the Forester of Drum, the Steward of Menteith, and other discontented personages, were grouping and whispering together.

The king was seated in the great chair, under the purple cloth of estate; near him stood John Abercrombie, the learned Benedictine, and they were examining with deep interest Lorenzo della Magna's edition of Dante's *Inferno*, which had been printed at Florence seven years before, and had thirteen illustrations engraved by Baldini. This had been a gift to James from the Papal ambassador, the Bishop of Imola; and the almost unlettered Angus gazed with wonder and pity at a king whose mind was so narrow that he could feel interested in a trifle so pitiful as a printed book!

The usually stern expression which clouded the dark face of this great lord of Galloway was partly concealed by the visor of his helmet; but the excitement under which he laboured was evident, for he frequently approached James, and withdrew again, as if irresolute how to broach the subject that oppressed him.

Lord Drummond and Rothesay were equally excited, and their emotion was balm to the gloomy soul of Sir Patrick Gray who accompanied them, and who, with his pale thin lips and fine but sharp teeth, his small wiry hands and cold delusive smile, seemed to be the evil genius of them all.

'My Lord Angus,' said the Constable of Dundee, 'dost think this king of ours will ever prefer the marshalling of hosts to the making of books and ballads—the clank of armour to rustle of silk—or the jangle of spurs to the patter of cork-heeled shoon?'

'We shall soon see,' replied Angus, hoarsely, through his clenched teeth, as he darted a savage glance at the Duke of Montrose.

'It would seem not,' added the warlike Constable, who, when a mere youth, had slain the aged Earl of Crawford at the battle of Arbroath; 'he is overmuch of a clerk and carpet squire for me.'

Neither Angus nor this Lord of Dudhope had much love for each other, but like many of the hostile nobles, they cordially agreed in keeping an iron hand over the poor king, and in resolving to defeat his projects, whether wise or unwise, and to destroy every favourite chosen from 'the herd,' as they designated the people, from whom unfortunately the favourites of the Stuart princes were generally chosen.

'Fool-king!' growled the furious earl, 'while thou toyest with some wretched ballad-book, I hold in my hand that which shall startle all Scotland like the note of the last trumpet.'

'Yea,' responded the Constable of Dundee, 'these balladeers and book-makers remind me of so many birds of prey hovering about the throne.'

'These carles in iron seem like so many crocodiles watching the poor king,' whispered the Benedictine at the same moment to William Dunbar, the sweet author of the *Thrissel and the Rois*, for there was then a feud between the men of the sword and the men of letters, as it was not an age when they could entertain a high veneration for each other.

Rothesay's excitement at last became insupportable. Pale and trembling with grief and anger, he approached the royal chair, and stretching out his hands, with his fine eyes full of fire, tears and unbraiding, said to the king:

'Father, is it thus thou hast deceived me!'

'Deceived thee—in what?' asked the astonished monarch.

'Yea, deceived me. The Lord Drummond told thee how I loved and was wedded to his daughter, and you gave me hopes of clemency and forgiveness, while knowing that overnight she had been most cruelly and foully abducted—torn away from me—from me who loved her better than my own soul!'

It is impossible to describe the astonishment that was visible in the faces of all who heard this startling avowal and charge; but in no face was it more strongly impressed than the king's, and his silence appeared to Rothesay the dumb confusion of discovered guilt.

'Father and king,' said he, firmly, 'where is my wife, the Duchess of Rothesay?'

'Rash monarch!' added Lord Drummond, with a hand on his sword, 'I, too, demand, where is my daughter?'

'By my soul as a man—by my honour as a king, I know not!' replied James, with dignity and indignation, as he rose from his chair, and threw the poems of Dante on the dais.

'Restore her to me!' continued the young prince, frantically, while his dark eyes sparkled through their tears; 'restore her, or in three days I will set all Scotland on fire!'

''Tis a wile of the English faction to further their Tudor marriage,' said Lord Lindesay, an opinion in which many nobles concurred; 'beware, my lord, beware of what you say and do!'

Angus stood silent and confounded by this double revelation.

''Tis enough to weep *once* over those we love,' said Lord Drummond; 'I have wept for my lost daughter, for she was my dearest and best beloved, the most gentle and bonnie of five; and now I shall think of vengeance! None but thee, James Stuart, could have an interest in removing or destroying her, so restore her, dead or alive, or vengeance will be the occupation of my life! The honour of a Scottish noble cannot be trifled with, even by a Scottish king; so beware that, when plunging into the abyss of rebellion, I do not drag thy throne down with me!'

Stunned by this terrible and, at such a time, most dangerous accusation—dangerous the more so that it came from the lips of his own son, the good and amiable king gazed irresolutely among the nobles, and read a threatening expression in all their clouded brows; even Montrose, his most trusty councillor, cast down his eyes in doubt, and now the stern face of Angus, who stood close by him, leaning on his sword, riveted his wondering gaze.

'My lord earl,' said he, 'what is the matter? Why

approach me in harness, and almost in a close helmet?
Say, dost thou believe me capable of a deed so vile?'

There was a solemn silence, for it was known that the
majority would adopt the opinion of this potent military
chief.

'I do deem thee guilty of this most cruel abduction;
yea, and of worse!' replied the stern Earl, as he threw up
the barred umbriere of his black helmet with a jerk, and
drew from his gauntlet a letter which was folded with care
and tied by a ribbon, sealed with purple wax, and inscribed
*secret, with care.'   'And to prove how far the bitter memory
of our raid at Lauder, and the love of the faithless and vile
will carry thee, I will take the liberty of reading to this
most illustrious audience a letter which is addressed to
his Grace of Montrose, but which, by a blundering pikeman,
was brought to my secretary, who made himself master
of its contents. My lords, these are terrible! Strict
honour required that it should have been forwarded to the
Earl of Crawford—pardon me—(with a sneer) I mean your
Grace of Montrose; but the common safety of the First
Estate required its immediate publicity.'

The stealthy eyes of Sir James Shaw sought those of
Gray, and an icy smile was exchanged; but to others,
their faces seemed imperturbable. A commotion immediately pervaded the hitherto still assembly; and the old
Duke of Montrose, with his sword half-drawn, was approaching Angus, in great wrath, when his arm was grasped by
the king. Seeing a storm impending, several of the peers,
the Sieur de Concressault, the Lord Lindesay, and Ramsay,
Lord Bothwell, drew near the throne, while the malcontent nobles
drew near Angus, while the pale and irresolute Rothesay
stood like a statue between them.

'You know this signature, my lords,' said Angus, displaying the latter.

'It is the king's,' said Shaw, almost the only man among
them who could read or write with ease.

'And this seal, *bearing two rocks in the centre of a stormy
sea*, with the motto " DURABO "?'

'The king's private signet,' said Sir Patrick Gray; 'we
all know that as well as our own faces.'

'Read, read, my lord,' cried twenty voices; and with
some trouble, though the handwriting of this document
of Borthwick, which is now before us, is very plain, Angus
sternly and emphatically read as follows:

'To his Grace the Duke of Montrose and Earl of Crawford, our trusty and heartily beloved friend, Lord Great Chamberlain, etc., be this delivered.

'Montrose, we greet you well. The help of the same blessed God, who has delivered us from many perils, will, I doubt not, with the assistance and advice of such powerful and zealous subjects as your grace, soon free our unhappy realm and oppressed people from that cruel nobility who tyrannize over all. I have now all prepared for the great banquet to be given in the Castle of Edinburgh, where, when Angus, Hailes, Home, and all that party, are birling the wine pot, we shall show them the *Black Bull's Head.* Fail not to come with all your most trusty adherents—men who will close their hearts to every emotion of pity and remorse, and who will have no thought but the wish to save Scotland by extirpating a traitorous nobility, who in all ages have been ready to sell their souls and bodies to the English kings for gold. With the fathers, all the sons above the age of twelve years should also be invited, and such I think was the suggestion of your grace at our last meeting. It now remains but to fix the time of this auspicious banquet. What say you to the feast of St. Monina—that evil day of July? From our Castle of Stirling, the 7th day of May, 1488.   JAMES REX.'

Exclamations of anger and astonishment burst from every lip, for this letter contained some artful hits, such as the Bull's Head, which was the signal for the murder of the Earl of Douglas in 1440, and Monina's day, which was the anniversary of the raid of Lauder.

The king was fearfully pale. 'My lord Earl of Angus,' said he, controlling his righteous indignation, 'on your allegiance as a subject, I command you to surrender up this tissue of falsehood—this infamous forgery.'

'Nay,' replied the earl, with a grim smile; 'if your Majesty wishes it consigned to the custody of the Lord Clerk Register, let him and other parasites seek it at my Castle of Thrieve, in Galloway, where, by the cannon's mouth, it shall be faithfully delivered to them or their messengers.'

'Beware, Archibald Douglas, lest ye overtask my patience.'

'Beware, James Stuart, for thou playest a perilous game! So this precious banquet is to be on Monina's day in July. I trust *that party* will all come with their best swords by their sides.'

'The anniversary of the raid of Lauder,' said the governor of Broughty; 'an ominous day.'

'This is infamous—this is intolerable!' exclaimed the white-haired Duke of Montrose, unsheathing his sword.

'So say I,' added Angus, with a bitter laugh.

'All who dare aver that the king wrote such a letter to me,' continued Montrose, 'or that such was the intention of our state banquet at Edinburgh, lie foully in their throats, and are false cravens! Let us betake us to our swords at once, for the sword alone can wrest a charter for the people's liberty from this subtle and tyrannical nobility.'

'Duke,' said James, 'liberty is the inherent right of the people. They give us prerogatives, but it is not in the power of princes to give a people what they possess by right of inheritance—liberty.'

'Montrose, thou sayest well,' said Angus, who did not understand the hint conveyed by the king's reply; 'the sword, the sword, so be it then,' he added, with lofty pride and stern joy; 'and with God's blessing, let the battle field decide whether this kingdom of Scotland shall be governed by its hereditary peers or the parasites of a king. James II. slew two earls of my house; one was murdered in the castle of Edinburgh in the midst of a friendly feast, another was stabbed to the heart by a dagger in the Castle of Stirling—stabbed by the royal hand, and then was flung over the chamber window upon the rocks below, like the body of a slaughtered hound rather than the corse of William Douglas, Duke of Touraine, and Lord Supreme of Galloway. I shall be wary how your father's son adds a third to the number.'

Angus glared with hatred at Montrose, who was the first subject in Scotland after the little Duke of Ross, being the first of the nobility who attained a ducal coronet, a distinction quite sufficient to gain him the enmity of all the earls of the Douglas faction.

'Oh, Angus,' said James, reproachfully, 'thou art a fierce subject, in whose lawless heart uncurbed ambition rages like a devouring flame; but wouldst thou have thy king to stoop to thee?'

'And why not, if that king hath erred?' asked the earl, bluntly.

'God be the judge between us,' said James, raising upwards his hands and tearful eyes.

'Decide, decide,' said Angus, whose anger was increasing every moment; 'banishment to evil councillors as Montrose, and death to all ignoble favourites—or death to the peers of Scotland; and here, at the foot of that throne for which I and ten generations of my house have often shed the Douglas blood, I throw down the gage of battle!'

With these daring words Angus drew the steel gauntlet from his right hand, hurled it at the foot of the throne, and withdrew, followed by Drummond, Hailes, Home, Gray, and others, who led the bewildered Duke of Rothesay away with them. The young Lord Lindesay, and his father the venerable Montrose, both sprang forward to pick the gauntlet up, but the latter was successful, and both these loyal nobles, with several others who loved and pitied the king, followed him to his private cabinet, to which he immediately withdrew.

'Said I not that I would put all Scotland in a flame?' whispered Borthwick to Sauchie, as he put his foot in the stirrup to mount at the palace gate.

'Yea, and verily thou shalt have, as I promised, three of my best tenements in Stirling, by deed of a notary's hand,' replied the Laird of Sauchie.

Abercrombie the Benedictine, William Dunbar the poet, and other literary men, were left behind in the hall. The angry altercation had somewhat scared them, but they could not resist an expression of pleasure at the prospect of their enemies, the military nobles, confronting each other on the field of battle.

'I would not, for a king's ransom, be in the boots of him who penned this specious forgery!' said the chief of our ancient poets, in his East Lothian patois.

'Ay, Willie Dunbar,' said Father Abercrombie, 'with the nobles it proposed to slay their eldest sons—no bad hint.'

'Why, this would make our poor king a heathen, like the Jews of old,' replied Dunbar.

'Yea, and it reminds me of a passage in the first act of the *Electra* of Sophocles.'

'You remember of the pagan emperor, who amused himself catching flies?' said the translator of Sallust, laughing.

'I warrant you, Brother Barclay,' replied Dunbar, 'the king will find these carles increase like unto so many wasps.

But hint not that, even in jest, our blessed king conceived
a thought so vile as that banquet of blood.'

' Alas ! ' said the young poet Henrison, sorrowfully, ' who
among us can foresee the end of all this ?   Life is unstable as
sunshine on the water.'

' Yes, my good master of arts,' replied Barclay, ' it is
even as our friend Dunbar sings in his sweet *Lament*—

> Our pleasaunce here is all vane glory,
> This false world is but transitory ;
> The flesh is bruckle, the fiend is slee—
> *Timor mortis conturbat me !* '

Dunbar gave a gratified smile at this quotation from his
poem, and bowed to the learned Benedictine.   At that
moment the clatter of hoofs drew them all to the north
windows of the hall, and they beheld the noisy train of
Angus gallop along the street with lances uplifted, and his
banner with the *red heart* displayed.   The earl, with the
Duke of Rothesay and others, were with them, and, save the
prince, all were brandishing their drawn swords, and crying,
' A Douglas ! a Home ! to arms !   Remember the raid of
Lauder !'

To these tumultuous cries many added others, such as,
' No English alliance, no invasion of Bretagne !   Remember
Andrew Barton ! ' And making a terrible din as they poured
along the narrow street, Angus, with five hundred armed
men, issued from the western gate of Dundee, and, conveying the young heir of Scotland with him, took the road direct
for the royal burgh of Stirling.

CHAPTER XXII.

THE SILKEN CORD.

WE must go a little back in this our history, to inform the reader how the daughters of Lord Drummond received his proposition of making one of them Lady of Home and the other Lady of Hailes. He did not find them quite so pliant or acquiescent as the noble lords for whom he destined them.

In the morning, before Margaret's abduction had been discovered, and when the cold roasted beef, the venison pies, and tankards of hot spiced ale, on which the good folks of those days breakfasted, were awaiting them in the dining-hall, he sent impatiently for Euphemia and Sybilla, and announced his views regarding them, simply saying that the safety of the state in a struggle which all men saw approaching required many bonds of union among the nobles, and that the bonds of matrimony being the surest, it was requisite, by an alliance with these two military chiefs, to strengthen his house, as he was now well up in years, had many enemies, and so forth.

Poor Sybilla, whose lover had avowed his passion to none save herself, and whose claim upon her love and honour were known to her only, received this startling announcement with terror and dismay ; for it crushed and bewildered her like a sentence of death. But Euphemia, who was proud and fiery, and the day of whose marriage with Robert Barton had been already named, and was now only postponed in consequence of his father's death, received the proposal with astonishment, and with the indignation it merited.

'My father, this cannot be!' she exclaimed, setting her pretty foot firmly on the floor, and nervously adjusting her satin hood ; ' you know that I am solemnly, and by a ritual of our Church, promised and affianced to Robert Barton. My uncle, the Dean of Dunblane, heard my *trothplight* at the altar, when I received this betrothal ring ; our promise

of marriage is sanctioned and blessed by the Church, and
can no more be broken than the band of marriage itself,
without committing sacrilege and sin.'

The old lord fidgeted about, for he felt the truth of what
she said.

' Oh think again, dearest father, of what you require of
us ? ' added Euphemia.

' Us—*us* ? I address myself to you, in the first place,
Dame Euphemia. The noble lovers I provide for you are
not to be trifled with, and will assuredly brush from their
path the son of Barton the merchant——'

' Sir Andrew Barton, the knight and admiral,' interposed
Euphemia—' Barton the Laird of Barnton and Almondell ! "

' Barton umquhile skipper and trader,' said the father,
angrily, as he tore open the ribbons of his doublet and
walked hurriedly up and down the oak floor, stamping hard
on his red-heeled boots at every turn.

' Dear father,' urged the plaintive voice of Sybilla, ' bethink thee what our dearest mother would have thought of
such a proposition.'

' Just what she thought when such a proposition was
made to her thirty years ago—God assoilzie her ! She was
a good and loving wife to me, and yet—dost know how we
came to be espoused ? '

' Because you loved her, I would hope.'

' Loved—fiddlestick ! not a bit, at that time at least.
When I was a beardless young callant, the Murrays of
Athole marched into Strathearn, and came down by the
woods of Ochtertyre and Comrie, with pipes playing and
banners displayed, to harry the lands of Drummond of
Mewie, and levy at the sword's point the tiends of the kirk
of St. Ronan at Monzievaird. Mewie was slain by them—
shot dead by three arrows. This was not to be borne ! I
marched with all the stout lads of the stewartry against the
Murrays, but they were too strong for me then, and I was
obliged to *gang warily* until Lord Crawford offered to lend
me five hundred lances from Angus. We soon cleared all
upper Strathearn of the Murrays, and drove them through
Glenturrit and Glenlednock. We besieged them in St.
Ronan's kirk—fired its heather roof, burned one half of
them alive, and claymored the rest. In gratitude to Crawford, who had more daughters than he knew what to do
with, I married Elizabeth Lindesay, and a good wife and true
she was to me—although at first she made many a moan,

for she had been affianced to Drummond of Mewie ; but who cares for woman's tears when trumpets are blown ? '

' Father,' said Euphemia, ' thou forgettest that a woman has but one heart to lose—one heart to bestow.'

' 'Sdeath ! I shall lose my patience, and bestow my curse on some of ye. Some harper or balladeer, some tramper or Egyptian hath put this stuff into your head. Whoever heard of hearts or lovers standing in the way of great lords —of castles and broad acres—of bands of mail-clad men ? Stuff, I tell thee, Effie ; Hailes and Home will both be made earls, and you shall both become countesses. I swear by every altar in yonder kirk of Mary, you shall ! We have had a queen and a Lady of the Isles in the family, but never a countess yet ! '

' Father, this cruelty and sacrilege will break my heart —it will kill me.'

' I never heard of a lusty lass like thee being killed by marriage yet. Now do not provoke me, for my mind is made up. Come hither, Sybilla ; thou wilt not take a plaguey love-fit to vex thy old father ? '

' Alas ! father——'

' What ! 'sdeath ! hast thou no heart either, and wilt thou become a contumacious gipsy ? '

' Hear me, dear father——'

' I hear nothing but thy promise to be the bride of Hailes, or of Home, I care not which ; but one you shall have, so settle it between you. They are both brave and handsome gallants, with a good retinue at their cruppers. I have no time for more of this,' he continued, buckling on his enormous sword ; ' or for responding to the devil's litanies of such gadabouts as either of ye.'

The announcement of Lady Margaret's disappearance gave a sudden change to this extraordinary conversation, and springing at a wrong conclusion, Lord Drummond impetuously rushed away in search of Rothesay, whom, as already related, he met in St. Clement's Wynd, from whence they proceeded to the poor king, leaving Sybilla and Euphemia overwhelmed with grief and consternation by this new and sudden calamity ; for no trace of Margaret could be found, and the discovery of her poor little babe, concealed in the alcove of the turret, served but to augment their sorrow and perplexity.

Next morning the anchors of the frigate were barely down before Jamie Gair, who acted as pilot, and others

who came off in the shore-boats, informed those on
board of the strange rumours then current in Dundee.
One man informed Archy the boatswain of how the Lady
Margaret Drummond had been carried off by the king's
order, and drowned in the pools of Errol ; another told
Master Wad how Angus and Drummond had quarrelled
with the king, and would have slain him but for the timely
intervention of the French ambassador, the Mareschal de
Concressault, and the Lord High Constable ; a hundred
other stories, equally absurd and improbable, were heard
by other members of the crew ; and the excitement which
evidently prevailed ashore, caused some alarm on board of
the ships.

The admiral doubled the guard of arquebussiers on the
poop and forecastle, loaded the cannon, moored the ships
with a spring upon their cables, ordered that all boats should
be kept a bowshot off, and desiring the barge to be piped
away, hurried ashore with all her crew armed by jacks of
mail below their canvas gaberdines.

Falconer, Barton, and the admiral, were in half armour.
The latter hastened to the presence of the afflicted king,
whom he found highly excited by his late altercation with
Angus and Rothesay ; while the two companions—the
lovers—repaired to the mansion of Stobhall.

Borthwick, whom Sir Patrick Gray had desired to act
as a spy upon the inmates of that stately residence from the
moment the ships had been seen in the estuary, threw
himself, sans leave, upon a collier's horse, which he found
tethered to a ring in St. Clement's Wynd, and galloped to
Broughty, where the malcontent noblesse were assembled
in solemn but somewhat angry conclave ; and there he
informed Lord Drummond and his two intended sons-in-
law that the young ladies had visitors. Upon this, the
trio formed a little plot within their greater conspiracy, to
remove, or as Lord Drummond said, to brush Barton and
Falconer from their path for ever, and if possible to entrap
the good old admiral, and get the two king's ships into their
own hands ; for the *Yellow Frigate* and the *Margaret* were
then the flower of the Scottish fleet, which, in the infancy
of our maritime affairs, mustered only a few sail.

In that time England had no more ; for Henry VII. and
Henry VIII., when requiring ships for warlike purposes,
seized without ceremony upon the largest merchantmen
in their English ports. In 1512 the fleet of James IV. con-

sisted of forty-six sail, and was in no way inferior to the fleets of Henry of England or Don Emanuel, King of Portugal.

Borthwick, a wretch whose whole life had been a lie, a cheat, a web of mischief and infamy, informed the three lords that Robert Barton was in the house with Lady Euphemia, and that Sir David Falconer was in the garden with her sister. On this they all rushed to their horses, summoned the Lairds of Carnock and Balloch and other armed followers of trust, and left the tower of Broughty intent on some desperate outrage.

'So then, 'tis Falconer whom Sybilla loves,' said Hailes; 'and 'tis she whom I have made up my mind to win if I can. I have observed that in his presence she always became brighter and more beautiful. I was sharp enough to see that a *spell* was upon her; but I had no idea then that she would ever be more to me than her aunt, the old dame of Montrose.'

'Prick on! prick on!' urged Home, spurring his horse; 'we will soon teach these varlets the penalty of raising their eyes to noble ladies.'

Unaware of the coming storm, Barton sat with Euphemia in the chamber of dais; and Falconer with Sybilla in a summer house or alcove at the foot of the garden, the southern boundary of which was the bed of the Tay.

Shaded from the brilliant sun of noon by the trellis-work, the thick honeysuckle and the privet, the lovers sat within their bower. The shining river chafed the yellow sand at their feet; in all its greenness and verdure, the opposite coast seemed to palpitate in a blaze of light; and midway between, with all their yards squared by the boatswain's critical eye, their white sails neatly handed, and their great blue ensigns drooping listlessly over their carved poops, the stately caravels of the Laird of Largo rode at their moorings with their heads to the ebbing tide.

Believing that none were watching and that none could see them, Sybilla, in the excess of grief for her sister's mysterious disappearance, had thrown herself upon the breast of Falconer. All his whispers were full of hope and affection, and Sybilla wept while she listened. Confined in its caul of gold, her glossy hair hung in a heavy cluster on the shoulder of Sir David, and her hands were locked in his. The lover endeavoured to convince her that their sad and gentle Margaret was not, as the credulous burghers averred, destroyed by the king, but most probably was abducted by him or young Rothesay, and secured in some of the royal castles, but for what end none could then foresee; at all events, to be assured that her safety was certain, and that they would infallibly hear of her soon, as none could have a pretext for injuring a being so good and gentle. Sybilla allowed herself to be persuaded, and a faint smile began to steal over her soft and downcast face.

Never did the rich costume of the court of James III. appear to better advantage than on the fine form of Sybilla Drummond. Her kirtle was of green brocade, and an open robe of cloth-of-silver fell behind her, edged with fur and lined with white satin. Her girdle was of silver, and there, as at her white forehead, her swelling bosom and delicate little ears, hung long pearl pendants.

Women are said 'to love those who follow desperate professions;' but in those days, though the men of Scotland were all desperate fellows, they had no professions to follow save the church, the sword, or the sea; so it was rather the chivalric uprightness of his character, the gallantry of his bearing, and the superiority which his educated mind gave him over the brutal barons and unlettered lords of her time, that made Sybilla yield up her pure and simple love to this young soldier, who was one of James's favourites, and a protégé; for his father had died in battle on the deck of his ship defending the harbour of Blackness when assailed by the English fleet seven years before.

They did not speak much, this young and dreaming pair, for their hearts were too full of tenderness and hope, desperate hope, that their love might be successful; and being loth to pain unnecessarily the heart of her lover, Sybilla, unlike the haughty Euphemia, did not confide to him the intentions of her father regarding that young noble whom he had sworn to make his son-in-law at all hazards; but with the superstition incident to her time, rather than to herself, she enumerated a number of omens of impending evil which *now* can only excite a smile—and Falconer smiled at them even then.

Yesterday, when going to the chapel of the Grey Sisters in the Overgaitt, she had seen a single crow flying straight before her—an infallible omen of mischance; and this morning at sunrise, when watching the swans that swam on the river, one uttered a wild, wailing, and melodious sound, such as she had never heard before. She thought it was enchanted; but an hour after it was seen to float upon the water with outstretched wings, quite dead—another terrible omen.

'The swan was dying, dearest Sybie, and was singing its own sweet dirge,' replied Falconer; 'but thou hast heard what few have the fortune to hear—though there is nothing wonderful in it. If Archy of Anster, our wight boatswain, were here, he could tell thee of stranger things; of an ocean where the fish turn all manner of beautiful colours before they die; of gigantic plants that flower but once in a hundred years, and happy is he who beholds them then; of islands where every tree utters a melodious sound when the soft wind sweeps through their fairy leaves, and of birds that live for six long centuries, and having no mate burn themselves to death in a nest of spices, from whence a young one springs forth with all its plumage sprouting—the phœnix of Arabia! In the bosom of Nature, dearest, there is hidden many a secret of which we know nothing.'

'I have heard Father Zuill speak of such things to my sister Margaret,' said Sybilla, weeping at her name.

'Our chaplain—ah! he hopes one day to invent a mirror which will consume ships and cities, scorch forests to charcoal, and mountains to cinders, and put cannon and arquebusses quite out of fashion, like the mangonels and balistæ of the olden time. What would become of me then? I should have to learn some other trade than soldiering, or go to battle with a mirror on my back. It is the insanity of science.'

'Yet I have heard that your old Dominican is a famous preacher.'

'Ay, Willie Wad, our gunner, swears that when he expounded on the Deluge, one day, all the fishes arose from the water and sat upon their tails to hear his discourse, as they of old to St. Anthony, when he preached. But Cuddie, the admiral's coxswain, averred that it was only because they had more reason to be grateful than other animals, being the sole portion of the animated creation that escaped the great flood in the days of old Admiral Noah. But thou dost not smile, Sybie—sweetheart.'

Between these two there was a reciprocity of sentiment so complete that conversation was, perhaps, little wanted at that sad and anxious interview. Neither had a thought, a hope, or a fear, in which the other did not participate;

and now, for more than another hour they sat dreaming side by side, or only exchanging mute and little caresses, as Sybilla reclined her head on Falconer's shoulder. Her eyes were fixed on the still flow of the sunlit Tay, while his were gazing on the radiance and serenity of her pure and delicate face.

He thought that a time *might* come when this dear spell would be broken—when the tendril that clung to him, this gentle one who had entwined herself around his heart, and who loved him with all the purity and fervour of a young and confiding girl, would be torn from him and given to another. It might be; such things happened often in Scotland then; and at that foreboding thought, a frown wrinkled the brow of Falconer; a cold anguish entered his heart, and he was obliged to turn away, lest the timid Sybilla should see the expression of menace which he knew such a terrible anticipation wrought upon his features. Was this a foreboding of what was to come?

At such moments Falconer would feel the white straight brow of Sybilla come nearer his cheek, and her hand tighten its clasp in his; then his angry fears evaporated, in the tenderness that mute caress inspired.

Poor lovers! they heard not the stealthy steps that were creeping down the gravel walks; they saw not the fierce and mocking eyes of those who, from without the leafy bower, were watching, with mingled scorn and amusement, this interchange of endearments and this purity of soul, in which they could not share; for, acting on the information received from Borthwick, those inseparable companions, Hailes and Home, with the Lairds of Carnock, Balloch, and others, were all close by, armed and intent on some deed of cruelty.

Suddenly their ominous shadows darkened the sunny entrance of the bower! The lovers started, and beheld five or six pairs of eyes regarding them with expressions of menace and insolence.

'Villan, draw!' said Lord Hailes, imperiously.

''Pon my soul, you have a polite way of announcing yourself,' said Falconer, scornfully, as he drew his sword and placed himself before the terrified Sybilla, around whom he threw his left arm as a protection.

'I most humbly crave pardon for this unpleasant intrusion, Lady Sybilla,' said Hailes, uncovering his head, and bowing till his plumed bonnet swept the grass—but bowing with bitter irony : ' we must hale forth this man, whose presence disgraces you.'

' Fellow, come forth ! ' cried Home, unsheathing his sword ; ' the crows shall hold thy lykewake to-night.'

' Gie him Lauder Brig owre again,' said Drummond of Carnock, making a thrust, which drew a shrill cry from Sybilla, and a successful parry from Falconer, whose sword twisted the other's blade out of his hand, and sent it flying over a tree-top behind him.

' A devil of a fellow this ! ' said Balloch.

' An insolent churl ! ' added the two lords.

' Allow me to suggest to your lordships the cultivation of courage as a quality—the acquisition of politeness being an impossibility,' said Falconer, with a withering glance.

At this sneer the rage of his assailants knew no bounds ; and they lunged at him again and again severally and with all their swords together, but being within the bower he kept them completely at bay.

' Come forth, I tell thee, villan ! ' said Home, imperiously, ' that I may handsel a new sword on thy plebeian head.'

' Proud lord,' said Falconer, as by one well-directed thrust he pierced the sword arm of Hailes ; ' ere long we will teach thee, and such as thee, who fight only to uphold long pedigrees and overweening privileges, that the Scottish people will not submit to be trampled on by a horde of titled traitors.'

' May I die, fellow, but thou shalt eat these words,' cried Hailes, hoarsely, and still pressing on, while his sword-arm dripped with blood.

' I know one thing thou wilt never die of—shame,' said Falconer, laughing, as he thrust him back at full length on the sward. At that moment, the gallant young arquebussier, who was so fully occupied in front that he did not hear Borthwick breaking through the bower behind him, suddenly felt his arms seized by that personage ; and then his assailants, two of whom were infuriated by wounds, rushed upon him ; tore the screaming Sybilla from his arm, wrested away his sword, and dashed him to the earth. Now there was an ominous pause, as to whether or not they should despatch him at once.

' Gie him Lauder Brig, I tell ye ! ' cried Balloch again.

' Thou art right, laird,' said Home, fiercely ; ' but we have no tent cords.'

'But here is my scarf,' said Hailes, whose hands clutched the throat of Falconer like a tiger's fangs. 'Knot me a noose some of you, and pull with a will.'

'Quick,' added Carnock; 'pull—pull! By Saint Beelzebub, my fine fellow, thou wilt soon look like a gled nailed on a byre-door.'

In the hands of so many, Sir David Falconer, though young, powerful, and athletic, was completely overmastered; and now ensued one of those terrible scenes which so often darkened the annals of our country. The scarf, which was of soft silk, was tied round Falconer's neck in a slip-knot, with grim deliberation.

'Save me from this butchery, Lord Home—for *her* sake,' said Falconer, making tremendous efforts to free himself; 'or at least, remove her in pity. Hear me, Home—thou wert once loyal and gallant.'

'Peace, villan,' replied that ferocious peer, as he smote the brave suppliant full and heavily on the mouth with his hand.

'Mercy,' implored Sybilla, sinking on her knees, and clinging to the hand of Borthwick, who held her as in a giant's grasp; 'mercy for him, and for the love of God! Man—man—thou hast been a priest, and must yet remember that the merciful are blessed, for they shall obtain mercy. Have pity! O have pity; by the star of Heaven, by the Queen of Angels, I implore you to have pity.'

But Borthwick, who was wholly employed in looking down upon that snowy bosom, of which her kneeling position enabled him to see more than was ever meant for eyes like his, heeded her not; but grasped her with the strength and tenacity of an iron vice; and now, while her cries and entreaties would have melted the hearts of any men but those of the Scottish noblesse of 1488, these miscreants began to strangle and drag Falconer, by the knotted scarf, towards the river.

'For God's love—for her sake—gentlemen—my Lords —good sirs, do not murder me thus before her face—before her; remove her—beloved Sybilla—pity, pity—mercy, am I to die like a dog—for her—for her sake, monsters—God!——'

The tightening of the knot cut short the cries of Falconer, who in that terrible moment thought only of Sybilla; but dragged as he was by the throat, strangulation immediately ensued; his handsome features became swollen, livid, and frightful; his eyeballs protruded. He tossed his arms about him wildly; but the third time he was dragged round the bower, he was senseless, lifeless, and stiff; and the assassins, after bestowing a few parting kicks on the body, carefully sheathed their swords, which had been lying on the ground, and retired, leisurely and without precipitation.

'Adieu, lady,' said Lord Hailes, with a stern loftiness of manner; 'now we have revenged your honour on this presumptuous churl.'

'Farewell, and I give you joy of your leman, sweet madam,' said Borthwick, mockingly, as he released her.

With a shriek Sybilla sprang to the breathless body of her lover. Her fingers were trembling, weak, and powerless; thus she strove fruitlessly to loosen the hateful scarf which encircled his neck. The attempt was vain, for there was no strength in her.

Then, overcome by the frightful, swollen, and blackened aspect of that beloved face, she uttered another wild, despairing cry, and fell prostrate and senseless upon him.

So ended this scene of horror!

CHAPTER XXIII.

LORD DRUMMOND AND ROBERT BARTON.

WHILE this atrocity was acted in the garden, and about a pistol shot distant from the mansion, Robert Barton received from Lady Euphemia a sorrowful and excited explanation of her father's new and peculiar views regarding herself and her sister ; on hearing which the lover lost all patience, and said all one might be supposed to say on receiving such startling information.   David Falconer would, perhaps, have heard it in silent sorrow, for he felt himself poor and powerless ; but the wealthy heir of old Sir Andrew Barton had no doubt on the subject of his own conduct.

' 'Zounds, Effie, what is this you tell me ?   Would your father, Lord of that ilk, and Steward of Strathearn though he be, wrest thee from me ? thee whom the Church hath given me—who art all but my wife, and wear on that dear hand the betrothal ring, which soon must be a bridal one ? No, no !   Yonder lieth the frigate, and the barge's crew are at the Craig of St. Nicholas ; say but the word, and I shall place the broad waters of the Tay between thee and these Lords of Home and Hailes ! They may be the prouder and the sterner, but that they are either richer or better men than Robert Barton of Leith I deny.   'Sdeath, 'tis little I value such holiday loons !   Mass ! I would like rarely to see them both piped aloft in a close-reefed topsail breeze to send down the topgallant yard, or haul out a weather-earing !   On my faith, it would be a sight for old Andrew Wood.'

' Alas ! they have seldom less than each a thousand lances at their back ; and thou, dear Robert, hath none.'

' None, say ye, Effie ?   I have every man in yonder *Yellow Frigate*, and the *Queen Margaret* to boot ; I have every seaman in Leith and Dundee. Faith ! I would not lie in the hosen of him who wronged the son of Andrew Barton ; but to let these lordlings get the weathergage of me and Davie Falconer—Hailes and Home—two varlets only fit for carrying powder or wringing wet swabs—no, no, Effie, it never shall be !'

'But alack ! they are both brave and determined.'

'Likely enough—brave fellows in smooth water ; but I'll teach them how to dip their spoons in the captain's mess ; by St. Mary I will !'

Euphemia Drummond threw herself upon his breast and wept, as she said—'Surely, they will never have the evil heart to take me from thee ? Oh, were my uncle the dean, or our good friend the old bishop here, they dared not even to think of it.'

'But your uncle the dean is attending a chapter at Dunblane, and our good friend the bishop is drinking King Henry's sack in London Tower, to which he has been wantonly conveyed a prisoner, by those same Englishmen who quite as wantonly slew my poor father on the open seas. But some one approaches—'tis thy father, Effie ; leave me to speak with him on this matter for a moment only, my sweet one.'

As the old lord raised the arras at one end of the apartment and entered, his eldest daughter retired by a door at the other ; and Robert Barton, while his heart swelled with sorrow and honest indignation, approached with a lowering brow the father of the girl he loved, and one whom until now he had ever esteemed as a dear and venerable friend.

'Good my lord,' said he, 'I pray you to pardon me, if I intrude upon the grief occasioned by the disappearance of Lady Margaret, by making a humble offer of my services and assistance.'

'I thank you, *Master* Robert Barton,' replied Lord Drummond, with something of confusion and much of stern coldness in his manner; 'but I believe that to the king—and to him only—must I look for the restoration of my dearest and most gentle daughter.'

'To the king ?——'

'Ay, to the king ! I spoke plain enough. She is the wedded wife of his son, the Duke of Rothesay——'

'Rothesay !'

'Ay, ye well may start ; but James, still hankering after those grasping Tudors (may God confound them all !) liked not the match, and hath had her kidnapped. He hath dared to do this ; but the act shall cost him a crown, should I spend the last of my breath and the last of my blood to tear it from his brow. False king!' he added, apostrophizing the wall; 'didst thou forget even for a moment that she was a daughter of Lord Drummond?'

'Hark you, my lord; I am the king's liegeman, and deplore you should nurse thoughts of treason, or have such words of danger on your tongue; but still more do I deplore that you should harbour in your heart sentiments repugnant to the principles of honour, and to the happiness of your eldest daughter.'

A flush of anger reddened the brow of the proud old noble. 'What mean you, Captain Barton?' he asked.

'Why, my lord, have you proposed to cast me adrift— I who am affianced to Euphemia, and who love her with a true and honest heart? Come, my lord, be fair and above-board with me, remember that our dear Effie is my plighted wife—plighted and betrothed to me in happier times than these.'

'Pledges made in peace are often broken in war,' replied the noble, coldly, and without noticing a gesture of impatience which escaped the honest seaman; for he remembered how anxious the conspirators at Broughty were to obtain the king's ships. In his ambition to achieve this, and also obtain vengeance upon James, he condescended to subterfuge.

'Captain Barton,' said he in a low voice, 'all correspondence between the king and his nobles is at an end, and another day may see their swords unsheathed against him. Promise me, should this event occur,' he continued, sinking his voice into a whisper, 'that you will contrive to have yonder war ships delivered unto such captains and mariners as the vice-admiral who acts under his Grace the Duke of Albany may appoint; or that you will serve the nobles—and my pledge to you may yet remain inviolate.'

'*May?* God forgive thee, thou subtle old man, for such a cruel alternative,' replied Barton, with deep emotion, while his eyes filled and their lashes trembled. 'I love your daughter better than my life; Heaven knows how long I have loved your Effie, how dearly and how well; but I also love that good king who was ever my father's friend; and the curse of that dead father would arise from his grave in the Englishman's sea, and follow me to the end of my days on sea and on land, if I proved false to my allegiance. My dear Effie! accursed be the policy which would make thee the boon for which I am to barter name and fame, honour and soul ! '

Lord Drummond, whose perceptions of right and wrong (never too clear at any time) were somewhat clouded and warped by the quarrel of the barons and king, against whom he now felt a deadly hatred, witnessed this deep burst of feeling unmoved, for he had not the smallest intention of yielding up his daughter to her betrothed, even though the latter were base enough to betray the admiral and surrender those great caravels, which were the terror of the northern sea, and the flower of the infant navy.

' You will not join us, and deliver up two paltry ships,' resumed the politic tempter ; ' what ? not even for a bride so fair ? '

' No—not as the king's rebellious subject.'

' So, so,' muttered the lord, impatiently ; ' if you go from this on your feet, you may warn James of the cloud that gathers round his throne.'

' Alas ! I will never betray your lordship. As the father of Euphemia, I almost considered you mine. Heaven judge between us, my lord, for I love and revere you still ; natheless, this duplicity to me, and this falsehood to our beloved king.'

Instead of being touched by the depth of feeling displayed by Robert Barton, the cruel noble now only feared that in his efforts to serve that desperate cause in which he had enlisted himself, he had betrayed too much to the king's true man, and saw at once the danger thus incurred. Raising the arras, he whispered to young Drummond of Mewie, who stood without, and was in attendance upon him :

' Summon Carnock, Balloch, and their people ; they are loitering in the hall, the street, or garden. Tell them that this man knoweth more than should be risked with others than ourselves. Dost thou comprehend me ? '

Mewie, a savage-looking and unscrupulous young Celt from Strathearn, muttered something under the thick red beard that fell in shaggy volume under the brow of his steel cap, while he grinned and withdrew. Then Lord Drummond turned once more to poor Barton, who, under the old noble's calm exterior, could never have divined the deadly intentions of one he loved so well, but gazed sadly at him as if he sought to gather some new hope for himself and for Euphemia.

'Then in this approaching raid, Captain Barton, you will permit that long Toledo of yours to rust in its velvet scabbard?'

'Not if the king's enemies are in the field; but, good my lord, let us talk of that which is nearer my heart than broil or battle. Consider how this sudden enmity to me has filled my soul with sorrow. Oh, my lord, to say how much poor Effie and I have loved each other were a vain and useless task; but to reflect that the very day on which we were to wed was named—to think——'

'Come, come,' replied Drummond, with a lowering brow and a grim smile, as he heard the trampling of feet in the arcades below, and knew that his clansman, Mewie, and others were assembling there; 'this may not be; Cupid must not shoot his shafts amid a civil war, nor Hymen light his torch at the flame of burning towns. We can have no dalliance now; the dame to her bower, and the knight to his saddle. If, Robert Barton, thou wilt deliver up Sir Andrew Wood and the king's ships to the governor of Broughty, thou mayest yet have thy bride; if not, seek a mate in another nest than the house of Drummond, and as its foe *gang warily*. Fare ye well, sir,—ha! ha! my daughters shall wed with new made earls.'

''Tis true, my lord, I am no noble, and consequently I am the better Scotsman; but I believe I am rich enough to please even you. My father has left me a fair estate upon the Forth and Almond, where the land is so fertile that, as the old rhyme says,

> A rood of land on links of Forth
> Is worth an earldom in the north.'

'I care not,' replied Lord Drummond, doggedly; 'thou shalt never have daughter of mine, wert thou rich as James III., and rumour says his black chest in the castle of Edinburgh is brimming with ingots and precious stones. I will not wed a Drummond to the son of a merchant trader.'

'My lord——,' Barton began, proudly.

'Nay, nay,' interrupted the old lord, impatiently; 'get thee some huckster lass about the timber holfe, at Leith; she will better suit old Barton's son than will a daughter of the Steward of Strathearn.'

At this gross speech Barton grew deadly pale, and laid a hand on his sword, but immediately relinquished it, saying

with calmness, ' No insult will tempt me to forget that
you are the father of my dear Euphemia ; that your hairs
are grey as my poor father's were ; and more than all,
that (alas !) you loved me once ! '

' Zounds, fellow, I shall lose all patience ! ' replied the
lord, angrily, for, in truth, he felt ashamed of himself,
and wished to be worked up into a passion. ' Wouldst
thou place thyself in competition with the Lord Home,
the son of the Hereditary Bailie of Coldinghome, or with
the Lord Hailes, the son of that gallant peer who slew the
Lieutenant-general of England at the battle of Sark, and
won that glorious day for Scotland ? '

' The son of Sir Andrew Barton may compete with any
man ! True, *he* began life as a poor ship-boy and skipper's
varlet ; but he died a knight and Laird of Barnton. Woe
to both Home and Hailes, if they come within arm's-length
of me ; some day I may overhaul them, and show them
the foretop with a vengeance ! Farewell, my lord ; when
next we meet I will not trouble you with entreaties even
for your daughter ; and so, till then, God keep you.'

Barton bowed, and with a heart swollen almost to bursting with rage and grief, and a brain that seemed to swim
under the influence of his conflicting emotions, he staggered
from the chamber, and descended unattended to the outer
door, and with all the aspect of a man flushed with wine.
On gaining the pavement he saw the Drummonds of Carnock,
Balloch, and Mewie, all with the holly-branch in their
bonnets or helmets, loitering under the arcades in the
Fish Street, and all well armed. He was hurrying past
them towards St. Clement's Wynd, when some one called
aloud :

' Hallo !—Captain Barton ! '

Too much occupied by his own bitter thoughts, he did
not hear the cry, but walked hurriedly on.

' Dost thou not hear us, rascal ? ' cried several voices.
Barton now turned to discover who was addressed.

' Ah,' said Lord Hailes, who with Home and others issued
into the street, ' I thought he would know we meant *him*.'

' Villain ! ' said Barton, unsheathing his sword, and
trembling with a terrible joy ; ' what mean you by this ? '

' By the black rood, my fine fellow, but your tone is high
for a skipper of Leith ! ' said Home.

' It is the tone to which I am entitled.'

' Ah, we shall prove that,' said Borthwick, drawing his

sword, while his eyes gleamed with cruelty and malice ; and the rest, to the number of seven or eight, also unsheathed their weapons.

Barton did not wait for the attack but fell on bravely, dealing long and sweeping cuts with many a thrust between. One of the latter ripped up the sword-arm of Borthwick, and hurled him against the wall of a house ; one of the former fell full upon the harnpan which Lord Hailes wore under his velvet bonnet, and rolled him ignominiously in the gutter ; but the rest closed in, fighting in a circle, and notwithstanding his bravery, skill, and that strength of arm peculiar to all seamen, Barton would have been beaten down and slain without mercy had not the sudden arrival of old Sir Andrew Wood, Cuddie Clewline, the coxswain, and the whole barge's crew, armed with boatstretchers and poniards, given a sudden change to the aspect of the conflict. With a stentorian shout, such as only can come from the throats of those who are wont to out-bellow the wind and waves, they rushed into the fray, with cries of—

' Ho for Barton ! Clear the hause here, loons and lubbers ! Ware your gingerbread, masters—Largo for ever ! '

Barton, who had been driven back against the wall of a house, was soon freed, and his assailants put to immediate flight, but not before several severe blows had been given and received. With the admiral there was a tall and handsome man, who was clad in a coat of rich gold brocade, and whose face was concealed by a salade. This person immediately assailed Lord Home with great impetuosity, and at every blow cried :

' Down with the traitor nobles—perdition to the foemen of the king ! '

Home met him with great resolution, but on receiving from Cuddie a side blow, right in the pit of the stomach, this great lord of the Merse was doubled up, as the admiral said, ' like a bolt of old canvas,' and stretched without breath on the causeway.

' Now that we have cleared the fairway, let us trip our anchors and be off,' said the admiral, ' for Home has a hundred mosstroppers and more in the market-place. Away to the Craig of St. Nicholas, my lads, and shove off ! '

They soon reached the landing-place and sprung into the barge ; the oars were shipped, Barton grasped the tiller, and with the blue ensign trailing in the water astern, they pulled away towards the ships. In his excitement the captain forgot his poor friend Falconer; then suddenly the recollection flashed upon him; he turned to address the admiral, when lo! he found that the tall gentleman whose voice and sword had been so active in Fish Street, had now removed his salade, and was no other than the—king!

On recognizing him, the barge's crew suspended rowing for a moment, and doffed the bonnets amid deep silence, while Barton also uncovered.

'Give way, my lads,' said the admiral, smiling; ''tis his Majesty the King, who, finding only falsehood and rascality among the loggerheads ashore, is coming to sail merrily with us on the sea, where we shall teach him how to knot and splice, to grease a mast, to hand, reef, and steer, and to sleep in the top-gallant-sail, as soundly as in the Castle of Stirling. Barton,' he added, in a whisper, 'the nobles are rising in arms; the men of Angus are already mustering in the Howe, and the barons hold conclave at the Tower of Broughty. We are on the eve of a dark rebellion, and as yet nowhere hereabout could the king be safe but on board the *Yellow Frigate*.'

Barton bowed, for he had no words to reply in. His heart was already too full of anxieties of his own—anger, bitterness, and sorrow, not unmingled with fear for the persecution that might be endured by Euphemia, and the domestic tyranny to which he might soon be subjected.

In a few minutes they were close to the frigate. Cuddie caught the mainchains by his hook, and the boat steered alongside the steps. The boatswain's pipe was heard— the kettle-drum beat, and the arquebussiers stood to their arms as the king stepped on board, followed by Wood and Barton. He was then marshalled with great formality and the deepest respect to the great cabin.

Then the royal standard, the yellow banner with the red lion rampant, was hoisted at the mainmast-head, to indicate that the king was on board. On this appearing, a commotion was observable immediately on board the *Margaret*, which lay a bowshot further up the river; her drum was beaten and her barge's crew piped away, to bring old Sir Alexander Mathieson, '*the King of the Sea*,' on board the admiral, while all her port-lids were triced up, and the cannon run out.

The salutes of the two great ships, which fired each a hundred guns, announced to the people of Dundee and of the opposite coast, that the king was on board. Hence arose that rumour, which proved perhaps so fatal to the interests of James—*that he had abdicated*, and was going with Admiral Wood to Holland or Flanders. Circulated industriously by the highborn enemies of the throne, the report spread like wildfire, and though there were no means of travelling in those days but on foot or on horseback, it was known with many strange additions at the cross of the metropolis on the following day, and it gave a great impetus to the bad cause of the malcontent nobles.

CHAPTER XXIV.

DAVID FALCONER.

WITH the last words of Barton ringing in his ears and rousing a voice of reproach in his heart, Lord Drummond flung aside his velvet cloak and descended into the garden, which was at the back of the mansion, and lay between it and the margin of the river. Some remembrance of happier, and perhaps of less ambitious days came over his memory; he felt something of remorse for having so ruthlessly delivered over his daughter's plighted husband to the violence of his enemies; but as he had no wish either to alter the deadly cast of the die, or to hear the clashing of the assassins' swords in the street without, he walked through the garden hurriedly and muttered:

'I have done wrong—I have acted ignobly, and not as Robert Barton would have done by me, or to the meanest in Scotland! Yet I did not tell him to love my daughter Effie—and Home and Hailes shall both be earls, if swords and lances can make them so. Yet—yet—tush! I have behaved like an old wolf. But there was no remedy—I had betrayed too much to him; so cold steel must seal his lips for ever. And yet, alack! those lips have often been upon poor Effie's cheek. No—no—let me not think of it! ——But who is this? A captain of the king's arquebussiers—and Sybilla too;—pest! here is another lover!'

Beside the bower he saw Sir David Falconer lying upon the ground with the scarf of Hailes (which he knew well) twisted round his throat. The young man was not dead, but nearly strangled, and was now beginning to recover. Near him, on her knees in a stupor of grief, with blood-shot eyes, and with her dress disordered, Sybilla was sobbing. Powerless and unable to rise, she stretched her hands to her father, saying—'Save him, father—save him!'

For a moment the heart of the ambitious old man was touched, he forgot that he had basely surrendered Barton to destruction, or remembered it only with an emotion

of terror ; and now he hastened to save Falconer. He freed his compressed throat from the rich silk and golden scarf of Lord Hailes, and opened the collar of his velvet doublet to afford him air ; he bathed his face and hands in the bright salt water of the firth that was rippling on the yellow sands close by, and in a few minutes the rescued man was able to raise himself upon his hands and look around him. Sybilla, still kneeling beside him, placed an arm caressingly around his livid neck, and while glancing thankfully and imploringly at her father, placed her trembling lips to the distorted brow of her lover, murmuring—
' Joy, joy—oh, David, dearest David, thou art still spared to me ! '

' Good morrow, fair sir,' said Lord Drummond, grimly. ' Now what am I to understand by all this ? '

' That your lordship—has—has saved me from a cruel death,—from a death the coward hands of Home and Hailes destined for me—for me who never wronged them,' said Falconer, with difficulty, and at intervals.

Sybilla wept aloud, and again wrung her pretty hands.

' Hold, little one,' said her father ; ' this noisy exhibition of love and grief but little beseems a noble lady. Though one of King James's new-fangled knights, do you forget that this man is but the son of a merchant skipper ? '

Though this was said in a low voice Falconer heard it, and it gave him new energy. Slowly and tremblingly he rose to his feet and said :

' My lord, with your daughter's love and your esteem I could achieve anything—Yea, I could ennoble myself,— yet both were alone sufficient to ennoble any man.'

Unsubdued by this compliment, the proud old noble made a gesture of impatience. ' Another lover ! ' he muttered, stamping his spurred heel on the gravel walk ; ' was there ever a poor man so pestered by three gadabout daughters ? This will be another fellow for us to kill, I suppose.'

' Ah, my lord, if you knew how I love her, and how to me her love is a richer and a greater treasure than our good king's favour.'

' The king's favour ? Umph—a poor inheritance to-day, perhaps a poorer one to-morrow ! '

' How, my lord,' said Falconer, anxiously ; ' what is it you mean ? '

' You will soon learn, for this night perhaps may see those

standards which we furled at Blackness unrolled against the king. He who serves James is the foe of the nobility; he who is the foe of the nobility is also mine. So come, Sir David, get thee gone to thy ship, for the day wears apace, and I would not for the brightest jewel in my coronet have my daughter seen in this unseemly dress. Thou knowest this infernal king has stolen her sister, and that I'll have sure vengeance; yea, by Him who preached in Jerusalem and died on Calvary, I will! Come, madam, come——'

A shout interrupted the old lord's sudden burst of anger; bright dresses and glittering swords were visible among the shrubbery; Home, Hailes, and their friends, smarting with wounds, bruises, and anger, after their conflict in the adjoining street, came tumultuously towards the bower, for they had resolved on hanging Falconer's body at the market-cross, in reparation of what they termed their wounded honour.

Sybilla uttered a cry of terror; again her heart trembled and stood still; but she threw herself with outstretched arms before her still feeble lover, whom the ferocious assailants again recognized and greeted with a shout.

'How now, my lords and gentlemen,' exclaimed Lord Drummond, unsheathing his sword; 'would ye commit hamesücken? Respect my presence, my property, and authority, if you regard not the life of this man, or the powers of the Lord High Constable! Are the rights of the baronage and nobility to be infringed by the nobles themselves? In the streets or highways slay as many as you please; but here, even a dog's life is sacred.'

'We have sworn to hang this half-strangled parasite of James at the market-cross, and hanged he shall be!' replied Hailes, making a deadly thrust with his sword, which was skilfully parried by Lord Drummond, yet it passed within three inches of Falconer's heart.

'Thank you, my good lord,' said the latter; 'I am weak, but will rather trust to my own limbs than to your power of protection, or to their humanity. Adieu, dear Sybilla, and may God bless thee, kind one, for we may never meet again.'

He staggered towards the water, and rushed in until beyond his depth, and then struck out to reach the ship.

Like a herd of wild animals disappointed of their prey, his tormentors sprang after him, midleg into the water;

but he was already beyond the reach of their swords. They then hurled stones from the beach, and two tall Highland gillies, who had followed Balloch from Lochlomond side, strung their bows and shot their feathered shafts after him, but without success; for, weak as he was, Falconer was an expert swimmer, and was soon far beyond bowshot.

After all he had undergone, it was evident that he never could reach the ships without succour; but, fortunately, the uproar on the beach had been observed by the watch on deck; the fainting swimmer was seen to make signals of distress; a boat was piped away and lowered; and just as poor Falconer was slowly and despairingly relaxing his efforts, and sinking beneath the calm glassy current of the river, he was seized by the strong nervous hands of Willie Wad and Cuddie Clewline, and dragged on board.

Sybilla uttered a cry of joy and fainted, just as the first cannon of the royal salute pealed over the shining river.

CHAPTER XXV.

HOWARD AND MARGARET.

MARGARET had now been three days on board of the *Harry*, which, with her consorts, the *White Rose* and *Cressi*, had been vainly endeavouring to weather the dangerous Ness of Buchan, and gain the open German sea; but as Howard's evil fortune would have it, the stiff breeze blew right ahead, and they were forced to tack and tack again, running eastward and westward on the same line, like that fated ship which, in the nautical legend, is ever striving in vain to weather Table Bay.

Howard, on leaving England, had provided two attendants for Margaret—pretty young English girls, whose names are recorded as Rose and Cicely. They were gentle and attentive, and did all that their kind natures dictated to soothe the prisoner's grief, which, after the first wild paroxysm had subsided, became a calm and settled bitterness, sadness, and dejection; and her tears fell incessantly for her child, which had been left in the secret alcove, where, perhaps, none might discover it, and where its feeble cries might be unheard till it perished; but then she remembered that Rothesay would know and reveal the place, and save its little life at all hazards.

She was now aware of being in the power of Henry's agents, and that she would be removed in secret, to make way for an English princess.

Howard, a gallant and polished gentleman, had visited her twice; the first time she repulsed him with flashing eyes and wild upbraidings of inhumanity and cruelty; the second time she heard all he had to say in silence, remaining pale and immovable, with eyes downcast, weeping and inflamed, for her powers of utterance were almost gone, and despair was coming fast upon her. Her great beauty of face and grace of form, when united to her grief, touched the manly heart of Howard; deep and sincere emotions of pity were stirred within him; and soon a deeper and a softer influence began to steal into his breast, and he muttered to himself again and again, as he walked on the weather-side of his poop:

'By St. George, I would rather stand old Largo's heaviest broadside than the witching glance of this fair woman's eyes! If I could but teach her to love me, a double end would be gained: it would win me Henry's favour on one hand, and such a charming wife on the other, as never a Howard had in his bosom before.'

Then he longed to visit her again, and try his powers of consolation. He descended to the door of her cabin. 'How is the Scottish dame?' he inquired of little Will Selby, one of his pages, who remained below in attendance.

'Ill enough at heart, but pretty well in body, sir,' replied the lad, with an impudent smile.

'Pretty well, sir,' added his brother, tall Dick Selby the gunner, a strong and athletic son of old Father Thames; 'especially after parting with her loose ballast in the last night's breeze.'

Howard knit his brow at this coarse speech. 'Poor little thing,' he muttered; 'may the great devil take this pitiful errand, say I! By my soul, John o' Lynne,' said he to his sailing master, or second in command, 'I would rather walk over the standing part of the fore-sheet, with a shot at each heel, than do all this dirty work over again!'

He knocked softly at the cabin door, which was opened by Rose, one of the attendants. Exhausted and overcome, Lady Margaret had fallen asleep on one of the cushioned lockers; a velvet cloak was spread over her; one white hand, and her pretty feet in their red velvet slippers richly embroidered with gold, were only visible. Her face was deathly pale; her eyelids unusually swollen and inflamed, while their long lashes were matted by the bitter tears she had shed. Her rich soft hair was in disorder. It hung half in and half out of its gold caul, and Cicely was kindly and gently endeavouring to plait it into braids, while its owner, her new mistress, slept.

'Thou art a good girl, Cicely,' said the captain, 'and shalt have a ring of gold for this.'

Though he spoke in low voice, Margaret was roused from her uneasy slumber, and started into a sitting position. Cicely and Rose withdrew into the inner cabin, and their lady began, as usual, to weep in silence, for the tears, which she had not the power to repress, rolled in large drops slowly over her face.

'Still so sad, so sorrowful!' said Howard, as he knelt on one knee, and taking her cold white hand in his, gazed kindly into her fine blue eyes; 'still weeping, dear madam; still those tears, which, like your reproaches, cut me to the soul!'

'Alas! sir, what other solace have the wretched but their tears?'

'I am but a plain English seaman, lady; I have been somewhat of a courtier in my time, but the salt water, as it washed the perfume out of my doublet, obliterated also the fine speeches that were then at my tongue's end, and I may not now fashion soft nothings to suit a lady's ear; but I speak from my heart, and with all the sincerity of an honest purpose. Oh! would, lady, that I could find some means of serving you and drying those tears! I beseech you to be pacified, and to hope for while life remains to us, there is always *hope* to bear us onward like a fair good breeze.'

'If once I see your English shore, what hope shall I have then?'

'Heaven only knows what may happen before we have old England on our lee, lady. This head-wind freshens every minute, and you may see that the rocks of Buchan are still upon our starboard quarter, while the sea looks black to port.'

Margaret gazed anxiously from the cabin window, and saw the bold coast of Invercruden half shrouded in the haze of evening, as the sun sank behind it; she saw, also, the waves rolling in white mountains on the Bowness, the most eastern point of Scotland, where the rocks are so steep and the water so deep, that, in one of the rooms of the High Constable's castle, a glass of wine has been drunk from the top-gallant yard-arm of a vessel, as an old tradition tells us.

'If you would but land me, even on yonder stormy point, I know one who would lay an earldom at your feet —a Howard, an Englishman though you be.'

'I would not disobey my king or betray his orders for all the earldoms in Scotland, lady. My father was an English lord, true; but the English nobles are not a race of sordid slaves like the Scottish peers, lady, ever ready to barter their country and their service for foreign gold and gain.'

' Too true—too true!' said Margaret, wringing her hands; ' I feel myself the victim of this cupidity.'

' But I pray you to pardon my harshness of speech,' said the handsome Howard, with great gentleness.

Amid all her grief, Margaret had sufficient perception to observe Howard's modulated tones, and the full, earnest, and anxious expression of his eye, which indicated the emotion then stealing into his heart. At first, the idea flashed upon her mind that she would make the poor Englishman's dawning passion subservient to her purpose and the achievement of her liberty; but Margaret Drummond was too artless and too honourable for such a course, and at once repressed the thought; for there was so much of open candour on his manly brow, and so much of kindness in his fine eyes and well-formed mouth, that she could perceive, although *he* was the instrument of her wrong and misery, that he was at heart her friend, and might yet prove her most powerful protector. To such a man, she knew at once, all bribes would be offered in vain; and she knew that she had nothing to hope for but from his generosity, his pity, or his love.

She gazed fixedly and with agony at the lessening shore, as the *Harry* stood off with its head towards the German Sea, and a pause, filled up by sighs, ensued.

' You still refuse to restore me to liberty?' she said, while her tears fell fast again.

' Absolutely—once and for all.'

' For the first time in my life, I have received a refusal from a gentleman,' said Margaret, proudly and bitterly.

' Alas! that this unfortunate should be me!'

' But it matters not; we are still in the Scottish seas, and a time may come when you will be forced to listen to me.'

' Listen! oh, Lady Margaret! if you know the secret which is hushed in my heart!' replied Howard, who felt her reproaches deeply. ' I do beseech you to pardon me,' he continued, in a sad and earnest manner, ' for I obey the dictates of a cold and politic king, not those of my conscience or my heart.'

' A brave English gentleman should be above being the tool even of a king.'

' Madam, I would deem myself the most ungallant of Englishmen if I refused you anything that lay within my power to grant, but liberty must lie with Henry himself.'

' Liberty ! but I am not an English subject. Oh, Rothe-say, Rothesay ! ' continued Margaret, giving way to a fresh burst of grief ; ' what will be your thoughts on finding that I am gone ? '

' Believe me, Lady Margaret,' said Howard, in his saddest tone, and yet with somewhat of pique in his manner, ' you will recover your love for this boy prince, and King Harry may mate you to some gallant English courtier.'

' Thou thinkest me very facile,' said Margaret, coldly, and with a pout on her pretty mouth.

' Nay, lady, I only think you beautiful, gentle, good, and indeed, most lovable ; so I crave pardon if I view you like a court lady too. They easily forget an affection ; for women, alas ! *are* very facile—yea, variable as wind and weather.'

' Many women never loved at all, sir.'

' No woman ever had only *one* love, gentle lady,' replied the seaman, laughing.

Again Margaret renewed her entreaties to be set ashore ; but she no longer resorted to bribery, for she saw how the noble Howard was stung when she formerly did so. Now she appealed only to his generosity, his courtesy, and his chivalry, and she plied her cause with all the power and eloquence that grief inspired, but plied in vain, though Howard became fearful that he would not be long able to withstand her pleading tongue, when aided by two such speaking eyes ; he therefore begged permission to retire on deck, where his presence had long been required, for the south-east wind was increasing to a squall, and sail after sail had to be taken off the three English ships, which were now separated and far apart.

The dangerous coast of Buchan, of Cruden, and Peter-head, with all their bluffs, and reefs, and boiling caves, were on their lee ; half-veiled in watery clouds, the sun had sunk behind the hill of Bennochie—that landmark of the ocean—and an angry sea was rolling in huge billows on the stern and terrible shore. To increase Margaret's mental and bodily miseries, a severe storm came on, and she had only one thought in the intervals of her sickness, as she lay weep-ing and supremely wretched on a couch—one desire—that this hated English ship might be dashed upon her native coast, and that she might have one desperate chance of ending her sorrows—of being saved or drowned. She would freely have risked one for the other ; but then she remem-

bered the poor mariners, who in that event might perish ;
and she prayed God and St. Olaus, the patron of that rocky
shore, to forgive her evil wishes ; and, after reckoning on
her white fingers the hours she had been absent from her
poor babe, and after becoming totally exhausted, she fell
into a deep, deep sleep, and was long unconscious of all
that passed around her.

The English ships floated on the chaos of waters. With
evening a pale ashy hue stole over them, and the whole sea
darkened as the clouds lowered above it ; then the wind
swept past with its mighty breath, rolling the waves like
vast ridges of mountains crested with foam, and having long
dark vales of water between.

Meanwhile Howard, an able seaman, was using incredible
exertions to weather the storm and that deadly lee shore,
behind the bluffs and peaks of which the sheets of lightning
were reddening the cloudy sky. He reduced the sails to a
few strips of canvas, and lowered the top-gallant yards on
deck. Being ignorant of the strong currents, as the night-
cloud deepened and the hoarse thunder died away, he feared
much that some of his consorts might be stranded ; he could
see nothing of them, for, on hoisting a lantern at the mainmast head, no answering signals were returned. Every
wave that swept over the *Harry* bore something from her
deck ; and John of Lynne was ordered to cut away her two
large anchors, after which she rode more lightly over the
black tumbling billows, and lay a point nearer the wind.

But the increasing storm compelled Howard at last to
put his ship about, and away she flew like the wind itself,
round Rattray Head, a promontory of Aberdeenshire ; and
so he bore away towards the Moray Firth, in search of
shelter and of safety.

CHAPTER XXVI.

THE CHAPLAIN'S CABIN.

THE king remained on board of the *Yellow Frigate* for some days, during which the rumour that he had abdicated and retired to Holland, to avoid a new civil war, spread far and wide, from the gates of Berwick to those of Kirkwall. Meanwhile, the faithful Lindesays of Crawford and Montrose, with Thomas, Earl of Mar, and other loyal peers, were exerting themselves to raise an armed force for the protection of James, who appointed the tower of Alloa as the place of tryst; and thus, immediately after the storm, the *Yellow Frigate* and her consort weighed anchor, and bore away for the Firth of Forth.

All communication between the ships and shore had been cut off since the king's embarkation, as the town of Dundee was full of malcontents; and indeed there were great fears that an exchange of shots might take place as the vessels passed Sir Patrick Gray's garrison in the Castle of Broughty.

Falconer and Barton had no means of ascertaining what was passing at the house of Lord Drummond; but rumour reached them that he had sent his four daughters to his Castle of Drummond in Strathearn, under the escort of the Laird of Balloch.

It was a beautiful morning, about the last day of May; the river shone like a mirror, but its shores yet slept in the sunny summer haze when the frigates weighed anchor. The king was in his cabin, but he heard the din of preparation for sea, as Barton gave the order to 'ship the capstan bars!'

Then, while his pages dressed him, he heard the sound of the fife and the stamping of feet, as the sailors in their deerskin boots tripped merrily round the capstan to the old air of ' Trolee lolee lemane dou.'

' Away aloft,' cried Barton ; ' let fall.'

Then the sails fell, and filled as they were sheeted home,

on which the frigate gathered way. ' Set the fore-topmast staysail—quick there—up with it, out of the cat's cradle.'

Muffled in a surcoat of scarlet cloth trimmed with sables, King James came on deck as the vessels passed Tentsmuir Point, and all the seamen took off their bonnets, while the drummer beat a march, and the arquebussiers gave a profound salute.

' I feel now more keenly than ever how hollow is all this pomp of royalty,' said he, as he walked up the poop with the admiral, ' and how paltry the inheritance of pride ! The poorest archer or pikeman in any of my castles is happier than I who to-day am called a king. Believe me, admiral,' he continued, sadly, ' if my death would be a bond of peace between my divided subjects, I could die happily ! '

' And let those rapscallions get the weather-gage of you ? No, no—I would never die while I could live—never sink while I could swim, and that I consider good salt-water philosophy. Yet when the death-watch is piped, doubt not, your Majesty, that old Andrew Wood will be found at his post, though he would be sorry to strike his flag before he had brought a few of these traitors up all standing at the bar of Divine Justice. Your Majesty is only half my age—and to think of dying——'

' Father Zuill,' said James, turning to the chaplain, who at that moment came on deck ; ' in this matter, what opinion have you to offer me ? '

' We should remember the words of Seneca,' replied the priest, folding his hands on his breast, and looking down ; ' he says—it is uncertain at what place death awaits thee, so wait thou for him in every place. Before old age be careful to *live* well, and in old age be careful to *die* well— and herein Seneca gave sound advice.'

' Alas, good priest,' responded the sad king, ' art thou a Scottish subject, and yet forget that thy kings—unhappy race !—never live to become old men ? '

' But their virtues and honour survive the tomb,' replied the chaplain ; ' true philosophy can only be acquired by mental suffering. There was a learned Persian who was wont to aver that he who had not suffered knew nothing.'

Here the admiral, who had a great aversion for this kind of conversation, which he did not understand, hailed the maindeck. ' How is she going, Barton ? '

' Eight knots—clear off the wet reel, Sir Andrew.'

'Keep her away a point or two to the south, and close the lee ports, for now we are past the guns of Broughty.'

'We weary thee, worthy admiral,' said the gentle king; 'but I pray thee, Sir Andrew, to excuse my sadness.' Largo bowed, and reddened with a feeling of vexation, that the king had detected his impatience.

'I am a cold comforter for those who are in trouble,' said he, 'for I am but a plain-spoken mariner, who know of nothing beyond the ropes of a ship and the points of a compass; but we sailors, though our tongues may be less ready than our hands, have our hearts in the right place, our anchor is hope, and the blessed gospels our helm and compass—religion is our polestar, and loyalty our pilot.'

'I defy thee, Father Zuill, to have expressed this better,' said the king, with a smile; 'how many of those dog nobles who are the curse of Scotland could say as much?'

The sun was now above the sea, which rolled like a mighty sheet of light around each rock and promontory; the low flat shore of Angus slept in that sunny glow, but the bolder bluffs of Fife were slowly becoming visible as the morning haze drew upward like a curtain of gauze. The clear brilliance of the sea and sun made Father Zuill think of his burning-glasses, and he invited the king (who found a great pleasure in visiting every part of the ship) into his cabin, whither the admiral felt himself constrained to accompany them; for, as there were many points and features in the chaplain's studies which he did not admire, he never entered this cabin when he could avoid it.

Small, low, and panelled with oak, it was surrounded by shelves, laden with books, glasses, retorts, and chemical apparatus, stuffed animals, and various antiquities, fossils, and preparations, the use of which the simple-minded seaman could not divine.

From one of the beams overhead hung a Roman lamp of bronze, which had been found in the city of Camelon; and appended thereto were the egg of an ostrich, a large amber bead, used as a charm to cure blindness, and an amulet of green stone, the meaning of which, Sir Andrew, after some hesitation, inquired.

'It is an Egyptian Nileometer,' replied the priest; 'in hieroglyphics this was the symbol of *stability*, and as such was given of old to Pthah and Osiris.'

Sir Andrew, who did not appear to be much more enlightened on the subject, rubbed his short beard, and ventured on one other inquiry. 'What means this black devil imprinted here on stone?'

'It is the Scarabæus, the symbol of Pthah and the emblem of creative power, inscribed on a tablet, supported by Serapis and Anubis.'

'Fiend take me, father chaplain, if I understand all this!' said the admiral, testily; 'yet it may be all true as Barton's log-book, for aught that I know to the contrary. But were these persons you name demons like he who dwells at the Cape of Storms, and by one puff of his sulphurous breath blew old Barty Diaz on his beam-ends? or like the sea-ape—that scaly monster which hath the voice and figure of a man, yet is, after all, but a fish? or like the great sea-serpent whose yawning causes the whirlpool of Lofoden?'

'Nay,' said the king, 'they were the false gods of the pagan Egyptians.'

'Well, I do not like having their trumpery on board the *Yellow Frigate*,' replied the admiral. 'Do they not smell of witchcraft?'

'Nay,' replied the chaplain, angrily, 'not half so much as these two books behind you.'

The admiral turned abruptly, and perceived two gigantic volumes, bound in vellum and clasped with iron; they lay upon the stock of a large brass culverin, which, as the port was closed, was lashed alongside the *gun-wall*, or, as it is now named, the gunnel.

'And what may they be anent?' he asked. 'The writings of Joannes de Sacro Bosco, *De Sphra Mundi*, and the magic book of Kirani, King of Persia, with the four treatises of Sir Michael Scott of Balwearie, *De Secretis Naturæ*; his tracts on the transmutation of metals, chiromancy, and astrology.'

'Priest, I do not understand all this,' said the admiral, growing quite angry. 'Gadzooks! to me it would seem that thou speakest very much like a sorcerer, and all this place must be well swabbed out, for it hath a devilish odour of necromancy. But the gunner to his lintstock, the steersman to his helm, and the cook——'

'Sorcery!' interrupted the poor chaplain; 'Heaven forbid! Dost think, if these relics of the olden time had aught to do with sorcery, they would lie side by side with this holy volume?' he added, opening an oak-bound tome, containing St. Gregory's Homilies on the Four Gospels.

' Nay, this amber head and this hieroglyphical tablet would then explode like a bursting cannon.'

The admiral craved pardon, but mentally resolved that, in the first gale of wind, he would contrive to have the ship lightened of all these strange and mysterious wares.

' Dost thou speak Latin, admiral ? ' asked the chaplain.

' Latin,' reiterated the seaman, angrily, ' how should I speak Latin ? '

' With your tongue,' replied the chaplain, simply.

' Thou laughest at me, Father Zuill; dost take me for a puling student or a smock-faced friar, that I should know Latin ?   Nay, when such drones as thee were at the grammar schule, and trembling like a wet dog under a pedant's ferule, I was a bold sailor-lad, learning to hand, reef, and steer, and being made a man of, even while my chin was smooth as a lady's hand.'

' Father Zuill was merely about to refer to a certain learned writer, who wrote of the secrets with which Nature is filled,' replied the king, in a conciliatory tone.   ' Was it not so ? '

' Exactly, please your grace ; for with all his seamanship, he hath much yet to learn.   Now, admiral, with what is the water filled ? '

' Fish,' was the laconic reply.

The chaplain smiled, and pouring a drop into the palm of the admiral's hand, placed a magnifying-glass above it. ' Look now, Sir Andrew,' said he.

The admiral bent his eyes over it, and lo ! an unknown world of little monsters were crawling there !

' Now, by Our Lady of Pittenweem, there *is* sorcery here ! ' said he, aghast, as he flung the water on the deck, and rubbed his hand on his trunk hose, and examined it again and again, to see whether all were gone.

' Nay, nay,' said the king, with one of his sad smiles, ' thou wrongest our good friend ; for I assure thee, admiral, there is nought of sorcery here.   This will show thee, Sir Andrew, how unsafe it is to laugh at anything merely because we do not understand it.'

' Your Majesty is right,' said the chaplain, beginning to screw and unscrew the mirrors of his warlike machine ; ' thus the admiral laughs at me, because he knows not the theory of light, or the principles of its production.   Why do decayed wood and dead fish emit a light ?   You know not ; yet Pliny, who lived fourteen centuries ago, knew and wrote of these things.   Every earthly body will emit light when heated, for the particles on their surfaces shine by attrition, and light is the first principle of fire. Ah,' continued the learned projector, setting all the little mirrors in motion, and making them flash and glitter in a very alarming manner, ' if Heaven give me grace, I may yet achieve much by my burning-glasses.'

' Father Zuill,' said James III., who had been reflecting that this poor priest, in his realm of strange inventions and abstruse study, was much happier than a King of Scotland and the Isles, ' thou mightest achieve more by striving to develop the use of the magnifying-glass. Dost remember what Seneca says of crystal convexity ? '

' Yes; and of a glass globe filled with water, which maketh letters appear larger and brighter when viewed through it.'

' I pray your Majesty to excuse me,' said the admiral, bowing ; ' for, gadzooks, if this goes on for another ten minutes, he will give me a fit of apoplexy. By the sound on deck, I think the wind is dead off-shore ; and as we have not a king under our pennon every day, I beg leave to retire to the deck, and see how the land bears.'

CHAPTER XXVII.

THE ISLES OF FORTH.

ON rounding that long promontory known as the Ness of Fife, the wind, which had been upon the beam, became, of course, ahead, and as the frigates entered the mouth of that magnificent estuary, where the Forth, after a course of a hundred and seventy miles, joins the German Sea, they had to tack from shore to shore, consequently their progress became slow and protracted. The king, who loved to be among his subjects, to learn their wants, their wishes, and ideas, had been through every part of the ship between stem and stern, and had heard Willie Wad's explanations on various points of gunnery, and the boatswain expound on seamanship and the intricacies of standing and running rigging. He had been through the magazine, the bread-room, the hold, cockpit, and cable-tier, and amid the various new things he heard and saw, forgot for a time, perhaps, that he was the unhappy King of Scotland.

He rejoined Father Zuill and the admiral on deck, where the former told him many a tale and legend of the castled craigs, the isles and rocks they passed; and amid these stories of the olden time, the chaplain forgot his crotchets of burning-glasses and other learned absurdities, and all who were near, drew nearer still to listen.

About noon, they were between the Isle of May and the straggling town of Anster, with the castle of the Anstruthers of that ilk, and all its rough, brown, antique houses that cluster round the mouth of the Dreel-burn. Brightly on sea and river shone the unclouded sun, on the white cliffs of the isle, and the rugged shore of Fife, with all its caverns, rocks, and towers, its ancient burghs, with their pointed spires, and long and straggling fisher-villages that dot the sandy beach. The scene was lively and beautiful; but with saddened eyes and a sorrowful heart the thoughtful king gazed from Sir Andrew's lofty poop on the shores of his rebellious kingdom. The Forth shone like a stream of lucid gold;

the Bass Rock, in the vaults and towers of which so many a wretch has pined ; the Isle of May, with its priory and gifted holy well ; Anster, with the enchanted Castle of Dreel ; lonely Crail, with its Chapel of St. Rufus, and the Weem, wherein King Constantine was murdered by the Danes ; St. Monan's, with the cavern where that martyr-hermit dwelt in the ninth century, and where he was slain, on that day of blood when the Norsemen ravaged all the coast of Fife, and slew six thousand persons ;—all these were visible at once, and bathed in ruddy light.

Around the ships vast droves of porpoises were leaping joyously in the bright sunshine, and near the shore at least three hundred fisher-boats, with all their varnished sides shining in the noontide glow, were shooting their nets ; and now a cheer floated over the water from their crews, in greeting to the valiant Laird of Largo, whose *Yellow Frigate* was so familiar to them all. Above these boats the white sea-mews were flying in wild flocks, thus indicating where the droves of herring were.

Perceiving that the king gazed fixedly at the picturesque old town of St. Monan, with its venerable church having the walls of its steep-roofed chancel washed by the encroaching waves, the chaplain drew near, and pointed out a deserted path, which leads to this beautiful fane, by the side of a little stream that rushes through a ravine upon the beach. By that path King David II., when in sore agony from a wound received at the Battle of Neville's Cross, came humbly to crave the intercession of the dead St. Monan by praying at his shrine ; and even while he prayed, the rankling wound, which had defied the care of the most skilful leeches, became well and whole, for the barbed head of an English arrow dropped from the scar as it closed ;—so say the monks of old.

In the days of which we write, the bell that summoned the people to prayer hung upon a venerable yew, which stood in the churchyard, just where the saint had placed it seven hundred years before : but once in every year it was removed during the herring season, for the fishermen of the East Neuk averred that the tolling thereof scared all the fish from the coast.

In the roads of Leith the king was joined by the *Salamander* and several other armed ships, commanded by the admiral's brother, by John Barton, and other brave seamen whose names are distinguished in the annals of their country.

The western breeze blew down the Firth as the vessels tacked between the narrowing shores, and Father Zuill or the garrulous boatswain had a tale to tell the king of every rock and isle; nor was the legend of Alexander II. and the Hermit of Emona, who saved him from shipwreck, forgotten; and they showed a rock where the little prince his son was drowned, since named Inch nan Mhic Rhi; and before this story was finished the vessels were passing through the Ferry and standing slowly up the river, which there opens out like a vast lake, bounded by hills and wooded shores, between which its waters were rippling in the evening sun: but still the wind blew hard ahead, and Sir Andrew's ships lay as close to it as possible, being anxious to land the king at Alloa, the muster-place of the loyal barons. Repeatedly Captain Barton reported to him that he feared 'the tide would not serve, and the ships would run aground.'

'No matter,' said he; 'bear ahead at all risks, and remember our auld Leith proverb—Obey orders, though ye break owners.'

Next morning, when the pale and anxious monarch came on deck, the ships were at anchor off the town of Alloa, which lay on one side of them, while on the other stretched a number of beautiful isles or Inches, covered with the richest pasture, and among the sedgy banks of these the stormy petrels yet build their nests at times. It was one of those hot summer days, when a smokelike vapour seems to pass in the sunshine over the fields of ripe corn, and in that sunny haze the hills of Clackmannan and the fertile shores of Stirling were steeped. The water was then deeper at Alloa than it is now, otherwise the ships of Wood could not have come abreast of the town, even though favoured by St. Mungo's tide, of which the crews, who of course knew the river well, took due advantage. This double flow is somewhat remarkable, for when the tide appears full it suddenly falls fifteen inches, and then returns with greater force, until it attains a much higher mark.

Tradition accounts for this by stating that when St. Mungo, the tutelar saint of the district, was proceeding with certain missionary priests to Stirling, by water, their vessel ran aground, and could not be got off, as the tide was ebbing; but the Saint prayed, and lo! the ebb returned with greater strength to bear the holy freight on their way; and in memory thereof, a *double tide* rolls even unto this day on the beach of the ancient Alaune.

CHAPTER XXVIII.

THE FIRST SCOTTISH REVOLUTION.

It was the meridian of June 1, 1488.

Partial gleams of sunlight fell or died away and flashed again alternately on the ancient town and still more ancient tower of Alloa, the stronghold of the Erskines, which crowns those strata of rock that lie between the fertile carse and the higher grounds, and break off abruptly above the harbour. The narrow and irregular streets of this picturesque little burgh were clustered round the strong donjon, the walls of which are eleven feet thick, and more than ninety feet high, and had often in Scotland's braver times repelled the chivalry of the first Plantagenets. A few crayers and barks, with their brown pitched sides and browned sails, were lying beside the rough stone quay that forms the pow or creek into which a rivulet flows.

The old lime-trees and venerable avenues of hedge, closely clipped in the French fashion, were in thick foliage around the old grey walls; the tide was full, and the Forth ran slowly past, still, calm, and waveless, as, with an imperceptible motion, the tall ships of Sir Andrew Wood warped close towards the town.

The gleam of arms was seen in the quaint old streets; steel helmets and cuirasses glittered on the quay, for armed men were watching the approaching ships, and a blue banner with a pale sable was unfurled on the tower, where Thomas, ninth Lord Erskine and second Earl of Mar, a loyal and irreproachable noble, with a numerous band of men-at-arms, drawn from his barony of Alloa, his forestry of Clackmannan, his estates of Nisbet, Pit-arrow, and Newton, awaited the landing of the king.

The nobles were everywhere rising in arms, and repairing to various muster-places, some for the king, but many more to fight for Angus, and against the court, in vindication of their imaginary rights and assumed privileges; while the hearts of the people, like their liberties, were oppressed and cast down.

It was a peculiarly close and sultry month, the June of 1488, and on this day in particular the air was breathless, hot, and still. Lowering thunder-clouds, through the openings of which the sunlight shot in sickly flakes, obscured the summer sky. Omens of evil preceded the coming civil war. In the fertile Carse of Gowrie the peasantry had observed numbers of field-mice lying dead about the footpaths among the ripening corn—dead without any apparent cause.

A wonderful scorpion had been killed in the jousting haugh of Linlithgow; and a terrible comet—men called it a fiery dragon—passed over the Castle of Rothesay, from whence it was visible between the Polestar and the Pleiads, and for three nights this source of terror floated in the darkened sky. The stone unicorn on the cross of Stirling uttered a cry at midnight; the shadowy figures of armed knights were seen to encounter on the battleground where Wallace defeated the army of Edward I., under the brow of the Abbey Craig; the helmeted or hooded fish, called monachi marini, which never appear in the Scottish seas but as the presage of some terrible event, were seen to swarm in the firths and bays; and, to his great dismay, Jamie Gair had thrice netted an entire shoal of them. The minds of the people (naturally and constitutionally superstitious) became filled with the most dire forebodings of the great events that were at hand; and on the hearts of none did these omens fall more heavily than those of the two sisters, Euphemia and Sybilla Drummond, who were secluded in their father's solitary Castle of Drummond, where no tidings reached them of their missing Margaret, and where they could only hear vague and flying rumours of the great events which then convulsed the kingdom.

Their father's words when he left Strathearn for the insurgent camp had made them aware only of two things:— that he would fight to the death against the false king who had carried off his favourite daughter, and that *they*— on the rout of James's forces and the destruction of his favourite courtiers—should become, one Countess of Hailes, and the other Countess of Home, or he would never see their faces more.

At this time, it was not exactly known by the king and his court where the malcontent nobles held their tryst, or where the Crown Prince of Scotland was. Some said they

were in Stirling with Sir James Shaw; others said, at Linlithgow; and many asserted they had retired as far off as
the Douglasses' Castle of Thrave, in the wild and distant
province of Galloway.

Many loyal and gallant gentlemen were now flocking to
the royal standard with all the armed men they could muster;
and with his most faithful adherents, James held a solemn
conclave, or council of war, in the hall of the Castle of Alloa.
On this occasion he was accompanied by the old admiral, by
Sir Alexander Mathieson, Captains Barton and Falconer, than
whom there were none present more eager to meet the insurgent
lords in battle, that they might have an opportunity of avenging
on Home and Hailes their late atrocities at Dundee. There,
too, were Sir William Knollis, the preceptor of the Scottish
Knights of Rhodez; the old Marshal de Concressault; and
young Ramsay, Lord of Bothwell, with many gentlemen of
his band—the Royal Guard—who wore the king's livery—
red doublets, faced and slashed with yellow. These crowded
around James, and on their glittering arms and excited faces
the sunlight fell in deep broad flakes of hazy radiance,
through the grated windows of the old Gothic hall.

The sadness and dejection of James were apparent to all,
as the noble Earl of Mar, the captain of Dunbarton—a
peer whose family stood proudly pre-eminent in the annals
of Scottish loyalty—conducted him to a chair on a dais at
the end of the hall, over which hung a crimson cloth of state.

'On this unhappy day,' said the earl, 'your Majesty is
more welcome to my house of Alloa than if you came to me
flushed with the triumph of a hundred battles.'

'I thank you kindly, my Lord of Mar,' said he; 'you are
one of the few who know that through life I have struggled
against an untoward and unhappy fate—or, as it would seem,
an irrevocable destiny, which I can neither conquer nor
avoid. Gladly would I change my father's crown for a
shepherd's bonnet, and this lofty place for the sphere of those
happy peasants who, in their narrow world, seem to pass
through life without meeting an obstacle, simply because
they are without ambition, and have few enemies. I never
knew that the poor could be so happy till within these last
few days which I spent among the brave hearts of good Sir
Andrew's frigate.'

'Hard work maketh a light heart at times,' said the admiral, as his eyes glistened; 'and I can assure your Majesty,
that never shipmate of mine would turn landsman again, to

be bearded by every painted baron, and bullied by every cock-laird and cow-baillie whom he met at kirk or market.'

'Are there no tidings yet of Rothesay?' asked James.

'None on which we can rely,' replied the Earl of Mar.

'Or of Angus?'

'A body of horsemen, supposed to be his, marched eastward through the Torwood two days ago,' replied the Duke of Montrose; 'but whether bound for Edinburgh or home to Galloway, no man can say; but the loyal nobles are gathering fast, and seven are now in waiting to pay their duty to your Majesty.'

'Seven—only seven, of all the peers of Scotland!'

'But seven is a fortunate number,' said Father Zuill; 'and seven may prevail, when thirty might fail.'

'Admit them at once, Earl of Mar,' said James, 'for this is not a time when a king of Scotland can trifle with his friends.'

Marshalled by ushers, preceded by pages, and followed by esquires bearing their swords and helmets, there now entered seven nobles, all of whom the king knew well, and now they were the more welcome that they came completely armed. Among them were—Alexander, Earl of Glencairn, a Lord of the Privy Council, who had fought for James against the nobles in the Raid of Blackness; the aged Earl of Menteith, who in his youth had been a hostage for James I.; the Lords Graham, Ruthven, Semple, Forbess, and Gray, the High Sheriff of Forfar—a cousin of Sir Patrick, the infamous Governor of Broughty.

Though all unlettered and ignorant of scholar-craft as the most humble peasant of their time, all these lords had a high and noble bearing—for the age was one when pride of birth and long descent, with high military renown, were valued more than life; and, moreover, they were all hardy, strong, and athletic—browned by exercise, hunting, and hosting, and inured to war by the incessant feuds of the clans; thus, they wore their globular cuirasses, large elbow plates, and immense angular tuilles, or thigh-pieces, as easily as if they were garments of the softest silk. James rose up to welcome them, and each in succession knelt to kiss his hand.

'Welcome, my lords,' said he; 'what tidings bring you of our friends and foes?'

'I have brought your Majesty three thousand good infantry from Cunninghame and Kyle,' said Glencairn; 'the

same brave men who won me a coronet on the field of
Blackness.'

'A thousand thanks, brave Cunninghame! And thou,
Ruthven?'

'A thousand and three brave fellows on horseback, all
armed with morion, jack, and spear.'

'And I, fifteen hundred archers and claymores,' said the
Lord Forbess, a weather-beaten and long-bearded noble,
who wore the ancient Celtic lurich, with a plaid of his green
clan-tartan, fastened by a silver brooch, upon his left
shoulder; 'I would they were as many thousands, to conquer
or die in this good cause!'

All had a good report to make of their vassalage, and the
king's spirit rose on finding, by computation, that these
faithful peers had marched to Alloa somewhere about thirty
thousand horse and foot, with many Highland archers; but
these forces had very few cannon, and the only arquebussiers
on whom they could rely were those of Sir Andrew Wood's
ships.

'Montrose,' said he, 'mount messengers and despatch
letters to those lairds who are captains of the Border castles;
desire them to keep tryst at Melrose, and come in with all
their lances and archers without an hour's delay.'

Montrose, whose principal scribes were the poor poets
who hovered about the court—such as William Dunbar and
others—soon had the messages written and given to gentlemen of trust, who concealed them in the scabbards of their
swords and poniards; and after being landed on the Carse
of Stirling by the boats of the *Yellow Frigate*, they departed
on the spur towards the south.

While James was taking counsel of the loyalists on what
course he should pursue, the venerable Duke of Montrose-
Crawford entered again, with an expression of gloom and dejection so strongly marked on his face, that all the nobles
turned towards him inquiringly.

'What now, my good Montrose,' said the agitated king—
'you have bad tidings—but what other can come to me?
Have blows been struck, or has my poor son been slain?
Speak, duke, for this suspense is torture.'

'I have tidings, indeed, of double evil,' said the aged peer,
slowly, as if considering in what terms to impart them.
'The Earls of Huntly, Errol, and Marischal, and the Lord
Glammis, at the head of more than ten thousand men, have
crossed the Forth at Stirling——'

' To join me—well ? '

' Nay, to join the Earl of Angus, it is supposed ; for they marched right under the cannon of the castle, and took their route through the Torwood.'

' For where ? ' asked James, growing pale.

' None know. The prince——'

' Was with them,' said James, bitterly.

' Nay, God forbid ! He is said to be with Sir James Shaw, in the Castle of Stirling.'

' 'Tis well ; we shall join him there, and together march against these rebel peers,' said James, with flashing eyes. ' Errol shall tyne his constable's staff, and perhaps his head with it. It is agreed, my lords, that we march for Stirling, and leave the ships of Sir Andrew Wood to guard the passage of the Forth ? '

A murmur of assent replied. ' Let us to horse, then,' said the king ; ' I would the queen were here, instead of praying at St. Duthac's shrine, in Ross. But to horse, sirs ; and now what ails thee, kind Montrose ? ' asked James, placing a hand on the old man's shoulder, on perceiving that amid the general bustle which ensued, the donning of helmets and buckling of swords, this most faithful and aged noble stood irresolute, with sorrow impressed in his eyes and upon his face.

' Allace, your Majesty,' said he ; ' there are tidings of serious evil ; the queen——'

' Is ill—my dear and loving Margaret ; she left me sick and ailing sorely,' said James, clasping his hands ; ' she is ill, while I am loitering here to play for a glittering bauble ; she is ill, and where ? '

' Allace the day ! she is dead and in her coffin ! ' said Montrose, as he covered his kind old face with his hands and burst into tears. . . .

The unfortunate monarch was so crushed by these evil tidings, that his heart seemed almost broken, and his spirit sank lower than ever. His guiding-star was gone now, for she on whose advice he had ever relied as his most faithful friend and counsellor, during a stormy and unhappy life, was dead.

Margaret of Oldenburg, daughter of Christian I. of Denmark, Sweden, and Norway, had been a woman of great beauty and amiability, tact, and discernment, and their marriage had been a happy one, though at first purely political, having been brought about by Andrew, Lord Evandale,

High Chancellor of Scotland. James had loved well his beautiful Dane, and they had three children, Rothesay, Alexander, Duke of Ross, and the little Prince John, styled, for a time, Earl of Mar. For eighteen years she had been his chief comfort amid every affliction, and the partner and soother of his sorrows; for the gentle Margaret had been all to him that a wise and politic queen, a dear and affectionate wife, could be.

Mistrusting even the few nobles who had joined him (the faithful Montrose excepted), James lingered in deep sorrow another day at the old tower of Alloa, and then resolved to join the prince, his son, in the Castle of Stirling, there to assure him by the most solemn vows a heart-broken man might make, that he was innocent of Margaret Drummond's abduction, and would use every means to discover her. After that, he resolved to shut himself up in the fortress until the Highland clans—ever loyal and ever true—came down from the northern hills to his succour; for now rumour said that Grant of Grant, and Sir James Ogilvie of Lintrathen (afterwards the ambassador to Denmark), Hugh, Lord Lovat, with many of the Forbesses, Gordons, Keiths, and Meldrums had risen in arms, and were marching south to defend and enforce the royal authority on the rebellious Lowland lords.

By this time sure tidings were brought to Alloa, that the Earl of Angus, the Lords Drummond, Hailes, and Home, Sir William Stirling of the Keir, Sir Patrick Gray, and many others had set up the standard of REVOLT at the town of Falkirk, in the fertile Carse of Stirling, where all the discontented lords and landholders of the three Lothians, Galloway, and the Borders, had joined them, with all the armed men they could collect; and together they formed a league, which for strength and daring had no parallel in the previous history of the kingdom, save the raid of the Douglasses in the reign of James II.

Sir James Shaw of Sauchie, Gray of Kyneff, and their minion, the infamous Borthwick, were among the most active in creating this unwarrantable rebellion.

The ancient burgh of Falkirk, which is so beautifully situated among the lands of the now fertile carse, was *then* surrounded by a dense forest of oaks and beeches, and near it lay a great morass, through which the Carron—that stream so famed in Celtic song and Roman war—flowed past the old Castle of Callendar, whose lords were for centuries comptrollers to the king. This town was then little more than a village, and consisted merely of a High Street and the Kirk Wynd, which led to the church of St. Modan, the pointed spire of which rose above the antique tenements of the Knights of Rhodez, whose preceptor possessed most of the property within the rising burgh. It was surrounded by a fortified wall having ports, one of which is yet remaining in the Back Row. Being loftily situated, and commanding an extensive view in every direction, it was admirably adapted for the muster-place of the rebel lords, whose whole desire was now to lure the unfortunate king to try their strength in battle. The town was filled by their troops; the cavalry occupied the High Street and Churchyard, while the chiefs had their quarters in the Castle of Callendar, the family seat of James, Lord Livingstone, where they held council by day, and wassail by night, drinking the comptroller's wine, and broaching his Lammas ale, ' to the confusion of the king, and of his parasitical favourites.'

Here they were visited by the venerable and valiant Sieur de Concressault, who came alone, or at least attended only by three horsemen—one who bore his banner, a second who carried his helmet, and a third who sounded a trumpet; and, penetrating into the flushed, proud, and riotous company, who were drinking and roistering in the hall of Callendar, where they

> Carved at the meal with gloves to steel
> And drank their red wine through the helmet barred,

the marshal boldly announced to them what he had been desired to say by a mandate recently received from his master, the King of France. But before he spoke, this good soldier was shocked to perceive the young Duke of Rothesay (whom all the loyalists believed to be in Stirling) among these dark and fierce conspirators; for the false and subtle Shaw and others retained the heir of the crown among them, to give a colour and pretext to all their illegal actions—or, at least, that on his young head some of the blame of revolt, and shame of defeat, should fall. He seemed pale and sad, and crushed in spirit; for he now felt convinced—thanks to the reiterations of Borthwick, Shaw, and Gray—that his father had destroyed both Margaret and her child; and as he was one of those who think it ' better to have loved and lost, than never to have loved at all,' his bitterness was great indeed.

'Marshal de Concressault,' said he, 'how did the king, my father, receive the tidings that I had left Dundee with these noble peers, and that they were in arms?'

'He wept.'

''Twas well,' said Lord Drummond, sternly; 'kings weep but seldom, and their tears are precious.'

'Ay,' added the grim and bearded Steward of Menteith; 'and there be some in Scotland who shall yet greet tears of blude before this wark is owre! But what seek ye here, Laird of Pitmilly—speak! for our swords are longer than our patience.'

'My lords,' said the ambassador, 'the Kings of France and England declare that they consider it to be the common cause of all monarchs to protect the Sovereign of Scotland against you; for subjects must not be permitted to give laws unto a king, who, even although he were a tyrant, cannot be amenable to the authority of the people; for we have yet to learn that it is from *them*, rather than from God, he receives his throne and power.'

All laughed loudly at this, for the 'right divine' was never valued much in the Lowlands of Scotland; but Angus, who presided, struck his mailed hand like thunder on the table, and sternly imposed silence.

'Your king is not a tyrant, my lords,' continued the aged marshal, warming as he spoke; 'nay, we all know that no lady in the land was ever more good or gentle. And his errors, if he hath any, are the result of youth and evil counsellors——'

At this remark, a storm of angry mutterings pervaded the cuirassed and helmeted assembly.

'But suppose these men have done you wrong, my lords, is it wise, or is it noble, in a wild desire for vengeance, to endanger the safety of the most ancient kingdom in Europe, and the honour of its throne? These princes desire me to say, firmly and boldly, that no state can be so pure that corruption cannot creep into it; that you, my lords and gentles, should be cautious how ye shake the framework of the Scottish monarchy, and shatter its government, for they are ready to resent it; and, moreover, John, King of Denmark, Ferdinand of Spain, Maximilian of the Romans, the Dukes of Austria, Muscovy, Burgundy, and Brittany are ready to join France and England in punishing this revolt; and his Holiness Innocent VIII., by the voice of his legate, armed with full pontifical powers, will, ere long, pour the terrors of his indignation on all who are in rebellion against the Scottish crown.'

Many a brow was knit, and many a sword half-drawn at this bold speech; but Angus waved his mailed hand, and again the multitude were still.

'Go back, De Concressault—go back to those false carles who sent you here,' said he; 'or, further still, to all those barbarous dukes and foreign kings, and tell them that the sacred rights of an old hereditary nobility shall not be shared with, or trampled on, by clodpoles and merchant-skippers, by hewers of wood and drawers of water, by men accustomed less to the sword than to the plough and hammer, the handloom and the tiller. Begone, I say, my Lord of Concressault; for if within another hour you are found within a mile of Callendar Yew, by the bones of St. Bryde, and by the soul of the *Dark Grey Man*, from whom my blood is drawn, I will hang you on its highest branch, as the taghairm of victory to our cause!'

'Be it so,' replied the Sieur de Monipennie, as he drew himself up with an air of scorn and military pride, and closed the umbriere of his helmet, as he donned it in defiance of them all. 'On a coming day, I hope to requite this foul insult, and teach thee, Lord of Angus, that a Scottish gentleman —a Marshal of France—is as good as any peer that ever came of the Douglas Blood, and better, it may be.'

Turning from the hall, he left Callendar with all speed, and crossed the Carse in the direction of the Forth, to rejoin the king at Alloa.

'How happy all these titled villans will be now,' said the marshal to his esquire, who was no other than David Falconer.

'Nay, they may be *glad*, but scarcely *happy*,' he replied. 'There are our ships. Barton sees us, and sends off a boat.'

'Say naught about our having seen that madcap prince among the rebels,' said the old soldier; 'for his father the king hath over many sorrows already to thole.'

The moment the ambassador left Callendar, Sir James Shaw summoned Borthwick, who had been duly infeft in his three tenements in the burgh of Stirling.

'Mount,' said he; 'mount and ride, with forty chosen men, to Linlithgow, and thence to Edinburgh; display our banners at the burgh crosses—rouse the Gutterbloods of the Good Town, and the Whelps of the Black Bitch; say that the Falkirk Bairns and the vassals of Carse and Callen-

dar have joined us to a man. Rouse one, rouse all against
the parasites of James! those base-born courtiers who
oppress the people—shout fire and sword, horse and armour!
It is easy to gather the rascal mob, and raise an outcry.
Here are a hundred lyons and rose-nobles——'

'English?'

'Ay, English rose-nobles,' replied the subtle Laird of
Sauchie, with one of his snaky smiles; 'scatter them among
the rabble; say they are from the good and charitable
nobles—ha, ha! from Angus and from Drummond. Bait
and draw on the *canaille;* threaten them with war and
pestilence; foretell the ruin of the burghs and the invasion
of their privileges. Select villans—thou knowest many—
harangue and arm them; say blood must flow. To arms
by tout of horn and tuck of drum—against the court—
and the muster-place is Callendar Wood. Say, to arms with
Angus! who, like Warwick the Englishman, will become a
maker of kings and a breaker of crowns in more ways than
one. Tell the people and the poor that they must no longer
be the stock-fish and foot-balls of the rich and noble; tell
the rich and great that the base multitude have risen for
plunder and the assumption of absurd privileges. Here,
take my sword, it is a good Banffshire blade, and away to
Edinburgh; see Napier, the provost, and say all I have said;
for the papal legate is coming, and if once he sets his red
legs on Scottish ground, the burghs are lost to the nobles
for ever!'

While Sauchie repaired to his governorship in the Castle
of Stirling, the firebrand Borthwick departed on his rebellious
mission; for the revolted peers dreaded that, on the arrival
of the Legate Adriano di Castello, who was hastening from
Rome, the burgesses, and all who feared the censures of the
Church, might join King James before a decisive battle
was fought or a Revolution achieved.

The artful minion was very successful in his mission, and
soon after, the flower of the Lothian spearmen—the finest
infantry in Scotland—joined the rebel lords at Falkirk.

CHAPTER XXIX.

THE MARCH TO STIRLING.

ON a glorious morning of the first days of June, James III. began his march for Stirling, once the El Dorado of the Scottish nobles during his reign, as Linlithgow was in the time of James IV., and Falkland in the time of James V.

The gentle breath of the morning stole along the heather braes, and the sound of the river was heard as it murmured on its yellow shores. Above the hills the sun was rising in his summer splendour, and the winding Forth blushed red as the shades of night retired. The peaks of the Ochil mountains glittered as the mist rolled away from their summits; the mavis and merle sang among the woods of Alloa; but the dew lay long in the grassy haughs and hollows, where the peaceful shepherds, who heeded little the godless strife of lords and earls, were winding their horns, while the colley dogs barked and yelled when herd and hirsel came forth from bught and penn.

Though less accustomed to armour than most of his turbulent subjects, James was attired in a heavy suit, which he valued highly for having been worn by his father at the sieges of Thrave and Roxburgh. It was gorgeously inlaid with ornamental and religious devices; the back and breastplates were composed of several pieces, to render them flexible, and the thighs were defended by an apron of chain mail. Above his salade (a peculiar headpiece, first introduced from Germany during the reign of James II.) he wore a cap of maintenance, surmounted by the imperial crest, the lion *in defence;* while the royal arms, the lion rampant, within the double tressure, were everywhere emblazoned on the caparisons of his horse, the head of which was encased in a chanfron of tempered steel.

Another helmet for battle was borne behind the king by the Laird of Touch, who was hereditary armour-bearer and esquire of the royal body; his standard was borne by Scrimgeour, the Constable of Dundee, also its hereditary bearer. The lances of the Royal Guard, under Ramsay, Lord Bothwell, wearing over their armour scarlet jupons, trimmed with yellow (the royal livery), rode close around, in front and in rear of the king, near whom were Sir William Knollis, preceptor of Torphichen, wearing the black côte d'armes of his order, with its white cross of eight points; the old Sieur de Concressault, clad in a gorgeous suit of Milan plate, with his orders of knighthood sparkling on his breast, his swallow-tailed pennon borne before him by one esquire, and his helmet behind him by another. With this group rode the venerable Montrose, the king's first counsellor, attended by many gentlemen, among whom were Sir David Falconer, who, as a soldier, had resolved to share the dangers of the campaign; while the admiral, Barton, and Mathieson, had returned to their ships to guard the passage of the river below Alloa.

The royal army was nearly thirty thousand strong, and gathered strength at every tower and hamlet as it marched westward, by the margin of the Forth, towards Stirling. There were the well-accoutred horsemen and spearmen of the North Lowlands, in their steel caps and buff coats, with iron gloves and gorgets; Highland archers in their long lurichs of chain and conical helmets of steel, with short bows and ponderous swords—all brave and determined, but unruly and, unfortunately, inferior in equipment to the fine troops of the revolted nobles. The cannon were few and small, their principal one being the *Lion*, a brass gun, cast in Flanders for James I., in 1438; it weighed 3000 lb. and was inscribed with a long Latin legend.

Save the hum of the marching squadrons as it rose on the morning air, the tramp of horses, and the tread of feet, the rustle of the many-coloured banners and pennons of baronial families, clans and burghtowns, or an occasional word of command, there were no sounds of military triumph accompanied this march to Stirling. In respect for the king's sorrow and recent bereavement, no Lowland drum was beaten, no trumpet blown, or bagpipe gave a note to the breeze; and most of the peers and gentlemen were thoughtful and downcast, or conversed only in low and subdued tones; for it was an age of omens, and many portending evils had been seen; and thus, their minds, being as were forewarned of unhappy results, attended to the most trivial things, and drew from them dark and mighty conclusions.

Passing through the woods of Tullibody, the forces crossed the beautiful Devon, which is fed by a hundred streams that pour down from the Ochils, and rush united through a channel of rock, among wild, romantic, and richly-wooded glens, towards the Forth. The royal troops passed through the little village of thatched cottages, from the low chimneys of which the smoke of fires, that were fed with fir and oak from the neighbouring bog, was curling high above the rich green foliage. The cottars stood at their doors, and held up at arm's-length their little ones, to see the passing king, and in the hope, perhaps, that they might catch a glance of the royal eye ; men, old and bent with age, stretched their thin hands towards him in blessing, and the tears came into the eyes of James when, after a long silence, he turned to those about him, and said :

' It is these poor people, and such as these, I love : and it is at such a time as this I feel myself a king. Believe me, my good Montrose, the prayers and wishes of the lowly reach Heaven more readily through these roofs of thatch, than those that rise from baron's halls and great cathedral aisles ; for, as Saint Mungo said of old, the poor are the children of God. I would that all Scotland were as single in purpose and as true in heart as these poor cottars now.'

To this no one replied, and after another silent pause, James continued, in the same bitter strain :

' How many of my forefathers have shed their blood for this ungrateful people, who will slay me, even as they slew James I. at Perth ? Fighting for Scotland, my father fell at Roxburgh, by a cannon, in the very armour I now wear ; yet how few of her nobles have one drop of blood for me ? Like the very demons of violence, crime, and ambition, they will traverse all the land in arms ; burghs will be sacked, and homesteads laid in ashes ; towers stormed and battles fought, for there is no hand can restrain them but *One*, and even that seems armed against me now ! '

' Alas ! ' said the Treasurer Knollis, in a low voice, as he laid a hand on the cross of his order ; ' alas ! that your Majesty should speak thus ; doth not the Holy Writ tell us, that " man is born to trouble, even as the sparks fly upward ? " '

' Where, beyond the little band here, have I a friend ? '

The Lord of St. John of Jerusalem pointed upwards, saying,

'The wisdom and the repining of man are alike folly in the sight of Heaven.'

'I beseech your Majesty to be of good cheer,' said Montrose; 'thirty thousand loyal hearts are under your royal banner; and another day may see your enemies routed, baffled, and destroyed.'

'Duke, I have ever heard it said that the most noble way of destroying one's enemies was to make them friends; but in every attempt to gain these hostile peers, I have signally failed. Our long projected banquet, which was to cement the bonds of friendship——'

'For God's love, speak not of that,' said Montrose, betraying a storm of anger in his eye and manner; 'for never shall I know one hour of peace until I have discovered and nailed on Stirling cross the hand which forged the letter proud Angus so exults in!'

And now old Stirling's 'towers and town' arose before the marching troops, all steeped in summer haze and brilliant sunlight—that gorgeous palatial fortress, so rich in statues, ornament, and carving—so lofty and so strong, rising tower above tower, and rampart over rampart, on that stupendous rock that terminates the steep on which the quaint old burgh clusters, with all its gable-ended houses, its grey turrets, and antique courts, its shady wynds and masses of fantastic masonry, with gardens all around, and orchards in full bloom; while, seen at intervals, the winding Forth swept through the fertile vale below, so rich in dark green coppice and golden fields of corn, and teeming all with natural loveliness—bounded by the dark and purple peaks of the mighty Ochils and the mightier Grampians—by a thousand hills and more, that look down on plains where Scotland fought three of her most glorious battles.

By old Stirling bridge, so famed in the annals of the past for pageantry and strife—so narrow and so steep, with its deep-ribbed arches that span the river Forth, the king crossed at the head of his troops, and for three hours they continued to defile along that lofty gangway of stone, with banners waving, and spears and helmets shining in the sun. Strong walls and fortified portes then enclosed the town. Its eastern barrier, 'a formidable arch of ponderous masonry, sprung from columns of basaltic rock, twenty feet in diameter. A jagged portcullis and solid gates closed the path by night, and their state keys of solid silver are yet preserved in the town-house.'

No provost, bailies, or dean of guild, in furred gowns, appeared on bended knee to present these keys to James as he passed through the arched portal which then secured the centre of the bridge ; and the streets beyond it were silent and deserted, for the people were stricken with fear and awe, as his forces marched through towards the Torwood ; for he had resolved to encamp beyond the walls, and thus relieve the burgesses of his favourite town from the presence of the wild and unruly northern clans who adhered to his cause and crown.

Intending to remain in Stirling until more of the Highland chiefs could join him, and being anxious to meet the prince his son, whom he believed to be in the castle with Shaw the governor, of whose defection he was still ignorant, James rode up the Broad Wynd, attended by a few of his guard, by Bothwell, its captain, Montrose, the Sieur de Monipennie, Sir David Falconer, and others who were his best friends, and who formed a glittering troop as they approached the castle, which was James's favourite residence, and which he had greatly embellished, having built therein a parliament-house, the magnificent oak roof of which was but recently and recklessly torn down by the British government, and sold for firewood !

As the cavalcade advanced up the hill, they were surprised to find a strange banner—the red heart of Douglas—flying upon the castle in place of the blue national ensign, while the gates were closed, the drawbridge up, the walls lined by the garrison, and the cannon pointed against them.

Glances of inquiry and suspicion were exchanged by the attendants of the king, whose pale face was turned with stern scrutiny upon the armed ramparts, so he ordered a trumpet to be sounded, and with the umbriere of his salade up rode forward boldly to the edge of the ditch.

' Is the Laird of Sauchie, my captain of Stirling, within your gates ? ' he asked, in a firm and haughty manner.

' I am here, at the service of your grace,' replied that arch-conspirator, as he appeared all armed, save the head, at the wall above the portcullis.

' Thou false traitor and mansworn subject,' said James, ' why am I received in this fashion at my own castle-gate ? Do ye not see the royal banner and the guard in our livery ? '

' As plainly as may be,' replied Sauchie, with the coolest assurance ; ' and what of it ? '

8

James thought of his dead queen, and controlled th
gust of proper indignation that swelled within him at th
insolent bearing of his subject.

'Am I to understand that you decline us entrance here ?'

'I regret to say that your Majesty surmises justly.'

'Soldiers!' he exclaimed, 'I am James, your king
Lieutenant-governor, Allan Cochrane of Dundonald, arres
the traitor Sauchie, and lower the bridge; arrest him,
command you all on your allegiance.'

The Laird of Dundonald curled up his mustachios i
silence, while Sauchie laughed aloud; but no man stirre
upon the walls, though all gazed upon each other in eviden
doubt and trepidation.

'Will no man there desire the prince, my son, to appea
before me,' said the poor king.

Then Sauchie answered : 'The prince, your son, is wit
the lords, in arms, beyond the Torwood, and is birling hi
bicker in Callendar Hall.'

This intelligence cut James to the soul, and he turned t
Concressault, with a glance full of reproach and inquiry.

'I could not tell your Majesty such evil tidings,' replied th
old soldier ; 'though I saw the prince, pale, sad, and I an
glad to say it, looking miserable enough, among those evil
minded lords.'

'And thou, David Falconer ?' said the king.

'I was silent for the same reason.'

'It was kindly meant, sirs—kindly meant ; but it make
the blow more heavy to-day. Wifeless and sonless, in on
week—I may well be crownless and lifeless the next. Oh
who that could have a crust and cup of water in peacefu
obscurity would be king of Scotland ? One word ere w
go, Sir James of Sauchie, and answer me truly on your sou
as a Christian man, is my son in arms against me of his ow
free will ?'

'I know not ; but the nobles, now in arms to deman
justice, took him away with them.'

'Justice is in the hand of Heaven ; and yet these rebe
lords would seek it at the head of forty-thousand spears.'

'I know not in whose hand it may be, and care not,
replied the insolent Shaw ; 'but time will prove all.'

'Time will also avenge thy perfidy !' said James, wit
great bitterness ; 'fie on thee, traitor ; fie ! But I sha
neither curse nor ban thee, for thy father was a good knigh
and loyal man ; and this conduct in thee is enough to mak

his bones shake in their coffin in Cambuskenneth aisle. Foully and basely hast thou deceived me, for to thee were entrusted alike the custody of this my royal castle and of my eldest son ; but I shall yet be avenged, and have thee rewarded as thou deservest.'

It is related that James then shook his clenched hand at the subtle traitor on the battlement above him ; and all his train made the same menacing gesture, as they wheeled their horses round and descended into the town.

CHAPTER XXX.

THE GOOD SHIP 'HARRY.'

THE evening was cold and grey; the shrill wind swept over the German sea, tearing the surf here and there from the crests of the murky waves, which reflected the colour of the inky scud that traversed the lowering sky heavily and swiftly in flying masses overhead.

Scattered far apart, three English ships are striving to make headway against the freshening gale that blows from the east, and at every fresh gust strains their almost close-reefed canvas as if to blow it out of the bolt-ropes; and seizing their ponderous spars, their intricate top-hamper and heavy-towering poops, every moment careens them over to leeward. Hardly they beat, and bravely too; for a foreign, and it may be a hostile shore is lying with all its rocky terrors on their lee, for these ships are the *Harry*, the *Cressi,* and *White Rose*.

They dared not signal for pilots as they passed the little fisher-towns that nestle in the creeks and crannies of that tremendous coast, which rises like a wall of rock along the northern sea; and if they had fired guns and shown their colours, it may be doubted whether a pilot could have come off in such tempestuous weather.

'It freshens fast, this plaguey breeze,' said John o' Lynne, turning his weather-beaten face to windward; 'but ere this I have weathered many a tough Levanter, and seen St. Elmo's light lay the spirit of the storm, as it burned blue for half a fathom or so below our maintruck, and along the topsail-yard.'

'Ay, John,' responded Howard, 'thou mayst have been all round the world, and outside it too—yea, have doubled the Cape of Storms, and yet never have seen a more dangerous or damnable coast than this of Buchan here!'

'Should we not take a reef in that foresail and the main-top-sail?'

' 'Nay—ouf! what a mouthful of salt water!—nay, stand on; see, the rocks fall back and the land opens! Ho!—St. George for England! we may yet get into safe riding, and thank God and St. Mary we have neither started tack nor sheet.'

'Or had aught carried away from truck to keel—from sprit-sail to poop-lantern.'

'A board of the forechain-plates hath been torn off; but we will plank it anew in Scottish fir,' said Howard, with a smile. 'The old *Harry* hath carried her canvas and shipped her seas most nobly; she is the most manageable craft 'tween Thames and Humber, and though we have not a dry hammock or doublet on board, we will be all right and ataunto ere long. Will Selby, pass the word forward for a posset of sack, and then wear the ship round, John o' Lynne, for that bight on the lee bow opens fast; and though I never was but once in these seas before, I remember me of finding safe anchorage hereabout. Get ready a culverin, as a signal to our craft to windward, and run up St. George's cross, but for a minute only; lest the gimlet eyes of some wary Scots may espy it from yonder devilish bluff, as we wear ship and make to port.'

'I hear a strange sound,' said Dick Selby, putting a tarry hand behind his red, weather-beaten ear.

' 'Tis the storm fiend laughing,' said John o' Lynne.

'Nay,' said Howard, ' 'tis the waves roaring in a cavern, and mingling with the boom of breakers on the beach; and now we should see Phillorth Church and sands; and lo! there they are to leeward—let her fall off a few points— so—yare—John, yare, and bravely!'

Rattray Point, that low and dangerous promontory, with its burgh town, not a vestige of which now remains, were left astern, and soon Kinnaird, that tremendous headland on the Buchan coast reared its weatherbeaten brow above the foam, where the wave that rose upon the far Norwayn shore breaks upon its iron front; and now, as Howard said, Phillorth opened its friendly bay, overlooked by an ancient castle belonging to the Frazers, and its kirk of St. Modan, the confessor of King Couran.

The *Harry* fired a gun as a signal to her consorts, and right before the wind they stood in between the foam-drenched promontories of Cairnbulg and Frazerburgh, and came to anchor in the bay or roads, where, as the high bluffs protected them from the fury of the sea, they rode in safety.

' Thank God and St. George our anchor is down, and seems to hold bravely too ! ' said Howard, as the ship swung round and everything was furled, fore and aft.

' But how fareth this dainty Scottish dame to-day ? ' asked John o' Lynne. Howard coloured deeply, and pretending not to have heard, looked fixedly at the bluff of Cairnbulg. ' Dost thou affect her, shipmate o' mine ? '

Still no answer.

' Ahoy, my captain ! thou'st seen her to-day, I warrant.'

' Who ? ' asked Howard, fretfully.

' The lady—our prisoner, who hath never set her pretty foot on our wetted deck since that misty night we were off Taymouth.'

' How could she do so, when the wind hath blown a tempest since, and we have shipped an ocean and more of this bitter Scottish sea ? She is low in heart, and sunk in health and spirit—poor little damsel—my heart bleeds for her ! '

' And yearns for her too—is it not so, Edmund Howard ? '

' It yearns in vain, then,' said Howard, with a sigh ; ' for she is impregnable.'

' Faith, she must be if *thou* hast failed in getting the weathergage of her ; thou hast been kind to her as father, brother, and lover, all in one,' continued the talkative lieutenant ; ' and I doubt not, she will make such a report of thee to old King Harry as may win thee a pair of golden spurs.'

' A stout fellow who wears a sword and faces salt water —a Howard least of all—should not owe his spurs to a petticoat, John o' Lynne,' said his captain, coldly ; ' but I would to Heaven she had never set foot on board the *Harry ;* and I hope its heaviest malison will fall on yonder villanous Scots who are plotting this poor girl's ruin, and who brought her to us—on Borthwick more than all ! That night his face was white as our flag ; but one day I hope to see it turn blue as a Scot's one ! '

Then, the coast which is now covered by one of the most thriving burghs of regality in Scotland, was lonely and somewhat bare. The high promontories, the level shore, the old castle of the Lairds o' Phillorth, the older church which was their burial place ; the green Mormond Hill, with thickets of fine oak and dense clumps of red stemmed Scottish firs, composed the scenery of the bay, in which the waves rolled blue and calmly, notwithstanding the storm that flecked with foam the sea without.

For several days the gale continued, and for these days the English ships rode at their anchors, without their crews molesting the shore, or being molested from thence: for it happened that the old Baron of Phillorth was marching with his chief, the Lord Lovat, and all his retainers, to join the king's host; so that none were left behind to guard his lady and their tower but old men and boys. Moreover, although Barton had been slain in the Downs, and Lord Angus had ravaged all Northumberland, the kingdoms of Scotland and England were rather in a state of suspicion and alarm, than of war, as the wary Henry VII. had no wish for that event, being anxious to cement the bonds of an offensive and defensive alliance by the projected marriage of Rothesay with his daughter, the voluptuous Margaret Tudor.

Howard knew nothing of all that had been passing at Dundee, Stirling, and elsewhere, during these several days of stormy and arduous beating to windward; and Margaret Drummond, his prisoner, knew of course no more. She had now become somewhat composed, and ceased alike to threaten, to entreat, and to weep, save when she thought of her motherless and abandoned infant.

While thus compelled by the stormy eastern wind to loiter off the Scottish coast, the amiable and gallant Howard became deeply impressed by the beauty, the gentleness, and sadness of Margaret Drummond; and he felt all this the more keenly, because he was too well aware that he was the contemptible instrument of causing sorrow and distress to one so beautiful. Daily he resolved never more to enter her cabin, and hourly he broke the resolution; for the charm of her presence was too strong for his heart to resist.

Frequently in his secret thoughts he cursed the cruel and subtle policy of his king, and the cupidity of the infamous Scottish traitors who pandered to him, and sold for English gold their faith and services.

At one time he had almost resolved to land her on the coast, near some seaport town or baronial castle, and then bear away for the Thames, and surrender himself to Henry's wrath; or to quit his ships and seek a shelter among the wild Northumbrian mosstroopers. Thus, fearful of adding fresh poignancy to her grief by commencing his homeward voyage, he loitered in the bay near Frazerburgh, while the gale moderated and veered round favourably to the north-west; while water, wine, and provisions became scarce on board the ships; while tall Dick Selby the gunner, An-

thony Arblaster, captain of the crossbows, who had lost an
eye at the Battle of Bosworth, and others of the crew, looked
strangely in each other's faces, and muttered under their
bushy beards; and John o' Lynne, who had been gruffly
told to 'haul taut and belay, and to mind his own affairs,'
strode sulkily up and down the larboard side of the poop,
with his hands thrust far into the pockets of his coarse blue
gaberdine, shouldering master Quentin Kraft, for whom he
had no great love or liking, and whistling to console himself,
as he sipped a peg-tankard of sack that stood on the binnacle-
head, and looked crossly from time to time at the flying clouds,
and the long whiplike pennon that streamed towards old
England.

In deep thought, poor Howard often walked quite as
hurriedly on the other side of the poop, and was frequently
heard to mutter—'Alas, for thee, Eddy Howard—thou art
a lost and ruined man!'

'Ruined people are dangerous,' grumbled John o' Lynne,
under his long wiry mustachios, which were always encrusted with saline particles; 'misfortune is infectious, and
I would fain see the ship cleared of this here piece of Scottish
trumpery.'

'And bearing away for the Nore and Thames, which we
are never likely to see again if this work lasts,' added Dick
Selby, emptying the lieutenant's posset in pure inadver-
tence. 'St. Mary be praised, we gave these Buchan-bouillars
a wide berth, though! else we had all found our graves in
the Scotsman's sea.'

'I would rather you had taken a pull at your slack jawing
tackle, than my sack posset, Master Selby,' said the lieutenant, gruffly; 'so please to sheer off when next it stands
here, and before you come aft again, give one look at the
Book of Good Manners.'

On this day the weather was calm and clear; the wind had
almost died away, and for the first time since she came on
board, Margaret had ascended to the poop, supported on
the arm of Howard, and well muffled in rich Muscovite
sables, for the muffly (or muff and tippet) were then worn
by the ladies in Scotland. Howard dared scarcely look his
own lieutenant in the face; for now the weather had cleared
so completely that he was at last deprived of every vestige
of excuse for lingering off the Scottish coast.

Upon that coast—on the granite brows of Cairnbulg and
the loftier bluff of Kinnaird with its cavern a hundred feet

in depth, on old Phillorth with its woods, and the Mormond Hill covered to its summit with green moss and purple heather, on the sandy beach in front and the flat champaign beyond, Margaret bent her sad and anxious eyes. Round them the blue bay shone like a mirror; but not a Scottish ship was near. Close by were the consorts of the *Harry*, lying at anchor, with their yards braced sharply up and their heads to the wind, and in the open sea without were a number of those Dutch vessels called bushes, which, until the beginning of the seventeenth century, were permitted by the Scottish government to fish in the Loch of Strathbeg, which was *then* an arm of the sea, though now it is more than a mile from it.

Howard saw the expression of Margaret's dark and beautiful eyes, as she gazed in silent sorrow on the shore and on the narrow strip of water, little more than half a bowshot, that separated her from the yellow beach on which that water rippled, and as she turned pleadingly and reproachfully to him, he felt that his own gaze became disordered; and dreading that she would renew those earnest entreaties with which he dared not comply—entreaties to be landed on any point or place from whence she could make her way to the nearest hut or house—he begged her to be seated, and to excuse him, and hurried to the fore-part of the vessel on some pretended duty, despatching to her the pretty Cicely and the black-eyed Rose, who were gaily chatting with Dick Selby and Anthony the archer, in the waist, and in the sunny side of the starboard gun-tier, and were looking as spruce and charming as the hideous dress then worn by the women of England would permit; for their gowns were cut square at the neck, with enormous sleeves confined at intervals from the elbow to the wrist, or worn like 'bishop's sleeves,' as they were named in London. On their heads were flowing capuchons turned back, as we may still see them in some of Holbein's portraits.

Finding herself an object of attention and considerable speculation among the crew, who (honest souls!) knew little of the mission and less of the object which had brought them into Scottish waters, the sensitive Margaret soon retired again to her cabin, and there Edmund Howard followed her, by a temptation which he could not resist—lured by the sound of her voice, and the soft expression of her eyes; for these, though speaking only of sorrow and reproach, were too powerful and too seductive to be easily withstood.

Though his visit had been respectfully heralded by little Will Selby, the gunner's brother, Howard found Margaret seated in a chair near the cabin windows, still watching the shore, then shining in the meridian sun. She had thrown aside her hood, and wore only her caul of gold, under which her soft fair hair fell in a shower of glittering curls down her back,—for such was then, and for long after, the fashion. The sunlight streamed through the cabin windows, and Margaret's bright tresses seemed to form a glory round her mild Madonna face, which was so pure, so fair, and exquisitely soft ; while the deep sadness and solemn thoughts that hovered in her heart, made her eyes seem of a darker and a deeper blue than they really were.

She gave Howard but one glance as he entered, and turned again to the stern windows, from whence the bright water rippled away like lines of light towards the pebbled shore, from which she deemed herself about to be taken as a punishment for having violated the laws of the Church, and brought discord into the royal family.

‘ You have soon quitted the deck, lady,’ said Howard, on whose handsome face there were impressed all the doubts and hesitation which now rendered strange and abrupt his usually open-hearted and elegant manner ; ‘ would not a little more of the breeze that blows from yonder waving woods have revived you, after such long confinement in this close cabin here.’

‘ Not unless I was under their branches, sir, which I am not likely to be while you are captain of this caravel,’ replied Margaret, without raising her eyes.

Howard then pressed her to partake of a luncheon of preserved strawberries, quince marmalade, macaroon biscuits, hippocrass and orange wine, which stood untasted on the cabin table ; but she coldly declined. He stood silent for a minute, and his heart swelled under his well-embroidered doublet, as he leaned over her chair and gazed upon the bright soft tresses that fell on the girl's neck,—for Margaret was yet a girl, though maternity had given a roundness to her beautiful form, even as premature sorrow had given a sadness to her charming face and manner.

Of that maternity and her marriage Edmund Howard was ignorant, but knowing that the heir of Scotland loved her, he dared not speak of his own growing passion ; for what had he to offer, compared with all of which he was depriving her. Yet Margaret could read that rising sentiment in his speaking eye and kind persuasive voice, and in his softened manner,—it fretted and provoked her. A woman has an intuitive or instinctive perception when a man is in love with her, let him do ever so much to conceal it; and in the present instance Howard was too much of an English sailor, and too little of a courtier, to show false colours.

'For the hundredth time, lady,' said he, 'I beseech you to be assured that if your fate was in my own hands, you would be conducted to any part of Scotland you desired; and there would I leave you, though in doing so my heart should break for ever!'

Margaret smiled bitterly, but did not reply.

'Alas, lady, think better of me,' urged Howard, sighing deeply; 'think better of me than to believe me a mansworn wretch like Sir James of Sauchie, or a sordid slave like those other Scots who have betrayed you to Henry of England. Lady, I see a cloud now gathering on your beautiful brow; I am but a plain-speaking English seaman (somewhat of a courtier once, it might be); I have no wish to take the wind out of any man's sails, but I do think, that while so many rascals tread her soil, this same Scotland of yours is not worth mourning for.'

'And dost think I have only the woods and mountains to weep for? Have I not my father—my four sisters, and my——' she dared not add 'child!'

'Lady, the love of kings and princes is like foam on the sea—a thing that comes and goes with every puff of wind, and so passes away for ever. Kings are but a hollow-hearted race at best; their lives and their loves are made alike subservient to policy and statecraft; and your Scottish kings have ever, as it were, been among breakers and shoal water since Scotland had a name; for her nobles are a race of hereditary traitors, such as have no parallel in Europe—men ever ready to sell her liberty and barter her honour for foreign gold.'

'Who spoke of kings or princes,' asked Margaret; 'not I surely, sir—my lips never uttered the name of king or prince?'

'But your heart did, madam,' said Howard, sadly. 'Oh, do not conceal your secret thoughts from me. My own sentiments enable me to sound the depth of yours too surely for my own peace.'

'I think, sir captain, I might have wearied you by this time.'

'Nay, lady, nay; does the miser ever weary of his treasure?' continued poor Howard, getting into deeper water every moment. 'I count not the hours you are with me, unless to reckon how long it may be till we are separated by King Henry, and my sun sets in a dark and hopeless sea.'

'And when will this happen?' asked Margaret, making a violent effort to control a rising sob.

'When we drop our anchors by the Tower of London.'

'Oh, thou art a wretch—a minion—the slave of servile slaves!' said Margaret, covering her face, and giving way to one of those wild bursts of grief which always convulsed her when the memory of the babe from which she had been so cruelly torn arose more poignantly within her; 'begone, and leave me to the horror thou hast wrought me.'

'Madam,' said Howard, with increasing sadness, 'I take kind Heaven to witness, that I seek no higher ornament than the admiration you withhold from me; no greater glory than the love I can never win. You have thrice held out bribes to me, as if I were some sordid Scottish lord or servile English clown, instead of being a gentleman of spotless coat-armour and reputable bearing. I have not deserved contempt thus, even at your hands, for your presence here has wrecked my peace as surely as it has wrecked your own; but alas! from very different causes. Dearly as he loves you, madam—and God who hears him only knows how dearly,—Edmund Howard will never again ask grace of one who has stigmatized him as a king's minion and a sordid wretch. I dare not land you on the Scottish coast; and I have now but one hope—that we shall fall in with old Andrew of Largo, and that after I have died fighting on my deck, you may be given to those whom you love by the lads I leave behind me; though I fear much that bold Dick Selby would rather throw a match in his magazine and blow the old *Harry* up, than see St. Andrew's cross above St. George's ensign! Farewell, madam—I will never trouble you more.'

Repenting her harshness, and impressed by Howard's calm and noble demeanour, Margaret would have called him back; but he sprang upon deck, and summoning John o' Lynne, ordered him to prepare for sailing—to man the windlass and heave short, and to cast loose the courses, while Dick Selby fired a culverin as a signal to their consorts the *White Rose* and *Cressi*, to put to sea.

'I will no longer act the traitor to my king,' thought Howard, 'or be the plaything of this proud beauty, who wrongs me in her heart, and treats my honest passion with the cold indifference of an anchor-stock. Too long have I been the laggard and the lover, and now the play is ended!'

'Ho! for England—cheerily, my hearts!' cried the gunner as he summoned a squad, who cast loose and loaded a culverin; 'I thought we should have ridden in this here cove till our anchors rusted and our cables rotted—or till the hungry devils of the Scottish sea had picked our ribs as clean as ivory. Ready the match! we have cruised long enough in these here northern latitudes to wish for home again!'

The culverin flashed redly from the dark porthole; the woods of Phillorth, the cave and rocks of Kinnaird, and the shores of the bay, gave back the report, and a hundred reverberations as the courses fell and swelled out in the western breeze, when the anchors were apeak, and the topsails sheeted home, and the white flags with St. George's red cross were displayed from the gaff-peak and mainmast-head, as the stately *Harry* moved slowly out of that lonely northern bay, and once more began to roll upon the stormy waters of the Scoto-German sea, which broke in foam above the ghastly reefs then known as Phillorth Briggs.

CHAPTER XXXI.

THE TORWOOD.

It is recorded in history that James III. made a second effort to overcome the treason of Shaw, but in vain. The message delivered by Sir David Falconer and Lord Bothwell, commander of the Royal Guard, was received with derision and contempt ; and for the evening and night the king remained in the town of Stirling, with all his troops around it, and fully resolved to fight the insurgents on the morrow, if they advanced against him.

Rumours of their great strength made the few faithful nobles who adhered to James doubtful of victory and fearful for his safety ; thus the good old Duke of Montrose desired Sir David Falconer to bear a message to Sir Andrew Wood, who was still anchored off Alloa, requesting him to have his boats along the beach and near the Carse, to take off all fugitives and wounded men of either party who might pass that way. As the Torwood—a vast forest of primeval oaks which covered most of the Carse to the eastward of Stirling—was full of wolves, wild deer, and, worse than these, the hunting and wandering parties of the insurgents, this duty was a task of no ordinary danger ; but the gallant captain of the king's arquebusses prepared for it with alacrity ; resolving, if molested, to trust to a steady hand, a sharp sword, and a swift horse.

Accoutred in his harness, back, breast, and head-pieces, armlets and gloves, or, as the Acts of James I. say, 'weel horsed and weel harnished as gentlemen oucht to be,' with lance, sword, dagger, and a hand-gun at his saddle-bow, Falconer quitted his lodgings in the Friars' Wynd, near the Meal-Market, and rode down the steep streets of Stirling on his mission, just as the sun was setting afar off behind the mountains of the Highland frontier. He had wisely taken from his helmet the knot of *red* and *yellow* ribbons—the royal colours—which the Duchess of Montrose and her *dames d'honneur* had prepared and bestowed upon the gentlemen of the royal army; thus he had nothing to distinguish him as he rode on his solitary mission, and he could pass for loyalist or traitor, according to circumstances.

He passed out of Stirling by an ancient porte near the Wolf's Craig, where, in the war of Donald V., a sentinel, when asleep, had been awakened by the growl of a wolf, and started to his sword just in time to find a horde of Saxon invaders close by; they were routed; and to this day we may still see on the old burgh seals a wolf, recumbent on a rock, with seven stars above it in the sky, in memory of how the town was saved. As Falconer gave his steed a draught of the pure spring that flows from St. Ninian's well, a dark frocked figure—an Augustine of Cambuskenneth apparently—was similarly occupied in watering his nag, a stout Galloway cob.

' Good morrow, father; I hope you are come to bless the cause of the king,' said Falconer. But he received no answer; so leaving the well and chapel behind, he wheeled off to the left, between the deepening shadows of the Torwood and the stupendous eminence crowned by the town; and at a rapid trot pursued the old Roman route towards the north-west.

The time-worn path was solitary and deserted; at such a crisis none were abroad save well-armed men, and now all these in the neighbourhood were within the walls of Stirling or cantoned around it. In the stillness of the summer eve, he heard the cattle lowing in the Queen's Haugh, where the herds of the queen were grazing, for the lordship of Stirling was the dowry of the queens-consort of Scotland.

The summer moon rose clearly and brightly above the dark foliage of the Torwood, and its silver light mingled with the yellow flush of the western sky, and threw forward in black and bold relief the sharp ridge of Stirling, with its castled rock, its turreted chateaux and old square Gothic spire; the wooded Abbey Craig, on which were the ruins of a castle, with the Forth winding like a gigantic snake of silver between thickets of beautiful coppice, and forming those green links of rich alluvial land, which, in all ages, have been so proverbial for their pasture and fertility. Above these towered the lofty Abbey of St. Mary of Cambuskenneth—massive, rich, and strong, as when King David built it three hundred and forty years before; and lights began to twinkle in the painted windows of its church and dormitories as the daylight faded behind the gigantic Ochils, and as the river that swept around it turned from silver to a cold, yet bright star-studded blue; and the mighty bell which swung in the highest tower was tolling the hour of ten, and summoning the Augustines to prayer, as the arquebussier rode on, and passing the Abbey and river on his left, dipped into the wood. The head of this great abbey was usually a powerful and wealthy lord. Henry, the then abbot, was sent ambassador to England a few years after the period we write of.

As the last note of its melodious bell—which, strange to say, is yet lying in the Forth, just where the Reformers sunk it—died away upon the wind, and the road grew dark as the lofty oaks of Torwood arched their branches over it, forming, as it were, a lofty tunnel of twined and matted foliage, Falconer thought he heard the hoofs of a horse behind him: he checked his own for a moment, and looked back. He saw only the monk mounted on his stout little cob, and well muffled up in his black gown and cowl; so the soldier turned and rode on, though it was evident that the stranger had also for a moment checked his speed.

As Falconer crossed the Bannock he again looked back; the monk was still in sight, preserving his distance, and pursuing at a trot the old Roman way. Falconer turned to ride back and meet this follower, who immediately wheeled round and galloped in the opposite direction to avoid him.

'Poor friar—my harness frightens him,' thought Falconer, as he resumed his way. 'By my faith, but these are sharp times, when peaceful monks and men of God tremble at the sight of their own countrymen!'

He soon dismissed the circumstance from his mind, on remembering that it was a peculiarity of the Augustines or Canons Regular, that they took charge of parish churches and performed ecclesiastical functions in any place, whereas the contemplative orders never left their convent walls. As he passed Polmaise (or the Pool of *Rotting*, so named from the thousands of bodies that lay unburied there after the Battle of Bannockburn), he again heard the hoofs of the priest's cob following closely and warily behind him.

''Tis intolerable, this!' said Falconer, as ideas of spies and assassins were suggested to his mind, and he remembered that twice he had recently escaped a barbarous death. 'Come on, good father,' he cried, 'come on, and fear nothing, for I am a peaceful man, though armed, as you see.'

To this the priest made no response, but again wheeled his horse to the right, and dashed into the recesses of the Torwood.

' Suspicious, this ! ' thought Falconer ; ' and if I find thee tracking me again, I will try the effect of a hand-gun shot on thee, were thou the last of all the friars in Scotland.'

He listened for a time, but all was still, save some distant and uncertain sound that arose from the recesses of the forest and floated in the still air overhead ; but whether these were the notes of hunting horns recalling straggling parties or wild wolves baying at the summer moon, seemed uncertain ; so once more he resumed his way, and at a hand-gallop passed the manor of Throsk, crossed the fertile Carse, turned round a link of the Forth, and descended to the Craigward or King's Ferry, where the river is still crossed by a boat.

Here the Forth is only half a mile broad at high water. Opposite lay dusky Alloa, with its lights twinkling among masses of quaint old buildings, and the smoke of their chimneys ascending into the pure still air of the evening, which had now almost blended with the dewy night. The woods, the castle, and the town were reflected downward in the stream, in the mid-channel of which were the *Yellow Frigate* and *Queen Margaret*, with their consorts, lying at anchor, with all their boats hoisted in, their courses loose, the upper portlids triced up and the guns run out ; strong watches were on deck, with battle-axe, and arquebuss, and all ready for sea and service at a moment's notice.

Dismounting, Falconer took his horse by the bridle and led it close down to the water-edge at the Craigward, and selecting a place where the boor-trees grew thick and mingled with the wild Scottish roses and the woodbine in a matted screen, over a scaured bank which the river had scooped as if to form a place of concealment, he looked cautiously round and listened for a moment, and all was still, save the ripple of the stream as it flowed towards the sea. He placed to his mouth a silver-mounted bugle that hung at his girdle, and blew one low, winding, and peculiar note. It floated away over the river, and ere it died in the distance, the shrill whistle of Archy the boatswain was heard on board the admiral's ship—a boat plashed as it was lowered into the moonlit water, the crew were seen to drop lightly down from the chains, and the oars gleamed, as Cuddie the coxswain pushed off from the carved and painted side of the high and formidable caravel.

At that moment Falconer heard something crackling among the boor-trees above his head, He looked upward suspiciously, but could perceive nothing.

' Tush,' thought he, ' I have scared some red fuimart or todlowrie from its lair—yet every leaf that stirs startles me to-night.'

He had forgotten the suspicious friar ; but had he looked more narrowly, he might have seen that respectable personage, with his head uncowled, with neck outstretched, with a hand behind one ear to let not a sound escape, and with grey, malignant eyes, half starting from their sockets, while, screened among the leaves, he bent over the bank to see and hear what this bugle-sound, the answering whistle, and shore-rowed boat portended—for our monk was a spy !

CHAPTER XXXII.

THE DOUBLE BRIBE.

'WELCOME as a fair wind!' said Barton, leaping lightly ashore, though he was heavily armed in a suit of black unpolished armour, and carried in his hand a Jedwood axe—'Welcome, doughtie Davie,'

'And welcome thou, my comrade and shipmate,' replied Falconer, as they drew off their steel gloves, and shook hands, but without a smile, for their hearts were full of stern thoughts.

'What tidings are there 'long shore, eh?' asked Barton.

'Evil enough—the lords are all in arms in the Carse, and to-morrow we hope to give them battle.''

'Would I might leave the ship and share it with thee!'

'And why not?' asked Falconer.

'The admiral——'

'True—true.'

''Tis said these lords have a hundred thousand men under their banner.'

'Rumour says even more,' added Falconer.

'But rumour is a landlubber, and often lies: and the king, how many?'

'Only thirty thousand men to my certain knowledge, but all good men and true, and God will bless their cause. Have any tidings of Howard's ships reached thee yet?'

'Not a whisper—nor has a boat boarded us since the king marched west from Alloa. On board we hear no more than a deep-sea lead, when down. Would that we could meet him!' added Robert Barton, twisting his mustachios. 'To me the opening cannon of that English fleet were welcome as a peal of merry marriage bells. Any message from the fair sisters in Strathearn?'

'Alas, none! and I suppose there is no intelligence of the lost Lady Margaret?'

'None—a strange mystery!'

'Can she be with Rothesay among the rebel lords?'

'Impossible! for Rothesay then would leave their banner. Hostility, despair, and old Lord Drummond's wiles alone detain the prince among them: for Sir James Shaw, who twice to-day bent the cannon of Stirling against the king, and also Sir Patrick of Kyneff, declare aloud that James has hidden or poisoned her.'

'I should like to meet, on clear deck or open field, an armed man who would say so much to me!' said Barton, grasping his Jedwood axe.

'Dost think we will have a fair day for the battle to-morrow; for the rain so bedevils our gun-matches.'

'Fair—I think so,' said Barton, looking at the starry sky. 'As Archy the boatswain says:

> When the mist takes to the German sea,
> Fair weather, shipmate, it will be;
> But when the mist rolls owre the land,
> The rain comes pouring off the sand;

so the mist took to the sea this morning. And now, shipmate of mine, what errand brings thee to the Craigward to-night?'

'A message from the Duke of Montrose to the admiral.'

'Well, and what is his grace's desire?'

'That, as we have, perhaps, more chance of being vanquished than victorious on the morrow, he will keep his boats along the shore here, to take off all fugitives and wounded men, and so provide a safe retreat for the king, who in case of reverse (which God avert!) will be conveyed by faithful friends this way.'

'So James retreats *this way!*' said the lurker overhead.

'And how shall we know him?' asked Barton.

'By the Lord Lindesay's famous grey horse, which he is to ride on the morrow, and by a yellow plume in his helmet.'

'Good,' said Barton; 'I shall note them in the log-book of my memory.'

'Good,' and so shall I,' muttered the friar, overhead. '*A grey horse and a yellow plume* will be readily known on the morrow.'

'Hark,' said Barton, as the listener withdrew; 'dost thou not hear something?'

'Can we be watched?' exclaimed Falconer, grasping the hand-gun at his saddle-bow. 'A muffled man—one at least in a friar's cowl, followed me to-night, pace for pace, from the Wolf Craig to the Polmaise,'

'Cuddie—ho, there!—keep the boat close in,' cried Barton,

looking sharply round him. ' A friar, said ye—and there is one, even now, at the top of the Craigward ! '

Barton sprang to the summit of the bank with all the agility of a sailor, and grasping the lurker by the frock, as he was crawling away, dragged him roughly down to the beach.

' How now, sir friar, what seek you here ? ' asked Falconer, recognizing the priest he had met at the Wolf Craig. ' A passage across the ferry.'

' Then you are not likely to get it, for the rebels have burned the boat, and the oarsmen have fled,' replied Barton, releasing him, and half ashamed of having shown so much warmth before a clergyman. ' Why did you not come boldly forward and say so at once, good friar, instead of crawling about there like a parboiled parton—eh ? '

' This is not a time to venture rashly among armed men.'

' The friar is right,' said Falconer ; ' and such was perhaps his reason for avoiding me in the Torwood.'

' Moreover, I am a friend of the Lord Drummond, bound on a peaceful mission to two gentleman of the king's ships,' said the friar, the upper and lower parts of whose face were concealed by his hood.

' We know most of the men in the king's ships, father,' said Barton, in an altered tone, ' and for whom may your message be ? '

' Robert Barton, captain of the *Yellow Frigate*, and Sir David Falconer, captain of the king's arquebussiers.'

There was a pause, during which the persons mentioned gazed at each other and then at the friar.

' Priest, thou gibest us,' said Barton, bluntly ; ' for we are the men you speak of.'

' How shall I be assured of that, sirs ? '

' Ask our names of the boat's crew, if you doubt us,' said Falconer.

' It is enough—I now recognize ye both, sirs.'

' A sudden recognition ! '

' Well, friar, thou'st the weather-gage of us, and knowest our rank and rating now ; but what would the Lord Drummond with us ? ' asked Barton.

' Step a little this way ; what I have to tell must not be overheard,' said the friar, drawing them a few paces from the boat. ' Sir David Falconer, you love the Lady Drummond's daughter, Sybilla ? '

Falconer was silent, for the sound of that beloved name made his heart leap under his cuirass.

'And you, Robert Barton, love her sister, Euphemia?'

'Silence, friar,' said Barton, angrily; 'what hast thou to do with this?'

'Thus much, that the Lord Drummond, the High Steward of Strathearn, sent me to say, that if you will make the admiral prisoner, seize his ships, and deliver them to the lords, ye shall yet win your brides; but refuse, and you shall never see them more.'

'Villain monk, thou liest!—the Lord Drummond is a gentleman!' said Falconer, furiously.

'He is more,' said the monk, sneeringly, 'he is a Scottish noble.'

'In that word *noble* lies a world of treason,' said Barton, 'but he was wise to send a priest on this infernal mission, for with this axe I would have cloven a layman to the chine.'

'Very likely,' sneered the monk again; 'for useful and honourable men are never appreciated in this world—they are ever unfortunate.'

'Such priests as thee will be fully appreciated in the world to come,' said Falconer.

'Do not let us quarrel, sirs,' said the tempter, with assumed meekness, crossing his hands upon his breast; 'I am but the Lord Drummond's mouthpiece; and he said, Sir David, that your pay as captain of the king's arquebussiers would go but a short way, with a houseful of little Davies and Sybies crying for bannocks, cheese, and Christmas boxes.'

This sneer enraged the soldier, but he heard it with apparent disdain. 'So you will not win your brides, fair sirs—yea, with as many gold pieces each as would fill a Linlithgow firlot.'

'English, no doubt,' said Falconer.

'Of course,' added Barton; 'what other coin could pay for Scottish treason? No—we will not win our brides thus, but by lance and sword will we win them on the morrow; so, base slubberdegullion, slip your cable and sheer off—begone, or by my father's bones, now bleaching in the English Downs, I will tie thee in thy friar's frock as in a sack, and sink thee with a whinstone bullet; though thou art more likely to die with a fathom of rope than a fathom of water over thy shaven crown! Away; ship your oars, my hearts,' he added, springing into the boat, as Falconer leaped on his horse; 'Farewell, gossip Davie—God speed thee back to Stirling, and give us victory on the morrow. I will not forget **to look for the yellow plume**, though I pray it may never come here on the head of a fugitive king.   Give way, lads ; we have been off a full hour by the glass ;—give way for the ship.'

The boat shot off from the shore into the stream, the rowers keeping time with Dalquhat, who pulled the stroke oar, and all their blades flashed in the moonlight, as Sir David Falconer, without bestowing a word or glance on the recreant friar, galloped up the slope and along the Carse by the old Roman Way that led to Stirling.

The moment they were gone, the friar threw back his hood and displayed to the white moon, then sailing high aloft in the clear blue sky, the evil visage of Hew Borthwick, over the deep sinister eyes and hateful mouth of whom a laugh spread as he said :

'Fools ! The bodachs of Angus, the men of the Mearns, the Whelps of the Black Bitch, and the Souters of Selkirk— yea, even the canny folk of Aberdeen—are in arms against you, and yet ye hope for victory !   I am now a Stirling laird, duly infeft and seized with earth and stone.   Well, well ! they laugh merrily who laugh the last.   A little more of Henry's gold, and my fortune is made !   In the battle of to-morrow, a crown will be lost and won ; and I shall gain a thousand *crowns* if I can bear to Berwick Gate sure tidings of King James's death !   *The yellow plume—the yellow plume,*— I shall watch for it in yonder field to-morrow as one who is d——d watches for the first blink of redemption ! '

CHAPTER XXXIII.

THE GREY HORSE.

THE morning of June 11, 1488, rose brightly over Stirling and its magnificent scenery.

Almost with dawn, tidings reached King James that the insurgent nobles, at the head of a vast force, had left Falkirk some hours before daybreak, and were on their march through the Torwood to attack him. The unfortunate monarch now found himself peculiarly situated.

His Castle of Stirling, the only adjacent place of security in case of reverse, was closed against him; while the nobles as they marched by the old Roman road which ran through the recesses of the Torwood, barred the only route to the capital. Thus, in the event of defeat, James could turn nowhere for succour but to the admiral's boats at the Craigward, as arranged by the faithful Falconer.

He summoned a council of his chiefs—Montrose, Glencairn, Menteith, Ruthven, Semple, the Preceptor of Torphichen, and others; and they were unanimously of opinion that he should commit their cause and fortunes to the hazard of a battle. Immediately on this decision being come to, the steep streets and old fantastic alleys and wynds of Stirling echoed to the brattle of drums, the clang of trumpets, the twang of Border horns, and the yelling of the mountain pipe, as the royal troops, horse and foot, spearmen, archers, and knights—all sheathed in mail, with horses richly trapped; burgesses and yeomen in splinted jacks, steel gloves, and morions; and clansmen with their long linked lurichs, tuaghs, and two-handed swords, marched past its walls and barrier-ports, by the ancient road, which then, as now, led towards the rampart that extended from the Forth to the Clyde, and advanced eastward in three heavy columns, all animated by enthusiasm for the royal cause, and by the highest spirit and determination.

At that time the insurgents were passing the Carron, so

famed of old in our Highland songs and Lowland history as
the scene of many a bloody contest with ' the kings of the
world ; ' for there the wings of their pride were shorn, and the
line of their conquests marked for ever by the swords of
the Scottish Gael.

The vast extent of the Torwood—the Sylvæ Caledonia of
antiquity—and all the foliaged hills that rise around the
' Bulwark of the North,' were clad in the richness of their
summer beauty. The air was laden with perfume exhaled
from the waving woods and teeming earth ; the sky was
without a cloud, save where a few specks of gold or fleecy
white floated in the distant east. The dew was glittering on
everything, from the topmost leaves of the Torwood's
giant oaks to the little mary-flower and red-eyed daisy that
grew below them. All nature seemed fresh and bright and
beautiful. The wild violet and the mountain roses that grew
thickly by the wayside scented the air, and its purity was
enchanting. It seemed rather a morning for a merry hunting
or hawking party, than the stern debate of Scottish civil
war ; and as pipe and trumpet, with the tramp of barbed
horses and the tread of heavily-armed men, rang on the
pavement of the Roman Via, and awoke the leafy echoes of
the forest, the wild erne screamed in the oaken glade, and the
cushat dove fled from the hateful sound.

After hearing mass in the Dominican church, and confessing himself to Henry, Abbot of Cambuskenneth, the king
mounted his horse amid a flourish of trumpets. He was a
peaceful and amiable prince—one more suited to our own
civilized time than that age of blood and cold iron ; and thus
he felt somewhat unused to the ponderous but gorgeous suit
of armour in which he was cased and riveted ; and all un-
cheered by the enthusiasm around him, the flashing of arms,
and the braying of martial music, as the drums and fifes, horns
and trumpets, of Lord Bothwell's guard (first embodied by
James II.), played merrily,

> Cou thou the rashes greene O,

or by the historical memories of the ground over which he
marched, for the Scottish Marathon lay close at hand ; he
rode silently and moodily on, with his helmet closed, to
conceal the tears that came unbidden to his eyes, as he
thought of his dead wife, his son's desertion, the unjust
accusations against him, and the coming slaughter which
nothing but his own death could perhaps avert.

'Another hour will bring us in sight of the foe,' said the old Duke of Montrose, whose armour was richly ornamented, though somewhat old-fashioned ; for his head-piece had the oreillets and long spike worn in the days of Murdoch, the Regent Duke of Albany, and his horse was gaily housed in his colours ; *gules*, a fess checque *argent* and *azure*, the bearings of the Lindesays of Crawford ; ' and in one hour after that, your Majesty will find yourself enabled to punish and repay the treason of Sauchie. I would give my best barony to see his head rolling on the Gowling Hill of Stirling !'

'Time will show, duke,' said James, with a sigh. 'God wot, I have no wish to shed the blood of my people ; but I never liked this Laird of Sauchie ; his soul was an abyss, and I never could fathom his thoughts.'

'His chief friend and follower—a man named Hew Borthwick—was in Stirling last night, disguised in a friar's frock. This man is a spy and traitor ; yet he escaped us, and took the eastern road, doubtless to tell what he has seen ; and for all the Howe of Angus, I would not have lost that fellow's head.'

'Borthwick ! have I not heard that name before ?'

'Doubtless ; he is a well-known bully, pimp, and brawler, who hovers about the discontented lords.'

'Is he well-born ?'

'Hell-born would be nearer truth, if rumour pedigrees him right,' replied Montrose ; 'but what aileth your majesty ?' he asked, perceiving the king to shudder so much that the joints of his armour rattled.

'A *grue* came over me,' said the poor king, and Montrose was silent, for neither were above the superstitions of the time ; and in Scotland people still believe that an involuntary shudder is caused either by a spirit passing near or when we tread upon the ground which is to be our grave.

A shout, a clamorous hurrah from the vanguard, announced that the foe was in sight ; and as the king, with his forces, debouched from the Torwood, he came in view of the long array of his insurgent lords ; and Falconer, who rode with the royal guard, shook his lance aloft in fierce ecstasy, as he thought the moment was now approaching when he might meet Hailes and Home, singly or together, in close and mortal combat.

The insurgents were posted at the bridge over the Carron, and were formed in three strong columns, the whole strength of which has been variously stated, for their exact number has never been ascertained. Some historians have estimated them at one hundred and eighty thousand, which is doubtless a great exaggeration. Their force, however, was sufficiently formidable to appal the mind of the heart-broken king.

The Lords Hailes and Home commanded the first column, which was composed of the men of Berwickshire and East Lothian; and Falconer's quick eye soon distinguished the chevron of the first and the green banner of the second, with its yellow lion waving above the flower of the Scottish spearmen.

With this body rode the traitor Borthwick, armed like a simple knight, and wearing a close helmet.

The second column was composed of the fierce clans of Galloway and the hardy Bordermen from the Liddel, the Annan, the Tweed, and the Teviot, all clad in jacks of splinted steel, with long lances and two-handed swords, well mounted, and ranged under the terrible Red Heart of Angus—the banner of a thousand battles, a thousand crimes and glories!

In the third column, led by the Lord High Constable, were the men of the central Lowlands (under the nominal command of the Duke of Rothesay), and in this column the insurgents had the hardihood to display the royal standard of the kingdom. Lord Drummond, the Steward of Menteith, Sir Patrick Gray, the Forester of Drum, Sir William Stirling of Keir, Sir James Shaw, who had come from Stirling Castle with many more malcontent noblesse, were around the prince, as guards and spies upon his conduct.

The aspect of these long triple lines as they stood in order of battle by the banks of the Carron, with their deep masses of long spears that vibrated like the stalks of a ripe cornfield, their many silken standards waving in the wind, and all their bright harness shining in the meridian sun, as knight and noble galloped from troop to troop and band to band, was too formidable to leave the unhappy king the shadow of a hope that he could ever come to an amicable arrangement with them, which he would gladly have done had his forces been the most numerous.

He formed his little army of thirty thousand men into four columns. The first was commanded by the aged Earl of Menteith, under whom were the banners and vassals of the Lords Erskine, Gray, Ruthven, Graham, and Maxwell; the second was led by the Earl of Glencairn, and consisted chiefly of the western clans ; the third was led by the Lord Boyd and the young Lord Lindesay, who carried the gauntlet of Angus on his spear.

The main body, in which was the royal guard under Lord Bothwell, was led by the king and Montrose. It consisted principally of men from Fife, Angus, and Stormont. In front were the Great Lion and a few other pieces of cannon. James III. rode at the head, distinguished above all around him by the loftiness of his stature, the brilliancy of his armour, the collar of the Thistle, and his towering *yellow plume*.

On both sides all were well armed according to the fashion of the time and country, for the Scots excelled in the manufacture of weapons ; and at that time every gentleman possessing ten pounds' worth of land was compelled to have a complete suit of harness, with sword, spear, and dagger ; every yeoman, a basinet, steel gloves, bow, shafts and buckler, sword and dirk. From an early period the nation were good gunners ; they first used cannon in the war against the English in the year 1340 ; and in after years the Parliament ordered that every proprietor whose lands were a hundred pounds of new extent should provide a hack-but, while every hundred-merk-land should equip two field-pieces ; consequently, the nobles had plenty of cannon in this fatal field of Sauchieburn.

As the lines were approaching each other, the faithful Lord Lindesay of the Byres rode up to the king, attended by an esquire who led a grey horse of beautiful proportions— one which was deemed unrivalled in Scotland for beauty, strength, and fleetness. ' I beg,' said he, ' that your Majesty will accept of this steed from me ; should we lose this eventful field—which God and St. Andrew avert—your Majesty may fully trust your sacred life to this animal's agility and sureness of foot ; for if you can but keep your saddle, my favourite grey will never fail you.'

' He has been carefully bred,' said the Duke of Montrose, ' and possesses the fifty-four gifts of a good horse.'

' Fifty-four, Duke ? ' reiterated the king, stroking the fiery animal as it pressed on the powerful curb, and caracoled from side to side ; ' on my faith, a goodly number.'

' Examine him, please your Majesty,' continued the handsome young donor, throwing up his umbriere ; ' he hath a woman's breast, with a lion's courage ; the eye of a bull with the patience of a sheep ; the strength of a Spanish mule, with the fleetness of a Scottish deer ; and the ears of a wolf ! You will find him no cutter of gowans. Keep his head well up, and, by the faith of Lindesay, he will never fail under you ! '

How fatal a gift this fiery horse proved will be shown in the sequel.

CHAPTER XXXIV.

THE BATTLE OF SAUCHIEBURN.

THE hostile lines were drawing nearer and more near ; the shouts of the wild clansmen of Galloway mingling with the slogans of the Merse-men, who shouted, ' A Home ! a Home ! ' were borne on the wind across the fertile fields that lay between the approaching columns.

A loud report pealed upon the stillness of the sky. It was the Great Lion, a ball from which made a gap in the ranks of the foe ; others followed from a green knoll on which the royal culveriniers had posted themselves, but slowly and laboriously, for the gunners of the fifteenth century were somewhat less expert than those of our own day. James gazed fixedly and anxiously at the insurgent bands. He was looking for the prince, his eldest son.

' No victory can come to a heart filled with dark forebodings such as mine,' said he to Montrose. The Duke's reply was lost in the hollow of his helmet.

' No doubt young Rothesay is surrounded by a flattering crowd, all anxious to hail him as *James IV.*'

' Ah, say not so, sire,' said the faithful old peer, with a sigh ; ' yet such, alas, is perhaps the fate of kings.'

' The fate of kings ! thou thinkest so ?—to see their own flesh and blood rise in rebellion up against them,' replied James, incoherently ; ' yet is there not an old proverb—a prophecy—which says—what said it ? '

Montrose did not reply.

' What said it ? ' repeated James, impatiently.

' That in Scotland *This year a lion shall be slain by its whelps.*'

The king grew pale as death, for at that moment the wind blew out the banner of the third division of the insurgents and above their long lines of shining helmets he recognized his own imperial flag, with the red lion rampant in its golden field

'If I this day am slain, and the boy, my son, made king,' said he, huskily, ' Scotland—Scotland—what will become of her ? Lord of St. John, doth not the scripture say, " woe unto the land whose monarch is a child ? " and my simple-hearted Rothesay is but little more in years.'

At that moment a number of arrows and caliver-shots whistled past them, and the battle began in earnest, just as the distant bell of St. Ninian's Church tolled twelve.

The scene of this sanguinary encounter was the tract of land now known as Little Canglar, upon the east side of a brook called the Sauchieburn, about two miles from Stirling. A number of weeping-willows—called in Scotland sauch-trees —drooped over the water, and gave a name to the place, as they did to Sir James Shaw's barony. The birds were carolling aloft in the blue welkin ; the air was pure, the sunshine bright and warm ; the fragrance of the flowers and bearded grass was wafted on the soft summer wind ; the mavis sang among the pale green sauches, and the cushat dove sent up its cry from the Torwood shady oaks. Grey Stirling, the wooded brow of Craigh-forth, and the Ochil peaks, rose on the north, all mellowed in the summer mist ; all nature looked beautiful and smiling ; but herd and hirsel fled as the brass cannon opened on the adverse lines, and the shout and shock of the furious onset made the poor shepherd who stood afar off on the lone hill-side hold his breath and bend his head in prayer—for when Scot met Scot, right well he knew how deadly and how deep would be the sacrilegious slaughter !

The king's vanguard, which was of course composed of his own clan, the gallant Stewarts and other Highlanders, armed with swords, long daggers, bows, and axes, led by John Stewart, Earl of Athole,—the conqueror of the Lord of the Isles—rushed upon the insurgents with a loud yell, such as can only rise from a Celtic throat. This attack was well supported by the king's left wing, composed of five thousand Perthshire spearmen, led by Lord Ruthven.

The Merse-men met them with their levelled lances— those pikes so terrible in warlike annals, ' six Scottish ells in length,' and an awful conflict took place ; while the shouts of ' A Home ! a Home !' on one side, and the shrill cathghairn of the Athole Stewarts, were often turned into the shriek of agony or the groan of death, as the lance was thrust through the Highland lurich, or the claymore found a passage through the Lowland jack ; while weapons broke and throats were

grasped and daggers driven through plate and mail, through
plaid and buff, or the swaying axe splits helmets of tempered
steel and targets of tough bull's-hide like withered nutshells.

'The first charge was valiantly given,' says Drummond of
Hawthornden, 'launce meeting with launce; so the vanguard
of the lords began to yield ground, and was strongly repulsed.'

The men of West Lothian shot showers of arrows, to which
the Highland archers replied; and for a few minutes the
air was darkened by the passing flights, while men fell fast
on both hands, and pressing on, pikemen and archers came
closing up on every side with axe and sword, till a deadly
and disastrous *mêlée* began between the royalists and insurgents, who rushed upon each other like two torrents broken
loose.

On one side was the poor bewildered king, driven forward
with this armed tide, confused, sorrowful, and irresolute,
with the royal standard borne over his head by the Constable of Dundee; on the other was the heir of Scotland,
agitated also by painful irresolution, by remorse and shame,
and also having the royal standard above him, but surrounded
by a brilliant band of nobles, all shining in polished steel,
gold, plumage, and embroidery; and towards that quarter
of the enemy's line, young Ramsay, Lord of Bothwell, at
the head of the royal guard, made incredible exertions to hew
a passage for the purpose of ridding the king, with his own
hand, of as many high-born traitors as possible.

James sat motionless on his magnificent grey charger,
with this forest of lances and sea of helmets flashing
round him; and not one blow did he strike, but kept his
eyes fixed with a species of despair on the banner of his son.

Conspicuous among the press of rebel lords and vassals
towered the gigantic Earl of Angus, mounted on a powerful
Clydesdale horse, and clad in fluted mail, his vizor up, and a
profusion of beautiful feathers streaming from his helmet
almost to the crupper of his steed. Aloft his mailed hand
brandished, with deadly execution, a sword which for length
and strength few men could wield, and he sent his voice
before him like a trumpet; thus it needed not the scarlet
heart on his golden surcoat to proclaim the terrible Angus
—the representative of his lord and chief, the captive Earl of
Douglas.

By one blow he drove the Earl of Glencairn through casque
and gorget to the breast, and still pressing forward—

'On, on, my wild men of Galloway!' he cried: 'a Douglas! a Douglas! on, on, for I have sworn to ride through this rabble rout *red wat shod and mair*' (i.e., above the feet in blood).

'See ye the Lord Angus, with his helmet open?' cried Sir David Falconer, to a Highland bowman; 'shoot, my brave Celt, with a will!'

The Gael—a MacRobert of Struan—shot an arrow, which glanced off the helmet of Angus.

'Shoot again,' exclaimed Falconer; ''sdeath, fellow, wert thou a king's archer, I would hang thee in thine own bowstring for such a glee'd shot.'

Again the Atholeman shot, and slew the standard-bearer of Angus instead of his lord.

Undaunted by the terrible aspect of this potent and herculean lord, many knights and gentlemen of the royal army pressed over the crowd of shrieking men and falling horses—over all the wild débris of a hand-to-hand combat to reach him; but the most successful was Ramsay of Balmain, captain of the guard, and recently created Lord Bothwell. Though young, slight, and athletic, he rushed upon the formidable Angus, and intent only on killing him, rained his blows thick and fast upon the coat of fluted armour, from which the sparks of fire were driven by every stroke.

'False fool and plebeian villain!' said the disdainful Angus, parrying the blows skilfully with his long Banffshire blade; 'methinks ye seem better used to the porridge spurtle than the knightly sword—but die, fellow, die! 'tis the hand of an earl that slays thee,' he cried, as his long weapon found entrance under the left pass-guard of Bothwell's armour, and pierced him to the heart. With a wild cry he fell into the seething mass of death and life below. 'Next time you meet me in Stirling streets, false loon, you will not pass me unveiled, I wot,' added Angus, as he pressed on, cleaving helmets like pippins, and shredding away the tough ash-spears like reeds by a winter brook.

'My God—my God—look on me!' cried the poor king, on seeing this terrible episode, which, more than the thousand others occurring round him, cut him to the soul. Intent on avenging his many wrongs on this imperious rebel, he now for the first time that day drew his sword and put spurs to his horse; but a furious rush of mounted men-at-arms, on both sides, separated them hopelessly.

These were led by Home and Hailes, who, having recognized Falconer, though in plain armour, by the silver falcon which adorned his helmet, and had a knot of scarlet and yellow ribbons in its beak, pressed on to slay him; while the wretched Borthwick, with Sir James Shaw, Sir Patrick Gray and Sir William Stirling of the Keir, disdaining all such humble antagonists, reserved alike their swords and strength for the king, whom the arch-traitor, their tool, had already indicated by the yellow plume in his head-piece; and towards him, and him only, they pressed surely and warily on.

Falconer, by one stroke, cut the reins of Lord Hailes's horse and so rid himself of one enemy; by another blow he struck Lord Home's casque from his head; yet, bareheaded and half-blinded by pride and fury, the noble pressed on, standing high in his stirrups, and showering blows on every side.

'A Home! a Home! By Saint Anne, fellow,' cried he, 'thou hadst better been tending the sheep on yon brae side than here in knight's armour.'

'Better for you, perhaps, my Lord of Home,' said Falconer, as by one skilful thrust, full upon the tempered gorget, he shot him out of his saddle on the heap of men below.

'*Gang warily!*' thundered a voice in his ear, and now the vengeful sword of one whom he trembled to encounter— old Lord Drummond—was flourished above him.

Covering himself, parrying thrusts and warding blows, poor Falconer sought only to escape from an antagonist whom he dared not assail, and for whose safety he would have laid down his life—for he was the father of Sybilla. But the fiery blood of the old noble was at boiling heat; he had seen 'this skipper's son' defeat two chiefs of name, to whom he had promised his daughters, and a storm of feudal pride and aristocratic hatred of the king's humble favourite was swelling up within him, and the arquebussier would undoubtedly have been slain, had not Drummond of Mewie, who was hewing away on foot, with a Lochaber axe, hamstrung his horse; and as the snorting animal sank under him, Falconer fell heavily to the earth. His armour protected him from serious injury, but the horses of Borthwick, Shaw, Gray, and Keir, as these worthies spurred on, trampled him down; thus he was stunned, and became unconscious of all that passed over and around him.

A deadly conflict, hand to hand and horse to horse, ensued around the unhappy king, as these four infernal spirits

followed by a thousand others, all superbly mounted and
accoutred, left the Duke of Rothesay far in the rear; and
though archers and pikemen, troopers and knights, nobles
and burgesses, pressed on with straining eyes and noisy
tongues, with swords flashing and uplifted, to kill, to capture,
or to overbear the most hapless monarch, save one, that ever
sat upon the Scottish throne, the four ruffians were ever the
nearest to him, but failed to reach him; for old Montrose,
Lindesay, and all the loyalists fought nobly in a circle round
the yellow plume; and there fell by James's side the Lord
Erskine, who was slain by a Drummond; Sir Thomas Semple
of Eliotstoun, who was pierced through the heart by a Border
spear; William Lord Ruthven, the heritable sheriff of
Perth; the Laird of Innes; Alexander Scott, director of
the chancery, whose head was carried off by a cannon-ball,
and many more gentlemen, with their friends and followers.
The royal standard was beaten down and its bearer unhorsed; the cannon—the Great Lion—and all the ensigns
were taken, and when the sun of that long summer day was
sinking behind the Grampians, and the shadows of the
Torwood were deepening on the plain, the king's troops,
overborne by numbers, after a long and gallant conflict,
gave way, and a total and irreparable rout ensued.

'God help your Majesty,' said the young Lord Lindesay,
as, pale, excited, without a helmet, and with his face
streaked by blood, he took the king's by the bridle;
'the day is lost, yet all is not lost with it while your
sacred life is safe. No horse in the field can overtake
this grey I gave you. Ride—ride north, and swiftly—the
admiral's boats await you at the Craigward—farewell!'

'Ay, farewell, Lindesay—a long farewell to Scotland and to
thee—for France or Holland now must be my home.'

Thus urged, and knowing that alone and unattended he
might escape more easily and unnoticed, than if followed
by a train, James turned his grey horse's head towards the
north, and gladly left behind that bloody and corpse-
incumbered plain.

Thousands of arrows, with their feathers uppermost,
planted all the turf around him; here the earth was torn
by hoofs, and there it was furrowed by cannon-shot. Men
and horses, dead or wounded, or writhing and dying, lay
singly or in piles and heaps together, among a vast débris
of broken helmets, torn standards, and bloody pennons,
splintered spears, swords, scarfs, and bucklers, near the

260 THE 'YELLOW FRIGATE.'

Sauchieburn, which yet gurgled placidly along under its pale green willows, as the king leaped his fiery and unwearied horse over it, and with a breaking heart rode towards the banks of the Forth, while night and sorrow descended together on that disastrous field. On, on he rode with a breaking heart, as he hoped, unnoticed and unknown—but hoped in vain; for close behind, and tracking him like blood-hounds, as history tells us, were Sir Patrick of Kyneff, Sir James of Sauchie, Stirling of Keir, and Borthwick, the apostate monk of Dunblane.

CHAPTER XXXV.

UNDER the Duke of Montrose, Lindesay his son, the Earls of Mar, Athole, and others, the main body of James's forces retired slowly through the Torwood, by the old Roman Way, still fighting with obstinate valour, and protracting the struggle until the long and lingering eve of June had faded into night, and darkness spread a veil over the horrors of the battle, when the royalists, as usual with all hastily collected levies, retired into the mountains, and disbanded.

The victorious lords, with the young prince still in their possession, passed that night near the field, and next day marched to the town and palace of Linlithgow.

The moon was shining in the summer sky, when Sir David Falconer freed himself from the bodies of three slain men, who lay heavily and coldly above him ; rising from the field, he was able to look after his own safety—for many of the border prickers were hovering abroad in search of rings and jewels, or gold-handled daggers and embroidered belts. A body lay near him sheathed in bright armour ; its gauntleted hands clutched the earth, the vizor of the casque was up, and the dead man's eyes glared horribly in the pale moonlight. Between his teeth were some blades of grass, which, when dying, he had bitten in his agony. On his breast sparkled the diamond jewel of the Thistle—for this was the corpse of Alexander Cunningham, the noble Earl of Glencairn. This brave warrior lay above the blue silk banner of his house, charged with its shakefork *sable*—the same pennon which his bride, fair Margaret of Hailes, had woven for his lance in their Castle of Kilmaurs.

Most of the wounded had been removed by their friends or by the merciful ; others had been speared by the moss-troopers of Hailes, Home, and Buccleuch ; thus, thick as grain on a harvest field, the bodies of the dead—white-visaged, and gleaming blue in their coats of mail—strewed all the plain ; but they were quiet and still as the leafy woods or the azure sky of that sweet summer night.

Ignorant of where the royal forces had retreated, and anxious only to ascertain the fact of the King's safety—of which he had great doubts on beholding the number of the guard who were lying dead three and four deep, and whom he knew easily by their scarlet surcoats trimmed with yellow,— and being anxious to rejoin the frigate, Falconer arose with difficulty, and after refreshing himself by a draught of pure water from the Sauchieburn at a place *above* where the dead lay in it, he took his way towards the north, and fortunately found a stray horse saddled and bridled, grazing in a field, near the gate of which its rider, a trooper, with the laurel of the Grahams in his morion, lay dead. This animal with great docility permitted Falconer to seize the reins and leap on his back ; thus mounted, he soon left the fatal field behind, and rode through the scattered oaks of the Torwood towards the ferry by which the Forth was crossed opposite Alloa.

The whole country appeared deserted ; he saw no one, and heard not even a dog bark ; thus the stillness became oppressive after the storm of war, the strife of wounds and agony, the carnage and horrors of the day that was past. He soon reached the boor-tree thickets at the Craigward, and saw the beautiful river with the Clackmannan hills and old Alloa rise before him in the moonlight, with the King's ships at anchor in the stream, with courses loose and a spring upon their cables. Half a bow-shot from the beach were several well-oared boats, full of armed men, and by their garb Falconer recognized his own arquebussiers and the King's seamen, while the royal standard drooped from the boats' sterns, and swept the water.

' Ho—boat yoho ! ' cried he, leaping from his horse.

' David Falconer, at last ! ' cried a number of distant voices, as the oars dipped, and the boat shot in. ' Welcome in safety, messmate o' mine,' said the bluff admiral, who was clad in his helmet and suit of steel ; ' we heard you had parted your cable in yonder devilish field.'

' Only unhorsed, Sir Andrew.'

' Any planks stove in, or timbers started ? '

' None, thank Heaven ! though I received a blow that must have killed me, had I not——'

' Like most Scotsmen in these troublous times, been well used to cuts and blows,' interrupted Barton. ' So the battle was fairly fought ? '

'Yea, fairly as the Ball of Scone, as the saw hath it—fairly fought and most unhappily lost. Alas! yonder field of battle is the very Garden of Death!'

'And what of the king?' asked several voices.

'The king—is he not on board the *Yellow Frigate?*'

'No,' said the admiral; 'I would to God he were, for then he would be in safe anchoring ground. Which way did he ride?'

'I know not, for I fell by his side in the middle of the battle——'

'Happy thou, my good Falconer, to share that day's vengeance with the king,' said the admiral; 'but that I had other ropes to splice, I had assuredly been with thee. Well?'

'The Lord Lindesay gave him a horse of matchless blood and speed, whereon, if evil happened or the day were lost, he might reach you here at the Craigward——'

'We have never sighted him once, though many a fugitive hath crossed, for we have been little better than ferrymen since the gloaming fell. The auld Earl of Menteith, in his battered harness; the Preceptor of Torphichen, with three other knights of Rhodez; and many of the Ogilvies, as we knew by their tartan plaids and the hawthorn in their helmets; and Murrays, with the juniper twig;—most of them pricked with spears or slashed by sword cuts, have we taken across the river; but nought have we seen of the king, though the Preceptor averred that he saw him ride towards the north.'

'What if he should have fallen from the Lindesay's fiery steed, and now be lying in the Torwood?'

'St. Mary avert it!' said Falconer. 'Yet, when I bethink me now, I saw more than one dead man, lying in his armour on the sward, between this and the field.'

'Sayest thou so?' exclaimed the admiral, leaping lightly ashore, despite his years, and rotundity, 'and we are loitering here like so many hag-ridden lubbers! Barton, do thou keep the boats here for us; and, Falconer, take twenty of thine arquebussiers and come with me; we'll bear up towards the battlefield a little way, and see if aught may be descried of the king; come on shore with your flasks, forks and arque-busses, heave a-head, my men, and quickly.'

The soldiers hastened up the bank, and Falconer would have resigned his horse to the admiral, but the latter declined, saying 'that he always lost some of his outer-sheathing when perched on horseback.' So Sir David drew his sword, and led the way back to the field of battle.

They marched three or four miles without finding any trace of him they sought. At last the sound of hoofs was heard near the milltown of Bannock.

'Hist—tarry a bit,' said the admiral. 'Lie to, sirs.'

'Halt!' cried Falconer, in a soldierly tone; 'plant your forks and wind up your spanners! Be ready to fire at a moment's notice.'

Four heavily-armed horsemen, all riding furiously, the last, however, a long way behind his companions, dashed along the road, and though repeatedly required to stop, they rode recklessly on, with their armour flashing, the horsehoofs striking fire, and disappeared among the Torwood oaks.

'Fire on the sternmost, and make him bring to,' cried the admiral, angrily; 'throw a shot across his forefoot.'

An arquebussier fired: the bullet whistled close to the horseman's casque, and panting and breathless he reined up, while his horse plunged and reared fearfully. 'Hallo! haul taut your reins or braces! don't miss stays!' said the admiral.

'From whence come you, sir?' asked Falconer, confronting him.

'From the field, as you may see,' he replied, showing a drawn dagger in his right hand.

'Know you aught of the king?'

The other gave a diabolical laugh. 'Elsewhere I have heard that laugh!' said the admiral, advancing a step with his Jedwood axe in his hand.

'Are you not the Admiral Wood?'

'Yes; and thou——'

'Sir Hew Borthwick, at your service.'

'Villain!' began Falconer; but the admiral stayed him.

'Saw ye the king to-day?'

'Yes—and moreover I saw him not a minute since.'

'Where—where?'

'In yonder mill.'

'And is he there now?'

'No,' replied the subtle assassin; 'he is one of yonder horsemen before me, and now rides hard to reach the *Yellow Frigate*.'

'Say ye so;—about ship, my lads, and after him,' said the admiral, as they hastily began to retrace their steps; while Borthwick, driving spurs into his horse, with a shout —but whether of fear or triumph it is impossible to say— dashed along the road after his three comrades.

The dagger in his hand was wet with James's blood!

On regaining the Craigward, the admiral and his companions found that they had been deceived, for neither the king nor any one else had approached the ferry since they had left it.

Many days passed away, yet no tidings were heard of the unfortunate king.

CHAPTER XXXVI.

THE MILL ON THE BANNOCK.

ALL unaware that he was singled out and tracked, James rode from that lost battle-field at a rapid trot, to reach the boats of Sir Andrew Wood; and every sound that rose from the Roman Way and woke the echoes of the Torwood —every shout and random shot of cannon or of hand-gun, made his heart vibrate and leap within him; for even as his own children did this good king love the people of his kingdom. His heart was full of prayer and sorrow, and the resolution which he had so often announced, of retiring to the court of his ally, Charles VIII., was now stronger than ever within him. As he thought of this, his saddened spirit rose, and he felt soothed by the beauty of the evening. The gorgeous sunset shot upward with a thousand golden rays behind the green peaks of the fertile Ochils, piercing the saffron clouds like veils of shining gauze; the giant oaks of the Torwood, many of them thirty or forty feet in circumference were rustling their heavy foliage; the solemn Scottish firs were shaking their wiry cones; and the perfume of the wild Gueldre roses loaded the evening air.

The coo of the cushat dove, the plashing of the Bannock under its pale green sauch-trees and white-blossomed hawthorns, the rocks spotted with grey lichens and green moss, the flowers, the birds, the foliage, the blue sky, the balmy air, and the beautiful mountains, all spoke to the poor king of his native home and that beloved Scotland which he had now resolved to leave for ever; and as he approached the Bannockburn he leaped the grey charger—Lindesay's last and fatal gift—across from bank to bank, and it cleared them by one furious bound. This was near Beaton's Mill, which still remains about one mile east from the field.

The mill was a strongly-built and old-fashioned house with crow-stepped gables, a heavily thatched roof, deep windows obscured by flour; a square ingle-lum, over which the green ivy clustered, stood at one end, while its huge wooden wheel revolved merrily at the other. Its snug and quiet aspect made the king think, with a sigh (as he shortened his reins and rode on), how much the contented and unambitious life of the occupant was to be envied.

Now it happened most unfortunately that Mysie Beaton, the gudewife of the Milltoun, was filling a pitcher with water from the dam; and on seeing an armed knight riding at full speed towards her, she uttered a shriek of terror and tossed away the tin vessel, which clattered noisily along the road, while she fled into her cottage adjoining the mill.

Terrified by the rolling pitcher and the foolish woman's sudden cry, the fiery grey horse swerved furiously round and threw his royal rider heavily on the road, close to one of those boor-trees hedges which generally in those days enclosed old gardens and barnyards in Scotland.

Gawain Beaton, the miller, a stout ruddy man about forty years of age, clad in a buckram gaberdine, which, like his beard and bonnet, was whitened by flour and meal, sprang to the door on hearing his wife cry and the armour clatter.

' Deevil mend thee, Mysie ! ' said he, angrily ; ' for thine eldritch scraigh hath scared the horse and slain this comely gentleman ! '

' Oh ! I trow not,' said the woman, in great terror.

' Weel may ye trow sae,' said the miller, in some consternation on beholding the excessive richness of the king's armour ; ' for if his vassals come this gate they will level the mill to its grundstane ; we shall tyne our a', and hae to flee like maukins when the bratches are on the bent.'

' Rise, sir—oh ! rise ; for the love of St. Mary and St. Ringan say where are ye hurt ? ' cried the miller's wife, kneeling down by the prostrate man ; but there came no reply from him, though she placed her ear close to the barred umbriere of the closed helmet.

' Hoolie,' said the honest miller to his buxom wife, from whose usually pink cheeks the roses had now fled and left them white as her coif of Mary of Gueldres' time ; ' Hoolie, gudewife, see ye nocht the knicht is feckless and weak ? Let us bear him in ayont the hallan, and get ye the flask of usquebaugh and mak' him a milk posset.'

While the fatal steed was galloping over the Carse, the miller and his wife raised the body of the inanimate man ; and bearing him in, closed the mill-door, carefully secured

its tirling-pin, and laid him on their humble box-bed ; and
then while the kind and sympathizing Mysie busied herself in
making up a posset, the miller, her husband, undid the clasps
of the gorget and the back and breast-plates, removing
them all after taking off the helmet, which he did with ease,
as it was opened simply by throwing up the metonniere
which guarded the chin and throat, and which turned on
the same screw with the vizor.

On doing this the miller saw a pale and handsome face,
surrounded by thick, dark clustering hair, and a well-trimmed
beard ; but the stranger was still senseless, and a streak of
blood was flowing from his mouth. On beholding so much
manly beauty, the sympathy and remorse of the miller's
wife were greatly increased ; and on her knees she took the
gauntlets off his hands and assisted Gawain to chafe them,
and to lave the patient's brow with cool water which he
brought from the Bannock in a black leather jack, about
sixteen inches high ; and then slowly the object of their
care began to revive.

' Eh ! sirs—oh ! sirs—St. Mary sain us !—to see that
comely face sae pale and sad)' exclaimed Mysie ; ' oh !
withered be my tongue for uttering that doolfu' cry ! '

' And dule it may bring to us, Mysie, my doo,' said the
miller ; ' if some o' his lances pass this way—for his friends
may slaughter us, or their enemies may slaughter him—
for we kenna whether he fought this sorrowfu' day for the
king—whom God bless—or the black-hearted nobles ; but
his degree is doubtless high ; look at that armour, Mysie ;
ilka stud on't is pure gold, and the diamonds shine like
stars on his baldrick and dudgeon knife ! '

' Alake, alake ! ' mourned Mysie, who deemed herself the
source of all, and whose sympathies were more and more
excited by the apparent rank of the unknown ; ' the sicht
o' this winsome gentleman wi' his silken hair bedabbled in
bluid wad melt the heart o' a nether mill-stone.'

' 'Od, Mysie, I ken mine is loupin like a mill happer, and
I wuss we were weel clear o' this ravelled hesp.'

' And some fair lady in Lawder or Angus will be sitting
on the tower-head wi' a fan in her hand, looking sadly owre
moss and muirland for you, my puir sir,' said Mysie, passing
her hand timidly and kindly through James's silky hair.
And now his sense began to rally. ' I am richt glad,
Gawain dear, I hid *your* steel bonnet and harness this
morning——'

'And kepit me frae fechting for our noble king—mair shame to you, Mysie lass.'

'Thanks, good people, thanks,' murmured their patient, rising up slowly on his elbow, and gazing about him with sad and heavy eyes. He passed a hand across his damp and blood-stained brow, and looked again at the low-roofed and clay-floored cottage, with its bunkers or window-seats, its fir ambres and girnels, its Scottish fauldstools and wide fire-place, before which lay the half of a cart-wheel as a fender, and within which, though the month was June, there blazed a fire of turf and bog-fir under a huge three-legged kail-pot that hung on one of those wooden crocans, or crooks (last used in the Hebrides), and then he turned again with surprise to his attendants. 'Honest people, accept my thanks, I pray you, for this great kindness—but say, where am I?'

'In the milltoun o' Bannock, gentle sir,' said Mysie, making a low courtesy.

'How far from this day's field of sorrow?'

'Little mair than a mile, sir.'

'He *is* a king's man,' said the miller, with satisfaction.

'And who, gudeman, are you?' he asked with mild dignity.

'Gawain Beaton, a puir miller, at your honour's service,' said the host, removing his dusty bonnet; 'and this is Mysie, my gudewife, sir.'

'Here, then, I am safe. Thank God, I have not fallen among those who boast of gentle blood and heraldic blazonry,' replied the other, while his eyes flashed.

'Gentle bluid—I dinna understand ye, sir. I am a far awa' cousin o' the Beatons o' Balfour,' said Gawain, proudly.

'What, art thou, too, infected by this absurdity? But, Gawain Beaton, and thou, too, gudewife, if I live, shall find this service faithfully and thankfully remembered; but I fear me my days cannot be many now, for that fall from my horse has been a dreadful shock to me.'

'Oh, say, gentle sir, what can we do for you,' said Mysie. 'Command us—we are at your bidding.'

'Then get me a priest, that I may confess.'

'There is none nearer than Cambuskenneth or St. Ninian's Kirk,' said Gawain, taking his walking-staff and dagger; 'yet I can soon reach either; but may we ask your name, sir?'

'My gudeman, this day, at morn, I was YOUR KING,' said

James, with a hollow voice and sorrowful emphasis, as he sank back on the coarse box-bed.

Gawain stood as one terrified and confounded on hearing this; but Mysie, his wife, burst into tears, and wringing her hands in great fear and excitement, ran out upon the roadway as she heard hoofs approaching.

'A priest,' she cried, 'a priest, for God's love and sweet St. Mary's sake; a priest to confess the king!'

'To confess whom say ye?' cried the headmost of four armed horsemen, who, with helmets open and swords drawn, galloped up to her in the glooming.

'The king, the king, gude sirs—our puir and sakless king!'

'And where is he, gudewife?'

'Lying in our puir bed—here, in here, ayont the hallan in my gudeman's mill. Oh, sirs, for a priest!'

'Hush, woman, I am a priest,' said the first, who was no other than *Sir* Hew Borthwick, with a glance of infernal import to his three companions, as he leaped from his horse; 'lead me to the king.'

Borthwick entered the lonely mill, and his three companions, who were no other than Sir Patrick Gray of Kyneff, Sir William Stirling of Keir, and Sir James Shaw of Sauchie, after fastening their horses to the hedge without, followed him beyond the *hallan*, or wooden partition, which formed the inner apartment.

CHAPTER XXXVII.

THE REGICIDES.

THE poor miller was inexpressibly alarmed on perceiving the four armed knights enter; the richness of their armour and accoutrement impressed him still more, and he hastened to say in an explanatory manner—

'His horse threw him at our door—a wicked horse, sirs; —we have done a' we could—on my life, sirs, I assure you —my gudewife and I—that the horse——'

'Enough, enough, fellow,' said Sir Patrick Gray, gruffly. 'Stir up that fire, for this den of thine is as dark as a dungeon. Let us see where this king of ours is lying.'

Though shocked and startled by the bearing of his visitors, Gawain hastened to throw a quantity of fir-apples on the fire, where they blazed and crackled and diffused a brilliant light throughout the humble apartment, and the highly polished suits of the ruffians shone like silver as they stooped over the bed of the hapless and helpless king, who was 'covered by a coarse checked rug,' and on whom they gazed with eyes as pitiless in expression as their hearts were in feeling.

'Does your Majesty fear death?' asked Gray.

'Nay, it never was my fear, and *now* it is my only hope,' replied James, in a low voice. 'But I asked for a priest, sirs——'

'Well—here I am—a priest, though cased in iron,' said Borthwick.

'And for whom fought you to-day, false priest?'

'By the cross of Macgriddy! I fought for my own hand —as Hal o' the Wynd fought, in old King Robert's time; but I am, nevertheless, a priest—behold my tonsure—or what remains of it.'

'It is enough—even the unworthy is better than none. And you will hear my confession?'

'Yea,' answered the bantering ruffian, 'wert thou as great a clown as ever played at Hogshouther.'

'And who are ye, sirs?' asked the king, turning uneasily from this disrespectful person.

'I am William Stirling of the Keir,' hissed one through his teeth.

'And thou art the Lord Gray?' said James to a second, his brow darkening, as he saw the scarlet tabard-coat, which had a lion within its engrailed border, and was worn above the armour of the wearer.

'Nay, I am only the Lord Gray's near kinsman, and captain of your Majesty's castle at Broughty.'

'Leave me,' said James, bitterly; 'I will confess myself —and oh, bless me, father, for I have sorely sinned.'

A terrible smile spread over Borthwick's face, as he grasped his dagger, and saw the poor king, after three futile attempts to rise, sink powerlessly down on the miller's humble pallet. Gawain and his wife drew aside, awestruck and silent; Mysie held her apron to her mouth with one hand while the other clasped her husband's arm; but the Lairds of Keir, Kyneff, and Sauchie, stood a little in the background, and conferred together in whispers on what should now be done, for their minds were agitated by a slender doubt, though the viler slave of English Henry's gold felt none.

'Dost thou expect to recover?' he sneered.

'I trow I might,' sighed the poor king, 'if I had a physician.'

'How long dost thou expect to live?' he asked again, playing with his victim as a cat does with a mouse.

'Alas! priest; He who numbereth the leaves in the Torwood, and every blade of grass in the Carse of Stirling, alone can tell.'

'I never numbered either; yet I think thou'lt be a dead man in ten minutes.'

A flush passed over James's pallid brow. 'Be it so, father; the world and all its vanities are nothing now to me;— wifeless, childless,—or worse, for my own son is in arms against me; my soul hovers, as it were, between this world and the next. Oh, would, father, that I might cure my soul at the expense of my body!'

'Pythagoras——'

'He was a pagan.'

'Well, what matters it,' said Borthwick, becoming deadly pale, while his eyes gleamed with fire, and he felt himself endued with a demon's strength of mind and body, by the very magnitude of the crime he was about to commit ; ' what matters it,' he continued, drawing one of those long Scottish dirks, such as are still worn with the Highland garb ; ' Pythagoras said that the eyes could not be cured without the head, nor the head without the body, nor the body without the soul ! I am not now a priest, and cannot shrive thee ; so by this stroke—and this—*and this*—I destroy both body and soul together ! '

And with these terrible words the merciless ruffian buried his dagger ' many times,' says Lindesay of Pitscottie, in the breast of the unfortunate king, who expired without a sigh.

Thus perished James III., in his thirty-fifth year.

Terrified on beholding the committal of a deed so awful, the poor miller and his wife abandoned their mill and cottage, and fled into the recesses of the Torwood, where they lurked many days.

When they ventured to return with some of their neighbours, the body of the king was *gone*, and no trace of it remained, save the blood encrusted on the bedding where it had lain.

*   *   *   *   *   *

' Thou hast done it at last, ruffian ! ' said the grim Sir Patrick Gray ; ' such a deed hath not been seen in Scotland since that night in the Black Friary at Perth, when James I. was stabbed in Jane of Beaufort's arms. And now, sirs, what shall we do with this royal piece of carrion ? '

' Let us fire the house, and leave *it* here to be consumed,' said Shaw.

' Not a bad idea ; but then consider the alarm it would raise.'

' Let us fling it into the dam, then.'

' Nay—toss him into the adjacent fields ; there it will be found and buried as the corpse of some one slain in the battle of to-day,' said the barbarous Laird of Keir.

' Then so be it ; help me, sirs,' said Borthwick, panting fiercely as he spoke ; ' for o' my soul, dead flesh is heavy to bear. I am sorry we allowed yonder hagridden fools, the miller and his wife, to escape us, though.'

The assassin and his companions dragged the gashed and bloody corpse irreverently out upon the clay floor, and carried it in the moonlight across a neighbouring field, and there flung it into a ditch beside a thorn-hedge.

Ere he left it, Borthwick tore off the third finger of the

right hand a large signet-ring, on the native amethyst of which was engraved a vine tree, fading and withered, because the current that flowed around was supposed to be wine instead of water. This strange device, which was adopted by the king (says Abercrombie) 'when he saw his son in arms against him,' bore the legend:

Mea sic mihi prosunt,

and the wretch placed it on his own finger. They again thought of firing the cottage; but the sudden appearance of Sir Andrew Wood's party made them think of providing for their own safety.

Their interview is already related.

Keir, Kyneff, and Sauchie took the road for Linlithgow, but Borthwick rode on direct to Berwick—as the king's private signet, when transmitted to Henry VII., would be the best assurance that the King of Scotland was slain.

Had the admiral arrived fifteen minutes sooner, he might have saved James's life, and spared Scotland the disgrace of one more historical atrocity.

The house in which this cruel regicide occurred is still in existence, and is yet named *Beaton's Milne,* and the traditionary account of the murder preserved by the inhabitants of the *town* or hamlet closely resembles that given in history, and reverently the good people still lower their voices, when pointing to the corner where their king was murdered. In 1667, as a date shows, the house of Gawain Beaton had been somewhat modernized; but it yet bears the aspect of antiquity and strength.

It stands about one hundred and fifty feet eastward of the road from Stirling to Glasgow; and though thatched, is yet as snug a little dwelling as when Gawain attended the *happer* and Mysie's spinning-wheel birred by its ingle in the days of the unhappy king, James III.

CHAPTER XXXVIII.

THE HOUSE OF THE BARTONS.

THE insurgent lords had marched from Linlithgow to Leith, but had not as yet obtained possession of the capital or its fortress, which the provost and governor maintained against them. They had established themselves in the seaport, and the house of the late Sir Andrew Barton was assigned to the young Duke of Rothesay and his suite.

It was the 18th of June. The sun was as bright, the sky as blue, and the atmosphere as pure, as they ever are in that delightful month. The broad Forth, with its anchorage full of crayers, pincks, and caravels ; its green isles and winding bays—the surf-beaten rocks and fertile promontories of Fife, with the fertile shores of Lothian, were glowing in sunny light.

The seaport was still, perhaps, in its infancy, though Sir Andrew Wood, Sir Andrew Barton, Sir Alexander Mathieson, and Sir William Merrimonth, all brave knights, who received their spurs on their own decks, and who had fought their way at sea as merchant-skippers, had given to the burgh a wealth and importance such as no port in the kingdom had hitherto known ; and though its wynds, alleys, and closes were quaint, small, and irregular, with all their gable-ends towards the street, though the shore was encumbered by boats, anchors, kailyards, and gardens, where *now* broad moles of stone bulwark in the river ; and though its pier was of wood, without either lighthouse or martello tower, the stately argosies and gay caravels of these fighting merchant-traders, and of many others, gave a gay aspect to the harbour ; though, as usual still, at this season, it was the least busy time, for the Baltic ships had not returned.

At anchor in the stream, or moored beside that wooden pier, which was burned by the English, 1544, lay those quaint old merchantmen, with their basketed tops, their lofty poops, and pinck-built or square projecting sterns, which were retained until lately by some of the Leith whalers, and may yet be found among our Orkney shipping.

Leith was full of armed men ; the nobles and their forces thronged every street and alley ; their banners waved over the houses they occupied, and armour, spears, swords, and axes flashed incessantly in the sunshine, especially in the Wynd of St. Nicholas and the vicinity of the house of the Bartons. This was a lofty, strong, and turreted mansion, situated near the site of the present Custom-house, on the west bank of the Leith ; and in after years, Henry VIII. gave the admiral of England special orders to cannonade and destroy it, during Hertford's invasion.

In the hall or chamber of dais of this noble dwelling of the old merchant, whose son and heir was then on board the *Yellow Frigate*, the Duke of Rothesay was seated in council with the victorious insurgent lords ; and the splendour and luxury with which the enterprising trader (a man far in advance of them in ' the march of intellect ' and civilization, and far in advance of the age) was enabled to decorate the dwelling his industry had won, must have formed a strong contrast to their rude stone-halls and the wooden benches of their secluded towers on the braes of Angus, or in the dells of Galloway ; and so, no doubt, each earl, lord, and laird thought, as they twisted their wiry mustachios under their steel caps, and surveyed the apartment in which they held council—the dining hall of a Leith merchant, in the year of the first revolution.

It had six tall windows, each barred with iron and latticed with brass ; the roof was arched with stone ; but the walls were hung with pale brown leather, richly stamped with thistles and silver fleurs-de-lys. The oak furniture was enormously massive and strong ; all the chairs were quaintly and grimly carved, and had arms with great knobs and square cushioned seats of blue Utrecht velvet. The fire-irons were chained to the jambs of the fire-place ; for our forefathers, honest souls ! being somewhat short-tempered, were wont to have disputes when they sat round the fire at night. In the recesses of the carved stone ambres and quaint old knobby cabinets, were many articles of vertu and rarity, which the taste of umquhile Sir Andrew Barton, when homeward bound, had made him select for his good dame in happier days. There were Turkish carpets, African skins, and Persian bows ; Venetian crystals, Japanese canisters (brought by the way of the Red Sea), Muscovite bowls, and

Italian bronzes ; a plump Cupid sprawling on a dolphin's back ; a St. John asleep ; the model of a ship, and several Egyptian gods and goddesses, minus ' pantaloons and bodices,' on which the noble lords looked somewhat dubiously, ' as smelling of sorcery and damnable idolatry ; ' but the late Sir Andrew was a pious and upright man—one who would rather have died than withheld a plack of the cess due to kirk or king ; and in his mercantile days he never omitted to pay regularly to the Hospitallers of St. Anthony at Leith the kain to which they were entitled by law—a Scottish quart from every tun of wine that passed the Beacon Rock ; and of all the fighting merchant-mariners of the time, none had paid more liberally the *primo gilt*, as it is still named—a duty paid from time immemorial, to aid ' the poor, old, and infirm mariners of Leith.'

The southern windows of the hall, showed the ancient bridge of the burgh, the old Gothic Hospital and Church of St. Nicholas, with its burying ground (on which, in after years the citadel was built), and the Links of North Leith, a green and level plain, which has now entirely disappeared, and become an irreclaimable waste, flooded at every tide. The eastern windows showed the opposite bank of the river, with the quaint shipping, the Beacon Rock, the wooden pier, the steeple of St. Anthony, and the picturesque outline of the old Timber Holfe, or bourse, where the Memel and Riga wood was sold, and where traders generally met for the transaction of business.

Sad, pale, and thoughtful, with a heart crushed between sorrow for the disappearance of his beloved Margaret, and the new mystery which involved the fate of his unhappy father, who had not been seen since the day of the battle, young Rothesay sat at the table, in a raised seat of honour : and his dark, melancholy eyes wandered alternately over the sunny landscape without, and the crowd of steel-clad, stern, and proud landholders who sat around the board or thronged the apartment, conversing and laughing, all very much at their ease—for they were not the men to be awed by the presence or opinions of a spirit-broken boy, even though that boy was the heir of the throne.

On one side of him stood the Earl of Errol, the Lord High Constable of Scotland, with his white ivory baton of office ; on the other sat the gigantic Earl of Angus, Lieu-enant-general of the realm, clad in his dark armour, with he *Red Heart* crowned and emblazoned on his surcoat, and his gauntleted hands crossed upon that terrible weapon, which had slain Glencairn and many a gallant man. Of all the poor men of letters who thronged the court of James III. not one was present here; but in the sunny recesses of the windows were Catherine Stirling of the Keir, Countess of Angus, Beatrix Douglas, Dowager of Errol, wearing on her espousal finger a bone ring, to which the wedding-ring of her late lord was attached by a cord; Elizabeth Douglas, Lady Lyle, and other dames of the rebel faction, among whom were the sad and shrinking daughters of Lord Drummond—Sybilla and Euphemia—who fixed their eyes, furtively, however, on the *Yellow Frigate* and her armed consorts, now many in number, which were all riding at anchor, under the admiral's flag, in the roads, about two miles distant, after scouring the surrounding shores, and sinking every ship whose crew adhered to the insurgent lords. The latter had offered the most splendid bribes to the Leith masters, if they would arm ships and attack the Laird of Largo; but not one would sail against him, were a ducal coronet the reward of conquest.

Seven days had now elapsed since the battle of Sauchie had been fought; yet, in all that time, no tidings had been heard of James; for the poor miller, Beaton, had not yet dared to relate the terrible scene he had witnessed; and those who could have given the best information, viz., Gray and Stirling, stood by the prince's council board, exchanging those deep smiles that villans can only read.

'Everywhere we have offered bribes to those who may bring us sure tidings of your royal father,' said Angus, 'by twang of trumpet at every burgh cross; I have proffered brave propines for drinking, and many a rich largess, yet no news hath come in.'

'Rumours are current that the king has been assassinated,' said the Lord Hailes, bluntly.

The young prince grew ghastly pale, and started with horror at the remark. 'By God's love and the Virgin's purity, I pray you, do not say so!' he exclaimed, imploringly.

'By both, I assure you, it is said so,' returned the coarse, unfeeling noble.

'Rumour ever lies,' said Sir Patrick Gray, angrily; 'for on one hand 'tis said he has fled to England—on the other, to Holland; and there are many who maintain that he is on board the ships of that contumacious loon, old

Largo, whose boats plied at the Craigward the live-long battle day, ferrying over the wounded and the fugitive.'

'From my soul, I thank you for the hope, my good Sir Patrick,' said the prince, mournfully.

Until the king's flight or safety—his death or abdication are known, my lords, we can decide on nothing,' said the constable.

'Save that we must keep together in arms,' added Angus, till Parliament meets, and we are voted scathless for the raid of Sauchie.'

'We have gained a battle,' said old Lord Drummond, in a growling whisper to his daughters : 'we have routed our false king—slain his minion Ramsay of Balmain, whom some styled Lord of Bothwell ; we have cut to pieces his red-doubleted guard ; yet I am not one inch nearer discovering where the foul villans of the late court have hidden or murdered your sister Maggie, to further their English alliance.'

Crushed by their own sorrows, the poor girls did not reply to this vituperation, save by the tears which fell silently over their cheeks. Young girls in general look to the bright side of everything : thus the sisters were full of hope ; and they loved their lost Margaret so much, that they shrunk, instinctively, with dismay from the rough inferences of their father ; and from the idea, that any one could injure a being so gentle and so harmless.

'Listen to me, Effie Drummond,' resumed the old lord, through his long mustachios, which resembled those of a walrus : 'look a little more at the quarterings on Lord Hailes' tabard-coat and a little less at yonder devilish ships ; and thou, too, Madam Sybilla—what, the fury ! hath this skipper's son gained more influence over thee in one year than I have done in eighteen ? '

Still they wept silently, for none had spoken to them kindly save young Rothesay, and he knew not their secret ; but now the sudden entrance of Lord Home, with his mail covered by dust relieved them of their father's persecution, for all now turned to him.

'Welcome, Bailie of Coldinghame ! ' said Angus, who by his loftiness and confidence seemed more like a king than a mere peer ; 'what tidings—hast heard of our missing *nan ?* '

'Nought, save that he hath fled ; but I have been harrying the lands of the *malcontents*, his people.'

' And now many castles hast thou burned ? '

' At the head of a thousand Border spears, I have ridden through all the Howe of Angus, where men shall long remember the slogan of *a Home!*' replied the chief, who was a very good type of those feudal nobles, who never bowed to religion or to law, and who never knew remorse for crime, or fear of God or man, and were generally as destitute of pure patriotism as ever Scottish peers have been in later years. ' I have sacked twenty farm towns on the baronies of the so-called Duke of Montrose ; I have ruined and dismantled ten castles in the Carse of Gowrie, and laid all the towns of Fife under heavy contribution.'

' Ye have done well, by St. Bryde ! ' said Angus, giving a glance of stern curiosity at Rothesay, who had listened with stolid apathy.

And now entered, quite as hastily, Robert, Lord Lyle ; he was one of James's most faithful servants, and had recently returned from an embassy to England, concerning the slaying of Barton.

' How now, Lyle—what news ? ' asked Angus.

' Men say the king is dead—murdered, and that the Lord Forbess hath risen in the north, and ridden from Aberdeen to Elgin o' Murray, displaying a bloody shirt upon a spear, and summoning all the Gordons, the Forbesses, and Leslies to rise in arms against you, and for vengeance ! My lords, alake ! this soundeth like evil.'

' Let him do so ; we may meet him and the northern clans by Sauchieburn, perhaps,' said Angus ; ' but I would we knew the verity, whether or not the king is on board the ships of yonder stubborn admiral.'

' Another messenger with tidings,' said Lord Hailes ' my kinsman, Adam Hepburn, of the Black Castle, ha come in from the east country, and would speak with hi grace.'

' Admit him,' said Rothesay ; ' he may have news of th king my father.'

Hepburn, a hardy and sunburned south-country laird accoutred in a very plain and somewhat rusty headpiece corslet, vambraces, and steel gloves, with an enormou sword, dagger, and wheel-lock caliver at his girdle, no pushed his way unceremoniously forward, but bowed lo on perceiving the young prince, whom he knew at onc by the richness of his dress—being without armour, an having on a short crimson velvet tunic, girdled tightly about the waist, long hose of spotless white silk, a violet-coloured cloak lined with white satin, and on his breast the sparkling collar of the Thistle.

'What news, laird? If of my father, by my soul, you shall have the best of all the forfeited baronies.'

'Would I had such tidings to give,' replied the soldier-like laird, who having *no title* was the truer Scotsman; 'but I have merely come in on the spur, with a message from the captain of the king's Castle of Dunbar.'

'Anent what?'

'Five English ships, which, after having lain wind-bound for many days in Phillorth Bay, have appeared off the Firth of Forth, and avoiding our cannon at Dunbar, now hover thereabouts, plundering the coast, cutting away our fishers' nets, firing on their boats, and taking every advantage, after their old fashion, of these our present hapless broils.'

'What can we do, my lords?' said the prince, whose patriotism was fired by hearing this news, which made Gray and Shaw exchange glances of anger and disappointment.

'Nothing that I know of, for Wood and all his people remain sullenly and proudly aloof from us, acknowledging no authority but that of James III.,' said Angus.

'My father's good and faithful subject!' said Rothesay, with honest ardour.

'I will wager my coronet against a jester's cap, that old Largo will sail against these Englishmen, if we do but ask him,' said Angus.

'I say nay,' said Sir Patrick Gray.

'I say *yea*,' added Angus, frowning.

'If this English churl is yet tarrying in Scottish waters, we may be totally ruined,' whispered Shaw to Gray.

'It cannot be he; this breathless courier speaks of *five* ships; now young Howard had but three.'

'True; yet I quake at the suggestion of sending out Wood against him.'

In less than half an hour several urgent messages of similar import came from the Whitefriars of Aberlady; from the provost of North Berwick, and the prioress of the Cistercians there, all complaining of ravages committed along the coast of Eastern Lothian; and by the prince's desire the Albany herald was despatched to Admiral Wood, requesting him to come on shore, for the double purpose of discovering whether he knew anything of the king's safety, and if he would sail against the enemy.

Too wary to trust himself among these barbarous nobles, Sir Andrew 'refused (says Abercrombie) to comply with the request unless good hostages were delivered to him for his security,' thus, two of the peers volunteered for this service, George Lord Seaton and John Lord Fleming, both men of great integrity. They were sent to the fleet as hostages, and were received with all honour on board the *Yellow Frigate*, where they were put in ward in one of the great cabins, under the care of Willie Wad, the gunner, who voluntarily bound himself to drink an unlimited quantity of bilge should they escape.

In one hour after this, the great barge of the admiral, having his banner, *azure*, charged with a tree, *or*, and pulled by sixteen well-armed oarsmen, with Cuddie in the prow, and Robert Barton and Sir David Falconer, both sheathed in armour and accoutred to the teeth, swept past the Musselcape, and through the old harbour, with oar-blades flashing in the sunshine. They landed at the ancient bridge which crossed the Leith, near where a chapel of St. Ninian was erected soon after by an abbot of Holyrood, with consent of his chapter. It was removed about seventy years ago, and nothing remains of it now but an arched door. At the other end of the bridge was a miraculous well, which belonged to the Bailie of St. Anthony.

Accompanied by all his barge's crew, armed with their boat-stretchers, and having daggers and wheel-locks at their belts, the old admiral, with no other ornament above his armour than the *silver whistle*, which was the badge of his rank, strode through the Wynd of St. Nicholas, and entered the house of Barton, where ensued one of the most interesting interviews recorded in the history of those stirring times.

CHAPTER XXXIX.

UNDAUNTED by the presence of so many enemies, Sir Andrew Wood and his two faithful followers ascended the great turnpike stair of Barton's house, and were ushered by pages, esquires, and heralds into the presence of the young prince and the chief conspirators, several of whom were grouped in the recesses of the hall windows, conversing earnestly. Others sat in corners, drinking the right Rhenish, the Canary, and Bordeaux with which the cellars of the wealthy Laird of Barton had been stored.

' Robbie Barton,' said the admiral, as they pushed their way towards the dais ; ' by St. Anthony, 'tis enough to make thy father's bones start from their coral bed in the English sea when so many deil's buckies and gilded sharks hold wassail under his old rooftree ! God sain thee, old shipmate o' mine,' sighed Sir Andrew, as he cast his eyes over the hall ; ' many a long wine horn hast thou and I birled here, over our old yarns of lee shores and cannon-shot.'

Barton felt his heart stirred doubly by grief and indignation ; for every feature of this hall reminded him of his brave old father, and he was exasperated to find so many of his enemies installed there, all very much at their ease, and drinking from his cellars as if the contents thereof were their own.

' My lords and gentlemen,' said he, sternly ; ' by my faith, ye reck little of hership and hamesücken.'

' These are but the spray of the great wave, Barton,' said Sir David Falconer, ' and are small items in the great amount of treason and rebellion.'

' And see,' added the admiral, ' on yonder window-bunker sprawls the traitor Sauchie, full to the beams with thy father's wine. Ah, false villan, one day, I hope to see thee spritsail-yarded by three feet of a good rapier ! '

By this time they had reached the presence of the prince, and his vicinity was fortunate for them, as the freedom of their remarks was such that several poniards were drawn, and there was every prospect of their being assailed, though the two noble hostages were certain to dangle from the *Frigate's* yardarm in an hour after. The young prince stood up, and coloured deeply as they appeared before him, and various whispers went round that otherwise silent circle of proud, ferocious, and unscrupulous peers ; for, owing to the loftiness, dignity, and high bearing of Wood, there ran from tongue to tongue a suggestion that ' he was *the king*—James himself ; ' and then a thrill pervaded all present, for he was the only one of three who wore a close casque, the rivets of the vizor having been secured before he came ashore, and his armour having gilded passguards on the shoulders, and puckered *lambeaux* similar to a suit frequently worn by the king on state occasions. The same resemblance occurred to Rothesay, who, looking up with eyes full of hope and timidity, said in a low and agitated voice :

' Sir, are you the king my father ? '

The artlessness of this question, and the touching accent of the young prince, smote the veteran admiral to the heart. He burst into tears, and replied, says Pitscottie—' I am not your father, sir ; but I am his true servant, and the sworn enemy of those who have occasioned his downfall.'

Though Lord Lyle and some of the nobles were touched by the pure, honest, and generous loyalty of Wood, his words kindled the rage and scorn of Angus and others. In the grief of age and manhood there is something very impressive ; and thus, when that brave mariner wept there was a dead silence in the vast apartment ; Rothesay covered his face with his violet-coloured mantle, while Barton and Falconer cast down their eyes, for they were deeply moved. But now that stately bearing, which made so many suppose the closed helmet concealed the face of James, kindled the pride of the nobles, who muttered among themselves, and to those who adhered to them.

' I would give three of my best crofts to see old Tarry-breeks, and these saucy tarpaulins, his comrades, with their master in yonder ditch beside the Bannock,' said Sir James Shaw, who was somewhat tipsy, to Gray, who grasped his arm, and gave him a fierce and significant glance ; for, in that iron age, banter (as we now understand it) was unknown in Scotland. Every man wore a sword and dagger ; so jesting was perilous work at all times.

'You speak somewhat loftily, *Master* Wood,' said Angus, with a haughty frown on his dark and commanding face.

'I am Andrew Wood, *knight*, my Lord Earl of Angus,' he replied, firmly ; 'I received that title from a king's hand on my own deck, abaft the mizen-mast—a deck drenched with foreign blood ! From my father, who was an honest and hard-working merchant-mariner of this good port of Leith, I inherited nothing but a bold heart, and my sturdy legs and arms. I have had to work my way through the voyage of life, with no compass but honesty and no convoy but faith in God ; and since I was an idle brat, who spent the day in fishing for podleys out of the forechains, I have never owed or wronged any man the value of a ropeyarn or a herring-scale—least of all do I owe any merit to a dead ancestry—thof most here, my lord, owe mickle mair to their ancestors than they owe to themselves, God wot ! But enough of this ; the gunner to his lintstock, the——'

'Remember, Laird of Largo,' said Lord Drummond, with a darkening brow, 'thou speakest to the Lieutenant-general of the kingdom, and to men who will not stoop to monarchs, for 'tis beneath the dignity of true nobility.'

'Then why should I stoop to such as thee, an old jack-feather, when 'tis beneath the dignity of true manhood ?'

'Let us have no brawling here, sirs,' said the High Constable, stepping forward, as he saw the admiral disposed to 'come to close quarters ; ' 'remember my office, its high prerogative, and this presence.'

'Know ye aught, Sir Andrew, of the king my father ?' asked Rothesay.

'Alake ! I do not,' replied Wood, mournfully.

'Will you swear on your honour as a knight, that he is not on board your fleet ?'

'There are over many knights here for me to be believed,' replied Wood ; but I pledge you my faith and troth as a seaman, that he is not on board of any of the ships now under my broad pennon.'

'Who were those you took off after the battle ?'

'My Lord St. John of Jerusalem, the High Treasurer, the Mareschal de Concressault, and a few more loyal men ; but as for the king,—God bless him, and confound his enemies !—of him I know nothing ; even rumour hath not reached us in the Firth. My shipmates and I were ready to have risked our lives in his defence; and we landed many times on that evil day, yet saw him not, though duly warned by his Grace of Montrose that James would wear a yellow plume, and ride a grey charger.'

Here Sir James Shaw gave a peculiar snort, and blew his nose to conceal his malicious laughter.

Then (as Buchanan records) Sir Andrew added: ' If the good king is alive, I am resolved to obey *none* but him; if he is slain, I am ready to *revenge* him!'

At this Gray almost clutched his dagger, and felt assured he would never be safe while such a man as Wood lived.

' Would to St. Mary he had never left our ship!' said Barton, who had hitherto remained silent, ' for then he would have been in safety from those false traitors, whom I hope to see one day rewarded as they deserve, by having their dog-throats cut from clew to ear-ring.'

Perceiving that these rough speeches were rousing the anger and apprehension of the insurgent lords, and moreover that they were making too favourable an impression on Rothesay, who never forgot the three leal and true men who now so boldly confronted so many enemies—for Scotland's truest sons were seldom men of noble birth—Lord Angus said:

' Sir Andrew Wood, news hath come in, within this hour, that five English ships are plundering all the coast about Dunbar, so that men can neither fish at sea, nor plough upon the shore, for the shot of their cannon and arquebusses. They have burned many homesteads in the night, and harried the hirsels of the friars at Aberlady; so, if you will not serve *us*, you may, at least, serve Scotland, by ridding her of these gnats, who sting her in her time of toil and trouble.'

' That will I do blithely, lord earl! I searched all the coast from the Red Head to Dunbar Sands, and yet saw nought of these English craft, which were off Taymouth last month. What say ye, Barton, if it should prove to be Eddy Howard?'

' That I will found an altar to St. Clement in Mary's Kirk of Leith, where, if we are victorious, masses shall be said till the day of doom.'

' Where were these crafts last seen, lord earl?'

' Cruising between the Isle of May and the Craig of Bass,' answered Hepburn of Blackcastle; ' there are five in all, and three have their forecastle guns *en barbette*.'

' With red crosses in their topsails ? ' asked Falconer.

' The same.'

' 'Tis Howard!' exclaimed Sir Andrew Wood, striking his hands together with joy ; ' let us unmoor, and be off, lest we miss them again. Farewell, your grace and lordships—come, Davie Falconer, and thou, too, Barton ; let us go.'

' You will take one cup of wine ere you leave us, admiral,' said Angus.

' I crave leave to be excused,' said Wood ; ' I have drunk many a pot of wine here with my auld messmate, Andrew Barton ; but I will never bend a bicker with those who are in arms against his master—for had puir Andrew been alive, he had stood by my side to-day ; so let us bear away, then—the sky is clear, as the saw saith :

> When the clouds spread like a feather,
> Mariner look for fair gude weather.

We'll sight these Englishmen to-night, and overhaul them before morning.'

Glad to be rid of one whose loyalty and inflexible truth were likely to prove troublesome, and perhaps infectious, the barons in reality cared very little whether Sir Andrew vanquished the English or was sunk by them ; for, like true Scottish peers, the national honour to them was nothing when conflicting with their own private ends. As the three kingsmen left the house, they saw two ladies at one of the lower windows waving their handkerchiefs through the basketed grating, careless whether pages, grooms, or men-at-arms observed them. These were Sybilla and Euphemia Drummond. For a minute the lovers loitered to exchange a word and glance.

' Thou art welcome, thrice welcome to my father's house, Lady Effie,' said Barton ; ' and one day I hope to see its porch bedecked with white garlands in thine honour, when coming home as its lawful mistress ; but that must be when the tide of fortune turns, for sorely hath it now set in against the loyal and true ; so we, dear Effie, must thole it with the others. I see how the land lies still with the old lord, thy father ; but we'll weather the reefs yet, please God, Effie.'

Poor Falconer could only kiss the soft white hand of Sybilla, and give her one deep and sorrowful glance, when

Lord Home, who would gladly have fallen on him, sword
in hand, but for the safety of their hostages, came furiously
forward, and the two lovers hurried after the admiral, who
was impatiently waiting for them at the outer gate.

'Bear on, Robbie,' said he, 'we have no leisure now for
backing and filling, or toying and kissing hands. Doth
not thy heart glow with a double hope of vengeance at the
sight of thy father's rooftree and wasted substance? Well-
a-day,' he added, as they hastened through St. Nicholas
Wynd, 'our poor king, after beating to windward all his
life against the dark current of adversity, perhaps is gone
now, as his grandsire went before him—sain him God! And
though I will rather scuttle the old frigate than lower my
colours or nail my topsails to those sharks of barons, yet
thou seest, messmate, we must e'en bear up before this civil
tempest, and scud under bare poles, for fear of losing all;
but were I sure that the king was in life, by the bones of
St. Rule, I would not lift tack or sheet to humour the best
lord in the land!'

'But then the English fleet?'

'Ay, true, there thou hast the weathergage of me; yes,
we must fight in honour and conscience, whether lord, earl,
or laird, king or chancellor commanded us or not; ship
your oars, my lads, and shove off for the ship,' he cried,
as they sprang on board the barge, just in time to prevent
a violent collision between some of her crew and the Angus
spearmen, who had been provoked by the taunts and abuse
of Cuddie Clewline the coxswain. This 'ancient mariner,'
whose weatherbeaten visage was puckered up like a knot
on an oak tree, possessed a vocabulary of abuse that was
pretty extensive; and he had been perambulating the pier,
spitting on his hard horny hands, and throwing mortal
defiances right and left among the vassals of the Lord of
Galloway, boasting that he did not value 'their steel trap-
pings or iron jacks a rope's end or a brass bodle.'

As the barge, with its colour waving, shot out of the
sunny harbour, the crews of the merchant craft and Hanse
traders gave the well-known admiral a hearty cheer, and
his oarsmen, as they bent to their task and almost lifted
their light craft out of the water, sung that merry old
Scottish sea-song, which is mentioned in the prologues of
Bishop Gawain Douglas:

> The ship sails owre ye saut sea faem,
> Yat rowes on ye rocks o' our native hame;

while Cuddie sat in the prow, flourishing his boat hook in defiance to the soldiers on the bridge and pier.

Ere the last notes of the song and the plash of the oars had been lost in the boom of the surf that broke on the reefs then known as the Musselcape and Beacon Rock, Sir Patrick Gray rushed down St. Nicholas Wynd, crossed the bridge, and hurried to the Kirkgate, where, in the *Bell of St. Anthony*, a well-known hostel, he found his minion, Sir Hew Borthvick, whom he scarcely knew, so splendidly was he attired; for the price of James's signet-ring (long since transmitted by the Governor of Berwick to London) had lined his pockets with something better than pebbles, and enabled him to ruin all the pages, pimps, and bullies about the prince's court at tric-trac and shovel-board.

'Ride, Borthwick, ride,' said Gray, breathlessly, as he roughly drew him into a corner; 'for death and life ride to Dunbar; here is money—six half lions (about thirty shillings); get thee a skiff, and seek the English Captain Howard. Warn him that Wood is putting to sea—say his fleet is overwhelming. Anathema! Oh, the fool, the half-witted English lurdane, to be loitering yet in Scottish waters with that devilish damsel in his possession! If she is taken, her tongue will destroy us all; she must be flung overboard, with all the ciphers of Quentin Kraft, the *Harry* is captured; see to this on your life, Hew Borthwick, see to it! Away, while there is yet time—away!'

In ten minutes after this the regicide, well mounted, left Leith by the Porte St. Anthony, and crossing the Links, struck eastward by the dreary Friggate Muir, riding at headlong speed towards Dunbar.

It was about four o'clock in the evening, and as these Scottish worthies' separated, each mentally bequeathed the other to the infernal shades.

CHAPTER XL.

CLEARED FOR ACTION.

As his barge glided into the stream, and Leith with its pie
spires, and sandy links, melted into the sunny haze;
the harbour closed and narrowed astern; the admiral, aft
remaining long silent, exclaimed :

' Well—split my topsails, if I would not rather endu
the English fire, yardarm and yardarm for eight glasse
than overhaul all this talk again with these herring-fac
lordlings; but one day, gadzooks! I hope to make t
best among them lower his ancient at the king's name.'

' They have cast a glamour over the Lord Drummon
said Barton, with a gloomy expression in his eyes; '
was kind to me once, and but for my father's death and t
unhappy strife, I had been ere now his son-in-law, a
holding a banquet, perhaps, in yonder hall, where all th
rabble rout of hostile peers hold council.'

' Thy fair weather and smooth anchorage are comi
Robert,' said the admiral; ' and what sayst thou, Da
Falconer ? '

' That fickle fortune, I fear me, will never tire of per
cuting one who ever courts her smiles; though sooth
say, I never fear her frowns. Poor Lady Sybilla, how s
how pale she looked ! '

' Be not cast down, Falconer,' continued the kind
Laird of Largo, on seeing the arquebussier gazing dream
at the tall house of Barton, which stood like a watch-to
on the left bank of the Leith; ' be not heavy o' hea
because thy purse is at low water; thou shalt have
winsome bride yet, my lad ! And if the king gives t
not land, thou shalt never lack siller while auld And
Wood hath a shot in his locker. Thy father's son, Da
shall beat to windward, and keep in the line of battle w
the best craft in the fleet. The happiest occurrence in
voyage of life is to be brought to by a bonnie young lass

'How woebegone young Rothesay looked to-day,' said
Falconer.

'Ah! there our king (God bless him!) was wrong,' said
the admiral; 'he should have given the lad a longer swing
to his cable, or a little more headway, in the matter of
running after the winsome dames at court, as young princes
will do at times. The tide of experience would soon have
brought him into deep water. I know that, though an
auld sailor, who (St. Mary be thanked) knoweth as much
anent courts and cities as a seaman may; but hilloh! what
is astir here?' he added, as the barge sheered alongside
the *Yellow Caravel*, and two very ominous loops were seen to
dangle from her foreyard-arms.

History informs us that the admiral had just returned in
time to save his two noble hostages from being hung; for
the crew having become alarmed by his long stay on shore,
were preparing—by order of Sir Alexander Mathieson,
who took command in his absence—with great deliberation
to run George Lord Seaton and John Lord Fleming to the
yardheads; and the poor nobles (both good and worthy
men) were in the very act of making their peace with Heaven,
through the intervention of Father Zuill, when the admiral
stepped on board, and at once despatched them on shore;
where the account they gave to Angus and others of their
treatment, made the peers more than ever dread and abhor
the Laird of Largo and his crews.

'Tell the spearmen o' the Lord Angus,' shouted Cuddie
over the side, as their boat was shoved off, 'that d——n
my auld buits if——'

'Peace, coxswain,' said Barton; 'thou ever becomest
rank when lacking ballast, or when thine orlof is overflowed with usquebaugh; so, silence—man the tackles,
and hoist the boats on board.'

'Lords, indeed!' muttered the admiral, as he walked
aft; 'were my honour not pledged, I would fain have be-
layed the dogsons to the whipping-post, and given them a
round dozen with a rope's end, just as a fare-ye-well. But
heave short on the anchor, Barton—cast loose the courses,
and make sail on the ship.'

History (to which in these chapters we are obliged to
have constant reference) informs us, that though the admiral
had several ships at his disposal, and the English squadron
consisted of five sail, he somewhat unwisely resolved 'to
take *only his own two*,' meaning the *Yellow Frigate* and the

Queen Margaret, which had been built at the Newhaven, under his own eye; and so, after desiring the other armed vessels, whose captains adhered to him and the cause of the missing king, to cruise between Leith Roads, St. Margaret's Hope, and Alloa, to cut off the communication of the insurgents with Fife, he weighed anchor, and stood down the river about six in the evening, favoured by a gentle south-west wind.

There were great preparations made for battle on board these two stately ships, as under a press of canvas they bore down the Forth, between Inchkeith and those two reefs known as the Briggs and the Craigness, and steered for the Isle of May, which lay north-east by east, but was not visible from that part of the river. The admiral and his officers remained in their harness. Willie Wad and his yeomen hoisted powder up from the magazine; the boatswain was preparing all the culverins on the long and clumsy slides then in use; the arquebussiers put fresh matches to the serpentine cocks of their firearms; filled their priming horns, and buckled on their bullet-bags, which were hung at the right hip, and all were on deck in their jazarine jackets and steel caps, swords, and daggers. The seamen were accoutred in nearly a similar manner, and armed themselves from the racks of Jedwood axes, hand-guns and boarding-pikes, that were framed round the masts and the bulwarks of the poop. All were noisy, loquacious, and enthusiastic, save a few of the quiet married men, whose wives and little ones were watching their departure from the shore.

'Away aloft, Cuddie—get into the fore-crosstrees,' said the admiral, 'and thou shalt have a can of egg-flip and three silver bonnet pieces the moment ye sight these English ships. Will she not carry more, Barton?'

'Not without leaving Sir Alexander too far astern; but we may try: master boatswain, rig me a guy on the spanker boom; sheet home the mizen-staysail, and up with the cross-jackyard a bit.'

This primitive contrivance has now been replaced by the gaff, and to the lower end of it the staysail was then bent on. Though the summer evening was then bright on shore, a thick white haze arose from the broad estuary, and hid the land on both sides. The admiral became merry as the river widened, and the May arose in a faint blue line at the horizon; and he said to the gunner:

' Pass the word, Willie, to Father Zuill, to quit the mass-book—to overhaul his hurdy-gurdy, and ship on its mirrors, for gadzooks, we will be aboard the English in another hour or two.'

' Carry those shot to their guns, Willie Wad,' said Barton, kicking away some balls that were rolling about the deck ; no iron should ever come within seven feet of a binnacle.'

The wind soon became lighter and more aft ; and as the yards were squared more, the staysails began to shiver. The vessels were now going slowly through the water, and cleaving a shining passage that left a long wake astern. The sun of June set brilliantly behind the distant Ochils ; the shores were mellowed in haze ; but above it, the peculiar hill of North Berwick rose on the starboard bow, gleaming in the western light like a volcanic cone of flame. As the glow faded on the waters, a light, like a gigantic star, began to beam among the hills astern.

This was Saint Anthony's Light—a beacon which was burned by the good and charitable Hospitallers of St. Anthony upon the tower of their hermitage on the rocks above Holyrood. This tower was then more than forty feet high, and thus its light was seen far down the estuary, in which it was the only beacon in those days ; for there was then no Pharos on Inchkeith (which belonged to *Keith*, the Earl Marischal), and was without a night-beacon until the early part of the seventeenth century. The island, in the time of James III., was a place of compulsory retirement for lepers and other sick persons ; and was a famous resort of water-cows and kelpies ; and on the rocks there the mermaids, with curling tails, a looking-glass in one hand and a comb in the other, are *still to be seen*, as more than one hardy boatman of Newhaven, and pious elder of the Fishwives Kirk, are ready to aver on oath, especially when the moon is S. by W., and the tide is full between Granton and Kinghorn.

CHAPTER XLI.

THE ENGLISH BOAT.

MEANWHILE, the worthy messenger of the worthy knight
Sir Patrick Gray, captain of Broughty, was riding hard
towards the east. To avoid question by the gateward
who kept the bridge and toll of Musselburgh, he swam
his horse through the river, near the church of St. Micha
the Archangel, and dashed through Pinkie woods, over
Tranentmuir and Hoprigmains, and never drew his bridl
until King David's royal burgh of Dunbar and the massiv
towers of that noble fortress, which was then considere
the key of East Lothian, rose before him ; and from th
higher ground, as he approached the bare and sea-beate
promontory on which they stand, he could perceive fiv
English vessels cruising in the offing, or deep water, an
almost becalmed between the mainland and the May.

Three of these were indeed the vessels of Howard, wh
when on his homeward voyage, had been joined off Ho
Island by two large armed vessels, under Miles Furniva
sent by Henry VII. from the Thames with orders to pilla
the coast of Scotland, and (in fulfilment of the old and i
variable policy of the English kings) to take every advanta
of the intestine broils of Scotland to distress and harass th
people, that they might the more willingly listen to h
proposals, when the project of the prince's marriage wi
Margaret Tudor was revived—a foolish and mistaken polic
as the Scots were ever the last people in the world to l
wooed by cold steel and gunpowder.

Feeling appetized after his long ride, Sir Patrick's me
senger reined up his foam-flecked charger at the *Dunt
Arms*, an hostel in the Highgate, where he ordered a c
of Malvoisie, a pair of roasted plovers, and a quail, wi
sweet sack, for he felt able to devour a horse, after his lo
ride near the seacoast ; and he resolved, that though t
evening was drawing on, affairs of state should wait h
pleasure.

'How happy are the rich,' thought he, with a sigh of enjoyment, after he had drained the last of his sack, and picked the last bone of the quail; 'how often have I fed my hopes when I had little wherewith to feed my stomach,' he added, clinking the English gold pieces, with which his purse was now so well lined, and which went current in Scotland as Scottish coins did in England, for then the coin of all nations was circulated everywhere; 'but this country will grow too hot for me ere long, so I must e'en turn spy on Henry, and win in England the lyons, louis, and angels of the new king, James IV.—ugh!' and he smiled a ferocious smile, 'he owes his crown to *me!* But now to reach these devilish ships anent that damsel, who I would with all my soul was sleeping with her fathers.'

He now went on foot to the harbour, where, though the sea was calm, there was considerable agitation in the water, for Dunbar is the most bleak and stormy headland on the coast; but he found that no money would tempt the fishermen to put him on board of any of those English vessels, which were lying, almost becalmed, about two miles off; and he soon ceased to ask them, as their suspicions were readily excited, and there were not a few who threatened to drag him before the provost, that he might be forced to declare what manner of business he, a Scot, had on board these hostile craft.'

This threat made him tremble, for now he had three tenements in Stirling, with a remarkably well-lined purse; and if 'the sudden possession of gold will make a brave man cautious,' how much more so will it render timid a dastardly regicide?

Hastily leaving the fishermen, he walked for nearly a mile along the sands, on which the surf was rolling with considerable force, and gazed anxiously at the English ships, which were all within two miles of each other, with their high lumbering poops, their carved and gilded quarter-galleries, and the muzzles of their brass cannon shining in the last rays of the sunlight that lingered in the west; and Borthwick stamped his feet with anger, for he supposed that Wood's ships must, by this time, have dropped far down the river, and that shots would soon be exchanged.

Upon the level shore, close to the seamark, there stood in those days the chapel of St. Bey, who was daughter of a certain Saxon king. This princess, according to local tradition, had emigrated among the Scots with her two

sisters, St. Abb and St. Helen, who, being meek, gentle,
and pious, were disgusted with the world and the barbaric
pomp of their father's petty court, and resolved to spend their
dowers in the erection of churches, and their lives in devotion.   All these three votaresses, having a curious predilec-
tion for salt water, endeavoured to find sites as near the sea
as possible.   St. Helen built her oratory on a plain, near the
beach, and St. Abb raised hers on that high rock which overhangs the German Ocean, while St. Bey succeeded in founding her fane so close to the floodmark that at every full tide
the waves washed its massive walls.

Thinking little of St. Abb, St. Helen, or St. Bey, Hew
Borthwick, on passing the chapel of the latter, suddenly
found himself seized by a party of seamen, whom, by the
fashion of their gabardines, and the sound of their voices
he knew at once to be English ; and close by was a large
boat, well laden with several sacks of flour, three sheep
and a quantity of vegetables, all taken from an adjacent
farm ; for this foraging party were numerous and well
armed.

' Yoho, brother ; whom seek ye ? ' demanded one, who
grasped Borthwick by the throat—yet the craven dared not
to draw his sword.

' I seek some one who will take me on board the *Harry*
for I have an urgent message to the captain.'

' Concerning the damosel aboard, I have little doubt
replied the seaman, who was no other than Dick Selby
the gunner ; ' I ever said little luck would come to Edd
Howard by having this painted galley in tow.'

' Nay, Dick,' said another, ' she be no galley, but
noble lady.'

' A Scots one, though.   Well, and what want ye with th
captain, eh ? '

' How can the Scot answer thee, Dick,' interfered anothe
' when thou'st twisted his mouth all to starboard ; wh
'tis all on one side, like the ballast-port of a timber-ship.'

' Teach thy grannum to make sackwhey !   I warran
thee I'll make the Scot find his tongue.   Speak ! ' roared th
gunner, giving Borthwick a furious shake.

' I have an urgent message for your captain, which non
must know but he,' gasped Borthwick, in a half-strangle
voice ; ' look at me, sirs—some of you must have seen n
on board before now ? '

' Tarry a minute, gunner Dick,' said a soldier who wa

in half mail, and had but one eye; ' I *have* seen this man before, methinks.'

' Off Taymouth—at night,' said Borthwick.

' I remember me now,' said the soldier, who was Anthony Arblaster; ' unhand him, Dick, ere worse come of it, for the captain's temper hath been truly devilish of late.'

' We have had a long spell on this here shore,' growled the gunner, as he released the throat of Borthwick, whose lace doublet was no way improved by the application of such a hard and tarry hand as Dick's ; ' we have turned our best barge into a bumboat, as ye may see, so come aboard and let us shove off, before some of your furious Scots come after their flour sacks. I would to St. George they were all, for the trouble they give us, steering in the latitude of purgatory ! '

' Or a warmer latitude still,' added Anthony Arblaster, rubbing his blind eye.

' Avast,' said an old sailor, ' and remember there is a Scot here, and that he be but one among many.'

But the said Scot, though boiling with rage at his treatment, cared little for national reflections ; yet had these honest English hearts known the actual character of the wretch they had on board, they would have flung him into the sea, lest they should never more have fortune on its waters.

' Ship your oars, my hearts,' said the gunner ; ' and harkee, Arblaster, bear a-hand, old dead-eye, and belay these here quadrupeds to the thwarts, or we may lose them in the surf.'

The boat was bluffly built, and being full of men, and moreover heavily laden, she laboured through the breakers which roll for ever on those sands, and shipped a great quantity of spray before her head was fairly turned towards the *Harry*, which was astern of all the other vessels, all of which were lying with their heads towards the river. The uneasiness manifested by Borthwick, as the spray flew over his rich cloak and doublet, afforded extreme gratification to the hardy seamen who had nothing to spoil, and whose oars bent almost to breaking, as they strained between the tholing-pins, and shot the heavy barge from one long roller to another.

After they had pulled a mile from the shore, and saw the castle of Dunbar rising with all its strong red towers and crenellated ramparts in many a frowning row, bristling with

cannon and black loop-holes, the one-eyed archer, who wa
seated in the stern, uttered a shout of astonishment:

'Hilloah, old Buff,' said the gunner; 'what is th
matter?'

'There are two large ships standing down the river?'

'Sir Andrew Wood, for a thousand rose nobles!' sai
the gunner, slapping his thigh; 'thou hast the true ey
of an English archer, Tony, thof thou'st but one; well,
thought we should not make out two days of a quiet cruis
here. Give way, my hearts—give way! odds firkin, the
are bringing down both wind and tide with them—yare-
yare—stretch out!'

'It _is_ the Admiral Wood,' said Borthwick, with gloom
spite, 'and my message to your captain concerns him.'

'They are hull down as yet,' said the gunner, as he stoc
up and shaded his weather-beaten visage with his thic
knotty hand; 'well—odds my life, bold as he is—and
better seaman never spliced a rope, Scot though he be—
do not think Sir Andrew with only two ships will ventu
to attack us; and we'll see him haul his wind ere anoth
half-glass is run.'

The ships of Wood were about nine miles off, bei
abreast of North Berwick, and they loomed large throu,
the haze of the summer gloaming, which, however, w
rising from the water as the moon, which was round a
full, soared into the clear blue sky, above the hills of E;
Lothian. The Ness of Fife was not visible in the haze, :
at this extreme point the noble Forth is more than twer
miles broad.

CHAPTER XLII.

THE LOVER AND THE SPY.

THE approaching vessels had been descried already from the ships of Howard, who fired a cannon to quicken his boat; and the moment it was on board and hoisted in, with his provisions, he desired all to be cleared away for battle, and ordered Borthwick to attend him in his cabin.

'Well, thou bird of ill omen,' said he, while arming himself, 'what evil wind hath blown thee on board the *Harry* to-night? Speak out, and briefly, too; try none of thy nobler tricks with me.'

'I have come with a message from the Lords at Leith——'

'Ah! they are there, then: and the rumours we have heard are true: has the King of Scotland fought a battle and been defeated?'

'Yes, and hath fled no man knows whither,' said Borthwick, with a dark smile on his pale face, while he could not repress a twinge of uneasiness at the mention of the king's name, for he saw ever before him—when alone for a moment —that ghastly corpse, lying where he had flung it, in the ditch beside the Bannock.

'And so young Rothesay now is king,' said Howard, coldly, and pausing while he braced his corslet.—'No—nor can be, until we ascertain that the king, his father, is dead.'

'Of course; well, and what want your rebel lords with me?'

'I should have said Sir Patrick Gray.'

'Well, well—speak quickly; for the foe comes on. Your message——'

'Concerns the Lady Margaret Drummond, and your bond in cipher with the Scottish friends of King Henry.'

'Well,' said Howard again, buckling his waist-belt with a furious jerk; 'what of them?'

Wood is about to attack you, and you must be well

aware that if the *Harry* is taken, and these are found on board—the lady and the bond—the hope of Henry's alliance will be crushed by her being discovered, and the safety of his allies in Scotland will be compromised by the documents.'

'The curse of all the saints be on King Henry's plots and on those Scottish cravens who pander to the pay, the wiles, and selfish ends of England!' said Howard, with great bitterness. 'Well, fellow, and what would your Laird of Kyneff advise?'

'That this troublesome dame be hove overboard, with Master Kraft's writings and the deep-sea lead tied together to her neck——'

'Confound thee, thou limb of Satan!—thou infamous and lubberly lurdane!' cried Howard, in a tempest of rage at this terrible proposition. 'Begone,' he added smiting Borthwick on the mouth with his steel glove; 'begone sheer off; or by all that is sacred in heaven, I will have thee bound to a kedge, and flung overboard like St. Clement. Yoho there, Will Selby!' he said to his page, who stood without the cabin, 'is that fisherboat, which we took off Tyningham sands, astern yet?'

The page replied that it was.

'Then see this ruffian put into her; give the two fishermen a handful of tokens, and bid them cast off and begone in the devil's name, lest I hang this recreant Scot where fain would hang his masters.'

In two minutes after this our knight of the scarlet mantle found himself hustled over the side of the *Harry* into shore-boat, in which were two poor fishermen, who, after receiving a handful of those leaden pledges which the English used in the time of their seventh and eighth Henries in lieu of copper coinage, gladly pulled away for Tyningham Sands, where their wives and children had been waiting for them in sore apprehension and weeping the livelong day. Anxious to get clear of the engagement which was to take place, they stepped their mast, hoisted their sail, and prayed hard to St. Bey for a favourable breeze; but little wind came, and even that was against them; so they bequeathed the poor saint to the devil, spat on their hands, and betook them to their oars, like men.

'Thank Heaven, my ship is freed from the contamination of such a wretch,' said Howard; 'though 'twere not worth while to lose my temper with him. By St. George, I profit little by old Caxton's *Book of Good Manners*; thou

I have studied it more than stars or compass since Margaret Drummond came on board.'

The handsome Howard was now completely armed, and presented himself at the cabin of Margaret, whose attendants, Cicely and Rose, had acquainted her of the dire preparations making on deck overhead. Sorrow and confinement had rendered her so pale that she was like a beautiful marble statue, and her exceeding fairness was rendered stronger by her dark purple dress, and the triangular cap of the same material which shaded her fine hair, the locks of which shone like golden tresses in the light of the cabin lamp. On beholding Howard in his armour she started forward to meet him.

' Dear madam,' said he, ' I am come—to—to——'

' To restore me to my family,' said Margaret, with sweet earnestness; ' is it not so ? you will—you will do so now; for I have been told that the king's admiral approaches to demand me.'

' Nay, lady, I came but to convey you to a place of safety,' said he ; ' you are misinformed, for none in Scotland (three villans excepted) know that you are here, or that you are in the land of the living. The king was accused of abducting you, and he has lost a bloody battle near Stirling, fought by the nobles.'

' And my father fought against him ? '

' Very probably.'

Margaret clasped her white hands in fear and misery. ' And what tidings are there of the Duke of Rothesay ? '

' I have heard of none,' said Howard, on whom that name, when uttered by her lips, fell as a mortal blight. ' Lady Drummond, we are about to engage in a close, and, it must be, desperate conflict, with the king of the Scottish mariners, and it may be that you will never again be troubled by the voice or presence of Edmund Howard. Oh, think over all I have dared to urge, during the many days it has been my happiness to know you and to seek your esteem. You know my secret ; say, if I survive to-night, may I hope for something more than friendship ? '

' Your secret,' reiterated Margaret, as her fine blue eyes filled with tears ; ' alas, fair sir, you know not *mine*. I admire and most sincerely respect you, Edmund Howard ; but more I dare not say—so, I beseech you, cease to urge me further on this most painful subject.'

' True, true,' said Howard, beating his breast, ' I have

indeed but little to offer you compared with what you have lost.   It may be weakness——'

' The weakness of the strong man and of the gallant heart.'

' Alas ! in love we ever carry more sail than ballast—who can control the heart in love——'

' If you knew *all*, you never again would address me thus. Oh, talk not of love to me—it is in vain, nor dare I listen.'

' Alas, that I should hear this doom from your own lips at last, lady !   I will quit this wandering life of mariner, for I have one of those happy homes that are only to be found in England ; where the woods are green, and our painted windows open down to soft and sunny lawns, instead of iron grates that grimly peer through deep fosses and guarded barbicans, as here in Scotland, lady.   There no rude barons or lawless lairds, ride from tower to tower with spears and torches in their train, no hostile clansmen wage eternal war, making their life but a mission of military vengeance and feudal hatred ; and there no venal peers are ever ready to sell their country and their king, her rights or her honour for foreign gold.   Oh no ; in merry England we know nothing of transmitted hatred, of Highland raids and border forays.   I love you, lady, well, and, with you, I fain would share that quiet English home ; I love you passionately, and denial is death, and worse than death to me ! and I say so now when on the eve of battle with one who was never foiled or vanquished on the sea.   In that happy home if spared to see it, I could worship you as a monk who serves his altar, and treasure you as a miser hoards his treasure.   Oh, do not turn from me as if I was hateful,' continued Howard, borne away by his passion and finding eloquence in the very depth of it ; ' 'tis true I am an English man, lady, and that you are a Scot—but can a few miles of land or of water make such an evil difference in our temper or our race——'

' Oh no, it is not hate that makes me turn away, but true sorrow for yourself, my good and noble Howard,' said Margaret, as she pressed his hands in hers ; for his honest passion and gentle bearing touched her to the soul, and no woman ever hears a man say he loves her without feeling a more than common interest in him ; but happily for both this painful interview was cut short by the stentorian voice of John o' Lynne, who cried through the poop door :

' Yoho, Captain Howard ; the Scots are within a mile

of us, and bring down the breeze with them, and it freshens
fast.'

This reminded Howard of what he had forgotten—that
he had come, not to make love, but to conduct his fair prisoner and her two pretty attendants, Rose and Cicely, to
a place of security, which he now proceeded to do.   They
were accordingly conducted between-decks, amid a tremendous uproar, for in one quarter Dick Selby was hoisting up
shot and powder from the magazine, in another, boxes,
chests, and bulkheads were going down, and hammocks
being triced up, while the shrill whistle of the boatswain,
the swearing and noise of the seamen, made the place
terrible to them; and from the lower deck they descended
by a ladder and the light of a lantern into a dreary and
Cimmerian gulf, from which arose the combined odours of
bilge and rancid beef, stale cheese, tarry ropes, and other
agreeable perfumes, such as usually pervade the region of
the cock-pit.   And there, in a curtained and cushioned
berth, below the water-line, he left them to their prayers,
and with a sigh ascended to the maindeck of the *Harry*;
and then his spirit rose as he breathed more freely.

' Dick Selby—up with the battle-lanterns, and beat to
quarters!' said he : ' John o' Lynne, make sail on the ship;
the *Cressi* will first engage these petulant Scots; stand
to your culverins, my lads, fore and aft, if you would not
look a Scottish prison, oatmeal, and iron fetters, before we
see merry England again!'

And bravely every man in the good ship *Harry* stood
by his gun, and drew tighter the buckles of his helmet and
girdle.

CHAPTER XLIII.

THE BATTLE OFF THE MAY.

THE wind had freshened as the *Yellow Frigate* and her
consort bore down the river, and confident in the great
size, heavy armament and complete equipment of those
vessels which Sir Andrew Wood was so fond of styling ' his
own two,' he walked to and fro on the poop, whistling for
more wind, and all undaunted by the reported strength of
the enemy, though Barton, Falconer, and Sir Alexander
Mathieson deemed him rash and unwary in leaving so many
of his vessels to cruise idly in the river. As the land lessened
Preston Bay opened out on one side and the far-stretching
bight of Largo on the other. By this the five English vessels
were in sight, scattered considerably apart, but their white
sails were distinctly visible on the dusky blue of the darkening sea and sky. Falconer and Barton were accoutred in
polished steel, and were armed with Jedwood axes, sword
and dagger. After having inspected the culverins, moyennes
and sakers with which the forecastle, poop, and main-deck
were mounted—after having seen that the bores were clear,
the wadding tight, and tackles clear—Willie Wad was
placidly regaling himself on cold salt junk and a can of beer
with the coxswain of the barge, who was drinking ale from an
old gallipot.

Archy the boatswain, and his mate (or yeoman as they
were then named), worked at a grindstone, putting a keen
edge on their two-handed swords, axes, and boarding pikes
while they whistled and sang as the sparks of the grinding
steel flew to leeward through the open ports ; and close by
them was a grim old arquebussier, who had served at the
siege of Lochmaben, under James II., against the Douglases
at Brechin, and at the Bog of Dunkinty, notching his
leaden balls with a cross for good luck ; and now the admiral
whose mind was occupied by the hope of victory, was joined

by Father Zuill, who under his cassock wore a jazarine jacket and steel gloves, which he was at no pains to conceal.

'Harkee, timoneer,' said the admiral, 'keep her head away a point or two towards the north. Yonder headmost ship I take to be the *Cressi*, and if so, I will play her a trick I have not tried since we fought the Portuguese under Antonio de Belem, and sunk his *Lady of Sorrow*. Gadzooks! that Englishman saileth as if he would poke the wind's eye out! We will have a brave moonlight night, Father Zuill; see how brightly she rises above the Lammermuirs.'

'Yet I would rather this bout took place by sunlight.'

'Why—what! art at thy plaguey burning-glasses again?'

'Thou knowest, admiral, that Marcellus used his mirrors both in summer and winter——'

'Nay, I know nothing of the kind.'

'Unless they were to trim his beard by,' said Falconer.

'Out on thee, Davie,' said the admiral; 'don't mock our friar, though he hath more crotchets in his poor head than there be strands in a nine-inch cable.'

'Yes,' mused the priest; 'he used them even in the coldest winters against the ships of an enemy; but there is no record of moonbeams setting aught on fire.'

'Odds life! I should think not, friar,' said the admiral, looking aloft, and watching the sails of the frigate.

'Would that I could assure thee, Sir Andrew, how a combination of mirrors, all reflecting heat on one point, could set the great globe itself on fire; then how much more so a miserable caravel?'

'Let me see the caravel set on fire first, and I will consider about the world after. So-ho, Barton, the wind is veering round upon our quarter.'

'And thou shalt see it, admiral; for when I construct my parabolic speculum to burn at ten paces, one ten times its size shall consume everything to cinders at a hundred paces. 'Tis plain as a pikestaff.'

'Look ye, shipmate,' said the admiral, impatiently, 'stick to thy mass, and leave burning and cannonading to those whose trade it is; the gunner to his lintstock, the steersman to his helm——'

'And the cook to the foresheet,' interrupted the friar, petulantly finishing the admiral's invariable proverb, which he had picked up in his old skipper days. 'Yet a time shall come when thou and all here shall behold with wonder the effect of my parabolic speculum, when it reflects the fierce solar rays to that point of fire which is the true focus of the parabola.'

' Perhaps so,' replied the admiral ; ' but I never mean to watch thy devilish hurdy-gurdy again. Dost remember when we were off Cape Ushant, how nearly I was brained at the taffrail by the jibbing of the mainboom, when watching these plaguey glasses with which you promised to burn me a hole in the sails of a Spanish lugger ? '

' Alas ! Laird of Largo,' said the learned chaplain, sorrowfully, ' thou knowest nought of this noble science—nothing of optics ; nothing of epicycles, whose central circle is the circumference of a greater ; and nothing of crystalline spheres.'

Hillo ! thou'rt at thy magic again,' said the admiral, angrily ; ' all this is too deep for me, Father Zuill ; I am out of soundings, look ye ; and if I dived into the abyss of this learning, I should never come up again. Look to the staysails, Barton——the wind cometh more upon the beam.'

The *Margaret* was now half a mile astern. After passing the Bass Rock, they found the wind coming freshly from the south, and saw the English ships closing up fast as they caught the breeze ; but still the *Cressi* was far ahead of the *Harry*, and though a small vessel, which mounted only twenty pieces of ordnance, with a crew of about two hundred men, she stood boldly towards the taller and heavier Scot, with which her crew were intent on grappling—a *tactique* peculiar to that age ; but Wood had no intention of letting her do so, and resolved to rid himself of her company, by serving her as he had served the Admiral of Portugal, when he fought him off the Rock of Lisbon, a few years before.

The light haze had now cleared away from the bosom of the estuary ; from a clear, unclouded sky, a gorgeous moon shed a flood of brilliant light upon the wide blue waters, on the coast of East Lothian, that lay sleeping in the silvery distance ; on the nearer bluffs of the castled Bass and the low, flat isle of May, that lay far off towards the north and east. The waves were dancing in green light tipped with silver foam, as they rolled between continent and isle, and the English vessels, with all their canvas set, as they stood towards the foe, looked like gigantic swans or sea-birds floating on the deep.

A red flash from the high forecastle of the *Cressi* was followed by a gush of pale blue smoke, and then the iron ball of a carthoun howled through the rigging of the frigate, and plunged into the water far off. This irritated the old Laird of Largo, who always loved to have the first fire ; and now he blew his whistle—the signal for battle.

' Let fly at her tophamper, Willie Wad,' he cried, as a line of lights glittered along the gun-deck ; ' give us moonlight through her canvas,—cut her cordage and unreeve her rigging.'

Simultaneously a flood of red fire and white smoke burst from the low waist and towering fore and *after-castles* of the two ships, and a storm of shot flew over each, the balls of the *Cressi*, many of them stone bullets from King Henry's quarries at Maidstone, knocked great white splinters from the painted hull and carved galleries of the *Yellow Frigate*, and killed and wounded many of her men ; while she in turn cut to pieces the rigging of her enemy, and thus rendered her motions slow and her management difficult.

' We must rid ourselves of this hornet before we engage her companions,' said Sir Andrew ; ' put the ship about, Barton, and remember our prank with the Portuguese.'

' 'Bout ship,' cried Barton, after a few preparations, putting the trumpet through his open helmet ; ' helm's a-lee ; —let go, and haul ! '

Round swung the ponderous ship, while loose shot and everything else rolled from windward to leeward, as she stood off on the opposite tack, as if about to creep in shore and fly ; and now the increasing breeze filled her canvas, and careened her gracefully over on that bright moonlit sea, which her bows cleft as an arrow cleaves the air. Astonished to find the dreaded Laird of Largo fly before them, the crew of the *Cressi* gave three hearty English cheers, and had the hardihood to make all sail in chase, firing the light falcons of their forecastle as fast as the cannoniers could bring them to bear upon the towering stern and quarter of the Scot, who, while returning the fire, tacked twice, as if to escape.

' Barton, take thou the helm,' said Wood, ' and keep at your quarters, my yeomen of the sheets and braces. Yo-ho, boatswain ! take in all the small sails.'

On seeing this, in their nautical or national confidence on the sea, the English crew again believed that now Wood was about to grapple with them, and natheless his superior size, they had no doubt of being âble to engage and retain him valiantly until the *Harry* which was a mile astern, came up.

Though it was an age in which navigation was destitute of many modern inventions and appliances, Wood was as

famous for the skilful manner in which he handled his ship
as for the bravery with which he fought her, for under his
orders, her vast hull, with its towering rigging and cloud of
sail, was like a toy.   Thus, after a few manœuvres, the *Cressi*
lay to, and continued firing briskly at the *Yellow Frigate*,
which her crew believed was about to run alongside ; but
in rounding to, her captain, though a brave mariner, had
given Wood the advantage of the wind, and while her crew
poured in their missiles, cannon and arquebuse-shot, with
those cloth-yard shafts so famed in English war, Barton
suddenly put the helm hard up, at a sign from the admiral,
who cried with the voice of a stentor :

' Yeomen of the braces and bowlines, let go ! slack off
your sheets and tacks,—yare, my hearts,—yare, and square
the yards.'

It was all the work of a moment ; the blocks creaked, the
cordage whistled, the canvas flapped heavily, and filled again,
as the tremendous bow of the Scottish Caravel was suddenly
brought to bear directly upon the broadside of the *Cressi*,
whose captain had no time to fill his yards or forge ahead
again, for dire confusion and dismay pervaded his crowded
decks, from which a hundred mingled cries of rage, wonder,
and defiance arose.   And there she lay, in the deep valley
formed by the long-swelling waves, while her crew bravely
fired their culverins at the *Yellow Frigate*, which bore down
under a cloud of canvas, looming like the shadow of death
between them and the brilliant moon.

On, on she glided, almost noiselessly.

One wave alone separated them !

Then down she came thundering with her iron beak upon
the enemy's vessel, striking her right amidships.   The wild
shriek of rage that rose on one side was mingled with a
shout of triumph on the other.   The *Yellow Frigate* scarcely
felt the shock, as she rode over the low waist, and crashed
through the torn rigging of the *Cressi*, the lofty poop and
forecastle of which fell inwards, as the hull was cloven in
two, and sunk for ever into that brilliant sea, the vortex of
which sucked down two hundred gallant men.

' For God's love, Sir Andrew, lower the boats,' cried Falconer, looking into the foam-covered whirlpool, where a few
spars and casks, with an occasional head or a hand, were
rising and sinking.

' Impossible—even our pinnace would sink with her ;
but God sain them,' said the old admiral ; ' there hath gone

down many a brave fellow, who will never more lift tack or sheet in this world ! '

A loud cheer now rose close astern ; it came from the crew of the *Queen Margaret ;* and both ships then bore on towards the enemy, leaving the sea covered with the débris of the wreck ; and as the old ballad says :

> Many was the feather bed,
>   That fluttered on the foam ;
> And many was the gude lord's son,
>   That never mair came home.

> The ladies wrang their fingers white,
>   The maidens tore their hair ;
> A' for the sake o' those true lovers,
>   They never shall see mair.

' May they sleep as soundly in the Scottish sea as my father sleeps in their Kentish downs,' said Barton ; ' but many a blue corpselight will dance on these waters ere the sun of to-morrow rises.'

' To your guns again, my merry men all,' cried the admiral, ' they are two to one against us ; but if we put them not to rout we were no better than Gordon gowks, and there will be many a toom bowie and kirn in Fife and Lothian. Heed not King Henry's bitter almonds, for I swear by my honour as a seaman and faith as a knight that every shipmate o' mine who loseth a fin, shall swing his hammock for life in Largo Tower, and share the goods kind God hath given me ; he shall never lack a brass bodle or a can of ale while auld Andrew Wood hath both to part with him fairly over the capstan head ; so stand every man to his quarters—put your faith in God and St. Andrew, and fight, my lads, as you have often fought before, for auld Scotland and her glory ! '

This characteristic harangue was answered by a hurrah, and many a weatherbeaten and well-bearded visage glowed redly along the gun-deck when the matches were blown, and the waves sparkled in the moonlight, as they ran merrily past the triced-up lids of the open ports through which the brass culverins and guns of Scottish yetlin were run and pointed, after being primed and shotted for battle.

' Sir David Falconer, send thine arquebussiers aft, line the taffrail and fill the tops with them—away aloft ! ' cried the admiral, ' and shame be on the last who is through the lubber's hole or over the foot-hook shrouds ! '

The arquebussiers clambered up the ratlins, and our marines of the present day would be rather amused could they see such a sight as those soldiers presented ; heavily accoutred with back, breast, head, and thigh pieces, bandoliers, flasks, and swords—and, more than all, their long arquebusses, crawling like scaly armadilloes up the black rigging. However, they soon reached their perches, and levelled their barrels over the little wooden battlement which then surrounded the tops. As it was now intended to come to what was termed ' close battle,' there was no more manœuvring ; and all the adverse ships bore down upon each other, firing their cannon briskly ; while arquebusses, pistolettes, and calivers, with many a shaft from bow and arblast were levelled from the tops, the poops, and forecastles—for the brilliant moon enabled aim to be taken with precision ; and as the wind was again becoming light, the courses were drawn up, and all reduced their sails.

' Stand by with the grappling-irons,' cried Barton, whose bright armour and conspicuous figure made him the mark of many a missile ; and in obedience to his order a number of bold fellows leaped into the chain-plates to throw them on board the foe, the moment the vessels came near enough. The sides of the English ship were similarly supplied. These grappling-irons were composed of five or six branches, bent round and pointed, with a ring at the root to which is fastened a rope to hold on by when the grapple is thrown and catches the object. Thus they closed in upon each other—these six hostile ships ; the two Scots running (as our annals relate) right in between the four English ships ; the left centre being the *Harry*. All were pouring their missiles upon each other with fearful rapidity, and the English were so reckless that their shot must have killed many of their own men, after piercing the Scottish hulls. By somemis management, the *Harry's* spritsail-yard became entangled with the mainshrouds of the *Yellow Frigate*, which forged a little a-head, and dragging round the *Harry* with her, by one broadside she swept her deck like a tempest, and breached to ruin the towering poop beyond.

' Half-an-hour of a true parabolic speculum were worth a year of this work ! ' said Father Zuill, who now appeared in a coat of mail, with a poleaxe which he handled as well as ever he had done his rosary.

' Boarders, away fore and aft ! ' cried Sir Andrew Wood, through his trumpet, as he stood above the clouds of smoke at the edge of the poop, towering like an iron statue, while the chain-plates crashed as the ponderous hulls sheered alongside of each other in rasping collision ; and in hundreds the boarders swarmed on the bulwarks, while the English grappling-irons clutched the Scottish ships, whose sailors worked side by side with the foe, in lashing the shrouds together below and the yard-arms aloft, until the six vessels formed, as it were, one broad platform, for a scene of melancholy butchery, which we have but little heart and less taste for describing.

The Scottish mariners, armed with their two-handed swords and Jedwood axes, and all accoutred in steel caps and jacks or doublets of escaupill, led by Sir Andrew Wood on one side, poured from the bows and spritsail-yard of the *Yellow Frigate* upon the decks of the *Harry*, and drove the enemy across the forecastle and along the larboard gangway, while Barton, sheathed in full armour, and wielding a deadly ghisarma in both hands, led another band through the fire, smoke, and infernal uproar, hewing a passage, hilt to hilt, to the forecastle of the other ship, desperately forcing a passage through a hedge of gallant billmen, into the waist.

The crew of the *Queen Margaret*, under Sir Alexander Mathieson, after succeeding in repelling the English boarders, were similarly employed elsewhere ; and there, under that placid summer moon, were Englishmen and Scot fighting like tigers, all mingled in a wild *mêlée*, while their firmly-grappled ships were committed to the mercy of the waves and currents. Save the flash and boom of a cannon or saker from the poops, or the bang of a pistolette or arquebuse from the tops, there were no other sounds heard now, but the rasp of steel gleaming on steel, the twang of the English bows, and the crash of the Scottish axes on helmets and bills ; the cries and shrieks of the wounded, and the yells of pain and defiance, drowned in a gurgle, as many a man was driven, fighting, overboard, and drowned or crushed to death between the grappled ships. The decks were encumbered by killed and wounded, and repeatedly the Scots were driven back over their own bulwarks, and had to fight the English on the decks of Wood and Mathieson.

'St. Andrew ! St Andrew ! A Wood ! a Wood !' on one side, were met by 'St. George for England !' on the other, mingled with many a furious epithet and ferocious expression of that deep-rooted national animosity, which the infamous wars of the Plantagenets had created between two nations, who, if allied, might then—as they have since—defied the world in arms.

Overhead the arquebussiers blazed at each other from the tops, and sent an occasional bullet into the mass of combatants below.

After various turns of the conflict, Robert Barton found himself fighting hand to hand with the crew of the *Harry*, close to her poop, and attended only by Willie Wad and a few seamen. With these he strove to join the admiral, who had already penetrated into the vessel *beyond*, and was maintaining a desperate and most unequal conflict with her crew.

While Barton fought his way up the starboard side of the *Harry's* deck, his boatswain, with a band of Jedwood axes, hewed a passage along the larboard, and, owing to the heavier weapons, and perhaps greater number of the Scots, the *Harry's* crew were driven into the poop, where they hewed and shot in the dark ; thus many a brave man perished by the hands of his own shipmates. Here Barton, when just at the poop door, encountered a gallant English gentleman, who had repeatedly cut a passage through the frigate's men, by knocking them down like ninepins ; and, recognizing Howard by the heraldic cognizance on his surcoat, the Scottish captain uttered a cry of triumph, and rushed upon him, to revenge Lord Howard's recent victory in the Downs ; and then forgetting all but their personal animosity, they engaged hand to hand with sword and dagger, at every blow and cut making the sparks fly from their coats of tempered steel ; and thrice during the conflict old Anthony Arblaster wound up his weapon, and sent a deliberate shot at Barton's head, and was preparing a fourth when a blow from an axe ended the poor man's shooting for ever.

' Haloo, auld junk,' cried his slayer, ' may I drink bilge, but thou'rt fitted for foreign parts at last ! and by St. Andrew gaffer Englishman,' he added, turning upon Howard, ' I'll cloure thy harnpan too, double caulked wi' wadding and sheathed wi' steel though it be ! '

The short squat gunner was rushing on with uplifted axe, when Barton threw himself forward, and on his own sword caught the descending blow.

' Sheer off, Wad, sheer off, this man is mine, and I must slay him myself, were it but to soothe my slaughtered father's soul ; so leave us, I command you ! '

Wad soon found another antagonist in tall Dick Selbv,

who gave him more than enough to do. Meanwhile the combat continued between Howard and Barton, till a passing bullet broke the sword of the latter, and he stood disarmed and at the mercy of Howard, who merely uttered a bitter laugh, and scornfully dropped the point of his sword, saying :

'How now, my bonnie Scot; wilt beg thy life at an English hand ?'

'I could beg it of none more noble than Howard's; but strike, if you will, for never will I beg life or quarter of a living man, and least of all from the brother of him who slew my father!' said Barton hoarsely.

At that moment Wad returned with an armed tide of seamen flushed with blood and victory; the noble Howard was beaten to the deck, and despite all Barton's efforts, would have been slain, had not the cry of a woman been heard, and Margaret Drummond, fearless of the surrounding carnage, the whistling shafts, the ferocious visages, and uplifted steel, threw herself on her knees beside him, and spread her white arms over him in protection.

The terror she had experienced in the cockpit was so great, that, regardless of the hideous grating and crashing below and the awful tumult above, she resolved to make an effort to reach the Scottish ships, which, as little Will Selby had informed her, were lashed alongside. Thus had she come so opportunely—and thus, with these two acts of mercy, will we gladly veil the horrors of this midnight conflict.

The Scottish seamen, who knew her not, and deemed she was the wife of Howard, drew back and spared him at once ; for none are more merciful, albeit their roughness, than those honest souls who live by salt water; but Barton was confounded, and gazed upon her in astonishment and silence, while the din of battle died away around them, and it became known that the English ships had hauled down their colours. So, thanks to the bravery of Sir Andrew Wood, old Sir Alexander Mathieson, 'the King of the Sea,' David Falconer, and a certain valiant mariner of Leith, named William Merrimonth, sailing master of the *Margaret*, who received a desperate wound, ' ye foure Inglish shippes were takin',' and all their crews disarmed, according to the records of the Scottish Admiralty, after a deadlier conflict than these waters had witnessed since the Knight of Dalhousie fought King Edward's fleet at Tweedmouth and sunk eighteen of his galleys.

CHAPTER XLIV

WHEN the sun rose from the ocean, the appearance of these six ships was wofully changed. The waves were rolling in brilliant green and gold, and the yellow sands of Tyningham, the red towers, the deep caverns and surf-beaten rocks of Dunbar were glistening in the morning beams ; the gannets, the cormorants, and gigantic solan geese on their snow-white pinions, were wheeling merrily in the welkin above the summer sea ; but the state of the hostile ships, which, while they were all lashed together, had drifted hither and thither at the mercy of the wind and tide, was deplorable. Their decks were crowded by killed and wounded, especially round the scuttle-butts, to which many had crawled for the purpose of allaying their burning thirst ; the bulwarks were splashed with blood, and it oozed or dropped in curdles from the scuppers : boats, booms, and spars were riven and splintered ; sheets and tackles were streaming loose upon the breeze ; the yards were out of trim and lowered upon the caps, while the canvas was pierced and torn ;—but still the *blue ensign* was flying over all.

The ships with which Sir Alexander Mathieson had grappled were almost complete wrecks, for all his cannon were great earthouns or forty-pounders—prodigious guns for that age. The *Yellow Frigate*, like her chief adversary, had lost all her trim neatness ; some of her yards were shot in the slings : her rigging hung in loops and bights, and blood was trickling down the masts and stays, or dropping from the tops upon the battered deck and white courses ; for many of Falconer's arquebussiers lay there slain, or bleeding through the gratings, from the wounds of bullets and arrows.

Sir Andrew Wood, before loosening a buckle of his harness, now ordered the prisoners to be secured, and crews put on board the prizes ; their damages to be partly repaired, and sail to be made on them all. The grappling-irons were cast off; the ports lowered; the decks swabbed, and the dead sent ashore; shot-holes were plugged and caulked; loose ropes coiled up, the sails trimmed, and before a favourable breeze from the south-east, the six vessels bore away for Largo Bay, as the admiral had no intention of taking his prizes into Leith, until he knew to whom they should be delivered; for he considered the victorious barons as no better than rebels.

The dead were buried in two trenches in the cemetery of the old collegiate kirk at Dunbar, where the mound which covered the ' Englishmen's grave ' was long an object of interest to the people.

In getting the ships clear of the horrid débris of the battle, and in attending to the wounded, English and Scots worked side by side with hearty goodwill, and only relaxed their sailor-like indifference when they drank their cans of brown ale together, and passed the blackjack of whisky-and-water from man to man;—for now, when that deadly strife was over and their fury had expended itself, enmity was at an end—for a time at least,—and Willie Wad and Dick Selby, the rival gunners, carved at the same junk with their jockte-legs (or clasp-knives), and the latter sang when the former produced his fiddle; while the boatswain spun some of his wonderful yarns to amuse the prisoners. All on the gundeck of the *Yellow Frigate* seemed merry enough, the maimed excepted, but there were lowering brows and heavy hearts in the cabin of her admiral.

This apartment had four windows which overlooked a gallery; and the morning sun shone brightly through them as he rose from the amber-coloured sea. Along the sides were the culverins of their carriages, and on the rudder-case were the arms of Wood—*argent*, an oak tree growing out of a mount, with two bears for supporters; and to this two ships were afterwards added, as we find in Sir David Lindesay's *Book of Blazons*, in memory of his victory near the Isle of May.

The frank Laird of Largo had doffed his helmet and much of his iron panoply, and at two bells (nine A. M.) was entertaining to a sumptuous breakfast (as sumptuous at least as could be prepared on board of ship) his officers and some of the English prisoners—Captain Howard, John o' Lynne, Miles Furnival, and two other English captains whose names are not recorded, with Falconer, Barton, and other gentlemen of the Scottish ships. All sat side by side at Largo's long and hospitable board, the place of honour being assigned to Lady Margaret Drummond and her two attendants, Rose and Cicely.

The three looked pale, jaded, and weary, for the terrors of the past night and the horrors of the dawn had impressed them deeply—the more so, as they had been attending to some of the wounded, who had no other leeches than the ship's barber-apothecary and their messmates. The breakfast consisted of several joints of mutton, cut in collops, with roasted capons, dishes of roasted chickens, eggs broiled in their shells on large platters—or as they are named in Scotland and France, assiettes,—cakes, manchets, and jugs of ale, with several sack possets, each formed of twelve eggs put into a Scottish mutchkin of sack with a quart of cream, well sugared and boiled together for fifteen minutes ; and there were hippocrass of milk and cherry wine for the ladies. Such was the repast to which fair justice was done by all save Howard and Margaret Drummond—or as we should perhaps style her—the Duchess of Rothesay.

Entreaty and remonstrance had proved alike futile when Howard was pressed by Barton and Sir Andrew Wood to explain how and why this missing daughter of the Lord Drummond—she whose strange disappearance was one of the secret springs that rolled a civil war against the throne— was found on board his vessel ! He flatly and firmly declined to answer ; and Margaret herself could not very clearly inform them as to her abductors ; for she knew of none save Borthwick, against whom, for want of a better object, Barton resolved to turn the whole current of his wrath.

However, all King Henry's plot with the Scottish traitors was nearly being discovered about the time the ships surrendered, by Master Quentin Kraft, the notary, who was dragged abaft the mizenmast of the *Yellow Frigate* by Cuddie Clewline and Dalquhat the seaman, who had found him ensconced in the cable-tier of the *Harry*, where he had repeatedly offered them a certain iron-bound volume, with which they would have nothing to do, believing by its aspect that it must be a book of magic, else wherefore that lock and all these bands of steel.

' Slue him round—heave ahead, master,' said the coxswain, giving him a push ; ' haud up your face, auld dog-fish —you are before the admiral ! '

The dapper attorney, in his black cassock-coat, looked very much scared, and said in a quavering voice :

'I crave your mercy, Sir Andrew Wood—I can pay a small ransom if it be wished; I am Quentin Kraft, a gentleman of the law—an attorney—a notary, if it please you—one well known about Westminster Hall and Lincoln's Inn—London.'

'A what, sayst thou?' demanded the admiral.

'A notary public, at your service—and secretary to the noble Captain Howard.'

'A scurvy rogue, Sir Andrew Wood,' said Howard disdainfully: 'one who hath been stripped of his gown and coif in Westminster Hall, and cast adrift by the benchers at Lincoln's Inn. But men who can handle the quill are scarce—so I was e'en forced to content me with such a secretary, for lack of a better.'

'It is false—I am a man of repute,' said Kraft.

'Yea,' said Howard; 'but a devilish one, sirrah.'

'And if the Scottish admiral,' added the spiteful notary, 'will accept *this volume* at my hands, promising that my life, limbs, and goods shall be respected, it will make his fortune.'

'Wretch and villan, wouldst thou betray the secrets of King Henry?' cried Howard, as he rushed upon Kraft, and wrenching away the volume, flung it through an open porthole; and being iron-bound, it sunk like a stone into the sea.

'It was well done, Captain Howard,' said Sir Andrew Wood; 'I ken little and I care less what yonder black tome contained; but I honour thee for destroying it, as much as I despise this miserable notary for proffering it as the price of a life that is not worth taking. Away with him, Cuddie, and though such lubberly land-loupers are gude for nocht but to drink the king's ale and lollop in the afterguard or ship's waist, see that no man molests him.'

The breakfast was dispatched with great relish. Men were used to hard knocks, cuts, and slashes in those days; and, though many at the table had their heads and arms bandaged up, from the effect of their late conflict, they passed the ale-cans and frothing possets merrily from hand to hand; and already Father Zuill, who had donned his friar's frock, was explaining to John o' Lynne the powerful results that would ultimately accrue to an astonished world by a properly developed parabolic speculum; and John listened with a smile of perplexity to what he considered the freak of a learned madman.

Barton sat silent, and gazed from time to time at Howard, as if he was pondering whether it was a dream or a reality, that they both had their legs under the same friendly table. Falconer, too, was somewhat silent, or only addressed the fair Margaret, in whose soft eyes and pale Madonna face he was tracing the expression of her darker sister Sybilla. Howard was also reserved, for the waves that ran so brightly past the cabin windows were bearing him further from his home ; and he felt himself disgraced in being captured by a force so inferior to his own, and being the subject of a narrative that would sound but ill on Paul's Walk, in London; and he was aware, too, that with Margaret's release all hope of his gaining her affection would pass away for ever, for now she would be restored to that gay young prince whom, as yet, he conceived to be her lover only.

Wood observed that the brave Englishman was low-spirited, and that a peculiar sadness hovered over his fine features, so he begged him to be of good cheer ; ' for I doubt not,' said he, ' that the Governor of Berwick will have in ward some of our mosstrooping lairds, for whom to exchange thee ; at all events, we may fairly set thee off against the Lord Bishop of Dunblane, whom your king still detains in London. Come, shipmate, fill the foreyard ; the sea is yet under thee—and life in thee is young yet ; for I am more than twice thine age, and am a canty auld carle yet.'

' True, admiral,' said Howard, with a glance at Margaret; ' but the charms of life have been doubly destroyed at the very time I was beginning to find there was another to live for than myself.'

The admiral rubbed his beard uneasily, for he detected the glance of Howard, and saw how Margaret's cheek reddened, though Falconer was speaking to her of other things ; and, as he afterwards said to Barton, he ' knew in a moment which way the wind was setting in,' but he veiled his correct suspicions, and said :

' Of course it is sad to lose one's old shipmates and a battle too ; but what o' that ? we lose to-day and win to-morrow, for we cannot be always victorious. Twelve years ago, the ships of stout Andrew Barton (who never was beaten before) were overwhelmed by the Admiral of Portugal, though, as the song says, he was

The best sailor that ever sailed the sea.

But, gadzooks, he soon after cleared off that score with the skippers of the King of Portugal.'

' True, admiral,' said Howard, glad to grasp at anything which might serve to explain his melancholy ; ' but of all those whom you have sent ashore to be entombed, and of those who in the *Cressi* have sunk to feed the hungry serpent of the sea,' he continued, for that nautical personage now so familiar to us as Master David Jones was then unknown, ' I regret none more than brave Anthony Arblaster, the captain of my archers.'

' Ah—and how fell he ? '

' A blow from a poleaxe took him right amidships, and slew him ;—poor Tony ! '

' And thus he went to foreign parts—God bless him ! we'll remember him when masses are said and the sance-bell tolled in Largo Kirk,' replied the admiral. ' And now, madam,' he added, turning to Margaret, to change the subject, ' now that the smiles are coming back to your sweet face (I am an auld carle, and may say so)—now that you have got all your gear rove and your golden hair braided, by my faith, I would scarcely know you to be the same wild dame who rushed from the *Harry's* poop last night, all pale, like a white spirit or weird woman, with your hair dishevelled and canvas loose in the brailes, to save this gallant gentleman ! I' faith ! 'twill be a strange story to tell the old Lord Drummond, though darkly enough he looked on me, when, yesterday at noon, we stood in the prince's presence. I think that now I may win his good-will, unless his heart be tough as a nine-inch cable or hard as a cannon-ball.'

' You have indeed a claim on my father's everlasting gratitude—and on one greater even than he,' said Margaret, as tears filled her eyes, and she paused, lest too many thanks should sound reproachfully to the gentle Howard.

' Ay, the good king,' said the admiral, partly mistaking her ; ' yet I would to St. Andrew we could hear aught of him, for he must be in Scotland still, and they are false traitors who say he hath fled to Holland, England, or any other foreign country ; for there are too many brave clansmen in the north to make flight necessary after *one* battle ! But of these matters of statecraft I ken little ; kings and lords ride in owre deep water for me ; so the gunner to his lint-stock and the steersman to his helm, say I.'

About noon the ships passed the basaltic promontory and low, flat, sterile links near Elie—or, as it was then named, Ardross, with the houses of its bleak old burgh standing upon sea-dykes of black round stones, on which the ride was

roaring with a peculiar sound, which ever betokens bad
weather. Thus, the fisher-boats were all creeping under the
lee of the bluff, into that little harbour which is still named
from our admiral, Wood's Haven ; and as the mist was beginning to roll round the green and conical hill of Largo, he
ordered that on coming to anchor in the bay, the topmasts
should be struck, the topgallant-yards sent down on deck,
and all the ports secured, for now the sky had overcast, and
as the old sea rhyme says :

> When Largo Law the mist doth bear,
> Let Kelly Law for storms prepare.

Thus, both wind and rain were expected.

The coast of Fife looked close and gloomy, the headlands
were drenched in foam ; the fir woods and deeply caverned
shore of Kilconquhar were black and dreary ; the sun became
fiery and red, while the wind came in hollow, sudden, and
furious gusts, as the vessels ran into the broad and beautiful
Bay of Largo, and came to anchor abreast of the little town,
which was then thriving under the fatherly care of the noble
merchant-skipper, and was protected by the strong castle he
had built with the royal permission, on becoming the king's
chief admiral, and being made a knight and baron of Parliament.

As the summer sky was darkening fast, and some of the
ships were injured in their hulls, Sir Andrew ordered all the
hammocks to be stowed below ; the culverins to be double-
breeched, the deadlights to be shipped, and the sheet anchors
to be let go, as the vessels had to ride on an ebb and lee tide.
He then conveyed Lady Margaret and her two English
attendants, with Howard, Miles Furnival, and all the gentlemen of their squadron, ashore, and conducted them to his
Castle of Largo, the gates of which were barely closed behind them before the summer storm burst forth with all its
fury, and its drenching rain that sowed the sea and smoked
along the shore, while the chill east wind swayed the heavy
woods and made the ships careen in the bay as it swept
round each bare headland, and the rifted nesses of Fife.

'Truly Horace was right,' sighed Father Zuill, as he saw
the squadron straining on their cables, 'when he said that
"he who ventured first to sea had a soul of triple brass." '

CHAPTER XLV.

ST. ANTHONY'S BELL.

NEXT day it became known among all the ports on both sides of the Forth, that Admiral Wood had won another victory—that his three favourite followers, Mathieson, Barton, of Leith, and Falconer of Bo'ness, had escaped without scaith, and the bells in more than a hundred steeples rang joyously, while the ships hoisted all their colours and streamers in the roadstead, at the Hope, and in the harbours.

In the house of Barton, the insurgent nobles held a deep carouse, and drank the Rhenish and Malvoisie of the umquhile Sir Andrew with a relish all the greater that it cost them nothing. Among the company were four persons, at least, who would rather have hailed a disastrous defeat than this unexpected victory.

These were the Lords Home and Hailes—who had great hopes that their troublesome rivals might have been sent to a better world ; but chiefly Sir Patrick Gray and Sir James Shaw, with others of their servile and infamous faction, who were thunderstruck by the intelligence; for they had never doubted, when the admiral dropped down the river with two vessels only, that he was running into the jaws of destruction. But it is strange that Wood, in all his naval battles, had to contend against great odds, yet never *once* was beaten. And now the cosmopolitans of the English faction trembled, as they remembered their bond with Henry, and feared that unless the lips of Margaret Drummond were sealed for ever, their projects would all be revealed to Rothesay, of whom, boy as he was, they knew enough to be assured of a terrible retribution.

Lord Drummond—that irascible old patrician—had peremptorily warned his daughters Euphemia and Sybilla to prepare for being espoused by Home and Hailes, whose new patents of nobility, he believed, would be issued as soon as the king's *flight*—his murder was yet unknown—was ascertained, and as soon as Rothesay was proclaimed king. Their uncle, the Dean of Dunblane—a facile priest, in all things subservient to his brother as chief of the clan Drummond, and, like most Scottish churchmen of that age, bent solely on the aggrandizement of his family—was to perform the ceremony, which was fixed to take place on an early day. And as the venerable dean had long since been abstracted from all human sympathies, and become a mere mummy in a cassock and scapular, the poor girls had now no hope in anything, and no resource but their tears, which were likely to avail them little ; for in Scotland, in those days, the rights of women were as little known, or nearly as ill defined, as among the Asiatics in the present ; for cruel coercion and abduction at the sword's point were of daily occurrence, as the criminal records show, until the middle of the last century.

The presence of the prince's court and insurgent army was a harvest to the keeper of the tavern or hostel, already referred to, as being situated in the Kirkgate—*the Bell*,—so named in honour of the hospitallers of the ancient and wealthy preceptory of St. Anthony, whose establishment stood on the east side of that venerable thoroughfare, and who wore a *bell*, sewn in blue cloth on the breast of their gowns. This signboard gave the said tavern respectability, while the keeper was ensured protection by paying an exorbitant yearly fee to the Laird of Restalrig for the privilege of keeping it open ; for that turbulent and avaricious little potentate was lord superior of Leith; and though King Robert I. had granted the harbour to the citizens of Edinburgh, they had still to purchase from the family of Logan the right of erecting wharves and houses upon the sandy banks of the river, which for ages had flowed into the Forth between heaps of sand and knolls of whin and broom.

On the second day after the naval battle, about six o'clock, when the great bell of St. Anthony had rung the hospitallers to prayer, in an upper chamber of the hostel (the east windows of which overlooked the drear expanse of the sandy links and the Figgate-muir, on the verge of which the waves were rippling) sat Sir James Shaw of Sauchie, Sir Patrick Gray, and their brother assassin, Sir William Stirling of Keir, all armed as we saw them last at Beaton's mill, save their helmets, which, with their scarfs, swords, and wheel-locks, lay on a bench, which stood on one side of the wainscoted room. On the mantelpiece were shells, stuffed fishes, and sea eggs. There was no fire on the hearth, of course, for the month of June; and the recess was destitute of a grate, for such things were expensive. The furniture consisted of a large table, and fauld-stools seated with leather. Comfort was considered unnecessary in a hostel, consequently the room looked bare and dreary, and the governor of His Majesty's Castle of Stirling was, as usual, a little tipsy; for after their early supper of fried flounders, buttered crabs, and eggs in gravy, each had imbibed more than a Scotch pint (equal to an English quart) of Rochelle wine, then sold at eightpence; and a fresh supply was ordered, for they had thirst and doubt, spleen and, it might be, some small remorse to drown. And the pewter stoups of the last supply had just been placed upon the black oak table, when Hew Borthwick, in his rich attire, stood before them, and carefully locked the door on the inside.

'By my soul, sir, but you are bravely apparelled,' said the grim Baron of Sauchie with a drunken leer. 'What sayeth the Act of '71?—that none wear silk except knights, minstrels, and heralds——'

'King James and his acts——'

'Are lying together in a slough ditch,' said the Lord of Keir, interrupting the pale and sneering Borthwick. 'But we have other matter in hand; you have just come from the east country?'

'I left Dunbar this day, at morn.'

'Be seated. Here, take a stoup of the Rochelle. Well, is not this accursed intelligence?' said Gray, grinding his teeth. 'What! Howard, with five great ships, to be beaten by this old seahorse of Largo, this presumptuous Leither, with only two!—and Kraft, that damnable secretary, he may ruin us all!'

'Think of three Scottish barons being at the mercy of an English notary!' said Borthwick, scanning them maliciously over his winepot, as it rose to the angle of forty-five degrees above his mouth.

'And his book—and the bond in cypher,' added Gray.

'God confound his evil fortune!' growled Sir James Shaw. 'To be at the beck of a smock-faced driveller! The thing is not to be borne, sirs; we must stop his mouth, by fair means or by foul.'

'Art certain, Hew, these rumours of victory are not exaggerated?'

'There remains not the shadow of a doubt. With hundreds more—yes, thousands—in East Lothian I saw at dawn yesterday but two flags flying, as the six ships stood under sail for Fife, and these were the blue ensigns, with the white cross of Saint Andrew.'

'We must sleep in our harness, and keep fleet horses saddled day and night,' said Gray; 'and let spies be set to watch what messages come hither from the admiral.'

'Angus may see us clear of it,' suggested Keir.

'Angus knows nothing of our deeper plots,' said the more politic and subtle Gray; 'moreover, he abhors an English match as much as we pretend to hate a continental one——'

'Among ourselves.'

'Of course. He cares not for rank—he is an earl; he cares not for pay—he is Lord of Galloway, and owns more land and lances than any four earls in Scotland.'

'He is well off. I' faith, I have been spending four thousand pounds yearly, out of a barony that yields but one thousand Scottish crowns per year,' said Shaw. 'Henry of England will deem us fools for having our plots marred, and in revenge may tell the whole to Rothesay, and then we shall be lost men.'

'Well, well,' said Shaw, draining his huge tankard; 'after all his gold spent and ships lost, it must be rather provoking to find that James III. is only removed to make little Maggie Drummond Queen of Scotland.'

'I urged Howard to throw her overboard,' said Borthwick, lowering his voice, while that snaky gleam which his eyes often wore passed over them.

'And what said Howard then?' asked Gray impatiently.

'The Saxon pockpudding! he smote me on the mouth with his steel glove, and styled your knighthoods a pack o' "Scottish hounds,"' replied Borthwick, whose sinister brow grew dark with ferocity; 'and he threatened to make a martyr of me, like St. Clement.'

'Would to thy master the devil that he had done so,' grumbled the drunken Shaw; thinking of his share in that dark deed in Beaton's mill.

Gray muttered an impatient and unmeaning malediction

'What said ye then?' asked Keir, with a cold smile, as he played with his dagger.

'I said little, but I thought much.'

'What thought ye?' asked Gray, fiercely.

'Merely that this Englishman was not yet on his own

side of the border,' said Borthwick with a deep smile, as he took the last drain of his wine-pot.

' Angus still acts the bearward to this beardless princeling Rothesay,' said Gray ; ' and so is occupied by matters of his own ; but the tide of events on which we have ridden so bravely seems setting in against us now ; all we can do is to watch, and watch well ; let us be assured in the first place, of what messengers come from the fleet, and whether they say aught of Margaret Drummond ; for if she once gain Rothesay's ear, our cause is ruined and for ever lost ! '

Borthwick bit his tongue with anger, for he trembled for himself alone.

' Get thee spies,' said Keir ; ' and let Barton's house, where Rothesay lodges, be watched both day and night. Watch all who come from thence, and from the Laird of Largo.'

' But spies must be paid, Sir William, and I am short of money.'

' Already ! ' cried Gray ; ' curse thee, fellow ; dost think we keep a coin house ? Short again, after all received from Howard, from Henry VII., and from us ? '

' All gone, sirs,' he added, doggedly ; ' patriotism is expensive work.'

' Here are eight fleurs-de-lys, and not another coin shalt thou have, were it for thy mass when *in articulo mortis*. So away to thy task, while we will watch and deliberate.'

The worthy functionary of the English faction swept the Laird of Keir's money into the velvet pouch which hung on his right hip beside his poniard, and then quitted the presence of his employers. As he descended the stair of the hostel, a gentleman in black armour touched him roughly on the shoulder. Borthwick grew pale, and clutched the dagger at his girdle ; and then perceiving that the iron plates of this personage were somewhat rusty, he said with haughty insolence :

' Who may you be ? '

' Your better man, sirrah—therefore attend.'

' What want ye, sir ? ' he asked, rather abashed by the other's air and determined manner.

' Nothing,' was the blunt reply ; ' that is, personally I seek nothing of such fellows as thee ; but the right honourable my very good lord and chief requires your presence in his chamber, here, without delay.'

Borthwick still kept a hand upon his poniard, as he scanned the speaker's sunburned face.

'And who are you ? ' he asked, after a pause.

'One of the Hepburns—Adam of the Black Castle.'

'Then your chief is the Lord Hailes ? '

'I have just had the honour of hinting as much,' replied the other, with an irony which Borthwick dared not resent.

'Lead on, then, laird ; I follow you,' he said ; and then they ascended another of the turnpike stairs with which this ancient hostel was furnished.

CHAPTER XLVI.

THE GUNNER.

At this time, when the sun had set enveloped in clouds—when the Forth was breaking in foam over the black scalp of the Beacon Rock, and while its billows boomed along the dreary ridges of the Musselcape and the far expanse of desert sand that bordered the Figgate-muir,—Euphemia and Sybilla Drummond occupied a seat near the beach at Barton's house, where they sat hand-in-hand, and bathed in tears; for their sky, to speak figuratively, was as much overcast as that which yesternight had warned old Andrew Wood to drop his anchors and make all snug for riding out a gale in the bonnie Bay of Largo. But it was not the sullen chafing of the waves, the darkening of the inky sky, the foam-flecked river, or the flying scud, that brought those tears to the hazel eyes of these two gentle and loving sisters, for they feared not for the safety of their lovers; they wept alone for that unhappy fate to which they seemed abandoned; for ambition or avarice had steeled the heart of their father against them; and family pride and priestly austerity had withered up the soul of their uncle; and hope they had none.

Callous, proud, and cold, Hailes and Home seemed bent on espousing them in a spirit of mere opposition or convenience—if not with something of revenge, for their rejection of an absurd and insulting suit which had been coarsely pressed upon them, while it was known that their affections were secured by others, and that their hearts were swollen with sorrow by the strange disappearance of their sister; and young Rothesay, who for her sake loved them well, and who might have unravelled one part of her story—viz., the discovery of the poor little babe in the alcove—was yet, by the lawless detention of the Bishop of Dunblane in England, obliged to seal his lips as to an espousal which he dared not acknowledge to the nation.

Two large willows, shaded, and a thick boor-tree hedge

screened this old garden seat, on which a hundred lovers had
cut their names or initials ; and on the soft rind of the willows
Sybilla soon discovered the date 1486, between the letters
D. F. and S. D.—the initials of herself and Falconer, who in
that year had first seen and learned to love her, and, like a
true Orlando, had cut them there,—thus revealing, as it
were, to the spirits of the air and the sea, that love which he
dared hardly acknowledge to himself as yet.

' Poor dear Falconer ! ' said Sybilla, patting the rind with
her pretty white hand ; ' thou lovest me well and truly ! '

Since their separation at Dundee, she had never heard
his voice ; nor since that horrible day had Euphemia an
opportunity of addressing Barton, her betrothed, save for
one brief moment the other evening, when with the admiral
he left that house of which the prince and nobles had un-
lawfully possessed themselves ; so both the poor girls were
very sad and miserable, and the communings of each served
but to feed rather than soothe the sorrow of the other.

Euphemia, who, as the eldest, had learned to act with
more decision than her sister, had written and had now
concealed in her bosom a letter for Robert Barton, relating
to him the desperate crisis that was coming ; and boldly
saying, that unless he and Falconer rescued and concealed
them from Hailes and Home, they would be compelled to bend
before the overweening influence of their father, especially
if united to the preaching and stern presence of their uncle,
the dean, of whose arrival from the cathedral city of Dunblane
they were hourly in terror.

' It is here, you see, sister Sybie,' said Lady Euphemia,
opening two little pearl buttons of her bodice, and discovering the corner of a square epistle, tied with blue ribbons ;
' but how we are to get it conveyed to Robert's hand, I know
not—for of all the hundreds about us, is there one we can
trust ? They are all Hepburns devoted to Hailes, Homes
devoted to Home, or Drummonds who tremble at our father's
name.'

' There is young Mewie, or Balloch,' said Sybilla ; ' both
smile in the silliest way, and blush from their bonnets to
their red beards, when I address them. What think you,
Effie, of trying them ? '

' I think it would be most unwise. Two cock-lairds, who
are good for nothing but hunting the deer and hewing down
the clan Donnoquhy, or any other tribe on whom our father
unkennels them and their followers, like a pack of hungry

hounds ;—men who drink all day and sleep all night in their plaids under the hall tables, or anywhere else, like gillies or trenchermen. You will find a hundred men as good in our father's band, yet there is not one I dare entrust with *this !* '

' Would not some old Franciscan or Hospitaller convey it, as an act of mercy ? ' said Sybilla, weeping bitterly.

' They dare not, sister, for the terror of our father's name is great ; and through the dean, his wrath might reach even them,' said Euphemia.

' And in three days at furthest, this terrible dean will be here, with his stern brow and cunning cold grey eye. Oh ! Effie, would not the young prince find us a messenger ? '

' Nay, he has not a friend himself on whom he can rely. Young Lindesay, his dearest gossip and companion, fought against him in the king's ranks ; and moreover, Rothesay seems as crushed in heart and broken in spirit as ourselves, for strange whispers are abroad anent our poor king's life and some old prophecy ; and these rumours sorely wound the prince's happiness and honour.'

' I believe thee, sister. Then hedged in, watched, begirt, and attended as we are, how can we communicate ? ' asked Sybilla ; ' Heaven only knows ! ' she added, lowering her head on her sister's breast, and giving way to tears again ; ' Poor David Falconer—so sad, so gentle ! so full of kind and affectionate thoughts !—perhaps I shall never see him more ! '

' Come, sister Sybie,' said Euphemia, ' take an example from me. Do I weep like a child, as little Beatrix would do ? No, no ; I gather courage as the storm darkens. Barton——'

' Barton is rich ; he possesses this lordly house and that noble barony on the Almond. He is very rich, dear Effie, so I do not pity him as I do David Falconer, who is poor, and hath nothing but what his sword wins.'

' And, Heaven knows, it would win him more in any land than here in Scotland ; for there are over many false traitors and hypocrites, envious detractors and jealous lords among us, for truth, honour, or patriotism to be justly appreciated ; and so will it ever be.'

' I long so much once more to speak with David ! ' said Sybilla ; ' to lay my cheek where it has never lain—on his kind breast, and tell him—tell him all the horror we endured, dear sister, on that last awful day at Dundee.'

' True,' said Euphemia, as her hazel eyes flashed fire, and she shook the pearl pendants in her velvet cap ; ' and that day of crime broke all truce for ever between our father's friends and us ; and so, this letter——'

' Would it were away—or that I were a pigeon, and could fly with it under my wing.'

' If I could meet the poor poet Dunbar,—you remember William Dunbar, who sent us the staff of sweet verses— the kind young Franciscan ?—I think we might trust him safely.'

' A poor fisherman, rather ! ' said Sybilla ; ' he comes from Lord Hailes' country, and yet hath fled to England in dread of the nobles.'

The sisters relapsed into silence for a time, and sat observing a brown fisher-boat, which, with its dark chocolate-coloured lug-sail set, was running swiftly towards the old harbour, with its sharp prow dashing the dingy water of the river in white spray on both sides, till it was almost abreast of the west bank of the Leith—i.e., between the old wooden pier and the sandy promontory occupied by the garden and mansion of Robert Barton. Then one of two men who were in her shortened sail, while the other (who was none else but our former friend, Jamie Gair) put the tiller hard up, and brought the little vessel sheering close by where the sisters were seated.

The person who had taken in the sail was a short, thickset man, clad in a rough grey gaberdine, girt with a belt at which hung a pouch and poniard ; on his head was a blue bonnet ; round his neck was a steel gorget, and his legs were encased in long boots which had never been blackened, and seldom oiled. He now sprang ashore by wading through the rippling surf, which came nearly up to his knees, and advanced straight towards the sisters, who, by his attire, knew him to be a seaman of the *Yellow Frigate*. He approached with diffidence, and, removing his bonnet from his round and well-thatched head as he bowed, made one of those scrapes with the right foot which we suppose have been peculiar to all seamen since the ark first got under way.

' Weel, may I drink bilge, ladies, but I have gude luck to-day,' said he.

' I hope you may have it every day, sir,' said Lady Euphemia. ' I suppose you are——'

' Wad—madam ; Willie Wad, gunner to the Laird of Largo.'

Sybilla held her breath as she listened to him.

' It came on foul weather after our tulzie with the English-

men off Dunbar, and so we ran owre to Largo Bay, where the
squadron rides wi' head to wind and topgallant yards on
deck ; while the admiral, and a' our gallant gentlemen—
English as weel as Scots—are safely moored in Largo House ;
but as soon as I could leave the ship, the gude Captain Barton
and Sir David Falconer sent me across the Firth in Jamie
Gair's boat, wi' some sma' bits o' remembrances to you ladies,
and to let ye be assured that they are baith sound and tight,
and had never a plank started or spar knocked awa', though
shot and shaft the other night flew about us thick as hail in
February.'

'And so they are safe !' said the impulsive Euphemia,
taking a silver chain from her neck, and throwing it over the
head of the gunner.

'Gentle madam,' said the sailor, with another scrape of
the right foot ; ' I couldna' decline the honour you do me—
I would rather drink bilge ! but what is a puir fellow like me
to do wi' a gaud sae braw as this ? '

'You have some bonnie lass who loves you, I doubt
not.'

' I have had many, but they aye parted their cables and
got adrift someway or other ; yet there is a braw bonnie
craft at Largo, that may yet come under my lee,' replied
Wad, who had grown tender with English Rose ; ' but the
captain gied me a silver pound to pay expenses, though his
shipmate. I hae here a packet addressed to you, Lady
Euphemia, and another for the Lady Sybilla ; I ne'er kent
muckle o' crocans and crooks, being better leared in the
weight o' shot, the charges o' powder, wi' knotting and
splicing ; so I desired that the big packet from Captain
Barton should be for the tallest lady, and the next, from the
captain of our arquebussiers, for you, Lady Sybilla.'

' How fortunate that we were here ! watched as we are,
you could never have reached us.'

' They have braw news, ladies, to tell you,' said Willie,
gathering courage as he spoke, and ceasing to twirl his
bonnet, or shift from foot to foot ; ' for what think ye ?
We found your fair sister, the Lady Margaret, a prisoner on
board the English *Harry*.'

Astonishment and joy fettered the tongues of the sisters
at this intelligence. ' Ay, ladies ; and noo she is wi' the admiral in Largo Tower, and I would ye were moored in as
safe riding ; for by what the captain told me, there are owre
many gilded sharks and perfumed pirates hovering about ye

here ; and by my father's grave, I see twa coming this way noo !'

The sisters did not hear this exclamation, or did not understand it, for they were weeping and joyfully embracing each other, being highly excited by the intelligence which the short squat gunner imparted to them with the most perfect stolidity ; and while they addressed each other, he continued to smooth his thick shock hair and gaze with suspicion upon two richly-attired gentlemen, who were in half armour, and who loitered near the back porch of the house, where they were closely observing him ; for they were no other than the two lords, Hailes and Home.

Those who are in the habit of plotting and deceiving, usually suspect others of doing the same. Thus, the moment these noble suitors (who had come to visit the sisters) perceived Euphemia and Sybilla conversing with an armed seaman, they paused to watch for what might follow, as they had no doubt he belonged to one of the admiral's ships.

To the eager questions of 'How—why—and wherefore their sister Margaret came to be an English captive ?' Wad replied, again and again :

' I ken nae mair, ladies, than the man in the mune, and neither do the admiral nor Robert Barton ; for the English captains, who alone may ken, are vowed to silence. We opine there has been dark treachery at work, but why or how is owre deep for us to fathom ; but noo I maun e'en be sheering off, for two armed gallants are heaving in sight, and Barton warned me that this was dangerous ground. These are the letters, whilk will gie a necessary account of our battle ; and lest ye havena time to read and answer them—for I must cut my cable and run—just say, madam, where it will please you to meet the captain and Sir David who hae muckle to say that none but you maun hear !'

' Oh, we cannot have more to hear than we have to say and ask !' said Euphemia, who had already made herself mistress of Barton's loving epistle, while Sybilla was bending her streaming eyes over Falconer's, who had sent her a handsome gold cross which he had found in one of the captured ships while Barton had enclosed a book—then a priceless gift—which he had found in the *Harry*.

' Is the admiral coming over to Leith ?' they asked.

' No ; his hard-won prizes will he yield to none but to the king ; and the king is not here.'

'I have a letter ready written for Barton, and in a moment will add where we can meet him; but my poor brain is a chaos now,' said Euphemia. 'Where shall we say, sister— St. Magdalen's Chapel?'

'On the Figgate-muir—it is so lonely.'

'And on what pretence can we visit it?'

'A pilgrimage to pray,' said Sybilla.

'People do not believe in pilgrimages now. Hailes would laugh, and our father would storm and refuse——'

'Then where else shall I say?' said Euphemia.

'The Rood Chapel in Leith Loan.'

'Their lives would be in peril there,' said Willie Wad, who still kept his eyes fixed on the eavesdroppers, who had resolved to waylay him as he passed through the garden, and force him at the sword's point to say from whence he came, or be slain.

'Say, say,' urged Euphemia, bewildered, as she produced a pencil of pointed lead.

'I know not where to say—but oh, speak lower, lest we be overheard.'

'Oh, will you be wary, Willie, for we have none to trust but you?'

'I will stick to you like a burr on a bonnet,' replied Wad, with energy; 'and may he that would wrong ye ne'er drink aught but bilge in this world, and boiling water in that to come!'

'We will meet them at Loretto,' said Sybilla.

'Loretto! that is beyond the Eskwater, and further off than St. Magdalene's.'

'True, sister; but it is a place of such holiness that none will molest us there.'

'May Heaven forgive our duplicity—but what *can* we do without it?' sighed Euphemia.

'We can meet them there, and pray too, sister.'

'We shall go on horseback, accompanied only by women and pages. The place is quiet; our meeting once achieved, and arrangements made, perhaps for a flight to our dear Maggie at Largo, we must trust to Providence for the rest. I am happier now, that this is decided on,' continued Euphemia, as she wrote—'Post scriptum: We will meet you at the Chapel of Loretto, beside the links of Musselburgh, on Friday, in the evening; for there we mean to spend the whole night in vigil and in prayer. Till then, may God and the Blessed Virgin take you into their holy keeping.—E. D.'

'Friday will be the day after to-morrow—may no unhappy event intervene to prevent our keeping the tryst,' she added, folding the letter, and tying the ribbons, after which she gave it to Wad, who placed it in the tarpaulin pouch at his girdle; and making a low obeisance, by scraping his left foot and pulling his forelock with the right hand, retired, *not* by the garden, as the two loitering lords expected, but by wading through the water, and stepping on board of Gair's boat. Then he and the proprietor thereof betook themselves to the oars, and pulled into the crowded harbour, where they were soon lost in the dusk, amid the maze of boats, barges, crayers, and caravels, which filled it on both sides; for, as there were then no wet-docks or stone quays, all vessels were moored by the sides of the Leith, or in the midstream.

With one or two followers, Home hurried away by St. Nicholas Wynd to intercept the gunner, while Hailes advanced to meet the two ladies, who, with flushed faces and sparkling eyes, were retiring into the house.

'I fear, madams,' said the proud lord, sarcastically, 'that our appearance in the garden has interrupted your conference with a salt-water friend.'

'I knew not that your lordship was watching us,' replied Euphemia.

'Did yonder tarry rascal come from the ship of our contumacious skipper, the Laird of Largo?'

'Permit us to pass, my lord, and do not add one more insult to the many we have received at your hands.'

'I deplore that you should speak thus to me, madam; but your father is a noble, and I cannot see his honour trifled with by fishermen and merchant mariners, though the king may knight them, and set them to fight and man his ships. I pray you to pardon my curiosity—but you gave that seaman a letter, I think.'

'He gave me a packet, you mean,' said Euphemia, trembling with apprehension, as the calm, bold eye of Hailes scrutinized her beautiful face with more of pity than indignation.

'And this packet——'

'You are very inquisitive.'

'Your *betrothed*, the Lord Home, is my dear friend.'

Euphemia bit her lips with anger, while her eyes filled with tears.

'And this packet?' said Hailes again.

'Contained a book—only a book found in an English ship; and your lordship knows that a printed book is worth some crofts of corn.'

'It may be so, but I would rather have the crofts,' said Hailes, with a smile of scorn, as Euphemia opened the black-letter folio. 'Thank God, I have no need to write; for I can bite my thumb, and affix my seal, like the good lord my father before me, to aught that is requisite in peace, and with this—his sword—I make my mark, where it suits me, in time of war; but what is this most precious tome?'

'One, the perusal of which might be of infinite service to your lordship.'

'Indeed!—then what may it be—read, if it please you, fair madam.'

'"*The Book of Good Manners*,"' said Euphemia, with a smile, as she read the title page, which we give literally from the original now before us; '"*fynisshed and translated out of frensshe in to englisshe, the viiij day of Juyne, in the yere of our Lord, 1487, and the first yere of the regne of Kyng harry the vij*—compiled by the venerable *Frere Jacques le Graunt, an Augustine*," and the study thereof would, I am assured, benefit you much, so God keep you, my lord—and now, fare-you-well.'

Sybilla laughed, as Euphemia gave one of her lofty bows, and they swept past Hailes, into whose proud heart the broad taunt sank deeply, for he had perception enough to feel his own want of manner and of education: so he bit his nether lip as he muttered, 'I shall byde my time, and when I have either of you in my castle by the Tyne, her tongue shall be bridled, should a brank of iron be made for it!'

Then turning on his heel, he hurried after Home, to wreak his smothered wrath on the interloping mariner.

CHAPTER XLVII.

BORTHWICK'S NEW MISSION.

' I WOULD give ten of my best horses, if by so doing I could find this stunted vagabond in the grey gaberdine ! ' said Hailes to Home, as they met in the Broad Wynd ; ' and so he has escaped your lordship too ! '

' Yes, but we shall find him yet. Canst think of any one to employ, Blackcastle ? ' asked Home of a Hepburn who attended them.

' Nay, not I, my lords,' replied Hepburn ; ' I am but little used to the dirty work which seems the sole occupation of those who hover about the court of this poor prince ; and it would ill beseem a gentleman of name to be hunting for a seaman among yonder tarry wilderness of boats and booms, casks and anchors.'

Lord Hailes frowned at his retainer.

' Lady Euphemia Drummond gave this man a letter, and this letter we must have, should we burn Leith for it ! ' said Home.

' Whom shall we employ ? ' asked Blackcastle ; ' there are rascals and pimps in plenty about the prince's court, for the news of our rising seems to have gathered all the roguery in Scotland from the four winds of Heaven.'

His lord and chief frowned again, and said, ' You are over free with your tongue, Adam, and at this juncture I like it not. Art thou a king's man, eh ? '

' Though a landed gentleman, I am your lordship's vassal and near kinsman,' replied the laird, evasively ; ' but there is a fellow named Borthwick, a follower of Sir Patrick Gray of Kyneff, who is the best man to assist you in this matter, I think.'

' And where may he be found ? ' asked Home.

' At the *Tantony Bell* in the Kirkgate.'

' Let us seek him. Get us a room, Blackcastle, and see if this fellow be about the tavern.'

Thus it was that *Sir* Hew was accosted in the stair by the haughty lesser baron, who despised both him and his lord for the plots they had in hand ; and thus it was that the avaricious regicide found himself ushered suddenly into the presence of the two greatest military chiefs in the South Lowlands ; for Hailes was a warden of the Marches, and Home was steward of Dunbar.

The landlord in person brought them a supply of wine in a large Delft jug, with four silver-rimmed stoups of horn. The chamber was wainscoted, and its windows faced, on one side, the quaint and narrow Kirkgate, which became gloomy as the dusk deepened, and on the other, overlooked a narrow pathway called the Cotefield-loan.

'Fill thy stoup, my friend—'tis East-sea wine, this,' said the Laird of Blackcastle to Borthwick, who, he rightly conjectured, would be more likely to do his lord's behest if his heart were first warmed by wine.

'Thou art a gaily-dressed carle, on my faith !' said Hailes, who had not recovered his temper since Lady Euphemia's ill-disguised contempt had ruffled it, and he lacked an object on which to vent his spleen. 'Scarlet cloth and seed-pearls, velvet and passments,' he continued coolly surveying the gay attire of Borthwick ; 'though I have two thousand mailed horse in my train, and twice that number of spearmen on foot, I doubt mickle whether I can afford to win the service of a gallant so dainty !'

'Tush !' said Lord Home, more warily ; 'why should not an honest man dress him as he pleases ?'

'Well, sirs,' said the plain Laird of Blackcastle, 'to cross the Lammermuirs, or ride through the Merse, I would rather have my steel cap and rusty jack, with its plate sleeves, or it might be, a good coat of wambesan, than all this finery. But was it to appraise his attire, and to comment on the fashion of his cloak or the trimming of his doublet, you sent me for this person, my lords ? '

'Thou art the plainest of all plain-spoken fellows, Blackcastle,' said his chief ; 'but thou art the best lance that rides on the land of the Hepburns. Nay, we sent for him to have a pot of wine together, and a little conversation.'

'I shall be glad to talk of anything your lordship pleases, said Borthwick, rather impatiently ; 'that is, anything except the battle off the May, anent which all men now speak till I have sickened of it.'

'Well, then, canst thou——'

'Nay,' whispered the politic Home, 'do not *thou* him, lest we mar our purpose.'

' Can you keep a secret ? '

' Yes—if I am paid for it,' was the unhesitating reply.

' Can you also be sincere and of service ? '

' Yes—if I am *very* well paid for it.'

' Hech ! ' said Hepburn, ' I would take thee to be one of that English faction who have been Scotland's curse since the days of Alexander III. and will be so till we have a broader barrier than the Tweed.'

Borthwick gave him one of his sour and sinister smiles. ' Men must live,' said he ; ' but what do your lordships desire ? '

' Simply this. Within the last hour a seaman landed from the ship of Admiral Wood, and he hath in his gaberdine——'

' Nay,' said Blackcastle, ' you said before, his pouch.'

' Well, well, his pouch—a letter addressed we know not to whom ; but this letter we must have, and if you will procure it by fair means or foul, we shall pay you bravely.'

' You will easily discover him, for all in Leith know and love the shipmates of Wood; we had made short work with him else,' said Home, haughtily, ' for we have lances enough to level the burgh, but seek not a feud with the Logans of Restalrig ; thus I was half forced by Angus to hang a pikeman yesterday, in defiance of the law of *Burdingseck* which sayeth that no man shall be " hanged for stealing so much as he can bear on his back in a poke." '

' The devil seize all laws ! ' said Blackcastle.

' So say I,' added Borthwick. ' But what manner of man is this sailor ? '

' Short and square set,' said Home.

' With thick mustachios, a beard, and grey gaberdine ? '

' The same—a calfskin girdle and long boots like a horseman's gambadoes.'

' I have him—I know him ! 'Tis Wad, the gunner of the *Yellow Frigate*, one of Sir Andrew's prime seamen.'

' I would they were hung together over yonder steeple ! '

' I know his howff, and before midnight will undertake to have this letter, even should I use my poniard for it.'

' Use it freely, fellow,' said Hailes, putting a hand into the velvet purse which hung at his glittering girdle. ' My Castle of Hailes, near Linn-Tyne, is a sure hiding-place, and such as thee need not fear a feud with the overlord of this regality. We lodge with the Lord Angus in the King's

Wark ; bring us there this looked-for letter as soon as you find it, and heed not the hour of night.'

'We who bide upon the Borders are used to have our rest broken at all hours,' added the other peer.

'Blackcastle, hand these coins to our new ally ; and now let us begone, for there is here that horrid odour of sawdust and stale liquors which I never knew an hostel to be without.'

'Fare-you-well, Master Borthwick,' said Lord Home.

'God keep you, sir,' added Hailes, turning away.

Borthwick found himself mechanically counting the money as he descended the stair. He had received twenty half-lyons, or five-shilling pieces.

'St. Nicholas, patron of thieves, I honour thee!' thought he. 'What with the fleurs-de-lys of Sir Patrick Gray, the half-lyons of Lord Hailes, the rents of my three tenements in Stirling, and the rose-nobles of King Henry, which are ever descending on me in a golden shower, I shall die a rich man! *Die*—ugh!' he added, with something between a sneer and a shudder, while he shut his eyes like one who sees a horror; 'why should people die at all, especially when they have plenty of money?'

'When thou comest to the King's Wark, ask first for the Laird of Blackcastle,' said that personage, who had taken upon himself the task of seeing this pitiful swashbuckler clear of the tavern. 'And I pray to St. Anne,' thought he, 'that this poor mariner may steer clear of thee, and deliver the fair lady's letter to her lover—Robert Barton, if all tales be true—for he is a brave good fellow, and hath fought well for old Scotland, like his father before him ; and God bless all who do so, say I!'

HOWEVER, neither the interference of St. Anne, nor the good wishes of the honest Lothian laird, availed Master William Wad in the matter in hand, for in five minutes after the interview just related Borthwick saw him coming up the Broad Wynd, with his thumbs stuck in his girdle, his bonnet on the back of his head, and his thick crop of such beard and whiskers as sailors alone have a peculiar facility for raising encrusted with spray ; and he was whistling very loud as he rolled along, every moment hailing or being hailed by some acquaintance ; for Willie was bent on having a night's amusement before he went back to the ship.

It was now dusk, and though the little town was full of armed men, its narrow streets were becoming empty. They were then alike destitute of lamps and pavement, and darkened by many a heavy projecting timber front and turnpike stair or stone outshot. Thus Borthwick followed his victim unseen and with facility as he rambled along without any apparent object.

On the east bank of the Leith, the banner of Angus waved above the King's Wark, which stood on the north side of the Broad Wynd, the houses of which were occupied by his vassals ; while the Lairds of Glendonwyn, Heriotmuir, Bonjedworth, Glenbervie, and ten other powerful barons, making fourteen heads of houses, all bearing his surname of *Douglas*, were installed in the best adjacent mansions, *sans* leave and *sans* ceremony.

The King's Wark, which their haughty and presumptuous leader appropriated to himself (leaving the young prince to occupy the house of Barton), was a strong and ancient tower, in which the kings of Scotland occasionally resided —hence its name. It was surrounded by a spacious garden, with which it was bestowed by James VI. on a groom of the bedchamber, Bernard Lindesay, of Lochill, from whom the site is still named Bernard's Street, or Neuk.

The number of armed men, all wearing the Douglas badge, who hovered about the vicinity of this place, made the gunner avoid it, and he turned abruptly into a dark and narrow close, which led towards the Timber Bourse, where an old friend of his, Tibby Tarvet, whose spouse had been taken prisoner by the Turks, kept a change-house for mariners, locally known as Tib's Howff.

The alley which led to this place was dark as if the time was midnight, owing to the height and projection of the houses ; therefore, when Borthwick contrived to meet Wad face to face, he asked the question, which may still be heard at times in the same kind of closes in Scottish towns after nightfall :

' Is there any one coming ? '

' Yoho !—heave to, or port your helm,' cried Wad, who was already some ' sheets in the wind ' ; and he added, 'the channel's narrow, whereby I've to mak' short tacks, ye ken.'

' Then keep to your left hand,' said Borthwick, who, having some idea of using his poniard, wished his right hand free ; but then, on a moment's reflection, he feared to encounter a man so stout as Wad, and therefore altered his plan, and came roughly and rudely against him in the dark.

' D——n ye ! did I no shout " Port your helm ? " ' asked the gunner, angrily ; ' whereby we would baith have had sea-room enough to clear each other.'

' Upon my faith, I believe it is my good friend Master Wad !—Master Wad, good morrow,' said Borthwick, with well affected surprise and satisfaction.

' Yes, I'm Willie Wad, the Laird of Largo's gunner,' replied the seaman, rather sulkily ; ' I never sail under false colours, or cheat the king's collectors of dock dues or haven siller, so I value nane a rope-yarn. But yoho, brother, I have seen you before,' he added, as a light shone through a shutter and showed the gay dress of Borthwick ; so Wad therefore became more suspicious than pleased by his familiarity, and scrutinized him closely, although various drams he had imbibed rendered his faculties rather obscure and his temper somewhat fractious.

' You have seen me ! indeed—and where ? ' asked Borthwick, who was ready to assume any character Wad might assign him ; for old habit and experience made him aware

that it was safer to be any other person than *himself;* but
Wad dissipated this idea by saying: ' You boarded us off
Broughty, when last we came from Holland ? '

' True ; I had a message from the king to the admiral.'

' From the king ! ' reiterated Wad, dubiously ; ' and the
admiral—ken ye him ? '

' Well as I know good Robert Barton.'

' Then ye ken the twa best men that ever sailed on salt
water—except——'

' The king ? '

' Ay, the king, of course,' said Wad, touching his bonnet.

Borthwick, who always trembled at that name, now
said hastily : ' Are you a king's man ? '

' Ye donnart fule ! am I not the gunner o' a king's ship ? '
said the seaman, who was rather pugnaciously inclined,
and began to clench his hands ; ' you, who were ashore,
fought for the king, I hope ? '

' Bravely,' said Borthwick, in whose throat the word
almost stuck.

' Had you fought against him, I had brained you on the
first timber-head ! ' hiccupped Wad, making one or two
blows in the air.

' Tib Tarvet, the alewife's booth, is close by,' said Borthwick ; ' let us in, Master Wad, and we shall drink to the
admiral's health in a bicker of her best brown ale ; moreover, I would fain hear the story of this battle off the May.'

' Our boatswain spinneth a better yarn than I,' said the
gunner ; ' but as I feel drouthy, and Tib is an auld friend, I
care not if I shake out a reef for an hour or sae, so bear ye
ahead, sir.'

The alewife's house was soon found, for over her door was
the sign which all brewsters had to put forth under a penalty
of four pennies. An Act of the Parliament passed in those
days made it unlawful for a man ' to walk or travell in tyme
of nicht, unless he was a man of great authoritie or of good
fame ;' and recent outrages committed in her establishment
made the poor alewife somewhat reluctant to unbar her
door, until she heard the familiar voice of Wad ; on this
she at once admitted him and his companion, placed a fresh
candle in the tin sconce, which lit her low ceiled and clay-
floored apartment, one end of which was spanned by an
enormous fireplace, wherein, though the season was summer,
a fire of wood and turf was blazing. On a fir-table she
placed a trenplate of cakes, and two jugs of foaming ale,

which she brought from a secret place. The vicinity of so many lawless vassals and mosstroopers having made her house very unsafe of late, Tib had allowed her barrels to remain empty, there being neither wisdom nor thrift in filling them for soldiers who only paid her by ridicule or abuse. Some had vowed that she brewed ' evil ale, and should pay them the usual fine of eight shillings for having *drunk it ;* ' others swore they ' would have her put upon the cuckstule at Bonnington, and send her ale to the puir or the hospitallers,' and so forth, as Tib, who was a rosy and comely woman of some forty years, and who had long since contrived to console herself for the abstraction of her spouse ' by the infidel Turks,' informed Willie Wad, while Borthwick listened to the history of her troubles with great impatience.

While he plied the honest and unsuspecting gunner with Tib Tarvet's strongest beverage, we may imagine the affectation of interest with which Borthwick listened to his detail of action, in which he was painfully minute, and which he loaded with technicalities unintelligible as Greek or Hebrew to the cunning listener, who bit his lips with impatience while Wad ardently expatiated on the able manner in which the poor *Cressi* was run down ; and how the spanking *Yellow Frigate*, with every stitch of canvas set aloft and alow, was brought to bear in all her weight and strength on the doomed ship ; how, in rounding to, she won the advantage of the wind, and how the gallant Barton took her helm ; how the braces and bowlines were let go through the blocks like a whirlwind ; how the sheets and tacks were slacked off and the yards squared like lightning ; and how the sea smoked under her counter, as the heavy ship broke like a thunderbolt upon the foeman's hull, crashing through and over it ! Then how they all ranged up alongside of each other, Englishman and Scot—yardarm and yardarm—muzzle to muzzle—till their portlids and chainplates rasped together, and men slew each other at the lower deck ports; how iron grapnels were flung out and lashed to yard-head and gunnel ; and how thus, for so many glasses, they continued that deadly strife, pouring in the shot of carthouns, sakers, falcons, crossbows, and arquebusses, while two-handed swords, axes, and mauls, were plied like flails in a barnyard, and the steel blades rang on the helmets like a shower of iron hammers upon clinking anvils ; how many brave fellows had fallen in the battle ; how many had weathered it, and how many had died since of their wounds *when the tide ebbed*, the invariable time of death, according to an old superstition.

Tib, who was somewhat abashed by the gay apparel of Borthwick, sat knitting in the ingle seat of her wide chimney, and though far aloof, listening intently to the narration of Wad, in which, as a sailor's wife and a Scot—for in those days the Scottish women possessed even more patriotism than their countrymen—she was doubly interested.

Meanwhile the fire blazed on the hearth; the candle guttered and streamed in the currents of air, and Willie continued to speak, but thicker and more slowly, of course, while he quaffed pot after pot of ale; and now he began to remember that 'Jamie Gair was waiting for him at the auld Brig Stairs,' just when Borthwick (whose wolfish eyes were constantly fixed on the pouch containing the letter) resolved to give him a finishing stroke, by ordering Tib Tarvet to prepare for him a strong *hot* pint.

Now, we have elsewhere mentioned, the Scottish pint is similar to the English quart, and as the required draught consisted of strong ale, whisky, and eggs boiled together, and taken hot, it may easily be supposed that such a decoction was more than sufficient to lay the unwary gunner, as he afterwards said, 'on his beam ends.'

Some lingering recollection of where he was, and of the message entrusted him, flashed upon his memory through the thickening haze that was overspreading his faculties, and setting the hot stoup, half drained, upon the board, he reeled up from it.

'Where away?' said Borthwick; 'finish thy pot, man, where away so fast?'

'A lady—a letter,' muttered Wad, opening and shutting his eyes in succession, and rolling his head from side to side; 'she gied me a braw siller chain for my pretty Rose; yoho, brother gossip; I must trip my anchor now——'

'But finish thine ale, friend, to the health of Andrew Wood.'

'Weel, weel,—*there*,—it is a' stowed under hatch,' said Willie, as with a loud whoop he poured the last of the hot ale down his throat; 'and noo,' said he, flinging away the stoup, 'may I drink bilge, if I can stay a minute mair —I am getting slow in stays—I yaw and canna obey my helm—hard up—hard up it is—thou'st owrestowed me— I careen—hillo—oh!' cried Wad, as he lurched and rolled

about, and then sank prostrate on the bench from which
he had just risen.

In his eagerness to obtain the letter, Borthwick would
have sprung upon him and wrenched away his belt-pouch,
for every man wore one in those days, and the goat-skin
sporran of the Highland clansmen is but the remnant of
the fashion; the gunner, however, lay with his pouch under
him, and he muttered, ' Avast, billy, avast,' and snorted
like a pig, when the thief turned him over to reach it.

Perceiving that the alewife's attention was directed
another way, and that she was busy in heaping turf upon
the fire, he attempted to unbutton the pouch; but a gleam of
sense and suspicion made Wad place a hand heavily upon it.

Borthwick glanced impatiently at the hostess; she was
still bent over the hearth; he clutched his dagger, and then
withdrew his hand as if the hilt had burned him.

He had never unsheathed that fatal weapon since the
terrible night at Beaton's mill, and even now the blood of
him who was the heir of ' a hundred kings ' had glued the
blade in its velvet scabbard.

' I would soon end thee, fellow,' thought he, ' but I choose
not to risk my life for bubbles.'

Then finding the seaman sunk in a deep and helpless
sleep, he tore open the pouch, and inserting his hand, pulled
forth the letter from among the pieces of cord, gunmatches,
fragments of biscuit, cheese, and ropeyarn, a few coins and
other et cetera, which Willie Wad usually carried in this
repository; and then throwing a half-lyon on the table,
Borthwick told Tibby Tarvet to ' keep the change, for looking
after this drunken lurdane,' and wrapping himself in his
cloak left the house.

* * * * * *

Faint and grey the summer morning was stealing down
between the lofty houses of the narrow alley and straggling
through the rusty and cobweb-woven gratings of the windows,
into the outer chamber of the alehouse, when the gunner
awoke and started up, with heavy eyes and an aching head.
The apartment was dark and cold: the *gathering peat* was
smouldering on the hearth, and a full minute elapsed before
he remembered where he was, and how he came to be there;
then the two pewter flagons and the ale-slopped table
recalled his debauch over-night with some one—a stranger
—gaily attired in scarlet and velvet; and instinctively

diving a hand into his pouch, he found the lady's letter
gone !

Master Wad became sober in a moment.

Starting from his seat he examined the pouch ; shook
it, turned it outside in ; he then opened his gaberdine and
examined the lining of his bonnet; then he searched all
about the chamber, and became convinced that the letter
for his captain was lost—irretrievably lost.

' May I drink bilge, but it's clean awa' ! ' said he, and stood
for a time bewildered; ' and what shall I say to Robert
Barton, or to the winsome lady who gied it, wi' this handsome chain—that I've been drunk—drunk as a Sluys pilot !
Oh, Willie Wad, Willie Wad—dool be on thee for this.'

The gunner sat down for a moment, and his honest heart
was swollen by the mingled emotions of shame and anger.
He prayed for help to St. Barbara, who was the patron of
all cannoniers, and whose altar stood in St. Mary's Church
close by ; but she probably turned a deaf ear to him, for
praying did not mend the matter ; then starting up, he
stormed and swore roundly, shouting the while on Tibby
Tarvet, whom he roused without ceremony from her box-
bed in one of the lofty garrets, and whom he threatened with
the vengeance of the Baron Bailie and all the terrors of the
Burgh laws enacted ' anent evil alewives,' if his lost letter
was not forthcoming.

Then Tib stormed in turn, and reminded him that he too
was liable to a fine, or six hours' detention in the iron *jougs*,
for being intoxicated in an alehouse after ten o'clock at
night—for such was the law.

Finding thus that the hostess might in the end have the
best of the dispute, the poor gunner had to smother his
wrath and ' sheer off.'

CHAPTER XLIX.

THE KING'S WARK.

THE bell in the tower of St. Anthony's preceptory—a tower demolished by the English cannon in 1559—was just tolling eleven, when Hew Borthwick blew the copper horn which hung by a chain at the outer gate of the King's Wark, and hastily inquired for the Laird of Blackcastle, or for the Lords Home or Hailes. These names secured to him an immediate passage among the Douglases, Homes, and Hepburns who loitered about or slept on the floor or benches of the passages, hall, and vestibule, and two pages, having the Hepburn arms —two Scottish lions rending an English rose—ushered the bravo at once into a chamber, the walls of which were hung with old amber-coloured arras, sewn over with red stars and green thistles, the work, it was said, of Elizabeth, Duchess of Brittany, daughter of James I.

This apartment was encumbered by arms and armour; halberts and lances were piled against the walls; two large sconces of tin, having in each four candles, gave sufficient light to the two reckless young lords, who were playing at chess, and sipping wine from silver cups, while the pages were conveying away the remains of the baked chicken and pie of plumdames on which they had just made their rere-supper.

Their daggers, belts, and cuirasses were flung aside, and they wore loose ample gowns of dark woollen cloth, lined with brightly coloured silk, and edged with stripes of fine sable.

'Thou hast come betimes, sir,' said Hailes; 'and doubtless hast succeeded, too.'

'I seldom fail in aught I undertake, my lord. A ready wit, a clear head, a bold heart, and nimble hands, are ever required by those who have light purses and high ambition,' was the confident reply.

' Thou hast rather an active tongue too, sirrah,' said Lord Home, frowning.

' 'Tis the only inheritance my good mother left me,' said the unabashed Borthwick.

' Enough of this—the letter, if thou hast it ! '

Borthwick still lingered, till Hailes scornfully tossed to him a fleur-de-lys, and then he received the letter at once. He untied the ribbons, opened and scrutinized it with stern and curious eyes.

He then counted the lines repeatedly, and looked at the address—but of that and the contents neither he nor Hailes could decipher one word.

' Curse on this conjuror's art ! ' said he ; ' 'tis the Dean of Dunblane hath taught dame Euphemia and her sisters this clerkly craft. Had they learned how to make hippocras, to knead a pasty, to collar a pig, or to throw a hawk well off, it had been wiser ! Canst thou make out this devilish scrawl, my lord ? '

' Nay, not I, thank God ! If I can mumble *Kyrie Eleison*, or *Christi Eleison*, at Mass, 'tis all my book lear.'

' Ouf ! for a fair dame's epistle, what an odour it hath of herrings and tar ! '

And now there was a pause. Home thrust aside the chessmen ; Hailes took a sip at his wine-cup, and curled up his mustachios, while Borthwick stood by with a sneer on his face, and watched them, smiling in his heart at their absurd perplexity.

Now, although so early as the year 1173 the towns of Perth and Stirling, Aberdeen and Ayr, had their seminaries under the monks, and others were established in Roxburgh, St. Andrews, and Montrose during the thirteenth and four-teenth centuries, the Scottish nobles were so ignorant, that a law was passed at a period subsequent to the reign of James III. that every peer should send his eldest son to school. Thus, to the Scots, all of whom—even the lowest and poorest classes—are now so well educated, the ignorance of the good folks, their ancestors, must seem extraordinary, if not incredible.

Impatient that Borthwick did not offer to read it, and yet half ashamed of what the contents might be, Home turned to him with reluctance, saying :

' Master Borthwick, wert thou not somewhat of a monk in thy younger days ? '

Borthwick started, and his countenance flushed, as he

replied, ' To my shame I acknowledge that I was ; I am now a more useful man—but what of that, my lord ? '

' You can read, of course ? ' said Hailes, a little more gently, and with a bitter expression of eye, for he felt that he and his friend were at the mercy of a man whom they disliked and despised.

' Read, if it please you,' said Lord Home, and he whispered, while Borthwick took up the letter, ' Fear not its contents, Hailes ; if it contains aught unpleasant, we can stop this fellow's tongue by a gag of steel, and there are vaults in Home Castle where the light of day hath never entered : read on.'

' " *For Robert Barton of that Ilk—Captain to the Laird of Largo—be these delivered*——" ' began Borthwick.

' Of that Ilk ! ' exclaimed the two lords, together, with fierce and unutterable scorn ; and then they burst into a fit of laughter.

' By St. Anne, this amuses me ! ' said Hailes. ' Read on, good fellow ; of that Ilk—read on.'

The noble lord was not so much amused by what followed, for Euphemia expressed in strong language the horror she. and her sister Sybilla entertained of the two suitors whom their impetuous and ambitious father had thrust upon them ; the letter expressed their double dread of him and of their uncle, the dean ; it detailed the persecution they were subjected to, and the surveillance with which they were annoyed ; and ended by stating that their marriage days were fixed, but that they were resolved not to be wedded, at the sword's point, like two brides among the wild Redshanks who dwelt beyond the Grampians ; and so they begged that Barton and Falconer, if they loved them, would take measures to save them from such a fate, and become their protectors.

' 'Tis madness—'tis infatuation ! ' said Home, with something of pity ; ' and but for the honour of Lord Drummond's house, and the necessity for killing these scurvy companions, and preventing the daughters of our nobles from making alliances so degrading, on my soul I would leave Lady Euphemia to her lover, Master Robert Barton of—*that Ilk.*'

' And had I not a slender fancy for the pretty Sybilla, and a greater one for that slice of Strathearn which the old lord promised me, I would rest contented with the black-eyed dame to whom I am hand-fasted already ; but we must punish their contumacy ; and I doubt not they will become loving

wives enough, after we have given their gallants to feed the
gleds.'

' So, so ; is that all, Master Borthwick ? '

' There is a postscriptum, my lord.'

' Post—what ? is there more of this precious epistle ? '

' But a line or two, my lord, hastily pencilled.'

' 'Tis what we saw her writing,' said Home ; ' and faith,
she did look beautiful as she bent over her tablets, and her
heavy locks fell forward ; well, and what saith the postscriptum ? '

' " *We will meet you at the chapel of Loretto, beside the
Links of Musselburgh, on Friday, in the evening, for there
we mean to spend the whole night in vigil and in prayer,* etc.
—E. D.*" '

' At our Lady of Loretto ! what a place for an assignation
with these skipper varlets,' said Lord Hailes, ' those cul-
lionly mongrels ! '

' Art sure of this, sirrah ? ' asked Lord Home, with a
terrible frown.

' Sure as I now address your lordship—for I read word
for word as it is written.'

' At six in the evening ? '

' Six, my lord.'

' God's death ! ' said Hailes, with ferocious joy, ' if this
meeting take place, I would not wed the Lord Drummond's
daughter had she the crown of Scotland on her head.'

' Nor I her sister, with Brittany and Orkney to boot.'

' What then shall we do ? '

' Send their letter to its destination, my lords,' said Borthwick, who ever loved to ferment and further mischief ;
' permit the ladies quietly to ride forth, but attend the tryst
too—and let them find their lovers there, but less their
heads.'

' It shall be so ; we'll beset the place, Hailes, and cut
them into gobbets, by my father's soul we will ? '

' But Loretto is a holy place.'

' What ! art thou one of those who deem one place more
holy than another because a shaveling mumbles Latin
there ? Well, we will drag them forth and hang them at
the Musselburgh Cross, if you will. I'll take a hundred
horse and hide them in the woods of Pinkey. Enough,
enough, we'll see to it ; and now to send this letter to the
churls at Largo. The bearer——'

' I left him drunk as a Saxon, and snorting like a pig

n an alehouse near the Timber Bourse; day has not yet
broken, so I may easily restore it to his pouch without his
having missed it, perhaps.'

'Good—excellent! away, it lacks but a short time of
day-dawn; when all this matter is over and settled, when
the rooks of Pinkey Wood have gorged them to their fill
on those aspiring curs who cross our plans, I'll make thee,
Borthwick—a rascal though thou art—the richest varlet
n my new earldom—away, away!' and laughing and push-
ng, he almost put Borthwick out of the room. When he
was gone—

'Hailes, can we really trust this fellow?' asked Home.

'Trust him! For gold he would sell his father's bones,
and his own slender chance of salvation; but I'll have him
followed, and prove whether or not he plays us foul.'

The messenger of Home was no other than the unwilling
Laird of Blackcastle, who had been sleeping in his armour
on a stone bench in the upper hall of the King's Wark, and
who grumbled under his helmet as he followed Borthwick
through the dark and narrow streets of Leith in the grey
light of the morning.

Turning off towards the Timber Bourse he saw him enter
the narrow alley which led to Tibby Tarvet's alehouse,
and there he met Willie Wad in a high state of excitement.
'What ho, Master Wad,' said he, 'you are abroad betimes.'

'Abroad betimes, thou dog-thief and loon; thou'st
boarded me like a pirate in the night, and stolen a letter
frae me.'—

'Beware ye, sirrah, of what you say,' replied Borthwick,
making a show of dignified indignation; 'beware, for I
am a man of a good repute, that must not be impugned;
but if this be the letter you have lost——'

'It is—it is,' said Wad, almost dancing with joy as the
other displayed the missing article; 'and where got ye it?'

'Lying the close-head.'

'Say you so? Could I have dropped it?'

'You know best.'

'My deck was overstown wi' usquebaugh—donnart deil
hat I am, it must have been so!'

'This letter is of value then?'

'I would rather lose my starboard fin than it.'

'Then it is well worth a crown.'

'To those wha hae crowns to spare,' said the gunner.
Borthwick took a firmer grasp of the packet.

'What, will a gay gentleman in a scarlet cloak chaffer thus wi' a puir mariner like me?' asked Wad, with astonishment mingled with contempt.

'I have said the letter is well worth a crown.'

'Crowns hae I none—but I will gie what I have, and then let us part; sorrow be on the hour I met you.'

As money poured upon this wretched bravo, avarice grew and strengthened in his heart; and he omitted no opportunity of gathering all he could win; knowing well that ere long Scotland would be too hot to hold him.

'A' I hae is here,' said Wad, opening a secret nook in his pouch; 'three rose-nobles, and welcome you are to them.'

'Rose-nobles,' said Borthwick, suspiciously, and pricking up his ears at the sound; 'where got you them?'

'In the pouch of a dead Englishman. Take them: the letter, the letter!' said Willie, losing all patience, and beginning to grasp his knife with one hand, while by the other he angrily snatched away the billet. 'You are doubtna a thief and limmer to boot—despite your braw gear and laced mantle. But off! sheer off, I say, or may I drink bilge, if by one hearty kick I dinna double you up like a bolt of wet canvas!'

With these complimentary remarks Willie hastened down the Broad Wynd, crossed the ancient bridge of three arches, where a trifling toll was levied from every passenger, and reached the boat of Jamie Gair, who was just preparing to put off without him. A chill wind was blowing from the north-east and a white *harr* was setting in from the German Sea, so they buttoned up their gaberdines, betook them to the oars, shot the boat out into the midstream, and in a short time the old wooden pier of Leith, the Beacon Rock and Partan Craig, were left astern. Then they set their lug-sail, and keeping the boat close-hauled, bore away as nearly as her head would lie to the wind, for the beautiful Bay of Largo.

CHAPTER L.

THE fatal Friday was a dark and lowering day; the sun had been hidden in fiery clouds, and torrents of rain had fallen, swelling all the mountain streams. The minds of Euphemia and Sybilla Drummond, though joyful in the certainty of their loved sister's safety, were oppressed to some extent by vague forebodings of evil. Lord Drummond was still ignorant of his daughter's discovery, for he was absent on a mission of the insurgents, and was still nursing and maturing his plans of vengeance against James III., whom he deemed and styled ' a forfeited and fugitive king.'

Well attended, guarded, and surrounded as they were by many hundreds of faithful and obsequious vassals, whose adherence combined the love of the patriarchal clansman with the servility of the Lowland feudal serf, the two young lords had little difficulty in having the mansion of umquhile Sir Andrew Barton closely watched; and on the afternoon of Friday, Borthwick, who had been lying, *en perdue,* somewhere in the vicinity, announced to them that the two daughters of Lord Drummond had ' set forth on their pretended pilgrimage to Loretto.'

The two noble suitors hastened to assure themselves that such was indeed the case, and had the chagrin to see them pass out from Leith by St. Anthony's Porte, their cheeks flushed with fear and pleasure, and their eyes beaming, well mounted on ambling horses, with long and sweeping foot-cloths over their saddles, and each attended by a female servant, who rode on a pillion behind a page, and carried each a basket of offerings to the hermit.

' They ride fast,' said Home, as they whipped their horses across the level links.

' They will come less speedily back,' said Hailes, with his dark but courtly smile; ' a heavy heart makes a slow wayfarer, and their hearts I ween will be heavy enough.'

' Two women and two pages——'

' A slender escort this for noble dames.'

' Especially in such ticklish times as these.'

' True, my lord; but what will not women risk for a lover'
sake ? ' said Hailes.

' Two painted pages (I'll have the rascals scourged
may be guard enough in Lothian here; but in the Merse
or Teviotdale, a hundred spears were not a man too many
if one goes but a hundred yards from one's own gate.'

' They have left betimes,' said the chief of the Hepburns
looking up at a dial-stone that projected from the corner
of St. Anthony's Gate.

' And at what time shall we set forth to spoil their precious
pilgrimage—this dainty love-making ? '

' Somewhere about six at even,' said Hailes.

' Then we shall have the whole night before us.'

' All the better; I have directed Borthwick and Black
castle——'

' I doubt whether my kinsman would like such a conjunct
partnership.'

' Well, Blackcastle and Borthwick,' said Home, im
patiently, ' with twenty of my most unscrupulous moss
troopers—Johnstones, thieves of Annandale, men wh
would spear their own brother if I wished them—to be a
in their jacks betimes, and mounted to ride with us.'

' Pleasant and honourable company,' said Lord Haile
with a smile.

' But fitted for the occasion, my lord,' replied Home
firmly; ' we know not but those scurvy fellows, Barton an
Falconer, may have some of their ruffianly seamen wit
them; and if so, by my father's hand and by the cre
of Home, though it be beneath our rank to draw on varle
such as these, I'll not leave in all Loretto one alive to te
the story to their admiral ! '

As he spoke, Home clenched one hand, and with th
other thrust his furred cap of maintenance over his dar
and fiery eyes.

' Good, my lord; farewell until we meet again,' sai
Hailes; ' if to-day we do not teach these fellows a shar
lesson, this glorious raid against the court and king, an
that most signal triumph before the walls of Stirling, hav
been less than vain.'

And these two ferocious and unlettered nobles, thoug
bent upon committing one of those atrocities which occurre

aily among their proud, turbulent, and unpatriotic class in
cotland, bowed and parted as quietly and as pleasantly
s if their appointed tryst had been for a pleasant evening
de in some green lane, instead of one for sacrilege and
murder.

The troop of twenty men, who assembled near a gate of
he King's Wark, and from thence set forth under the
uidance of the two nobles, the Laird of Blackcastle and
heir new ally, Hew Borthwick, in their aspect and appear-
nce did full justice to that character for ease and flexibility
f conscience ascribed to them by Lord Home. They were
l strong, dark and sinewy men, whose forms were hardened
to mere bone and brawn, and were durable as iron ; for
hey were lawless mosstroopers, Scottish Bedouins, in fact ;
en who won every meal at the spear's point, and lived
a their harness ; men whose dwellings were among wild
orasses, pathless woods, and inaccessible mountains ;
here law was never known, and religion little heard of ;
ild and predatory warriors, who fought against their
ountrymen as readily as against the common enemy that
welt beyond the frontier ; for, like the Ishmaelites, their
ands were upraised against all men.

Their armour, which consisted of a splinted jack with
ate sleeves and steel gloves, head-piece and gourgerin,
as all rusty and well dinted by many a sword-cut and lance-
rust. Their beards and whiskers flowed out between
eir steel cheek-plates, ample and uncombed as the shaggy
anes of their strong and active border steeds. Well armed
d fleetly mounted, Home and Hailes, divested of every
stinguishing badge, rode together at their head.

Wheeling off the main street between the hedge-rows
the Cotefield-loan, the whole party crossed the green
d sandy links, and entered on the vast and purple expanse
the Figgate Muir, which was covered by the mossy stump
' an old druidical forest, whose roots are yet turned up
v the plough and spade.

Shrill blew the wind, and drearily boomed the waves
oon their left. The estuary of the Forth looked black as
k, and its billows rolled in white foam upon the lonely
each with a deep and hollow sound. The slanting aspect
the clouds showed that the rain, which had been pouring
l that morning in torrents, was again about to descend ;
d though the party rode fast to escape it, they had only
ached the little Chapel of Saint Mary Magdalene, which

stood among some coppice near a stream that poured through
a ravine into the sea, when it descended with such fury
as almost to blind even the border riders, and the wind
blew as if it would have blown its last, driving the sand
from the shore across the open moor, and forcing the horsemen to seek shelter in the grove, while the two lords dismounted and entered the chapel, the door of which stood open
and before the altar of which they made the usual involuntary genuflection, by half-kneeling and signing the cross
and this, with them, was a very useless piece of mummery

'How unlucky!' said Home, as the rain continued to fall
in torrents upon the stone roof of the little oratory, while
the stream beside it rolled in red foambells upon the beach,
'this devilish tempest may spoil all, and there seems little
chance of its lulling soon.'

'Had our meeting with these rascals been elsewhere than
at Loretto, there might not perhaps have been a storm.'

'Art really so weak as to think this?' said Home.

'I know not what to think—but I like it not,' replied
his companion, shrugging his shoulders; for he was not
without his share of the superstition incident to the time
and country.

'How,' continued Lord Home, with a lowering expression
in his keen and fiery eyes, as he seated himself on a stone
bench near the steps of the rude altar, and dashed the
water from his plume; 'your words would imply that
Heaven itself was against us.'

'I know not; but this sudden storm hath broken on us
with wondrous fury, and here we are forced to draw our
bridles within four miles of the place.'

'Rest assured, my good lord, that Heaven leaves you and
me to mind our own affairs. The elements would never
be at peace if storms were raised to cross every man's
purpose in Scotland; and least of all will they raise such
an infernal hubbub as this to save a couple of scurvy varlets
who must swing, even as their companions swung, over
Lauder Bridge, in our raid of '82. There is one comfort
however,' continued the practical but irreverent chief of
Homes, listening for a moment as the wind howled through
the unglazed windows of the edifice, and the rain drenched
the copsewood near it, and hissed along the beach till sun
and sand were smoking; 'we may be assured that the
same storm which stays us here must keep our fair dame
in shelter at Loretto, while it may also save us all trouble

y kindly sending their lovers to feed the fishes of the
irth.'

' But suppose we find the cockbirds flown ? '

' Think not of such a disappointment.'

' Yet such a thing is possible.'

' Remember that Lady Euphemia, in her precious post-
criptum, spoke of spending the night in vigil and in prayer.'

' Profound prayer no doubt it will be, with a couple of
aucy gallants to hold their tapers and turn the missal
aves,' said Hailes, with a smile of contempt. ' St. Mary,
ow the sky darkens ! '

' And how the rain comes down ! '

' This burn beside us is swelling into a perfect torrent.'

' How fare our rogues of Annandale in the thicket ? '

' Ill enough, I doubt not,' replied the Laird of Blackcastle ;
and methinks they were as well riding as standing there,
ke todlowries under a lynn.'

' You forget that no man could keep his saddle in such
tempest of wind,' said Lord Home.

' Of a surety it must portend some coming evil ; a pesti-
nce, or an English invasion,' added the superstitious
Hailes.

As the chapel of Loretto stood in a solitary place beyond
he eastern gate of Musselburgh, the two lords arranged
nat, on setting forth again, when once the Esk was crossed,
: should be surrounded, an alarm given, and that all should
e killed who issued forth—every man at least ; for they
ad no wish to incur the vengeance of a tyrannical hierarchy
vhich was full of power and strength, by actually slaughter-
ig their victims within the walls or precincts of a church,
f such a catastrophe could be possibly avoided.

But while, within a holy place, and close to the altar
f their religion and their God—the symbolical throne,
efore which they had each gravely, and not in the least
1 mockery, made a low reverence—they sat planning
his projected outrage, and combining with their own
iews such suggestions as the mischievous and blood-
hirsty spirit of Borthwick proposed, the storm still con-
inued to howl along the shore ; the rain still poured in
ne broad and blinding cataract ; and torn from the wood-
ands by the furious wind, the wet leaves were whirled and
wept in myriads across the moor, which at times was
hrouded in mist and spray ; and for hours this continued,
vith occasional gleams of lightning ; and the mosstroopers,

who had unsaddled their terrified horses and haltered them to the trees, now crowded, all drenched and disconsolate, into the dreary little chapel beside their leaders, where they grumbled and muttered under their thick beards, while drinking raw whisky from their portable leather flasks and horn quaighs.

As the evening drew on and the place grew dark, they were not without their own fears that the elements were indeed in league against them; and now, enraged that their well-matured stratagem should be crossed by an intervention so unlooked for, their lords sat in sullen silence listening to the din without; and the time seemed interminably long, for there were then no watches to mark the passing hours, and even had a dial been there, without the sun it had been useless.

'At last,' said Home, 'at last the wind lulls! Horse and spear, my Annan wight—let us mount, and begone!'

The horses were soon saddled and their riders mounted. Though the wind had lulled, the rain poured down as furiously as ever. The time was now past nine in the evening; but the gloomy aspect of the sky made the drenched landscape and the sea look very dark, for the sun had set enveloped in dense banks of opaque and murky cloud, behind the Ochill peaks, Dumiat, and the hills of Alloa.

The riders soon passed the hamlet named the Fisher Row, and reached the ancient bridge of the Roman Municipium, the arches of which still span 'the mountain Esk,' the opposite bank of which was covered with copsewood, where the dark and heavy oak mingled its thick crisp foliage with the lighter spray of the pale-green sauch and the feathery ash-tree. This venerable bridge consists of three quaint high and narrow arches, 'over which,' says one of our modern writers, 'all of noble or kingly birth that approached Edinburgh for at least a thousand years must have passed; which has witnessed the processions of monks, the march of armies, and the trains of kings; which has rattled beneath the feet of Mary's ambling steed, and thundered beneath the war-horse of Cromwell.'

Swollen by the summer flood, the Esk was found by our troopers to be rolling in one vast sheet of foam under the three arches, each of which are fifty feet in width; and in froth and spray its red current lashed furiously against their strong abutments, sweeping the mingled spoil of field and fell, uprooted trees, straw, hay, and grass, farm implements, rafters, and garden pales, with the rolling carcasses of sheep and cattle, into the harbour, which was *then* so deep as to admit the largest merchantmen of Norway, of Pomerania, and of Holland; and. many of these vessels, built in that quaint style which the Dutch have yet retained unchanged, were riding with all their anchors out, to stem the furious *speat*.

The narrow pathway of the bridge was then barred or banned by a transverse arch and an iron gate, traces of which are yet remaining in the parapets. The warder dwelt in a small house on the other side, and as the barrier was closed, the night darkening fast, and the rain still pouring down, the two lords and their drenched mosstroopers hallooed loudly and impatiently for passage through; but the keeper of the gate paid not the slightest attention to their loud and angry summons.

'Hark,' said Lord Hailes; 'what hour is that now striking?'

The mournful notes of an old bell were now heard, but faintly and far between, upon the gusts of wind.

'Ten by Musselburgh clock,' said Borthwick; 'ten, and we still loiter here!'

Above the trees they could discern, against the murky sky, the quaint steeple of the Town House, in which there yet remains a bell-clock of the fifteenth century, which was presented to the burgh by their High Mightinesses, the States of Holland.

The dusk was now so deep that the foliaged bank opposite seemed all black and solid; and the white and foaming river boiled and thundered past so rapidly and fiercely, that the boldest trooper among our adventurers shrunk from attempting to swim his horse across it; for if they essayed it above the bridge, they ran the chance of being brained against the arches, on which the stream had risen; and if below it, of being powerlessly swept with the débris of its banks among the boats and shipping. Red and fiery, the stars were seen to peep at times between the flying scud, while the dark trees tossed their foliage on the gusty wind, like the black plumes of our modern Scottish infantry.

At times a mournful cry rose amid the gloom that enveloped the rolling river, and the grim horsemen reined back their reeking steeds, and looked darkly and inquiringly in each other's faces.

'Hear ye that, sirs?' said the Laird of Blackcastle. 'What doth it sound like?'

'The monks chanting *De Profundis* in St. Michael's Kirk,' said Lord Hailes.

'God's malison on this base runnion of a warder!' cried Borthwick, impatiently.

'Hark!' said Hailes; 'there comes that wailing cry again!'

''Tis the Water Kelpie!' muttered the troopers, for the belief in that aquatic demon was yet strong in Scotland; and thus there was not a rider there who did not tremble at the idea of being drawn by that voracious fiend into his den below the flood.

'By my soul, I'll ride the river,' said Hailes, boldly; 'there should be a ford here, I think, but the darkness is such that I cannot see.'

'Beware, in Heaven's name, my lord,' cried Blackcastle, anxiously throwing his horse before the charger of his chief; 'beware, lest your life be needlessly perilled; for ever were the flood stemmed, ye may not abide the Kelpie's grasp. Listen to me,' he continued, speaking breathlessly, 'I had once a narrow escape from one at the Brig of Tyne, when last I crossed it during a Lammas flood. I had bought me a black horse from a strange-looking carle at the Haddington market; and at the sight of water, however far off, this horse became wild and frantic; it kicked, plunged, and neighed; and when we offered him drink, he dashed over the bucket, and laved its contents about him with delight. When I rode him along the bridge at the Nunraw, he uttered an awesome yell as he rose into the air with me, and sprang over the parapet; and lo! I found myself astride a kelpie in that black Lammas flood, at mirk midnight! He turned upon me with open jaws, and eyes that blazed with fire. But I signed the cross between us, and then he sunk from me, yelling like a fiend as he was; and drowned I had been assuredly, had I not caught the branch of a sauch-tree and reached the shore——'

'And thy devilish horse-couper, what of him?'

'He was never more seen.'

'St. Mary! he must have been the devil!' said Hailes.

'Or Michael Scott of Balwearie,' said Home.

'Blackcastle, blow thy bugle,' said his chief, 'and we'll crop the gate-ward's ears if they hear it not.'

'Woe to the loitering villan!' grumbled Home.

'His gudewife will be keeping him abed,' said the other lord; 'and perhaps the poor man dare not rise.'

'I *have* heard that the grey mare is the better horse here,' said Blackcastle, as he blew a startling blast; 'and I have seen good proof that the poor gate-ward is only Joan Tamson's man, as the saw hath it.'

'How——'

'The rosemary sprig borne at their wedding now flourishes in his kail-yard, like a green bay-tree.'

'The drowsy rascal; I'll strew its branches on his coffin-board. Blow again!'

Once more Blackcastle poured the notes of his horn to the wind; and as the echoes mingled with the roaring of the river and the moaning of the trees, that low wailing cry, so chilling to their hearts, was heard again; and now lights began to twinkle in the warder's cottage.

'Pest upon thee, villan!' said Borthwick; 'while we are detained here, our birds may indeed be flown from Loretto. He ought to know 'tis no ordinary errand that bringeth men abroad in weather such as this.'

As he spake a white figure, evidently that of a woman in a long dress, appeared on the opposite bank of the stream, and beckoned repeatedly to the troopers to attempt the ford.

''Tis the keeper's wife,' said one; 'I ken the carlin weel by her lang luggit mutch.'

''Tis the Kelpie—beware, beware!' said another, while their horses trembled, kicked, and plunged, and their eyes shot fire, as a deadly terror seemed to possess them—a terror easily communicated to their superstitious riders.

Still the figure pointed to the ford and beckoned impatiently.

'Thank you, mistress,' cried Hailes; 'but we would rather not attempt it; so instantly open the gate.'

But she continued to beckon, and her voice, if she used it, was lost in the howling of the wind and the hoarse roaring of the stream; so, finding their horses were becoming quite unmanageable, Lord Home lost his temper, a commodity which he was ever losing and long of recovering, 'Hag!' he exclaimed; 'undo the gate, or begone at once *to hell!*'

On this, it is related, a wild shriek was heard, and the white wavering figure disappeared. At the same moment, the warder came hurriedly and opened the barrier.

'Wretched varlet!' said the imperious Home, giving the

man a blow with his clenched hand; 'thou hast kept us waiting long enough; why did not that hag of thine open the gate, instead of seeking to wile us by the ford?'

'A thousand humble pardons, noble gentlemen,' stammered the poor warder; 'but—but—a hag, said ye?'

'Ay, thy gudewife, carle,' said Blackcastle; 'I know her well enough by her long-eared coif.'

'God assoil us! Ye have seen a spirit; for my wife was drowned at the ford this fatal morning, and noo we are streekin' her puir wat corpse for the burial! Oh! sirs,' wept the keeper, 'what is this o't—what is this o't?'

'By St. Mary! we have seen a spectre!' shouted Hailes, dashing spurs into his horse, and clearing the bridge at a bound; and furiously all the train followed him through the dark but wide street of Musselburgh.

This event shed a species of horror over the whole party, whose faculties, never very clear at any time, were past inquiring whether or not it was a supernatural figure they had seen; so they all spurred on to leave the bridge and stream behind, and to reach Loretto as soon as possible. But whether the delay which occurred at the gate was productive of good or evil consequences to the lovers at the Hermitage, another chapter or so will disclose.

CHAPTER LI.

LADY EFFIE'S LETTER.

THE weather had become gloomy, and continued so. Though the month was merry and sunny June, and all the woods of fertile Fife were then in their fullest foliage, the sky lowered heavily over the German sea, and the waves of the Firth broke sullenly on the pillared bluffs of Crail and Elie; and, driven by the east wind, the breakers of Largo Bay broke furiously upon the Dyke, and dashed their spray on the sandy shore beyond it.

This noble bay, in which the Scottish ships and their prizes were still at anchor, forms a semicircle of about ten miles of coast, marked by a peculiar ridge of sand, called by fishermen the Dyke; and old tradition says it was a wall or rampart, that ran from Kincraig, round all the bay, to Methul, and that it contained a forest, called the Wood of Forth. In corroboration of this, the anchors of ships have been known to drag up the roots of oaks from their beds in the sand below.

The *Yellow Frigate* and her consorts rode quietly there at anchor, and safe from every wind but a south one.

Meanwhile, in Largo House there was a gay and joyous company, for the hospitable old admiral made all welcome —Englishman and Scot—to the noble dwelling with which the grateful king James III. had gifted him. The castle was old, for in ancient times it had been a jointure house of the queens consort, and built, some say, for Jolande de Dreux, the bride of Alexander III. Northward of it rose the conical hill of Largo, green to its summit, which stands nine hundred feet above the yellow shore. Near the castle grew a pine coppice, in the centre of which yawned a wild and deep ravine, the *Keil's Den*, famous in the annals of sorcery and horror. Through this brawled a mountain burn, which rushed to meet the waters of the bay.

The noble barony of Largo had been granted by James III.

to his favourite admiral, because it was the place of his birth, the royal donor considering, 'Gratuita et fidelia servicia sibi per familiarem servitorem suum Andream Wod, commorante in Leith, tam per terram, quam per mare, in pace et guerra, gratuiter impensa, in Regno Scotiæ et extra idem, et signanter CONTRA INIMICOS SUOS ANGLIA, et dampnum per ipsum Andream inde sustenta, suum personam gravibus vitæ exponendo periculus 18 die Martii, 1482;' for thus runs his charter, which is yet preserved in the office of the great seal of Scotland.

The evening was grey; a mist was settling over the estuary, and the woods and hill of Largo looked dark and nigh; on the tower-head of the admiral's mansion, Barton and Falconer were pacing to and fro, with their quarter-deck step, conversing on their chances in love and war, and awaiting the return of Willie Wad, whom, as related, they had, on the previous day, despatched to Leith with letters to the sisters.

The admiral was on board the fleet, seeing after the repair of damages and awaiting tidings of the lost king or the rebellious barons.

Howard and Margaret Drummond were seated together on the cushioned seats of a deep window in the hall. It overlooked the wooden glen, through which the yellow sunlight straggled in the haze of the misty evening; and both were silent and sad, for their hearts were occupied by many heavy thoughts.

That of Howard was full of Margaret; but her heart was wandering away to Rothesay and their child.

She was very pale, yet a tinge of health had returned to her soft cheek; now that hope was reviving in her breast; now that she was no longer the secret prisoner of Henry and the victim of his cold intrigues; and now that she was about to be restored to the powerful protection of her father, and her youthful husband. With her white hand she playfully caressed a large Scottish staghound, which had ventured to nestle his great rough head upon her knees.

Her fine bright hair, which she had long neglected—at least during her sad sojourn on board the *Harry*—was now smoothly braided above her forehead, and it shone like threads of gold in the occasional sunbeams that stole through the deep embayment of the window; and nothing could be prettier or more becoming than the fashion of her blue velvet hood, with its white satin lining, tied by twelve little friars' knots of fine silver—a favourite ornament with the Scottish belles of the time.

Howard thought he had never seen her looking so beautiful or so seductive; and she believed that she had never seen him more sad and more silent.

The residence of a day or two in the lonely Castle of Largo, in the society of the gentle Drummond, with the painful certainty of a total separation now close at hand, had sealed the fate of the poor English captain, by destroying his happiness for ever.

'Then I have no hope now—none?' said he, gazing upon her tenderly and earnestly, as he referred to a previous and most anxious conversation.

'It is most painful, good Howard, that my lips should—' said Margaret, with hesitation, 'should ever confirm anything that—that is calculated to make unhappy a heart so kind, so noble, and so true as thine; but ho, I beseech you to be assured, that to love me is indeed a hopeless task.'

'Curse on our king's cold-blooded policy!' he exclaimed, in bitterness and sorrow. 'Had I known you under kinder and better auspices,—under any other than as the compatriot of infamous abductors, you had perhaps listened to me with more approbation. I am indeed unfortunate—more unhappy than the power of language can convey.'

He paused, and Margaret sighed with impatience. 'My heart, that never knew another love, is all your own, sweet Margaret; it became so from that time when over your senseless form I spread my cloak in pity; on that unfortunate night at Dundee; a night to me the source of mingled joy and woe, for then I knew you first.'

'Alas, poor Edmund Howard; you were indeed born under an evil star.'

'Madam, it had been well for me, if in our battle in the Downs a shot from Barton's ships had ended my career, before this northern mission was devised. I had then been spared the pain of losing you—of loving you in vain.'

He turned his eyes away and pressed his hand upon his breast, for the depth of his emotion was great.

Margaret gazed upon him with mournful interest; he was indeed most winning in manner and noble in aspect, for he was the stateliest captain in all King Henry's infant fleet.

His face and form were unexceptionable, and his attire was gorgeous. His tunic was cloth-of-gold, brocaded, and fastened by twenty little clasps, studded with diamonds, and on each breast were six slashes of blue silk. A collar of twelve pearls, with twelve medallions of the apostles, encircled his neck, and at the end of it hung his silver whistle, his badge of office and command. His cap was of scarlet velvet, edged with pearls; his long hose were of fawn-coloured silk, and his shoes of crimson leather.

'Captain Howard,' said Margaret, after a long and painful pause, 'I will make you the partner of a secret, if, on your honour, you promise me to keep it from others; for it is of mighty import to me,—a secret valuable as life, dear as honour.'

'Oh, command me, madam,' said Howard, kneeling down and removing his cap, full of that chivalric enthusiasm which was peculiar to the time as well as to the man. 'Your wish shall seal my lips as close as death himself.'

'Well, my kind, good Howard, imagine how I have suffered by your professions of love to me, and how much is the pity I feel, when obliged to acknowledge that I am the wedded wife of the crown prince, and am now, by virtue of this *his ring*, the Duchess of Rothesay, and Countess of Carrick.'

Howard was paralysed by this fatal intelligence; again he clasped his hands, and his nut-brown cheek grew ashy pale.

'Oh, madam,' said he, 'to me your secret is worse than death; for now I am indeed hopeless, crushed, and ruined! Honour and love are alike lost to me! The wife of Rothesay——'

'Wedded to him, Howard, a year ago, in my uncle's cathedral of Dunblane. 'Tis best to know the worst at once—ay, wedded!'

'Despite his betrothal to a princess of England?'

'Despite a more serious barrier—our ties of blood; and hence this fatal secrecy.'

'Oh, most fatal—fatal, at least to me! But say, dear madam, knew Henry our king of this espousal?'

He knew not, or, knowing, little cared: but the Bishop of Dunblane has been lawlessly seized on his way from Rome with our dispensation, and now well must Henry know this well-kept secret, which was hidden even from my father and my own beloved sisters.'

Now there was a long and sorrowful pause.

Howard felt assured that he could urge nothing more, and Margaret, after a time, spoke kindly to him of other things—but in vain; for his passion for her was the only idea that had soothed, or made him forget at times the mortification of being a prisoner, and of his late defeat— a defeat so remarkable, when the smallness of the attacking force is considered: but history shows us, that in all his battles Sir Andrew Wood never feared to encounter double his strength at any time, and never encountered without being victorious; so, on that score Howard had no reason for shame.

Meanwhile, the communings of Robert Barton and Sir David Falconer on the bartizan overhead were interrupted by the appearance of Master Wad, who, bonnet in hand, ascended to their lofty promenade by the narrow wheel-stair of a turret, that gave admittance to the battlement, and which yet overlooks the orchard of the house.

'Welcome, good shipmate,' said Barton.

'Well, what tidings, Willie?' added Falconer; for in Scotland it is still the kindly custom with persons in authority to address inferiors by their *Christian* name.

Not conceiving it conducive either to his interest or reputation to relate how he had lost, and so narrowly regained, the letter of Lady Euphemia, the gunner smoothed down his obstinate forelock, made the invariable scrape with his foot, and delivered the missive to Robert Barton; after which he hurried away to join one whom he deemed his own peculiar prisoner—the pretty English Rose, who had been also awaiting his return.

'It is from Euphemia!' said Barton, reading it hurriedly; 'from dear Effie; and she says it must equally suffice for one from Sybilla to you. It tells of close surveillance, of their father's roughness, and their new lovers' cool insolence and quiet pertinacity. 'Sdeath! would we were alongside of them for three minutes—only three minutes, Davie. A time has been fixed for their marriage——'

'Their marriage!' reiterated Falconer, stamping his heel on the bartizan. 'They dread the arrival of their uncle the dean——'

'A stern man—hard of heart and dark of brow; I know him well.'

'And implore us to find a place where they can be sheltered until these troubles are past, and the army of the insurgent lords is disbanded. Moreover, they promise to meet us on Friday evening at the Chapel of Loretto, beside the Links of Musselburgh—kind Effie!'

'We'll keep the tryst,' said Falconer; 'Loretto—know ye the place, Robert, for we must not wander much on yonder side of Forth?'

'I know it well; 'tis a run of eighteen miles across the river, and we'll take the ship's pinnace or the boat of Jamie Gair, which lies yonder, anchored by the Dyke; but to find them a place of shelter, that puzzles me sorely!'

'If dear Sybie would but marry me——'

'Perhaps she would, David, now, when matters are at the worst; but where would you place her, while you were afloat—eh?'

'Alas! I have neither house nor hold—nor any home, but the *Yellow Frigate*.'

'Nor I; for now these rebel lords have seized my manor of Barnton and my father's house in Leith; but I hope soon to make a clear ship of them.'

'Then all these dog-nobles would cry aloud for vengeance, at the sisters taking shelter with us.'

'Two jovial young bachelors.'

'Nay,' said Falconer, with a sigh of anger; 'as two plebeians, whose presumption brought dishonour on a noble house.'

'Let them cry; it suits their fancy.'

'But we must find a secret as well as sure place, lest they be carried off from us at the sword's point; for the Lords Drummond, Hailes, and Home could march with ease five thousand men to recover them. I know their power better than thee, Robert, the half of whose life, and more, has been spent upon the water. Besides, Lady Euphemia has written to you, perhaps when spurred on by some keen excitement; and it may so chance that when the time comes, they will shrink from committing themselves to our care.'

'What! Effie shrink from committing herself to the care of her betrothed? Thou art a timid lover, Davie.'

'I am crushed in spirit by my evil fortune.'

'When their hearts are touched, women (and to their glory be it said) scorn alike the vaunted rubbish of feudal pride and the cold north wind of worldly prudence! Besides, who has a better right to secure the safety of Lady Effie than I? Am I not her affianced husband, whose ring of promise is on her finger? Stay—thou knowest, Davie, that my aunt, Robina Barton, is prioress of the Grey Sisters at Dundee; and for the love she bears us, she will gladly keep the three sisters until this breeze blows past and the king's authority is enforced.'

' Right, Rob ; I would rather trust them with that reverend lady and her good Claresses, than in the strongest castle in Scotland. For these lords might storm and sack the stronghold—even the Bass itself—when they dare not molest the poor nuns ; but we must consult the admiral——'

' He is on board the ships in the bay.'

' Or Howard—but then he is an Englishman, and consequently knows little or nothing of Scotland or her customs.'

' But he is a brave fellow, a foeman though he be,' said Barton, with a darkening face ; ' and I might learn to love him had not my father fallen in battle by his brother's hand.'

Leaving the two friends and lovers to arrange, consider and reconsider their plans—leaving poor Howard to console himself the best way he can—leaving the admiral busied about his ships and their prizes, while his gunner and coxswain, though staunch Scotsmen, were yielding to English influence, like greater men in more modern times, but after a more honourable fashion, for they were lowering their colours to the pretty Cicely and the bright-eyed Rose, on whom their kind leader had bestowed two carcanets of silver, studded with those beautiful stones which are found upon the beach of Fife, and from their deep red colour are called Elie Rubies—leaving Father Zuill busied in the development of the great parabolic speculum—and leaving young Margaret sighing with impatience to rejoin her boy husband, we will change the scene to the other side of the river.

CHAPTER LII.

THE HERMIT OF LORETTO.

AMONG all the places esteemed for sanctity, at a time when a singular mixture of high religious veneration and a strong faith amounting to adoration and sublimity, united to gross superstition, existed in the land, there was none in Scotland so famous as the chapel and hermitage of Our Lady of Loretto, which stood a little way without the eastern gate of Musselburgh.

It belonged to the abbots of Dunfermline, and had been built in an age anterior to all written record ; so now, we know not when it was founded or by whom. The obscurity in which its early history was enveloped left fancy free, and thus the fane enjoyed a celebrity for holiness second only to the Cottage of the Nativity, like which it became famous for effecting supernatural cures and conversions on visitors and devotees.

The nuns of St. Catharine of Sienna patronized the cell and sought the prayers of the ascetic who dwelt in the hermitage. In August, 1530, before visiting France, James V. made a pilgrimage of more than forty miles on foot to Loretto. Ladies about to be delivered sent there their childbed linen, to obtain the ' odour of sanctity.' If they recovered, the hermit attributed it to the powers of the shrine; if they died, to their own evil and sin. Then, it was affirmed that sight had been restored to the blind, and strength to the lame ; but under the coarse and pungent satires of Sir David Lindesay of the Mount, and one in particular by John Knox, beginning :

> I, Thomas the Hermit, in Loreitte,
> Sanct Francis Order do heartillie greet,

the shrine ultimately lost all reputation and honour ; it was demolished, and its materials form the present Tolbooth of the town—little more being left of Loretto than the name and a vault under a wooded mound.

By the decline of the Church, and the general decay of religious sentiment before the Reformation, the pilgrimages to Loretto became mere scenes of debauchery and an excuse for licentiousness.

In the days of James III. the shrine enjoyed its ancient fame—pure and undefiled; and Father Fairlie, the Franciscan who then occupied the hermitage, afterwards attained a great age, for he was the immediate predecessor of the Father Thomas referred to in the pasquil of Knox. Though a pious enthusiast in some respects, he was not at all one of those who thought

To merit heaven by making earth a hell.

He had been a soldier in his youth, and fought in the Douglas wars; so he said his office daily and never omitted his prayers, or withheld kind advice from those who sought his shrine; and yet withal, he enjoyed the various good things of this life that came his way. Thus, though he went abroad barefooted and wore the grey woollen gown and cowl, with the knotted girdle prescribed by his patron St. Francis of Assisi, he was one of the most sleek and well fed of the brotherhood in Scotland.

It was towards the afternoon of that stormy day described in a recent chapter. From the Firth a cool wind blew over the sandy knolls and broomy hollows of Musselburgh Links; the old woods of Pinkey and the venerable oaks around the Chapel of Loretto moaned in the rising wind, and their damp foliage whistled drearily. The sky wore a dingy grey hue to the eastward, darkening as it approached the horizon, which served as a background, and against which the white curling waves of the Firth rose and fell, while the bitter surf boomed far along the echoing shore.

No less than three substantial burgess-wives of the 'honest town' had been at the shrine on this morning, craving the prayers of the hermit; one for the recovery of her spouse, who was a leper on Inchkeith; a second that her child might be cured of the croup; and a third that her husband might escape from the Turks, who had taken him prisoner in the Levant, all of which Father Fairlie promised should be done ' without delay, if they had *faith* ; ' —however, each had what was of more importance to him, a basket of viands, ready cooked, which they deposited and departed.

The hermit, after a long and sorrowful contemplation of a daintily roasted duck and side of lamb, was compelled (the day being Friday) to content himself with a couple of pounds of kippered salmon, five or six buttered eggs, and a quart of Rhenish wine for dinner; after which he stroked his paunch, made a sign of the cross three times, and blessed the three burgess-wives in his heart. He then drew his grey cowl over his face, and walked forth upon the beach for the double purpose of gaining an appetite for supper and saying 'his office' or daily set of prescribed prayers in Latin; though some persons who were envious of the popularity enjoyed by Friar Fairlie among the maids, wives, and widows of the honest town—for so was Musselburgh named *par excellence*, by the Regent Randolph in 1333—averred that he knew no more of Latinity than a few scraps, with which he incessantly interlarded his conversation; and as the said scraps sounded very mysterious and holy, they were not without having a due and potent effect upon the simple-minded folks who heard them. Some were rash enough to assert that at vespers he had been heard in his hermitage singing, 'Jollie Martin,' and that old ditty which became so famous in the time of James V.:

> Bill, wilt thou come by a lute
> And belt thee in Sanct Francis cord;

but all this we verily believe to have been mere scandal, raised by the chaplains of other oratories in the burgh, who belonged to rival orders, and were envious of the fame enjoyed by the poor Franciscan hermit and his shrine at Loretto, without the gate.

The attention of our new friend the recluse was divided between his daily office, which he repeated drowsily and mechanically, and in watching the lowering of the sky and sea, on which a boat with her large lug-sail squared was running straight for the beach which bordered the links.

She cut through the water, riding over, or cleaving asunder the waves with her sharp prow, and throwing on each side a continual shower of spray; the helmsman steered her straight for the shore, and being aware that the tide was ebbing, beached her firmly into the soft sand, while at the same moment two companions whom he had on board reduced the sail, hauled down the yard, and struck the mast. They then threw over the anchor, to keep her fast when the tide floated her again; and stepping into the surf in their long boots which came above the knee, they crossed the links (or downs, as they would be called in England) and approached the observant friar.

The latter was glad to perceive that one of the trio carried an ample basket on one arm and had a small keg under the other; and these—as there were no smugglers in those primitive times—he fondly believed were dutiful offerings for himself.

The three men, who came straight towards him, wore the coarse grey doublet, cloak, and short trews then worn by the Scottish seaman, with long fisher-boots; but under this plain attire, the quick eye of the hermit detected in each the upper rim of a gorget of fine steel, and other indications which led him to suspect that two of them, at least, were gentlemen, who under their humble garments had each a good coat of mail; and such was really the case, for the three mysterious boat voyagers were none else than Robert Barton, Sir David Falconer, and Willie Wad, who had boldly run across that morning from Largo in a fisher-boat, all undeterred by the threatening aspect of the sky and weather, and still less by terror of the insurgents—for each had with him his sword, dagger, and handgun.

'Good-morrow, father,' said Barton, with a profound salutation; 'we presume you are the Franciscan Father of Loretto.'

'Dominus vobiscum—gude-morrow, my bairns,' said the hermit, waving a blessing to them with his fat fingers; 'come ye here to pray?' he added, eyeing with affection the basket and barrel.

'We have run in here and anchored, good father, for the double purpose of avoiding the black squall now coming on, and of offering up a small orison at the shrine of Loretto, where—much as I have heard of it—I never, to my shame, have been before,' said Robert Barton.

'Come ye here, sirs, to pray alone?' asked the hermit, inquisitively.

'Alone,' reiterated Falconer, puzzled by the question; 'dost not see there are three of us?'

'Benedictus dominus Deus,' said the friar, shrugging his shoulders, over which his grey cowl hung, for by past experience, he had a shrewd guess that ladies would soon arrive. 'This is the way to my hermitage—enter, and the blessings of the day be on ye, for every day is blessed.'

'The eleventh of this month, for example?' said Falconer. 'Nay, in all his wickedness, man cannot curse it; but our poor king—are there yet no tidings of him?'

'None; and awful rumours are abroad anent his fate.'

'Our pilgrimage here is dark and devious,' sighed Father Fairlie, eyeing the basket again; 'yea, it is full of pitfalls, crooks, and thorns—Benedictus dom—— but take care, friend, that barrel will slip and the ale be spilled.'

'Wha tauld ye it was ale, friar?' asked the gunner, with a smirk; 'maybe it's only bilge.'

'What?' asked the Franciscan.

'Peace, Willie,' said Sir David Falconer; 'by my faith, priest, it is the best of French brandy.'

'Well, as I was saying, our path here in this valley of sorrow is indeed full of dangers and doubt. The poor king—(brandy indeed!—Causa nostræ lætitiæ!)—the king of the commons, alake!' and the friar beat his breast, through which a glow had spread on hearing with what the keg was filled.

They now approached the chapel, which was surrounded by a high stone wall, and stood amid a group of venerable oak trees, the branches of which were widely spread and entwined together. One of these bore the name of the Weirdwoman's Aik, from what circumstance it is now impossible to ascertain, but innumerable tales of terror were connected with it. There the souls of those who had committed acts of sacrilege during their lifetime had been heard to moan, and were seen to hover near the precincts of the holy place; there the Druids had performed their impious rites in the days of their awful rule; and there the gentle fairies yet danced in the bright moonlight, on the festival of St. John, as every hermit of Loretto had averred since the chapel was founded.

Moreover, more than one fugitive, who, unable to reach the sanctuary of the chapel, or, mistrusting its security, had clambered up the oak and taken shelter there, *had never more come down;* thus it was with something of the superstitious awe incident to their time and profession that Barton, Falconer, and the gunner gazed up at the dark, dense foliage of the Weirdwoman's Aik, and approached the chapel.

This venerable fane, which had been built by the *Kulden*

(corrupted Gaelic for 'the servants of God') at a time when sculpture was merely an adjunct to masonry, was massive and plain; for though erected for the simple form of worship those early priests performed within its walls, it exhibited the engrafted decorations of later times. Built of dark grey stone, it was a simple parallelogram, destitute of transept and of aisle. Its door and windows were arched, and the latter were small and placed high in the wall, having been for ages unglazed—the *Kuldee* architect had wished to screen the half-savage worshippers from the cold east wind that usually blows from the Forth, and from the sandy links; yet much of the solemnity and mystery peculiar to Catholic edifices were imparted to it, by a gilded figure of the Saviour on His cross, which stood above the altar; and before it, were daily offerings of flowers.

Above this image shone the letters I.N.R.I.; below was a niche covered by a grotesquely sculptured canopy of stone: here were the elements, within a gilded door, around which were the following words in old Gothic letters, cut in the stone, and flourished in blue and gold:

Hic Est Servatum Corpus ex virgine natum.

While the three visitors, after dipping their right hands in the font at the chapel door, proceeded, like good Catholics, to say a prayer or two on their knees before the carved stone rail which enclosed the altar, the hermit peeped into the basket which the gunner had left without (giving him a wink and nod as he did so); and the reverend father enumerated the contents with great satisfaction, muttering between many a scrap of pious Latinity:

'A goose, roasted—daintily, too!—*mater purissima!*— and stuffed with cloves and spices, doubtless; a pout pasty; three choppin flasks of Rochelle, as I live! good;—and a mutchkin of canary; a bag of maccaroons, with ten crowns, and five lyons—*Dominus vobiscum.* Master gunner, you are a worthy soul; and your masters are generous!'

The brevity of their prayers convinced the hermit that they had not come for religious purposes alone, and scrutinizing them he said, 'My gude sirs, your mariners' garb fails to conceal from me that you have iron harness below these gaberdines of frieze.'

'True, father,' said Barton, smiling; 'we are shelled

over like partans. But what of that ? In these desperate times men are not wont to go abroad unarmed.'

' Then who may ye be ? '

' We may be a couple of rascals,' said Falconer, laughing, in that free manner acquired by soldiering ; ' and would be traitors most likely, if our blood was noble ; but being of humble birth, or only the sons of our own deserts, we are the king's liege men, and true Scotsmen.'

' Benedictus dominus,' mumbled the hermit.

' This is Robert Barton, captain of the yellow caravel ; this is Master Wad, our gunner wight, and I am David Falconer, knight, and a captain of the king's arquebusses.'

The fat and full-faced hermit threw back his cowl, and taking each by the hand with warmth, said :

' God and St. Mary bless ye, sirs ; for though your fathers were but humble men, you are the sons of gallant deeds, and have stood nobly by our hapless king. Welcome to my poor cell, sirs, and to share the gude cheer ye have brought me. But hark—here are horses ! ' he added, as the sound of hoofs was heard without.

THE hermit's eyes were filled by a cunning leer, as two ladies, each followed by a page and female attendant, all mounted, rode down the pathway to the chapel, and, whipping up their nags as they passed the Weirdwoman's Aik, they alighted at the arched doorway, from which Barton and Falconer hurried forth to meet them, full of joy and ardour.

'Causa nostræ lætitiæ!' said the hermit. 'I kenned how it would be; the hen-birds are come at last!'

Now, as interviews between lovers are usually very delightful to young ladies in general, we might for their benefit narrate at great length all that was said and done by the two fair Drummonds and the brave loyalists who met them at Loretto; but a foreknowledge of the dire conclusion of their tryst has somewhat chilled us, and so we hasten to unfold the more important part of their adventures.

'So, so; Sancta Maria!' muttered the sleek hermit, as he reckoned on his fingers the sum given by the page of Lady Euphemia, and the contents of a basket given him by the other. 'Such is the fashion of prayer in these degenerate modern times, and such are the pilgrims who usually come to pray. Once it was not so. A pity, too, 'tis Friday! That pout pie will be quite stale to-morrow. But away with these thoughts, for here is a pie of buttered crabs, on which I can sup bravely, and with a clear conscience.'

'By my certie, Friar Fairlie, ye might victual a sea-going ship,' said Willie Wad. 'Here now are a cask, six flasks, and three baskets.'

'Well,' responded the hermit, sulkily, 'I shall have the more wherewith to feed the hungry, the puir headsmen and lamiters, who will be here betimes in the morning. King William the Lion ordained that "Kirkmen should live honestlie by the fruits and profits of their kirk;" even so, sir gunner, do I live by the profit and fruit of mine. I lippen to none, and none can say that while I have a drop to share or a crumb to divide, the poor or the hungry left the cell of Loretto uncared for.'

'How black it grows without,' said the gunner, somewhat abashed, as he hastened to change the subject, and the chapel became dark and gloomy, while the distant waves were heard to roll like thunder on the lonely beach. ⁰Those that are at sea to-night will hae about as mickle sleep as a weathercock may, in a close-reef-topsail breeze.'

⁰Then do thou take up the barrel and basket, while I take these, and come hither with me, master gunner. And you, gentlemen,' he added to the pages ; ' this stair leads to my cell. Let us leave these four friends to their prayers (prayers —mater purissima !), while we arrange for them something by way of repast. Look ye, sirs, and be quick. Hark ! is that rain ? '

Now the storm which swelled the Esk, and served to detain the would-be murderers in the chapel on the Figgatemuir, was beginning to descend in all its fury, and the grove of Loretto waved in the rising wind, while the deep heavy foliage of the weirdwoman's tree swayed mournfully in the gusty blasts.

Meanwhile, heedless of it (for perhaps they heard it not) the lovers poured out their hearts to each other ; for their cause was common, and Barton had nothing for the ear of Euphemia that Falconer might not hear, while he had no secret for Sybilla in which his friend had not an interest. It was their common safety, and the successful issue of their fortunes on which they now consulted.

Impetuous and impulsive, with all her firmness, Euphemia gave way to tears and wept bitterly ; and the breast of Sybilla was swollen by many a heavy sob. Falconer left nothing unsaid to console and to soothe her, while he gazed upon her tenderly, as if he would have said in the words of the poet :

> Would I were with thee every day and hour
> Which now I spend so sadly, far from thee !
> Would that my form possessed the magic power
> To follow where my heavy heart would be.
> Whate'er thy lot by land or sea,
> Would I were there eternally !

'My poor blossom, how faded and how pale ! ' said Falconer, encircling her by an arm. ' But take new courage, dear one, for be assured that happier days will come. God controlleth our destinies, and whatever is in store for you, Sybilla, must be happiness and peace.'

'I cannot, without presumption, assure myself of that. I have endured so much, Sir David, since that awful day at Dundee!' she added, closing her eyes for a moment as the scene in the garden came before her.

'Forget it, as I have forgotten it, my sweet one.'

'We have been so lonely and so isolated, Euphemia and I, that—that——'

'Thou hast missed me, then, beloved Sybilla!'

'Oh yes, as a bird misses the sunshine,' said she, with a bright smile through her tears.

A mute caress was the only reply of Falconer.

'And this may be the last time we shall ever meet!' said Sybilla, clasping her hands.

'Unless we find a safe harbour for you,' said Barton.

'And found it must be, Robert,' said the firmer Euphemia; 'for if we return to place ourselves under the authority of our father, and—and the influence of our uncle, that cold and determined dean, we will be hopelessly separated from you; for, women though we be, we dare not refuse to wed those facile fools of Angus, Hepburn of Hailes, and Home of Home.'

Barton uttered a bitter laugh, which almost burst the braces of his cuirass.

'What say you to this, Sybilla?' asked Falconer, with a mournful smile.

'I have nothing to urge,' said she, gently; 'my mind has long been without hope, and my heart is so crushed by sorrow that I have now less courage than a child.'

'Has the Lord Drummond forgotten altogether that you are my plighted wife, Euphemia?' asked Barton, in a mingled tone of tenderness and anger.

'He forgets all—everything—or despises to remember——'

'And faith! I had almost forgotten to give thee that particular kiss our dear Margaret sent thee.'

'Stay—the friar——'

'Oh, the hermit—he is busy overhauling our baskets; well—and so Lord Drummond forgets, eh?'

'Everything of the past; and now sees nothing but two earl's coronets and clumps of Border spears; and hears nothing but the whispers of envy, anger, and restless ambition——'

' Ay—and treason and rebellion.'

' Hush, Rob,' said the less confident Falconer : ' bethink you he is *their* father ? '

' Poor infatuated old lord,' continued Barton, pursuing his own train of thought ; ' in these times it may be rash to wed, when one half of Scotland has unsheathed the sword against the other ; but why may we not bring in the hermit ; here is an altar (in the kingdom we have none holier), and we have witnesses enough—the pages, the tirewomen, and the gunner. Father Fairlie will splice us all in half the time a reel would run ; what say you, dear Euphemia ? '

Sybilla coloured deeply at this proposal, while her sister waved her hand in dissent and said : ' Nay, nay, Robert Barton ; say no more of that, or this instant we mount and ride westward again ; shelter we must have—a sanctuary —but not such as you would propose.'

' Then for the love she bears me, my aunt, the old Claress of Dundee, will gladly receive you both.'

' Such was our wish ; but how to reach her ? '

' By horse or boat—which you will. Sauchie's soldiers guard the Bridge of Stirling ; but the king's ships keep the passage of the river at Alloa. At present neither mode can be thought of—to-night at least ; for we shall have a blast that will furrow up the very bottom of the sea, and show old wrecks that lie among the weeds and waste below ; yet we shall be happy enough here, whate'er betide without.'

' I often think, dear Robert, that happiness has left us for ever ! ' said the elder sister, with a sigh.

' Heaven hath its own ways, Effie, of working out its own ends ; and thus it may be all for the best of purposes that we now are beating against a head-wind with the ebb-tide of misfortune to boot.'

' Circumstances are seldom so bad, Lady Euphemia, that they might not be worse,' said Falconer, cheerfully ; ' we might both have been maimed or slain outright in our last battle with the English——'

' Oh, that would have been a scene of horror ! ' said Sybilla, wringing her hands.

' Horror, indeed, dearest Sybie ! When the ships crushed together till the muzzles of their cannon rung, and the boarders were brayed to death between them, as their sides thundered in collision.'

' Yea, David,' said the captain ; ' many a brave fellow found a watery grave that night, and is now lying in pickle off the Isle of May. But let us visit the Father Hermit in his cell; after having a slice of meat and a bicker of wine we shall be better able to arrange our thoughts. And hark! By my soul, what a blast! How the gale rises as the spirits of the air pipe up fresh gusts of wind; all at sea must keep sure watch to-night!'

The tempestuous state of the evening prevented the chapel being favoured by any more visitors; and the whole party (including the four attendants of the ladies), making ten persons in all, sat on the stone benches of the Hermit's cell, and by the light of a lamp supped pleasantly enough; though the wind howled through the trees, and moaned in the openings of a burial vault close by, and the boom of the sea resounded on the beach, while the glare of the lightning reddened at times the two narrow slits which served as windows to the recluse's dormitory, and on the coarse glass of which the heavy rain-drops pattered and hissed.

Willie Wad, having nothing else to do (for the ladies' attendants seemed more occupied by the gaily-dressed pages than with him), coiled himself up in a corner, and knowing that he would have to keep the harbour-watch on board to-morrow night, had gone to sleep with that sailor-like facility which defies all discomfort.

The attendants were awed into silence by the reputed holiness of the place; the aspect of the cowled hermit, in his grey Franciscan frock, sitting silent and reserved, as he always did before strangers; and by the grim aspect of the cell, which was all built of bare hewn stone, and darkened by age.

In a recess on one side lay the bed of the recluse; on the other was a rudely sculptured niche, before which projected a little stone font for holy water; within it was a coarse crucifix of black-thorn and a bare skull, well polished by long use; and having inscribed on its blanched bony temples a pious legend.

CHAPTER LIV.

THE WEIRDWOMAN'S TREE.

THE evening was growing into night.

The conversation at Loretto had been maintained in broken and unconnected sentences, or in low whispers; the hermit had retrimmed his lamp, removed the remains of the supper, and composed himself to finish that part of his 'office' which yet remained unsaid; and then he told the maids and pages many a wonderful story of the miraculous cures effected at the shrine: how the blind had recovered their sight, the sick their health; how the lame had left their crutches and wooden legs behind them; and how, when an impious boy had cast a stone at the image of Our Lady, blood dropped from her nostrils, to the horror of the beholders, and how that wild little boy died the mitred Abbot of Dunfermline.

Then the gunner, who had wakened up, told many a story of a somewhat different character: of the achievements of Andrew Wood, and of brave old Andrew Barton; and how, in the old war waged by Scotland against the Dutch and Portuguese, he had swept all the ocean of their ships, from the Fortunate Isles to the swamps of the Zuiderzee; capturing, sinking, or burning their gilded argosies and noble carracques, to avenge the murder of some Scottish mariners on the high seas in time of peace; and how he had barrelled up their heads in brine, and sent some scores of them to Stirling (to the no small horror of the good King James) as the best proof of how he was discharging his duty—and as the records of the Secret Council still remain to show.

The wind had gone down as the night darkened; the rain had ceased, and now little more was heard than the roar of the billows on the level shore; but the lovers were thoughtful and silent, for the time of separation was approaching, and no definite plan had been resolved on.

Amid this silence the tread of an armed man—if one might judge by the jangling rowels of heavy military spurs—was heard to cross the chapel floor above them; for the hermitage was in one of the numerous vaults below the edifice.

'Gate of Heaven—a visitor!' said the hermit, closing his book, and softly ascending the narrow stair to the chapel. Falconer followed with his sword half drawn, and prepared for any meeting of emergency.

The chapel was empty; there was no one there, and the door was still closed, lest the wind might extinguish the six tapers that were always burning before the little altar.

'This is most strange!' said the fat hermit, with an expression of perplexity on his sleek round face. 'No man can have crossed the chapel, and closed the door too, before we could see him.'

'Some one may be without,' said Falconer.

'Sancta Maria! it may be a warning of approaching evil; keep back, Sir David, a little way, while I look without; for none dare meddle with me.'

Setting down his lamp, the hermit softly opened the chapel door, slipped out, and looked round him; the wind had sunk into a low, moaning sough; the stars were shining through the gaps in the flying clouds. These gaps revealed patches of blue, occasionally; their ragged edges were tinged by the moon; and a lurid light was visible at the horizon. The night was still wild-looking; but the storm was evidently past.

On the pathway which led to the chapel, he saw a group of mounted horsemen, one of whom was giving directions to the rest, and in about half a minute after, they separated and formed themselves in a circle round the edifice, with the unmistakable design of surrounding and entrapping its unwary inmates.

The friar softly and hastily closed the door, and drew across it the ponderous oak bar by which it was secured.

'How now, Father Hermit?' said Falconer, startled by the pale and excited aspect of his usually rubicund visage; 'what is the matter?'

'Matter! Sancta Maria ora pro nobis—the chapel is beset!' he cried, rushing down stairs to alarm still more the startled inmates, 'we are surrounded, hemmed in on all sides!'

'By whom?' asked Falconer, furiously.

'Men——'

'The devil, friar! I scarcely expected it would be by wild beasts.'

'You may find them little better, perhaps. They are a band of armed horsemen, who must be in pursuit of you, and who have heard our voices or seen the light through this small loop of glass.'

'Horsemen!' said Euphemia; 'they must be the moss-troopers of Lord Home, or of Hailes. Alas! Robert Barton, we—*we* have lured you to this destruction!'

'Ora pro nobis,' mumbled the bewildered hermit, looking upward imploringly; 'alack—is this a time for wretched men to wage a strife amongst themselves, when the elements are at war with us all!'

'Away, away, dearest David,' said Sybilla, throwing herself into the arms of Falconer; 'reach your boat, and trust to the waves rather than to them. They dare not harm *us*—but you and Robert Barton—oh, Mother above, have mercy on us!'

At that moment, the two female attendants unwisely began to utter noisy cries of terror, while the startled pages, though but boys, grasped their poniards; then a knocking, like thunder, shook the chapel door, and a fierce laugh was heard without the little painted window of the cell, at which Sybilla saw a grim and bearded face appear, with its eyes glittering under the peak of an iron morion; for there stood Borthwick, with his brazen visage, and heart as hard as steel.

'Be calm,' said Barton—'be silent all,' he added, with a voice of authority; 'take courage, and remember that this is a sanctuary—a holy place.'

'You should have remembered that before making it the scene of amorous assignations and unholy dalliance,' said the hermit, with something of anger.

'Pardon us,' said Barton; 'yet it is not the less a sanctuary.'

'But, I fear me, these masterful limmers would violate the blessed sepulchre itself,' replied the friar, bitterly, as he hastened to conceal the barrel, the two baskets, and the six flasks, in the niche beyond the crucifix and skull.

'Violate it! dost thou think so?' asked Barton, drawing his sword.

At that instant, again the thundering knocks rang on the chapel door, and shouts were heard.

'A Home! a Home!'

'Dost think they will commit sacrilege?'

'What dare they not do? Hear ye not they are Homes?'

'True—true,' said Falconer, biting his nether lip; 'hark to the slogan of the Border-men.'

'Ay,' quoth Master Wad; 'but mony a gay galley saileth under fause colours; mony a muffled man and mony a lord baron when his helmet is closed, if bound on a deed of ill, crieth the slogan of another house than his own, to mislead the people.'

'A shrewd suggestion, Willie; but no other men have such an interest in the shortening of our lives as Hepburn of Hailes and——'

'*Keepe tryste!*' cried a voice without.

'That is the cry of Hailes—so both are there!' said Falconer, with fiery joy.

''Sdeath,' said Home; 'open, false priest! Is the chapel of Our Blessed Lady a place for these cushat doves to coo and bill in? By Saint Ringan, Father Hermit, the Lord Abbot of Dunfermline and the Archbishop of St. Andrews shall know of this, and dearly shall it cost thee!'

'Now we know our enemies,' said Falconer, as he and Barton exchanged a dark glance of intelligence; 'off with these vile disguises, Robert,' he added, throwing aside his grey gaberdine and short trews, below which appeared a handsome coat of mail; 'if we must die, let us do so like the men we are, not garbed like guisards on the night of Hogmenai.'

'Oh, Father Hermit—oh! is there, is there no avenue—no mode of escape for them?' said Euphemia, while pale and trembling she clung with her white hands to the friar's coarse grey cassock.

'None—none; there is a passage through the burial vault, towards the links——'

'And that—and that——'

'Is guarded;—hark how they hammer at it now.'

'Saint Mary and Saint John! then the place is surrounded.'

'On every side.'

The wretched sisters wrung their hands in an ecstasy of grief; while Wad began to tighten his waistbelt, draw his bonnet over his brow, and spit with terrible deliberation into the palms of his brown hands, as the preliminaries of attempting something desperate.

'We have but one way,' said Falconer.

' And that ? ' asked Barton.

' Is to sally out and die boldly,' said he, as he pressed h
lip to Sybilla's cold white cheek.

' To climb the wall of the precincts is impossible,' sai
the priest ; ' it is ten feet high, and its gate is guarded b
eight spearmen at least. I could reckon their lance-head
when glittering in the starlight.'

' Eight, and we are but three men on foot,' said Barton.

' If we could but slip out and reach one of these trees
said the gunner, ' there we might sit perched up and undi
covered till the burgesses of Musselburgh were roused wit
their axes and staves.'

' St. Mary forgive me for engaging in this matter ; but
is most just to defend the innocent, to punish the sacrilegiou
and prevent the effusion of Christian blood,' said the poo
hermit, with a sigh of anger, as he brought up from his ce
the cask of brandy, and staved in the head thereof by on
blow of his sturdy hand. ' Now, friend gunner, lend me
match from that pistolette of thine, and while I souse th
leading varlets in burning liquor, do you three take shelte
in the weirdwoman's tree, for the gate beyond is guarde
Among its branches you will be safe from molestation, an
perhaps from discovery.'

' Good—thou counsellest bravely,' said Barton ; and a
the while the incessant din continued at the door without.

The three shipmates stood ready, with their swords an
daggers drawn ; the hermit dipped the flaming match into th
brandy, from which the fire arose in red and bluish lambe
light. The ladies shrunk back towards the altar-rail, whi
Wad flung open the chapel door. Then, as four or fiv
armed men rushed forward to enter :

' Malediction !' cried the hermit, and dashed the flamin
spirit full into their faces ; while Barton, Falconer, and Wa
charged them sword in hand, and broke through at the sam
moment. Some of the assailants had the aventayles
their helmets shut, thus the hot spirit passed through th
eyelet-holes, and half or wholly blinded them for the tim
There was a momentary shock—a clashing of blades, and emi
sion of sparks, as two men were hurled to the earth, and or
run through the body by our fugitives, who, being well awa
that the outer gate of the precincts was securely guarde
hastened to the weirdwoman's tree, and with no other foo
ing on its rough and gnarled bark than such as desperatio
and the fierce energy of the moment supplied, they clamber

p, all heavily accoutred as they were. Wad was first secure
among the branches, and Barton next. Less accustomed to
climbing and wholly unused to 'going aloft,' poor Falconer,
but for the assistance lent by their proffered hands, would
have failed to attain the same secure elevation, and must
infallibly have been sacrificed, but soon they all three clambered up together among the damp leaves, and in the heart
of the thick dark foliage attained a perch where even spearmen on horseback would fail to reach them.

'Art thou secure and firmly anchored, friend David?'
asked Barton, in a whisper.

'Yes, I am astride a great branch here, like a French
juggler in a *cheval-de-bois*,' said he, laughing.

'Hush!—here come those runions now, so let us take to
our hand-guns, and make service against them. My flask—
I have left it in the chapel! Falconer, I trust thine is at thy
belt?'

'Nay, I unstrapped it at supper; but perhaps Willie
Wad——'

An imprecation from the gunner now increased their
alarm.

'God's mercy!' said Barton; 'is thine missing too?'

'No, sir; but I have only three charges of powder in it.'

'Well, these are three men's lives. Charge home, Willie,
and fire surely, for here they come.'

In the fitful moonlight, Falconer being the last, had been
seen to scramble up the oak; and now, with drawn sword
and brandished lance, Home, Hailes, Borthwick, and even
honest Blackcastle, whom the infectious spirit of mischief had
seized, and who was still smarting from the burning brandy,
some of which had been dashed in his face, with all the rest
of their party, surrounded the stem of the great tree, with
threats, jibes, and cries of anger and defiance.

'Ha, ha!' laughed Hailes; 'so the cock-pigeons, whose
cooing we spoiled, are all roosted in this tree.'

'Unwind me your hand-guns, some of ye, sirs,' said
Home; 'try a shot ere they take wing.'

'Blithely, though I wad rather hae ane gude straik wi' a
lethart staff than sax shots wi' thae *war-cracks*,' said a grim
mosstrooper, who gave his weapon the local name by which
these primitive firearms were then known.

This simple gun, which first made its appearance in Scotland about 1450, in the time of James II., who received it
from the Italians, was at first a mere iron tube, with little

trunnions at its sides. By these it was secured to a wooden stock. The touch-hole was first on the top; but as the priming was liable to fall off, or be blown away, the vent was transferred to the right side, where a pan held the powder and over it was a cover which opened on a pivot; such was the first germ of our modern musket.

Two or three horsemen who were furnished with these then formidable weapons, opened their pans, and levelling at the heart of the tree above their heads, applied the matches. There was a triple blaze—a simultaneous report and three bullets whistled harmlessly through the foliage of the oak, cutting its leaves, and whitening the branches but far apart from the three fugitives; for the troopers fired unsteadily, and at random.

The night was still dark; the moon glinted uncertainly at times, and the foliage was dense and thick.

' Again, and again,' said Home; ' fire while there is a charge in your flasks or a ball in your bags; and I will give ten crowns to the first who brings down his bird like a capercailzie.'

At that moment there was a flash in the heart of the black foliage; a ball grazed Lord Home's shoulder and killed a mosstrooper beside him. The man's morion and iron jack rang heavily as he fell to the ground, and almost without a cry; for Wad's aim was a sure one.

' Fire at the spot that flash came from,' cried Lord Hailes ' and I swear by St. Serf's ram, and St. Anthony's pig, to add twenty crowns to thine, Home, as the guerdon of our best gunner.'

' 'Tis said that some have gone up this tree and never more come down,' said Blackcastle.

' Well, it would matter little if it happens again in the present instance,' said Borthwick, on seeing how the superstitious mosstroopers shrunk back at this remark; ' but we shall soon bring them down, I warrant. Let the chapel door, however, be well guarded, lest the hermit or his ladies rouse on us the burgesses of Musselburgh, which their tongue will assuredly do, if this unwonted firing doth not.'

Again three bullets were fired into the tree, and as the flashes broke from the iron muzzles of the hand-guns, the murderers—for such they were by intention—could see each other's brown visages, wiry beards, and rusty morions, and the green leaves and rough bark of the enchanted oak—but for an instant only.

These three balls were as harmless as their predecessors; and while the slow process of loading from a flask, putting in wadding, bullets, and priming, was resumed, a shot came from the tree, and with a cry of agony another borderer fell at the side of Lord Home.

'On my soul, thou'st the cry of a screech-owl! Where the devil art thou hurt, fellow?' asked the lord, with considerably less of sympathy than anger in his tone.

'In the left cuit. Oh, my lord, I shall never, never ride again, and wha will gie me meat and fee?'

'Ha, ha!' laughed Wad from his perch; 'I have pinked this one on the larboard side.'

'He'll have a heel to port for the remainder of his days,' said Barton; 'fire again, Willie.'

'What if yonder white figure by the stream was the weirdwoman, and *not* the ghost of the warder's wife?' suggested Blackcastle.

'Gomeral!' cried Home, furiously; 'I care not if she were the devil, and——'

Wad's last shot, for (as the reader is aware) he had unhappily but *three*, grazed the cheek-plate of the noble's helmet, and so discomposed him that he forgot what he meant to say; but now doubly alarmed by their superstitious fears, and by finding themselves exposed, under an increasing moonlight, to the deadly aim of those they could not see, the two lords and their fellows withdrew a little to consult on their future measures.

Meanwhile those who had been left within the chapel heard the uproar without, and the reports of the hand-guns, which filled their hearts with terror; for these weapons were little known in Scotland, and were deemed more deadly in effect than they really were.

'Let us kindle a fire round the tree,' said Borthwick, whose wits were sharpened by the prospect of gaining thirty crowns; 'this will soon bring them all down among fire and smoke.'

'Good!'

'Admirable!' said the lords. 'But where is the fuel?'

'Here; this shed, wherein this rogue of a hermit stables his visitors' horses, will provide us; alight, my Annandale thieves—off with your steel gloves, and unroof the stable,' said Borthwick, setting the example; 'pile sticks and straw, roof and rafters, round the stem, and throw in your lighted matches—quick!'

The little edifice to which he referred adjoined the chapel and was meant to receive the horses of pilgrims and visitors. It was heavily roofed with warm thatch, which was quite dry below the coating of emerald green moss which covered it. Well used to such work, the strong mosstroopers in two minutes tore down the rafters, broke up the hack manger, and one or two old corn casks that lay in the stalls, and piled them with all the straw round the stem of the oak tree ; and then, sprinkling powder over all, threw in their lighted matches.

The flame smouldered a little, and then shot up and licked the thick-seamed bark of the ancient tree.

' Bring more fuel,' cried Hailes, ' even though we tear down the provost's house for it ; quick, my bold mosstroopers, so ready of wit and stout of heart.'

Two little stacks, one of heather, from which the poor hermit made up his bed, and another of peats, which supplied him with fuel, and both of which, like everything else he had, were the gift of visitors, were torn down and added to the pile with all the fallen branches and green saplings that could be collected ; and now the wavering fire began to ascend and blaze in a fiery circle, twisting itself into a column around the stem of the strong oak tree.

The forky flames shot high and higher among the foliage, hissing against the wet branches, and scorching off those that were crisped and dry ; the old knots and gnarls began to crack and burn ; and as the sheet of fire deepened and gathered strength, it became evident that the three lurkers, even if they failed to be suffocated, would soon be compelled by the heat to fall on the spears of those who watched and waited below, while others were constantly employed in seeking the means necessary to maintain and augment the fire !

' It burns well,' said Borthwick, with grim complacency while poking it up with his sword-blade.

' These varlets have given us more trouble than their miserable lives can ever atone for,' said Hailes, in an undertone.

' Lives ! on my soul, they seem to have as many each as a cat,' replied Home.

' With the power of making the most of each of them.'

' On my faith, were not my pride and obstinacy enlisted in this cause, I would counsel that we should wear the willow in our bonnets, Hailes, and bequeath these Drummond

ames to their salt-water lovers, with the devil's benison on
heir bridal.'

'Let us first see each gay lemane with his head under his
rm. Halloa, fellows, art not yet coming down? By my
oul, ye must be birselled in your iron coats like winter
pples or roasted crabs by this time!'

The flames had now reached the middle of the tree, and in
heir blaze the whole band could see each other's flushed faces
nd fiery eyes; their rusty accoutrements and glittering
veapons; and their two comrades stretched on the ground,
ne with upturned eye and jaw relaxed, but placid and still,
ke all who die by gunshot wounds; the other still bleeding,
nd writhing in pain. On one side rose the façade of the
ncient chapel with its low-browed Roman doorway and
leep-sunk windows, on the other were the sturdy stems and
reakish branches of the patriarchal tree which shaded its
ime-worn walls.

Up and farther upward shot the flames, and in half an hour
very leaf, save those upon the extremity of the branches,
vas gone; the whole foliage had been scorched off; the large
cnotty limbs were blackened and burned, or the smaller
ntirely consumed; the whole of that magnificent oak was
livested of bark, cracked, calcined, and half consumed by fire.

Still the three prisoners had neither cried once for mercy,
ior fallen down by being overcome by heat or exhaustion;
nd *now*, those who thirsted for their blood below, began
o look rather blankly in each other's faces, while fear and
vonder grew together in their hearts.

The flames around its mighty stem sunk low, and died
way as morning brightened in the east; and there stood
he giant tree, with its trunk, nearly nine feet in diameter,
he bare and blackened ruin of its former self—a smoking
nd sable skeleton; but there was no trace, not even a
vestige of the fugitives!

It was impossible that the fire could have consumed them
nd their apparel too.

It was equally impossible that they could have descended
nd escaped through the flames, for their intended destroyers
stood around them in a circle.

'By St. Mary, there hath been magic or a miracle at work
iere!' said Hailes, on being convinced that, beyond a doubt,
the *three* had vanished from their lofty perch.

''Tis said that some who have ascended this tree did never
nore come down,' said Home.

' May the Blessed Virgin not have borne them away to punish us for violating the sanctity of Loretto,' said the superstitious Laird of Blackcastle, in a low voice.

' May not the devil or the weirdwoman have done the same thing ? ' asked Borthwick, scoffingly, with a scowl in his eye.

' Peace,' said Hailes, with an irrepressible shudder, caused either by fear or the chill morning air ; ' I have heard of strange things for good or evil happening here,' he added, putting a foot in his stirrup to remount ; ' and *now* I am not ashamed to say that I repent me sorely of following those rascals into consecrated ground; so let us to horse and begone, lest the burgesses of the honest town betake them to axe and stave to punish this raid of ours before we cross the Esk again ; for *they* will not thole the sin, though our gentler Lady of Loretto may.'

CHAPTER LV.

THE ESCAPE.

IN no way satisfied by the result of their expedition, the two nobles and their followers galloped from Loretto, and repassed the Bridge of Musselburgh just in time to avoid the wrath of the burghers, who had displayed their standard with its *three mussels* and the proud motto, 'Honesto,' and were preparing to punish severely the sacrilege of the night; but Borthwick, as his companions retreated across the bridge of the Esk, locked the iron gate on the western side, and tauntingly, in sight of all their pursuers, flung the key 'to the Kelpie's keeping,' in the swollen river, the deep and rapid torrent of which barred all passage; and thus in safety the whole band—two excepted, who were afterwards hanged at Musselburgh Cross—'the quick and the dead'—reached the King's Wark at Leith, the headquarters of the insurgent lords.

'Mater purissima!' exclaimed Father Fairlie, as well he might, on leaving his chapel door next morning, and seeing the débris of the operations we have just described; the roofless stable; the rifled stacks; the torn shrubbery; the scorched sward; the black skeleton of the burned oak, and the two men who lay upon the ground in their armour, one dead and the other nearly so.

'Heaven will assuredly punish this sacrilege,' said Euphemia to Sybilla, as a smile of triumph struggled with the fear and sorrow impressed upon her pale face by the events of the past night. 'Bring forth our horses,' she added to the pages, 'and let us also begone, for I fear me, holy friar, you will deem your cell but little favoured by the presence of those who have been the innocent, though certainly the primary cause of this atrocious outrage and bloodshed. In our purses, which we have left upon the altar, you will, I hope, find more than enough to repay you for all you have suffered or lost; and be assured we will never forget you.'

The friar did not reply.

Poor man—he was astounded by the whole affair; and crossing his hands upon his paunch, rolled his round eyes, and continued to mutter involuntarily, 'Benedictus Dominus Deus!' and other scraps from the canticle of Zachary, while the pages prepared the horses in haste; and with all speed the ladies departed, expressing the most lively and heart-felt gratitude to the hermit, who retired to begin his daily 'office,' and once more investigate the contents of the two baskets and six flasks.

'But the barrel, alas!' said he, with a sigh of anger, though its contents had been spent or spilt in furthering the escape of Barton, Falconer, and their faithful follower from the barbarous fate to which this luckless tryst had lured them; 'the brandy—the barrel—*miserere nostri*—'tis lost!'

Their disappearance was brought about in the following manner:—

When our three fugitives found that their ammunition was expended—that day was breaking, and yet there came no signs of rescue—that the tree remained environed by armed men on every side—and that the fire which begirt it was mounting up the stem, despair and horror began to seize their hearts, and, creeping close together in the dark among the rising smoke and withering foliage, they were about to adopt the proposal of Robert Barton—that the whole three of them should leap down, sword in hand, on three different sides, and die under the steel of these vindictive enemies, if they could not baffle or surmount them, when, lo! to their astonishment, they heard a fourth voice beside them, and the bald head of the hermit appeared close by, projecting from a hole in the enormous trunk of the tree, which by age was quite hollow, and by decay had become a mere wooden tube.

'Mater purissima,' said he; 'quick, my bairns, quick! descend this way, while there is yet time.'

'Descend—but to where?' The smoke hath made me blind as a bat,' said Barton; 'but how, in the name of Saint or Satan, came you here, most reverend Father?'

'Up the hollow trunk of this old oak, with which a stair below communicates,' replied the priest, whose voice was almost lost amid the crackling of the flames; 'this has proved a hiding-place to more than one in time of broil and trouble; but descend, and, in the name of Our Lady, quickly. Give me thy hand—thy foot, I mean—place it *here*, so—this

s the first step hollowed in the trunk—now thy hand, so—
this is the next, and thus we descend ; one of my predecessors
constructed this stair, that he might say his prayers on the
tree-top, in imitation of St. Simon Stock, who lived in a tree
in Kent ;—down—down—yet, carefully now.'

The friar disappeared, and Barton and Falconer followed ;
but the latter, missing a footstep, fell heavily to the bottom,
and found himself underground, on the soft, damp mould
of the burial vault.

Dumbfounded by the sudden and mysterious disappearance
of his companions, poor Willie Wad paused for a moment in
great irresolution.

' Avast, Sir David—belay there,' cried he ; ' hallo, gude
Father Fairlie, in the name o' Our Leddy, dinna leave me here
in stays ! O-ho—I see how it is ! ' he added. Ignorant of
the mode of descent, and not wishing exactly to drop into
the dark hole below, he resolved to ' go down by the run.'
After reflecting for a moment, Willie pulled out of the pouch
which has been so often already referred to, a few fathoms
of what a seaman is seldom without—stout cord, and looping
it round a branch, lowered himself into the hole, from the
bottom of which he heard Captain Barton anxiously shouting,
and describing the mode of descent.

While the fat, pursy friar was clambering slowly and
laboriously up to his assistance, he was unexpectedly met by
the broad end of the short, squat gunner, who, as the cord
slid through his hands, descended upon his shaven crown with
all the force of a steam-hammer or a battering-ram, and shot
him at once to the bottom ; nearly ending there his orisons
and feasts of every kind, spiritual and temporal.

' O Mater castissima, you have slain me ! ' he cried, as he
rose with difficulty from the floor of the vault ; ' *Miserere
nostri Domine !* '

' Mercy on us ! ' said the startled gunner ; ' look ye,
shipmate—holy Father, I mean——'

' Heaven send that no more pilgrims such as you come
here,' said the hermit, peevishly ; ' and now, for your own
sakes at least, begone ; I shall be blessed by the sight of
your backs.'

' May we not see the ladies ? '

' Impossible, Sir David ; they are above in the chapel,
at some distance, for this is but an old burial-vault, where
the lairds of Fawsyde lie. Ye have suffered enough for cooing
and billing here, instead of confessing and praying ; so get

ye gone, sirs, in the Holy Virgin's name,—away, by yonder outlet, which will take you to the beach; away, ere worse come upon you.'

'Friar, may we not take them with us?' asked Sir David Falconer.

'Four women in an open boat—and in this weather?' exclaimed the priest, polishing his bald crown with his wide sleeve, and giving the penitent gunner a glance of very mingled cast.

'True—true,' said Barton; 'it is impossible.'

'With a fresh breeze perhaps coming on,' said the gunner, rubbing the nether end of his galligaskins.

'Heaven knoweth I would be the last man to keep fond hearts asunder; but, once again, I implore—nay, I command you to begone, before your blood desecrates these holy walls for ever!'

After this, further parley was useless, and through a suite of vaults—only one of which now remains—they were led by the friar for about forty yards, till he reached a little door, which on the outside was half buried by drifted sand. He opened it, and they soon found themselves beyond the precincts, and free.

'Gude be thankit, we are fairly under way,' said Willie Wad; 'may I drink bilge, if such a hellicate job was ever mine before! noo, sirs, let us haul off on the larboard tack and reach our boat.'

They hurried across the sandy knolls and broomy hollows of the links and reached their boat by wading to her through the full tide. Taking the kedge on board, they stepped the mast, half hoisted the lugsail, and betaking them to their oars, bore away into the river just as the dawn began to streak the eastern sea with light. But still the wind was blowing hard.

'I have but one sorrow,' said Barton, as he relaxed the braces of his armour and bent to the oar; 'we have left our ladies in their hands—but by Tantony's bell, they have had a hard fight for them!'

'If I thought Sybilla's chances of happiness were greater with the powerful Lord of Hailes than with the king's poor arquebussier, by my word, Barton, I would yield her to him, though my heart should break in doing so.'

'Wherefore and why so benevolent?'

'Because it would best prove the strength and purity of my love for her to yield her up, rather than by prosecuting my humbler suit to the injury of her worldly interest and commoditie—thus throwing my own happiness overboard to secure hers.'

'Hailes could neither secure her happiness nor value your sacrifice. You heard his sentiments under that flaming oak?' said Barton.

'Alas! I cannot blame Lord Drummond for his hostility to me. Unlike Hailes, I cannot offer poor Sybilla the rank, the power, the splendid gifts of feudal fortune possessed by the House of the Hepburns.'

'Thou canst give her far more—a brave and honest heart, and a name unstained by crime and *treason*. Of that few Scottish noble names are free! Ouf—there was a mouthful of salt water! Willie, mind ye the tiller, my lad.'

The chapel wherein the events of this chapter occurred was demolished at the Reformation, and no vestige of it now remains save the name—Loretto—and a little cell, which measures about twelve feet by ten. Herein were found a number of skulls lately.

From the materials of the edifice, the present Tolbooth of Musselburgh was built in 1590, during the reign of James VI.; and for this signal act of sacrilege, the burgesses of the 'Honest Town' were regularly excommunicated annually, by bell, book, and candle, at Rome, until within the last few years, when his Holiness perhaps grew tired of it.

CHAPTER LVI.

THE UNICORN LOOSE.

The Lords still remained at Leith, where they took all measures and precautions necessary to strengthen their power and increase their forces, in case the missing king should appear at the head of the Highland clans, or perhaps a foreign army, to vindicate his rights and those of Scotland; for they still remembered the threats uttered by the Mareschal de Concressault in the Castle of Callendar; but an end was put to all their arrangements and surmises by the discovery of James's body, which was found by the sleuth bratches of the old Steward of Menteith when tracking some robbers through the Torwood, all gashed and bloody, blanched and soiled by a week's exposure in a field-ditch near Beaton's mill on the Bannock; and now a thrill of sorrow went over all their land, for even the most barbarous of that nobility who have ever been so false, so treacherous, and so base to Scotland—who have usually been the first to abandon her on the field, and assuredly *not* the last to betray her in the cabinet—had not contemplated an issue so terrible!

The young prince was filled with horror and remorse, which even the tidings of Lady Margaret's safety with the admiral could not alleviate: for now he recalled with the keenest sorrow, how bitterly he had accused his poor father of abducting her, and how, led away by passion and despair, he had permitted himself to be the tool, the dupe, and the plaything of the turbulent and ambitious noblesse.

From that hour he began to shun them, and to seek for his father's oldest and most faithful friends. The first he thought of was the trusty Laird of Largo, to whom he despatched the Snowdon Herald and Unicorn Pursuivant, announcing the awful intelligence of his royal father's murder (the news of which was already pretty well known at the court of England), and requiring his presence at Leith. Then full of rage and sorrow the admiral put out of Largo Bay, and with all his ships and prisoners, stood with all sail set up the river, and anchored off the seaport of the capital, where all the vessels in the harbour and roadstead showed their ensigns half hoisted—the blue Scottish flag with its white saltier, which is the groundwork of the modern Union Jack; and which is still retained unchanged by the Old Shipping Company of Leith.

The same flag was hoisted on the English prizes, one of which, say the Admiralty records, as she came abreast of the town, had her keel knocked away upon the Gunnel. The latter is a dangerous sunken rock, which is yet unmarked by a buoy, though it has only eight feet of water over it at ebb tide.

In the large hall of Barton's house at Leith, on a bright and sunny morning, the prince was again seated at the table, where a grave and melancholy council had just been held on what should *now* be done to heal the dissensions which were likely to break out anew, as a cry 'for vengeance on the king's murderers' was going throughout the land. The council had been broken up without a decision being found. The prince was pale, sad-eyed, and downcast, and left almost alone: for in the deep recesses of the hall windows, Angus, Home, Hailes, the Heritable Forester of Drum, and others, with many lords of the noble faction, were conversing, or gazing dreamily at the sunlit river and the ships which came to anchor near the shore.

Sir Patrick Gray of Kyneff had retired to the Castle of Broughty; Sir James Shaw of Sauchie had repaired to his fortress of Stirling, and Sir William Stirling of the Keir, animated by the same wisdom and prudence, had retreated to some fastness in the Highlands of Perthshire; while their worthy compatriot, Hew Borthwick—though as yet unsuspected and unknown—had concealed himself in Berwick, which was then garrisoned by English troops, and had been so since its betrayal by Alexander Duke of Albany, who was then an exile in France.

Above the prince's chair was a coat of the royal arms, in which the chains of the unicorns were represented *loose*, as we may still see them.

Lately by the voice of Heralds, by the sound of trumpets and by the boom of brass artillery, he had been proclaimed at the crosses of all the adjacent burghs, King of Scotland and the Isles, by the title of James IV.; but he felt as if a curse had come with it upon him, for the crown had been drenched in the blood of his father.

'Betouch us, too!' said old Lord Drummond, to whom Home and Hailes related the mysterious disappearance of the three fugitives from the tree. 'Well, it matters not whether the spirits of the air, the earth, the gude wichts, or the weirdwoman herself hath made away with them; they are gone, and St. Mary be praised, there is an end of them now. But please you, my good lords, bruit not abroad this scandalous tryst of my runagate daughters.'

'I shall speak with the Abbot of Dunfermline anent this runion of a hermit, however,' said Home, angrily; 'by Heaven I will!'

'The friar; yes, we shall have him unfrocked for abetting assignations under the colour of pilgrimages, and bringing scandal upon holy places,' added Hailes, as he joined Lord Lyle and turned to another window to watch the ships of Wood.

Observing his daughter Sybilla similarly engaged with her pale cheek resting on her hand, Lord Drummond approached her, with his brows knit, and said in a low voice: 'Art prepared now, Sybie, to seek my blessing, and to win forgiveness for this most shameful visit to Loretto, by wedding at once this gay young Lord, whose Earl's patent hath all but passed the seals?'

'Oh, father, I never could love him.'

'Why not? hath he not as many legs and arms, eyes and ears, as other men—and what more dost thou want—eh?'

'Oh, Mother Mary!' sighed Lady Sybilla, 'teach me what to say.'

'A truce to prayers,' said the old Lord, spitefully, while his eyes kindled; 'prayers, indeed! had we not enough of that ware at Loretto?'

'I have ever striven to please you, dear father,—to be dutiful and kind—but—but——'

'But me no *buts*—thou silly giglet.'

'Father, I am your child——'

'I hope so, though of late I've had my doubts of it. Well, then, as my child thou art bound to obey me.'

'But surely not in all things?' said Sybilla, whose tears fell fast.

'In all things!' reiterated this despotic old baron, who had the power of life and death, pit and gallows, over all in Strathearn, and yearly took by force the best horse and fattest cow from every tenant there as a herezeld : ' if the greatest of my vassals is bound to obey me to the death— yea, to obey or swing on the nearest branch,—how much more ought thou and Euphemia who are my own daughters ! A curse on the hour such brittle ware as daughters came into the house of Drummond ! '

' I have no desire to wed,' said Sybilla, making a violent effort to control her tears, for many eyes were upon her, ' none ! let me abide with you, dearest father, and little Elizabeth and Beatrix, in bonnie Strathearn ; for I have no wish to leave your hearth and home ; I have no wish for wealth, and no desire for rank.'

' Rank—what do you mean by rank ? *My* daughters require not *that*,' said the old chief, clanking his enormous spurs on the floor.

' But if you think over-many of us are growing up to woman's estate, let me retire into a convent, where, by teaching others to embroider, to illuminate, and to write, I may maintain myself with utility ; hear me, dearest father ! '

' A convent, Sybie ? '

' Yes—yes ; there are the Grey Sisters at Dundee, all of whom are pious, good, and kind, and know me well.'

' Enough, thou cunning minx, enough ! the superior of those Claresses is aunt to Robert Barton, the skipper's son ; nay, I see how the wind sets, as *he* would say. 'Tis a conspiracy against me,' added the old lord, furiously ; ' but let all plotters *gang warily*, for by the arm of St. Fillan I'll have a deep revenge and a sure one ! But hush now, lassie, for here cometh the Admiral Wood and his English prisoners, with Margaret—my daughter Margaret, as I am a living man ! '

' And two spruce English damsels,' said Hailes, who like Home was astonished on beholding Falconer and Barton, both of whom accompanied the admiral.

' On my soul, this Laird of Largo hath no small assurance, to bring all this rabble of fellows into the prince's presence,' said the Earl of Angus, knitting his brows as he surveyed the numerous group surrounding Sir Andrew Wood, whose friends were all in armour, and who had brought with him Willie Wad and Cuddie Clewline, his coxswain ; while Edmund Howard, conspicuous by his noble bearing and rich costume, was followed by John o' Lynne, Dick Selby,

his tall gunner, and the principal officers of the captured
ships; all of whom were without swords or armour, and
were graciously received by the sad and thoughtful prince
—now James IV.—after he had sprung forward, and heedless
of the assembled crowd, knelt down with that enthusiastic
gallantry for which he was so celebrated, and kissed both
the hands of Lady Margaret Drummond. He then placed
her by his side, where her sisters hung around her neck.

James then asked Howard with something of sternness,
'how she came to be found on board of the *Harry*, and why,
in time of truce, such war was levied on the Scottish people?'

Howard, who had beheld this meeting with a keen emotion
that amounted almost to agony, replied with grave but
respectful firmness:

'I can assure your Majesty, that in the matter of having
this noble dame on board my ship I shall answer no questions,
and though you should tear me limb from limb, I would
rather die than betray the secrets of my royal master!'

'Hah—is it so? then here, as usual, have been at work
dark England's cursed gold and Scotland's ready treason,'
said the young king, striking his spurred heel on the floor;
'but a time shall come for unravelling all this! Welcome,
brave Andrew Wood, my dear dead father's firmest friend;
his first and last, his noblest and most true!'

A tear came zigzag down the furrows of the old mariner's
face as the young monarch spoke, and he answered in a
broken voice:

'I have striven ever to do my duty to Scotland and her
king, like a sailor and a man, and so God has blessed and
prospered me. Weel, weel, it's a' owre noo; our gude king
is, I doubt not, safely moored in a blessed anchorage, and
lest he may not lie in the smoothest riding, I will lay out a
thousand crowns in masses for his soul in Largo Kirk and at
Mary's Altar in Leith, just to make his anchor hold. Let
us hope that the evil currents, the rocks and shoals he came
through in life, will all be taken into account aloft, when he
comes to reckon up his variation and leeway, and shall secure
him everlasting peace in the blessed latitudes above; for a
braver or a better man never faced wind or water, shot or
steel! Well fare thy soul, King James; in thee puir auld
Andrew Wood has lost a kind and faithful master, such as he
never more may see!'

'This may savour more of truth than politeness to his
successor,' said the haughty Angus, who disliked this out-

burst of feeling, which quite unmanned James IV.; 'but I say welcome to thee from battle, stout Largo, and there is my hand to thee in all amity and friendship.'

The giant earl drew off his glove, and they shook hands; the noble with an air of courtly condescension, and the seaman with blunt cordiality.

Many now expressed the pleasure it gave them to see the admiral once more in safety, but he received their advances with coolness and evident distrust.

'I am safe and sound and well, thank Heaven, my lords and gentles,' said he, 'and have neither had a hole punched in my ribs, nor a butt nor bolt started; but here I bring your Majesty four gallant ships and much warlike gear, all marked with the broad arrow of England' (the badge of the Edwards was then, as now, a government mark). 'Would that I could have laid their white colours at the feet of that brave monarch over whose devoted head the stormy sea of this world has closed for ever!'

After a few words with Barton, Falconer, John o' Lynne, and others, the young monarch, for whom 'woman's face was never formed in vain,' suddenly perceived Rose and Cicely, and desired them to approach. As the old admiral led them both forward trembling and blushing, to a close observer it would have been evident how nervously Cuddie Clewline and Willie Wad fumbled each with his ruff and waistbelt, twirled his bonnet, and hitched up his short wide trews, or chewed the ropeyarn lanyard of his jockteleg, i.e., clasp-knife.

'And so, my pretty damsels,' said James IV., 'you also were found on board this great ship, the _Harry_?'

'They were my attendants,' said Margaret, 'and most kind and faithful have they been to me.'

'What is thy father in his own country, maiden?' James asked of Rose,—a shade coming over his face as he thought of his own sire. But poor Rose blushed and hesitated, for she had never stood in such a presence before; and a simple English girl of those days had about as much conception of what like a Scottish king might be as of the Khan of Tartary;—indeed, the unlettered English are not very clear in their ideas of Scotland yet, for two acts of the British parliament have recently described it as an _island_.

'Speak, my pretty one; and be not alarmed,' said the handsome young king.

' My father is Abel Eyre, a fishmonger in the Knight-Rider Street,' said she, gathering courage at the gentle voice of James; 'my mother is the sister of Peter Puddle, who keepeth a wharf westward of Baynard Castle, upon Thames; so please you. Alas!' she continued, still keeping her eyes and their long dark lashes downcast; 'I know not how to see them all again; I never was so far, far away from the sound of London bells before!'

' And *thou*, maiden, with the dark brown braids, eh?'

' I am an orphan,' said Cicely, as she was about to weep; ' my father was a poor cottager of Liverpool.'

' Liverpool—where may that place be; dost know, admiral?'

The Admiral expressed ignorance, as well he might, for it was then, as Leland terms it, a small ' paved towne with a chapel,' in the parish of Walton.

James gave each of the girls a gold chain and a purse of money, and perceiving that Howard was without a sword, presented him with his own, which, with an expression of sadness and gratitude, this brave English gentleman received on his knees. He felt his heart beating keenly all the time, for the eyes of Margaret were fixed upon him with kindness and regret.

At her intercession and request, James gave him liberty to return to England whenever he pleased; but added, that so severe had been the ravages committed along the coast between Berwick and Dunbar, by the ships under his command, that their crews must be considered as ordinary prisoners of war, and be committed to some royal castle, until John, Prior of St. Andrews, the new secretary of state, arranged for their exchange or transmission home.

Howard gave a silent bow of acquiescence.

Barton now whispered to Sir Andrew Wood, who, with a half smile, in his own fashion of phraseology, informed the young king, that his ' gunner and coxswain had conceived certain matrimonial designs against the two English prizes, and that if these fair damsels would bring-to under their lee, he would give each of them a cottage, a cow, and a cow's mailing, at least, for their dower, by the shore of Largo Bay.'

At this speech, Cuddie and the gunner gave their foretops a tug, and scraped with their right feet; while the two girls cast down their eyes and again blushed furiously, for there was a numerous circle around them; but none of these

four had a word of thanks to offer, so completely were they
abashed by the presence in which they stood; for there was
many a dark and hostile eye bent on one portion of the
group, because they were English; and on the other portion,
because they were the late king's faithful subjects.

'Come, Cuddie Clewline, stand forward,' said the admiral;
'lay alongside thine own prize, man; show thyself a sailor.
And thou, gunner o' mine, heave ahead, sirrah; let not
the king's presence abash one who hath so often looked
grim death in the face and never blanched. I assure thee,
Willie,' he continued, as the king put Cicely's hand into the
gunner's, 'there's not such another bride on this side of
Cape Non. Rogue, sawest thou ever such swelling bows
and a run so clean under the counter? I trow not. Hold
up thy head, man, for thou and that lumping varlet, Cuthbert Clewline, are the only two among us who may recall
with joy that night's hard battle in the Firth.'

'God bless your Majesty,' said Wad, 'and may my drink
be bilge in this world, and waur in that to come, if I keep
not a clear conscience and a fair reckoning, having sic a
consort to sail through the voyage o' life wi'.'

'And friend coxswain,' said James, with a smile, 'hast
thou no thanks?'

'Tickle my timmers, but I say wi' the gunner,' said Cuddie,
as they backed through the gay crowd not very ceremoniously,
and at that moment the eyes of poor Falconer and Sybilla
met, with a glance that seemed to inquire, 'Were there no
other hearts here—whom the king's influence might render
happy?'

'Now, thanks be to Heaven, all this is over, Robbie
Barton,' said the admiral; 'for when among lords I always
lose my temper, and yaw in my speech. Gadzooks, courts
are not for me; the gunner to his lintstock, the steersman
to his helm.'

'Saw you how sternly the Lord Drummond regarded
us?' said Robbie, gravely.

'Let him glower his een out, Robbie—an obstinate old
snatchblock!'

So ended this interview, and the whole issue of it tended
somewhat to soothe the excited minds of those who were
present.

That stringent act of the Scottish parliament, which
ordained that 'none of his Majestie's subjectes marrie
with any Englishwoman,' was not passed for a hundred

years *after* the time of our history; thus the espousals of the gunner and coxswain were duly celebrated by Father Zuill at the capstan-head of the *Yellow Frigate;* the admiral gave them each a piece of land at the mouth of the Keil Burn; and it is a curious fact, that most of the inhabitants of the thriving village of Lower Largo have descended from these two marriages.

Barton, in the religious spirit peculiar to the time, founded and dedicated an altar to St. Clement, according to his vow, and there solemn masses were said till the times of Knox and Wishart.

Two days after the marriages the admiral parted with Edmund Howard, who returned to England sorrowfully, for he had left both fame and happiness behind him. The chivalric Barton escorted him to the Borders.

'Adieu, captain,' said Howard, 'until we *meet again;* and believe me, that when in merrie England I reckon up the days of my captivity among you, I will omit the happy ones I spent in Largo House in Fife.'

The wardens of the marches soon achieved the exchange of Miles Furnival, John o' Lynne, Dick Selby, and other prisoners, who, strange to say, are all designated as ' English *pirates*' in the royal charters of land given to the admiral, who received the island of Inchkeith, the estate of Dron, and the lordship of Newbryne for his bravery.

Still poor David Falconer was forgotten; and he and Robert Barton, by the determination, vigilance, and assiduity of Lord Drummond, found themselves as far as ever from all prospect of successfully winning their brides.

CHAPTER LVII.

CAMBUSKENNETH.

PREPARATIONS for the young king's coronation were suspended until after the interment of his father, whose body had been conveyed to Cambuskenneth Abbey; and also until after the general pacification of the kingdom. All the realm south of the Tay acknowledged him as king; the Castles of Edinburgh and Stirling were surrendered to him; and now he began the task of rewarding his father's friends, and punishing his own pretended adherents, by appointing Sir John Lundie of that Ilk, governor of Stirling, and the Laird of Balgillo, captain of Broughty. On this Sir Patrick Gray, and Sir James Shaw, and others of their party, retired to their own houses, and brooding on revenge, entered into a closer correspondence with the agents of Henry VII.

Thus did James punish Shaw for shutting his father out of his own castle.

Dissension for a time seemed to be suspended around the coffin of the murdered king, whose remains were borne with all the pomp of regality, and all the solemnity of the Romish faith, from the Abbey to the great Church of St. Mary of Cambuskenneth; and there those grasping lords and loyal chiefs, who had so lately crossed their swords in mortal strife at Sauchieburn, met side by side, in secret prayer and sorrow—or making an outward show of both: the tall and dark-browed Angus; the good and pious Montrose; the brave hero of Rhodez, the Preceptor Knollis, in the robes of his order; the veteran Lord of Concressault; the ambitious Drummond; the turbulent chiefs of the Homes and Hepburns; the half-savage Steward of Menteith; the rough Forester of Drum; and all the great officers of the state and household, gorgeously apparelled and carefully armed.

The heralds and pursuivants, the guards and beadsmen, with the prelates of the then powerful but withal crumbling hierarchy; the Archbishop of St. Andrews, primate of the kingdom, with the *ten* other bishops (the Right Reverend Lord of Dunblane was still a prisoner in England), with their mitres, crosiers, and cross-bearers, attended by many a relique, censer, banner, and taper, were also there.

These prelates really sorrowed for the king, unless where family influence and rank curbed or warped their natural feelings ; but the majority of the temporal lords, while wearing armour, a strong evidence of their mutual distrust of each other, contrived to veil all emotions under a calm exterior ; and with their heads bent low, and bearing lighted tapers in their gauntleted hands, they followed through that long and lofty aisle the purple-velvet coffin in which their slaughtered monarch lay, with the crown of ' Fergus, father of a hundred kings,' the sword and sceptre above him; and there, to the sound of trumpet, bell, and organ, amid the half-hushed murmur of a thousand tongues that prayed, they lowered him into his narrow home, beside his wife, the queen, Margaret of Oldenburg.

As the vault closed over him, faint and distant came the boom of the minute-guns, as they rang from the dusky towers of Stirling, where the royal standard hung, half hoisted, in the sunny air.

Sir Andrew Wood, Barton, Falconer, and their barge's crew, stood by the closing grave, and there was not an eye unmoistened among them when Rothesay dropped the velvet cord that lowered down his father's head ; but the admiral could not repress his inclination to compliment Lord Drummond and other nobles ' on the great *fortitude* they displayed on this sorrowful occasion,' a jibe which made them knit their brows.

But now none may say where James III. of Scotland and the Isles, or his queen, Margaret of Oldenburg, are lying ; for the noble Abbey of St. Mary has been swept from its foundations ; one remnant alone survives—a lofty tower ; and though the peasants still pretend to remember the royal grave, and point it out to visitors, not a stone remains to mark the tomb of the murdered monarch, for the place is now a bare greensward.

The sorrow and remorse of the young prince, his successor, were long and deep ; and it was by the advice of the good abbot, Henry of Cambuskenneth, he resolved to atone for the part he had taken against his father by wearing next his skin a belt of iron, to which every year he should add a weight, while he shortened it by a link.

While this remarkable belt was preparing,—while Gray and Shaw were plotting with England,—while Borthwick lurked in Berwick, and rewards were offered in vain for the murderers of the king,—while Sir Andrew Wood busied himself in preparing a fleet to meet one which Henry VII. was said to be secretly preparing against Scotland, while openly he avowed his intentions of pressing by diplomacy the long projected marriage of the Duke of Rothesay, now James IV., with his daughter, Margaret Tudor, of dubious reputation,—while the Bishop of Dunblane was still detained in England, in defiance of international law—while all these events were passing, or in progress, measures were taken by Lord Drummond to have his daughter Margaret—now restored to her family—acknowledged as queen-consort by the king, who spent much of his time in the charm of her society at Dundee and Dunblane. But fresh delays occurred, for the late king's loyal adherents had risen in arms, inspired by that wild inborn love of justice so natural to the Celt—for every Scottish Lowlander has, more or less, Celtic blood in his veins.

Beaton, the miller of Bannock, now related the barbarous manner in which James III. had been butchered. Lord Forbess, in armour, rode through the clans on the northern slopes of the Grampians, displaying upon his lance a bloody shirt, said to have been taken off the king's body; the venerable Earl of Lennox joined him at the head of five thousand Highlanders; but the Lords Drummond, Home, and Hailes marched against them with all their vassals. Favoured by information received from a deserter named Alexander Mac Alpine, Lord Drummond surprised these loyal insurrectionists in their camp at the Moss of Sassentilly, near Stirling, and routed them, after a brisk engagement, with great loss of life.

Pushing on from thence, he took the Castle of Dunbarton, which the Earl of Lennox and the Lord Lyle endeavoured in vain to defend.

For these services Drummond received a grant of Lennox's forfeited lands in the lordship of Menteith; Home was appointed Lord Warden of the Eastern Marches and High Chamberlain of Scotland. In the same month, Hailes obtained the Earldom of Bothwell, with all the forfeited estates of John Ramsay, the loyal Laird of Balmain, who had fallen at Sauchieburn when charging at the head of the royal guard; he was, moreover, made Lord Warden of the

Western Marches, High Admiral of Scotland, and master of the young king's household; so old Lord Drummond returned to court in excellent humour with himself, and highly delighted to find that a shower of favours had descended upon his two intended sons-in-law.

James IV. had painful doubts regarding the fight at Sassentilly; for the men who were defeated there had been his father's dearest friends, and the banner they fought under was no feudal flag or royal standard, but the gory garment borne on the lance of the Lord Forbess.

He asked his father-in-law if there was anything he could bestow upon him.

'I seek naught,' said he; 'I am a lord of that ilk, and the Drummonds have no need of titles; terror and antiquity had caused their name to be venerated enough in the land.'

This was but a species of the pride that aped humility; but it was so peculiar that the young king laughed. Without much pressing, the old lord accepted the office of Justice-general of Scotland—and a dear office it proved to most of his enemies; but 'the contumacy of those gipsies,' his daughters, proved a source of continual annoyance to him.

As corruption and bribery were (and not unfrequently are still) the highway to public offices in Scotland, it is wonderful that we do not find Shaw or Gray installed as lord advocate; but that official was merely a lawyer then, without any pretence of being a statesman, and so the post was not held in great repute.

The reader may marvel whether Master—we beg pardon—Sir Hew Borthwick was troubled by his conscience; but it must be borne in mind, that those facile Scots, who from time to time (since the days of Sir John Menteith down to a very recent period) have sold themselves to English ministers, never had a conscience to trouble. Besides, a few acts of slaughter, more or less, in a lifetime, were of little consequence in those days; thus any twinges experienced by our Scottish cosmopolite were principally those of fear.

One fact is *certain;* there is no record of Stirling, Shaw, or Gray ever having been punished for abetting him in the barbarous assassination of the king; and though even *he* escaped all judicial penalties, his ultimate fate was not a happy one, as shall be seen in the sequel to the events we have narrated.

As time progresses and the world turns round, even the

most serious events are fated to be faintly remembered or soon forgotten: thus, the grave of the unhappy James III. was barely closed, when his young successor in the assembled parliament was forced to give his royal sanction to an act which was brought forward and carried by an overwhelming majority of the powerful lords and their adherents, the commissioners of shires and burghs—an act which declared that the slaughter of the late king and of his followers was the just reward of their own crimes and deceit; and that James IV., and the *trew* Lordis and Barronis that were with him in the same field were innocent, free and quyte of the slauchters'; and that copies of this deed, with their seals attached thereto, should be sent to the Vatican, to the courts of 'France, Hispanzie, Denmark, and other realmes as shall be expedient for the tyme.'

The old Mareschal de Concressault, who, as a Scottish baron, had a seat in the house, now demanded from the prior of St. Andrews his passport, with a safe escort back to France; and in addressing the three estates upon the late events, he adverted severely on the spirit of treason, conspiracy, and rebellion, which seemed to be spreading over Europe, every kingdom and state of which had been convulsed, as well as Scotland.

'To wit, my lords,' he continued, 'France under Louis XI., Flanders and Holland under Charles the Warlike, Gueldres under Duke Arnold, who is now imprisoned by his own son, and England under Henry VI. and Edward IV. But rest assured, my lords, that in each and all of these countries a just Heaven will punish those who have advanced, with swords drawn and banners displayed, against the Lord's anointed!'

'Laird of Pitmilly, this is but pyots talk,' was the insolent reply of Angus; 'for we remember, my lords, that Louis of France, Charles of Burgundy, John II. of Portugal, and Richard III. of England, have all endeavoured to play the tyrant in their own countries, as well as King James in Scotland; and if they have not been duly punished for it in this world, they will assuredly smart for it in the next!'

And then, as the veteran Concressault left the asembly for ever, the grim Scottish nobles only smiled as they played with their long swords, and remembered that they had forced James III. when seated on the same throne now occupied by his sad-eyed son, to *stitch* the patent of James Douglas, Lord of Dalkeith and Earl of Morton, the parch-

ment of which he had torn in a fit of just indignation at the
'inordinate royalties and privileges it contained.'

Though no declaration of war had been made—for Henry
had yet hopes of achieving an alliance by marriage—political
relations between Scotland and England were somewhat
dubious. Thus, to prevent any hostile interference with the
French ambassador, Sir Andrew Wood, with the *Yellow Frigate*
and a ship named the *Flower*, was ordered by the Lord High
Admiral Hailes, now Earl of Bothwell, to convey the Sieur
de Monipennie to Brest; and thus he prepared for sea with
all speed.

CHAPTER LVIII.

SINCE the day when the English prisoners were presented to James IV. at Leith, Euphemia and her sister Sybilla had no opportunity of meeting, or even seeing Barton, or Falconer. They were kept in strict seclusion at their father's mansion in Dundee, while their lovers were compelled to remain as much as possible on board their ships, owing to the dangers that menaced them ashore; for the unscrupulous emissaries of Drummond, Home, and the new-made Earl of Bothwell, were ever on the watch for them; moreover, their presence was constantly required during the refitting consequent to the late engagement and the projected voyage to Brest.

These repairs were conducted at the New Haven above Leith, where the king's dockyards were then established.

James IV., about 1512, had no less than forty-six ships of war built here and elsewhere; one of these, the *Great Michael*, was the largest vessel in the known world; she carried a thousand men, was two hundred and forty feet long, and cost £40,000—an enormous sum in those days. For the accommodation of the workmen, at Sir Andrew Wood's suggestion, he built a chapel dedicated to Our Lady and St. James, the eastern window and gable of which are yet remaining in the Vennel of New Haven. If Scotland, in 1512, could equip such a fleet, before the value of her vast iron mines, her forests of fir and oak, and the convenience of her deep bays and salt lakes were known, what a noble armament could she now launch upon the waters of the Tay and Clyde!

Margaret Drummond, though happy in her restoration to her royal husband (who was making every requisite preparation for espousing her publicly on his coronation day, after the arrival of the papal dispensation), never mentioned that her sisters had lovers of more humble preten-

sions, who were known only to their own family circle.
Her father had laid her and them under the most stern
injunctions of secrecy, and thus the young king believed that
his two beautiful sisters-in-law were the affianced brides of
Home and Bothwell ; and though he had no great admiration for the characters of those turbulent and unlettered
lords, he had no desire to excite dissension anew by seeking
other spouses for Euphemia and Sybilla.

Thus overawed by their parent, the sisters locked the
secret in their own breasts, and were miserable ; for this
old, habitual terror of their father mingled with the love
and respect which were due to him, and united to a long
foreknowledge of his unbounded pride, his imperious spirit,
his calculating ambition, and his haughty will, which had
never, since the hour of his birth, been thwarted, and which
made him follow to the death any man who dared to mar,
in the most trifling manner, the plots he wove and the plans
he laid for the aggrandizement of himself and his family.

Confident in the young king's chivalric and generous
character, Barton and Falconer, with the natural bluntness
of their profession, would at once have sought an interview,
told their story, and claimed his patronage and protection ; but the king was at Stirling one day, at Falkland the
next, at Dundee the third, and thus no proper opportunity
was afforded to them ; the ships were soon reported as
ready for sea; De Concressault came on board, with all his
train, under three salvoes of cannon, as ambassador of
France ; and the *Yellow Frigate* and the *Flower* got under
way ; and the reader may easily conceive the emotions of
Barton and Falconer when sailing on this expedition, and
leaving their loves behind them while so many evil influences
combined to cast a shadow on their hopes.

Indeed, both sailed with the most firm and melancholy
conviction that, long before their return, either by fear,
coercion, or despair, or by all three combined, Euphemia
would be Lady Home, and Sybilla Countess of Bothwell.

Their growing sadness and their many communings
could not escape the quick eyes of the old admiral, who had
been closely observing them, one day in particular, as he
was taking an observation with the cross-staff, during a
bright sunshine that equally favoured the operations of
Father Zuill, who was hard at work levelling his lenses,
mirrors, and parabolic speculum against the sails of a fisher-
boat, which he was vainly endeavouring to ignite, an ex-

periment which, if successful, would no doubt have excited considerable surprise and consternation in the mind of the unconscious proprietor thereof.   The kind admiral, who knew well the secrets of the two friends, endeavoured to reassure them, and laugh their fears away.

'Alas, admiral,' said Falconer, 'I never can forget that all my fortune is in my scabbard; that my prospects of success at home are now more dim and distant since the late king's death, and how can I hope to be the brother-in-law of his son?   Oh, it is all vanity and madness in me—this passion for Lord Drummond's daughter!   Yet I know that Sybilla loves me; thus I cannot abandon her while life remains, otherwise, I would not return with you from France, but would enlist in the Scottish archers, or offer my sword to Robert of Patulloch, or the Mareschal de Concressault, and seek fortune in the wars of Charles VIII.   These nobles at home will prove too strong for us in the end, Barton!'

'In their eyes no deed, however brave, can gild a humble birth; and no shame is so deep as a lowly name!' said Barton.

'Well, and is not this a wisdom in the titled blockheads, after all,' said the admiral; 'for they know that, in respecting high birth and sounding titles, they are but paying a compliment to themselves and enhancing their own value.'

'To conceive it possible that my gentle Sybilla may be *forced*—yea, in free Scotland, forced like a Danish serf, to marry a man who cannot appreciate her goodness and excellence.'

'There is no man so low in the scale of humanity—not even among the rebel lords,' said Barton.

'Poor Sybilla—how I love her!'

'This were vast presumption in Strathearn, Davie,' said the admiral; 'but here, on the deck of the *Yellow Frigate*, is only natural and just,—a great lord's daughter though she be.   But tush, man! is this the way for a stout fellow to pule and sadden like a pitiful scaramouche?   If these damosels wed in your absence, my lads, remember there are gude fish in the salt sea, as ever came out of it; a rusty anchor and a rotten cable are not worth the upheaval; and so, gadzooks! if they miss stays and get stranded in your absence, let them e'en go, with God's blessing, and bear ye away for a fairer haven and more seaworthy consorts.'

Consolation of this kind was about as good as none; but time wore on—day succeeded day.   After passing the straits of Dover without seeing any sign of a hostile English fleet, which rumour said was preparing to intercept them, and after running down the English Channel, the two Scottish caravels doubled the point then named by the French the *End of the World*, as no land was known to the westward of it, and arrived in safety at Brest in Brittany.

This, though one of the best harbours in Europe, was then but a small seaport or village, dependent on the town of Sainte Renan.

After exchanging salutes with the Castle of Brest, and being royally feasted by the abbot and monks of its rich Benedictine abbey, the Scottish admiral bade adieu to the Sieur de Concressault (who began his journey to court), and again put to sea.

Passing between the Isle of Ushant and the mainland, he bore away for Sluys, on another mission from the court of Scotland to the Flemings, concerning that commercial dispute, which, natheless the casks of Dutch heads, pickled by Andrew Barton, it was believed no man in Scotland was better able to adjust than Sir Andrew Wood of Largo.

CHAPTER LIX.

REUNITED.

MEANWHILE treason was not idle at home.

Sir Patrick Gray and Sir James Shaw, exasperated by the turn affairs had taken against them, and by finding, that instead of having their petty lairdships erected into lord-ships and earldoms, with many a fair slice of the lands of the Crawfords, the Erskines, the Stewarts, and others, to whose confiscation and forfeiture they had fondly looked forward, and being no longer able to exact kain and here-zelds at the sword's point again and again from the hapless rentallers of the king's castles, they entered into a closer compact with Henry for the removal of Margaret Drummond, and with Master Quentin Kraft, who, eluding the chain of guards and close watch kept upon the Borders between Tweedmouth and Solway Sands, had the hardihood to re-enter Scotland disguised, and he, together with Borthwick, who still lurked about the town and Castle of Berwick, were, as before, their ready means of communication with the court of London.

The two anti-national knights had both conceived a mortal grudge against Sir Andrew Wood, for no other cause, perhaps, than his being a sterling and unflinching patriot, who, by taking the English ships, had restored Margaret Drummond to her princely lover. Thus they had many a long conference, and one in particular on the very day after he sailed for Brest.

Shaw, as usual,, half intoxicated,—and Gray, nervous, grim, and fiery as ever, sat over their wine in the half-naked hall of Kyneff, where Kraft, the notary, or attorney —for he was called both—prepared a statement of the number of ships, men, and guns carried by Admiral Wood. With this paper he departed on the spur to Berwick, from whence Borthwick conveyed it to London (then a four-

weeks' journey at least,) and there he informed the Bishop
of Winchester, the secretary of King Henry, who was then
residing at Baynard Castle, that on leaving Brest, the
Scottish admiral would sail for Sluys ; and that by having
a powerful fleet to intercept him, he might easily, at one
and the same time, crush one of the young king's most
gallant subjects, assert the superiority of England on the
sea, and revenge the affront so lately put upon her arms
in the battle of the Firth of Forth.

Though kings had generally as little power of choice in
love, then as now, and had to submit to the wishes and will
of their subjects, and to the interests of their country,
James IV., after striving to banish from his mind the gloom
his father's fate had brought upon him, and after exiling
from his presence most of those who had been the cause
of that hapless father's downfall, gave himself up to the
joy and intoxication of his passion for Margaret Drummond
—a passion all untrammelled now by secrecy, and uncurbed
by caution.

The whole nation knew that he loved her now—that they
were secretly married, and that a little daughter had been
born, to secure whose legitimacy and regal rights the dispensation of the Pope alone was wanting ; and the Lyon
King of Arms had gone to England, empowered to demand
the instant liberation of its bearer, or denounce war by sea
and land. But though anxious to destroy Sir Andrew
Wood and his companions, and also to detain the Bishop
of Dunblane, the subtle Henry VII. had no intention, if it
could be avoided, of having a crisis so fatal to his darling
matrimonial projects ; and he still resolved, that by fair
means or foul, Lord Drummond's daughter should be removed, to make way for an English princess.

It was now the beginning of August : the birds had ceased
to sing, and were training their newly-fledged broods ; the
swallows were gathering for their long and mysterious
journey, and the ripe corn waved in heavy ear.

The sun was setting beyond the fertile carse of Gowrie
and the evening was warm and balmy in bonnie Dundee.

The last of the traders had left the meal-market, and the
lorimers, the bonnet-makers, the websters, and cordiners
had closed their booth about the old Salt Iron. The various
bells were ringing for the vesper service, and the broad blue
river, with its picturesque craft, lay sleeping in its beauty between the yellow sands and fertile slopes of Fife and Angus

Dreaming little of the tangled web of trouble, care, and sorrow Scottish guile and English gold were weaving round their young and loving hearts, James and his fair-haired consort occupied the old Palace of St. Margaret, of which we gave the reader a description in the earlier chapters of this history.

The royal guard had been re-established under another captain ; the town was occupied by a great number of armed men—Drummonds, Homes, and Hepburns,—all flushed with their recent victory at Sassentilly, and these were quartered on the wealthy citizens, among whom they remained at free quarters to be ready for any emergency, as the country was far from being quiet or settled.

The young monarch gave himself up to all the joy of a complete reunion with his youthful consort ; but she was unusually sad and thoughtful, as if a foreboding of approaching evil hovered in her heart and clouded her open brow.

' Dearest,' said she, after a long pause, as they sat together in a recess of one of those deep old windows which were so well calculated for a quiet *tête-à-tête*, ' how deeply am I indebted to you for your tenderness, which gratifies all my wishes, and anticipates all my thoughts. Oh, my dearest—my best beloved one ! ' she continued, clinging to him like a child ; ' let me creep closer to you.'

' Sweet Maggie,' said the handsome young king, as he passed a hand fondly and caressingly over her bright-coloured hair, which looked indeed ' as if powdered with gold dust '—and this was the same stout hand which was afterwards hewn off his stiffened arm at Flodden,—' every moment we are separated seems an age, and yet the while my heart is full of thee ! But a time is coming, when in the presence of all Scotland, we shall stand side by side upon the throne, and the greatest peers shall kiss this pretty hand, as their queen's.'

' When our good bishop returns—but not, alas ! till then ! ' she murmured, looking upward, as her soft cheek fell upon his shoulder ; ' he is a weary time away.'

The brightness of pure love shone in her fair face ; and this young queen—for a queen, indeed, she was, though the Church would not yet acknowledge her—seemed enchanting in her beauty and her innocence.

' Fools speak of the right divine of kings,' said James, gazing tenderly upon her. ' By my soul, dear Margaret, the power of a beautiful woman is the only one that comes direct from heaven.'

Margaret only sighed at this compliment, and her eyes filled with tears.

'Still nursing thine old sadness, Margaret!'

'Ah, call me pet names, as you were wont to do.'

'Well, then, Maggie, why so sorrowful?'

'My aunt, the Duchess of Montrose, told me that there is a rumour going abroad—that——'

'That what?'

'That an old prophecy of Thomas of Ercildoune says:

> When Pausyle and Tweed meet o'er Merlin's grave,
> Scotlande and Englande one king shall have.'

'There they can never meet, thank God!' said the king, laughing: 'though Merlin lies buried in Drummellier, by Tweedside; for there I have seen his tomb. But what doth an old rhyme matter to us, Maggie?'

'They say moreover——'

'Who are *they?*'

'The people,' said Margaret, giving way to tears, 'that this prophecy will be accomplished by your wedding the daughter of Henry VII.'

'Those who say so are fools! Has not this cunning old Tudor a son, who will be Henry VIII.? No English king can reign over Scotland, and I would not sit on the English throne were I its heir to-morrow; for who, then, would be king of broad Scotland, Margaret? and who would be a barrier between her people and the tyrannical nobility? Besides, tidings must long ere this have reached the English court that we are married, and well must Henry know that thus all hope of fulfilling the terms of that state betrothal, which assigned *another Margaret* to me, is at an end for ever.'

Margaret only sighed, and her tears continued to fall.

'My bounibel,' said James, 'here are luxury, wealth, grandeur, rank, and greater are yet before thee; yet thou art not happy.'

'Oh, pardon my ingratitude; but I have such strange dreams by night, and such dark forebodings by day! Something is always wanting to complete happiness.'

'That is the curse of life, Margaret.'

'Of mine at least,' said she, folding her soft little hands.

'And that want——'

'Is security,' said Margaret, sighing.

'Thou wilt always be loved and respected, Maggie,' said her boy husband, as he caressed her; 'for thou art not valued by the dimness or splendour of thy fortune, but for thy sweetness and piety, thy goodness of heart and purity of soul, rather than imaginary nobility of name.'

'But your Majesty must be ever watchful and ready to defend from danger your poor Margaret, who loves you so well—better than all the world beside;—yea, better even than her little babe—*ours*; and you must not leave me so often and so long for those meetings of council and affairs of state, for dire forebodings of evil crush me whenever I am left alone.'

'Why so fearful of plots and wiles, sweet Maggie? But take courage, for I would defend you against a world in arms; and fear not either for our fair-haired little one, who may one day wed some gallant king of France or Spain, when she is beautiful as thyself, my kind-eyed Maggie!'

Such was one of many similar conversations which took place between the young king and his secretly wedded wife, while they awaited the bishop's return and the coming coronation; but whether the dark presentiments that hovered in Margaret's timid mind and saddened her winning manner were false or true, a little time will now serve to show.

CHAPTER LX.

LONDON IN 1488.

SAINT SWITHIN'S DAY in 1488—fortunately a fair and sunny one—was the busiest ever witnessed in the good city of London, if not since the English capital had a name, at least since the mayoralty of the loyal and wealthy Sir William Horne, whom King Henry VII. had knighted in the preceding year at Hornsey Park ; and from its countless wooden thoroughfares—bricks were only beginning to be used about thirty years before—she poured forth her thousands, to witness the departure of a gallant admiral against the Scots.

' The first article of an Englishman's political creed,' saith my Lord Halifax, ' must be that he believeth in the sea ! '—and a very good article it is.

Hence Henry VII. was so deeply concerned by the humiliation of Howard, that he summoned the most expert and experienced mariners in his kingdom, ' and after exhorting them to purge away the stain cast upon the English name,' he offered the then handsome pension of a thousand pounds yearly, to any man who would undertake to bring before him, dead or alive, Sir Andrew Wood of Largo, though it was now a time of truce, and actually of treaty between the two nations ; but such were the anomalies of an age when no man was particular about anything but the length of his sword and the trim of his beard—if he had one.

In his new project Henry had many difficulties to encounter, for at that time, England was almost destitute of a navy. ' Before the reign of Queen Elizabeth,' says Fuller, ' the ships-royal were so few that they deserved not the name of a fleet, and our kings hired vessels from Hamburg, Lubeck, yea, from Genoa itself.' The *Great Harry*, his first ship, cost him one hundred and fourteen thousand pounds ; before this, he used to seize or press merchant vessels for warlike purposes when he required them.

The celebrity for skill and valour enjoyed by Sir Andrew

Wood, caused him to be so much dreaded by the English, Dutch, and Portuguese, that some time elapsed before a volunteer was found. At last Sir Stephen Bull, a naval captain of known talent and well-tried courage, offered his sword and services to the King, who accepted them with joy; and three vessels, the largest and strongest that England could furnish, well-manned by chosen men, and mounted with heavy cannon, were placed at his disposal by John de Vere, Earl of Oxford, who was Lord High Admiral of England from the year 1485 to 1512, and who spared no pains to fit out this half chivalric and wholly vindictive enterprise,—for to their glory be it said, the English nobles —unlike the Scottish—have always been distinguished by a high degree of patriotism and love of the honour and interests of their native country; identifying themselves with both in all ages.

The chief of these three ships was the *Unicorn*—the caravel of the late Sir Andrew Barton.

Sir Stephen had been a merchant-trader of London, and was well known at Staple Inn, where the dealers of those days exposed their samples of wool, cloth, and other commodities for sale; and no vote had more influence than his at Aldermanbury, where the Guildhall was then situated, and where the council met; but fired by a laudable and honourable desire for upholding the glory of ' Old England,' he had buckled on his armour, and left his buxom dame and comfortable mansion with its *glazed* windows— then no ordinary luxury—at the corner of Fenchurch Street, near the Aldgate, to wage battle against ' the hot and termagant Scots.'

To the great, or uneducated mass of the English people, even in the present age, Scotland is a country of which but little is known. *Then* it was deemed a distant and remote, as well as hated land, and all expeditions against it were fraught with danger and death.

In those ' good old times ' there were no electric telegraphs; no mails, rails, or ' own correspondents,' and no resident ambassadors or consuls. Every Scot entering England became a prisoner; every Englishman entering Scotland might be lawfully killed or captured by whoever could catch him. There were pleasant times withal; and thus, though it was a season of peace between the two countries, Henry, after wisely considering the recent convulsion in Scotland, and the new King's extreme youth, thought he might risk a little to punish the bold Scottish mariner, in the same fashion in which he had overwhelmed Sir Andrew Barton ; and if war was declared by Scotland thereanent, he might easily contrive to repudiate the whole affair as a military quarrel between two rival knights—a passage of arms upon the sea.

Sir Stephen Bull had hoisted his flag on board the captured *Unicorn,* and he had spared no pains or expense in fitting her up ; thus, not content with all the King gave him, he had borrowed largely from the opulent money-lenders in Lombard Street.

Edmund Howard was his captain.

The second ship was commanded by Miles le Furnival, son of the Lord of Farnham in Bucks—an ancient house, whose tenure it was to find the King of England a right-hand glove on his Coronation day, and to support his right arm when he held the sceptre. Their town residence, still known as Furnival's Inn, stood on the north side of Holborn.

The third ship was under the orders of the wealthy Fulke, Lord of Fulkeshall (now better known as Vauxhall), who is said to have been an ancestor of Guy of notorious memory.

Immense quantities of iron balls and stone shot—the latter from the royal quarries at Maidstone in Kent—had been put on board of these vessels, and they were crowded by the best marksmen of the ancient Fraternity of Artillery, or Gunners of the Tower ; and the chief of these was our old friend, tall Dick Selby, the best cudgel-player that ever broke a head at Moorfields, or tossed the bar at Finsbury, and who, moreover, was the blithest toper that ever tossed off a horn, as the bluff host of the *Belle Sauvage* on Ludgate Hill was ready to testify.

Many brave volunteers accompanied Bull ; these were all members of noble families—some of them gay fellows, whose white feathers and laced mantles would long be missed by many a bright blue eye in Paul's Walk, as the aisle of the great cathedral was named, being the favourite place of the Londoners for gossip and promenades ; many, too, would prance no more among the horsemen at the Smoothfield, on Friday, or lounge at the Priory of St. John, at Clerkenwell, where the Sacred Mysteries were performed in the fine summer evenings.

Thus, the three ships were manned by mariners of tried skill, and soldiers of proved courage ; but among them

vere not a few desperadoes from that sanctuary of miscreants, St. Martin's-le-Grand.

'Bring ye back my daughter, Captain Howard,' cried
old Abel Eyre, the stout fishmonger of Knightrider Street,
as he came off to the *Unicorn* in a wherry, from the Old
Swan Stairs; 'bring her back to me, from yonder distant
country, and I will give thee a pair of the best gold spurs
Giltspur Street can furnish.'

'Restore my niece, Rose,' added Peter Puddle, of Puddle
Wharf, 'for, by my troth, I would rather she had turned
cut-purse, or wedded the greasiest scullion of Pie Corner,
than become the wife of a rough-footed Scot.'

'If I ever return, good citizens,' said Howard, through
his open helmet, as he looked over the buckler-ports of the
Unicorn; 'thy daughter will be by my side. I took her
away with me, and it is but fair I should restore her, if I
can. Farewell, sirs, and remember me at vespers to-night,'
he added, with a sadness that chilled the hearts of the two
portly citizens; 'for sorely my mind misgives me, I shall
never hear the English curfew bell again!'

Never had the banks of Thames seen a sight so gay or
so busy, since London Stone was first placed by the verge
of the old Prætorian Road!

In a gorgeous barge, covered by an awning, decorated by
pennons and rowed by men in the royal livery, Henry VII.
was on the river, accompanied by the Lord Mayor and com-
monalty, all in smaller barges, garnished with streamers
and surrounded by a swarm of lesser boats, crowded by
knights, courtiers, citizens, and beautiful women, all wearing the gayest of colours.

He wore his royal robes—a kirtle and surcoat, with his
furred hood and mantle, and the George upon his breast.
A smile of gratification lit up his usually grave face from
time to time, as he caressed his chief favourite—an abomi-
nable monkey.

As he stood up in the barge to bow in return to the people,
whose shouts rent the sunny air, his tall thin figure was
conspicuous above his courtiers, 'among whom we observed,' as the newspapers would have said had there been
one in this year of grace, 1488, Sir William Stanley, Lord
Chamberlain of England, wearing his gold key of office;
Robert Lord Brook, Knight of the Garter, and Lord Steward
of the Household; Sir Richard Crofts, the King's Treasurer,
and Sir Richard Edgecumbe, his comptroller, each bearing

a white wand ; Berkely, the Earl Marshal ; Lord Dinham
the Treasurer of England ; and Gerald, Earl of Kildare, the
newly appointed Governor of Henry's lordship of Ireland
all attired in gorgeous costumes, while the fifty Yeomen
of the Guard—a body established only two years before—
clad in scarlet cloaks and black velvet caps, and armed with
partisans and swords, were in the king's great barge, with their
captain, Sir Charles Somerset, afterwards Earl of Worcester.

It was quite a gala day in London. The beautiful cross
in Cheapside, and the Conduit, recently built by the Sheriff
Thomas Ilam, were covered with garlands of flowers ; all
the bells were tolling, and the houses which faced the river
had their windows crowded with heads, and their horn
lattices open,—for glass was not common in England until
the middle of the sixteenth century, and even in 1558
when the 'proud Earl of Northumberland' left Alnwick
Castle for a time, the glass windows were carefully taken
out, and thriftily replaced by plain wooden boards.

The culverins and bombardes of the Tower thundered
out their farewell salute as the ships got under way ; flags
were displayed on the old Church of St. Katharine, where
now the Docks are ; and all the foreign argosies and the
corn traders from the Cinque Ports, which in those days
were compelled to land their cargoes at Queenhithe, the rival
of Billingsgate, were bedecked with banners and streamers
while many a broad piece of tapestry floated from the keep
of the Tower, and from Baynard Castle, which had been
rebuilt about sixty years before by the Duke of Gloucester.

The roofs and windows of quaint Old London Bridge
through the narrow arches of which the ebb tide was rushing, displayed a thousand faces and waving caps. It had
then a grotesque row of houses and shops, forming a narrow
street across the river, with a gothic Chapel of St. Thomas
à Becket ; an embattled drawbridge-tower, on which Hentz-
ner, one fine morning, counted no less than thirty human
heads, all of which had been carefully cooked and parboiled
according to act of parliament, in the kitchen of the said
tower.

At last the topsails were sheeted home, and while their
ordnance, amid clouds of smoke, replied to the farewell
salutes of the Tower and the deafening cheers of the people,
St. George's red cross was thrice lowered in adieu to the
king, and the vessels began to drop down the river, while
a fry of wherries pulled by bare-footed and bare-legged

watermen shot after them, their occupants cheering with delight at the anticipation of pelting with the mud of the then unpaved streets ' the rough-footed Scots ' of Andrew Wood ; for those of Andrew Barton, when marched in chains through the thoroughfares of London, obtained some weighty marks of the goodwill borne by the citizens to foreigners in general, and the abhorred Scots in particular.   In the days of Henry VII. and Henry VIII., we are told the London streets ' were very foul, and full of pits and sloughs,' and thus, plenty of muddy ammunition lay always at hand.

On board the ship of Miles Furnival sailed Hew Borthwick, bound to Scotland on another mission of infamy.

A deadly and subtle poison had been prepared by a certain Master Kraft, an herbalist whom Henry VII. patronized, and who was a brother of Quentin the Notary.   This personage kept an apothecary's booth in Bucklersbury, a street which, from a very early period, until the great fire of 1666, was inhabited solely, or nearly so, by vendors of simples, medicines, cosmetics, and deleterious drugs.

This poison had been delivered by Henry's agents to Borthwick, who was to leave nothing untried, by its means, to remove Margaret Drummond for ever from the path of Margaret Tudor.

Thus Hew Borthwick had embarked on board the caravel of Miles Furnival, being too wary to show himself near Captain Howard, who he knew would indubitably fling him overboard, without mercy or remedy.

Cheer after cheer continued to be interchanged as the vessels dropped down Thames with the ebbing tide, and with their white sails and silken streamers shining in the sunny evening light.   The bank near East Smithfield, known as the Red Cliff, which gave a name to the ancient village of Ratcliffe Highway, was crowded by spectators, who waved their adieux to the tall and stately caravels—the hope of so many hearts.

The sun was sinking now, and soon the merry chimes of St. Clement Danes, and the deep ding-dong of the Bow-bell in the spire of St. Mary de Arcubus, with the smoke and steeples of London, the din of its streets with the voices of their assembled thousands, and the huge square tower of old St. Paul's lessened and faded together in the distance, as the vessels stood down the widening and winding river, on their bold expedition to intercept Sir Andrew Wood of Largo on his return from Sluys.

CHAPTER LXI.

THE ADMIRAL'S STORY—THE LEGEND OF CORA LYNN.

WHILE the two Scottish caravels (such was the name usually given to all large ships) lay at Sluys, the admiral left nothing unsaid, in his rough, hearty fashion, to rouse the spirit and fan the hopes of David Falconer and Robert Barton; but both sank lower, they grew weary of the flat shores of Dutch Flanders, with their gaudy houses, closely clipped hollies and stiff tall poplar trees; and of the sluggish Scheldt that flowed so noiselessly to the sea in slime and sunshine; and of rambling among the grass-grown fortifications of Cadsandt, the cannon of which commanded the navigation of the river; they were wearied, too, by the endless interviews and diplomacy of the slow, pompous, and full-fed burgomasters of Bruges, Sluys, and Ardenburg, with their vast circular hats, great bombasted breeches, and long iron spadas; and heartily they longed to weigh anchor for home.

'Take courage, and be men,' said the Laird of Largo to his two friends and companions, as they lingered over their wine, one sunny afternoon, in that famous old hostel on the quay at Sluys, the 'Yung-fraü,' kept by Dame Gudule Snichtercloot, who wore a cap with long ears, a score of petticoats, and had a long-legged stork sitting dreamily on each of the six steep gables of her house. 'Take courage, carles; gadzooks! had I lost heart thus every time fortune gave me a head-wind, I had never gathered leeway in life, or been Laird of Largo and Newbyrne.'

'True, true, Sir Andrew,' said Barton, gnawing the ends of his mustachios; 'but had the stout old skipper, my father, been a lord of that ilk——'

'He would have kent to a plack the price of Scottish honour and of the favour of foreign kings,' said the admiral, bitterly; 'but being a humble man, he deemed that Scotland was the Scotsman's gift from God—for the poor man's ole inheritance is his country, and so, he fought and died or her. Were I the Lion King of Arms, I would enact a law of heraldry that every Scottish peer and placeman should have his shield powdered with English rose-nobles, as indicative of the fealty they are ever ready to transfer for lucre. But were there two Adams in the Garden of Eden, and two Eves to mate with them, Father Zuill? I trow not. Gadzooks! one man's blood is as good as the blood of another, whatever his soul may be. But enough of this—I could spin you a yarn to the point, though I usually leave that task to the boatswain. Heard ye ever the story of King Malcolm's daughter Cora and Mac Ian the royal huntsman?'

'No.'

'No,' were the replies from each side of the table.

'And of how she wedded a youth of low degree?'

'Cora! I have heard of her,' said Father Zuill, who was making a focus with his glass in the sunshine, and endeavouring to burn a hole in his cassock; 'she was drowned in the Falls of Clyde.'

'So sayeth old history, but old history is wrong. 'Twas a tale my poor mother was wont to tell me, when I was a wee halfling callant that spent the lee lang summer day in fishing for podleys at the auld wooden pier of Leith, and rambling on the Musselcape; and many a time have I thought of it after I became a sailor, like my father before me; and the auld woman's kind voice came to me in dreams, when the wind rocked me asleep on the swinging topsail-yard. Well, fill up the bickers—summon another stoup of Dame Snichtercloot's best Bordeaux, and I'll tell you the tale, for it may give you heart to bear up against your present crosses, and show how a sair broken ship may natheless come merrily to land.'

After a few more preambles, the admiral began as follows —and although we have shown hitherto that he spoke in his own dialect, and mingled his phraseology with many a nautical simile and salt-water metaphor, lest the reader should tire of these, we have rendered his story into proper language, and in short preferred to tell it in our own way :—

Malcolm II., King of Scotland, surnamed Mac Kenneth (his father, the victor of Luncarty, being the third of that name), was a wise, just, and valiant monarch, who divided his realm into provinces, putting over each a governor or sheriff to restrain the turbulent and lawless; he encouraged the commons to become skilful husbandmen and tillers of the soil, and to become merchants and traders on the sea. Under his rule all the arts of peace flourished, while those of war were not forgotten; for by his valour he spread his conquests far beyond the Saxon border, and by the annexation of the northern counties of England obtained the additional surname of

Rex Victoriosissimus.

Hence it is, that for many years after, the eldest sons of the kings of Scotland bore the title of Prince of Cumberland; and hence it is that we find the inhabitants of these northern counties of England so Scottish in aspect, dialect, and character. Malcolm had no son; but he had four daughters, all famous for their charms: the Princess Beatrix, wife of Crinian Abthane of the Western Isles; the Princess Doacha, wife of the Thane of Angus, and consequently mother of the terrible Macbeth; Muriella, married to Sigurd Earl of Orkney; and lastly, the Princess Cora, the most beautiful lady in the land.

Many powerful thanes and chiefs sought her hand in marriage, but the principal competitors were Kenneth, a Lord of the Isles; Græme, Thane of Strathearn; and Dunbar, Thane of Lothian: and so anxious was the king to secure by her means the firm adherence of one of these influential nobles, that he would not have hesitated to employ force and severity, but that he loved the gentle Cora with the tenderest love that can fill a human breast; for he had transferred to her, in another form, all the regard he had borne the queen her mother, who had now passed away to the company of the saints, and whose remains lay with those of her fathers, among the royal tombs of Iona.

Yet, when this good king waxed old, when his brow became lyart and his beard grew white, and when he saw that Cora, his youngest born, had expanded into a beautiful woman—full-bosomed, graceful, and tall, with snow-white skin, soft eyes, and golden hair, he thought in his secret heart, how gladly he would see her some bold warrior's bride; lest, when the time came that he too should be borne through the valley of corpses in Kilmalie, that some of his bearded thanes and ferocious chiefs might decide the prize of her hand by the sword, and so deluge the land in Scottish blood.

Many of the great lords were more than usually importunate, because Malcolm's grandchildren, little Duncan, the son of Beatrix, and the boy Macbeth, the son of Doacha, might both die in infancy, or when they grew older, might perish in war, or in the forest, which was then fraught with danger to the hunter; for the woods were full of white mountain bulls, bears and wolves, elks, and other wild animals, that the old Scots of those hardy times loved to encounter and subdue, for wild sports were their chief pastime.

None of King Malcolm's court loved the chase like the Princess Cora, and she was ever the foremost of the hunters, mounted on a beautiful horse, which Gregory, Bishop of St. Andrews, had procured for her in Arabia Petræa, with its bridle of silver, at which hung thirteen blessed bells; and as she gave each of these as a prize to the best horseman successively in racing round the ring, the proverb first came among us of ' bearing away the *bell*.'

The old king spared no cost in the decoration of her chamber, which was entirely hung with bright-coloured silk, and its windows were glazed with clear beryl, though he and his courtiers contented themselves with beds of soft heather, and had nothing in their windows save the iron gratings which gave them security. Moreover, the floor of her chamber was laid with the softest furs, and her bed and her pillows were the finest feathers, all procured by Mac Ian Rua, the Forester of Dunfermline, and favourite huntsman of the king, in an age when luxury was almost unknown.

She was an expert citharist, and none in Scotland sang more beautifully; thus, each night by the royal couch she sat with her harp on her knees, and sang the old king to sleep by rehearsing the lay of Aneurin, describing the great Battle of Cattraeth, which was fought in Etterick Forest, where, five hundred years before, the men of Dunedin were almost exterminated by the Saxons of Deiria; and this war-like song made the old king's heart leap within him, and he would beat time with his fingers, and thus sinking to sleep, would dream of his early days, of the field of Cramond, the flight of flanes and shock of spears, and his battles with Danes by the Earn and the Tay. But his chief favourite was the low sad song of ' The Owl,' which our Highlanders yet sing when the cloud of night descends upon the darkening mountains, word for word as Ossian sang it in Selma, many a long and misty year ago.

Yet it was strange that three chiefs so powerful, so handsome, and so valiant as the Thanes of Lothian, Strathearn, and the Isles, should be without interest in the eyes of the young princess—for a day seldom passed without their laying some offering before her. Græme brought from the Perthshire mountains the snow-white hide and sable horns of the mighty Scottish bull, the tusks of the savage boar, the antlers of the elk, and the claws of the red-mouthed wolf ; to evince his prowess, Dunbar of Lothian laid before her the painted banners, the steel helmets, and white linen surcoats of the yellow-haired Saxons whom he had slain in many a field between the Tweed and Ouse ; while Kenneth of the wave-beaten Isles brought a hundred bearded harpers, each of whom could frame a hundred songs in her praise, and the charms of whose united voices filled the air by day and the halls by night with melody ; while by the number and splendour of their retinues, the usually sequestered court of the good King Malcolm was a scene of constant gaiety and delight ; for the merriment of the palace seemed to grow apace with the years that grew upon him.

Still the princess remained unwedded, and the bells of many a church and chapel had rung on her twenty-third birthday, before the king began to lose patience ; but whenever he waxed wroth, or even serious, Cora spread her white hands over her harp, shook back her long golden locks from her smiling face, and sang the song of ' The Owl ' with an eye so bright and a voice so sweet, that the kind king laughed at her drollery, kissed her, and was pacified.

Pondering on her opposition to his dearest wishes, one evening when the sun was low in the west, Malcolm II. left the old tower in the woods by a secret door and wandered into the deep dark glen of Pittencrief.

The sunlight streamed along the wooded hollow, and tinged with many a brilliant hue the topmost branches of the tallest trees and the red battlements of the old tower which crowned the summit of the *Dun*,—a steep and lofty rock, at the base of which flowed a stream. The brown fox shot across the leafy dell, the dun fuimart peeped from among the long grass, and the cushat dove cooed on the branches of the ivied oaks, as the king walked slowly and thoughtfully on, until he reached a nook in the copsewood, where a pair of lovers were sitting side by side and hand in hand, with the arm of the man around the white neck of the maiden, whose soft cheek rested on his brown and sunburned face.

Then the old king paused, with a finger on his bearded lip, and held his breath, for their figures seemed familiar to him.

The maiden wore a mantle of yellow linen, with a tunic of scarlet silk that reached to her ankles, according to the fashion of the time; and instead of sleeves, this tunic had openings for her arms, which were white as hawthorn flowers, and were encircled by bracelets and armlets of fine silver. After the custom of all unmarried women, her hair, which was of the brightest golden colour, was uncovered, untied, and flowed in ringlets over her neck; and a brooch, which the king recognized to have been a gift of his own, beamed on her left shoulder.

Roused by a step among the last year's leaves, she started, and turned her beautiful face from her lover's breast, in fear and confusion.

'Cora!' said the king, in a breathless voice, and stood as one transfixed.

The youth wore a lurich of linked mail, with a cap of steel, and an eagle's wing therein. In his hand was a boar-spear, and on his back a short bow and a quiver of arrows; at his belt hung a knife and silver bugle—for he was no other than the king's own huntsman, the son of Red John, and usually named Mac Ian Rua.

Malcolm stood silent for a minute, full of anger, grief, and scorn, for he now knew how her heart by pre-engagement had become invulnerable, and why the compliments of her princely suitors—the hardy Kenneth of the Isles, the gallant Græme of Strathearn, and the splendid Dunbar, who ruled all the fertile Lothians, from the sands of Tyningham on the east to the Torwood oaks on the west, were heard in vain.

'My own huntsman, by the holy crook of Saint Fillan! Have I lived to see my daughter in the arms of Mac Ian Rua?' exclaimed the old king, bitterly, as he strode forward, with his walking-staff clenched in his hand.

'Mac Ian,' he exclaimed, 'thou black-hearted traitor and presumptuous churl, what punishment is due to one who dares as thou this day hast dared?'

'Death,' replied Mac Ian, without hesitation, yet pale as ashes, and laying a hand upon his breast, while with the other he handed his sword to the king; 'death, Malcolm Mac Kenneth; and I am ready to die; strike and rid me of a life, that, since the hapless hour I dared to lift my eyes and heart so high, has been to me a burden and a toil; for I lived as one who was in daily dread of losing his all—his life, his sun, and glory! God made thy daughter beautiful, O king, and if to love her was presumption, strike, strike *here*—one thrust, and all will be over!'

Pale as a statue, the Princess Cora stood between her incensed father and her humble but handsome lover, but not one word fell from her quivering lip, for her tongue was chained by love for both, by fear and by a pride that was not unmingled with shame, that her father, the proud old Malcolm II.—Rex Victoriosissimus—should have seen her hanging like a wanton on a common huntsman's neck.

But if the king was proud, he was also generous, and with dignity gave back the proffered sword to Mac Ian Rua.

'Mac Ian,' said he, ' thou hast wickedly betrayed the trust I reposed in thee, in common with all my people; yet will I forgive thee. Take up thy bow and hunting-spear and begone; if within three days from this, I find thee within thirty miles of Dunfermline Tower, by the Stone of Fate, I will have thee torn asunder by wild horses—away!'

Thus commanded, Mac Ian Rua gave the princess a glance of sorrow and agony, and taking up his spear and bow, made a low reverence to the king, who watched him with a stern yet glistening eye, as he strode down the wooded glen and disappeared; for he had ever been his favourite hunter, and the old monarch had loved well to see Mac Ian bend that bow against the eagle, as it cleft the azure sky, or launch that spear against the wild boar, while its angry bristles stood erect, and its small and sunken eyes shot fire as it whetted its foam-covered tusks on the stump of some sturdy oak; and well had the good Malcolm loved to hear his favourite huntsman's bugle waking the wooded echoes of Pittencrief; and he now reflected almost with sadness, that he would never hear that ringing horn more.

' And as for *thee*, Cora,' said the king, ' the Black Abbess of Iona shall soon have thee under her care; thou knowest her? Muriella Mac Fingon—stern, ascetic, cold as ice, and immovable as the black stones of the isle; well, she shall have thee, if not as a nun, at least as one who requires much good guidance, wise counsel, and purification by prayer.'

In a chamber of the old tower, Cora secluded herself from all, and wept over this discovery and separation with shame, anger, and grief; but none shared the emotions of the king, save the young Macbeth, the son of Doacha, and *his* anger had no bounds; for he swore by the pillow of Jacob, on which our kings are crowned, and by the black rood of Scotland, that no mercy should be shown to Mac Ian; and for three days this furious boy scoured all Fife in search of him, beating every thicket and wood between Ardross and the Castle of Lindores.

But who could baffle the pursuit, or trace the steps of a hunter so wary, so bold, and expert as Mac Ian Rua? He had gone off towards the woods and mountains of the south and west; he crossed the Forth at Stirling Bridge, not the present one, but the more ancient, which was built in the days of Donald V., and inscribed:

> I am free to march, as passengers may ken,
> To Scots, to Britons, and to English-men;

and passing through the mighty forest of Torwood, he went no man knew whither; at least, the fiery young prince and his followers could never discover him, though a hundred head of cattle were offered for him, dead or alive.

Notwithstanding his indignation, and the justness thereof, the old king soon missed his favourite huntsman sorely, for he loved all manner of forestry and venery, and Mac Ian had vigorously enforced all the laws of the woods; but now these were outraged and broken daily; for there was none so faithful to the king as he had been. So all the ancient rules of the forest were violated; stray droves of cattle broke through the royal wood at the time of St. John's Feast; men with horn and hound passed the night there; no longer did three blasts of a bugle announce to the keeper of the royal kitchen that Mac Ian had found a stray cow or flock of sheep, lawfully escheat to the king; goats rambled through the parks, and the new huntsman omitted to hang up one by the horns, according to the ancient use and wont; carts and wains passed through, and if the fine of thirty silver pence was exacted, the new forester spent them at the ale-brewster's, while the keeper of the king's wood and grass declared by all the devils he could no longer preserve either, for one was cut and the other eaten,—for waife-beasts rambled, and wild men hunted with spear and horn, and laughed at the rangers, for they now feared none, since Mac Ian Rua was gone.

Rumours of these things reached Cora in her bower; her colour came and went, and her eyes brightened as her old nurse told them; for these acknowledgments of her lover's courage and gallant bearing pleased and gratified her; but now, more than ever incensed against his daughter, the old king resolved to consign her, for a time at least, to the care of the rigid and reverend mother, Muriella, among those servants of God, the canonesses of Saint Augustine. There he hoped by prayer and solitude, by the force of good example and of pious precept, that Cora would be led into a proper train of thought; that the low-born churl, Mac Ian, would be banished from her memory; and that in good time she would accept as her husband one of those noble thanes or earls, who, in their love for her and jealousy of each other, were ready to clutch each other's beards.

Malcolm loved this bright-haired daughter—his last and youngest—dearly; yet he steeled his heart against her sorrows and reluctance to be immured in that lone Hebridean Isle, and with a train of faithful attendants departed from his Tower of Dunfermline in the woods of Fife, towards the Clyde, where Gillespie Campbell, the great Lord of Lochawe, was to have one of his largest birlinns in waiting to convey the royal train from the wooden bridge of Glasgow in all safety to the Port-na-curragh of Iona; and this birlinn was to be steered by one who had thrice, in the name of the Blessed Trinity, stretched his hand over the *Black stones* of the isle; for it was an old superstition—yea, old as the days of the Druids, that the timoneer who did so would never fail in his steering; and that the vessel he guided would assuredly come safe to land. But vain were all their reckonings, and vain their preparations.

Among the apple groves and oaken woods of Clydesdale the king and his train lingered long, for he loved well the free greenwood, and at every turn of the old paved Roman Way by which they traversed that long and lovely dale, the great Scottish bull with its snow-white mane and sable horns, shot past, crushing the trees in his path, and making even the ravening wolf and stubborn boar fly before him. Thus, as the king's train rode on, many a *détour* was made, many a shaft was shot, and many a lance was flung; but he saw none whose hand was so perfect or whose aim was so true as those of Mac Ian Rua had been; and the beautiful princess smiled brightly at their discomfiture as she rode by the margin of the descending Clyde, making her fine Arabian horse caracole and paw the soft air of the warm summer morning.

And now the ceaseless din of falling water was heard, where the stream rolled over a linn of tremendous height and breadth.

There, roaring and rushing between their wooded shores, the whole waters of the Clyde, in one mighty volume, poured over a sheer precipice of four-and-twenty feet, down, down below, into a black and weltering pool, from whence the foam arose like smoke, but tinted by a hundred rainbow hues, in the hot sunshine that fell between the jagged rocks and tangled woods like a steady flood of light, to brighten the gushing flood of water.

Bewildered by the whirling and screaming of the wild birds, by the grandeur and sublimity of the scene, and almost stunned by a dreamy sense that stole over him while listening to the endless roar of that tremendous linn, cascade, or deluge that thundered down between the shattered woods, and boiled in foam against the upheaved crags till it shook the very shore, King Malcolm, with his white locks streaming on the wind from under his cap of steel, which was girt by a crown of golden trefoils, reined in his horse upon the brink, with his shrinking daughter by his side, and gazed over the natural rampart into the wild confusion of waters that hissed and boiled in the gulf which yawned far down below.

' Look down, dear Cora,' said he kindly,—for his soul was awed ; ' look down if thou darest ; for in all my kingdom, from Caithness to the Tyne, there is not such another linn as this. The very spray, as it cometh upward from that dark pool beneath, hangs on our hair like dew ! '

At that moment, a cry broke from all the royal attendants, for scared, some say, by a loud blast from a bugle which sounded like that of Mac Ian Rua,—others say by the din of the mighty waterfall, the fiery Arabian steed of the princess reared up on the very verge of that tremendous brink— reared until its sable mane was mingling with its rider's golden hair, and wildly shook its head, till every silvery bell at its bit and bridle jangled, and with Cora on its back, plunged headforemost down into that deep and awful den, the depth of which no mortal hand had fathomed, and which the boldest eye shrunk from contemplating !

In a moment Cora—the laughing and beautiful Cora, and her fiery horse, had vanished into that hideous maelstrom, which for ages had swallowed up rocks, trees, and herds, with all the débris swept down by that mighty stream from Clydesdale and the Western Lowlands !

The poor king closed his eyes in horror ; he stretched his trembling hands to Heaven in silent agony, and by the quivering of his bearded lips his nobles knew that he was praying devoutly; and after commending his soul to God, he uttered a cry of despair, and was urging his steed towards the brink, when Græme, Kenneth, and Dunbar, the three lovers of his daughter, with Duncan, Earl of Caithness, Hugo of Aberbuthnoth, old Thomas of Errol, with his three sons, whose sturdy hands and hearts in former years had turned the tide of battle at Luncarty, flung themselves before him, and dragged his terrified horse from the giddy verge, and forcibly conducted him from the terrible scene.

Far down below the fall, where, calm and blue and shining, the broad majestic river rolled between its thick dark woodlands to the sea, three days after, the Arabian horse was found, swollen and drowned upon the sand, with its silver bridle and all its tinkling bells; but no trace appeared of the poor princess, from whom that fall upon the Clyde, even to this day, bears the name of *Cora Lynn.*

Long and deep was the sorrow of the old and lonely Malcolm, who returned to his grim and gloomy tower among the woods of Dunfermline, and committing the care of the kingdom to Dunbar, the justiciar of Lothian, Duncan, the chancellor, and Nicholas, the secretary, he gave himself up to grief and contemplation, prayer, and long communings with Gregory the Bishop of St. Andrews, who made him found and endow thirteen chapels to St. Mary, in thirteen different districts; a proceeding which, if it failed to ease the mind of the king, at least eased his treasurer of all the superfluous cash in his exchequer.

CHAPTER LXII.

Now, when too late, the bereaved king thought he could willingly have bestowed his Cora upon even the humble huntsman, and believed he could happily have seen her the wife of Mac Ian, or of any honest man who would love her as she deserved to be loved ; but now he had lost her in a moment, and in a manner so terrible that it seemed like a judgment direct from the hand of Heaven upon him, for his pride and severity ; for, thought he :

' I may control the bodies of my subjects, or those of my children, but God hath given me no power over the hearts or consciences of either. Woe is me ! for the brightest diamond has fallen from my crown, and never more will my old bosom swell while she strikes her harp to the " Battle of Cattraeth," or never more will she soothe me to sleep with the low sad song of " The Owl," when the north wind soughs down the leafless glen, and the frozen lynn hangs owre the beetling crag like the beard on an auld carle's chin. Oh, Cora, Cora ! '

And the old king kept poor Cora's harp in his bed-chamber, and often in the stillness of midnight he wept, while his thin and wrinkled hands wandered among the strings, and woke their old familiar sounds again and again, till her voice seemed to mingle with them.

Now it happened that although her Arabian steed was drowned, the Princess, by some blessed miracle of Providence, escaped ; for she had been caught in her descent by one of the spouts or boiling streams that ascended upward from the bottom of the den, and unseen among the clouds of light and vapoury spray was flung far over a ledge of rocks into the smoother water beyond ; and while the king, her sire, and all his bearded thanes, in their steel caps and iron lurichs, were beating their breasts, calling upon all the saints, and fixing their eyes upon the hazy horrors of the gulf below the lynn, she was swept gently onward, in a dream as it were ; and then the hands of some one seemed to buoy her up ; then she felt herself conveyed into a dark and shady chasm of rock, overhung by a gorgeous mass of wild-roses and ivy, honeysuckle and sweetbrier, and there, upon a bank of daisies and violets, kind hands laid her gently down—a hot breath came upon her cheek, as some one tenderly parted her soft and wet dishevelled hair from her chilled and pallid cheek ; and after remaining long insensible, she opened her eyes to meet the enraptured face of the bold Mac Ian Rua, for he it was who had saved her.

No other leech than love was necessary to bring the half-drowned princess to life. Her heart soon beat with joy, and amid the double raptures of her escape, and reunion with her lover, she forgot the sorrow of her bereaved father, and the terror of her friends on the summit of the cascade, from which she had been so awfully precipitated and so miraculously saved ; and for the fleeting hours of that soft summer day till the sun sank behind the hills of Lanarkshire, she listened to the adventures of her banished lover, and heard him repeat a hundred times over all he had endured in danger, absence, doubt, and grief, while hovering in disguise near the court of the king ; how he had accompanied her step by step from the palace in Fife to the banks of the Clyde ; and how by the goodness of Heaven he had chanced to be at hand, and ready to save her from a death so terrible, by plunging boldly into the fierce and seething flood beyond the water-fall.

Love, like death, levels all distinctions,—and indeed he knows of none ; thus, the daughter of the king assured Mac Ian that her passion was yet unchanged ; and laving their clasped hands in the water that flowed at their feet—that perilous water from which Cora had so wondrously escaped—after the old fashion of Scottish lovers, they vowed to be leal and true, and wished that if one deserted or forgot the other, that God and the saints might so desert and forget the faith-less and untrue.

Now this wish was doubtless very wrong, yet they were not punished for it, neither were they again separated ; but to reward them for all they had suffered during Mac Ian's exile, and to seal their faith for ever, they received the nuptial blessing from a poor Gillie Dhia—that is, a culdee, or servant of God—who dwelt in a cell of rock in the wood of Cadzow ; and then, to avoid all discovery, they crossed the

Forth, the Tay, and Don, and travelled far north till they reached the forest of Glenfiddich. There Mac Ian built a bower, over the door of which he placed the antlers of a stag; and their daily food was furnished by his spear and bow, while the princess spun with her own white hands to clothe herself and the bright-haired children with which God had blessed them; and thus, far from courts and camps, and the troubles of council and debate, they lived in happiness, in peace, and in seclusion.

Eight years passed away, and though the poor old king had never forgotten his lost daughter, he had learned to think calmly over the events of that terrible day at Cora's Lynn, and eight times as the mournful anniversary returned he shut himself up in a chamber, darkened and hung with sackcloth; and there he repeated those solemn prayers which the Church ordains shall be said for the dead; and solemnly he rehearsed them while the hot tears coursed over his silver beard; they were for the soul of his daughter, who was yet living in her birchen bower, and singing to her little ones among the woods that shroud the rolling Fiddich.

Aged though he was, the din of war now summoned Malcolm II. to the field, against those common foemen of the British Isles, the half-pagan and wholly barbarous Danes.

Sueno, King of Denmark, who then reigned in England, having driven Ethelred, monarch of that country, into Normandy, had an implacable hatred at Malcolm for yielding succour and assistance to the English, whom the Danes were rapidly crushing; and he resolved to send an army which should assail in his own dominions the King of the Scots, of whose title—Rex Victoriosissimus—he was jealous and impatient.

Landing in Murrayshire, under Enotus, in the year 1009, the Danes overthrew in battle the Scottish forces which opposed them; they took the Castle of Nairn, and cutting through the neck of land on which it stood, brought the sea round it, and named it Burg for the time; the fortresses of Elgin and Forres were next taken, and for nearly a year they held them; being the longest period that those invaders retained possession of Scottish earth, while alive, at least. They also took the Castle of Balvenie, and therein Enotus built a great chamber, which is still named the Danes' Hall. In the following year Malcolm marched against them in person with a powerful army, formed in three great columns, under Kenneth, Thane of the Isles; Græme, Thane of Strathearn;

and Dunbar, Thane of Lothian ; for they were yet feal men and true to the old king whose daughter they had loved so well.

Clad in a byrne, formed of steel rings, which were sewn flat upon a leathern tunic, and having on his head a square helmet, like those last worn by the guards of Charles the Bald, surmounted by a diadem, the venerable monarch rode at the head of his troops, who—although he wore a tunic of blue silk crossed by a white St. Andrew saltire of the same material (which was then so rare and costly)—were mostly clad in long lurichs, with helmets of iron, and carried targets and swords, axes and mauls of ponderous weight, with bows and spears, having leaf-shaped blades of bronze or tempered steel. The wild clans of Galwegia marched beneath the banner of their lord, all clad in tartans, dyed with checks of purple and dark red, violet and blue, while their long locks flowed under their caps of iron ; and they had their sturdy arms bare, as well as their legs, which were kilted to the knee. *Albyn! Albyn!* was their battle cry, and with the sound of the harp, the horn, and pipe, they roused their fiery hearts, when, after a march of some weeks' duration, they came in sight of the foe, drawn up in array of war, near the old Pictish town of Balvenie, then named the House of St. Beyne the Great—which stands on a high green bank overlooking the Fiddich, and the rich landscape through which it wanders, where the dark firs cast the shadow of their solemn cones upon its lonely waters.

South-west of the castle the barbarous Danes were formed in deep ranks, all mailed in byrnes of iron rings, and bosses sown upon cloth or leather, with hauberks and painted surcoats to the knee, with spears and axes of steel and bronze, and ponderous iron maces that swung at the end of clubs and chains ; while above their heads waved the enchanted banner with the Black Raven, which had never been unfurled without ensuring victory.

The mighty scalp of Benrinnes was shining in the warm glow of the rising sun ; the snow-white mist was rising from the side of Corriehabbie, and the valley, the wood and water, rock and heather, all that make the scenery of the Fiddich so wild, so bold, and beautiful, were glowing under a warm summer sun ; while the yells of the red-haired Danes on one side, the braying of mountain pipes on the other, the twanging of bows, and hiss of passing arrows announced that the battle was beginning.

The lonely heron and the mountain eagle were scared from rock and river by the flashing of the steel; but the cries of the combatants brought the gled and the hawk from the four winds of heaven, and high in mid-air, with outstretched wings, they overhung the nearing hosts, expectant of their coming feast—the flesh of horse and man.

This was the anniversary of the day on which he had lost his daughter, and the heart of Malcolm II. was oppressed, and full of dark and dire forebodings: so he anticipated both defeat and death.

The first charge was a furious one, and the onset was deadly and disastrous. The Danes plied the poleaxe, their national weapon, with savage fury; the Scots charged with their long pikes and two-handed swords, while swift and surely shot the archers on both sides from the rear ranks of the closing columns. Steel helmets and byrnes of shining rings, bucklers of tempered iron, and targets of thick bull-hide were cut by the sword, cloven by the axe, or pierced by the barbed arrow, or by the spear that was launched from afar; and unhappily in the early part of the battle, Kenneth of the Isles, Græme of Strathearn, and Dunbar of Lothian, fell from their horses, each struck by a mortal wound; for the first had the axe of Enotus the Dane driven through the brass umbo of his shield and the iron cone of his helmet, sheer down to his teeth; the second had his heart pierced through, byrne and buff, by a leaf-shaped javelin; and the third had a double-edged *seax* driven repeatedly through his body.

Valiantly fought the venerable king, and as fast as men fell, their places were supplied; but disheartened by the sudden loss of the three greatest chiefs in the land, his soldiers began to give way, and with a triumphant yell the heavily-armed Danes pressed on them—their eyes sparkling with rage and the lust of blood, while the horsehair of their helmets mingled with their long and tangled locks and the wild volume of their shaggy beards.

Enotus, the Danish general, a powerful and gigantic warrior mounted on a white charger, and clad in a hauberk of burnished rings, with the skin of a bear floating from his shoulders, on which the claws rested, while the skull of the monster grinned above his basinet, soon singled out the King of Scotland, whom he knew by his venerable aspect, his silver beard, and the diadem of golden trefoils that encircled his helmet, which had three upright feathers of the iolar—for the Scottish king is the chief of all the Scottish chiefs;—and (though around him fought Gillemichael, Earl of Fife; Alan, Thane of Sutherland, who defeated the Danes on the muir of Drumilea; Hugo of the Rütherford, whose ancestor twelve hundred years before had conducted King Reuther through the Tweed against the Britons; Crinian, Thane of Dunbar, and others, the very flower of the land), with his tremendous mace, the Dane, by one blow, dashed out the brains of the royal charger, and by a second would assuredly have slain the king had not a sturdy warrior of the Murrayland, clad in striped breacan and wearing the long Celtic lurich to his bare knees, at that moment cloven the mighty Scandinavian almost in two by one stroke of his tuagh, or Scottish battle-axe.

'Well fare thee, my stalwart soldier,' cried Malcolm; 'for thou hast saved thy king!'

His protector re-mounted him on the white steed of the slaughtered Dane, and, blowing his bugle to collect the scattered Scots, plunged into the thickest of the conflict, parting the foes before him like a field of corn.

'By the stone of Fate,' cried the king, shortening his reins and grasping his sword, 'yonder blast never came from other horn than the bugle of Mac Ian Rua!'

So said all who heard it.

'And if yonder fellow proved to be Mac Ian?' said the king's secretary, wiping his bloody sword in the mane of his horse, 'what then, sire?'

'Then he should have the best earldom in the north, were it but for the sake of her he loved and lost,' said the brave old king, as he spurred once more to battle; but alas! disheartened by the loss of three of their greatest leaders, despite the bravery of Malcolm, and the fiery example of this warrior of the Murrayland, the Scots began to give way and retreat, but with their faces and weapons to the foe, until they gained an old rampart formed of turf, trees, and stones, the relic of former wars.

There the king's preserver encountered Enrique, the second Danish leader, and, under Malcolm's eye, cut off his head, and holding it aloft with one hand and his dagger with the other, cried, in Gaelic:

'*Eris-skene!*—by this knife I did it.'

'Eriskene, my brave man, thy name shall be,' said the king; but natheless these valiant deeds, the Scots were still borne back in disorder.

Malcolm was swept away with the crowd of fugitives, who were all wedged in a narrow valley, till he found himself near an old chapel at Mortlach, which was dedicated to Saint Molach, the bishop and confessor, a Scot who, in the seventh century, was the assistant of St. Boniface of Ross, and whose bones lay in that sequestered fane.

Here the king raised his gauntleted hands to heaven, and prayed that the holy saint would intercede with God and St. Andrew for Scotland and her people, vowing that, if they obtained a victory, he would increase the chapel by three lengths of his spear, and make the church of a bishoprick dedicated to Heaven and its service. Wheeling round at that moment, he found a third Danish captain close by him, and slew him by one thrust of his lance, and restored courage to the Scots.

' Victory ! Victory ! ' cried Malcolm ; ' God and St. Andrew for Scotland ! '

Like a torrent the Scots again rushed through the narrow vale, and again many a tartan plaid and many an eagle's wing was dyed in the reddest blood of Denmark. So furious was their new onset, that the Danes were swept along the valley like dry leaves before a stormy wind, and, over a field strewn with gashed corpses and bleeding men, were driven in headlong flight towards the sea. The slaughter was terrible !

Not a man of them saw the sun sink behind the great ridge of Benrinnes ; and when daylight faded in the west, the king found himself breathless, weary, and alone in a silent and sequestered place, where a brawling stream, flowing from a deep copse-wooded glen, mingled its waters with those of the Fiddich, which roll from the mountains down to the Lowlands of Banffshire.

The gloomy pines were shaking their wiry cones in the soft evening wind ; a deep blue, darkening into a dusky purple, tinted the distant hills ; the evening star was glimmering amid the blush that lingered in the west ; and the king sat down by a tree to think and to pray.

After the fury, the excitement, and slaughter of the past day, his heart felt oppressed by its own thoughts, and a glow of rapture struggled with his sorrow, for Heaven had that day accorded victory to his people ; and kneeling on the grass, there, in solitude and unseen, he raised his aged eyes and hands in thanksgiving and in prayer to God and the patron saint of Mortlach.

While he was praying thus, there came a child with a pitcher to draw water at the stream—a little golden-haired girl of eight years, whose face was beautiful as that of an angel, and whose bare feet, as they brushed the heather-bells, seemed white as new-fallen snow. She did not perceive the king as she stooped over the water in a cool and shady spot, and sang while her vessel filled.

'What is this that stirs within me,' sighed the king, who was troubled by the sight of this child, and whose heart yearned for her; for the fairness and the beauty of her face, with the brightness and softness of her eyes, reminded him of Cora, when she was a child; and, that nothing might be wanting to complete this dear illusion, the girl sang the soft, low song of 'The Owl'; and as the poor old king, still remaining on his knees, listened breathlessly, he almost seemed to hear the voice of Cora mingling, as of old, with the notes of her harp; 'but Cora,' thought he, 'is sleeping in her grave among the unblest waters of the Clyde, and her harp is in her silent chamber, far away beyond the mighty Grampians and the broad Firth of Tay, in the lonely Castle of Dunfermline.'

The king now called the child to him, and though her first impulses were fear and flight, on hearing his voice, and beholding a stranger so brilliantly armed, the reverence of his aspect and the kindness of his manner soothed and delighted her, and she approached with timidity and curiosity mingled in her charming little face. The eyes of Malcolm filled, and his heart swelled as he gazed on her, and would fain have kissed, but feared to alarm her.

'Child,' said he, 'ken ye where I may find a bield wherein to rest me for the night; I am an auld man and a weary one, for I have fought in battle this lee-lang summer day.'

'My mother bydes on Fiddich side,' replied the child, 'and though she dreads all strangers, she cannot fear you, for ye are auld and kind; and my father is a strong man whom none dare wrong, for he is the boldest archer on the Braes of Auchindoune.'

'My name is Malcolm Mac Kenneth,' said the king; 'auld I trow I be—yea, ten times your age, my bairn, but give me your hand in mine and lead on.'

Leaning on his long sword, with his silver tresses floating over his mailed shoulders, the king walked along, led by the smiling child, who peeped upward at him timidly from time to time through her clustering curls, as they went through a daisied haugh, and among the sweetly scented hawthorn birks. She soon prattled and talked to the *auld knycht*, as if she had known him for all the years of her little life; and when the good king felt the warm glow of the evening on his cheek, and saw the bright flowers that spangled the banks of the stream, and when he heard the rustle of the summer leaves, and the merry brawl of the mountain burn mingling with the glad voices of children, he felt himself young again, and his heart grew light and joyous as he forgot the corpse-strewn field that lay near the old tower of Balvenie and all along the shore of the rushing Fiddich.

'Little one,' said the king, 'who taught thee the song of " The Owl " ? '

'My mother,' replied the child.

The king sighed heavily; then, after a pause, he asked, ' And thy name, little one—what is it ? '

' Cora——'

' Cora ! ' he reiterated, and bursting into tears, pressed her to his breast; ' I might have guessed it—Cora ! what other name could be borne by one so bright, so beautiful, and so innocent; but be not alarmed, my poor little one, for I once had a Cora like thee.'

' Oh, here we byde, and yonder is my mother ! ' said the child, who was terrified by the stranger's emotion; and now they found themselves before a hunter's cot, the walls and roof of which were formed of turf and clay; and over the door of which were the branching antlers of a stag. Around it was a thicket of dark hawthorns, with all their white blossoms in full and fragrant bloom,—for as the reader has no doubt long since surmised, this was the humble dwelling of Mac Ian Rua which the king approached, and the beautiful matron who stood at its lowly door, with two babies at her knee and one in her arms, was his daughter Cora; yet the king, whose mind was full of her, knew her not; for she no longer wore the rich attire, the garments of many-coloured silk, the jewels and golden armlets of old, with which he had last seen her; but a homespun kirtle and linen tunic with sleeves that reached only to her white elbows; and about her tresses, which once waved round her head like a golden halo, was plaited a plain linen fillet—the *heafodes rægel*, or headrail of the Lowland peasant woman— an adoption from the Saxons—who dwelt beyond the English border.

The king gazed upon her earnestly, yet he knew her not ; and though he was older and his face was more wrinkled,—though his eyes were sad, and haggard, and his hair, which had been grey, was now white as the snows of Ben Mhor, Cora knew her parent—that princely sire who had loved her so well of old—and all the daughter gushed up in her heart ; yet not a word could she say, but gazed upon him trembling with sorrow and remorse, with fear, with love, and hope, while her children clung to her skirts, and she pressed to her bosom their youngest born—the child of Mac Ian Rua, the banished huntsman.

' Good woman, I seek but a night's shelter in your sheiling, till my train can join me,' said the king ; ' be not alarmed, I am a Scottish soldier, and have been fighting all day down the water-side. The foes are vanquished, and the king is safe. Allow me to enter ; and believe that kindness will not be unrewarded. My name is Malcolm Mac Kenneth.'

The tongue of Cora was without words. Silently she led Malcolm into her humble hut, and silently placed a seat for him, spreading the softest deerskin under his feet,—for her gentle heart was full of old thoughts and loving memories that came crowding fast and remorselessly upon her—summoned back, as it were, by the sound of her father's voice ; yet that voice was sadder in tone, and more tremulous than it was wont to be of old ; and that conviction stirred her heart of hearts, and crossing her hands upon her bosom, she thought, ' Oh, pardon me, God—for it is I who have caused this ! '

' Hast thou no words to welcome me, good woman, or does this armour, even when on an auld man's back, so scare thee ? ' said the king, kindly taking one of the children on his knee, as he perceived that she was gazing eagerly, mournfully, and with awe upon him, as he sat near the little window, with his silver tresses glittering in the light of the west, and his wrinkled hand resting on the flaxen head of his little conductress.

Cora could control her emotions no longer.

' Father—sire ! ' she exclaimed, wildly, as she threw herself upon the clay floor and embraced his knees ; ' oh, father ! dost thou not know me ? Have these few years so sorely changed me ? I am Cora—thine own Cora, who was swept down the Lynn of Clyde. Beloved father and king—behold me at thy feet ! Oh thou whom I have so cruelly and so wickedly forsaken in thine old age, pardon and forgive me,

lest these younglings should forsake me in turn; forgive me
and bless me, though I have sinned against God and thee ! '

These words terrified the old king as if a spirit had spoken
them. He held her from him at arm's length, and his eyes
wandered over her face and person with an expression of
fear and wonder.

' I am Cora, the little child that clambered at your knee,
and nestled in your bosom, in old Dunfermline Tower,' she
exclaimed, passionately ; ' I am Cora whose cheek was once
so dimpled—whose hair was so bright—whose little mouth
you kissed so often and so kindly——'

' Cora was drowned ! oh day of horror—horror—horror ! '
replied the troubled king ; ' she is dead and at rest.'

' She is not, for I am she.'

' Thou ? ' he exclaimed.

' I.'

' Impossible ! '

' I. Oh father, am I indeed so changed ? '

A glare shot over the king's keen eyes ; he trembled, and
stretching out his hands, drew her towards him, but a cloud
came over his brow, and pausing, he said : ' And these
children ? '

' Are the offspring of Mac Ian Rua.'

' Born of thee ? '

' My father,—oh, my father ! '

' Born of the daughter of Scotland ? ' he added bitterly.

' My heart, long steeped in sorrow, will burst at last. In
pity, father, have mercy on us.'

' And where is the lawless traitor who stole thee from me,
and hath concealed thee for these many long years, my
daughter ? '

' Say rather, where is he who saved me when the greatest
and noblest in the land—yea, even Kenneth of the Isles and
Dunbar of Lothian—hung back.'

' Kenneth of the Isles and Dunbar of Lothian are both
lying dead in their armour by the walls of Balvenie ;—God
rest them ! they fought and fell for our dear Scotland.
But Mac Ian ; where is he ? '

' Yonder he comes down the glade, with a stag on his
back,—your favourite huntsman, so ready of hand and true
of aim ; the same Mac Ian Rua as of old,' said Cora, in a
trembling voice.

' Heaven be praised, my daughter, I have found thee ;
yet oh, to find thee thus ! '

'Oh, embrace me, or I shall die: let me feel your cheek on mine once more, my father!'

'Come then—come to my old heart,' said the king, as he sobbed; for it was a rude old age, when even kings had human hearts, and nobles were not without them.

'Forgive me my sins against thee,' said Cora, in a choking voice. .

'They are forgiven.'

'And my husband—Mac Ian Rua.'

'Even he, too, is forgiven,' said the king, as the door of the hut was thrown open and the tall huntsman, fresh from the pursuit, and still clad in his lurich—the same stalwart warrior who had that day slain Enrique and Enotus, and saved his monarch's life, and whose loud bugle blast had rallied the Scottish bands—stood before Cora and her father, with astonishment and fear in his eyes, while one hand grasped his axe, and the other the antlers of the stag, and his ruddy children clung joyously to his sturdy legs.

To dwell longer on this scene would mar its effect.

The huntsman was forgiven, and the old king spent the happiest night of his long life with his daughter on one side of him, and her husband on the other, while his grandchildren clambered about him, and in wild glee rolled about the floor the glittering helmet which was encircled by a diadem.

He told them how he had pined and sorrowed, and how deep his grief had been—for Cora was ever the subject around which all his affections had been entwined—and how desolate his heart, his hearth, and home had been since her loss.

Then Cora related, that with the exception of bitter remorse at times, how happily they had dwelt in this green bower beside the Fiddich, far away from courts and kings, with their children budding round them, maintained by the fruit of her own industry and the skill of Mac Ian's hand.

They supped that night on venison broiled on a wooden spit, with cakes of Cora's baking, and nut-brown ale of her husband's brewing. When the old king was disencumbered of his armour, Mac Ian and he sat over their cans and fought the battle thrice again; and when he lay down to sleep on a soft bed of freshly-pulled heather and smooth skins—the spoils of fell and forest—Cora produced a clairshach, or harp of humble form, and once more sang him to sleep, as of old, by the warlike lay of the king of bards ; that soul-stirring lay he loved so well—' The Battle of Cattraeth ' ;—and often, as his eyes were closing, the old man raised himself with a flush of ardour, as she related the slaughter of the men of Dunedin in Anuerins' burning words, which told how, among the Pagan Saxons, ' were three hundred warriors arrayed in gilded armour—three loricated bands, each with three commanders wearing torques of gold.'

With early morning came the king's train. They had traced him to the hut, and all flushed with victory, pursuit, and slaughter, Duncan, Earl of Caithness, Nicholas, the secretary, Hugo of the Rütherford, Crinian, Thane of Dunbar, Gillemichael, Earl of Fife, and others, stood by his humble couch of skins, and after reporting the utter extermination of the Danes, heard him relate the joyous and wondrous discovery he had made overnight.

In Scotland there were great rejoicings for the restoration of the long lost Cora, and there could no longer be competition or discord about her hand ; for Græme, Dunbar, and Kenneth lay dead on the field of Mortlach, and she was now a wedded woman. For his bravery in saving first the life of Cora from the waters of the Clyde, and secondly the life of the king in battle, the huntsman, Mac Ian, was made thane of a thanedom in the shire of Rhynfrew ; and Malcolm gave him a coat of arms, which his descendants bear to the present time. Moreover, he nobly fulfilled the vow he had made to St. Molach, by adding to the chapel thrice the length of his long Scottish spear ; thus it became, as we may still see it, a church, and he made it the cathedral of the diocese of Mortlach, of which St. Beyne was the first bishop, and Nechtan the last, when the see was translated by King David I. to Aberdeen, and enriched in all its revenues : and in memory of the bloody field so auspiciously won by the saint's intercession, he desired that the heads of Enrique, Enotus, and another valiant Dane, should be built into the wall, and there *to this hour* we may still see them, bare, white, and ghastly, with their teeth grinning from the stonework, and in the brow of each is the broken mark of the blow under which he died.

In that church is the shrine of St. Molach, whose festival was held on June 25, and who became famous all over Scotland, but especially in Ross-shire and Argyle, where another church was built in his honour at Lismore.

Such was the story of the princess and the huntsman; and the moral of it is, that we should never despair, for the spokes in the wheel of fortune follow each other so fast that all are uppermost in their turn. Thus, the once despised Mac Ian Rua became the head of a great house, still named ERSKINE, in memory of his words at Mortlach; and Malcolm II. gave him for his cognizance a hand holding a dagger, with the motto, ' Je pense plus,' and a shield *argent*, with a pale, *sable;* then as Mac Ian loved the Clyde—for there he had won the beautiful Cora—Malcolm gave him the lands, barony, and castle of Erskine, and from his marriage sprung a race that never failed their king or country—the loyal and noble Earls of Mar.*

Such was the story of the admiral, an old legend, which as before mentioned, I have given in my own words rather than his; for many parts of the narrative, as *he* told it, would not have been over-intelligible to landsmen.

* The death of Cora, at Cora Lynn, is an ancient legend, still remembered in Clydesdale. The scene of the Battle of Mortlach is still marked by many sepulchral mounds, full of bones and broken armour. The bishopric is said to have originated in the king's vow, and it was confirmed by a bull of Pope Benedict VIII. The charter of erection by the king is still preserved in the chartulary of Aberdeen. It begins in the usual form ' Malcolmus Rex Scottorum,' and consists of only five or six lines, and ends with ' Teste meipst apud Forfar, octavo die mensis Octobris, anno regni mei sexto.'

CHAPTER LXIII.

THE BROKEN WEDDING-RING.

WHILE all these events which have been narrated had taken place, Jamie Gair, the fisherman of Broughty-point, had been quietly fishing and selling or selling and fishing, and while battles were won and a kingdom lost, he had nothing to agitate his mind of greater importance than an occasional foul wind, or an evil omen, such as meeting a cat, a pig, or an old woman, when about to embark, or seeing two crows flying together—an infallible sign of misfortune; or losing a net, and being unable to settle his twine bill— a serious matter for a poor fisherman.

During the last days of July, he had suffered so many omens to deter him from putting to sea, that the imperative necessity for braving all such absurd dangers and superstitious fears, and of departing for the fishing ground, made Jamie prepare his nets and floats, though advised by his companion and partner in the boat, John o' the Buddonness, that the weather, which had been squally for some days past, was likely to become more so.

'Toots, carle,' said Jamie, as he knotted the last brown bladder to the net; 'the Crail fisher that passed in here yestreen said the sea had been roaring at Kincraig, a sure sign o' fine weather; so let us trip our anchor, and hie awa', John, for the last cogfu' o' meal is in Mary's girnel, and I daurna' byde langer by the ingle cheek, like a lubberly land-louper.'

'E'en as ye please,' replied John, drawing on his long rough boots; 'he that will to Cupar, maun to Cupar.'

'But Mary, my doo, what is asteer, lass, and wherefore greet ye?' asked Gair, whom John's proverb annoyed.

'Oh, Jamie, look on *this*, and then say whether you suld gang to the fishing this day!' replied Mary, showing her wedding ring, which by some fatal mischance had been broken in two ; and in Scotland this is deemed an invariable sign of approaching separation. People lived in an atmosphere of omens in those days ; thus Jamie was sorely staggered : but he had been inert so long, that to linger longer on shore was to ruin himself. He held his cottage from the castellan of the king's castle, and its rent had to be punctually paid when the time came. For many days his kain of fish had not been delivered at the barbican gate, and though the new governor, the Laird of Balgillo, was a man of a very different character from Sir Patrick Gray, yet he could be trifled with no longer ! And now the herring droves were sweeping down from the Northern Ocean ; and seaward Jamie Gair resolved to go, though John o' the Buddon-ness looked stern and gloomy, and Mary wept and held up their little son and heir for the last kiss of his father's rough and bearded cheek,—and a *last* kiss it proved indeed to be ! But let us not anticipate.

' The ring will mend, Mary,' said Jamie, as he kissed away the tears from her blooming cheek ; 'and bethink ye, lass, can an omen o' evil ever be shown by a ring that was blessed by the auld Monk o' Sanct John at the Sclaitheughs ?   I trow no.'

After a breakfast of peasebannocks, cheese, and hot Lammas ale, thickened by eggs, the fishermen embarked, trimmed their boat, braced the yard sharp up to the north wind, and bore down the estuary.

There was a grey sky overhead, and a rolling sea below ; the horizon looked dark where it met the line of ocean, and the waves lifted their white tops between.

The wind whistled drearily along the shores of the Firth ; the breakers boomed on the low flat sands of the Buddonness ; the gusts that came at times strained the braces of the brown lugsail, and while they lifted the boat's sharp prow above the water, they tore the white spray off the dancing waves, and threw it far along the sea, like heavy rain or mist.

Mary's form in her mantle and lowland wyliecoat had faded to a speck on the sand, and now the square tower of Broughty and the Hill of Balgillo began to sink among the grey vapour that crept along the shore. The cottage on the beach was all the world to Jamie Gair, and the boat that was dwindling into a black spot in the grey and dusky offing, was all the world to Mary.

Jamie whistled and sang, as the waves rolled past.

' There will be a grand haul o' herrings to-nicht ! ' said he ; but his partner, John o' the Buddon-ness, made no reply, for his keen eyes were fixed to windward. He had an uncomfortable feeling in his breast—for old seamen have secret instincts about the weather, instincts of which a landsman knows nothing, and in which he cannot share ; but the evil foreboded by this old man's heart was different, perhaps, from what he anticipated.

' Tak' a pull o' the sheet, John,' said Jamie ; ' though the weather looks grey, we are as safe as our neighbours— be a man—trust in God and St. Mary ! '

' I do trust in them,' said the old man, touching his bonnet with reverence as he looked upward ; ' but neither God nor St. Mary have said men shall no be drooned. I can face saut water and the northern scud, Jamie, as my faithers did before me—and face them like a man as ye say, and neither blench nor quail.'

' Keep her away another point or sae,' said Jamie, ' for the glare o' the kelpfires and the saut pans have scared the droves frae this part o' the shore,—and mairower, the *waterburn* has been here for a week and mair.'

This is a luminous appearance of the sea, which, like lightning, has the effect of scaring the herrings from the coast.

It is usually about this season—the end of June or middle of July—that the great *heer*, or shoal of herrings from the north, appears at the extremity of the northern isles of Scotland.

Where they come from, no man knows ; but a surface of many hundred square miles of water becomes literally alive, and teeming with this prodigious body of fish. All the ocean seems to ripple around them, while whales are tumbling and myriads of porpoises surging and plunging through them, and clouds of gulls and gannets accompany them, screaming and in full flight.

The Scottish fishermen aver that they can scent this mighty drove from afar off, by the strong oily smell with which the air becomes impregnated. This yearly invasion divides into two bodies, one of which seeks the Ebudœ and the Irish Channel ; the other keeps along the eastern and western coasts of Scotland till October, and then, from her countless creeks and harbours, she sends forth her clinker-built fleets to net the annual mine of wealth with which her waters teem.

By sunset Jamie Gair and his companion reached the

herring ground, where the gulls were screaming and the porpoises dancing through the short foamy waves, but still
the sky was cold and lowering, and the sea was inky black;
yet though the breeze was freshening, they shot their net,
with inward hopes and a half muttered prayer—for they are
pious souls, those hardy Scottish fishers—that a night of
success might reward a day of toil amid the drenching
spray.

Their boat, the *Mary*—for so she was fondly named—
they denuded of her sail, and hooked on to the net, allowing
her thus to drift before wind and tide. They were the
farthest off shore, for more than a hundred boats were all
drifting in the same fashion, between them and the land.

Night came on, and to prevent any chance of their being
run down, each boat's crew lit their dim horn lantern;
then a quaighful of whisky went round; and still the darkness deepened on the silent sea; still the boats drifted by
their heavy nets, and still the breeze was freshening from
afar.

Midnight came. Black, dense, and furious, a gust came
with it—a fierce and heavy squall, sheer from the icy north,
that scattered all the little fleet and nearly swamped the
boat of Gair.

It was the turn of the tide now, and from their fishing
ground a strong current runs from the north-north-east
towards St. Andrews stormy bay, and all along that bleak
and iron shore.

'Awa' wi' the net, Jamie!' cried old John o' the Buddon-
ness, furiously, through the roaring wind and hissing sea;
and he held up a hand to the side of his mouth.

Jamie lingered, for the sacrifice was great. 'Awa' wi't!'
cried John; 'awa' wi't, or the boat is swamped in a minnit
mair!'

Jamie sprang to the leeward gunnel, knife in hand, and
a sore pang shot through his heart, as he thought of the
unpaid twine bill—for he yet owed the price of the net to
the rope-makers in Tindall's Wynd; but go it must. One
slash of the knife, and net and floats, with all their scaly
cargo, were swept away like a gossamer web. Half the boat-
lanterns around them were tumbling hither and thither on
the crest of the waves, or deep in the trough of the sea; the
other half had vanished, for many a boat had gone down
with all her hands on board!

And now nothing can save their frail shallop but running

before the wind, and the close-reefed foresail strains on the mast of tough Scottish larch as it lifts the boat of the bold fisherman over each hoarse wave of that black and gurly sea.

Nor kith nor kin has poor John o' the Buddon-ness to weep for him, if his corpselicht dances on the waves to-morrow night ; for his father and seven brethren had all perished at sea.

Jamie thought of Mary and of their babe—of the broken ring—of the lost nets, and of his older friend's foreboding, and their present danger ; and, while his strong heart swelled with agony, his iron hands grasped the wet tiller, and kept the lug-sail full.

On, on flew the sharp boat before that furious wind ; and now faint lights were seen to twinkle amid the darkness and the flying scud to starboard ; then the poor Scottish fishermen, while tears of hope and reliance mingled with the bitter spray that drenched their faces, put their trust in God and St. Andrew, and a hope arose that all might yet go well ; for those lights were twinkling in the aisles of that glorious cathedral church upon the promontory—the work of a hundred and fifty years ; and their prayers were heard ; for morning came, and still their boat was sea-worthy, and as the dawn brightened, both sea and wind went down ; the water was covered with foam—but not a trace was seen of that little fleet, among which they had shot their nets over-night.

As the sun rose through a hazy veil of vapour, Jamie found the Isle of May lying right ahead, and discovered that he had been blown far past Fife-ness, for now the distant spire of Crail and the faint blue Craig of Kilmeinie were gilded by the rising beams ; and, now that all danger of being drowned was past, Jamie thought bitterly of his losses over-night.

Toil-worn and disappointed, the two fishermen were about to haul up for the shore and run into Crail Harbour, when the sudden apparition of three large vessels, under easy sail, bearing straight towards them, from under the lee of the Isle of May, where doubtless they had lain secure all night at anchor, arrested their attention ; for at a glance Gair and John o' the Buddon-ness perceived they were English ships, heavily armed and full of men.

These vessels were little more than a mile distant, and the fishermen knew that a run of four miles would bring them

into the nearest harbour, where their boat—their little all—
would be safe. The time was one of truce between the two
countries; but recent events had proved that the warlike
skippers of King Henry were not over-particular in respecting
strangers at sea.

The breeze was still fresh and keen; the fishers stepped
their mast, hoisted so much of their lug-sail as they dared,
and, favoured by a side wind, bore away for Crail; but one
of the English caravels followed them, and only a short time
elapsed before a puff of smoke curled from her bows, and
a cannon-shot boomed over the water close by, and plunging
into the slope of a wave, raised it like a spout ahead of the
boat.

'Ablins, they lack a pilot, Jamie,' said John o' the
Buddon-ness; 'let us lie-to; they canna' hae the hearts
to harm twa puir dyvour shields like you and me.'

'May my een melt in their sockets when I undertake to
pilot an Englishman!' said Jamie; 'but, by my certie,
here comes another shot—douk doon, John, douk doon!'

This time it was the ball of an arquebuse, levelled through
an iron sling attached to the ratlins.

The warning words had scarcely left Jamie's lips before
the boat yawed round furiously, and his poor old companion
fell dead across the thwart, for the same bullet that cut the
halyard had pierced his heart, and in another minute the
startled Gair found the English ship cleaving the billows
close by him, and her hull towering from the sea as her mainyard was backed, and she lay to.

'Come on board, thou rascally Scot,' cried a voice;
'and marry! come quickly, lest we fire again!'

'Fling me owre a rope, then,' replied Jamie, who, but
for the sake of Mary, would have jumped overboard rather
than obeyed.

A rope was thrown to him, and in another moment he
found himself standing on the deck of the stately ship commanded by Sir Stephen Bull, and he was roughly dragged
before that portly commander, who appeared in half armour
at the door of the poop, which contained the principal cabins.

'Thou hast given us trouble enough, in all conscience,
fellow!' said he, angrily; 'why laid ye not to?'

'Because Sir Andrew Wood is not in these waters; the
ships of Sir William Merrimonth and John Barton are all
in the western seas, and we have none to protect us now,'
said Gair, with a sigh of bitterness as he looked after his

boat, now cut adrift and tossing on the sea with the dead
body of his companion in it.

' Ah ! and so Sir Andrew Wood is not in the seas ? '

' No, sir ; but is daily expected,' said Gair, spitefully.

' Good,' said Sir Stephen, with a smile of gratification
on his broad and bearded face ; ' that is the reason, Scot,
which brings us here.'

' I pray you to release me, gude sir,' implored Jamie, as
he stood, bonnet in hand, amid a circle of armed Londoners,
who stared at the ' rough-footed Scot ' as if he had been a
wild animal ; ' I am but a puir fisher carle, wi' a wife and
a wean to support in these hard times of civil war and trouble ;
I lost my nets yesternicht in the squall, and ye have cut my
boat adrift this morning—I am a ruined man ! ' he added,
as he almost wept in the agony of his spirit.

' A ruined man, indeed ! so much the better for our purpose, perhaps,' said Sir Stephen Bull, with an icy smile ;
' wouldst know the ships of Sir Andrew Wood if you saw
them now ? '

' Yes, sir, as well as my ain cottage lum.'

' Cottage what, sirrah ? '

' Lum, sir ; lum.'

' 'Tis well,' said Bull, turning to Captain Edmund
Howard, who had recognized the poor fisherman of Broughty-
point, and who had been standing somewhat aloof ; ' let
this man be well watched, and call me the moment a sail
appears in sight ; for Scot though he be, his eyes may serve
us here better than our own.'

' But he may escape,' suggested Howard, who half hoped
he would.

' Escape ! nay, nay ; let his legs be secured in fetterlocks,
then he'll not drag his anchor, I warrant.'

Strictly guarded, Jamie was kept for three days on board
of the *Unicorn*, the ship of Bull ; and though he knew not
exactly for what purpose, he feared it would prove of no good
ultimately to himself. In these three days which succeeded
the midnight storm, what would be the thoughts, the surmises of poor Mary, and how great would be her terror at his
disappearance ; how much greater, too, if his boat was
picked up, or cast ashore, with the body of his slaughtered
friend in it ! The poor man covered his brown visage with
his rough hands, and endeavoured to shut out sight, sound,
and reflection, but such thoughts would come again and
again.

Edmund Howard treated him with the greatest kindness, and endeavoured to raise his drooping spirits by promises that he would soon be set on shore, with gold sufficient to buy ten such boats and nets as those he had lost ; but Jamie ever replied :

' Na—na, sir ; I want nane o' your siller, for English gold works Scotland ever dule and wae ; and may my fingers be blistered if I touch it ! '

Then Howard questioned him about the family of Lord Drummond ; but Jamie could only say that ' it was commonly bruited abroad that his daughter, the Lady Margaret, the king's gude cousin, was to be Queen of Scotland, and that a winsome young pair they would be.'

Had honest Jamie Gair been less occupied by his own thoughts than he was, he could not have failed to observe how these tidings—though expected, sank into poor Howard's brave and noble heart.

Meanwhile the English ships never molested the coast, for it was not the purpose of Sir Stephen Bull to create an alarm, so he continued to cruise off the mouth of the Firth, within a space of twenty miles or so, running southward as far as Dunbar, and northward as far as the Carr Rock ; but generally hovering about the Isle of May, to the great anxiety and discomposure of the secluded priests of Pittenweem, who dwelt thereon, and traded by shipping with France and the Baltic.

About dawn, on the fourth day after Jamie's misadventure, two large vessels were descried at the horizon, like black specks, for the clear streak of the coming day was astern of them, and their outline was darkly and strongly defined. They loomed large ; and from the lofty poop of the *Unicorn* Sir Stephen Bull reconnoitred them with some anxiety, for the Scottish admiral was said to have but two ships with him ; and so he despatched a boat to the vessel of Miles le Furnival, to bring on board the Scottish spy he had brought with him from London.

' Is it *thee*, thou hell-begotten wretch ? ' exclaimed Howard, as Hew Borthwick, gaily attired, stepped confidently along the deck of the very ship which had been captured by his treachery ; ' by St. Paul, I would give something handsome to see thee rove up to the foreyard-arm ! '

Borthwick gave the speaker a dark and furtive glance, but made no reply.

' Thou art sure, sirrah, that Andrew Wood hath but two

ships with him ? ' asked Stephen Bull, imperiously, contempt and scorn curling his full, ruddy lip as he spoke.

' Sure as I have now the honour of addressing you.'

' Wouldst know them if ye saw them ? '

' Not unless within half-a-mile or so.'

' That were somewhat too close for my purpose,' said Bull ; ' remove this shabby lubber, this skulking lurdane, from the quarter-deck, and bring aft the fisherman.'

Borthwick, who had repeatedly begged to be placed ashore, but in vain, was now roughly removed, and poor Jamie Gair, with his legs stiff by four days' and nights' retention in fetterlocks, was brought before Sir Stephen Bull, around whom all his officers and gentlemen volunteers were crowding, with kindling eyes and open ears.

' Wouldst thou know the ships of Sir Andrew Wood, sirrah ? ' asked Sir Stephen, whose pages were arming him in a brilliant coat of mail.

' Well as I wad ken the dear face o' my ain wife ! ' replied the prisoner with ardour and sadness.

' Never mind thy wife's face, Scot ; but answer me.'

' So far an honest man may, I will, sir.'

' Then, are these his vessels—away there to windward ? '

Gair looked there for a moment ; his eyes flashed and his cheek reddened ; but he hung his head with an emotion which did not escape the keen and penetrating eyes of the English captain.

' Speak, sirrah ! ' said he, imperiously, as he grasped his poniard.

' They are hull down, sir.'

' Well, but ye may know the trim of his sails, and the fashion of his gear aloft.'

' I—I dinna ken, sir.'

' Answer me, fellow, at once ; are these, or are they *not*, the caravels of Sir Andrew of Largo ? '

' I am no free to say.'

' Trifle not ; answer me at once, or, by the head of King Henry, I will lash you at the gunner's daughter, and fling you overboard after ! '

' I daurna trifle, noble sir, I who am but a puir fisherman, with you, an armed knight ; but I too can swear, and by the head of King James, I sall rather dee than tell ye.'

' Then die, fellow ! ' said the knight, furiously ; ' Dick Selby, tie a ball to his heels, and trice him by the armpits up to the yard-arm ; while there, he will have a better view

of these coming craft.   Knot the rope round in a fisherman's
bend—he may like it the better.'

It was all done in the time we have taken to write it;
the ball of a carthoun—about thirty-six pounds in weight—
was attached to his ankles, which were tied together; a
rope was passed round his body, and he was run up to the
arm of the maintopsail-yard, where he hung with outspread
hands.   A shudder, but partly subdued by anger at his
obstinacy, passed over all on deck.   A culverin was prepared, and the seamen in the waist, who had 'triced'
the poor fisherman up, held in their hands the line on which
his life depended.

'Answer me now, Scot—are yonder craft the ships of
Sir Andrew Wood?' cried Stephen Bull, who was a stern
and uncompromising as well as a cunning and reckless man;
'answer!'

'Never,' cried Gair, though ye should wrench me bone
frae bone!'

'You may as well tell the truth,' said Howard, 'and save
your life, for it will be all the same for your admiral in the
end.'

'I ne'er say aucht but truth,' replied Gair; 'but ye sall
get nae information frae me.'

'Then take thy last look of yonder rising sun, my brave
fellow,' said Howard, with deep commiseration; 'for in
one minute more thou'lt be lying at the bottom of thy
native sea.'

'Oh, my sakeless wife and bairn!' cried the poor fisherman: 'but in life and death, I commit you to the care of
God!'

These words struck a chill on all who heard them, and the
brave English gentlemen and mariners of Bull grew pale as
they looked on each other.

Twice Sir Stephen repeated the question, and on receiving,
for the last time, the same reply, he cried, furiously: 'Thy
blood be on thine own head, fellow!—fire the gun!'

The white smoke gushed from the gunport through the
black rigging; the sharp report pealed over the morning
sea, and ere it died away the rope had whistled through the
block, as the sailors cast it from them like an instrument of
murder, and poor Jamie Gair had vanished from the yard-
arm of the *Unicorn*.

'Oh, Sir Stephen Bull,' cried Howard, as he rushed to the
vessel's side; 'what is this thou hast done?'

Drowned a pitiful Scot, whose obstinacy may mar our morning's work,' was the dogged reply, as a few bubbles that rose to the surface were all that remained to show where the fisherman had sunk. Sir Stephen walked aft hastily, but was evidently dissatisfied with himself, for he returned, and said :

' Why this regret, Edmund Howard ; was not the man only a Scot ? '

' For that reason I commiserate his fate the more,' said Howard, who was no doubt thinking of Lady Margaret Drummond.

' Tush ! display the signal to clear away for battle, and hoist the French ancient, for I have no doubt these are the ships of him we are in search of. If they were not, our defunct fisherman would soon have said so.'

' God will not bless the course we thus begin,' said Howard ; and if yonder ships are indeed those of Sir Andrew Wood, the weepers of Saint John, by London Wall, will be singing dirges for some of us ere long.'

' I care little whether or not God blesses it, if Henry our king is pleased,' said Sir Stephen, with a glance of pride and anger ; ' but peace with this croaking, Sir Captain of mine—'tis a new thing in thee. To your arms and to your quarters, fore and aft—sound trumpets, and load culverins and arquebusses ! Dick Selby, open the magazine ; John o' Lynne, see the fire's out ; beat to quarters, and set abroach three runlets of canary. Fight to the death, my merry men all, for if you fall into the hands of the Scots they will chain you to work on their castles and highways, and feed you worse than Charterhouse monks—so every man to quarters, and St. George for Merry England ! '

CHAPTER LXIV.

THE BATTLE OFF FIFENESS.

AFTER nearly bringing to a successful issue his diplomatic mission concerning the quarrel between the Scottish, Dutch, and Flemish merchants—though the latter remembered bitterly the various barrels of pickled heads despatched by the umquhile Sir Andrew Barton to the Privy Council of James III.—Sir Andrew Wood had left the port of Sluys, or Sluice, which is one of the best harbours and strongest frontier towns in Dutch Flanders, and from the Bailiff and Echevins of which he received a gold cup and silken banner. Sailing with a fair wind, he soon lost sight of the low flat shores of Batavia, and bore away for the Firth of Forth.

The voyage across the northern ocean was rough, and more than once his Scottish caravels rolled their lower yard-arms in the water ; but their trip of five hundred miles was drawing to a close, and on the morning mentioned in the preceding chapter the crews of the *Flower* and *Yellow Frigate* hailed with satisfaction the black rugged scalp of St. Abb, as it rose above the summer sea.

The *Flower* was commanded by Sir Alexander Mathieson, the Auld King o' the Sea,' whose former ship, the *Margaret*, had been given by the young king to John, the younger brother of Robert Barton. John was also a brave mariner, and well known in Scottish history.

The vessels were going under easy sail ; morning prayers were over ; the crew were lying in groups between the guns on deck, resting themselves after the recent gale. Willie Wad was plying on the fiddle ; Father Zuill was of course engaged in the further development of his parabolic speculum ; the admiral was writing in his cabin ; Falconer and Barton were on deck, talking no doubt over the chances of good or evil tidings awaiting them from the fair daughters of Lord Drummond, and of their aversion for the new Lord High Admiral of Scotland—Hailes, now Earl of Bothwell ; old

Archy, the boatswain, was 'spinning a yarn' to some idlers who were clustered near the capstan, and assuring them that in some parts of the Northern Sea, he knew with certainty there was a fiend who was often seen astride the bowsprit or the spritsail-yard on the eve of a hurricane, with blue flames coming out of his hawseholes, and wearing a conical hat tipped with fire; and there he rode, leading the vessel to destruction; for if the storm was weathered, she would run into the down-hill at the back of the world, where she might beat and tack in vain, for her crew could never gather leeway until the day of doom. This, and much more to the same purpose, was listened to, in the most perfect good faith by the hearers, and was corroborated by some of them, who had seen the identical demon referred to, when they were wrecked near the English Castle of Bamborough in '72, in the great ship of James Kennedy, Bishop of St. Andrew's, when all perished, save a few who escaped in a jolly-boat with the holy Abbot of Inchcolm, whose case of reliques—but at that moment a voice was hailing the deck.

'Hollo,' cried Barton, 'who hails?'

'Captain of the maintop, sir—sail ho!'

'Sail ho!' was echoed from the deck.

'Why, thou gomeral, there is nothing wonderful in seeing a sail off St. Abb's head.'

'But there are three o' them, Sir Captain,' cried the sailor, looking over the basket-work of the top; 'war-ships to my eye.'

'Oho—that alters the case entirely!'

Barton sprung into the main-rigging, and ran up aloft to take a view; when he descended, the admiral, whom some rumour had reached, was on deck.

'What dost make them out to be, Robert?'

'Three full-rigged ships, standing straight towards us; coming down with a fine breeze, and everything set aloft that will catch it.'

'Didst make out their colours?'

'They have none hoisted as yet; but, by St. Andrew, they are war-ships, or I have the eyes of a mole!'

'They may be English——'

'Or Portuguese caravels on some roving commission; but both are alike dangerous. To be forewarned is to be forearmed.'

'Right,' said the admiral; 'so beat the starboard watch to quarters; Willie Wad, out with all lights, and open the magazine! To your armour, gentlemen; Sir David Falconer, order your trumpeter to sound, and line the poop with arquebussiers.'

'That puff of smoke,' said Falconer, as he buckled on his splendid baldrick, 'is very like the discharge of a culverin.'

And such it was, being the death-knell of Jamie Gair, the unfortunate fisherman.

As the vessels neared each other, the two Scottish caravels were cleared for action, and every man armed himself; the cannon was served with shot and powder; the arquebussiers manned the tops and taffrails; the cannoniers stood by their guns, with tackle, sponge, and rammer; the lines were laid along the deck, and the ports were triced up.

'By my soul, Robert Barton,' said the admiral, as he scanned the strangers; 'I think I should know the hull of yonder craft and the rake of her masts. Gadzooks! look at her now, as her sails lift in the breeze.'

'And the fashion of her topsails, too,' said Barton, observing her with kindling eyes, and a darkening brow.

''Tis the *Unicorn*—as I am a living man!'

'Either thy father's spirit, or an English foe, is under sail on these waters. It *is* the *Unicorn*, Robert. But hah —what is this? Up goeth her pennon and ensign. French, gadzooks! Now what may this portend?'

''Tis all a wile,' said Barton, as Sir Stephen Bull, the further to deceive them, as he hoped, hoisted the white flag with the fleur-de-lis, a flag then as familiar to the Scottish people as their own; and as the oriflamme swelled out in the breeze, Sir Stephen fired a gun to leeward.

'Up with St. Andrew's cross,' said the admiral; 'if these are not three English ships, may I skulk in the lee scuppers of fortune to the end of my days. Up with our ancient, quartermaster; and Wad, fire a gun to *windward*.'

It is recorded that immediately on the hostile signal being given, the oriflamme went down, and up went the white flag with the red cross of England, while the bright heraldic pennons of the many gentlemen who served in the ships for glory and honour, or in sheer hatred of the Scots, were displayed in the bright sunshine. The adverse ships, now about half a mile apart, were nearing each other fast, and every heart on board beat high.

In our account of this battle, we will follow briefly and strictly the relation of Dalzel, Pitcairn, Buchanan, the Laird of Pitscottie, and others. The quaint chronicler Lindesay gives us the characteristic address of his contemporary, the Scottish admiral to his crew, while every man received a stoup of wine at the capstan-head.

' My lads, these are the men who would seek to convey us in fetters to the foot of an English king as they did the shipmates of stout old Andrew Barton; but, by the help of God and your bravery, they shall fail! Shipmates, set yourselves in order; every man to his station; the gunner to his lintstock, and the steersman to his helm! Charge home, cannoniers—crossbowmen, to the tops—pikes and two-handed swords to the forerooms. Down with the bulkheads, up with the screens, reeve tackle, and ram home. Be stout men and true, for the love of your kindred, and the honour of old Scotland—hurrah!'

A loud cheer responded; the poops, tops, and forecastles were bristling with cuirassed and helmeted men; the yeomen of the sheets and braces stood by their stations, the gunners by their guns, and all were armed to the teeth, with swords and daggers, pikes, axes, ghisarmas, and hand-cannons.

The sun was clear and the sky brilliant; the waves rolled like crystal in long glassy swells; the bellying canvas was white as snow, and the gaudy pennons waved from mast-head and yard-arm, like long ribands of many coloured silk on the gentle wind. The sides of all the ships, but more especially their towering poops and ponderous quarter-galleries, were gay with carving and gilding, and grim with the flashing of sharp weapons and the brass-mouthed tiers of their pointed artillery; and a thousand bright or gaily tinted objects were thus reflected in the clear waves as they rolled past in slow heaving ridges that glistened in the sun.

In a few minutes the guns of Bull commenced firing, and their balls whistled through the rigging of the *Yellow Frigate* as she closed up, but without firing a shot, for, breathless and impatient, her crew were waiting for the sound of the admiral's whistle.

One ball splintered the mizenmast near Sir Andrew, and another stretched Cuddie Clewline, his coxswain, on the deck.

' My poor Cuddie,' said he, rushing forward; ' how art thou, old shipmate?'

' Ill enough, Sir Andrew,' groaned the seaman, from the sleeve of whose doublet the blood was gushing; ' my best spar is knocked away.'

'Poor carle—thy right arm?' said Barton.

'Never fear ye for me, sirs, I'll weather the gale yet,' he answered, as he crawled along the deck, leaving a long trail of blood, till he reached the main hatchway, where Father Zuill, relinquishing an immense parabolic speculum, received him in his arms, and conveyed him below.

'Hollo! Saints and angels, what clattering is that?' he asked, as a heavy shot tore its way between decks.

'An English bullet through the magazine,' said some one.

'Damnation,' cried Wad, plunging down the ladder to ascertain the damage.

'Peace,' said the chaplain; swear not, friend gunner; it is forbidden.'

'The shot is through thy laboratory, Father Zuill,' said the boatswain, ascending; 'and if it hasna smashed your hurdy-gurdy to splinters, may I never mair see Anster kirk!'

'Hell's fury! sayst thou so?' cried the chaplain, losing all patience, as another of King Henry's pills came crashing through the timbers, killing and wounding all in its way.

'Oho! may I drink bilge but a friar can swear as well as a poor gunner, though it is forbidden,' said Willie Wad, as he hoisted up case after case of shot; but the unhappy chaplain, rendered furious by the destruction of his life-long labours, flung off his frock, under which he wore a jazarine jacket, seized a sword, and rushed on deck intent on vengeance.

The *Yellow Frigate* and *Unicorn* were now less than a musket shot apart, when Sir Andrew blew his silver whistle; and then the former poured her broadside of 'pestilent' carthouns, sakers, and serpentines into the latter, exchanging fire with her on opposite tacks, while the arquebussiers and crossbowmen aloft and below volleyed at each other as fast as they could cast their weapons about.

'By the soul of King James, that broadside will cost ye a few bolts of canvas, my friends!' said Wood, with a smile; and bearing on, by his great seamanship he continued to keep the weather-gage of Bull; while Sir Alexander Mathieson, with the *Flower*, followed close in his wake, they each exchanged broadsides with the three English ships, whose triple fire cut up their rigging, battered their gay bulwarks, and wounded a vast number of their men; but few were killed, though all the scuppers ran with blood and water.

These brave adversaries saw not the days that were to come, when 'Duncan, Nelson, Keppel, Howe, and Jervis, under a *united* flag, would lead their descendants side by side to sweep Scotland's ancient ally from the ocean.

' Tack,' cried the admiral to Barton again, as the cannon were charged for the fourth time; ' tack again, and range up on the weather quarter of the sternmost ship.'

By this manœuvre he almost blew to pieces the poop of Miles Furnival's caravel; he then gave the order to ' close in and grapple.'

' A narrow escape, David,' said Barton, as an English bullet tore the crest off Falconer's headpiece.

' A little lower, and it would have ended all my cares to-day,' replied Sir David, with a sad smile; ' and believe me, Barton, I would rather die here than land to-morrow, and learn that Sybilla has become the countess of the high admiral.'

The five vessels now simultaneously shortened sail, and, according to the tactics of the day, grappled with each other; and there was a frightful rasping as they closed in muzzle to muzzle with their yard-arms tearing each other's canvas to rags and ribbons.

Alas! we need scarcely advert to the *desperation* of the conflict which ensued—a conflict from which we recoil; for it was Englishmen and Scotsmen who then fought against each other, and fought as they alone can fight.

The yetlan guns soon became so hot that Wad reported to the admiral, ' that they were bouncing off their stocks, and tearing their breechings like pack-thread.'

We are told that, fearless of the numerical force and superiority of the enemy, old Andrew Wood led the way to the ' Inglish deckis with his twa-handed quhinger,' and that for twelve hours, with sword and pike, crossbow and battle-axe, a deadly conflict was maintained; and that they had often to retire from sheer exhaustion, and to free their blood-stained decks from the dead and wounded; ' and there they fought,' saith Pitscottie, who knew the admiral well, ' frae the rising of the sun till the going down of the same, in the long summer's day, while all the men and women that dwelt near the coast-side stood and beheld the fighting, which was terrible to see.'

The sun sank behind the hills of Fife, and those persons who crowded on the steeple of Crail and the summit of Kincraig saw the five grappled ships abandoned to the wind and current drifting off towards the north. They saw the blue flag of Scotland and the white English ensign floating side by side;

they could see the incessant gleaming of steel, and the pale smoke that broke upward in white curls from time to time, but they knew not how the tide of battle turned, or to whom red Victory held out her bloody wreath.

Night came down on the echoing deep, and when morning dawned the good folk of the East Neuk, pale with watching, and fired by expectation, could see no trace of the hostile ships ; for by that time they had drifted like a huge and gory raft, or a floating hecatomb, to the mouth of the Tay.   There, after casting off to refit and reeve anew their cut and torn rigging, again the trumpets sounded, and again they grappled at sunrise ; and Wood ordered that the English ships should be lashed ' with cables ' to his own—that they should all go down together rather than any one should escape.

The Scots and English were repeatedly in possession of each other's decks, and incredible valour was exhibited in the many hand-to-hand conflicts that ensued amid the general *mêlée* ; many a Scottish mariner was ' spritsail yarded,' as they termed it, by being pinned in the head or breast by the clothyard shafts of Sir Stephen's archers, who shot from the tops and poops ; and many an Englishman was *scotched* (i.e., cut or slashed by the sword or Jedwood axe), a phrase we first find in Shakespeare, but which had long previously been common in England for a wound received in the Scottish wars.

Tall Dick Selby, with his poleaxe, displayed to advantage the agility and prowess which made him the lion of the Moorfields and Finsbury ; and strong in the belief of a blessed Paternoster, bought in the Row beside St. Paul's, and bound about his better wrist, he had hewed a way almost to the poop of the *Yellow Frigate*, when he was killed by Sir David Falconer, who there recognized Edmund Howard fighting bravely against great odds, and keeping his back to the mizenmast ; and there, after doing all in his power by voice and deed to save him, he had the mortification of seeing him hewn almost to pieces by the crew of the *Flower*.

Sir Fulke of Fulkeshall was also slain, and there was scarcely a noble or wealthy family in London that did not lose a relative in this desperate conflict.

Sir Stephen Bull, tall, powerful, and brave as a Hector, sought everywhere for old Sir Andrew Wood, reserving his sword and strength for him alone ; and they encountered each other no less than six times, but were always separated by the furious pressure of those around them; for Miles le Furnival, John of Lynne, and others, on one side, Sir Alexander Mathieson, Robert Barton, and Falconer, on the other, were always rushing on, and taking part in the bloody game, though all of them were severely wounded, and covered with blood and bandages.

'Had we no better cast off the grapples,' cried Archy of Anster, rushing to the admiral, who was leaning, breathless, against the taffrail of the *Unicorn*, with his sword in his hand.

'Wherefore?' he said.

'We are close on the Buddon-ness—in shoal water,' exclaimed the boatswain; 'and will strike in three minutes or less.'

'Let us take our chance,' answered Wood, grimly; 'I will rather knock the old ship to pieces than see her an English prize; but, alas! honest Archy—art thou wounded?'

'My mainyard is shot in the slings,' groaned the old boatswain, as a ball struck him near the shoulder, and he fell heavily on the deck, with his right arm broken.

At that moment there was a tremendous shock; the masts nodded like willow wands, and several topmasts, with all their yards, sails, rigging, and hamper, came thundering down on the still contested decks; and then a hoarse shout of rage and despair arose from the English ships, for their crews were aware that they were all ashore, or wedged on the shoaly sands together.

To shorten this account, which, as it may be found in many old histories of Scotland, need not be longer dwelt on here, the English trumpets sounded a parley, and the brave Sir Stephen Bull, now thoroughly crestfallen and dejected, surrendered his sword to Sir Andrew Wood; but without shame or dishonour, for he and his crews had done all that brave men might do.

The ships were all floated off by the flood tide; the grapplings cut, jurymasts were rigged, and sails set on them, and before midnight they were all safely anchored in the harbour of Dundee, within the protection of the cannon of Broughty.

CHAPTER LXV.

THE ENGLISH PRISONERS.

THE tidings of this victory, notwithstanding the slaughter by which it was gained, caused the greatest rejoicings over all Scotland, for her people were proud of their country, and were then sensitively jealous of her honour; thus, the excitement in Dundee, on the day after the battle, was tremendous.

Sir Andrew Wood took Sir Stephen Bull and all the officers and English gentlemen volunteers ashore to present them to King James IV. When the barge of this fine old Scottish mariner left the ships, the seamen of the *Yellow Frigate* and *Flower* swarmed up the rigging, manned the yards, and gave him three hearty cheers.

' God bless ye, my brave callants,' said the good admiral, as he stood up in the boat, bowed his silvery head, and waved his blue bonnet.

A similar greeting awaited him at the rock of St. Nicholas, and in the streets of Dundee, where, giving his arm in token of amity to his late adversary, the haughty and resentful Stephen Bull, and followed by the principal prisoners, and surrounded by Falconer's arquebussiers, to guard them from insult, he went straight to the little palace of St. Margaret, where the young king, who had been apprised of his coming, awaited him. Vast crowds followed the vanquished and the victors; the lances of the Provost guarded them, and in front rode the Laird of Blackness, bearing the banner of the Burgh, argent, with a pot of lilies, or—the emblem of the Virgin—supported by two green dragons, with enormous twisted tails; and many an unsophisticated Englishman, who had never seen a Scot before, gazed about him with emotions of wonder and hostility; for the towns and dresses of the Lowlanders were very different from those of the English, to whom the architecture of the Scottish streets and houses has still a strange and foreign aspect. In those days, the peasantry of the Lowlands all wore rough brogues of deerskin, with the hair outwards; hence they were named rough-footed Scots by the people of England, where the peasantry were all barefooted, and even bare-legged, as some writers of the time of James IV. say.

Accompanied by the venerable Duke of Montrose-Crawford, the young Lord Lindesay, in his scarlet mantle, and his tall mother, the Duchess, by Robert Lord Lyle, and many other friends of his unhappy father, mingled with a few of the Angus faction, James IV., with his half-acknowledged queen by his side, received the victorious admiral and his bold prisoners in one of the finest chambers of this old country palace.

The walls were hung with green and gold arras; the oak ceiling was divided into square compartments, and in the centre of each was a royal or heraldic device, the arms of the house of Stuart, of their alliances with foreign reigning families, and their many ennobled descendants. Above the carved stone fireplace hung the celebrated picture of the murdered James III., with his queen, in which he is represented in a lilac-coloured robe, trimmed with ermine, and wearing a vest of cloth of gold; Margaret of Oldenburg is attired in a blue robe, with a Scottish kirtle of cloth of gold, and a headdress blazing with jewels. This picture, which now hangs in Kensington, is probably one of the many valuable portraits of which the avaricious James VI. stripped the Scottish palaces, on his succession to the English crown in 1603.

Crestfallen and silent, the proud and brave English captain stood within this noble apartment.

James frankly and kindly shook the hand of the vanquished mariner, and complimented him on his bravery, in terms similar to those with which he favoured Wood.

'Sir Stephen,' he added, 'I will restore to you and to your followers your swords, arms, and armour, your ships, and liberty, because I ever love brave men who fight—not for gain—but for glory. Go, sirs, you are free; but I trust that never again you will trouble the Scottish seas with your presence or your piracies, else another fate may await you.'

Before presenting his own officers and shipmates to their young sovereign, Sir Andrew courteously introduced Miles de Furnival, John o' Lynne, and all those Englishmen who had distinguished themselves most in the recent battle; he also deplored the death of Captain Edmund Howard; 'for,' said he, ' he was a brave man, and a true English seaman, whom I respected, though his brother, the admiral, slew my old shipmate, Barton, on that day of sorrow in the Downs —but woe is for women, and masses are for monks—the gunner to his lintstock, and the steersman to his helm, say I.'

Margaret Drummond heard these tidings with a pang, for the noble and gentle Howard had won her whole esteem, though he could win nothing more.

' Thou art so rich in honour, and, men say, in money too, Robert Barton,' said the king, ' that I am sorely puzzled how to reward thy bright career of faithful service ; but thou shalt be the captain of my *Great Michael*, as soon as that stately ship is launched and fit for sea. And as for thee, my honest Davie Falconer, the gentle and the brave,' he added, taking both Sir David's hands in his, ' what shall I say to thee ? As an earnest of better things, let me hang this gold medal, the gift of our Holy Father Innocent VIII., to the golden chain my father gave thee, when last we were all under this old roof-tree together. May the good God bless thee, Davie Falconer ; for, on the last day of that poor father's life, thou didst fight nobly by his side, where I too should have been, but for evil fortune and most accursed counsel ! '

Falconer's heart swelled with mingled joy and sadness as the young king attached the medal to his chain, and he gazed imploringly at Margaret Drummond, with an expression that seemed to say, ' Oh, speak for us—for Sybilla and for me—you know our secret well ;' but terror of her father, on whose face there was a scornful smile, repressed any such thought in her mind.

' I have ever done my duty as a subject and a leal Scotsman,' said Falconer ; ' but in this presence I dare not say all I think, or all I feel, lest the Lord Drummond and others deem me bold ; for other inheritance than my sword and an honest name, have I none.'

' Nay, by my soul, David Falconer, Drummond will never deem thee over-bold,' said the old lord, with a sudden emotion of generosity, ' for the sword is ever the Scotsman's best, and often his *last* inheritance, as many a foreign field can show ; and well I know, that it was not when treading on a silken carpet you won the spurs you wear.'

These were the first kind words the father of Sybilla had ever addressed to him, and they raised in his warm heart a glow of hope and gratitude.

That evening there was a grand banquet served up amid a flourish of trumpets ; Sir Stephen Bull sat on the king's right hand, the Laird of Largo on his left ; and the English and Scots, oblivious of yesterday's strife and slaughter, pushed the stoups of Malmsey and Rochelle, Canary and Bordeaux, as busily as of late they had plied cannon and arquebuss, eghisarma and hand-gun. Sir John Carmichael of Netheton and Hyndford—the same who, with Swinton of Dalswinton, slew the Duke of Clarence at the Battle of Verneuil—was chief carver ; the Laird of Southesk was cup-bearer, and the kirk bells of ' the Blessed Virgin Mary-in-the-Fields ' rang their matin-chime before the carousers drank the voidée, or parting-cup—the signal for retiring.

The dead were buried in two large graves, within the old cemetery of St. Paul's Church, between the Sea Gate and the Murray Gate of Dundee. Sir Fulke of Fulkeshall was interred alone ; and his remains, with a large sword with the blade full of notches, and several silver coins (which the Scots always interred with the dead—a strange remnant of paganry) were found in a large stone coffin, when the foundations of the East Church of Dundee were being dug in 1842 ; but poor Howard had found a grave among the waves that dash upon the shoals of the Buddon-ness.

In less than a week the English ships were refitted, and began to drop down the Tay, to sail for London.

On blue Peter being displayed at the masthead by Sir Stephen Bull, and the fore-topsails being cast loose— announcing that they were about to depart—the crews of all the Scottish war-ships, about fifteen or twenty of which had now mustered near Dundee—manned the yards, and gave them a parting cheer, while the Laird of Balgillo saluted St. George's cross by a salvo of guns from the battlements of Broughty ; and thus they separated—those hostile ships —with farewell compliments and mutual expressions of amity and good-will.

Bull had on board the Montrose Herald and Garioch Pursuivant, who were the bearers of a letter to King Henry.

This document demanded the immediate release of the Bishop of Dunblane, and begged Henry to accept of his own ships back again as presents, and enjoined him to reward nobly the brave men who had fought them so skilfully and well ; and also recommended him to remember for the future, ' that Scotland could boast of warlike sons by sea as well as land, and that he—King James—trusted the piratical ship

men of England would disturb his coasts no more, for it
micht be, they would not be so weel entertained, nor loup
hame so dryshod.'

King Henry (add Buchanan and Lindesay) dissembled his
anger and mortification, saying that he ' accepted the
kindness of the young King of Scotland, and could not but
applaud the greatness and the chivalry of his soul.'

The Nethertoun of Largo was bestowed by James upon
the admiral, together with the Green Ribbon of the Thistle,
an Order in which the death of the loyal Glencairn at Sauchieburn had made a vacancy ; for this naval victory, on which
innumerable ballads were made, was of infinite consequence
to Scotland, as it spread abroad the terror of her name by sea
at a time when the warlike skippers of France, England,
Portugal, and Spain, when sailing in their lumbering argosies,
with their cumbrous tops and gigantic poop-lanterns, were
not over-particular in distinguishing friends from foes, when
they met each other, far from human aid or justice, on the
broad and open arena of the ocean.

CHAPTER LXVI.

THE STONE BICKER.

EVERYTHING being quiet now, at home and abroad, Lord Drummond proposed the completion of his old arrangement for wedding his daughters to Home and Bothwell; and as the Bishop of Dunblane was returning through England—ready excuses having been found for his unlawful detention—the scheming and ambitious old noble contemplated a grand and triple ceremony; the coronation of one daughter and the marriage of the other two, and spent much of his time among monks, minstrels, heralds, and other devisers of pageantries.

Henry had released the poor bishop, and satisfied him that his detention had been all a mistake; and in proof thereof, committed his secretary of state to the Tower—craved the reverend Father's blessing, kissed his episcopal ring, and so forth, and thus dismissed him with all honour; but, cunning as a lynx, and still following the insidious policy of his family and his time, he hourly expected tidings from Shaw, from Gray, or Borthwick, of whom more anon; for that worthy had contrived to keep himself concealed in the ship of Bull during the engagement, having not the slightest interest in its issue, and feeling only a laudable spirit of economy with regard to risking his own precious person. Thus, on the ship's anchoring off Dundee, favoured by the darkness and confusion, he lowered himself into the water by one of the starboard gunports, swam safely ashore, and made his way with all speed to the house of the traitor Gray of Kyneff, which lay several miles distant, beyond the Howe of Angus, and there he remained for some time in concealment and consultation.

Brown autumn came; the birchen leaves turned yellow in the russet woods of Angus; the hills looked dark and close at hand; the black corbie and the greedy gled croaked on the fauld dykes and on the bare branches of the loftiest trees, and the swallows had long since departed on their yearly journey to the sunny lands of the South.

All taut and trim as ever, the *Yellow Frigate*, with her carved and painted sides that shone with gilding, still lay inactive in the harbour of Dundee, with her long blue pennon dipping in the glassy water alongside.

The Bishop of Dunblane (James Chisholm, chaplain to the late king) had now reached his episcopal palace on the banks of the Allan Water, and from Strathearn, Lord Drummond had brought his two beautiful daughters, with a glittering escort, to Dundee; but now Home and Bothwell, their intended spouses and their double terror, were loitering on the borders, concerning some dispute in which they had—fortunately for those in whom we are interested—become involved with the Wardens of the English Marches.

Barton and Falconer hovered about the mansion of Lord Drummond, and watched its walls, till they knew every stone in its quaint arcades and broad round towers; they loitered in Tyndall's Wynd and the Fish Street daily—each like an Adam near his Eden; but never once at the windows, on the bartizan, nor in the street on foot or on horseback, nor at church during morning mass or evening vespers, had they been favoured by a sight of the sisters; neither did they receive any message, which only convinced them how strictly the poor girls were guarded, for Drummond of Mewie and a band of his men from Strathearn garrisoned the house, and warded, like wakeful hounds, every avenue to it.

In Dundee, in those days, there was a famous hostel and tavern, named the Stone Bicker, which had been established by the provost and magistrates in the time of James I., in obedience to the law of 1424, which required all burgh towns in the realm to have at least one comfortable "hostellrie," with stables and chambers. This was a quaint old house, having many crow-stepped gables, square ingle-chimneys, and deep shady galleries of wood, which stood upon columns of stone. Above its door was carved in stone a bicker—with the legend

PAX INTRANTIBUS, 1424.

In form, this stoup or bicker was identically the same as that now used in Scotland; and the name is derived from the same source as the German *becher*.

Behind the house was a spacious green, smooth, grassy,

and surrounded by various little bowers trimmed over with
Gueldre roses, sweetbriar, and woodbine. Here the soldiers of
the king's guard, the cannoniers of Broughty Castle, the seamen of the ships, pages of the court, and other idlers—not a
few of the latter, knights and gentlemen—loitered and played,
or observed others playing, at long-bowls, at chess, or cards,
or shooting at the butts with bow and arquebuse, to encourage
the use of which, James I. put down the games of golf and
football by Act of Parliament in 1424.

On a warm evening about the end of August, Barton and
Falconer sat moodily over a stoup of Bordeaux, in one of
these bowers ; close by them on the green was a knot of
their sailors, lounging at full length, drinking ale from pewter
flagons of that form which we find still retained in the
metal gill and mutchkin stoups in Scotland : they were all
talking and laughing with their bonnets off and gaberdines
unbuttoned, for they had just ended a tough game at bowls ;
Cuddie Clewline, the coxswain, with his arm still in a sling,
old Archy of Anster, the boatswain, and Master Wad, the
gunner, were among them ; and placing his short squat
figure against a cask, Willie began to scrape and screw up
his fiddle, preparatory to favouring the company with an
air.

'How happy seem those honest souls of ours,' said Falconer ; 'no thought of to-day, and less care for the morrow.'

'True, David ; and all are happy whose wants and wishes,
hopes and ambitions, are small—for contentment is great
wealth.'

'Hark,' said Wad, lowering his fiddle-bow as a bell tolled ;
'what's o'clock ? '

'It is Sanct Clement's Kirk, but tak' nae heed what's
o'clock, sae lang as ye are happy, Willie,' said Cuddie. 'We'll
hae another stoup, and pay the score wi' the fore-topsail.'

'And are you sae happy awa' frae your bonnie English
wife ? '

'Yes, I am—happy as a cricket ; but do the folk no say
that bell tolled o' its sel on the nicht the king was slain ? '

'There can be nae sic thing in nature, coxswain,' said a
seaman.

'But there may be out o' nature,' replied the coxswain,
sharply ; 'how the black de'il can you ken aucht aboot it—
you that hae been but a month at sea ? '

'I hae heard o' mony queer things in my time, Cuddie ;
but I never heard o' a bell that rang o' its ain accord.'

'Weel, I *have*,' said the old boatswain, solemnly; 'and if ye wad like to hear a bit yarnie spun anent it——'

'Coil away, boatswain,' said one, clinking his stoup.

'Pay it out, carle Archy,' said another.

'My faither, honest man, in his young days was master o' the *Saint Denis*, a pinck of Kinghorn,' began the boatswain, 'and had three times the honour o' sailing to France wi' knights and ambassadors, anent the marriage o' King James wi' the daughter o' Duke Arnold and Catharine the Duchess o' Cleves. Weel, on the third time, in the year '48, as he was bearing awa' for hame, and had left far astern the free port o' auld Dunkerque, wi' its basin, sluice, and batteries, he found a dismasted and abandoned caravel floating on the sea; and lang she seemed to have been dismantled and unmanned, for seaweed and barnacles grew thick on her gaping planks and rusty chainplates, and it was next thing to a miracle that she floated at all. He boarded and overhauled her, but name, mark, or trace found he none, to indicate whose she might be, or where she cam' frae. A fine bell, wi' a clear siller tone, rocked on her forecastle, and this he unhooked and brought awa'; and the moment his boat pushed off, the bell gied a clink wi' its tongue, and the auld battered wreck gaed down wi' a sough, and half swamped the boat in its swirl as the waves yawned and closed owre it. The sailors looked ilka man in the other's face, and there seemed whisper in their hearts, that there was something about that auld and nameless wreck that was strange and eerie.

'My faither hung the bell in his forecastle—for its tones were clear and ringing, like a siller horn in a summer wood, or a young lassie's laugh when her heart is full; but my certie, there were soon terror and dismay on board the brave pinck *Saint Denis*, of Kinghorn; for the bell o' the nameless wreck was bewitched, and rang a' the watches itsel', and untouched by mortal hand; and in the deid hour o' the mirk nichts its full clear notes vibrated through every plank and stanchion in the ship, and through every sleeper's ears and heart; for never before had a bell wi' sic a sweet yet terrible tone flung its sound upon the waters. It was thrice thrown overboard, and thrice it was found hanging on its old neuk in the forecastle; and when the *Saint Denis* came home, far and wide spread the terror o' her story through a' the seaport towns o' Lothian, Fife, and Angus; so the owners had to break up the pinck, for nae man would bide aboard o' her, and

minstrelsy,' said a gentleman who had loitered near, tossing into the coxswain's bonnet a golden louis, a donation which immediately drew all eyes upon him.

He was a handsome man, young apparently, and wore a rich sword and scarlet mantle, with a jazarine jacket and salade, which concealed his face, or at least hid so much of it that recognition was impossible. He had lingered near Falconer and Barton, and now resumed his place in a seat adjoining theirs, and if he was not eavesdropping his conduct looked very much like it; but it was unmarked by them, for they were too full of their own thoughts.

'Well fare thee, Scotland,' sighed Falconer, draining his wine-horn, 'and many such battles may ye win by land and sea. But much as I love thee, thou art no longer a home or a place for me; France—France or Italy, and their battlefields, must now be the place where my life and its sorrows may be ended together.'

'Why so, brave Falconer?' asked a familiar voice, as a hand was laid on his shoulder. 'What melancholy crooning is this?'

Sir David turned, and his eyes met the face of the young king—for he it was who wore the scarlet mantle, and had now laid the salade aside.

The two gentlemen started to their feet, and uncovered their heads with reverence.

'Nay, nay, sirs; put on your bonnets,' said he. 'I am the younger man by a few years, and, though a king, have not risked my head so often in my country's service; but a time may come. And now answer me truly, gallant Falconer—why didst thou not tell *me* of this old love of thine for our pretty Sybilla Drummond?'

'I dared not.'

'Dared not! art thou not a brave fellow?'

'I am a poor one. Alas! your Majesty cannot know the miserable timidity of the poor.'

'Then what fettered thy tongue, stout Barton, eh?—thou who art laird of manors and acres, ships and stores, enow to make a monarch envy thee?'

'Because—dare I say it?'

'My true friends may say whatever they please to me.'

'Because, your Majesty, deep though my love, I dared not aspire to wed the sister of one who—who is to be our queen.'

The young king coloured deeply, and paused for a moment, as if some such thought had now struck himself for the first time ; then he thrust the idea aside, and said :

' Your fears were foolish, sirs ; ye had won those ladies' love, and surely that was winning the main part of the battle ; for, if the song says rightly, when a woman's heart is won, there is nothing more to achieve in this world.'

' Save fortune and rank ; and dare I, the son of a poor skipper of Borrowstounness, who have neither, compete with long descended peers who have both ? '

' Yes, Falconer,' said Barton, proudly ; ' for thou hast that which we seldom find among our nobles—a right true Scottish heart, that would peril all for the weal and honour of the land God gave our fathers.'

' By Heaven and by my father's bones, you say well, Robert Barton !' said the young king, with a sudden emotion of generous enthusiasm : ' and men who have hearts so tried and so true as yours, may well be the brothers of a Scottish king ! and mine you shall be, or this proud old lord—John Drummond of Stobhall and that ilk—must tell me better why not ! Come with me then—his house is close by ; let us have this skein unravelled, for to make my loyal subjects happy is the best tribute I can pay to the memory of that dear departed sire for whom you fought ; he who lost his life in upholding the rights of the people against the monstrous privileges of a race of titled tyrants.'

However reluctant Barton and Falconer might be to thrust themselves upon the presence of Lord Drummond, while the barbarous treatment they had so lately experienced there was fresh in their minds, and being aware that the Laird of Mewie, with a band of wild Celts from the Highlands of Perthshire, guarded the passages and ambulatories of the house—the generous energy of the young king, the protection his presence could afford, his desire, which was law, and the happiness his intervention might procure, together with the wish for meeting once again with those they loved so well—were all too powerful to be resisted ; and in silence the two gentlemen followed King James down the main street of Dundee, through Tyndall's Wynd, where Lord Lindesay and part of the royal retinue joined them, and together they all proceeded straight to visit Lord Drummond, the copper horn at whose gate young Lindesay blew lustily. And the old baron's half anger, half astonishment, and entire perplexity at the visit and its object, we will leave to the reader's imagination, and thus close this eventful chapter — eventful, at least, to the two lovers who accompanied the King of Scotland.

CHAPTER LXVII.

THE MAUCHLINE TOWER.

WHAT followed this happy interview with the leal and true-hearted James IV. may be gathered from the following conversation, which took place next day, in the Mauchline Tower, between three Scottish worthies who have already occupied a prominent place in the annals of their country, as well as in this more humble narrative. The Mauchline Tower, which had the honour of being the residence of Sir Patrick Gray of Kyneff, when that personage afflicted Dundee with his presence, stood at the south-west corner of the Murray gate, and obtained its name from the Campbells of Loudon and Mauchline, to whom it once belonged. It was of such strength as to become in after years a bastel-house of the town wall, but is now removed, and no trace of it remains save its name, which is still retained by a court or alley that opens off the Murray gate.

In the roughly-arched and stone-paved hall of this ancient mansion, the windows of which had stone seats and iron gratings, the furniture was of an old and barbarous aspect, and consisted only of a great standing-table, forms and cupboards all of black old Scottish oak, with five or six enormous armchairs. In stone recesses were the wooden bowls, the tren-plates and luggies used at meals; for the half-bankrupt baron's silver tankard and pewter dishes were all carefully put away in lockfast almries.

The wide fireplace was without a grate, and over it was carved the escutcheon of the Grays—a lion rampant, within a border engrailed; the emblem of hope upon a wreath, and the motto 'Anchor, fast anchor,' being the cognizance of the first of the race in Scotland—Sir Hugh de Gray, Lord of Broxmouth, in the days of Alexander II.

On the day after the interview between James IV. and

the two officers of the *Yellow Caravel*, Sir James Shaw of Sauchie and Sir Patrick Gray had a meeting with Hew Borthwick, in the upper hall of this ancient structure.

Gray and the regicide had been in close consultation, when Sir James Shaw, a little intoxicated, though the hour was early, hastened in, with his face inflamed, and expressive of high excitement.

' Here are tidings, with a vengeance ! ' said he, dashing his blue velvet bonnet on the paved floor.

' What's astir now ? ' asked Gray, knitting his dark eyebrows. ' If it be the reading of the papal dispensation in the cathedral kirk of Dunblane to-morrow, I know of it already, for our friend Hew Borthwick has just informed me thereanent.'

' The king, with Margaret Drummond, Sir David Falconer —the same runnion who is captain of Wood's arquebussiers —and Robert Barton, with the Lord Drummond, and the ladies Euphemia and Sybilla—all smiles and merriment, and riding side by side, with hawks upon their dexter wrists, each lover by his lemane, and guarded by the lances of the Royal Guard—have left Dundee within this hour.'

' Which way—east or west ? ' asked Gray, starting to his feet.

' By the western gate, and past Blackness.'

' For Dunblane ? '

' Yes ; and the Constable of Dundee carried the royal pennon on a lance.'

' Damnation ! '

' So say I—doubly,' stammered Shaw.

' On what errand have they gone ? '

' Men say variously,' replied the Laird of Sauchie, opening and shutting his bloodshot eyes ; ' but I overheard that venerable foutre whom the courtiers call Duke of Montrose, tell his son—that fop the Lord Lindesay—that the king was gone to hear the sentence of excommunication fulminated against those who slew his father.'

' That concerns thee, Master Hew. *Sir* Hew,' sneered Shaw.

Borthwick winced, and smiled bitterly. ' He said, moreover, that James was to receive from the bishop's hand, an iron belt, to be worn for ever under his shirt, in memory of the day he drew his sword against his father.'

' Few who were at Sauchie, on either side of the burn, will be likely to forget the day, Sir James. Well—and is there anything more?' asked Gray, biting his glove and rasping his steel spurs on the pavement.

'Yes—chief of all—that Margaret Drummond will there be crowned as Queen of Scotland, at the same time as her husband, and that the Lord Lyon, with all his heralds and pursuivants, the chancellor and all the great officers of state, are appointed to keep tryst at Dunblane.'

'What—the reading of the papal letter, the crowning of a king and queen, and a sentence of excommunication, all to be performed in one day—not omitting this freak of the iron belt—pshaw! thou ravest, man; and I will not believe it.'

'And why not?'

'Because, since Scone became old-fashioned, every coronation must take place at Holyrood. A rare bundle of news thou'st brought us, gossip.'

'I have not yet told thee all—for the best of the pudding is still in the pot.'

'Well, say on,' said Gray, shrugging his shoulders with something between a smile and a frown on his face.

'I heard Sir Andrew Wood say to the Constable of Dundee that Falconer and Barton were to be wedded by the bishop to old John Drummond's daughters—and by the king's express command; but thou wilt not believe *that* either, perhaps?'

'Wedded—is he as mad as his father was before him? Will he wed one sister himself, and in the person of others raise those traders' sons—loons whose ancestors are buried in obscurity, and whose fathers brought salted hides and tallow, tar and hemp from Memmel, cartwheels and saddles, iron pots and pewter pans, from Flanders—to a close alliance with the Scottish crown? God's death, it's monstrous—pshaw! and cannot be! Our peers and barons are not so low in pride or poor in spirit as to brook such an outrage——'

'Unless King Henry paid them for it—which he is not likely to do.'

'But what will the Lords Home and Hailes—Bothwell, I mean—say to this?'

'The constable put the same question to yonder gorbellied admiral, who replied that the king had undertaken to pacify them; but it was no business of his—a mariner's—to study such ware; then he added something about a gunner and his lintstock, a steersman and his helm, which I did not understand, but conceived to mean something insolent to the nobility.'

'And doubtless it was so—the tarry varlet!' said Gray, stamping his armed heel on the paved floor; 'Sir James, thou amazest me by all this! but where tarries now the Lord Angus?'

'He is hunting the red deer on the wild Rinns of Galloway,' replied Shaw, with a reckless laugh.

'I might have shrewdly guessed he was not on this side of the Howe of Fife.'

'Are there any fresh tidings from Henry of England?'

'Henry expects them from us,' said Gray with one of his hissing whispers and deep satanic smiles.

'True—I am forgetting our fair stipulation, penned by Master Quentin Kraft, and of which there are duplicates in London, to the effect that he—that is, King Henry—shall use all interest with our king to have my barony of Sauchie erected into an earldom——'

'And *my* barony of Kyneff and estate of Caterline erected into a lordship; I do not see why I should not have put in for an earldom too—but I shall content me if made as good as my chief, Kinfauns; though I would make as noble a Scottish peer as most of them.'

For once in his life, Sir Patrick Gray spoke truth.

'But instead of gaining these things, sirs,' said Borthwick, who had listened in attentive silence to all the foregoing, 'ye have lost your governorships of Stirling and of Broughty, with all their attendant customs, kains, and powers, and now——'

'The marriage on which these airy coronets depend will never happen, I fear me,' said Shaw, seating himself with a groan.

'It shall happen,' said Gray, furiously, as he took a huge tankard of wine and three flagons from a side press; 'we have made but one or two false moves, Sir James; next time we'll have better luck; and the tables will turn when we have Margaret Tudor for queen. She is said to be not over-handsome; but 'twill be all the same to King James when the candles are out in Linlithgow Bower. So Margaret Drummond must be removed,' he added, filling up the silver-rimmed horns with Rochelle.

'We have each said so a thousand times, sirs,' said Borthwick, 'and yet she still remains.'

'This removal must then be thy task, Master Hew,'

said Shaw, setting down the pot, in the purple contents of which he had dipped his wiry mustachios; 'get thee a nag at the *Stone Bicker*, or anywhere else; hie thee away after these galliards to Dunblane, and learn what can be done; for nothing but desperate measures can save us now, as we are desperate men; one may see that by these bare walls and these half mutchkin stoups of sour Rochelle.'

'Thou hast still the powder of Kraft, the London apothecary?' asked Gray, in a whisper.

'Yea,' answered Borthwick; 'and it is said to be so potent, that I have borne it about me in great fear, though it is carefully sealed and waxed all over.'

'Draw closer,' hissed the voice of Gray, as he sunk it into an almost inaudible whisper.

The reader is already aware that Borthwick had been originally a priest of Dunblane, and, consequently, he knew well the whole cathedral and its locality. It was therefore agreed that he should disguise himself in any manner he deemed most fitted for the occasion; that he should depart for that secluded little city, and endeavour to put to some deadly use the poison with which he was entrusted.

It was, moreover, arranged that at midnight, on the second day from this one, they should both meet him at the Bridge of Dunblane, and hear what his success had been. Gray supplied this trusty ruffian with a horse, and Shaw gave him gold, for he had about seventy miles of a rough and devious road to travel, and so they separated; the two barons to prepare and mount, for any emergency, all the armed retainers they could collect; and the regicide to execute his terrible mission.

'This object once achieved,' said Gray, '*we must rid ourselves of Borthwick*—for he knoweth over many secrets to make our heads secure on our shoulders!'

CHAPTER LXVIII.

DUNBLANE.

THE information of Sauchie was all correct, save in that part which referred to the coronation of Margaret, which James intended should take place at the same time as his own, not in the little episcopal city of Dunblane, but in the capital city of Edinburgh, amid all the splendour with which he could invest it; and already the Lord High Treasurer, Sir William Knollis, better known as Lord St. John of Jerusalem, being Preceptor of the Scottish Knights of Rhodez, the Lord Chancellor, the Secretary of State, and the Lords of the Privy Council, were making the necessary arrangements for the great ceremonial at Holyrood.

The king's influence, united to Barton's acknowledged worth and landed possessions, operated so far on Lord Drummond, as to make him sullenly acquiesce in the marriage of Euphemia to one whose betrothal could not, in a Catholic age, be broken without incurring the penalty of sin; and, in the same spirit, he permitted arrangements to be make for Sir David Falconer, whom James called 'the gentlest and the bravest knight at court,' wedding Sybilla; meanwhile the old lord consoled himself for thus stooping to the royal will by reflecting that he still had two other daughters growing up—Beatrice and Elizabeth—who should be forced bongré malgré to marry the first eligible earls upon whom he could lay the hands of a father-in-law.

The king's train was received with all honour by the Baron Bailie of Dunblane, and Sir Edmund Hay of Melginch, the chamberlain of the diocese, who marshalled them to the palace of the good old bishop, James Chisholm, whose name must not be confounded with that of his successor, William Chisholm, a base and irreverend prelate, who robbed the see of its revenues to maintain his children, and desecrated the episcopal palace by scenes of licentiousness.

This palace stood to the southward of the magnificent cathedral, on the edge of the declivity which slopes down towards the river Allan. It was surrounded by thick old copsewood and by striking and picturesque scenery; but it has long since fallen into shapeless ruin, and now only a few vestiges of its lower apartments can be traced.

The four lovers were so happy that we shall not presume to intrude upon them, or attempt to transfer to paper any description of their joy, but will leave them to their quiet and dreamy rambles, arm in arm, or hand in hand, in that deep and finely wooded glen below Dunblane, where the precipices overhang the Allan, and the windings of the dell give so many lovely glimpses of foliaged scenery; and to their sport of shooting at the butts with feathered arrows, in the smooth park without the old cathedral walls, where many hundred years of careful pasturage and mowing had made the green grass as smooth as velvet; for now it was never brushed by other feet than those of the gliding deer or the lighter-footed hares and rabbits; and there the young king, and even the kind bishop, with some of the prebends, drew the bow to please the three beautiful Drummonds; and Margaret, with her blonde hair and sweet blue eyes, was voted the best shot of them all—for James and his two favourite subjects were too gallant to beat her shooting, and the most reverend father, by Divine permission Bishop of Dunblane, was somewhat too stout and pursy to draw a shaft like her.

They were all happy, and pure joy beamed in their eyes; it glowed in their young hearts and mantled in their cheeks.

Two alone were grave; viz., old Lord Drummond, because he was somewhat perplexed or felt that he cut rather a foolish figure, and was about to have for sons-in-law two men on whom James dared not yet bestow nobility for fear of raising the anger of older patentees; and on the young king's brow a cloud was resting, for on the morrow he was to receive from the bishop's hand 'the sackcloth shirt and iron belt,' which he was to wear as the self-imposed penance of filial disobedience;

> While for his royal father's soul,
> The chanters sung, the bells did toll;

and kindly and consolingly the white-haired bishop sought to soothe the sorrow and disperse the gloom which the young monarch strove in vain to overcome.

Could it be that a mysterious presentiment of approaching evil was hovering in his heart? In Scotland, we often hear of such forebodings still.

On the day following the intended sentence of excommunication, Margaret was to behold one sister wedded to Robert Barton and another to David Falconer; and on that day the *Yellow Frigate* and her consorts would startle the broad blue Firth that rolls before Dundee by a loud and merry salvo from their brass culverins and iron arquebusses à croc.

Already had each beautiful bride playfully tried the espousal ring—the emblem of eternity—upon her pretty finger—that third finger of the left hand from which, according to an old superstition, there ran one mysterious fibre directly to the heart; and now we may inform our fair readers, whom such items may interest, that the said rings were not the plain hoops used in our own day, but each was massive and chased, inscribed by a holy legend, and having on it two ruby hearts, surmounted by a little crown of diamonds, for such was the fashion in the olden time.

And now, as the day on which the sisters were to receive communion at mass in the cathedral dawned in sunny glory and splendour, lighting up the painted lattices, the grey walls, and green woods of the old episcopal palace, and tinting with its brightest hues the rapid waters of the Allan, the old bishop patted their silken tresses, and called them his 'good children,' as they knelt to receive his morning blessing in the dining-hall, reminding them with a smile, that 'happy was the bride whom the sun shone on, and that he hoped the god of day would not rise less brightly on the morrow.'

And they all smiled to each other timidly and fondly, for, alas! they little knew that for some of them to-morrow was—eternity.

Margaret, the Queen of Scotland—for such indeed was she now—was to receive the communion with her sisters; but Barton and Falconer having, we may suppose, obtained it but recently, or for some other reason now unknown, *did not* share it with them, which will account for their escaping the perilous web which English guile and Scottish treason were weaving around them all.

CHAPTER LXIX.

THE MIDNIGHT TRYST.

True to his appointment, about twelve o'clock, ' that hour o' nicht's black arch the keystone,' on the night before the important day of the three solemnities, when the papal dispensation was to be read, an excommunication to be pronounced, and that Iron Belt, so famous in the history of James IV., to be consecrated and bestowed—Hew Borthwick, the fell spirit, the evil genius of Margaret Drummond —or rather, the vile slave and tool of villans more subtle than himself—appeared at the ancient bridge of Dunblane; the same which is mentioned in the introduction to this work as being the erection of the Bishop Findlay Dermach, in the year 1406.

The stillness of midnight reigned in and around that diminutive cathedral city. As Hew Borthwick, the outcast of nature, loitered on the old and narrow bridge which spans the Allan, and lingered under the gloom of some enormous alder or boor-trees that grew out of the rocks and threw their shadow on the path, some strange ideas began to hover in his mind.

Save the rush of the river over its rocky bed, the rustle of the autumn leaves in the coppice, or the bay of a sheep-dog on the distant muirlands, there was no sound in the air; but there came many an imaginary one to the ears of Borthwick. At one time he thought a wild cry went past him on the wind; at another, he was certain that voices were lamenting among the copsewood by the river side.

He listened breathlessly! All was still, save the beating of his own heart.

Was conscience beginning to be stirred at last within that arid, cruel, and stony breast, or were these ideas the mere result of the dark and midnight hour, the place, the time, and the solemn and awful superstitions incident to the age and the nation?

Swinging high aloft in the beautiful square tower of carved stonework, the cathedral bell tolled the hour of twelve. The first sonorous note, as it rolled away upon the trembling air, made Borthwick's coward heart leap within him; and he listened to each stroke in breathless agony, as a wretch might listen to his death-knell, and when the last and twelfth had boomed away upon the darkened sky, he breathed more freely, but the perspiration hung in drops upon his clammy brow, for that bell had roused old memories in his heart, and called back the days that were gone, as an old familiar voice or song might do.

'Tush!' he muttered; 'let me not be now white-hearted and a fool, when the last die has been cast in this infernal game—the last scene prepared in this tremendous drama. Twelve has struck, but there is no appearance of them yet!'

Faint and flickering lights shot over the tall and many-coloured windows of the cathedral, and played between the slender tracery of their shafted mullions, or died away in the recesses of the church. Those were the tapers of monks who had received a penance of midnight prayers to say at certain tombs or shrines; and our lurker remembered the time when he too—but he turned on his heel, and strove to forget those better days and that embittering memory. 'Would the tryst had been anywhere but here.'

Rays of light were streaming more brightly from the smaller but strongly grated windows of the bishop's palace, and they played on the brown foliage of the woods below, and on the rushing surface of the river in the dell. One by one these rays of light faded away; at last darkness reigned in the mansion, and Borthwick shuddered, for he knew that Margaret Drummond and her sisters would then be a-bed.

He was deadly pale; and had any one passed him casually on that high and narrow bridge, his aspect, even at night, must assuredly have startled them.

To him it was strange and almost irritating, that all the life he had passed, with many of its minuter and long-forgotten incidents, should now rise before him like a long unfolding scroll, strongly, darkly, and fearfully, as it might do before one who is about to die; and a terrible tissue it was!

He recalled the awful name and fate of his parents, and the promises he had made to the humane old priest who had saved him doubly as he was wont to say, 'like a brand from the burning,' and the vows he had made in youth, in that cathedral aisle, to spend a life of holiness, of usefulness, of purity, and of prayer, to atone for the real or traditional atrocities of Ewain Gavelrigg and his wife among the Sidlaw hills; and how he had kept these vows?

'Accursed be these thoughts!' said he, as he walked to and fro, and bit his nether lip, as if to control the growing fear and bitterness of his heart. At that moment something struck his face, and he sprang aside in terror uncontrollable.

'Pshaw!' said he, 'a bat!'

Everything was fraught with some old memory to him now, and he remembered the old story of its origin to which he had often listened, as the monks sat round the refectory fire in the cold winter nights, when the Allan was sheeted with ice, and the blast of the snow-clad Grampians moaned in the leafless woods of Dunblane; and the voice of his old patron came back to his ears in the accents of awe with which he used to tell the story:—of how, when a boy of seven years of age, the Saviour of mankind was at play in the streets of Jerusalem, with other little Jews, and in sport they fashioned various birds and animals of clay, and then the children quarrelled among themselves, each preferring his own workmanship, and all united in laughing to scorn an uncouth bird made by the little hands of the golden-haired boy, the son of Mary, till the tears fell from his eyes; and as they dropped upon the little image, lo! it expanded its wings of clay and flew from hand to hand, and after fluttering over his head, soared into the air and became a veritable *bat*. On beholding this, the children fled, and on relating the story to their parents, were by them forbidden to play again with that bright-haired little boy, whom they stigmatized as an embryo sorcerer; and Borthwick remembered with mingled pity and envy the good faith, the awe, and holy interest with which the old and silver-bearded priests bent their heads around the winter hearth, and listened to legends such as this; for it was indeed an age 'when old simplicity was in its prime.'

At last his reveries were interrupted by perceiving at the other end of the bridge two men on foot; they had been there for some time conversing and regarding him, but unobserved by Borthwick, whose eyes and mind were turned inward, if we may say so; and now by their height, bearing, and stealthy motions, he was convinced that they were no other than Sir James Shaw of Sauchie and Sir Patrick Gray of Kyneff.

' Well met, fair sir,' said the latter, with his usual courtly sneer.

' Good-morrow, Master Borthwick,' added Shaw, whose incessant intoxication was quite visible, even in the dark.

Both were well armed in cuirasses, gorgets, and plate sleeves, with swords and daggers in their belts, and they bore on their heads French salades which completely concealed their faces, forming at the same time a defence which no sword could cleave or poleaxe break.

' You have good tidings, I opine, sir,' said Gray.

' Alas ! what leads you to infer so ? '

' Your keeping tryst so faithfully,' said he, again.

' Is this troublesome dame disposed of ? ' asked his companion, with a hiccup.

' To-morrow will tell—— '

' To-morrow, and why to-morrow ? ' demanded Shaw, angrily.

' God's death, fellow ! have we ridden a matter of seventy miles, from the Mauchline Tower to the Brig of Dunblane, only to hear this ? '

' Hear me, sirs, and be patient,' said Borthwick, who, to their astonishment, seemed to be as crushed in spirit as he was pale in face and trembling in speech; ' I have essayed a hundred modes of obtaining access to the bishop's palace, that I might reach Dame Margaret's room, which is in the north-east corner thereof, for I know every nook and cranny of that house of old, as if it were my own.'

' And with what intent ? '

' To poison the holy water font, which I understand hangs at the head of her bed.'

' A rare idea,' hiccupped Shaw, ' provided King Henry's powder be strong enough.'

' 'Sdeath, the young king likely dips his dainty fingers too therein, so that would only mar King Henry's matrimony for ever—well.'

' The king's pages and attendants, archers, esquires, and priests, thronged every avenue, so all attempts to reach the room were vain. By the way of the bishop's kitchen, I had less hope; for though I might dose a dish strongly enough to poison a score, yet how could I be assured that Dame Margaret would eat of it ? '

' True ; then by the Holy Father, we have come but to hear of difficulties.'

'And to learn that nothing has been done,' grumbled Sir James Shaw; 'a pestilent humbug!'

'Patience, sirs, patience,' groaned Borthwick; 'failing about the palace, I resolved to try what could be achieved by the way of the cathedral.'

'Hah!' said Gray, starting.

'I know its avenues well——'

'Ay, you were a monk, and snuffled Latin there for many a year—well.'

'I begin to breathe again—so——' muttered Shaw.

'I had heard with certainty that the three sisters were to receive the Blessed Sacrament there to-morrow from the hands of the bishop, with all solemnity——'

'Well, well, what then?' asked Gray, impatiently.

'Yes, what then?' repeated the Laird of Sauchie, whose eyes were always closing.

'I stole the vestments of the sacrist who hath charge of the altar vessels, flowers, and ornaments, and whose duty it is to provide candles, bread, and wine for the communion. Well I knew where old Father Duncan's cassock hung when the good man was a-bed; and I knew the pocket too wherein he kept the key of the iron-doored niche containing the cruets of wine, beside the great altar. I donned the gown, I found the key—with eyes half blind, with ears that tingled, and a heart that trembled at every fancied sound, I glided through the long aisle of yonder silent church, and sought the niche, unchanged as when I saw it last, some sixteen years ago! I opened it—softly—slowly—fearfully, and the cruets of wine were before me—to-night, sirs,—only to-night—yea, only an hour ago were they before me, in my hands—and—and——'

'My God! thou didst not poison the wine—the wine about to become——'

'Hush, oh hush, in pity now; I poisoned one of them at least.'

'Horror!' exclaimed Gray of Kyneff; 'I foresaw not this. I would have cared little about the poisoning of some vulgar wine-pot, suppose that all Dunblane had died o' the dose; but the Communion—the Holy Eucharist——'

'*I poisoned it!*' groaned Borthwick, while his teeth chattered; 'and to-morrow will solve a grand and awful mystery.'

'And gain me an earldom,' said Shaw.

Gray placed a hand upon his mouth. There was a pause

during which the three wretches gazed upon each other in silence ; for it would require a Catholic, and more especially a Scottish Catholic of that age, to feel the full effect of the chilling awe and dread the act of this apostate priest produced upon himself and his two companions. Even *their* hearts quailed and trembled at it ; for though the infamous and unjust conduct of the popes to Scotland, in early times and during the Crusades, made the people value lightly the bulls of the Vatican—so lightly, indeed, that more than one papal legate, natheless his purple cope and scarlet stockings, has been assaulted, stripped, and driven across the English frontier, with the nation in arms, and the country flaming at his heels ; still the influence of religious sentiment, whatever its phase, was, as it has ever been, strong in the hearts of the Scots ; but now with Shaw and Gray it was mingled with an overpowering superstition, and veneration for ancient, incomprehensible, and mysterious rites.

A holy horror curdled all their blood ; and thus for some minutes none of them spoke.

' This sacrilege is awful ! ' said Sir Patrick.

' But the Holy Eucharist will *not* poison,' said Shaw, whom the communication had completely sobered ; ' so thou hast, perhaps, but fooled thyself as well as us, Master Borthwick.'

' What is this, Laird of Sauchie,' asked Borthwick, with gloomy fury ; ' art thou so dull as to think so ? was there not William Comyn, the Lord High Chancellor of Scotland, in the days of King Malcolm IV.—a consecrated bishop too —who was poisoned by the wine of the Eucharist, and fell stone dead, in rochet, cope, and stole, on the steps of the altar ? '

Another long pause ensued, during which Gray whispered to Shaw, ' We must now close this fellow's mouth for ever ; a dagger stroke, and over the bridge with him. Be ready when I say, " Let us part, Sir Hew." '

' May the blessing, or invocation, render this poison, if not altogether null in effect, at least less fatal than death ? '

On this important point, Borthwick dared not reply, and they could hear his teeth chattering.

' Where is there a leech ? ' asked the ex-governor of Stirling.

' There is none nearer than Perth—at least none that I wot of.'

' How, Ninian the barber-chirurgeon in the Speygate ? '

'The same; and he is too far off to be available,' said Borthwick.

'He is the only one on the south side of Tay, except the Highland seers and crones,' said Shaw, loosening his dagger in its sheath of velvet.

'Ah,' continued Gray, conversing in the assumed tone of ease, to throw their intended victim off his guard; 'did he not nearly slay the Lord Angus by piercing him too deep with his phlebotemus?'

'Missing the vein and cutting the artery—a very fool.'

'For which, if he had failed to stop it, the Master of Angus would have hung him over his own stair-head. He knoweth the signs and stars,' continued this cold-blooded ruffian, looking casually, as it were, over the bridge to measure the height by his cold and stern eye; 'but who save asses employ him, Master Borthwick?'

'Oh, many,' continued Shaw, laughing, as they drew nearer their victim; 'husbands, to have doses for scolding wives, and expectant heirs whose purses are empty, for old and doting uncles; in short, any one who wishes to be rid of any one else; for he enjoys pretty much the reputation of your friend the apothecary at—how name you the place —oh yes, Bucklersbury, in London, ha! ha! is it not so, Master Borthwick?'

He made no reply, for their ghastly merriment chilled him.

'Such a leech will not do for the daughters of the Lord Drummond,' resumed Shaw; 'but the night wears apace.'

'*Let us part, then, Sir Hew!*' said Gray, and at the same moment both their daggers clashed together in the breast of Borthwick, whose hot blood spirted horribly through his pyne doublet, over the hilts, and over their fingers.

The first blows failed to kill him, and he sank heavily against the parapet of the bridge.

'Mercy,' he sighed; 'mercy—God—mercy!'

'Such mercy as thou gavest King James,' replied the villains as an apology to themselves, while they buried their poniards again and again in his heart, with a heavy and awful sound.

'Tis but an act of self-defence, this!' said Gray.

'True—true—of course it is—he might have destroyed us, else,' added Shaw, in a breathless voice.

'He is gone now—so over with him!' replied the other.

Lifting the heavy, and yet warm body of the regicide,

they shot it over the steep bridge into the rapid stream below, where it fell with a loud splash. As it was swept down the current, they sprang upon their horses, which were haltered under the boor-trees.

'Now, Sir James, away for Kyneff or Caterline!' cried Gray, as they dashed through the dark streets of Dunblane, and at full speed took the road towards that great and fertile plain which lies between the northern bank of the Tay and the base of the Sidlaw hills, and is known so well in song as the Carse of Gowrie.

CHAPTER LXX.

THE IRON BELT.

PONTIFICAL high mass was performed with unusual splendour in the cathedral church of Dunblane. On this occasion the bishop, preceded by his cross-bearer, and the banner of the diocese, borne by Sir Edward Hay of Melginch, by all the prebends of the cathedral, with choristers and singing-boys, passed in procession through the centre aisle to the altar, having on his head a mitre blazing with jewels, gorgeous robes on his shoulders, and wearing scarlet gloves on his hands, which bore the identical crook by one touch of which Saint Blane restored sight to the blind, and life to the dead heir of Appilby, as we may still see recorded in the fifty-seventh folio of the Breviary of Aberdeen.

The king was on a royal seat, surrounded by the lords and ladies of the court and household, and many of the great officers of state; the Captain of his Guards, Lord Drummond, Falconer, Barton, and many more, all richly dressed in the gaudy costumes of the time, when fancy and fashion ran riot among silk and satin, velvet and miniver, feathers, jewels, and lace. Bright steel cuirasses, cloth of gold, satin doublets and velvet mantles, with the silver stars and green ribands of the Thistle, or the escallops of St. Michael, and the crosses of many a foreign Order of knighthood, made the group around the young monarch alike gay and splendid.

The entire population of the little city and of the adjacent district crowded the triple aisles of the magnificent church; and on groups of these, all of them attired in varying colours, and various fashions—for Dunblane approaches the Highland border—long hazy flakes of light fell inward from the three tall lance-headed compartments of the great western window, in which were a thousand prismatic tints, as martyred saints, crowned kings, and pallid Virgins stood amid pious scrolls and gaudy flowers, green foliage and bright armorial bearings, all woven in the brilliant glass, filling up the double mullions and grotesquely twisted tracery.

This beautiful church is less richly decorated than many others in Scotland; its mouldings and clustered capitals are without flowering; yet from the loftiness of its window, and the general symmetry of its proportions, this effort of the architectural taste and piety of King David I. is full of grandeur and dignity. From its walls hung the banners and scutcheons of the once powerful Earls of Strathearn, with the sword of Malise, who fought at the Battle of the Standard; and the helmet of Sir Maurice of Strathearn, who was slain at the Battle of Durham; there, too, hung the trophies of the Lords of Strathallan, and the Drummonds of Drummond. Beneath the pavement, which was lettered with epitaphs, and rich with graven brasses, their bones were reposing, cered in lead, deep in the Gothic vaults below; and there their effigies may yet be seen, with shield on arm, with sword at side, and hands upraised as in prayer.

The light stole through the windows with a chastened effect, and so many tapers burned upon the great altar, that with all its gilding it seemed a pyramid of flame; and in front of it were the floating garments of the bishop and his attendant priests, with the thin white smoke of the censers rising among them; while the full-toned organ, with its trumpet sound, and the harmony of a hundred voices, all melodiously attuned, rolled along the high-arched roofs, and went at once to the depth of every soul and the inmost chords of every heart—calling, as it were, to prayer and to enthusiasm, the whole being of every listener.

On the altar lay two bridal wreaths, and a peculiar belt of iron.

The wreaths were those to be worn on the morrow by Euphemia and Sybilla Drummond; the iron belt was to be the life-long penance of King James.

In the lower aisles 'a dim religious light' brooded over all; and in the solemnity of devotion, every knee and every head were bowed, and, outwardly at least, all was hushed and humble meekness.

Before the carved oak rail of the sanctuary knelt the three sisters, with their bright hair confined in golden cauls, and their faces bowed before the venerable bishop—an old man, whose days went back to those of the Regent Murdoc Stuart, and the wars of James I. with Alaster of the Isles.

Mass was performed with great solemnity; and though few Catholics—perhaps none—will believe what ensued, or that blessed wine would poison, yet we have it on record, that a Scotsman, who was Bishop of Durham in 1153, was destroyed by the wine of the Eucharist, in which a deadly drug had been placed by his enemies, some English priests.

From the prelate's hand the three fated sisters received the communion, of which he had himself partaken, impregnated as it was with a poison as deadly as ever human science or human villany prepared.

' *Corpus Domini nostri,*' etc., etc., prayed the poor bishop, with reverence, and eyes half closed as he signed the cross in blessing over their fair foreheads, and placed between the lips of each the wafer which he had dipped in the poisoned wine, of which he had himself partaken!

The poor girls, with their white hands crossed upon their fluttering breasts, and their young hearts full of pious joy, returned to the crimson canopied stall, over which their father's feudal banner, with the three bars, wavy, hung beside the royal standard, with the lion, gules, and there again they knelt in prayer beside the youthful king.

When mass was over, the bishop ascended the altar, still robed in full pontificals, with his mitre on his head, and resigning his crook to an assistant priest who waited on the steps, he opened the famous letter of Dispensation.

' The Most Holy Father in Christ our Lord, Innocent the Eighth, by Divine Providence, *servus servorum Dei,* to his dearly beloved brother James, also by Divine mercy, Bishop of Dunblane, and to all others, etc., etc., wisheth health and benediction in the Lord.'

Beginning thus, he read, in pure and sonorous Latin, the Papal authority, removing the guilt and sin committed, and absolving, dissolving, and annulling the ties of blood between James, by the grace of God, King of the Scots and his cousin, the Lady Margaret Drummond; and thus, by the apostolical power confided to the Holy see, removing every hindrance and impediment to their lawful marriage, ' dated at Rome, on the festival of Corpus Christi, and of our Pontificate then fourth year.'

The bishop closed the letter which he had brought from such a distance, and which had involved him in so many personal perils, and then resumed his glittering crozier from its bearer.

Then Margaret, whose small white hand the young king

had pressed repeatedly, and whose agitated heart had beat wildly, felt as if a mountain had been lifted off it; for fondly, fully, and devoutly she believed in the annulment it announced, and the authority from which it came; and her soft blue eyes beamed under her velvet hood and gold-fringed caul with the most beautiful joy, and with the purest and holiest of rapture as they met those of the young king, her husband—ay, her husband now, without secrecy, or fear, or sin.

'Margaret—my own beloved Margaret!' he whispered, and tremblingly kissed her brow, an act of respect and tenderness which stirred the hearts of all the people.

Honest Barton was spelling away industriously at his missal, content, as he thought, and said inwardly, ' that Euphemia was alongside of him, and that, on the morrow, with a fair wind and a friar's blessing, they would cast anchor together in smooth riding, and in the sunny haven of matrimony;' but Falconer and Sybilla knelt hand in hand behind the high oak-screen, and deeply thanked God and the good young king, who had brought to this happy and most unexpected issue the long hushed secret of their ardent hearts.

Would that we could leave them thus; but the ways of fate, and the course of unforeseen events, are inexorable.

James IV. now received from the Bishop's hand the penance-girdle—that *Iron Belt*—to which he added every year a weight to be worn in memory of his father's fall, and which he never laid aside either by day or by night, until the morning of the fatal ninth of September, 1513, thirty-five years after; and *on that day* he perished at Flodden, with ten thousand Scottish hearts as brave as his own!

Now old Duncan, the sacristan, supplied innumerable torches and tapers to the people, giving one to every man, woman, and child. The whole church became filled with light—a blaze, a flood of flame, till the eyes ached, and the beautiful lines of St. Paulinus seemed to be realized in the old aisles of Dunblane:

> With crowded lamps are these bright altars crowned,
> And waxen tapers shed perfume around,
> From fragrant wicks beams calm and scented ray.
> To gladden night, and brighten radiant day.

> Meridian splendours thus light up the night,
> And day itself, illum'd with sacred light,
> Wears a new glory, borrowed from those rays,
> That stream from countless lamps in never-ending blaze.

But this unusual glory chilled the hearts of the vast congregation who filled that great cathedral church; for now
the bishop prepared to pass upon the murderers of the
late king and their abettors the heaviest fulminations of
the Vatican; and in that age, when churchmen united
spiritual with temporal power, everything in nature, from
the king on his throne to a caterpillar on the leaf of a tree,
were liable to anathema. To men, its sentence was armed
with a thousand terrors. The excommunicated person was
shut out, cut off, as it were, from all social life; his servants,
his wife—even his dearest children, dare not come near
him, or relieve his most urgent wants by a crumb of bread
or a drop of water; for he had forfeited all claims on
humanity, all natural rights and legal privileges.

Any man might slay him, and under this inhuman law,
even his body was denied proper burial; in some sequestered or hated, at least unconsecrated spot, it was flung
aside, and covered up with stones; and now the bells of
Dunblane began to toll a solemn peal, and the inmost
hearts of all the people, surrounded as they were by that
blaze of light, became appalled, as the bishop, in a loud but
melancholy voice, poured forth against the regicides the
sentence of Pope Innocent VIII.: ' In nomine Patris et
Filii et Spiritus Sancti, et benedictæ nostræ Dominæ Sanc-
tissimæ Mariæ, atque virtute angelorum archangelorumque,
etc., à sancte matris Ecclesiæ græmio segregamus ac per-
petuæ *maledictionis anathemate condemnamus!*'

The three sisters felt a sleep stealing over their humid
eyes and hushing their beating hearts, as they nestled close
together, as if in terror of the spiritual thunder that rang
over their heads in a language they could not comprehend;
but, perhaps, it was excess of happiness at their own position—or, perhaps, the blaze of light oppressed them, for
they were silent, motionless, and still.

Timidly they cast a furtive glance at their father, Lord
Drummond, as he stood near them, sheathed in the same
armour he had worn at the Battle of Sauchieburn, with a
wax taper clutched like a lance in his gauntleted hand; unsubdued by the terrible anathema, the proud noble heard it

with constitutional indifference, or concealed his inward fear under an outward smile of scorn.

But his daughters felt sick and faint.

Margaret closed her eyes and drooped her head upon the shoulder of Euphemia, whose hand was now clasped by Sybilla.

As the bishop concluded he extinguished his taper, and every one in the church followed his example—the prebendaries and others treading their torches vigorously under foot, and Lord Drummond crushed his under his armed heel with as much animus as Sir Andrew Wood might have done ; while the bells continued to toll the knell of the doomed souls, at long and solemn intervals, in the towers of the cathedral, the interior of which seemed to become suddenly dark and gloomy, for the day without had overcast, and dense autumn clouds, charged with mist and rain, came rolling from the Grampians across the lowering sky.

A chill—a horror of the scene, this solemn cursing with bell, book and candle—had fallen upon the people, who were stealing softly and hastily away ; while the poor old bishop, exhausted by the long service and its exciting nature, and more than all by the poison he had imbibed, tottered into the arms of Sir Walter Drummond, the dean, and was borne out by a side door, with all the air of a dying man.

The three sisters, as if absorbed in prayer, were still leaning forward against the oak rail and kneeling on the velvet cushions ; they remained thus very long after all the congregation had dispersed ; and loth to disturb them, their happy lovers lingered in the aisle with the king and his attendants, till Lord Drummond lost all patience, and roughly summoned them.

' Effie—Maggie—by my soul, ye have gone to sleep, I think—come, arouse ye there ! ' he exclaimed.

Then the young king went softly over and touched Margaret on the shoulder.

She did not stir ; neither did she seem to feel him.

' Sybilla—Euphemia ! ' said he.

But there was no answer.

For those three kneeling figures were stone dead !

*   *   *   *   *   *

CHAPTER LXXI.

CONCLUSION.

LORD DRUMMOND lived to see one of his daughters become a countess, and the other in a fair way to wear a coronet; for little Lady Beatrix grew a beautiful woman, and in after years became the Countess of James Earl of Arran, commander of the Scots in the French and Danish wars; while Elizabeth was wedded to the warlike Master of Angus, who fell at Flodden with two hundred knights and gentlemen, all of the great and gallant Douglas' name; and could the proud old lord have had a vision of *her* descendants, his ambitious heart would have swelled with joy, for her grand-daughter, Margaret, became the mother of Henry, King of Scotland, from whom the kings of Britain, France, Spain, Prussia, and the emperors of Germany, are descended.

After the horrible catastrophe which closed our last chapter, we at first intended to have said no more; but as this narrative has partaken much more of the character of a veritable history than a romance, a few parting words are necessary before we say farewell to those who have accompanied us so far.

The historians of later times have revealed to us what was then unknown—that the unhappy Margaret Drummond was, as Robert Douglas has it, '*taken away to make room for a daughter of England*,' and that her two elder sisters perished with her.

In their bridal wreaths and veils each was interred, with a golden chalice on her breast, in that old cathedral aisle; and there they sleep, side by side, where for many years solemn masses were said over them, until the belief in such things passed away.

Three blue slabs cover them, and mossy ruins and grassy graves are around them. The Allan murmurs by unchanged; but the trees that shade it are old now, and they moan as they shake their rustling leaves in the wind that comes from the distant Grampians. Few now know the stones that mark the graves of the three hapless sisters—the three beautiful Drummonds; for it is often the way of the world that those whose couch in life has been decked with every splendour, have their bed of eternity forgotten and neglected.

Neither David Falconer nor Robert Barton died of broken hearts, as the heroes of romance might have done; but broken hearts were as little in fashion then as now. They sorrowed long and deeply, like noble and true-hearted men, and they never married.

Barton was knighted, and became comptroller of the royal household; the arquebussier, as we are informed by Buchanan, was slain at the head of the Royal Guard, of which he was captain, when covering the retreat of the king's artillery at the siege of Tantallon. He was then a man well up in years, being past his seventieth birthday; and when his body was stripped and plundered by the Douglas troopers, there were found, in a little bag at his neck, an Agnus Dei, a lock of hair, a ring, and a medal.

The ring and the lock of hair belonged to Sybilla Drummond, and the medal was the gift of King James IV. Some monks of North Berwick found the body as it lay on the highway; and though it had ever been Sir David's wish to lie in Dunblane, they buried him in the Auld-kirk close by the sea, which is now washing its burying-ground away.

The reader will naturally suppose that after achieving the long-desired wish of the English faction, in removing the unfortunate Margaret, the enterprising Lairds of Sauchie and Kyneff ultimately obtained their peerages; but such was *not* the case—*why*, we are not in a position to state, for no doubt they or their descendants would have shone conspicuously in that black list of political traitors who broke the heart of King James V.

Sir Andrew Wood of Largo survived to see the early part of the reign of James V. He was then in extreme old age; and after a long career of faithful service and brilliant achievement, and after fighting his old ship, the *Yellow Caravel*, as long as her timbers held together, he retired to the Castle of Largo, in and around which Cuddie Clewline, the coxswain of his barge, Willie Wad, the gunner, Archy of Anster, the boatswain, and nearly all his crew, were located; for the Scottish Nelson lived in his old age and died, when the hour came, like a true Scottish Trunnion.

When he grew feeble and unable to ride to Largo Kirk, where Father Zuill was chaplain, and where he long strove in vain to achieve the development of the parabolic speculum of Marcellus, it was proposed to make a litter, wherein his old shipmates might convey him on their shoulders.

'Nay, nay, Robbie Barton,' said he, 'I ken nothing of how to navigate such a craft; every man to his trade—the gunner to his lintstock, the steersman to his helm, and the cook to the foresheet. Gadzooks, I shall be rowed in my barge as of yore!'

From the northern gate of Largo Castle he had *a canal* cut through a wooded hollow to Largo Kirk, and along this he was rowed every Sunday by his old barge's crew, with Cuddie in the prow, bearing a boat-hook, and keeping a look-out ahead, and an admiral's broad pennon floating in the water astern.

The remains of this canal are still distinctly visible at Upper Largo; and along that watery path, when his years were full, his remains were rowed by torchlight to the venerable fane where his tomb is yet to be seen; and where now he sleeps, with his compass, his cross-staff, sword, and whistle, in his coffin; and so he passed away, 'believing and hoping,' as he said to those who wept around him, 'that when piped up aloft at the last muster-day, he would be able to give as good an account of his steerage, variation, and leeway in life, as ever he had done in the longest voyage of the dear old *Yellow Frigate*—God bless every plank of her!'

Such were the last words of the brave old Laird of Largo.

NOTES.

1. Concerning Lady Margaret Drummond, a long and interesting note will be found in Tytler's admirable *History of Scotland*, vol. iv. The king became deeply attached to her at an early period. In his first Parliament she was voted an allowance for dresses. Douglas, in his *Peerage*, stated that she was poisoned in 1501; 'great mystery,' says Mr. Tytler, 'hangs over the death of this royal favourite.'

In Moreri's *Dictionary*, it is stated that John, first Lord Drummond, 'had four daughters, one of whom, named Margaret, was so much beloved by James IV. that he wished to marry her; but as they were connected by blood, and a dispensation from the Pope was required, the impatient monarch concluded a private marriage, from which clandestine union sprang a daughter, who became the wife of the Earl of Huntly. The dispensation having arrived, the king determined to celebrate his nuptials publicly; but the jealousy of some of the nobles against the house of Drummond, suggested to them the cruel project of taking off Margaret by poison, in order that her family might not enjoy the glory of giving two queens to Scotland.

'Certain it is, that Margaret Drummond, with Euphemia and the Lady Sybilla, her sisters, died suddenly at the same time with symptoms exciting a strong suspicion of poison, which it was thought had been administered to them at breakfast. Sir Walter Drummond, Lord Clerk Register, their paternal uncle, was at the time Dean of Dunblane, a circumstance which seems to have led to their interment there, the family having lately removed from Stobhall, their original seat, on the banks of the Tay, to Drummond Castle, where probably they had no place of internment.'

James IV. appears never to have forgotten her, for down to the end of his life are entries in the Treasurer's accounts of the payments made to the two priests who sung masses for her soul in Dunblane.

2. Concerning the story told by the boatswain in Chapter X., I may mention, that in Ogilby's *Africa*, a gigantic folio work, published in 'the White Fryers, London, 1670,' will be found a curious description of the Guanchos, and their mode of preserving the dead, which agrees entirely with the description thereof given by the shipmate of our admiral. The idea of the chalked ship sailing *off* the wall is not original, for I remember once hearing a soldier tell some such story to his comrades as they sat round a guard-room fire, on a cold winter night in North America.

3. I may remark, that though I have rather anticipated the time of Sir Andrew Wood's two battles, for the purpose of my own story, I have striven in the details of them, and everywhere else, to adhere closely to history, to character, and to costume, etc., and to those who

are curious in the matter, much information concerning the admiral
will be found in *Tait's Magazine* for April and May, 1852. ' He was,'
says Tytler, ' an enterprising and opulent merchant, a brave warrior
and skilful naval commander, an able financialist, intimately acquainted
with the management of commercial transactions, and a stalwart feudal
baron.' He died about the year 1540, and left several sons, one of whom
became a senator of the College of Justice. There is still remaining a
circular tower of the castellated dwelling erected by the brave old admiral.
A tablet, bearing an inscription to his memory, and an extract from his
charter, was inserted in the mouldering wall by the late General Durham ;
on the summit of the ruin was one of the iron thirty-two pounders recovered from the wreck of the *Royal George*, which pointed towards the
sandy shore and beautiful bay of Largo, and formed a characteristic
monument to the stout old captain of the *Yellow Caravel*.

The cannon is now placed in front of the modern mansion-house, but
the white marble slab yet remains above the door of the old one, and is
inscribed as follows :

This Tablet was placed by

GENERAL JAMES DURHAM, of Largo,

In the year M.DCCC.XXXII.
To remind posterity that
These are the remains of the Royal Residence,
Granted with the lands of Largo, by

JAMES THE THIRD

To His Admiral Sir Andrew Wood,

Who repaired and strengthened the Fortalice
By the hands of Englishmen captured by him.
This donation from his grateful Sovereign
Was the well merited reward
Of his brave and generous conduct,
In successfully defending,
At his own private expense,
The seas and shores of Scotland
From the otherwise unconquered Navy of England,
Or, as his charter bears :
' Propter servicia tam per terram quam per mare,
in pace et in guerra, gratuiter impensa.'

Sir Alexander Durham of Largo, Lord Lyon King-at-Arms, acquired
the estate of Largo Anno Dom. 1659.

PRINTED IN GREAT BRITAIN AT
THE PRESS OF THE PUBLISHERS